THE
COMPLETE NAPOLEONIC
STORIES

By Sir Arthur Conan Doyle

THE ADVENTURES OF SHERLOCK HOLMES
THE CASE-BOOK OF SHERLOCK HOLMES
THE MEMOIRS OF SHERLOCK HOLMES
THE RETURN OF SHERLOCK HOLMES
HIS LAST BOW
THE HOUND OF THE BASKERVILLES
THE SIGN OF FOUR
THE VALLEY OF FEAR
SIR NIGEL
THE WHITE COMPANY
MICAH CLARKE
THE   REFUGEES
RODNEY STONE
UNCLE BERNAC
ADVENTURES OF GERARD
THE EXPLOITS OF BRIGADIER GERARD
THE LOST WORLD
THE TRAGEDY OF THE KOROSKO
THE MARACOT DEEP

Omnibus Volumes

GREAT STORIES
THE CONAN DOYLE STORIES
THE SHERLOCK HOLMES SHORT STORIES
THE SHERLOCK HOLMES LONG STORIES
THE HISTORICAL ROMANCES
THE COMPLETE PROFESSOR CHALLENGER STORIES
THE COMPLETE NAPOLEONIC STORIES

THE LIFE OF SIR ARTHUR CONAN DOYLE
  by John Dickson Carr

THE EXPLOITS OF SHERLOCK HOLMES
  by Adrian Conan Doyle and John Dickson Carr

THE SHERLOCK HOLMES COMPANION
SHERLOCK HOLMES INVESTIGATES
THE MAN WHO WAS SHERLOCK HOLMES
FOUR SHERLOCK HOLMES PLAYS
  by Michael and Mollie Hardwick

The
Complete Napoleonic Stories

**UNCLE BERNAC
EXPLOITS OF BRIGADIER GERARD
ADVENTURES OF GERARD
THE GREAT SHADOW**

by
SIR ARTHUR CONAN DOYLE

JOHN MURRAY
FIFTY ALBEMARLE STREET
LONDON

First published in one volume 1956
Reprinted 1967

*This book is published by arrangement with the Estate of
the late Sir Arthur Conan Doyle*

**Printed in Great Britain by Butler & Tanner Ltd., Frome and London
and published by John Murray (Publishers) Ltd.**

AUTHOR'S PREFACE[1]

READERS of Marbot, de Gonneville, Coignet, de Fezenac, Bourgogne, and the other French soldiers who have recorded their reminiscences of the Napoleonic campaigns, will recognise the fountain from which I have drawn the adventures of Etienne Gerard. It was an extraordinary age, and produced extraordinary types. For twenty-three years France was at war, with one short breathing space of a few months. To Frenchmen war had become the normal and natural state. Children were born in war, grew up in war, fought in the war, and died in the same endless war without ever knowing what peace was like. Yet, as we read the memoirs of these fighting men, or if we consult the descriptions left by those who, like our own Napier, had met them in the field, we find that they were by no means brutalised by this strange experience, and that among them were knightly and gentle souls, playfully gallant, whose actions recall the very spirit of chivalry. A better knight than Marbot never rode in the lists, and what shall we say of that dragoon, described by Napier, who raised his sword, saluted and passed, on perceiving that his English antagonist in a fierce *mêlée* had only one arm, or that madcap officer of the cavalry who charged the whole English army single-handed. These are the men, glorious in their youth, and pathetic in their useless and poverty-stricken old age, of whom I desired to draw a type, noble, *debonnaire*, capable, self-sufficient, human, and garrulous. I may add that there has been some attempt to keep the military and historical detail correct.

A preface had always seemed to me an unnecessary impertinence, until I found by experience how easily one

[1] This Preface by Sir Arthur Conan Doyle is taken from his Preface to the limited 'Author's Edition' of his works published by Smith Elder (1902).

may be misunderstood, and so before I stand aside I am emboldened to say a few words as to my own conception of the art of fiction. That conception is that our treatment may be as wide as the heavens and as broad as the earth, if it does but attain the essential end of *interest*. All methods and schools, romance and realism, symbolism and naturalism, have the one object in view— to interest. They are all good so far as they attain that, and all useless when they cease to do so. The weary workers or the more weary idlers turn to the writer and demand to have their thoughts drawn away from themselves and the routine of their own lives. Within the bounds of morality all methods are legitimate by which we can effect this. Every school is right in claiming that it is justified, and every school is wrong when it tries to prove that its rival is unjustified. You are right to make your book adventurous, you are right to make it theological, you are right to make it informative or controversial or idyllic, or humorous or grave or what you will, but you *must* make it interesting. That is essential—all the rest is detail. There is nothing inconsistent in the same writer using every method in turn, so long as he can in each hold his reader and take his thoughts from his own selfish interests.

But there comes the obvious retort, 'You say "interesting"—interesting to *whom*?' The difficulty is not really a great one. The higher and more permanent work has always been interesting to all. The work which is the cult of a clique, too precious for general use, must be wanting in some quality. We know cases where obscurity of style has retarded the recognition of really great writers—but obscurity of style is not a virtue, and they were great in spite of it. Take the most honoured names in our literature, Scott, Thackeray, Dickens, Reade, Poe, they do not interest one or other social stratum, but they appeal equally to all educated readers. If you were to make a list of the works of fiction which have proved their greatness by their permanence and by the common consensus of mankind, you would find that no narrow formula would cover them. *Tom Jones, Don Quixote, Gulliver's Travels, Madame Bovary, Esmond, Pride and Prejudice, Notre Dame,* which shall we rule out as inartistic? And yet the only point which they have in common is that each of them holds the attention of every reader.

It is just this power of holding the attention which forms the art of story-telling—an art which may be developed and improved but cannot be imitated. It is the power of sympathy, the sense of the dramatic. There is no more capricious and indefinable quality. The professor in his study may have no trace of it, while the Irish nurse in the attic can draw out the very souls of his children with her words. It is imagination—and it is the power of conveying imagination. But we do not know what imagination is, and so all our definitions and explanations become mere juggling with words.

And still critics are found to write, 'The book is interesting, but we confess that we are unable to say what useful purpose it serves.' As if interest were not in itself the essential purpose! Ask the sleepless man worn with insomnia, the watcher beside the sick-bed, the man of business whose very sanity depends upon getting his thoughts out of one weary groove, the tired student, the woman whose only escape from an endless sordid life is that one window of imagination which leads out into the enchanted country—ask all these if interest serves any useful purpose. The life of a writer of fiction has its own troubles, the weary waiting for ideas, the blank reaction when they have been used, worst of all the despair when the thought which had seemed so bright and new goes dull and dark in the telling. But surely he has in return some claim to hope that if he can but interest his readers he fulfils the chief end of man in leaving others a little happier than he found them.

A. CONAN DOYLE

Undershaw, Hindhead

CONTENTS

Uncle Bernac

Exploits of Brigadier Gerard

Adventures of Gerard

The Great Shadow

UNCLE BERNAC

I. The Coast of France

I DARESAY that I had already read my uncle's letter a hundred times, and I am sure that I knew it by heart. None the less I took it out of my pocket, and, sitting on the side of the lugger, I went over it again with as much attention as if it were for the first time. It was written in a prim, angular hand, such as one might expect from a man who had begun life as a village attorney, and it was addressed to Louis de Laval, to the care of William Hargreaves, of the Green Man in Ashford, Kent. The landlord had many a hogshead of untaxed French brandy from the Normandy coast, and the letter had found its way by the same hands.

'MY DEAR NEPHEW LOUIS,' said the letter, 'now that your father is dead, and that you are alone in the world, I am sure that you will not wish to carry on the feud which has existed between the two halves of the family. At the time of the troubles your father was drawn towards the side of the King, and I towards that of the people, and it ended, as you know, by his having to fly from the country, and by my becoming the possessor of the estates of Grosbois. No doubt it is very hard that you should find yourself in a different position to your ancestors, but I am sure that you would rather that the land should be held by a Bernac than by a stranger. From the brother of your mother you will at least always meet with sympathy and consideration.

'And now I have some advice for you. You know that I have always been a Republican, but it has become evident to me that there is no use in fighting against fate, and that Napoleon's power is far too great to be shaken. This being so, I have tried to serve him, for it is well to howl when you are among wolves. I have been able to do so much for him that he has become my very good friend, so that I may ask him what I like in return. He is now, as

3

you are probably aware, with the army at Boulogne, within a few miles of Grosbois. If you will come over at once he will certainly forget the hostility of your father in consideration of the services of your uncle. It is true that your name is still proscribed, but my influence with the Emperor will set that matter right. Come to me, then, come at once, and come with confidence.

Your uncle,

C. BERNAC.'

So much for the letter, but it was the outside which had puzzled me most. A seal of red wax had been affixed at either end, and my uncle had apparently used his thumb as a signet. One could see the little rippling edges of a coarse skin imprinted upon the wax. And then above one of the seals there was written in English the two words, 'Don't come.' It was hastily scrawled, and whether by a man or a woman it was impossible to say; but there it stared me in the face, that sinister addition to an invitation.

'Don't come!' Had it been added by this unknown uncle of mine on account of some sudden change in his plans? Surely that was inconceivable, for why in that case should he send the invitation at all? Or was it placed there by some one else who wished to warn me from accepting this offer of hospitality? The letter was in French. The warning was in English. Could it have been added in England? But the seals were unbroken, and how could any one in England know what were the contents of the letter?

And then, as I sat there with the big sail humming like a shell above my head and the green water hissing beside me, I thought over all that I had heard of this uncle of mine. My father, the descendant of one of the proudest and oldest families in France, had chosen beauty and virtue rather than rank in his wife. Never for an hour had she given him cause to regret it; but this lawyer brother of hers had, as I understood, offended my father

4

by his slavish obsequiousness in days of prosperity and his venomous enmity in the days of trouble. He had hounded on the peasants until my family had been compelled to fly from the country, and had afterwards aided Robespierre in his worst excesses, receiving as a reward the castle and estate of Grosbois, which was our own. At the fall of Robespierre he had succeeded in conciliating Barras, and through every successive change he still managed to gain a fresh tenure of the property. Now it appeared from his letter that the new Emperor of France had also taken his part, though why he should befriend a man with such a history, and what service my Republican uncle could possibly render to him, were matters upon which I could form no opinion.

And now you will ask me, no doubt, why I should accept the invitation of such a man—a man whom my father had always stigmatised as a usurper and a traitor. It is easier to speak of it now than then, but the fact was that we of the new generation felt it very irksome and difficult to carry on the bitter quarrels of the past. To the older *émigrés* the clock of time seemed to have stopped in the year 1792, and they remained for ever with the loves and the hatreds of that era fixed indelibly upon their souls. They had been burned into them by the fiery furnace through which they had passed. But we, who had grown up upon a strange soil, understood that the world had moved, and that new issues had arisen. We were inclined to forget these feuds of the last generation. France to us was no longer the murderous land of the *sans-culotte* and the guillotine basket; it was rather the glorious queen of war, attacked by all and conquering all, but still so hard pressed that her scattered sons could hear her call to arms for ever sounding in their ears. It was that call more than my uncle's letter which was taking me over the waters of the Channel.

For long my heart had been with my country in her struggle, and yet while my father lived I had never dared to say so; for to him, who had served under Condé and fought at Quiberon, it would have seemed the blackest treason. But after his death there was no reason why I should not return to the land of my birth, and my desire was the stronger because Eugénie—the same Eugénie who has been thirty years my wife—was of the same way of thinking as myself. Her parents were a branch of the de Choiseuls, and their prejudices were even stronger than those of my father. Little did they think what was passing in the minds of their children. Many a time when they were mourning a French victory in the parlour we were both capering with joy in the garden. There was a little window, all choked round with laurel bushes, in the corner of the bare brick house, and there we used to meet at night, the dearer to each other from our difference with all who surrounded us. I would tell her my ambitions; she would strengthen them by her enthusiasm. And so all was ready when the time came.

But there was another reason besides the death of my father and the receipt of this letter from my uncle. Ashford was becoming too hot to hold me. I will say this for the English, that they were very generous hosts to the French emigrants. There was not one of us who did not carry away a kindly remembrance of the land and its people. But in every country there are overbearing, swaggering folk, and even in quiet, sleepy Ashford we were plagued by them. There was one young Kentish squire, Farley was his name, who had earned a reputation in the town as a bully and a roisterer. He could not meet one of us without uttering insults not merely against the present French Government, which might have been excusable in an English patriot, but against France itself and all Frenchmen. Often we were forced to be deaf in his presence, but at last his conduct became so intolerable that I determined to teach him a lesson. There were several of us in the coffee-room at the Green Man one evening, and he, full of wine and malice, was heaping insults upon the French, his eyes creeping round to me

6

every moment to see how I was taking it. 'Now, Monsieur de Laval,' he cried, putting his rude hand upon my shoulder, 'here is a toast for you to drink. This is to the arm of Nelson which strikes down the French.' He stood leering at me to see if I would drink it. 'Well, sir,' said I, 'I will drink your toast if you will drink mine in return.' 'Come on, then!' said he. So we drank. 'Now, Monsieur, let us have your toast,' said he. 'Fill your glass, then,' said I. 'It is full now.' 'Well, then, here's to the cannon-ball which carried off that arm!' In an instant I had a glass of port wine running down my face, and within an hour a meeting had been arranged. I shot him through the shoulder, and that night, when I came to the little window, Eugénie plucked off some of the laurel leaves and stuck them in my hair.

There were no legal proceedings about the duel, but it made my position a little difficult in the town, and it will explain, with other things, why I had no hesitation in accepting my unknown uncle's invitation, in spite of the singular addition which I found upon the cover. If he had indeed sufficient influence with the Emperor to remove the proscription which was attached to our name, then the only barrier which shut me off from my country would be demolished.

You must picture me all this time as sitting upon the side of the lugger and turning my prospects and my position over in my head. My reverie was interrupted by the heavy hand of the English skipper dropping abruptly upon my arm.

'Now then, master,' said he, 'it's time you were stepping into the dingey.'

I do not inherit the politics of the aristocrats, but I have never lost their sense of personal dignity. I gently pushed away his polluting hand, and I remarked that we were still a long way from the shore.

'Well, you can do as you please,' said he roughly; 'I'm going no nearer, so you can take your choice of getting into the dingey or of swimming for it.'

It was in vain that I pleaded that he had been paid his price. I did not add that that price meant that the watch which had belonged to three generations of de Lavals was now lying in the shop of a Dover goldsmith.

'Little enough, too!' he cried harshly. 'Down sail, Jim, and bring her to! Now, master, you can step over the side, or you can come back to Dover, but I don't take the *Vixen* a cable's length nearer to Ambleteuse Reef with this gale coming up from the sou'-west.'

'In that case I shall go,' said I.

'You can lay your life on that!' he answered, and laughed in so irritating a fashion that I half turned upon him with the intention of chastising him. One is very helpless with these fellows, however, for a serious affair is of course out of the question, while if one uses a cane upon them they have a vile habit of striking with their hands, which gives them an advantage. The Marquis de Chamfort told me that, when he first settled in Sutton at the time of the emigration, he lost a tooth when reproving an unruly peasant. I made the best of a necessity, therefore, and, shrugging my shoulders, I passed over the side of the lugger into the little boat. My bundle was dropped in after me—conceive to yourself the heir of all the de Lavals travelling with a single bundle for his baggage!—and two seamen pushed her off, pulling with long slow strokes towards the low-lying shore.

There was certainly every promise of a wild night, for the dark cloud which had rolled up over the setting sun was now frayed and ragged at the edges, extending a good third of the way across the heavens. It had split low down near the horizon, and the crimson glare of the sunset beat through the gap, so that there was the appearance of fire with a monstrous reek of smoke. A red dancing belt of light lay across the broad slate-coloured ocean, and in the centre of it the little black craft was wallowing and tumbling. The two seamen kept looking up at the heavens, and then over their shoulders at the land, and I feared every moment that they would put

8

back before the gale burst. I was filled with apprehension every time when the end of their pull turned their faces skyward, and it was to draw their attention away from the storm-drift that I asked them what the lights were which had begun to twinkle through the dusk both to the right and to the left of us.

'That's Boulogne to the north, and Etaples upon the south,' said one of the seamen civilly.

Boulogne! Etaples! How the words came back to me! It was to Boulogne that in my boyhood we had gone down for the summer bathing. Could I not remember as a little lad trotting along by my father's side as he paced the beach, and wondering why every fisherman's cap flew off at our approach? And as to Etaples, it was thence that we had fled for England, when the folks came raving to the pier-head as we passed, and I joined my thin voice to my father's as he shrieked back at them, for a stone had broken my mother's knee, and we were all frenzied with our fear and our hatred. And here they were, these places of my childhood, twinkling to the north and south of me, while there, in the darkness between them, and only ten miles off at the furthest, lay my own castle, my own land of Grosbois, where the men of my blood had lived and died long before some of us had gone across with Duke William to conquer the proud island over the water. How I strained my eager eyes through the darkness as I thought that the distant black keep of our fortalice might even now be visible!

'Yes, sir,' said the seaman, ' 'tis a fine stretch of lonesome coast, and many is the cock of your hackle that I have helped ashore there.'

'What do you take me for, then?' I asked.

'Well, 'tis no business of mine, sir,' he answered. 'There are some trades that had best not even be spoken about.'

'You think that I am a conspirator?'

'Well, master, since you have put a name to it. Lor' love you, sir, we're used to it.'

'I give you my word that I am none.'

'An escaped prisoner, then?'

'No, nor that either.'

The man leaned upon his oar, and I could see in the gloom that his face was thrust forward, and that it was wrinkled with suspicion.

'If you're one of Boney's spies——' he cried.

'I! A spy?' The tone of my voice was enough to convince him.

'Well,' said he, 'I'm darned if I know what you are. But if you'd been a spy I'd ha' had no hand in landing you, whatever the skipper might say.'

'Mind you, I've no word to say aginst Boney,' said the other seaman, speaking in a very thick rumbling voice. 'He's been a rare good friend to the poor mariner.'

It surprised me to hear him speak so, for the virulence of feeling against the new French Emperor in England exceeded all belief, and high and low were united in their hatred of him; but the sailor soon gave me a clew to his politics.

'If the poor mariner can run in his little bit of coffee and sugar, and run out his silk and his brandy, he has Boney to thank for it,' said he. 'The merchants have had their spell, and now it's the turn of the poor mariner.'

I remembered then that Buonaparte was personally very popular amongst the smugglers, as well he might be, seeing that he had made over into their hands all the trade of the Channel. The seaman continued to pull with his left hand, but he pointed with his right over the slate-coloured dancing waters.

'There's Boney himself,' said he.

You who live in a quieter age cannot conceive the thrill which these simple words sent through me. It was but ten years since we had first heard of this man with the curious Italian name—think of it, ten years, the time that it takes for a private to become a non-commissioned officer, or a clerk to win a fifty-pound advance in his salary. He had sprung in an instant out of nothing into everything. One month people were asking who he was, the next he had broken out in the north of Italy like the plague; Venice and Genoa withered at the touch of this swarthy ill-nourished boy. He cowed the soldiers in the field, and he outwitted the statesmen in the council chamber. With a frenzy of energy he rushed to the east, and then, while men were still marvelling at the way in which he had converted Egypt into a French department, he was back again in Italy and had beaten Austria for the second time to the earth. He travelled as quickly as the rumour of his coming; and where he came there were new victories, new combinations, the crackling of old systems and the blurring of ancient lines of frontier. Holland, Savoy, Switzerland—they were become mere names upon the map. France was eating into Europe in every direction. They had made him Emperor, this beardless artillery officer, and without an effort he had crushed down those Republicans before whom the oldest king and the proudest nobility of Europe had been helpless. So it came about that we, who watched him dart from place to place like the shuttle of destiny, and who heard his name always in connection with some new achievement and some new success, had come at last to look upon him as something more than human, something monstrous, overshadowing France and menacing Europe. His giant presence loomed over the continent, and so deep was the impression which his fame had made in my mind that, when the English sailor pointed confidently over the darkening waters, and cried, 'There's Boney!' I looked up for the instant with a foolish expectation of seeing some gigantic figure, some elemental creature, dark, inchoate, and threatening, brooding over the waters of the Channel. Even now, after the long gap of years and the knowledge of his downfall, that great man casts his spell upon you, but all that you read and all that you hear cannot give you an idea of what his name meant in the days when he was at the summit of his career.

What actually met my eye was very different from this childish expectation of mine. To the north there was a long low cape, the name of which has now escaped me. In the evening light it had been of the same greyish green tint as the other headlands; but now, as the darkness fell, it gradually broke into a dull glow, like a cooling iron. On that wild night, seen and lost with the heave and sweep of the boat, this lurid streak carried with it a vague but sinister suggestion. The red line splitting the darkness might have been a giant half-forged sword-blade with its point towards England.

'What is it, then?' I asked.

'Just what I say, master,' said he. 'It's one of Boney's armies, with Boney himself in the middle of it as like as not. Them is their camp fires, and you'll see a dozen such between this and Ostend. He's audacious enough to come across, is little Boney, if he could dowse Lord Nelson's other eye; but there's no chance for him until then, and well he knows it.'

'How can Lord Nelson know what he is doing?' I asked.

The man pointed out over my shoulder into the darkness, and far on the horizon I perceived three little twinkling lights.

'Watch dog,' said he, in his husky voice.

'*Andromeda*. Forty-four,' added his companion.

I have often thought of them since, the long glow upon the land, and the three little lights upon the sea, standing for so much, for the two great rivals face to face, for the power of the land and the power of the water, for the centuries-old battle, which may last for centuries to come. And yet, Frenchman as I am, do I not know that the struggle is already decided?—for it lies between the childless nation and that which has a lusty young brood springing up around her. If France falls she dies, but if England falls how many nations are there who will carry her speech, her traditions and her blood on into the history of the future?

The land had been looming darker, and the thudding

of the waves upon the sand sounded louder every instant upon my ears. I could already see the quick dancing gleam of the surf in front of me. Suddenly, as I peered through the deepening shadow, a long dark boat shot out from it, like a trout from under a stone, making straight in our direction.

'A guard boat!' cried one of the seamen.

'Bill, boy, we're done!' said the other, and began to stuff something into his sea-boot.

But the boat swerved at the sight of us, like a shying horse, and was off in another direction as fast as eight frantic oars could drive her. The seamen stared after her and wiped their brows. 'Her conscience don't seem much easier than our own,' said one of them. 'I made sure it was the preventives.'

'Looks to me as if you weren't the only queer cargo on the coast to-night, mister,' remarked his comrade. 'What could she be?'

'Cursed if I know what she was. I rammed a cake of good Trinidad tobacco into my boot when I saw her. I've seen the inside of a French prison before now. Give way, Bill, and have it over.'

A minute later, with a low grating sound, we ran aground upon a gravelly beach. My bundle was thrown ashore, I stepped after it, and a seaman pushed the prow off again, springing in as his comrade backed her into deep water. Already the glow in the west had vanished, the storm-cloud was half up the heavens, and a thick blackness had gathered over the ocean. As I turned to watch the vanishing boat a keen wet blast flapped in my face, and the air was filled with the high piping of the wind and with the deep thunder of the sea.

And thus it was that, on a wild evening in the early spring of the year 1805, I, Louis de Laval, being in the twenty-first year of my age, returned, after an exile of thirteen years, to the country of which my family had for many centuries been the ornament and support. She had treated us badly, this country; she had repaid our

13

services by insult, exile, and confiscation. But all that was forgotten as I, the only de Laval of the new generation, dropped upon my knees upon her sacred soil, and, with the strong smell of the seaweed in my nostrils, pressed my lips upon the gravel.

II. The Salt-Marsh

WHEN a man has reached his mature age he can rest at that point of vantage, and cast his eyes back at the long road along which he has travelled, lying with its gleams of sunshine and its stretches of shadow in the valley behind him. He knows then its whence and its whither, and the twists and bends which were so full of promise or of menace as he approached them lie exposed and open to his gaze. So plain is it all that he can scarce remember how dark it may have seemed to him, or how long he once hesitated at the cross roads. Thus when he tries to recall each stage of the journey he does so with the knowledge of its end, and can no longer make it clear, even to himself, how it may have seemed to him at the time. And yet, in spite of the strain of years, and the many passages which have befallen me since, there is no time of my life which comes back so very clearly as that gusty evening, and to this day I cannot feel the briny wholesome whiff of the seaweed without being carried back, with that intimate feeling of reality which only the sense of smell can confer, to the wet shingle of the French beach.

When I had risen from my knees, the first thing that I did was to put my purse into the inner pocket of my coat. I had taken it out in order to give a gold piece to the sailor who had handed me ashore, though I have little doubt that the fellow was both wealthier and of more assured prospects than myself. I had actually drawn out a silver half-crown, but I could not bring myself to offer it to him, and so ended by giving a tenth part of my whole fortune to a stranger. The other nine sovereigns I put very carefully away, and then, sitting down upon a flat rock just above high-water mark, I turned it all over in my mind and weighed what I should do. Already I was cold and hungry, with the wind lashing my face and the spray smarting in my eyes, but at least I was no longer living upon the charity of the enemies of my country, and the thought set my heart dancing within me. But the castle, as well as I could remember, was a good ten miles off. To go there now was to arrive at an unseemly hour, unkempt and weather-stained, before this uncle whom I had never seen. My sensitive pride conjured up a picture of the scornful faces of his servants as they looked out upon this bedraggled wanderer from England slinking back to the castle which should have been his own. No, I must seek shelter for the night, and then at my leisure, with as fair a show of appearances as possible, I must present myself before my relative. Where then could I find a refuge from the storm?

You will ask me, doubtless, why I did not make for Etaples or Boulogne. I answer that it was for the same reason which forced me to land secretly upon that forbidding coast. The name of de Laval still headed the list of the proscribed, for my father had been a famous and energetic leader of the small but influential body of men who had remained true at all costs to the old order of things. Do not think that, because I was of another way of thinking, I despised those who had given up so much for their principles. There is a curious saint-like trait in our natures which draws us most strongly towards that which involves the greatest sacrifice, and I have sometimes thought that if the conditions had been less onerous the Bourbons might have had fewer, or at least less noble, followers. The French nobles had been more faithful to them than the English to the Stuarts, for Cromwell had no luxurious court or rich appointments which he could hold out to those who would desert the royal cause. No words can exaggerate the self-abnegation of those men. I have seen a supper party under my father's roof where our guests were two fencing-masters, three professors of language, one ornamental gardener, and one translator of books, who held his hand in the front of his coat to conceal a rent in the lapel. But these eight men were of the highest nobility of France, who might have had what they chose to ask if they would only consent to forget the past, and to throw themselves heartily into the new order of things. But the humble, and what is sadder the incapable, monarch of Hartwell still held the allegiance of those old Montmorencies, Rohuns, and Choiseuls, who, having shared the greatness of his family, were determined also to stand by it in its ruin. The dark chambers of that exiled monarch were furnished with something better than the tapestry of Gobelins or the china of Sèvres. Across the gulf which separates my old age from theirs I can still see those ill-clad, grave-mannered men, and I raise my hat to the noblest group of nobles that our history can show.

To visit a coast-town, therefore, before I had seen my uncle, or learnt whether my return had been sanctioned, would be simply to deliver myself into the hands of the *gens d'armes*, who were ever on the look-out for strangers from England. To go before the new Emperor was one thing and to be dragged before him another. On the whole, it seemed to me that my best course was to wander inland, in the hope of finding some empty barn or outhouse, where I could pass the night unseen and undisturbed. Then in the morning I should consider how it was best for me to approach my Uncle Bernac, and through him the new master of France.

The wind had freshened meanwhile into a gale, and it was so dark upon the seaward side that I could only catch the white flash of a leaping wave here and there in the blackness. Of the lugger which had brought me from Dover I could see no sign. On the land side of me there seemed, as far as I could make it out, to be a line of low hills, but when I came to traverse them I found that the dim light had exaggerated their size, and that they were mere scattered sand-dunes, mottled with patches of bramble. Over these I toiled with my bundle slung over my shoulder, plodding heavily through the loose sand, and tripping over the creepers, but forgetting my wet clothes and my numb hands as I recalled the many hardships and adventures which my ancestors had undergone. It amused me to think that the day might come when my own descendants might fortify themselves by the recollection of that which was happening to me, for in a great family like ours the individual is always subordinate to the race.

It seemed to me that I should never get to the end of the sand-dunes, but when at last I did come off them I heartily wished that I was back upon them again; for the sea in that part comes by some creek up the back of the beach, forming at low tide a great desolate salt-marsh, which must be a forlorn place even in the daytime, but upon such a night as that it was a most dreary wilderness. At first it was but a softness of the ground, causing me to slip as I walked, but soon the mud was over my ankles and half-way up to my knees, so that each foot gave a loud flop as I raised it, and a dull splash as I set it down again. I would willingly have made my way out, even if I had to return to the sand-dunes, but in trying to pick my path I had lost all my bearings, and the air was so full of the sounds of the storm that the sea seemed to be on every side of me. I had heard of how one may steer oneself by observation of the stars, but my quiet English life had not taught me how such things were done, and had I known I could scarcely have profited by it, since the few stars which were visible peeped out here and there in the rifts of the flying storm-clouds. I wandered on then, wet and weary, trusting to fortune, but always blundering deeper and deeper into this horrible bog, until I began to think that my first night in France was destined also to be my last, and that the heir of the de Lavals was destined to perish of cold and misery in the depths of this obscene morass.

I must have toiled for many miles in this dreary fashion, sometimes coming upon shallower mud and sometimes upon deeper, but never making my way on to the dry, when I perceived through the gloom something which turned my heart even heavier than it had been before. This was a curious clump of some whitish shrub—cotton-grass of a flowering variety—which glimmered suddenly before me in the darkness. Now, an hour earlier I had passed just such a square-headed, whitish clump; so that I was confirmed in the opinion which I had already begun to form, that I was wandering in a circle. To make it certain I stooped down, striking a momentary flash from my tinder-box, and there sure enough was my own old track very clearly marked in the brown mud in front of me. At this confirmation of my worst fears I threw my eyes up to heaven in my despair, and there I saw something which for the first time gave me a clew in the uncertainty which surrounded me.

It was nothing else than a glimpse of the moon between two flowing clouds. This in itself might have been of small avail to me, but over its white face was marked a long thin V, which shot swiftly across like a shaftless arrow. It was a flock of wild ducks, and its flight was in the same direction as that towards which my face was turned. Now, I had observed in Kent how all these creatures come further inland when there is rough weather breaking, so I made no doubt that their course indicated the path which would lead me away from the sea. I struggled on, therefore, taking every precaution to walk in a straight line, above all being very careful to make a stride of equal length with either leg, until at last, after half an hour or so, my perseverance was rewarded by the welcome sight of a little yellow light, as from a cottage window, glimmering through the darkness. Ah, how it shone through my eyes and down into my heart, glowing and twinkling there, that little golden speck, which meant food, and rest, and life itself to the wanderer! I blundered towards it through the mud and the slush as fast as my weary legs would bear me. I was too cold and miserable to refuse any shelter, and I had no doubt that for the sake of one of my gold pieces the fisherman or peasant who lived in this strange situation would shut his eyes to whatever might be suspicious in my presence or appearance.

As I approached it became more and more wonderful to me any one should live there at all, for the bog grew worse rather than better, and in the occasional gleams of moonshine I could make out that the water lay in glimmering pools all round the low dark cottage from which the light was breaking. I could see now that it shone through a small square window. As I approached the gleam was suddenly obscured, and there in a yellow frame appeared the round black outline of a man's head peering out into the darkness. A second time it appeared before I reached the cottage, and there was something in the stealthy manner in which it peeped and whisked away, and peeped once more, which filled me with surprise, and with a certain vague apprehension.

So cautious were the movements of this sentinel, and so singular the position of his watch-house, that I determined, in spite of my misery, to see something more of him before I trusted myself to the shelter of his roof. And, indeed, the amount of shelter which I might hope for was not very great, for as I drew softly nearer I could see that the light from within was beating through at several points, and that the whole cottage was in the most crazy state of disrepair. For a moment I paused, thinking that even the salt-marsh might perhaps be a safer resting-place for the night than the headquarters of some desperate smuggler, for such I conjectured that this lonely dwelling must be. The scud, however, had covered the moon once more, and the darkness was so pitchy black that I felt that I might reconnoitre a little more closely without fear of discovery. Walking on tiptoe I approached the little window and looked in.

What I saw reassured me vastly. A small wood fire was crackling in one of those old-fashioned country grates, and beside it was seated a strikingly handsome young man, who was reading earnestly out of a fat little book. He had an oval, olive-tinted face, with long black hair, ungathered in a queue, and there was something of the poet or of the artist in his whole appearance. The sight of that refined face, and of the warm yellow firelight which beat upon it, was a very cheering one to a cold and famished traveller. I stood for an instant gazing at him, and noticing the way in which his full and somewhat loose-fitting lower lip quivered continually, as if he were repeating to himself that which he was reading, I was still looking at him when he put his book down upon the table and approached the window. Catching a glimpse of my figure in the darkness he called out something which I could not hear, and waved his hand in a gesture of welcome. An instant later the door flew open, and there was his thin tall figure standing upon the threshold, with his skirts flapping in the wind.

'My dear friends,' he cried, peering out into the gloom with his hand over his eyes to screen them from the salt-laden wind and driving sand, 'I had given you up. I thought that you were never coming. I've been waiting for two hours.'

For answer I stepped out in front of him, so that the light fell upon my face.

'I am afraid, sir——' said I.

But I had no time to finish my sentence. He struck at me with both hands like an angry cat, and, springing back into the room, he slammed the door with a crash in my face.

The swiftness of his movements and the malignity of his gesture were in such singular contrast with his appearance that I was struck speechless with surprise. But as I stood there with the door in front of me I was a witness to something which filled me with even greater astonishment.

I have already said that the cottage was in the last stage of disrepair. Amidst the many seams and cracks through which the light was breaking there was one along the whole of the hinge side of the door, which gave me from where I was standing a view of the further end of the room, at which the fire was burning. As I gazed then I saw this man reappear in front of the fire, fumbling furiously with both his hands in his bosom, and then with a spring he disappeared up the chimney, so that I could only see his shoes and half of his black calves as he stood upon the brickwork at the side of the grate. In an instant he was down again and back at the door.

'Who are you?' he cried, in a voice which seemed to me to be thrilling with some strong emotion.

'I am a traveller, and have lost my way.'

There was a pause as if he were thinking what course he should pursue.

'You will find little here to tempt you to stay,' said he at last.

'I am weary and spent, sir; and surely you will not refuse me shelter. I have been wandering for hours in the salt-marsh.'

'Did you meet any one there?' he asked eagerly.

'No.'

'Stand back a little from the door. This is a wild place, and the times are troublous. A man must take some precautions.'

I took a few steps back, and he then opened the door sufficiently to allow his head to come through. He said nothing, but he looked at me for a long time in a very searching manner.

'What is your name?'

'Louis Laval,' said I, thinking that it might sound less dangerous in this plebeian form.

'Whither are you going?'

'I wish to reach some shelter.'

'You are from England?'

'I am from the coast.'

He shook his head slowly to show me how little my replies had satisfied him.

'You cannot come in here,' said he.

'But surely——'

'No, no, it is impossible.'

'Show me then how to find my way out of the marsh.'

'It is easy enough. If you go a few hundred paces in that direction you will perceive the lights of a village. You are already almost free of the marsh.'

He stepped a pace or two from the door in order to point the way for me, and then turned upon his heel. I had already taken a stride or two away from him and his inhospitable hut, when he suddenly called after me.

'Come, Monsieur Laval,' said he, with quite a different ring in his voice; 'I really cannot permit you to leave me upon so tempestuous a night. A warm by my fire and a glass of brandy will hearten you upon your way.'

You may think that I did not feel disposed to contradict him, though I could make nothing of this sudden and welcome change in his manner.

'I am much obliged to you, sir,' said I.

And I followed him into the hut.

III. *The Ruined Cottage*

IT was delightful to see the glow and twinkle of the fire and to escape from the wet wind and the numbing cold, but my curiosity had already risen so high about this lonely man and his singular dwelling that my thoughts ran rather upon that than upon my personal comfort. There was his remarkable appearance, the fact that he should be awaiting company within that miserable ruin in the heart of the morass at so sinister an hour, and finally the inexplicable incident of the chimney, all of which excited my imagination. It was beyond my comprehension why he should at one moment charge me sternly to continue my journey, and then, in almost the same breath, invite me most cordially to seek the shelter of his hut. On all these points I was keenly on the alert for an explanation. Yet I endeavoured to conceal my feelings, and to assume the air of a man who finds everything quite natural about him, and who is much too absorbed in his own personal wants to have a thought to spare upon anything outside himself.

A glance at the inside of the cottage, as I entered, confirmed me in the conjecture which the appearance of the outside had already given rise to, that it was not used for human residence, and that this man was only here for a rendezvous. Prolonged moisture had peeled the plaster in flakes from the walls, and had covered the stones with blotches and rosettes of lichen. The whole place was rotten and scaling like a leper. The single large room was unfurnished save for a crazy table, three wooden boxes, which might be used as seats, and a great pile of decayed fishing-net in the corner. The splinters of a fourth box, with a hand-axe, which leaned against the wall, showed how the wood for the fire had been gathered. But it was to the table that my gaze was chiefly drawn, for there, beside the lamp and the book, lay an open basket, from which projected the knuckle-end of a ham, the corner of a loaf of bread, and the black neck of a bottle.

If my host had been suspicious and cold at our first meeting he was now atoning for his inhospitality by an overdone cordiality even harder for me to explain. With many lamentations over my mud-stained and sodden condition, he drew a box close to the blaze and cut me off a corner of the bread and ham. I could not help observing, however, that though his loose under-lipped mouth was wreathed with smiles, his beautiful dark eyes were continually running over me and my attire, asking and re-asking what my business might be.

'As for myself,' said he, with an air of false candour, 'you will very well understand that in these days a worthy merchant must do the best he can to get his wares, and if the Emperor, God save him, sees fit in his wisdom to put an end to open trade, one must come to such places as these to get into touch with those who bring across the coffee and the tobacco. I promise you that in the Tuileries itself there is no difficulty about getting either one or the other, and the Emperor drinks his ten cups a day of the real Mocha without asking questions, though he must know that it is not grown within the confines of France. The vegetable kingdom still remains one of the few which Napoleon has not yet conquered, and, if it were not for traders, who are at some risk and inconvenience, it is hard to say what we should do for our supplies. I suppose, sir, that you are not yourself either in the seafaring or in the trading line?'

I contented myself by answering that I was not, by which reticence I could see that I only excited his curiosity the more. As to his account of himself, I read a lie in those tell-tale eyes all the time that he was talking. As I looked at him now in the full light of the lamp and the fire, I could see that he was even more good-looking than I had at first thought, but with a type of beauty which has never been to my taste. His features were so refined as to be almost effeminate, and so regular that they would have been perfect if it had not been for that ill-fitting, slabbing mouth. It was a clever, and yet it was a weak face, full of a sort of fickle enthusiasm and feeble impulsiveness. I felt that the more I knew him the less reason I should probably find either to like him or to fear him, and in my first conclusion I was right, although I had occasion to change my views upon the second.

'You will forgive me, Monsieur Laval, if I was a little cold at first,' said he. 'Since the Emperor has been upon the coast the place swarms with police agents, so that a trader must look to his own interests. You will allow that my fears of you were not unnatural, since neither your dress nor your appearance were such as one would expect to meet with in such a place and at such a time.'

It was on my lips to return the remark, but I refrained. 'I can assure you,' said I, 'that I am merely a traveller who have lost my way. Now that I am refreshed and rested I will not encroach further upon your hospitality, except to ask you to point out the way to the nearest village.'

'Tut; you had best stay where you are, for the night grows wilder every instant.' As he spoke there came a whoop and scream of wind in the chimney, as if the old place were coming down about our ears. He walked across to the window and looked very earnestly out of it, just as I had seen him do upon my first approach. 'The fact is, Monsieur Laval,' said he, looking round at me with his false air of good fellowship, 'you may be of some good service to me if you will wait here for half an hour or so.'

'How so?' I asked, wavering between my distrust and my curiosity.

'Well, to be frank with you'—and never did a man look less frank as he spoke—'I am waiting here for some of those people with whom I do business; but in some way they have not come yet, and I am inclined to take a walk round the marsh on the chance of finding them, if they have lost their way. On the other hand, it would be exceedingly awkward for me if they were to come here in my absence and imagine that I am gone. I should take it as a favour, then, if you would remain here for half an hour or so, that you may tell them how matters stand if I should chance to miss them.'

The request seemed reasonable enough, and yet there was that same oblique glance which told me that it was false. Still, I could not see what harm could come to me by complying with his request, and certainly I could not have devised any arrangement which would give me such an opportunity of satisfying my curiosity. What was in that wide stone chimney, and why had he clambered up there upon the sight of me? My adventure would be inconclusive indeed if I did not settle that point before I went on with my journey.

'Well,' said he, snatching up his black broad-brimmed hat and running very briskly to the door, 'I am sure that you will not refuse me my request, and I must delay no longer or I shall never get my business finished.' He closed the door hurriedly behind him, and I heard the splashing of his footsteps until they were lost in the howling of the gale.

And so the mysterious cottage was mine to ransack if I could pluck its secrets from it. I lifted the book which had been left upon the table. It was Rousseau's *Social Contract*—excellent literature, but hardly what one would expect a trader to carry with him whilst awaiting an appointment with smugglers. On the fly-leaf was written 'Lucien Lesage,' and beneath it, in a woman's hand, 'Lucien, from Sibylle.' Lesage, then, was the name of my good-looking but sinister acquaintance. It only remained for me now to discover what it was which he had concealed up the chimney. I listened intently, and as there was no sound from without save the cry of the storm, I stepped on to the edge of the grate as I had seen him do, and sprang up by the side of the fire.

It was a very broad, old-fashioned cottage chimney, so that standing on one side I was not inconvenienced either by the heat or by the smoke, and the bright glare from below showed me in an instant that for which I sought. There was a recess at the back, caused by the fall or removal of one of the stones, and in this was lying a small bundle. There could not be the least doubt that it was this which the fellow had striven so frantically to conceal upon the first alarm of the approach of a stranger. I took it down and held it to the light.

It was a small square of yellow glazed cloth tied round with white tape. Upon my opening it a number of letters appeared, and a single large paper folded up. The addresses upon the letters took my breath away. The first that I glanced at was to Citizen Talleyrand. The others were in the Republican style addressed to Citizen Fouché, to Citizen Soult, to Citizen MacDonald, to Citizen Berthier, and so on through the whole list of famous names in war and in diplomacy who were the pillars of the new Empire. What in the world could this pretended merchant of coffee have to write to all these great notables about? The other paper would explain, no doubt. I laid the letters upon the shelf and I unfolded the paper which had been enclosed with them. It did not take more than the opening sentence to convince me that the salt-marsh outside might prove to be a very much safer place than this accursed cottage.

These were the words which met my eyes:

'Fellow-citizens of France. The deed of to-day has proved that, even in the midst of his troops, a tyrant is unable to escape the vengeance of an outraged people. The committee of three, acting temporarily for the Republic, has awarded to Buonaparte the same fate which has already befallen Louis Capet. In avenging the outrage of the 18th Brumaire——'

So far I had got when my heart sprang suddenly into my mouth and the paper fluttered down from my fingers. A grip of iron had closed suddenly round each of my ankles, and there in the light of the fire I saw two hands which, even in that terrified glance, I perceived to be covered with black hair and of an enormous size.

'So, my friend,' cried a thundering voice, 'this time, at least, we have been too many for you.'

IV. Men of the Night

I HAD little time given me to realise the extraordinary and humiliating position in which I found myself, for I was lifted up by my ankles, as if I were a fowl pulled off a perch, and jerked roughly down into the room, my back striking upon the stone floor with a thud which shook the breath from my body.

'Don't kill him yet, Toussac,' said a soft voice. 'Let us make sure who he is first.'

I felt the pressure of a thumb upon my chin and of fingers upon my throat, and my head was slowly forced round until the strain became unbearable.

'Quarter of an inch does it and no mark,' said the thunderous voice. 'You can trust my old turn.'

'Don't, Toussac; don't!' said the same gentle voice which had spoken first. 'I saw you do it once before, and the horrible snick that it made haunted me for a long time. To think that the sacred flame of life can be so readily snuffed out by that great material finger and thumb! Mind can indeed conquer matter, but the fighting must not be at close quarters.'

My neck was so twisted that I could not see any of these people who were discussing my fate. I could only lie and listen.

'The fact remains, my dear Charles, that the fellow has our all-important secret, and that it is our lives or his.' I recognised in the voice which was now speaking that of the man of the cottage. 'We owe it to ourselves to put it out of his power to harm us. Let him sit up, Toussac, for there is no possibility of his escaping.'

Some irresistible force at the back of my neck dragged me instantly into a sitting position, and so for the first time I was able to look round me in a dazed fashion, and to see these men into whose hands I had fallen. That they were murderers in the past and had murderous plans for the future I already gathered from what I had heard and seen. I understood also that in the heart of that lonely marsh I was absolutely in their power. None the less, I remembered the name that I bore, and I concealed as far as I could the sickening terror which lay at my heart.

There were three of them in my room, my former acquaintance and two new comers. Lesage stood by the table, with his fat brown book in his hand, looking at me with a composed face, but with that humorous questioning twinkle in his eyes which a master chess-player might assume when he had left his opponent without a move. On the top of the box beside him sat a very ascetic-faced, yellow, hollow-eyed man of fifty, with prim lips and a shrunken skin, which hung loosely over the long jerking tendons under his prominent chin. He was dressed in snuff-coloured clothes, and his legs under his knee-breeches were of a ludicrous thinness. He shook his head at me with an air of sad wisdom, and I could read little comfort in his inhuman grey eyes. But it was the man called Toussac who alarmed me most. He was a colossus; bulky rather than tall, but misshapen from his excess of muscle. His huge legs were crooked like those of a great ape; and, indeed, there was something animal about his whole appearance, for he was bearded up to his eyes, and it was a paw rather than a hand which still clutched me by the collar. As to his expression, he was too thatched with hair to show one, but his large black eyes looked with a sinister questioning from me to the others. If they were the judge and jury, it was clear who was to be executioner.

'Whence did he come? What is his business? How came he to know the hiding-place?' asked the thin man.

'When he first came I mistook him for you in the darkness,' Lesage answered. 'You will acknowledge that it was not a night on which one would expect to meet many people in the salt-marsh. On discovering my mistake I shut the door and concealed the papers in the chimney. I had forgotten that he might see me do this through that crack by the hinges, but when I went out again, to show him his way and so get rid of him, my eye caught the gap, and I at once realised that he had seen my action, and that it must have aroused his curiosity to such an extent that it would be quite certain that he would think and speak of it. I called him back into the hut, therefore, in order that I might have time to consider what I had best do with him.'

'Sapristi! a couple of cuts of that wood-axe, and a bed in the softest corner of the marsh, would have settled the business at once,' said the fellow by my side.

'Quite true, my good Toussac; but it is not usual to lead off with your ace of trumps. A little delicacy—a little finesse——'

'Let us hear what you did then?'

'It was my first object to learn whether this man Laval——'

'What did you say his name was?' cried the thin man.

'His name, according to his account, is Laval. My first object then was to find out whether he had in truth seen me conceal the papers or not. It was an important question for us, and, as things have turned out, more important still for him. I made my little plan, therefore. I waited until I saw you approach, and I then left him alone in the hut. I watched through the window and saw him fly to the hiding-place. We then entered, and I asked you, Toussac, to be good enough to lift him down—and there he lies.'

The young fellow looked proudly round for the applause of his comrades, and the thin man clapped his hands softly together, looking very hard at me while he did so.

'My dear Lesage,' said he, 'you have certainly excelled yourself. When our new republic looks for its minister of police we shall know where to find him. I confess that when, after guiding Toussac to this shelter, I followed you in and perceived a gentleman's legs projecting from the fireplace, even my wits, which are usually none of the slowest, hardly grasped the situation. Toussac, however, grasped the legs. He is always practical, the good Toussac.'

'Enough words!' growled the hairy creature beside me. 'It is because we have talked instead of acting that this Buonaparte has a crown upon his head or a head upon his shoulders. Let us have done with the fellow and come to business.'

The refined features of Lesage made me look towards him as to a possible protector, but his large dark eyes were as cold and hard as jet as he looked back at me.

'What Toussac says is right,' said he. 'We imperil our own safety if he goes with our secret.'

'The devil take our own safety!' cried Toussac. 'What has that to do with the matter? We imperil the success of our plans—that is of more importance.'

'The two things go together,' replied Lesage. 'There is no doubt that Rule 13 of our confederation defines exactly what should be done in such a case. Any responsibility must rest with the passers of Rule 13.'

My heart had turned cold when this man with his poet's face supported the savage at my side. But my hopes were raised again when the thin man, who had said little hitherto, though he had continued to stare at me very intently, began now to show some signs of alarm at the bloodthirsty proposals of his comrades.

'My dear Lucien,' said he, in a soothing voice, laying his hand upon the young man's arm, 'we philosophers and reasoners must have a respect for human life. The tabernacle is not to be lightly violated. We have frequently agreed that if it were not for the excesses of Marat——'

'I have every respect for your opinion, Charles,' the other interrupted. 'You will allow that I have always been a willing and obedient disciple. But I again say that our personal safety is involved, and that, as far as I see, there is no middle course. No one could be more averse from cruelty than I am, but you were present with me some months ago when Toussac silenced the man from Bow Street, and certainly it was done with such dexterity that the process was probably more painful to the spectators than to the victim. He could not have been aware of the horrible sound which announced his own dissolution. If you and I had constancy enough to endure this— and if I remember right it was chiefly at your instigation that the deed was done—then surely on this more vital occasion——'

31

'No, no, Toussac, stop!' cried the thin man, his voice rising from its soft tones to a perfect scream as the giant's hairy hands gripped me by the chin once more. 'I appeal to you, Lucien, upon practical as well as upon moral grounds, not to let this deed be done. Consider that if things should go against us this will cut us off from all hopes of mercy. Consider also——'

This argument seemed for a moment to stagger the younger man, whose olive complexion had turned a shade greyer.

'There will be no hope for us in any case, Charles,' said he. 'We have no choice but to obey Rule 13.'

'Some latitude is allowed to us. We are ourselves upon the inner committee.'

'But it takes a quorum to change a rule, and we have no powers to do it.' His pendulous lip was quivering, but there was no softening in his eyes. Slowly under the pressure of those cruel fingers my chin began to sweep round to my shoulder, and I commended my soul to the Virgin and to Saint Ignatius, who has always been the especial patron of my family. But this man Charles, who had already befriended me, darted forward and began to tear at Toussac's hands with a vehemence which was very different from his former philosophic calm.

'You *shall* not kill him!' he cried angrily. 'Who are you, to set your wills up against mine? Let him go, Toussac! Take your thumb from his chin! I won't have it done, I tell you!' Then, as he saw by the inflexible faces of his companions that blustering would not help him, he turned suddenly to tones of entreaty. 'See, now! I'll make you a promise!' said he. 'Listen to me, Lucien! Let me examine him! If he is a police spy he shall die! You may have him then, Toussac. But if he is only a harmless traveller, who has blundered in here by an evil chance, and who has been led by a foolish curiosity to inquire into our business, then you will leave him to me.'

You will observe that from the beginning of this affair I had never once opened my mouth, nor said a word in my defence, which made me mightily pleased with myself afterwards, though my silence came rather from pride than from courage. To lose life and self-respect together was more than I could face. But now, at this appeal from my advocate, I turned my eyes from the monster who held me to the other who condemned me. The brutality of the one alarmed me less than the self-interested attitude of the other, for a man is never so dangerous as when he is afraid, and of all judges the judge who has cause to fear you is the most inflexible.

My life depended upon the answer which was to come to the appeal of my champion. Lesage tapped his fingers upon his teeth, and smiled indulgently at the earnestness of his companion.

'Rule 13! Rule 13!' he kept repeating, in that exasperating voice of his.

'I will take all responsibility.'

'I'll tell you what, mister,' said Toussac, in his savage voice. 'There's another rule besides Rule 13, and that's the one that says that if any man shelters an offender he shall be treated as if he was himself guilty of the offence.'

This attack did not shake the serenity of my champion in the least.

'You are an excellent man of action, Toussac,' said he calmly; 'but when it comes to choosing the right course, you must leave it to wiser heads than your own.'

His air of tranquil superiority seemed to daunt the fierce creature who held me. He shrugged his huge shoulders in silent dissent.

'As to you, Lucien,' my friend continued, 'I am surprised, considering the position to which you aspire in my family, that you should for an instant stand in the way of any wish which I may express. If you have grasped the true principles of liberty, and if you are privileged to be one of the small band who have never despaired of the republic, to whom is it that you owe it?'

'Yes, yes, Charles; I acknowledge what you say,' the young man answered, with much agitation. 'I am sure that I should be the last to oppose any wish which you might express, but in this case I fear lest your tenderness of heart may be leading you astray. By all means ask him any questions that you like; but it seems to me that there can be only one end to the matter.'

So I thought also; for, with the full secret of these desperate men in my possession, what hope was there that they would ever suffer me to leave the hut alive? And yet, so sweet is human life, and so dear a respite, be it ever so short a one, that when that murderous hand was taken from my chin I heard a sudden chiming of little bells, and the lamp blazed up into a strange fantastic blur. It was but for a moment, and then my mind was clear again, and I was looking up at the strange gaunt face of my examiner.

'Whence have you come?' he asked.

'From England.'

'But you are French?'

'Yes.'

'When did you arrive?'

'To-night.'

'How?'

'In a lugger from Dover.'

'The fellow is speaking the truth,' growled Toussac. 'Yes, I'll say that for him, that he is speaking the truth. We saw the lugger, and some one was landed from it just after the boat that brought me over pushed off.'

I remembered that boat, which had been the first thing which I had seen upon the coast of France. How little I had thought what it would mean to me!

And now my advocate began asking questions—vague, useless questions—in a slow, hesitating fashion which set Toussac grumbling. This cross-examination appeared to me to be a useless farce; and yet there was a certain eagerness and intensity in my questioner's manner which gave me the assurance that he had some end in view. Was it merely that he wished to gain time? Time for what? And then, suddenly, with that quick perception which comes upon those whose nerves are strained by an extremity of danger, I became convinced that he really was awaiting something—that he was tense with expectation. I read it upon his drawn face, upon his sidelong head with his ear scooped into his hand, above all in his twitching, restless eyes. He expected an interruption, and he was talking, talking, talking, in order to gain time for it. I was as sure of it as if he had whispered his secret in my ear, and down in my numb, cold heart a warm little spring of hope began to bubble and run.

But Toussac had chafed at all this word-fencing, and now with an oath he broke in upon our dialogue

'I have had enough of this!' he cried. 'It is not for child's play of this sort that I risked my head in coming over here. Have we nothing better to talk about than this fellow? Do you suppose I came from London to listen to your fine phrases? Have done with it, I say, and get to business.'

'Very good,' said my champion. 'There's an excellent little cupboard here which makes as fine a prison as one could wish for. Let us put him in here, and pass on to business. We can deal with him when we have finished.'

'And have him overhear all that we say,' said Lesage.

'I don't know what the devil has come over you,' cried Toussac, turning suspicious eyes upon my protector. 'I never knew you squeamish before, and certainly you were not backward in the affair of the man from Bow Street. This fellow has our secret, and he must either die, or we shall see him at our trial. What is the sense of arranging a plot, and then at the last moment turning a man loose who will ruin us all? Let us snap his neck and have done with it.'

The great hairy hands were stretched towards me again, but Lesage had sprung suddenly to his feet. His face had turned very white, and he stood listening with his forefinger up and his head slanted. It was a long, thin, delicate hand, and it was quivering like a leaf in the wind.

'I heard something,' he whispered.

'And I,' said the older man.

'What was it?'

'Silence. Listen!'

For a minute or more we all stayed with straining ears while the wind still whimpered in the chimney or rattled the crazy window.

'It was nothing,' said Lesage at last, with a nervous laugh. 'The storm makes curious sounds sometimes.'

'I heard nothing,' said Toussac.

'Hush!' cried the other. 'There it is again!'

A clear rising cry floated high above the wailing of the storm; a wild, musical cry, beginning on a low note, and thrilling swiftly up to a keen, sharp-edged howl.

'A hound!'

'They are following us!'

Lesage dashed to the fireplace, and I saw him thrust his papers into the blaze and grind them down with his heel.

Toussac seized the wood-axe which leaned against the wall. The thin man dragged the pile of decayed netting from the corner, and opened a small wooden screen, which shut off a low recess.

'In here,' he whispered, 'quick!'

And then, as I scrambled into my refuge, I heard him say to the others that I should be safe there, and that they could lay their hands upon me when they wished.

V. The Law

THE cupboard—for it was little more—into which I had been hurried was low and narrow, and I felt in the darkness that it was heaped with peculiar round wickerwork baskets, the nature of which I could by no means imagine, although I discovered afterwards that they were lobster traps. The only light which entered was through the cracks of the old broken door, but these were so wide and numerous that I could see the whole of the room which I had just quitted. Sick and faint, with the shadow of death still clouding my wits, I was none the less fascinated by the scene which lay before me.

My thin friend, with the same prim composure upon his emaciated face, had seated himself again upon the box. With his hands clasped round one of his knees he was rocking slowly backwards and forwards; and I noticed, in the lamplight, that his jaw muscles were contracting rhythmically, like the gills of a fish. Beside him stood Lesage, his white face glistening with moisture and his loose lip quivering with fear. Every now and then he would make a vigorous attempt to compose his features, but after each rally a fresh wave of terror would sweep everything before it, and set him shaking once more. As to Toussac, he stood before the fire, a magnificent figure, with the axe held down by his leg, and his head thrown back in defiance, so that his great black beard bristled straight out in front of him. He said not a word, but every fibre of his body was braced for a struggle. Then, as the howl of the hound rose louder and clearer from the marsh outside, he ran forward and threw open the door.

'No, no, keep the dog out!' cried Lesage in an agony of apprehension.

'You fool, our only chance is to kill it.'

'But it is in leash.'

'If it is in leash nothing can save us. But if, as I think, it is running free, then we may escape yet.'

Lesage cowered up against the table, with his agonised eyes fixed upon the blue-black square of the door. The man who had befriended me still swayed his body about with a singular half-smile upon his face. His skinny hand was twitching at the frill of his shirt, and I conjectured that he held some weapon concealed there. Toussac stood between them and the open door, and, much as I feared and loathed him, I could not take my eyes from his gallant figure. As to myself, I was so much occupied by the singular drama before me, and by the impending fate of those three men of the cottage, that all thought of my own fortunes had passed completely out of my mind. On this mean stage a terrible all-absorbing drama was being played, and I, crouching in a squalid recess, was to be the sole spectator of it. I could but hold my breath and wait and watch.

And suddenly I became conscious that they could all three see something which was invisible to me. I read it from their tense faces and their staring eyes. Toussac swung his axe over his shoulder and poised himself for a blow. Lesage cowered away and put one hand between his eyes and the open door. The other ceased swinging his spindle legs and sat like a little brown image upon the edge of his box. There was a moist pattering of feet, a yellow streak shot through the doorway, and Toussac lashed at it as I have seen an English cricketer strike at a ball. His aim was true, for he buried the head of the hatchet in the creature's throat, but the force of his blow shattered his weapon, and the weight of the hound carried him backward on to the floor. Over they rolled and over, the hairy man and the hairy dog, growling and worrying in a bestial combat. He was fumbling at the animal's throat, and I could not see what he was doing, until it gave a sudden sharp yelp of pain, and there was a rending sound like the tearing of canvas. The man staggered up with his hands dripping, and the tawny mass with the blotch of crimson lay motionless upon the floor.

'Now!' cried Toussac in a voice of thunder, 'now!' and he rushed from the hut.

Lesage had shrunk away into the corner in a frenzy of fear whilst Toussac had been killing the hound, but now he raised his agonised face, which was as wet as if he had dipped it into a basin.

'Yes, yes,' he cried; 'we must fly, Charles. The hound has left the police behind, and we may still escape.'

But the other, with the same imperturbable face, motionless save for the rhythm of his jaw muscles, walked quietly over and closed the door upon the inside.

'I think, friend Lucien,' said he in his quiet voice, 'that you had best stay where you are.'

Lesage looked at him with amazement gradually replacing terror upon his pallid features.

'But you do not understand, Charles,' he cried.

'Oh, yes, I think I do,' said the other, smiling.

'They may be here in a few minutes. The hound has slipped its leash, you see, and has left them behind in the marsh; but they are sure to come here, for there is no other cottage but this.'

'They are sure to come here.'

'Well, then, let us fly. In the darkness we may yet escape.'

'No; we shall stay where we are.'

'Madman, you may sacrifice your own life, but not mine. Stay if you wish, but for my part I am going.'

He ran towards the door with a foolish, helpless flapping of his hands, but the other sprang in front of him with so determined a gesture of authority that the younger man staggered back from it as from a blow.

'You fool!' said his companion. 'You poor miserable dupe!'

Lesage's mouth opened, and he stood staring with his knees bent and his spread-fingered hands up, the most hideous picture of fear that I have ever seen.

'You, Charles, you!' he stammered, hawking up each word.

'Yes, me,' said the other, smiling grimly.

'A police agent all the time! You who were the very soul of our society! You who were in our inmost council! You who led us on! Oh, Charles, you have not the heart! I think I hear them coming, Charles. Let me pass! I beg and implore you to let me pass.'

The granite face shook slowly from side to side.

'But why me? Why not Toussac?'

'If the dog had crippled Toussac, why then I might have had you both. But friend Toussac is rather vigorous for a thin little fellow like me. No, no, my good Lucien, you are destined to be the trophy of my bow and my spear, and you must reconcile yourself to the fact.'

Lesage slapped his forehead as if to assure himself that he was not dreaming.

'A police agent!' he repeated, 'Charles a police agent!'

'I thought it would surprise you.'

'But you were the most republican of us all. We were none of us advanced enough for you. How often have we gathered round you, Charles, to listen to your philosophy! And there is Sibylle, too! Don't tell me that Sibylle was a police spy also. But you are joking, Charles. Say that you are joking!'

The man relaxed his grim features, and his eyes puckered with amusement.

'Your astonishment is very flattering,' said he. 'I confess that I thought that I played my part rather cleverly. It is not my fault that these bunglers unleashed their hound, but at least I shall have the credit of having made a single-handed capture of one very desperate and dangerous conspirator.' He smiled drily at this description of his prisoner. 'The Emperor knows how to reward his friends,' he added, 'and also how to punish his enemies.'

All this time he had held his hand in his bosom, and now he drew it out so far as to show the brass gleam of a pistol butt.

'It is no use,' said he, in answer to some look in the other's eye. 'You stay in the hut, alive or dead.'

Lesage put his hands to his face and began to cry with loud, helpless sobbings.

'Why, you have been worse than any of us, Charles,' he moaned. 'It was you who told Toussac to kill the man from Bow Street, and it was you also who set fire to the house in the Rue Basse du Rempart. And now you turn on us!'

'I did that because I wished to be the one to throw light upon it all—and at the proper moment.'

'That is very fine, Charles, but what will be thought about that when I make it all public in my own defence? How can you explain all that to your Emperor? There is still time to prevent my telling all that I know about you.'

'Well, really, I think that you are right, my friend,' said the other, drawing out his pistol and cocking it. 'Perhaps I *did* go a little beyond my instructions in one or two points, and, as you very properly remark, there is still time to set it right. It is a matter of detail whether I give you up living or give you up dead, and I think that, on the whole, it had better be dead.'

It had been horrible to see Toussac tear the throat out of the hound, but it had not made my flesh creep as it crept now. Pity was mingled with my disgust for this unfortunate young man, who had been fitted by Nature for the life of a retired student or of a dreaming poet, but who had been dragged by stronger wills than his own into a part which no child could be more incapable of playing. I forgave him the trick by which he had caught me and the selfish fears to which he had been willing to sacrifice me. He had flung himself down upon the ground, and floundered about in a convulsion of terror, whilst his terrible little companion, with his cynical smile, stood over him with his pistol in his hand. He played with the helpless panting coward as a cat might with a mouse; but I read in his inexorable eyes that it was no jest, and his finger seemed to be already tightening upon his trigger. Full of horror at so cold-blooded a murder, I pushed open my crazy cupboard, and had rushed out to plead for the victim, when there came a buzz of voices and a clanking of steel from without. With a stentorian shout of 'In the name of the Emperor!' a single violent wrench tore the door of the hut from its hinges.

It was still blowing hard, and through the open doorway I could see a thick cluster of mounted men, with

41

plumes slanted and mantles flapping, the rain shining upon their shoulders. At the side the light from the hut struck upon the heads of two beautiful horses, and upon the heavy red-toupeed busbies of the hussars who stood at their heads. In the doorway stood another hussar—a man of high rank, as could be seen from the richness of his dress and the distinction of his bearing. He was booted to the knees, with a uniform of light blue and silver, which his tall, slim, light-cavalry figure suited to a marvel. I could not but admire the way in which he carried himself, for he never deigned to draw the sword which shone at his side, but he stood in the doorway glancing round the blood-bespattered hut, and staring at its occupants with a very cool and alert expression. He had a handsome face, pale and clear-cut, with a bristling moustache, which cut across the brass chin-chain of his busby.

'Well,' said he, 'well?'

The older man had put his pistol back into the breast of his brown coat.

'This is Lucien Lesage,' said he.

The hussar looked with disgust at the prostrate figure upon the floor.

'A pretty conspirator!' said he. 'Get up, you grovelling hound! Here, Gerard, take charge of him and bring him into camp.'

A younger officer with two troopers at his heels came clanking into the hut, and the wretched creature, half swooning, was dragged out into the darkness.

'Where is the other—the man called Toussac?'

'He killed the hound and escaped. Lesage would have got away also had I not prevented him. If you had kept the dog in leash we should have had them both, but as it is, Colonel Lasalle, I think that you may congratulate me.' He held out his hand as he spoke, but the other turned abruptly on his heel.

'You hear that, General Savary?' said he, looking out of the door. 'Toussac has escaped.'

A tall, dark young man appeared within the circle of light cast by the lamp. The agitation of his handsome swarthy face showed the effect which the news had upon him.

'Where is he, then?'

'It is a quarter of an hour since he got away.'

'But he is the only dangerous man of them all. The Emperor will be furious. In which direction did he fly?'

'It must have been inland.'

'But who is this?' asked General Savary, pointing at me. 'I understand from your information that there were only two besides yourself, Monsieur——'

'I had rather no names were mentioned,' said the other abruptly.

'I can well understand that,' General Savary answered with a sneer.

'I would have told you that the cottage was the rendez-vous, but it was not decided upon until the last moment. I gave you the means of tracking Toussac, but you let the hound slip. I certainly think that you will have to answer to the Emperor for the way in which you have managed the business.'

'That, sir, is our affair,' said General Savary sternly. 'In the meantime you have not told us who this person is.'

It seemed useless for me to conceal my identity, since I had a letter in my pocket which would reveal it.

'My name is Louis de Laval,' said I proudly.

I may confess that I think we had exaggerated our own importance over in England. We had thought that all France was wondering whether we should return, whereas in the quick march of events France had really almost forgotten our existence. This young General Savary was not in the least impressed by my aristocratic name, but he jotted it down in his note-book.

'Monsieur de Laval has nothing whatever to do with the matter,' said the spy. 'He has blundered into it entirely by chance, and I will answer for his safe-keeping in case he should be wanted.'

'He will certainly be wanted,' said General Savary. 'In the meantime I need every trooper that I have for the chase, so, if you make yourself personally responsible, and bring him to the camp when needed, I see no objection to his remaining in your keeping, I shall send to you if I require him.'

'He will be at the Emperor's orders.'

'Are there any papers in the cottage?'

'They have been burned.'

'That is unfortunate.'

'But I have duplicates.'

'Excellent! Come, Lasalle, every minute counts, and there is nothing to be done here. Let the men scatter, and we may still ride him down.'

The two tall soldiers clanked out of the cottage without taking any further notice of my companion, and I heard the sharp stern order and the jingling of metal as the troopers sprang back into their saddles once more. An instant later they were off, and I listened to the dull beat of their hoofs dying rapidly into a confused murmur. My little snuff-coloured champion went to the door of the hut and peered after them through the darkness. Then he came back and looked me up and down, with his usual dry sardonic smile.

'Well, young man,' said he, 'we have played some pretty *tableaux-vivants* for your amusement, and you can thank me for that nice seat in the front row of the parterre."

'I am under a very deep obligation to you, sir,' I answered, struggling between my gratitude and my aversion. 'I hardly know how to thank you.'

He looked at me with a singular expression in his ironical eyes.

'You will have the opportunity for thanking me later,' said he. 'In the meantime, as you say that you are a stranger upon our coast, and as I am responsible for your safe-keeping, you cannot do better than follow me, and I will take you to a place where you may sleep in safety.'

VI. *The Secret Passage*

THE fire had already smouldered down, and my companion blew out the lamp, so that we had not taken ten paces before we had lost sight of the ill-omened cottage, in which I had received so singular a welcome upon my home-coming. The wind had softened down, but a fine rain, cold and clammy, came drifting up from the sea. Had I been left to myself I should have found myself as much at a loss as I had been when I first landed; but my companion walked with a brisk and assured step, so that it was evident that he guided himself by landmarks which were invisible to me. For my part, wet and miserable, with my forlorn bundle under my arm, and my nerves all jangled by my terrible experiences, I trudged in silence by his side, turning over in my mind all that had occurred to me.

Young as I was, I had heard much political discussion amongst my elders in England, and the state of affairs in France was perfectly familiar to me. I was aware that the recent elevation of Buonaparte to the throne had enraged the small but formidable section of Jacobins and extreme Republicans, who saw that all their efforts to abolish a kingdom had only ended in transforming it into an empire. It was, indeed, a pitiable result of their frenzied strivings that a crown with eight fleurs-de-lis should be changed into a higher crown surmounted by a cross and ball. On the other hand, the followers of the Bourbons, in whose company I had spent my youth, were equally disappointed at the manner in which the mass of the French people hailed this final step in the return from chaos to order. Contradictory as were their motives, the more violent spirits of both parties were united in their hatred to Napoleon, and in their fierce determination to get rid of him by any means. Hence a series of conspiracies, most of them with their base in England; and hence also a large use of spies and informers upon the part of

Fouché and of Savary, upon whom the responsibility of the safety of the Emperor lay. A strange chance had landed me upon the French coast at the very same time as a murderous conspirator, and had afterwards enabled me to see the weapons with which the police contrived to thwart and outwit him and his associates. When I looked back upon my series of adventures, my wanderings in the salt-marsh, my entrance into the cottage, my discovery of the papers, my capture by the conspirators, the long period of suspense with Toussac's dreadful thumb upon my chin, and finally the moving scenes which I had witnessed—the killing of the hound, the capture of Lesage, and the arrival of the soldiers—I could not wonder that my nerves were overwrought, and that I surprised myself in little convulsive gestures, like those of a frightened child.

The chief thought which now filled my mind was what my relations were with this dangerous man who walked by my side. His conduct and bearing had filled me with abhorrence. I had seen the depth of cunning with which he had duped and betrayed his companions, and I had read in his lean smiling face the cold deliberate cruelty of his nature, as he stood, pistol in hand, over the whimpering coward whom he had outwitted. Yet I could not deny that when, through my own foolish curiosity, I had placed myself in a most hopeless position, it was he who had braved the wrath of the formidable Toussac in order to extricate me. It was evident also that he might have made his achievement more striking by delivering up two prisoners instead of one to the troopers. It is true that I was not a conspirator, but I might have found it difficult to prove it. So inconsistent did such conduct seem in this little yellow flint-stone of a man that, after walking a mile or two in silence, I asked him suddenly what the meaning of it might be.

I heard a dry chuckle in the darkness, as if he were amused by the abruptness and directness of my question.

'You are a most amusing person, Monsieur—Monsieur —let me see, what did you say your name was?'

'De Laval.'

'Ah, quite so, Monsieur de Laval. You have the impetuosity and the ingenuousness of youth. You want to know what is up a chimney, you jump up the chimney. You want to know the reason of a thing, and you blurt out a question. I have been in the habit of living among people who keep their thoughts to themselves, and I find you very refreshing.'

'Whatever the motives of your conduct, there is no doubt that you saved my life,' said I. 'I am much obliged to you for your intercession.' It is the most difficult thing in the world to express gratitude to a person who fills you with abhorrence, and I fear that my halting speech was another instance of that ingenuousness of which he accused me.

'I can do without your thanks,' said he coldly. 'You are perfectly right when you think that if it had suited my purpose I should have let you perish, and I am perfectly right when I think that if it were not that you are under an obligation you would fail to see my hand if I stretched it out to you just as that overgrown puppy Lasalle did. It is very honourable, he thinks, to serve the Emperor upon the field of battle, and to risk life in his behalf, but when it comes to living amidst danger as I have done, consorting with desperate men, and knowing well that the least slip would mean death, why then one is beneath the notice of a fine clean-handed gentleman. Why,' he continued in a burst of bitter passion, 'I have dared more, and endured more, with Toussac and a few of his kidney for comrades, than this Lasalle has done in all the childish cavalry charges that ever he undertook. As to service, all his Marshals put together have not rendered the Emperor as pressing a service as I have done. But I daresay it does not strike you in that light, Monsieur— Monsieur——'

'De Laval.'

'Quite so—it is curious how that name escapes me. I daresay you take the same view as Colonel Lasalle?'

'It is not a question upon which I can offer an opinion,' said I. 'I only know that I owe my life to your intercession.'

I do not know what reply he might have made to this evasion, but at that moment we heard a couple of pistol shots and a distant shouting from far away in the darkness. We stopped for a few minutes, but all was silent once more.

'They must have caught sight of Toussac,' said my companion. 'I am afraid that he is too strong and too cunning to be taken by them. I do not know what impression he left upon you, but I can tell you that you will go far to meet a more dangerous man.'

I answered that I would go far to avoid meeting one, unless I had the means of defending myself, and my companion's dry chuckle showed that he appreciated my feelings.

'Yet he is an absolutely honest man, which is no very common thing in these days,' said he. 'He is one of those who, at the outbreak of the Revolution, embraced it with the whole strength of his simple nature. He believed what the writers and the speakers told him, and he was convinced that, after a little disturbance and a few necessary executions, France was to become a heaven upon earth, the centre of peace and comfort and brotherly love. A good many people got those fine ideas into their heads, but the heads have mostly dropped into the sawdust-basket by this time. Toussac was true to them, and when instead of peace he found war, instead of comfort a grinding poverty, and instead of equality an Empire, it drove him mad. He became the fierce creature you see, with the one idea of devoting his huge body and giant's strength to the destruction of those who had interfered with his ideal. He is fearless, persevering, and implacable. I have no doubt at all that he will kill me for the part that I have played to-night.'

It was in the calmest voice that my companion uttered the remark, and it made me understand that it was no boast when he said there was more courage needed to carry on his unsavoury trade than to play the part of a *beau sabreur* like Lasalle. He paused a little, and then went on as if speaking to himself.

'Yes,' said he, 'I missed my chance. I certainly ought to have shot him when he was struggling with the hound. But if I had only wounded him he would have torn me into bits like an over-boiled pullet, so perhaps it is as well as it is.'

We had left the salt-marsh behind us, and for some time I had felt the soft springy turf of the downland beneath my feet, and our path had risen and dipped over the curves of the low coast hills. In spite of the darkness my companion walked with great assurance, never hesitating for an instant, and keeping up a stiff pace which was welcome to me in my sodden and benumbed condition. I had been so young when I left my native place that it is doubtful whether, even in daylight, I should have recognised the country-side, but now in the darkness, half stupefied by my adventures, I could not form the least idea as to where we were or what we were making for. A certain recklessness had taken possession of me, and I cared little where I went as long as I could gain the rest and shelter of which I stood in need.

I do not know how long we had walked; I only know that I had dozed and woke and dozed again whilst still automatically keeping pace with my comrade, when I was at last aroused by his coming to a dead stop. The rain had ceased, and although the moon was still obscured, the heavens had cleared somewhat, and I could see for a little distance in every direction. A huge white basin gaped in front of us, and I made out that it was a deserted chalk quarry, with brambles and ferns growing thickly all round the edges. My companion, after a stealthy glance round to make sure that no one was observing us, picked his way amongst the scattered clumps of bushes until he reached the wall of chalk. This he skirted for some distance, squeezing between the cliff and the brambles until he came at last to a spot where all further progress appeared to be impossible.

'Can you see a light behind us?' asked my companion.

I turned round and looked carefully in every direction, but was unable to see one.

'Never mind,' said he. 'You go first, and I will follow.'

In some way during the instant that my back had been turned he had swung aside or plucked out the tangle of bush which had barred our way. When I turned there was a square dark opening in the white glimmering wall in front of us.

'It is small at the entrance, but it grows larger further in,' said he.

I hesitated for an instant. Whither was it that this strange man was leading me? Did he live in a cave like a wild beast, or was this some trap into which he was luring me? The moon shone out at the instant, and in its silver light this black, silent port-hole looked inexpressibly cheerless and menacing.

'You have gone rather far to turn back, my good friend,' said my companion. 'You must either trust me altogether or not trust me at all.'

'I am at your disposal.'

'Pass in then, and I shall follow.'

I crept into the narrow passage, which was so low that I had to crawl down it upon my hands and knees. Craning my neck round, I could see the black angular silhouette of my companion as he came after me. He paused at the entrance, and then, with a rustling of branches and snapping of twigs, the faint light was suddenly shut off from outside, and we were left in pitchy darkness. I heard the scraping of his knees as he crawled up behind me.

'Go on until you come to a step down,' said he. 'We shall have more room there, and we can strike a light.'

The ceiling was so low that by arching my back I could

easily strike it, and my elbows touched the wall upon either side. In those days I was slim and lithe, however, so that I found no difficulty in making my way onward until, at the end of a hundred paces, or it may have been a hundred and fifty, I felt with my hands that there was a dip in front of me. Down this I clambered, and was instantly conscious from the purer air that I was in some larger cavity. I heard the snapping of my companion's flint, and the red glow of the tinder paper leaped suddenly into the clear yellow flame of the taper. At first I could only see that stern, emaciated face, like some grotesque carving in walnut wood, with the ceaseless fish-like vibration of the muscles of his jaw. The light beat full upon it, and it stood strangely out with a dim halo round it in the darkness. Then he raised the taper and swept it slowly round at arm's length so as to illuminate the place in which we stood.

I found that we were in a subterranean tunnel, which appeared to extend into the bowels of the earth. It was so high that I could stand erect with ease, and the old lichen-blotched stones which lined the walls told of its great age. At the spot where we stood the ceiling had fallen in and the original passage had been blocked, but a cutting had been made from this point through the chalk to form the narrow burrow along which we had come. This cutting appeared to be quite recent, for a mound of debris and some trenching tools were still lying in the passage. My companion, taper in hand, started off down the tunnel, and I followed at his heels, stepping over the great stones which had fallen from the roof or the walls, and now obstructed the path.

'Well,' said he, grinning at me over his shoulder, 'have you ever seen anything like this in England?'

'Never,' I answered.

'These are the precautions and devices which men adopted in rough days long ago. Now that rough days have come again, they are very useful to those who know of such places.'

'Whither does it lead, then?' I asked.

'To this,' said he, stopping before an old wooden door, powerfully clamped with iron. He fumbled with the metal-work, keeping himself between me and it, so that I could not see what he was doing. There was a sharp snick, and the door revolved slowly upon its hinges. Within there was a steep flight of time-worn steps leading upward. He motioned me on, and closed the door behind us. At the head of the stair there was a second wooden gate, which he opened in a similar manner.

I had been dazed before ever I came into the chalk pit, but now, at this succession of incidents, I began to rub my eyes and ask myself whether this was young Louis de Laval, late of Ashford, in Kent, or whether it was some dream of the adventures of a hero of Pigault Lebrun. These massive moss-grown arches and mighty iron-clamped doors were, indeed, like the dim shadowy background of a vision; but the guttering taper, my sodden bundle, and all the sordid details of my disarranged toilet assured me only too clearly of their reality. Above all, the swift, brisk, business-like manner of my companion, and his occasional abrupt remarks, brought my fancies back to the ground once more. He held the door open for me now, and closed it again when I had passed through.

We found ourselves in a long vaulted corridor, with a stone-flagged floor, and a dim oil lamp burning at the further end. Two iron-barred windows showed that we had come above the earth's surface once more. Down this corridor we passed, and then through several passages and up a short winding stair. At the head of it was an open door, which led into a small but comfortable bedroom.

'I presume that this will satisfy your wants for to-night,' said he.

I asked for nothing better than to throw myself down, damp clothes and all, upon that snowy coverlet; but for the instant my curiosity overcame my fatigue.

'I am much indebted to you, sir,' said I. 'Perhaps you

will add to your favours by letting me know where I am.'

'You are in my house, and that must suffice you for to-night. In the morning we shall go further into the matter.' He rang a small bell, and a gaunt shock-headed country man-servant came running at the call.

'Your mistress has retired, I suppose?'

'Yes, sir, a good two hours ago.'

'Very good. I shall call you myself in the morning.' He closed my door, and the echo of his steps seemed hardly to have died from my ears before I had sunk into that deep and dreamless sleep which only youth and fatigue can give.

VII. The Owner of Grosbois

My host was as good as his word, for, when a noise in my room awoke me in the morning, it was to find him standing by the side of my bed, so composed in his features and so drab in his attire, that it was hard to associate him with the stirring scenes of yesterday and with the repulsive part which he had played in them. Now in the fresh morning sunlight he presented rather the appearance of a pedantic schoolmaster, an impression which was increased by the masterful, and yet benevolent, smile with which he regarded me. In spite of his smile, I was more conscious than ever that my whole soul shrank from him, and that I should not be at my ease until I had broken this companionship which had been so involuntarily formed. He carried a heap of clothes over one arm, which he threw upon a chair at the bottom of my bed.

'I gather from the little that you told me last night,' said he, 'that your wardrobe is at present somewhat scanty. I fear that your inches are greater than those of any one in my household, but I have brought a few things here amongst which you may find something to fit you. Here, too, are the razors, the soap, and the powder-box. I will return in half an hour, when your toilet will doubtless be completed.'

I found that my own clothes, with a little brushing, were as good as ever, but I availed myself of his offer to the extent of a ruffled shirt and a black satin cravat. I had finished dressing and was looking out of the window of my room, which opened on to a blank wall, when my host returned. He looked me all over with a keenly scrutinising eye, and appeared to be satisfied with what he saw.

'That will do! That will do very well indeed!' said he, nodding a critical head. 'In these times a slight indication of travel or hard work upon a costume is more fashionable than the foppishness of the Incroyable. I have heard ladies remark that it was in better taste. Now, sir, if you will kindly follow me.'

His solicitude about my dress filled me with surprise, but this was soon forgotten in the shock which was awaiting me. For as we passed down the passage and into a large hall which seemed strangely familiar to me, there was a full length portrait of my father standing right in front of me. I stood staring with a gasp of astonishment, and turned to see the cold grey eyes of my companion fixed upon me with a humorous glitter.

'You seem surprised, Monsieur de Laval,' said he.

'For God's sake,' said I, 'do not trifle with me any further! Who are you, and what is this place to which you have taken me?'

For answer he broke into one of his dry chuckles, and, laying his skinny brown hand upon my wrist, he led me into a large apartment. In the centre was a table, tastefully laid, and beyond it in a low chair a young lady was seated, with a book in her hand. She rose as we entered, and I saw that she was tall and slender, with a dark face, pronounced features, and black eyes of extraordinary brilliancy. Even in that one glance it struck me that the

54

expression with which she regarded me was by no means a friendly one.

'Sibylle,' said my host, and his words took the breath from my lips, 'this is your cousin from England, Louis de Laval. This, my dear nephew, is my only daughter, Sibylle Bernac.'

'Then you——'

'I am your mother's brother, Charles Bernac.'

'You are my Uncle Bernac!' I stammered at him like an idiot. 'But why did you not tell me so?' I cried.

'I was not sorry to have a chance of quietly observing what his English education had done for my nephew. It might also have been harder for me to stand your friend if my comrades had any reason to think that I was personally interested in you. But you will permit me now to welcome you heartily to France, and to express my regret if your reception has been a rough one. I am sure that Sibylle will help me to atone for it.' He smiled archly at his daughter, who continued to regard me with a stony face.

I looked round me, and gradually the spacious room, with the weapons upon the wall, and the deers' heads, came dimly back to my memory. That view through the oriel window, too, with the clump of oaks in the sloping park, and the sea in the distance beyond, I had certainly seen it before. It was true then, and I was in our own castle of Grosbois, and this dreadful man in the snuff-coloured coat, this sinister plotter with the death's-head face, was the man whom I had heard my poor father curse so often, the man who had ousted him from his own property and installed himself in his place. And yet I could not forget that it was he also who, at some risk to himself, had saved me the night before, and my soul was again torn between my gratitude and my repulsion.

We had seated ourselves at the table, and as we ate, this newly-found uncle of mine continued to explain all those points which I had failed to understand.

'I suspected that it was you the instant that I set eyes

upon you,' said he 'I am old enough to remember your father when he was a young gallant, and you are his very double—though I may say, without flattery, that where there is a difference it is in your favour. And yet he had the name of being one of the handsomest men betwixt Rouen and the sea. You must bear in mind that I was expecting you, and that there are not so many young aristocrats of your age wandering about along the coast. I was surprised when you did not recognise where you were last night. Had you never heard of the secret passage of Grosbois?'

It came vaguely back to me that in my childhood I had heard of this underground tunnel, but that the roof had fallen in and rendered it useless.

'Precisely,' said my uncle. 'When the castle passed into my hands, one of the very first things which I did was to cut a new opening at the end of it, for I foresaw that in these troublesome times it might be of use to me; indeed, had it been in repair it might have made the escape of your mother and father a very much easier affair.'

His words recalled all that I had heard and all that I could remember of those dreadful days when we, the Lords of the country-side, had been chased across it as if we had been wolves, with the howling mob still clustering at the pier-head to shake their fists and hurl their stones at us. I remembered, too, that it was this very man who was speaking to me who had thrown oil upon the flames in those days, and whose fortunes had been founded upon our ruin. As I looked across at him I found that his keen grey eyes were fixed upon me, and I could see that he had read the thoughts in my mind.

'We must let bygones be bygones,' said he. 'Those are quarrels of the last generation, and Sibylle and you represent a new one.'

My cousin had not said one word or taken any notice of my presence, but at this joining of our names she glanced at me with the same hostile expression which I had already remarked.

'Come, Sibylle,' said her father, 'you can assure your Cousin Louis that, so far as you are concerned, any family misunderstanding is at an end.'

'It is very well for us to talk in that way, father,' she answered. 'It is not your picture that hangs in the hall, or your coat-of-arms that I see upon the wall. We hold the castle and the land, but it is for the heir of the de Lavals to tell *us* if he is satisfied with this.' Her dark scornful eyes were fixed upon me as she waited for my reply, but her father hastened to intervene.

'This is not a very hospitable tone in which to greet your cousin,' said he harshly. 'It has so chanced that Louis's heritage has fallen to us, but it is not for us to remind him of the fact.'

'He needs no reminding,' said she.

'You do me an injustice,' I cried, for the evident and malignant scorn of this girl galled me to the quick. 'It is true that I cannot forget this castle and these grounds belonged to my ancestors—I should be a clod indeed if I *could* forget it—but if you think that I harbour any bitterness, you are mistaken. For my own part, I ask nothing better than to open up a career for myself with my own sword.'

'And never was there a time when it could be more easily and more brilliantly done,' cried my uncle. 'There are great things about to happen in the world, and if you are at the Emperor's court you will be in the middle of them. I understand that you are content to serve him?'

'I wish to serve my country.'

'By serving the Emperor you do so, for without him the country becomes chaos.'

'From all we hear it is not a very easy service,' said my cousin. 'I should have thought that you would have been very much more comfortable in England—and then you would have been so much safer also.'

Everything which the girl said seemed to be meant as an insult to me, and yet I could not imagine how I had ever offended her. Never had I met a woman for whom

57

I conceived so hearty and rapid a dislike. I could see that her remarks were as offensive to her father as they were to me, for he looked at her with eyes which were as angry as her own.

'Your cousin is a brave man, and that is more than can be said for some one else that I could mention,' said he.

'For whom?' she asked.

'Never mind!' he snapped, and, jumping up with the air of a man who is afraid that his rage may master him, and that he may say more than he wished, he ran from the room.

She seemed startled by this retort of his, and rose as if she would follow him. Then she tossed her head and laughed incredulously.

'I suppose that you have never met your uncle before?' said she, after a few minutes of embarrassed silence.

'Never,' answered I.

'Well, what do you think of him now you *have* met him?'

Such a question from a daughter about her father filled me with a certain vague horror. I felt that he must be even a worse man than I had taken him for if he had so completely forfeited the loyalty of his own nearest and dearest.

'Your silence is a sufficient answer,' said she, as I hesitated for a reply. 'I do not know how you came to meet him last night, or what passed between you, for we do not share each other's confidences. I think, however, that you have read him aright. Now I have something to ask you. You had a letter from him inviting you to leave England and to come here, had you not?'

'Yes, I had.'

'Did you observe nothing on the outside?'

I thought of those two sinister words which had puzzled me so much.

'What! it was you who warned me not to come?'

'Yes, it was I. I had no other means of doing it.'

'But why did you do it?'

'Because I did not wish you to come here.'

'Did you think that I would harm you?'

She sat silent for a few seconds like one who is afraid of saying too much. When her answer came it was a very unexpected one:

'I was afraid that you would be harmed.'

'You think that I am in danger here?'

'I am sure of it.'

'You advise me to leave?'

'Without losing an instant.'

'From whom is the danger then?'

Again she hesitated, and then, with a reckless motion like one who throws prudence to the winds, she turned upon me.

'It is from my father,' said she.

'But why should he harm me?'

'That is for your sagacity to discover.'

'But I assure you, mademoiselle, that in this matter you misjudge him,' said I. 'As it happens, he interfered to save my life last night.'

'To save your life! From whom?'

'From two conspirators whose plans I had chanced to discover.'

'Conspirators!' She looked at me in surprise.

'They would have killed me if he had not intervened.'

'It is not his interest that you should be harmed yet awhile. He had reasons for wishing you to come to Castle Grosbois. But I have been very frank with you, and I wish you to be equally so with me. Does it happen—does it happen that during your youth in England you have ever—you have ever had an affair of the heart?'

Everything which this cousin of mine said appeared to me to be stranger than the last, and this question, coming at the end of so serious a conversation, was the strangest of all. But frankness begets frankness, and I did not hesitate.

'I have left the very best and truest girl in the world behind me in England,' said I. 'Eugénie is her name, Eugénie de Choiseul, the niece of the old Duke.'

My reply seemed to give my cousin great satisfaction. Her large dark eyes shone with pleasure.

'You are very attached?' she asked.

'I shall never be happy until I see her.'

'And you would not give her up?'

'God forbid!'

'Not for the Castle of Grosbois?'

'Not even for that.'

My cousin held out her hand to me with a charmingly frank impulsiveness.

'You will forgive me for my rudeness,' said she. 'I see that we are to be allies and not enemies.'

And our hands were still clasped when her father re-entered the room.

VIII. Cousin Sibylle

I COULD see in my uncle's grim face as he looked at us the keenest satisfaction contending with surprise at this sign of our sudden reconciliation. All trace of his recent anger seemed to have left him as he addressed his daughter, but in spite of his altered tone I noticed that her eyes looked defiance and distrust.

'I have some papers of importance to look over,' said he. 'For an hour or so I shall be engaged. I can guess that Louis would like to see the old place once again, and I am sure that he could not have a better guide than you, Sibylle, if you will take him over it.'

She raised no objection, and for my part I was overjoyed at the proposal, as it gave me an opportunity of learning more of this singular cousin of mine, who had told me so much and yet seemed to know so much more. What was the meaning of this obscure warning which she had given me against her father, and why was she so frankly anxious to know about my love affairs? These were the two questions which pressed for an answer. So out we went together into the sweet coast-land air, the sweeter for the gale of the night before, and we walked through the old yew-lined paths, and out into the park, and so round the castle, looking up at the gables, the grey pinnacles, the oak-mullioned windows, the ancient wing with its crenulated walls and its meurtrière windows, the modern with its pleasant verandah and veil of honeysuckle. And as she showed me each fresh little detail, with a particularity which made me understand how dear the place had become to her, she would still keep offering her apologies for the fact that she should be the hostess and I the visitor.

'It is not against you but against ourselves that I was bitter,' said she, 'for are we not the cuckoos who have taken a strange nest and driven out those who built it? It makes me blush to think that my father should invite you to your own house.'

'Perhaps we had been rooted here too long,' I answered. 'Perhaps it is for our own good that we are driven out to carve our own fortunes, as I intend to do.'

'You say that you are going to the Emperor?'

'Yes.'

'You know that he is in camp near here?'

'So I have heard.'

'But your family is still proscribed?'

'I have done him no harm. I will go boldly to him and ask him to admit me into his service."

'Well,' said she, 'there are some who call him a usurper, and wish him all evil; but for my own part I have never heard of anything that he has said and done which was not great and noble. But I had expected that you would be quite an Englishman, Cousin Louis, and come over here with your pockets full of Pitt's guineas and your heart of treason.'

'I have met nothing but hospitality from the English,' I answered; 'but my heart has always been French.'

'But your father fought against us at Quiberon.'

'Let each generation settle its own quarrels,' said I. 'I am quite of your father's opinion about that.'

61

'Do not judge my father by his words, but by his deeds,' said she, with a warning finger upraised; 'and, above all, Cousin Louis, unless you wish to have my life upon your conscience, never let him suspect that I have said a word to set you on your guard.'

'Your life!' I gasped.

'Oh, yes, he would not stick at that!' she cried. 'He killed my mother. I do not say that he slaughtered her, but I mean that his cold brutality broke her gentle heart. Now perhaps you begin to understand why I can talk of him in this fashion.'

As she spoke I could see the secret broodings of years, the bitter resentments crushed down in her silent soul, rising suddenly to flush her dark cheeks and to gleam in her splendid eyes. I realised at that moment that in that tall slim figure there dwelt an unconquerable spirit.

'You must think that I speak very freely to you, since I have only known you a few hours, Cousin Louis,' said she.

'To whom should you speak freely if not to your own relative?'

'It is true; and yet I never expected that I should be on such terms with you. I looked forward to your coming with dread and sorrow. No doubt I showed something of my feelings when my father brought you in.'

'Indeed you did,' I answered. 'I feared that my presence was unwelcome to you.'

'Most unwelcome, both for your own sake and for mine,' said she. 'For your sake because I suspected, as I have told you, that my father's intentions might be unfriendly. For mine——'

'Why for yours?' I asked in surprise, for she had stopped in embarrassment.

'You have told me that your heart is another's. I may tell you that my hand is also promised, and that my love has gone with it.'

'May all happiness attend it!' said I. 'But why should this make my coming unwelcome?'

'That thick English air has dimmed your wits, cousin,' said she, shaking her stately head at me. 'But I can speak freely now that I know that this plan would be as hateful to you as to me. You must know, then, that if my father could have married us he would have united all claims to the succession of Grosbois. Then, come what might —Bourbon or Buonaparte—nothing could shake his position.'

I thought of the solicitude which he had shown over my toilet in the morning, his anxiety that I should make a favourable impression, his displeasure when she had been cold to me, and the smile upon his face when he had seen us hand in hand.

'I believe you are right!' I cried.

'Right! Of course I am right! Look at him watching us now.'

We were walking on the edge of the dried moat, and as I looked up there, sure enough, was the little yellow face turned towards us in the angle of one of the windows. Seeing that I was watching him, he rose and waved his hand merrily.

'Now you know why he saved your life—since you say that he saved it,' said she. 'It would suit his plans best that you should marry his daughter, and so he wished you to live. But when once he understands that that is impossible, why then, my poor Cousin Louis, his only way of guarding against the return of the de Lavals must lie in insuring that there are none to return.'

It was those words of hers, coupled with that furtive yellow face still lurking at the window, which made me realise the imminence of my danger. No one in France had any reason to take an interest in me. If I were to pass away there was no one who could make inquiry—I was absolutely in his power. My memory told me what a ruthless and dangerous man it was with whom I had to deal.

'But,' said I, 'he must have known that your affections were already engaged.'

63

'He did,' she answered; 'it was that which made me most uneasy of all. I was afraid for you and afraid for myself, but, most of all, I was afraid for Lucien. No man can stand in the way of his plans.'

'Lucien!' The name was like a lightning flash upon a dark night. I had heard of the vagaries of a woman's love, but was it possible that this spirited woman loved that poor creature whom I had seen grovelling last night in a frenzy of fear? But now I remembered also where I had seen the name Sibylle. It was upon the fly-leaf of his book. 'Lucien, from Sibylle,' was the inscription. I recalled also that my uncle had said something to him about his aspirations.

'Lucien is hot-headed, and easily carried away,' said she. 'My father has seen a great deal of him lately. They sit for hours in his room, and Lucien will say nothing of what passes between them. I fear that there is something going forward which may lead to evil. Lucien is a student rather than a man of the world, but he has strong opinions about politics.'

I was at my wits' ends what to do, whether to be silent, or to tell her of the terrible position in which her lover was placed; but, even as I hesitated, she, with the quick intuition of a woman, read the doubts which were in my mind.

'You know something of him,' she cried. 'I understood that he had gone to Paris. For God's sake tell me what you know about him!'

'His name is Lesage?'

'Yes, yes. Lucien Lesage.'

'I have—I have seen him,' I stammered.

'You have seen him! And you only arrived in France last night. Where did you see him? What has happened to him?' She gripped me by the wrist in her anxiety.

It was cruel to tell her, and yet it seemed more cruel still to keep silent. I looked round in my bewilderment, and there was my uncle himself coming along over the close-cropped green lawn. By his side, with a merry clash-

ing of steel and jingling of spurs, there walked a handsome young hussar—the same to whom the charge of the
prisoner had been committed upon the night before.
Sibylle never hesitated for an instant, but, with a set face
and blazing eyes, she swept towards them.

'Father,' said she, 'what have you done with Lucien?'

I saw his impassive face wince for a moment before
the passionate hatred and contempt which he read in
her eyes. 'We will discuss this at some future time,' said
he.

'I will know here and now,' she cried. 'What have you
done with Lucien?'

'Gentlemen,' said he, turning to the young hussar and
me, 'I am sorry that we should intrude our little domestic
differences upon your attention. You will, I am sure,
make allowances, lieutenant, when I tell you that your
prisoner of last night was a very dear friend of my
daughter's. Such family considerations do not prevent me
from doing my duty to the Emperor, but they make that
duty more painful than it would otherwise be.'

'You have my sympathy, mademoiselle,' said the young
hussar.

It was to him that my cousin had now turned.

'Do I understand that you took him prisoner?' she
asked.

'It was unfortunately my duty.'

'From you I will get the truth. Whither did you take
him?'

'To the Emperor's camp.'

'And why?'

'Ah, mademoiselle, it is not for me to go into politics.
My duties are but to wield a sword, and sit a horse,
and obey my orders. Both these gentlemen will be my
witnesses that I received my instructions from Colonel
Lasalle.'

'Tut, tut, child, we have had enough of this!' said my
uncle harshly. 'If you insist upon knowing I will tell you
once and for all, that Monsieur Lucien Lesage has been

seized for being concerned in a plot against the life of the Emperor, and that it was my privilege to denounce the would-be assassin.'

'To denounce him!' cried the girl. 'I know that it was you who set him on, who encouraged him, who held him to it whenever he tried to draw back. Oh, you villain! you villain! What have I ever done, what sin of my ancestors am I expiating, that I should be compelled to call such a man Father?'

My uncle shrugged his shoulders as if to say that it was useless to argue with a woman's tantrums. The hussar and I made as if we would stroll away, for it was embarrassing to stand listening to such words, but in her fury she called to us to stop and be witnesses against him. Never have I seen such a recklessness of passion as blazed in her dry wide-opened eyes.

'You have deceived others, but you have never deceived me,' she cried. 'I know you as your own conscience knows you. You may murder me, as you murdered my mother before me, but you can never frighten me into being your accomplice. You proclaimed yourself a Republican that you might creep into a house and estate which do not belong to you. And now you try to make a friend of Buonaparte by betraying your old associates, who still trust in you. And you have sent Lucien to his death! But I know your plans, and my cousin Louis knows them also, and I can assure you that there is just as much chance of his agreeing to them as there is of my doing so. I'd rather lie in my grave than be the wife of any man but Lucien.'

'If you had seen the pitiful poltroon that he proved himself you would not say so,' said my uncle coolly. 'You are not yourself at present, but when you return to your right mind you will be ashamed of having made this public exposure of your weakness. And now, lieutenant, you have something to say.'

'My message was to you, Monsieur de Laval,' said the young hussar, turning his back contemptuously upon my uncle. 'The Emperor has sent me to bring you to him at once at the camp at Boulogne.'

My heart leapt at the thought of escaping from my uncle.

'I ask nothing better,' I cried.

'A horse and an escort are waiting at the gates.'

'I am ready to start at this instant.'

'Nay, there can be no such very great hurry,' said my uncle. 'Surely you will wait for luncheon, Lieutenant Gerard.'

'The Emperor's commissions, sir, are not carried out in such a manner,' said the young hussar sternly. 'I have already wasted too much time. We must be upon our way in five minutes.'

My uncle placed his hand upon my arm and led me slowly towards the gateway, through which my Cousin Sibylle had already passed.

'There is one matter that I wish to speak to you about before you go. Since my time is so short you will forgive me if I introduce it without preamble. You have seen your Cousin Sibylle, and though her behaviour this morning is such as to prejudice you against her, yet I can assure you that she is a very amiable girl. She spoke just now as if she had mentioned the plan which I had conceived to you. I confess to you that I cannot imagine anything more convenient than that we should unite in order to settle once for all every question as to which branch of the family shall hold the estates.'

'Unfortunately,' said I, 'there are objections.'

'And pray what are they?'

'The fact that my cousin's hand, as I have just learned, is promised to another.'

'That need not hinder us,' said he, with a sour smile; 'I will undertake that he never claims the promise.'

'I fear that I have the English idea of marriage, that it should go by love and not by convenience. But in any case your scheme is out of the question, for my own affections are pledged to a young lady in England.'

67

He looked wickedly at me out of the corners of his grey eyes.

'Think well what you are doing, Louis,' said he, in a sibilant whisper which was as menacing as a serpent's hiss. 'You are deranging my plans, and that is not done with impunity.'

'It is not a matter in which I have any choice.'

He gripped me by the sleeve, and waved his hand round as Satan may have done when he showed the kingdoms and principalities. 'Look at the park,' he cried, 'the fields, the woods. Look at the old castle in which your fathers have lived for eight hundred years. You have but to say the word and it is all yours once more.'

There flashed up into my memory the little red-brick house at Ashford, and Eugénie's sweet pale face looking over the laurel bushes which grew by the window.

'It is impossible!' said I.

There must have been something in my manner which made him comprehend that it really was so, for his face darkened with anger, and his persuasion changed in an instant to menace.

'If I had known this they might have done what they wished with you last night,' said he. 'I would never have put out a finger to save you.'

'I am glad to hear you say so,' I answered, 'for it makes it easier for me to say that I wish to go my own way, and to have nothing more to do with you. What you have just said frees me from the bond of gratitude which held me back.'

'I have no doubt that you would like to have nothing more to do with me,' he cried. 'You will wish it more heartily still before you finish. Very well, sir, go your own way and I will go mine, and we shall see who comes out the best in the end.'

A group of hussars were standing by their horses' heads in the gateway. In a few minutes I had packed my scanty possessions, and I was hastening with them down the corridor when a chill struck suddenly through my heart

68

at the thought of my Cousin Sibylle. How could I leave her alone with this grim companion in the old castle? Had she not herself told me that her very life might be at stake? I had stopped in my perplexity, and suddenly there was a patter of feet, and there she was running towards me.

'Good-bye, Cousin Louis,' she cried, with outstretched hands.

'I was thinking of you,' said I; 'your father and I have had an explanation and a quarrel.'

'Thank God!' she cried. 'Your only chance was to get away from him. But beware, for he will do you an injury if he can!'

'He may do his worst; but how can I leave you here in his power?'

'Have no fears about me. He has more reason to avoid me than I him. But they are calling for you, Cousin Louis. Good-bye, and God be with you!'

IX. *The Camp of Boulogne*

MY uncle was still standing at the castle gateway, the very picture of a usurper, with our own old coat-of-arms of the bend argent and the three blue martlets engraved upon the stones at either side of him. He gave me no sign of greeting as I mounted the large grey horse which was awaiting me, but he looked thoughtfully at me from under his down-drawn brows, and his jaw muscles still throbbed with that steady rhythmical movement. I read a cold and settled malice in his set yellow face and his stern eyes. For my own part I sprang readily enough into the saddle, for the man's presence had, from the first, been loathsome to me, and I was right glad to be able to turn my back upon him. And so, with a stern quick order from the lieutenant and a jingle and clatter from the troopers, we were off upon our journey. As I glanced back at the black keep of Grosbois, and at the sinister figure who stood looking after us from beside the gateway, I saw from over his head a white handkerchief gleam for an instant in a last greeting from one of the gloomy meurtrière windows, and again a chill ran through me as I thought of the fearless girl and of the hands in which we were leaving her.

But sorrow clears from the mind of youth like the tarnish of breath upon glass, and who could carry a heavy heart upon so lightfooted a horse and through so sweet an air? The white glimmering road wound over the downs with the sea far upon the left, and between lay that great salt-marsh which had been the scene of our adventures. I could even see, as I fancied, a dull black spot in the distance to mark the position of that terrible cottage. Far away the little clusters of houses showed the positions of Etaples, Ambleterre, and the other fishing villages, whilst I could see that the point which had seemed last night to glow like a half-forged red-hot sword-blade was now white as a snow-field with the camp of a great army. Far, far away, a little dim cloud upon the water stood for the land where I had spent my days— the pleasant, homely land which will always rank next to my own in my affections.

And now I turned my attention from the downs and the sea to the hussars who rode beside me, forming, as I could perceive, a guard rather than an escort. Save for the patrol last night, they were the first of the famous soldiers of Napoleon whom I had ever seen, and it was with admiration and curiosity that I looked upon men who had won a world-wide reputation for their discipline and their gallantry. Their appearance was by no means gorgeous, and their dress and equipment was much more modest than that of the East Kent Yeomanry, which rode every Saturday through Ashford; but the stained tunics, the worn leathers, and the rough hardy horses gave them a very workmanlike appearance. They were small, light, brown-faced fellows, heavily whiskered and moustached, many of them wearing ear-rings in their ears. It surprised me that even the youngest and most boyish-looking of them should be so bristling with hair, until, upon a second look, I perceived that his whiskers were formed of lumps of black wax stuck on to the sides of his face. The tall young lieutenant noticed the astonishment with which I gazed at his boyish trooper.

'Yes, yes,' said he, 'they are artificial, sure enough; but what can you expect from a lad of seventeen? On the other hand, we cannot spoil the appearance of the regiment upon parade by having a girl's cheeks in the ranks.'

'It melts terribly in this warm weather, lieutenant,' said the hussar, joining in the conversation with the freedom which was one of the characteristics of Napoleon's troops.

'Well, well, Caspar, in a year or two you will dispense with them.'

'Who knows? Perhaps he will have dispensed with his head also by that time,' said a corporal in front, and they all laughed together in a manner which in England would have meant a court-martial. This seemed to me to be one of the survivals of the Revolution, that officer and private were left upon a very familiar footing, which was increased, no doubt, by the freedom with which the Emperor would chat with his old soldiers, and the liberties which he would allow them to take with him. It was no uncommon thing for a shower of chaff to come from the ranks directed at their own commanding officers, and I am sorry to say, also, that it was no very unusual thing for a shower of bullets to come also. Unpopular officers were continually assassinated by their own men; at the battle of Montebello it is well known that every officer, with the exception of one lieutenant belonging to the 24th demi-brigade, was shot down from behind. But this was a relic of the bad times, and, as the Emperor gained more complete control, a better feeling was established. The history of our army at that time proved, at any rate, that the highest efficiency could be maintained without the flogging which was still used in the Prussian and the English service, and it was shown, for the first time, that great bodies of men could be induced to act from a sense of duty and a love of country, without hope of reward or fear of punishment. When a French general could suffer his division to straggle as they would over the face of the country, with the certainty that they would concentrate upon the day of battle, he proved that he had soldiers who were worthy of his trust.

One thing had struck me as curious about these hussars —that they pronounced French with the utmost difficulty. I remarked it to the lieutenant as he rode by my side, and I asked him from what foreign country his men were recruited, since I could perceive that they were not Frenchmen.

'My faith, you must not let them hear you say so,' said he, 'for they would answer you as like as not by a thrust from their sabres. We are the premier regiment of the French cavalry, the First Hussars of Berchény, and, though it is true that our men are all recruited in Alsace, and few of them can speak anything but German, they are as good Frenchmen as Kléber or Kellermann, who came from the same parts. Our men are all picked, and our officers,' he added, pulling at his light moustache, 'are the finest in the service.'

The swaggering vanity of the fellow amused me, for he cocked his busby, swung the blue dolman which hung from his shoulder, sat his horse, and clattered his scabbard in a manner which told of his boyish delight and pride in himself and his regiment. As I looked at his lithe figure and his fearless bearing, I could quite imagine that he did himself no more than justice, while his frank smile and his merry blue eyes assured me that he would prove a good comrade. He had himself been taking observations of me, for he suddenly placed his hand upon my knee as we rode side by side.

'I trust the Emperor is not displeased with you,' said he, with a very grave face.

'I cannot think that he can be so,' I answered, 'for I have come from England to put my services at his disposal.'

'When the report was presented last night, and he heard of your presence in that den of thieves, he was very anxious that you should be brought to him. Perhaps it is that he wishes you to be guide to us in England. No doubt you know your way all over the island.'

The hussar's idea of an island seemed to be limited to the little patches which lie off the Norman or Breton coast. I tried to explain to him that this was a great country, not much smaller than France.

'Well, well,' said he, 'we shall know all about it presently, for we are going to conquer it. They say in the camp that we shall probably enter London either next Wednesday evening or else on the Thursday morning. We are to have a week for plundering the town, and then one army corps is to take possession of Scotland and another of Ireland.'

His serene confidence made me smile. 'But how do you know you can do all this?' I asked.

'Oh!' said he, 'the Emperor has arranged it.'

'But they have an army, and they are well prepared. They are brave men and they will fight.'

'There would be no use their doing that, for the Emperor is going over himself,' said he; and in the simple answer I understood for the first time the absolute trust and confidence which these soldiers had in their leader. Their feeling for him was fanaticism, and its strength was religion, and never did Mahomet nerve the arms of his believers and strengthen them against pain and death more absolutely than this little grey-coated idol did to those who worshipped him. If he had chosen—and he was more than once upon the point of it—to assert that he was indeed above humanity he would have found millions to grant his claim. You who have heard of him as a stout gentleman in a straw hat, as he was in his later days, may find it hard to understand it, but if you had seen his mangled soldiers still with their dying breath

73

crying out to him, and turning their livid faces towards him as he passed, you would have realised the hold which he had over the minds of men.

'You have been over there?' asked the lieutenant presently, jerking his thumb towards the distant cloud upon the water.

'Yes, I have spent my life there.'

'But why did you stay there when there was such good fighting to be had in the French service?'

'My father was driven out of the country as an aristocrat. It was only after his death that I could offer my sword to the Emperor.'

'You have missed a great deal, but I have no doubt that we shall still have plenty of fine wars. And you think that the English will offer us battle?'

'I have no doubt of it.'

'We feared that when they understood that it was the Emperor in person who had come they would throw down their arms. I have heard that there are some fine women over there.'

'The women are beautiful.'

He said nothing, but for some time he squared his shoulders and puffed out his chest, curling up the ends of his little yellow moustache.

'But they will escape in boats,' he muttered at last; and I could see that he had still that picture of a little island in his imagination. 'If they could but see us they might remain. It has been said of the Hussars of Berchény that they can set a whole population running, the women towards us, the men away. We are, as you have no doubt observed, a very fine body of men, and the officers are the pick of the service, though the seniors are hardly up to the same standard as the rest of us.'

With all his self-confidence, this officer did not seem to me to be more than my own age, so I asked him whether he had seen any service. His moustache bristled with indignation at my question, and he looked me up and down with a severe eye.

'I have had the good fortune to be present at nine battles, sir, and at more than forty skirmishes,' said he. 'I have also fought a considerable number of duels, and I can assure you that I am always ready to meet anyone —even a civilian—who may wish to put me to the proof.'

I assured him that he was very fortunate to be so young and yet to have seen so much, upon which his ill-temper vanished as quickly as it came, and he explained that he had served in the Hohenlinden campaign under Moreau, as well as in Napoleon's passage of the Alps, and the campaign of Marengo.

'When you have been with the army for a little time the name of Etienne Gerard will not be so unfamiliar to you,' said he. 'I believe that I may claim to be the hero of one or two little stories which the soldiers love to tell about their camp-fires. You will hear of my duel with the six fencing masters, and you will be told how, single-handed, I charged the Austrian Hussars of Graz and brought their silver kettle-drum back upon the crupper of my mare. I can assure you that it was not by accident that I was present last night, but it was because Colonel Lasalle was very anxious to be sure of any prisoners whom he might make. As it turned out, however, I only had the one poor chicken-hearted creature, whom I handed over to the provost-marshal.'

'And the other—Toussac?'

'Ah, he seems to have been a man of another breed. I could have asked nothing better than to have had him at my sword-point. But he has escaped. They caught sight of him and fired a pistol or two, but he knew the bog too well, and they could not follow him.'

'And what will be done to your prisoner?' I asked.

Lieutenant Gerard shrugged his shoulders.

'I am very sorry for Mademoiselle your cousin,' said he, 'but a fine girl should not love such a man when there are so many gallant soldiers upon the country-side. I hear that the Emperor is weary of these endless plottings, and that an example will be made of him.'

Whilst the young hussar and I had been talking we had been cantering down the broad white road, until we were now quite close to the camp, which we could see lying in its arrangement of regiments and brigades beneath us. Our approach lay over the high ground, so that we could see down into this canvas city, with its interminable lines of picketed horses, its parks of artillery, and its swarms of soldiers. In the centre was a clear space, with one very large tent and a cluster of low wooden houses in the middle of it, with the tricolour banner waving above them.

'That is the Emperor's quarters, and the smaller tent there is the headquarters of General Ney, who commands this corps. You understand that this is only one of several armies dotted along from Dunkirk in the north to this, which is the most southerly. The Emperor goes from one to the other, inspecting each in its turn, but this is the main body, and contains most of the picked troops, so that it is we who see most of him, especially now that the Empress and the Court have come to Pont de Briques. He is in there at the present moment,' he added in a hushed voice, pointing to the great white tent in the centre.

The road into the camp ran through a considerable plain, which was covered by bodies of cavalry and infantry engaged upon their drill. We had heard so much in England about Napoleon's troops, and their feats had appeared so extraordinary, that my imagination had prepared me for men of very striking appearance. As a matter of fact, the ordinary infantry of the line, in their blue coats and white breeches and gaiters, were quite little fellows, and even their high brass-covered hats and red plumes could not make them very imposing.

In spite of their size, however, they were tough and wiry, and after their eighteen months in camp they were trained to the highest pitch of perfection. The ranks were full of veterans, and all the under-officers had seen much service, while the generals in command have never been equalled in ability, so that it was no mean foe which lay with its menacing eyes fixed upon the distant cliffs of England. If Pitt had not been able to place the first navy in the world between the two shores the history of Europe might be very different to-day.

Lieutenant Gerard, seeing the interest with which I gazed at the manœuvring troops, was good enough to satisfy my curiosity about such of them as approached the road along which we were journeying.

'Those fellows on the black horses with the great blue rugs upon their croups are the Cuirassiers,' said he. 'They are so heavy that they cannot raise more than a trot, so when they charge we manage that there shall be a brigade of chasseurs or hussars behind them to follow up the advantage.'

'Who is the civilian who is inspecting them?' I asked.

'That is not a civilian, but it is General St. Cyr, who is one of those whom they called the Spartans of the Rhine. They were of opinion that simplicity of life and of dress were part of a good soldier, and so they would wear no uniform beyond a simple blue riding coat, such as you see. St. Cyr is an excellent officer, but he is not popular, for he seldom speaks to anyone, and he sometimes shuts himself up for days on end in his tent, where he plays upon his violin. I think myself that a soldier is none the worse because he enjoys a glass of good wine, or has a smart jacket and a few Brandenburgs across his chest. For my part I do both, and yet those who know me would tell you that it has not harmed my soldiering. You see this infantry upon the left?'

'The men with the yellow facings?'

'Precisely. Those are Oudinot's famous grenadiers. And the other grenadiers, with the red shoulder-knots and the fur hats strapped above their knapsacks, are the Imperial Guard, the successors of the old Consular Guard who won Marengo for us. Eighteen hundred of them got the cross of honour for the battle. There is the 57th of the line, which has been named "The Terrible," and there is the 7th Light Infantry, who come from the Pyrenees, and who are well known to be the best marchers and the greatest rascals in the army. The light cavalry in green are the Horse Chasseurs of the Guard, sometimes called the Guides, who are said to be the Emperor's favourite troops, although he makes a great mistake if he prefers them to the Hussars of Berchény. The other cavalry with the green pelisses are also chasseurs, but I cannot tell from here what regiment they are. Their colonel handles them admirably. They are moving to a flank in open column of half-squadrons and then wheeling into line to charge. We could not do it better ourselves. And now, Monsieur de Laval, here we are at the gates of the Camp of Boulogne, and it is my duty to take you straight to the Emperor's quarters.'

X. *The Ante-room*

THE camp of Boulogne contained at that time one hundred and fifty thousand infantry, with fifty thousand cavalry, so that its population was second only to Paris among the cities of France. It was divided into four sections, the right camp, the left camp, the camp of Wimereux, and the camp of Ambleteuse, the whole being about a mile in depth, and extending along the sea-shore for a length of about seven miles. On the land side it was open, but on the sea side it was fringed by powerful batteries containing mortars and cannon of a size never seen before. These batteries were placed along the edges of the high cliffs, and their lofty position increased their range, and enabled them to drop their missiles upon the decks of the English ships.

It was a pretty sight to ride through the camp, for the men had been there for more than a year, and had done all that was possible to decorate and ornament their tents. Most of them had little gardens in front or around them, and the sunburned fellows might be seen as we passed kneeling in their shirt-sleeves with their spuds and their watering-cans in the midst of their flower-beds. Others sat in the sunshine at the openings of the tents tying up their queues, pipe-claying their belts, and polishing their arms, hardly bestowing a glance upon us as we passed, for patrols of cavalry were coming and going in every direction. The endless lines were formed into streets, with their names printed up upon boards. Thus we had passed through the Rue d'Arcola, the Rue de Kléber, the Rue d'Egypte, and the Rue d'Artillerie Volante, before we found ourselves in the great central square in which the headquarters of the army were situated.

The Emperor at this time used to sleep at a village called Pont de Briques, some four miles inland, but his days were spent at the camp, and his continual councils of war were held there. Here also were his ministers, and the generals of the army corps which were scattered up and down the coast came thither to make their reports and to receive their orders. For these consultations a plain wooden house had been constructed containing one very large room and three small ones. The pavilion which we had observed from the downs served as an ante-chamber to the house, in which those who sought audience with the Emperor might assemble. It was at the door of this, where a strong guard of grenadiers announced Napoleon's presence, that my guardian sprang down from his horse and signed to me to follow his example. An officer of the guard took our names and returned to us accompanied by General Duroc, a thin, hard, dry man of forty, with a formal manner and a suspicious eye.

'Is this Monsieur Louis de Laval?' he asked, with a stiff smile.

I bowed.

'The Emperor is very anxious to see you. You are no longer needed, Lieutenant.'

'I am personally responsible for bringing him safely, General.'

'Very good. You may come in, if you prefer it!' And he passed us into the huge tent, which was unfurnished, save for a row of wooden benches round the sides. A number of men in naval and military uniforms were seated upon these, and numerous groups were standing about chatting in subdued tones. At the far end was a door which led into the Imperial council chamber. Now and then I saw some man in official dress walk up to this door, scratch gently upon it with his nail, and then, as it instantly opened, slip discreetly through, closing it softly behind him. Over the whole assembly there hung an air of the Court rather than of the camp, an atmosphere of awe and of reverence which was the more impressive when it affected these bluff soldiers and sailors. The Emperor had seemed to me to be formidable in the distance, but I found him even more overwhelming now that he was close at hand.

'You need have no fears, Monsieur de Laval,' said my companion. 'You are going to have a good reception.'

'How do you know that?'

'From General Duroc's manner. In these cursed Courts, if the Emperor smiles upon you everyone smiles, down to that flunkey in the red velvet coat yonder. But if the Emperor frowns, why, you have only to look at the face of the man who washes the Imperial plates, and you will see the frown reflected upon it. And the worst of it is that, if you are a plain-witted man, you may never find out what earned you either the frown or the smile. That is why I had rather wear the shoulder-straps of a lieutenant, and be at the side of my squadron, with a good horse between my knees and my sabre clanking against my stirrup-iron, than have Monsieur Talleyrand's grand hotel in the Rue Saint Florentin, and his hundred thousand livres of income.'

I was still wondering whether the hussar could be right, and if the smile with which Duroc had greeted me could mean that the Emperor's intentions towards me were friendly, when a very tall and handsome young man, in a brilliant uniform, came towards me. In spite of the change in his dress, I recognised him at once as the General Savary who had commanded the expedition of the night before.

'Well, Monsieur de Laval,' said he, shaking hands with me very pleasantly, 'you have heard, no doubt, that this fellow Toussac has escaped us. He was really the only one whom we were anxious to seize, for the other is evidently a mere dupe and dreamer. But we shall have him yet, and between ourselves we shall keep a very strict guard upon the Emperor's person until we do, for Master Toussac is not a man to be despised.'

I seemed to feel his great rough thumb upon my chin as I answered that I thought he was a very dangerous man indeed.

'The Emperor will see you presently,' said Savary. 'He is very busy this morning, but he bade me say that you should have an audience.' He smiled and passed on.

'Assuredly you are getting on,' whispered Gerard. 'There are a good many men here who would risk something to have Savary address them as he addressed you. The Emperor is certainly going to do something for you. But attention, friend, for here is Monsieur de Talleyrand himself coming towards us.'

A singular-looking person was shuffling in our direction. He was a man about fifty years of age, largely made about the shoulders and chest, but stooping a good deal, and limping heavily in one leg. He walked slowly, leaning upon a silver-headed stick, and his sober suit of black, with silk stockings of the same hue, looked strangely staid among the brilliant uniforms which surrounded him. But in spite of his plain dress there was an expression of great authority upon his shrewd face, and every one drew back with bows and salutes as he moved across the tent.

'Monsieur Louis de Laval?' said he, as he stopped in front of me, and his cold grey eyes played over me from head to heel.

I bowed, and with some coldness, for I shared the

dislike which my father used to profess for this unfrocked priest and perjured politician; but his manner was so polished and engaging that it was hard to hold out against it.

'I knew your cousin de Rohan very well indeed,' said he. 'We were two rascals together when the world was not quite so serious as it is at present. I believe that you are related to the Cardinal de Montmorency de Laval, who is also an old friend of mine. I understand that you are about to offer your services to the Emperor?'

'I have come from England for that purpose, sir.'

'And met with some little adventure immediately upon your arrival, as I understand. I have heard the story of the worthy police agent, the two Jacobins, and the lonely hut. Well, you have seen the danger to which the Emperor is exposed, and it may make you the more zealous in his service. Where is your uncle, Monsieur Bernac?'

'He is at the Castle of Grosbois.'

'Do you know him well?'

'I had not seen him until yesterday.'

'He is a very useful servant of the Emperor, but—but—' he inclined his head downward to my ear, 'some more congenial service will be found for you, Monsieur de Laval,' and so, with a bow, he whisked round, and tapped his way across the tent again.

'Why, my friend, you are certainly destined for something great,' said the hussar lieutenant. 'Monsieur de Talleyrand does not waste his smiles and his bows, I promise you. He knows which way the wind blows before he flies his kite, and I foresee that I shall be asking for your interest to get me my captaincy in this English campaign. Ah, the council of war is at an end.'

As he spoke the inner door at the end of the great tent opened, and a small knot of men came through dressed in the dark blue coats, with trimmings of gold oak-leaves, which marked the marshals of the Empire. They were, all but one, men who had hardly reached their middle age, and who, in any other army, might have been considered fortunate if they had gained the command of a regiment; but the continuous wars and the open system by which rules of seniority yielded to merit had opened up a rapid career to a successful soldier. Each carried his curved cocked hat under his arm, and now, leaning upon their sword-hilts, they fell into a little circle and chatted eagerly among themselves.

'You are a man of family, are you not?' asked my hussar.

'I am of the same blood as the de Rohans and the Montmorencies.'

'So I had understood. Well, then, you will understand that there have been some changes in this country when I tell you that those men who, under the Emperor, are the greatest in the country have been the one a waiter, the next a wine smuggler, the next a cooper of barrels, and the next a house painter. Those are the trades which gave us Murat, Masséna, Ney, and Lannes.'

Aristocrat as I was, no names had ever thrilled me as those did, and I eagerly asked him to point me out each of these famous soldiers.

'Oh, there are many famous soldiers in the room,' said he. 'Besides,' he added, twisting his moustache, 'there may be junior officers here who have it in them to rise higher than any of them. But there is Ney to the right.'

I saw a man with close-cropped red hair and a large square-jowled face, such as I have seen upon an English prize-fighter.

'We call him Peter the Red, and sometimes the Red Lion, in the army,' said my companion. 'He is said to be the bravest man in the army, though I cannot admit that he is braver than some other people whom I could mention. Still he is undoubtedly a very good leader.'

'And the general next him?' I asked. 'Why does he carry his head all upon one side?'

'That is General Lannes, and he carries his head upon his left shoulder because he was shot through the neck at the siege of St. Jean d'Acre. He is a Gascon, like myself, and I fear that he gives some ground to those who accuse my countrymen of being a little talkative and quarrelsome. But monsieur smiles?'

'You are mistaken.'

'I thought that perhaps something which I had said might have amused monsieur. I thought that possibly he meant that Gascons really were quarrelsome, instead of being, as I contend, the mildest race in France—an opinion which I am always ready to uphold in any way which may be suggested. But, as I say, Lannes is a very valiant man, though, occasionally, perhaps, a trifle hotheaded. The next man is Augereau.'

I looked with interest upon the hero of Castiglione, who had taken command upon the one occasion when Napoleon's heart and spirit had failed him. He was a man, I should judge, who would shine rather in war than in peace, for, with his long goat's face and his brandy nose, he looked, in spite of his golden oak-leaves, just such a long-legged, vulgar, swaggering, foul-mouthed old soldier as every barrack-room can show. He was an older man than the others, and his sudden promotion had come too late for him to change. He was always the Corporal of the Prussian Guard under the hat of the French Marshal.

'Yes, yes; he is a rough fellow,' said Gerard, in answer to my remark. 'He is one of those whom the Emperor had to warn that he wished them to be soldiers only with the army. He and Rapp and Lefebvre, with their big boots and their clanking sabres, were too much for the Empress's drawing-room at the Tuileries. There is Vandamme also, the dark man with the heavy face. Heaven help the English village that he finds his quarters in! It was he who got into trouble because he broke the jaw of a Westphalian priest who could not find him a second bottle of Tokay.'

'And that is Murat, I suppose?'

'Yes; that is Murat with the black whiskers and the

84

red, thick lips, and the brown of Egypt upon his face. He is the man for me! My word, when you have seen him raving in front of a brigade of light cavalry, with his plumes tossing and his sabre flashing, you would not wish to see anything finer. I have known a square of grenadiers break and scatter at the very sight of him. In Egypt the Emperor kept away from him, for the Arabs would not look at the little General when this fine horseman and swordsman was before them. In my opinion Lasalle is the better light cavalry officer, but there is no one whom the men will follow as they do Murat.'

'And who is the stern-looking man, leaning on the Oriental sword?'

'Oh, that is Soult! He is the most obstinate man in the world. He argues with the Emperor. The handsome man beside him is Junot, and Bernadotte is leaning against the tent-pole.'

I looked with interest at the extraordinary face of this adventurer, who, after starting with a musket and a knapsack in the ranks, was not contented with the baton of a marshal, but passed on afterward to grasp the sceptre of a king. And it might be said of him that, unlike his fellows, he gained his throne in spite of Napoleon rather than by his aid. Any man who looked at his singular pronounced features, the swarthiness of which proclaimed his half Spanish origin, must have read in his flashing black eyes and in that huge aggressive nose that he was reserved for a strange destiny. Of all the fierce and masterful men who surrounded the Emperor there was none with greater gifts, and none, also, whose ambitions he more distrusted, than those of Jules Bernadotte.

And yet, fierce and masterful as these men were, having, as Augereau boasted, fear neither of God nor of the devil, there was something which thrilled or cowed them in the pale smile or black frown of the little man who ruled them. For, as I watched them, there suddenly came over the assembly a start and hush such as you see in a boys' school when the master enters unexpectedly, and there near the open doors of his headquarters stood the master himself. Even without that sudden silence, and the scramble to their feet of those upon the benches, I felt that I should have known instantly that he was present. There was a pale luminosity about his ivory face which drew the eye towards it, and though his dress might be the plainest of a hundred, his appearance would be the first which one would notice. There he was, with his little plump, heavy-shouldered figure, his green coat with the red collar and cuffs, his white, well-formed legs, his sword with the gilt hilt and the tortoise-shell scabbard. His head was uncovered, showing his thin hair of a ruddy chestnut colour. Under one arm was the flat cocked hat with the twopenny tricolour rosette, which was already reproduced in his pictures. In his right hand he held a little riding switch with a metal head. He walked slowly forward, his face immutable, his eyes fixed steadily before him, measured, inexorable, the very personification of Destiny.

'Admiral Bruix!'

I do not know if that voice thrilled through every one as it did through me. Never had I heard anything more harsh, more menacing, more sinister. From under his puckered brows his light-blue eyes glanced swiftly round with a sweep like a sabre.

'I am here, Sire!' A dark, grizzled, middle-aged man, in a naval uniform, had advanced from the throng. Napoleon took three quick little steps towards him in so menacing a fashion, that I saw the weather-stained cheeks of the sailor turn a shade paler, and he gave a helpless glance round him, as if for assistance.

'How comes it, Admiral Bruix,' cried the Emperor, in the same terrible rasping voice, 'that you did not obey my commands last night?'

'I could see that a westerly gale was coming up, Sire. I knew that—' he could hardly speak for his agitation, 'I knew that if the ships went out with this lee shore——'

'What right have you to judge, sir?' cried the Emperor,

86

in a cold fury of indignation. 'Do you conceive that your judgment is to be placed against mine?'

'In matters of navigation, Sire.'

'In no matters whatsoever.'

'But the tempest, Sire! Did it not prove me to be in the right?'

'What! You still dare to bandy words with me?'

'When I have justice on my side.'

There was a hush amidst all the great audience; such a heavy silence as comes only when many are waiting, and all with bated breath. The Emperor's face was terrible. His cheeks were of a greenish, livid tint, and there was a singular rotary movement of the muscles of his forehead. It was the countenance of an epileptic. He raised the whip to his shoulder, and took a step towards the admiral.

'You insolent rascal!' he hissed. It was the Italian word *coglione* which he used, and I observed that as his feelings overcame him his French became more and more that of a foreigner.

For a moment he seemed to be about to slash the sailor across the face with his whip. The latter took a step back, and clapped his hand to his sword.

'Have a care, Sire,' said he.

For a few instants the tension was terrible. Then Napoleon brought the whip down with a sharp crack against his own thigh.

'Vice-Admiral Magon,' he cried, 'you will in future receive all orders connected with the fleet. Admiral Bruix, you will leave Boulogne in twenty-four hours and withdraw to Holland. Where is Lieutenant Gerard, of the Hussars of Berchény?'

My companion's gauntlet sprang to his busby.

'I ordered you to bring Monsieur Louis de Laval from the Castle of Grosbois.'

'He is here, Sire.'

'Good! You may retire.'

The lieutenant saluted, whisked round upon his heel,

and clattered away, whilst the Emperor's blue eyes were turned upon me. I had often heard the phrase of eyes looking through you, but that piercing gaze did really give one the feeling that it penetrated to one's inmost thoughts. But the sternness had all melted out of it, and I read a great gentleness and kindness in their expression.

'You have come to serve me, Monsieur de Laval?'

'Yes, Sire.'

'You have been some time in making up your mind.'

'I was not my own master, Sire.'

'Your father was an aristocrat?'

'Yes, Sire.'

'And a supporter of the Bourbons?'

'Yes, Sire.'

'You will find that in France now there are no aristocrats and no Jacobins; but that we are all Frenchmen working for the glory of our country. Have you seen Louis de Bourbon?'

'I have seen him once, Sire.'

'An insignificant-looking man, is he not?'

'No, Sire, I thought him a fine-looking man.'

For a moment. I saw a hard gleam of resentment in those changing blue eyes. Then he put out his hand and pinched one of my ears.

'Monsieur de Laval was not born to be a courtier,' said he. 'Well, well, Louis de Bourbon will find that he cannot gain a throne by writing proclamations in London and signing them Louis. For my part, I found the crown of France lying upon the ground, and I lifted it upon my sword-point.'

'You have lifted France with your sword also, Sire,' said Talleyrand, who stood at his elbow.

Napoleon looked at his famous minister, and I seemed to read suspicion in his eyes. Then he turned to his secretary.

'I leave Monsieur de Laval in your hands, de Meneval,' said he. 'I desire to see him in the council chamber after the inspection of the artillery.'

88

XI. *The Secretary*

EMPEROR, generals, and officials all streamed away to the review, leaving me with a gentle-looking, large-eyed man in a black suit with very white cambric ruffles, who introduced himself to me as Monsieur de Meneval, private secretary to His Majesty.

'We must get some food, Monsieur de Laval,' said he. 'It is always well, if you have anything to do with the Emperor, to get your food whenever you have the chance. It may be many hours before he takes a meal, and if you are in his presence you have to fast also. I assure you that I have nearly fainted from hunger and from thirst.'

'But how does the Emperor manage himself?' I asked. This Monsieur de Meneval had such a kindly human appearance that I already felt much at my ease with him.

'Oh, he, he is a man of iron, Monsieur de Laval. We must not set our watches by his. I have known him work for eighteen hours on end and take nothing but a cup or two of coffee. He wears everybody out around him. Even the soldiers cannot keep up with him. I assure you that I look upon it as the very highest honour to have charge of his papers, but there are times when it is very trying all the same. Sometimes it is eleven o'clock at night, Monsieur de Laval, and I am writing to his dictation with my head aching for want of sleep. It is dreadful work, for he dictates as quickly as he can talk, and he never repeats anything. "Now, Meneval," says he suddenly, "we shall stop here and have a good night's rest." And then, just as I am congratulating myself, he adds, "and we shall continue with the dictation at three to-morrow morning." That is what he means by a good night's rest.'

'But has he no hours for his meals, Monsieur de Meneval?' I asked, as I accompanied the unhappy secretary out of the tent.

'Oh, yes, he has hours, but he will not observe them.

You see that it is already long after dinner time, but he has gone to this review. After the review something else will probably take up his attention, and then something else, until suddenly in the evening it will occur to him that he has had no dinner. "My dinner, Constant, this instant!" he will cry, and poor Constant has to see that it is there.'

'But it must be unfit to eat by that time,' said I.

The secretary laughed in the discreet way of a man who has always been obliged to control his emotions.

'This is the Imperial kitchen,' said he, indicating a large tent just outside the headquarters. 'Here is Borel, the second cook, at the door. How many pullets to-day, Borel?'

'Ah, Monsieur de Meneval, it is heartrending,' cried the cook. 'Behold them!' and, drawing back the flap of the entrance, he showed us seven dishes, each of them containing a cold fowl. 'The eighth is now on the fire and done to a turn, but I hear that His Majesty has started for the review, so we must put on a ninth.'

'That is how it is managed,' said my companion, as we turned from the tent. 'I have known twenty-three fowls got ready for him before he asked for his meal. That day he called for his dinner at eleven at night. He cares little what he eats or drinks, but he will not be kept waiting. Half a bottle of Chambertin, a red mullet, or a pullet à la Marengo satisfy every need, but it is unwise to put pastry or cream upon the table, because he is as likely as not to eat it before the fowl. Ah, that is a curious sight, is it not?'

I had halted with an exclamation of astonishment. A groom was cantering a very beautiful Arab horse down one of the lanes between the tents. As it passed, a grenadier who was standing with a small pig under his arm hurled it down under the feet of the horse. The pig squealed vigorously and scuttled away, but the horse cantered on without changing its step.

'What does that mean?' I asked.

'That is Jardin, the head groom, breaking in a charger for the Emperor's use. They are first trained by having a cannon fired in their ears, then they are struck suddenly by heavy objects, and finally they have the test of the pig being thrown under their feet. The Emperor has not a very firm seat, and he very often loses himself in a reverie when he is riding, so it might not be very safe if the horse were not well trained. Do you see that young man asleep at the door of a tent?'

'Yes, I see him.'

'You would not think that he is at the present moment serving the Emperor?'

'It seems a very easy service.'

'I wish all our services were as easy, Monsieur de Laval. That is Joseph Linden, whose foot is the exact size of the Emperor's. He wears his new boots and shoes for three days before they are given to his master. You can see by the gold buckles that he has a pair on at the present moment. Ah, Monsieur de Caulaincourt, will you not join us at dinner in my tent?'

A tall, handsome man, very elegantly dressed, came across and greeted us. 'It is rare to find you at rest, Monsieur de Meneval. I have no very light task myself as head of the household, but I think I have more leisure than you. Have we time for dinner before the Emperor returns?'

'Yes, yes; here is the tent, and everything ready. We can see when the Emperor returns, and be in the room before he can reach it. This is camp fare, Monsieur de Laval, but no doubt you will excuse it.'

For my own part I had an excellent appetite for the cutlets and salad, but what I relished above all was to hear the talk of my companions, for I was full of curiosity as to everything which concerned this singular man, whose genius had elevated him so rapidly to the highest position in the world. The head of his household discussed him with an extraordinary frankness.

'What do they say of him in England, Monsieur de Laval?' he asked.

'Nothing very good.'

'So I have gathered from their papers. They drive the Emperor frantic, and yet he will insist upon reading them. I am willing to lay a wager that the very first thing which he does when he enters London will be to send cavalry detachments to the various newspaper offices, and endeavour to seize the editors.'

'And the next?'

'The next,' said he, laughing, 'will be to issue a long proclamation to prove that we have conquered England entirely for the good of the English, and very much against our own inclinations. And then, perhaps, the Emperor will allow the English to understand that, if they absolutely demand a Protestant for a ruler, it is possible that there are a few little points in which he differs from Holy Church.'

'Too bad! Too bad!' cried de Meneval, looking amused and yet rather frightened at his companion's audacity. 'No doubt for state reasons the Emperor had to tamper a little with Mahommedanism, and I daresay he would attend this Church of St. Paul's as readily as he did the Mosque at Cairo; but it would not do for a ruler to be a bigot. After all, the Emperor has to think for all.'

'He thinks too much,' said Caulaincourt, gravely. 'He thinks so much that other people in France are getting out of the way of thinking at all. You know what I mean, de Meneval, for you have seen it as much as I have.'

'Yes, yes,' answered the secretary. 'He certainly does not encourage originality among those who surround him. I have heard him say many a time that he desired nothing but mediocrity, which was a poor compliment, it must be confessed, to us who have the honour of serving him.'

'A clever man at his Court shows his cleverness best by pretending to be dull,' said Caulaincourt, with some bitterness.

'And yet there are many famous characters there,' I remarked.

'If so, it is only by concealing their characters that they remain there. His ministers are clerks, his generals are superior aides-de-camp. They are all agents. You have this wonderful man in the middle, and all around you have so many mirrors which reflect different sides of him. In one you see him as a financier, and you call him Lebrun. In another you have a gendarme, and you name it Savary or Fouché. In yet another he figures as a diplomatist, and is called Talleyrand. You see different figures, but it is really the same man. There is a Monsieur de Caulaincourt, for example, who arranges the household; but he cannot dismiss a servant without permission. It is still always the Emperor. And he plays upon us. We must confess, de Meneval, that he plays upon us. In nothing else do I see so clearly his wonderful cleverness. He will not let us be too friendly lest we combine. He has set his Marshals against each other until there are hardly two of them on speaking terms. Look how Davoust hates Bernadotte, or Lannes and Bessières, or Ney and Masséna. It is all they can do to keep their sabres in their sheaths when they meet. And then he knows our weak points. Savary's thirst for money, Cambacérès's vanity, Duroc's bluntness, Berthier's foolishness, Maret's insipidity, Talleyrand's mania for speculation, they are all so many tools in his hand. I do not know what my own greatest weakness may be, but I am sure that he does, and that he uses his knowledge.'

'But how he must work!' I exclaimed.

'Ah, you may say so,' said de Meneval. 'What energy! Eighteen hours out of twenty-four for weeks on end. He has presided over the Legislative Council until they were fainting at their desks. As to me, he will be the death of me, just as he wore out de Bourrienne; but I will die at my post without a murmur, for if he is hard upon us he is hard upon himself also.'

'He was the man for France,' said de Caulaincourt. 'He is the very genius of system and of order, and of discipline. When one remembers the chaos in which our poor country found itself after the Revolution, when no one would be governed and everyone wanted to govern some-one else, you will understand that only Napoleon could have saved us. We were all longing for something fixed to secure ourselves to, and then we came upon this iron pillar of a man. And what a man he was in those days, Monsieur de Laval! You see him now when he has got all that he can want. He is good-humoured and easy. But at that time he had got nothing, but coveted everything. His glance frightened women. He walked the streets like a wolf. People looked after him as he passed. His face was quite different—it was craggy, hollow-cheeked, with an oblique menacing gaze, and the jaws of a pike. Oh, yes, this little Lieutenant Buonaparte from the Military School of Brienne was a singular figure. "There is a man," said I, when I saw him, "who will sit upon a throne or kneel upon a scaffold." And now look at him!'

'And that is ten years ago,' I exclaimed.

'Only ten years, and they have brought him from a barrack-room to the Tuileries. But he was born for it. You could not keep him down. De Bourrienne told me that when he was a little fellow at Brienne he had the grand Imperial manner, and would praise or blame, glare or smile, exactly as he does now. Have you seen his mother, Monsieur de Laval? She is a tragedy queen, tall, stern, reserved, silent. There is the spring from which he flowed.'

I could see in the gentle, spaniel-eyes of the secretary that he was disturbed by the frankness of de Caulain-court's remarks.

'You can tell that we do not live under a very terrible tyranny, Monsieur de Laval,' said he, 'or we should hardly venture to discuss our ruler so frankly. The fact is that we have said nothing which he would not have listened to with pleasure and perhaps with approval. He has his little frailties, or he would not be human, but take his qualities as a ruler and I would ask you if there has ever been a man who has justified the choice of a

94

nation so completely. He works harder than any of his subjects. He is a general beloved by his soldiers. He is a master beloved by his servants. He never has a holiday, and he is always ready for his work. There is not under the roof of the Tuileries a more abstemious eater or drinker. He educated his brothers at his own expense when he was a very poor man, and he has caused even his most distant relatives to share in his prosperity. In a word, he is economical, hard-working, and temperate. We read in the London papers about this Prince of Wales, Monsieur de Laval, and I do not think that he comes very well out of the comparison.'

I thought of the long record of Brighton scandals, London scandals, Newmarket scandals, and I had to leave George undefended.

'As I understand it,' said I, 'it is not the Emperor's private life, but his public ambition, that the English attack.'

'The fact is,' said de Caulaincourt, 'that the Emperor knows, and we all know, that there is not room enough in the world for both France and England. One or other must be supreme. If England were once crushed we could then lay the foundations of a permanent peace. Italy is ours. Austria we can crush again as we have crushed her before. Germany is divided. Russia can expand to the south and east. America we can take at our leisure, finding our pretext in Louisiana or in Canada. There is a world empire waiting for us, and there is the only thing that stops us.' He pointed out through the opening of the tent at the broad blue Channel.

Far away, like snow-white gulls in the distance, were the sails of the blockading fleet. I thought again of what I had seen the night before—the lights of the ships upon the sea and the glow of the camp upon the shore. The powers of the land and of the ocean were face to face whilst a waiting world stood round to see what would come of it.

XII. The Man of Action

De Meneval's tent had been pitched in such a way that he could overlook the Royal headquarters, but whether it was that we were too absorbed in the interest of our conversation, or that the Emperor had used the other entrance in returning from the review, we were suddenly startled by the appearance of a captain dressed in the green jacket of the Chasseurs of the Guard, who had come to say that Napoleon was waiting for his secretary. Poor de Meneval's face turned as white as his beautiful ruffles as he sprang to his feet, hardly able to speak for agitation.

'I should have been there!' he gasped. 'Oh, what a misfortune! Monsieur de Caulaincourt, you must excuse me! Where is my hat and my sword? Come, Monsieur de Laval, not an instant is to be lost!'

I could judge from the terror of de Meneval, as well as from the scene which I had witnessed with Admiral Bruix, what the influence was which the Emperor exercised over those who were around him. They were never at their ease, always upon the brink of a catastrophe, encouraged one day only to be rudely rebuffed the next, bullied in public and slighted in private, and yet, in spite of it all, the singular fact remains that they loved him and served him as no monarch has been loved and served.

'Perhaps I had best stay here,' said I, when we had come to the ante-chamber, which was still crowded with people.

'No, no, I am responsible for you. You must come with me. Oh, I trust he is not offended with me! How could he have got in without my seeing him?'

My frightened companion scratched at the door, which was opened instantly by Roustem the Mameluke, who guarded it within. The room into which we passed was of considerable size, but was furnished with extreme simplicity. It was papered of a silver-grey colour, with a sky-blue ceiling, in the centre of which was the Imperial eagle in gold, holding a thunderbolt. In spite of the warm weather, a large fire was burning at one side, and the air was heavy with heat and the aromatic smell of aloes. In the middle of the room was a large oval table covered with green cloth and littered with a number of letters and papers. A raised writing-desk was at one side of the table, and behind it in a green morocco chair with curved arms there sat the Emperor. A number of officials were standing round the walls, but he took no notice of them. In his hand he had a small penknife, with which he whittled the wooden knob at the end of his chair. He glanced up as we entered, and shook his head coldly at de Meneval.

'I have had to wait for you, Monsieur de Meneval,' said he. 'I cannot remember that I ever waited for my late secretary de Bourrienne. That is enough! No excuses! Take this report which I have written in your absence, and make a copy of it.'

Poor de Meneval took the paper with a shaking hand, and carried it to the little side table which was reserved for his use. Napoleon rose and paced slowly up and down the room with his hands behind his back, and his big round head stooping a little forwards. It was certainly as well that he had a secretary, for I observed that in writing this single document he had spattered the whole place with ink, and it was obvious that he had twice used his white kerseymere knee-breeches as a pen-wiper. As for me, I stood quietly beside Roustem at the door, and he took not the slightest notice of my presence.

'Well,' he cried presently, 'is it ready, de Meneval? We have something more to do.'

The secretary half turned in his chair, and his face was more agitated than ever.

'If it please you, Sire——' he stammered.

'Well, well, what is the matter now?'

'If it please you, Sire, I find some little difficulty in reading what you have written.'

'Tut, tut, sir. You see what the report is about.'

'Yes, Sire, it is about forage for the cavalry horses.'

Napoleon smiled, and the action made his face look quite boyish.

'You remind me of Cambacérès, de Meneval. When I wrote him an account of the battle of Marengo, he thought that my letter was a rough plan of the engagement. It is incredible how much difficulty you appear to have in reading what I write. This document has nothing to do with cavalry horses, but it contains the instructions to Admiral Villeneuve as to the concentration of his fleet so as to obtain command of the Channel. Give it to me and I will read it to you.'

He snatched the paper up in the quick, impulsive way which was characteristic of him. But after a long fierce stare he crumpled it up and hurled it under the table.

'I will dictate it to you,' said he; and, pacing up and down the long room, he poured forth a torrent of words, which poor de Meneval, his face shining with his exertions, strove hard to put upon paper. As he grew excited by his own ideas, Napoleon's voice became shriller, his step faster, and he seized his right cuff in the fingers of the same hand, and twisted his right arm in the singular epileptic gesture which was peculiar to him. But his thoughts and plans were so admirably clear that even I, who knew nothing of the matter, could readily follow them, while above all I was impressed by the marvellous grasp of fact which enabled him to speak with confidence, not only of the line-of-battle ships, but of the frigates, sloops, and brigs at Ferrol, Rochefort, Cadiz, Carthagena, and Brest, with the exact strength of each in men and in guns; while the names and force of the English vessels were equally at his fingers' ends. Such familiarity would have been remarkable in a naval officer, but when I thought that this question of the ships was only one out of fifty with which this man had to deal, I began to realise the immense grasp of that capacious mind. He did not appear to be paying the least attention to me, but it seems that he was really watching me closely, for he turned upon me when he had finished his dictation.

'You appear to be surprised, Monsieur de Laval, that I should be able to transact my naval business without having my minister of marine at my elbow; but it is one of my rules to know and to do things for myself. Perhaps if these good Bourbons had had the same habit they would not now be living amidst the fogs of England.'

'One must have your Majesty's memory in order to do it,' I observed.

'It is the result of system,' said he. 'It is as if I had drawers in my brain, so that when I opened one I could close the others. It is seldom that I fail to find what I want there. I have a poor memory for names or dates, but an excellent one for facts or faces. There is a good deal to bear in mind, Monsieur de Laval. For example, I have, as you have seen, my one little drawer full of the ships upon the sea. I have another which contains all the harbours and forts of France. As an example, I may tell you that when my minister of war was reading me a report of all the coast defences, I was able to point out to him that he had omitted two guns in a battery near Ostend. In yet another of my brain-drawers I have the regiments of France. Is that drawer in order, Marshal Berthier?'

A clean-shaven man, who had stood biting his nails in the window, bowed at the Emperor's question.

'I am sometimes tempted to believe, Sire, that you know the name of every man in the ranks,' said he.

'I think that I know most of my old Egyptian grumblers,' said he. 'And then, Monsieur de Laval, there is another drawer for canals, bridges, roads, manufactures, and every detail of internal administration. The law, finance, Italy, the Colonies, Holland, all these things demand drawers of their own. In these days, Monsieur de Laval, France asks something more of its ruler than that he should carry eight yards of ermine with dignity, or ride after a stag in the forest of Fontainebleau.'

I thought of the helpless, gentle, pompous Louis whom

my father had once taken me to visit, and I understood that France, after her convulsions and her sufferings, did indeed require another and a stronger head.

'Do you not think so, Monsieur de Laval?' asked the Emperor. He had halted for a moment by the fire, and was grinding his dainty gold-buckled shoe into one of the burning logs.

'You have come to a very wise decision,' said he when I had answered his question. 'But you have always been of this way of thinking, have you not? Is it not true that you once defended me when some young Englishman was drinking toasts to my downfall at an inn in this village in which you lived?'

I remembered the incident, although I could not imagine how it had reached his ears.

'Why should you have done this?'

'I did it on impulse, Sire.'

'On impulse!' he cried, in a tone of contempt. 'I do not know what people mean when they say that they do things upon impulse. In Charenton things are doubtless done upon impulse, but not amongst sane people. Why should you risk your life over there in defending me when at the time you had nothing to hope for from me?'

'It was because I felt that you stood for France, Sire.'

During this conversation he had still walked up and down the room, twisting his right arm about, and occasionally looking at one or other of us with his eyeglass, for his sight was so weak that he always needed a single glass indoors and binoculars outside. Sometimes he stopped and helped himself to great pinches of snuff from a tortoise-shell box, but I observed that none of it ever reached his nose, for he dropped it all from between his fingers on to his waistcoat and the floor. My answer seemed to please him, for he suddenly seized my ear and pulled it with considerable violence.

'You are quite right, my friend,' said he. 'I stand for France just as Frederic the Second stood for Prussia. I will make her the great Power of the world, so that every monarch in Europe will find it necessary to keep a palace in Paris, and they will all come to hold the train at the coronation of my descendants'—a spasm of pain passed suddenly over his face. 'My God! for whom am I building? Who will be my descendants?' I heard him mutter, and he passed his hand over his forehead.

'Do they seem frightened in England about my approaching invasion?' he asked suddenly. 'Have you heard them express fears lest I get across the Channel?'

I was forced in truth to say that the only fears which I had ever heard expressed were lest he should not get across.

'The soldiers are very jealous that the sailors should always have the honour,' said I.

'But they have a very small army.'

'Nearly every man is a volunteer, Sire.'

'Pooh, conscripts!' he chided, and made a motion with his hands as if to sweep them from before him. 'I will land with a hundred thousand men in Kent or in Sussex. I will fight a great battle which I will win with a loss of ten thousand men. On the third day I shall be in London. I will seize the statesmen, the bankers, the merchants, the newspaper men. I will impose an indemnity of a hundred millions of their pounds. I will favour the poor at the expense of the rich, and so I shall have a party. I will detach Scotland and Ireland by giving them constitutions which will put them in a superior condition to England. Thus I will sow dissensions everywhere. Then as a price for leaving the island I will claim their fleet and their colonies. In this way I shall secure the command of the world to France for at least a century to come.'

In this short sketch I could perceive the quality which I have since heard remarked in Napoleon, that his mind could both conceive a large scheme, and at the same time evolve those practical details which would seem to bring it within the bounds of possibility. One instant it would be a wild dream of overrunning the East. The next it was a schedule of the ships, the ports, the stores, the troops, which would be needed to turn dream into fact. He gripped the heart of a question with the same decision which made him strike straight for an enemy's capital. The soul of a poet, and the mind of a man of business of the first order, that is the combination which may make a man dangerous to the world.

I think that it may have been his purpose—for he never did anything without a purpose—to give me an object-lesson of his own capacity for governing, with the idea, perhaps, that I might in turn influence others of the émigrés by what I told them. At any rate he left me there to stand and to watch the curious succession of points upon which he had to give an opinion during a few hours. Nothing seemed to be either too large or too small for that extraordinary mind. At one instant it was the arrangements for the winter cantonments of two hundred thousand men, at the next he was discussing with de Caulaincourt the curtailing of the expenses of the household, and the possibility of suppressing some of the carriages.

'It is my desire to be economical at home so as to make a good show abroad,' said he. 'For myself, when I had the honour to be a sub-lieutenant I found that I could live very well upon 1,200 francs a year, and it would be no hardship to me to go back to it. This extravagance of the palace must be stopped. For example, I see upon your accounts that 155 cups of coffee are drunk a day, which with sugar at four francs and coffee at five francs a pound come to twenty sous a cup. It would be better to make an allowance for coffee. The stable bills are also too high. At the present price of fodder seven or eight francs a week should be enough for each horse in a stable of two hundred. I will not have any waste at the Tuileries.'

Thus within a few minutes he would pass from a question of milliards to a question of sous, and from the management of an empire to that of a stable. From time to time I could observe that he threw a little oblique glance at me as if to ask what I thought of it all, and at the time I wondered very much why my approval should be of any consequence to him. But now, when I look back and see that my following his fortunes brought over so many others of the young nobility, I understand that he saw very much further than I did.

'Well, Monsieur de Laval,' said he suddenly, 'you have seen something of my methods. Are you prepared to enter my service?'

'Assuredly, Sire,' I answered.

'I can be a very hard master when I like,' said he, smiling. 'You were there when I spoke to Admiral Bruix. We have all our duty to do, and discipline is as necessary in the highest as in the lowest ranks. But anger with me never rises above here,' and he drew his hand across his throat. 'I never permit it to cloud my brain. Dr. Corvisart here would tell you that I have the slowest pulse of all his patients.'

'And that you are the fastest eater, Sire,' said a large-faced, benevolent-looking person who had been whispering to Marshal Berthier.

'Ohé, you rascal, you rake that up against me, do you? The Doctor will not forgive me because I tell him when I am unwell that I had rather die of the disease than of the remedies. If I eat too fast it is the fault of the State, which does not allow me more than a few minutes for my meals. Which reminds me that it must be rather after my dinner hour, Constant?'

'It is four hours after it, Sire.'

'Serve it up then at once.'

'Yes, Sire. Monsieur Isabey is outside, Sire, with his dolls.'

'Ah, we shall see them at once. Show him in.'

A man entered who had evidently just arrived from a long journey. Under his arm he carried a large flat wickerwork basket.

'It is two days since I sent for you, Monsieur Isabey.'

'The courier arrived yesterday, Sire. I have been travelling from Paris ever since.'

'Have you the models there?'

'Yes, Sire.'

'Then you may lay them out on that table.'

I could not at first imagine what it meant when I saw, upon Isabey opening his basket, that it was crammed with little puppets about a foot high, all of them dressed in the most gorgeous silk and velvet costumes, with trimmings of ermine and hangings of gold lace. But presently, as the designer took them out one by one and placed them on the table, I understood that the Emperor, with his extraordinary passion for detail and for directly controlling everything in his Court, had had these dolls dressed in order to judge the effect of the gorgeous costumes which had been ordered for his grand functionaries upon State occasions.

'What is this?' he asked, holding up a little lady in hunting costume of amaranth and gold with a toque and plume of white feathers.

'That is for the Empress's hunt, Sire.'

'You should have the waist rather lower,' said Napoleon, who had very definite opinions about ladies' dresses. 'These cursed fashions seem to be the only thing in my dominions which I cannot regulate. My tailor, Duchesne, takes three inches from my coat-tails, and all the armies and fleets of France cannot prevent him. Who is this?'

He had picked up a very gorgeous figure in a green coat.

'That is the grand master of the hunt, Sire.'

'Then it is you, Berthier. How do you like your new costume? And this in red?'

'That is the Arch-Chancellor.'

'And the violet?'

'That is the Grand Chamberlain.'

The Emperor was as much amused as a child with a new toy. He formed little groups of the figures upon the table, so that he might have an idea of how the dignitaries would look when they chatted together. Then he threw them all back into the basket.

'Very good,' said he. 'You and David have done your work very well, Isabey. You will submit these designs to the Court outfitters and have an estimate for the expense. You may tell Lenormand that if she ventures to send in such an account as the last which she sent to the Empress she shall see the inside of Vincennes. You would not think it right, Monsieur de Laval, to spend twenty-five thousand francs upon a single dress, even though it were for Mademoiselle Eugénie de Choiseul.'

Was there anything which this wizard of a man did not know? What could my love affairs be to him amidst the clash of armies and the struggles of nations? When I looked at him, half in amazement and half in fear, that pleasant boyish smile lit up his pale face, and his plump little hand rested for an instant upon my shoulder. His eyes were of a bright blue when he was amused, though they would turn dark when he was thoughtful, and steel-grey in moments of excitement.

'You were surprised when I told you a little while ago about your encounter with the Englishman in the village inn. You are still more surprised now when I tell you about a certain young lady. You must certainly have thought that I was very badly served by my agents in England if I did not know such important details as these.'

'I cannot conceive, Sire, why such trifles should be reported to you, or why you should for one instant remember them.'

'You are certainly a very modest young man, and I hope you will not lose that charming quality when you have been for a little time at my Court. So you think that your own private affairs are of no importance to me?'

'I do not know why they should be, Sire.'

'What is the name of your great-uncle?'

'He is the Cardinal de Laval de Montmorency.'

'Precisely. And where is he?'

'He is in Germany.'

'Quite so—in Germany, and not at Notre Dame,

where I should have placed him. Who is your first cousin?'

'The Duke de Rohan.'

'And where is he?'

'In London.'

'Yes, in London, and not at the Tuileries, where he might have had what he liked for the asking. I wonder if I were to fall whether I should have followers as faithful as those of the Bourbons. Would the men that I have made go into exile and refuse all offers until I should return? Come here, Berthier!' he took his favourite by the ear with the caressing gesture which was peculiar to him. 'Could I count upon you, you rascal—eh?'

'I do not understand you, Sire.' Our conversation had been carried on in a voice which had made it inaudible to the other people in the room, but now they were all listening to what Berthier had to say.

'If I were driven out, would you go into exile also?'

'No, sire.'

'Diable! At least you are frank.'

'I could not go into exile, Sire.'

'And why?'

'Because I should be dead, Sire.'

Napoleon began to laugh.

'And there are some who say that our Berthier is dull-witted,' said he. 'Well, I think I am pretty sure of you, Berthier, for although I am fond of you for reasons of my own I do not think that you would be of much value to anyone else. Now I could not say that of you, Monsieur Talleyrand. You would change very quickly to a new master as you have changed from an old one. You have a genius, you know, for adapting yourself.'

There was nothing which the Emperor loved more than to suddenly produce little scenes of this sort which made everybody very uncomfortable, for no one could tell what awkward or compromising question he was going to put to them next. At present, however, they all forgot their own fears of what might come in their interest at the reply which the famous diplomatist might make to a suggestion which everybody knew to be so true. He stood, leaning upon his black ebony stick, with his bulky shoulders stooping forward, and an amused smile upon his face, as if the most innocent of compliments had been addressed to him. One of his few titles to respect is that he always met Napoleon upon equal terms, and never condescended to fawn upon him or to flatter him.

'You think I should desert you, Sire, if your enemies offered me more than you have given me?'

'I am perfectly sure that you would.'

'Well, really I cannot answer for myself, Sire, until the offer has been made. But it will have to be a very large one. You see, apart from my very nice hotel in the Rue St. Florentin, and the two hundred thousand or so which you are pleased to allow me, there is my position as the first minister in Europe. Really, Sire, unless they put me on the throne I cannot see how I can better my position.'

'No, I think I have you pretty safe,' said Napoleon, looking hard at him with thoughtful eyes. 'By the way, Talleyrand, you must either marry Madame Grand or get rid of her, for I cannot have a scandal about the Court.'

I was astounded to hear so delicate and personal a matter discussed in this public way, but this also was characteristic of the rule of this extraordinary man, who proclaimed that he looked upon delicacy and good taste as two of the fetters with which mediocrity attempted to cripple genius. There was no question of private life, from the choosing of a wife to the discarding of a mistress, that this young conqueror of thirty-six did not claim the right of discussing and of finally settling. Talleyrand broke once more into his benevolent but inscrutable smile.

'I suppose that it is from early association, Sire,' said he, ' but my instincts are to avoid marriage.'

Napoleon began to laugh.

'I forget sometimes that it is really the Bishop of Autun

107

to whom I am speaking,' said he. 'I think that perhaps I have interest enough with the Pope to ask him, in return for any little attention which we gave him at the Coronation, to show you some leniency in this matter. She is a clever woman, this Madame Grand. I have observed that she listens with attention.'

Talleyrand shrugged his rounded shoulders.

'Intellect in a woman is not always an advantage, Sire. A clever woman compromises her husband. A stupid woman only compromises herself.'

'The cleverest woman,' said Napoleon, 'is the woman who is clever enough to conceal her cleverness. The women in France have always been a danger, for they are cleverer than the men. They cannot understand that it is their hearts and not their heads that we want. When they have had influence upon a monarch, they have invariably ruined his career. Look at Henry the Fourth and Louis the Fourteenth. They are all ideologists, dreamers, sentimentalists, full of emotion and energy, but without logic or foresight. Look at that accursed Madame de Staël! Look at the Salons of the Quartier St. Germain! Their eternal clack, clack, clack give me more trouble than the fleet of England. Why cannot they look after their babies and their needlework? I suppose you think that these are very dreadful opinions, Monsieur de Laval?'

It was not an easy question to answer, so I was silent.

'You have not at your age become a practical man,' said the Emperor. 'You will understand then. I daresay that I thought as you do at the time when the stupid Parisians were saying what a misalliance the widow of the famous General de Beauharnais was making by marrying the unknown Buonaparte. It was a beautiful dream! There are nine inns in a single day's journey between Milan and Mantua, and I wrote a letter to my wife from each of them. Nine letters in a day—but one becomes disillusioned, monsieur. One learns to accept things as they are.'

I could not but think what a beautiful young man he

must have been before he had learned to accept things as they are. The glamour, the romance—what a bald dead thing is life without it! His own face had clouded over as if that old life had perhaps had a charm which the Emperor's crown had never given. It may be that those nine letters written in one day at wayside inns had brought him more true joy than all the treaties by which he had torn provinces from his neighbours. But the sentiment passed from his face, and he came back in his sudden concise fashion to my own affairs.

'Eugénie de Choiseul is the niece of the Duc de Choiseul, is she not?' he asked.

'Yes, Sire.'

'You are affianced!'

'Yes, Sire.'

He shook his head impatiently.

'If you wish to advance yourself in my Court, Monsieur de Laval,' said he, 'you must commit such matters to my care. Is it likely that I can look with indifference upon a marriage between émigrés—an alliance between my enemies?'

'But she shares my opinions, Sire.'

'Ta, ta, ta, at her age one has no opinions. She has the émigré blood in her veins, and it will come out. Your marriage shall be my care, Monsieur de Laval. And I wish you to come to the Pont de Briques that you may be presented to the Empress. What is it, Constant?'

'There is a lady outside who desires to see your Majesty. Shall I tell her to come later?'

'A lady!' cried the Emperor, smiling. 'We do not see many faces in the camp which have not a moustache upon them. Who is she? What does she want?'

'Her name, Sire, is Mademoiselle Sibylle Bernac.'

'What!' cried Napoleon. 'It must be the daughter of old Bernac of Grosbois. By the way, Monsieur de Laval, he is your uncle upon your mother's side, is he not?'

I may have flushed with shame as I acknowledged it, for the Emperor read my feelings.

'Well, well, he has not a very savoury trade, it is true, and yet I can assure you that it is one which is very necessary to me. By the way, this uncle of yours, as I understand, holds the estates which should have descended to you, does he not?'

'Yes, Sire.'

His blue eyes flashed suspicion at me.

'I trust that you are not joining my service merely in the hope of having them restored to you.'

'No, Sire. It is my ambition to make a career for myself.'

'It is a prouder thing,' said the Emperor, 'to found a family than merely to perpetuate one. I could not restore your estates, Monsieur de Laval, for things have come to such a pitch in France that if one once begins restorations the affair is endless. It would shake all public confidence. I have no more devoted adherents than the men who hold land which does not belong to them. As long as they serve me, as your uncle serves me, the land must remain with them. But what can this young lady require of me? Show her in, Constant!'

An instant later my Cousin Sibylle was conducted into the room. Her face was pale and set, but her large dark eyes were filled with resolution, and she carried herself like a princess.

'Well, mademoiselle, why do you come here? What is it that you want?' asked the Emperor in the brusque manner which he adopted to women even if he were wooing them.

Sibylle glanced round, and as our eyes met for an instant I felt that my presence had renewed her courage. She looked bravely at the Emperor as she answered him.

'I come, Sire, to implore a favour of you.'

'Your father's daughter has certainly claims upon me, mademoiselle. What is it that you wish?'

'I do not ask it in my father's name, but in my own. I implore you, Sire, to spare the life of Monsieur Lucien Lesage, who was arrested yesterday upon a charge of treason. He is a student, Sire—a mere dreamer who has lived away from the world and has been made a tool by designing men.'

'A dreamer!' cried the Emperor harshly. 'They are the most dangerous of all.' He took a bundle of notes from his table and glanced them over. 'I presume that he is fortunate enough to be your lover, mademoiselle?'

Sibylle's pale face flushed, and she looked down before the Emperor's keen sardonic glance.

'I have his examination here. He does not come well out of it. I confess that from what I see of the young man's character I should not say that he is worthy of your love.'

'I implore you to spare him, Sire.'

'What you ask is impossible, mademoiselle. I have been conspired against from two sides—by the Bourbons and by the Jacobins. Hitherto I have been too long-suffering, and they have been encouraged by my patience. Since Cadoudal and the Duc d'Enghien died the Bourbons have been quiet. Now I must teach the same lesson to these others.'

I was astonished and am still astonished at the passion with which my brave and pure cousin loved this cowardly and low-minded man, though it is but in accordance with that strange law which draws the extremes of nature together. As she heard the Emperor's stern reply the last sign of colour faded from her pale face, and her eyes were dimmed with despairing tears, which gleamed upon her white cheeks like dew upon the petals of a lily.

'For God's sake, Sire! For the love of your mother spare him!' she cried, falling upon her knees at the Emperor's feet. 'I will answer for him that he never offends you again.'

'Tut, tut!' cried Napoleon angrily, turning upon his heel and walking impatiently up and down the room. 'I cannot grant you what you ask, mademoiselle. When I say so once it is finished. I cannot have my decisions in high matters of State affected by the intrusion of women.

The Jacobins have been dangerous of late, and an example must be made or we shall have the Faubourg St. Antoine upon our hands once more.'

The Emperor's set face and firm manner showed it was hopeless, and yet my cousin persevered as no one but a woman who pleads for her lover would have dared to do.

'He is harmless, Sire.'

'His death will frighten others.'

'Spare him and I will answer for his loyalty.'

'What you ask is impossible.'

Constant and I raised her from the ground.

'That is right, Monsieur de Laval,' said the Emperor. 'This interview can lead to nothing. Remove your cousin from the room!'

But she had again turned to him with a face which showed that even now all hope had not been abandoned.

'Sire,' cried. 'You say that an example must be made. There is Toussac——!'

'Ah, if I could lay my hands upon Toussac!'

'He is the dangerous man. It was he and my father who led Lucien on. If an example must be made it should be an example of the guilty rather than of the innocent.'

'They are both guilty. And, besides, we have our hands upon the one but not upon the other.'

'But if I could find him?'

Napoleon thought for a moment.

'If you do,' said he, 'Lesage will be forgiven!'

'But I cannot do it in a day.'

'How long do you ask?'

'A week at the least.'

'Then he has a respite of a week. If you can find Toussac in the time, Lesage will be pardoned. If not he will die upon the eighth day. It is enough. Monsieur de Laval, remove your cousin, for I have matters of more importance to attend to. I shall expect you one evening at the Pont de Briques, when you are ready to be presented to the Empress.'

XIII. The Man of Dreams

WHEN I had escorted my Cousin Sibylle from the presence of the Emperor, I was surprised to find the same young hussar officer waiting outside who had commanded the guard which had brought me to the camp.

'Well, mademoiselle, what luck?' he asked excitedly, clanking towards us.

For an answer Sibylle shook her head.

'Ah, I feared as much, for the Emperor is a terrible man. It was brave, indeed, of you to attempt it. I had rather charge an unshaken square upon a spent horse than ask him for anything. But my heart is heavy, mademoiselle, that you should have been unsuccessful.' His boyish blue eyes filled with tears and his fair moustache drooped in such a deplorable fashion, that I could have laughed had the matter been less serious.

'Lieutenant Gerard chanced to meet me, and escorted me through the camp,' said my cousin. 'He has been kind enough to give me sympathy in my trouble.'

'And so do I, Sibylle,' I cried; 'you carried yourself like an angel, and it is a lucky man who is blessed with your love. I trust that he may be worthy of it.'

She turned cold and proud in an instant when anyone threw a doubt upon this wretched lover of hers.

'I know him as neither the Emperor nor you can do,' said she. 'He has the heart and soul of a poet, and he is too high-minded to suspect the intrigues to which he has fallen a victim. But as to Toussac, I should have no pity upon him, for I know him to be a murderer five times over, and I know also that there will be no peace in France until he has been taken. Cousin Louis, will you help me to do it?'

The lieutenant had been tugging at his moustache and looking me up and down with a jealous eye.

'Surely, mademoiselle, you will permit me to help you?' he cried in a piteous voice.

'I may need you both,' said she. 'I will come to you if I do. Now I will ask you to ride with me to the edge of the camp and there to leave me.'

She had a quick imperative way which came charmingly from those sweet womanly lips. The grey horse upon which I had come to the camp was waiting beside that of the hussar, so we were soon in the saddle. When we were clear of the huts my cousin turned to us.

'I had rather go alone now,' said she. 'It is understood, then, that I can rely upon you.'

'Entirely,' said I.

'To the death,' cried Gerard.

'It is everything to me to have two brave men at my back,' said she, and so, with a smile, gave her horse its head and cantered off over the downland in the direction of Grosbois.

For my part I remained in thought for some time, wondering what plan she could have in her head by which she hoped to get upon the track of Toussac. A woman's wit, spurred by the danger of her lover, might perhaps succeed where Fouché and Savary had failed. When at last I turned my horse I found my young hussar still staring after the distant rider.

'My faith! There is the woman for you, Etienne!' he kept repeating. 'What an eye! What a smile! What a rider! And she is not afraid of the Emperor. Oh, Etienne, here is the woman who is worthy of you!'

These were the little sentences which he kept muttering to himself until she vanished over the hill, when he became conscious at last of my presence.

'You are mademoiselle's cousin?' he asked. 'You are joined with me in doing something for her. I do not yet know what it is, but I am perfectly ready to do it.'

'It is to capture Toussac.'

'Excellent!'

'In order to save the life of her lover.'

There was a struggle in the face of the young hussar, but his more generous nature won.

'Sapristi! I will do even that if it will make her the happier!' he cried, and he shook the hand which I extended towards him. 'The Hussars of Berchény are quartered over yonder, where you see the lines of picketed horses. If you will send for Lieutenant Etienne Gerard you will find a sure blade always at your disposal. Let me hear from you then, and the sooner the better!' He shook his bridle and was off, with youth and gallantry in every line of him, from his red toupet and flowing dolman to the spur which twinkled on his heel.

But for four long days no word came from my cousin as to her quest, nor did I hear from this grim uncle of mine at the Castle of Grosbois. For myself I had gone into the town of Boulogne and had hired such a room as my thin purse could afford over the shop of a baker named Vidal, next to the Church of St. Augustin, in the Rue des Vents. Only last year I went back there under that strange impulse which leads the old to tread once more with dragging feet the same spots which have sounded to the crisp tread of their youth. The room is still there, the very pictures and the plaster head of Jean Bart which used to stand upon the side table. As I stood with my back to the narrow window, I had around me every smallest detail upon which my young eyes had looked; nor was I conscious that my own heart and feelings had undergone much change. And yet there, in the little round glass which faced me, was the long drawn, weary face of an aged man, and out of the window, when I turned, were the bare and lonely downs which had been peopled by that mighty host of a hundred and fifty thousand men. To think that the Grand Army should have vanished away like a shredding cloud upon a windy day, and yet that every sordid detail of a bourgeois lodging should remain unchanged! Truly, if man is not humble it is not for want of having his lesson taught to him by Nature.

My first care after I had chosen my room was to send to Grosbois for that poor little bundle which I had carried ashore with me that squally night from the English lugger. My next was to use the credit which my favourable reception by the Emperor and his assurance of employment had given me in order to obtain such a wardrobe as would enable me to appear without discredit among the richly-dressed courtiers and soldiers who surrounded him. It was well known that it was his whim that he should himself be the only plainly-dressed man in the company, and that in the most luxurious times of the Bourbons there was never a period when fine linen and a brave coat were more necessary for a man who would keep in favour. A new court and a young empire cannot afford to take anything for granted.

It was upon the morning of the fifth day that I received a message from Duroc, who was the head of the household, that I was to attend the Emperor at the headquarters in the camp, and that a seat in one of the Imperial carriages would be at my disposal that I might proceed with the Court to Pont de Briques, there to be present at the reception of the Empress. When I arrived I was shown at once through the large entrance tent, and admitted by Constant into the room beyond, where the Emperor stood with his back to the fire, kicking his heels against the grate. Talleyrand and Berthier were in attendance, and de Meneval, the secretary, sat at the writing-table.

'Ah, Monsieur de Laval,' said the Emperor with a friendly nod. 'Have you heard anything yet of your charming cousin?'

'Nothing, Sire,' I answered.

'I fear that her efforts will be in vain. I wish her every success, for we have no reason at all to fear this miserable poet, while the other is formidable. All the same, an example of some sort must be made.'

The darkness was drawing in, and Constant had appeared with a taper to light the candles, but the Emperor ordered him out.

'I like the twilight,' said he. 'No doubt, Monsieur de

116

Laval, after your long residence in England you find yourself also most at home in a dim light. I think that the brains of these people must be as dense as their fogs, to judge by the nonsense which they write in their accursed papers.' With one of those convulsive gestures which accompanied his sudden outbursts of passion he seized a sheaf of late London papers from the table, and ground them into the fire with his heel. 'An editor!' he cried in the guttural rasping voice which I had heard when I first met him. 'What is he? A dirty man with a pen in a back office. And he will talk like one of the great Powers of Europe. I have had enough of this freedom of the Press. There are some who would like to see it established in Paris. You are among them, Talleyrand. For my part I see no need for any paper at all except the *Moniteur* by which the Government may make known its decisions to the people.'

'I am of opinion, Sire,' said the minister, 'that it is better to have open foes than secret ones, and that it is less dangerous to shed ink than blood. What matters if your enemies have leave to rave in a few Paris papers, so long as you are at the head of five hundred thousand armed men?'

'Ta, ta, ta!' cried the Emperor impatiently. 'You speak as if I had received my crown from my father the late king. But even if I had, it would be intolerable, this government by newspaper. The Bourbons allowed themselves to be criticised, and where are they now? Had they used their Swiss Guards as I did the Grenadiers upon the eighteenth Brumaire what would have become of their precious National Assembly? There was a time when a bayonet in the stomach of Mirabeau might have settled the whole matter. Later it took the heads of a king and queen and the blood of a hundred thousand people.'

He sat down, and stretched his plump, white-clad legs towards the fire. Through the blackened shreds of the English papers the red glow beat upwards upon the beautiful, pallid, sphinx-like face—the face of a poet, of a

117

philosopher—of anything rather than of a ruthless and ambitious soldier. I have heard folk remark that no two portraits of the Emperor are alike, and the fault does not lie with the artists but with the fact that every varying mood made him a different man. But in his prime, before his features became heavy, I, who have seen sixty years of mankind, can say that in repose I have never looked upon a more beautiful face.

'You have no dreams and no illusions, Talleyrand,' said he. 'You are always practical, cold, and cynical. But with me, when I am in the twilight, as now, or when I hear the sound of the sea, my imagination begins to work. It is the same when I hear some music—especially music which repeats itself again and again like some pieces of Paisiello. They have a strange effect upon me, and I begin to Ossianise. I get large ideas and great aspirations. It is at such times that my mind always turns to the East, that swarming ant-heap of the human race, where alone it is possible to be very great. I renew my dreams of '98. I think of the possibility of drilling and arming these vast masses of men, and of precipitating them upon Europe. Had I conquered Syria I should have done this, and the fate of the world was really decided at the siege of Acre. With Egypt at my feet I already pictured myself approaching India, mounted upon an elephant, and holding in my hand a new version of the Koran which I had myself composed. I have been born too late. To be accepted as a world's conqueror one must claim to be divine. Alexander declared himself to be the son of Jupiter, and no one questioned it. But the world has grown old, and has lost its enthusiasms. What would happen if I were to make the same claim? Monsieur de Talleyrand would smile behind his hand, and the Parisians would write little lampoons upon the walls.'

He did not appear to be addressing us, but rather to be expressing his thoughts aloud, while allowing them to run to the most fantastic and extravagant lengths. This it was which he called Ossianising, because it recalled to him the wild vague dreams of the Gaelic Ossian, whose poems had always had a fascination for him. De Meneval has told me that for an hour at a time he has sometimes talked in this strain of the most intimate thoughts and aspirations of his heart, while his courtiers have stood round in silence waiting for the instant when he would return once more to his practical and incisive self.

'The great ruler,' said he, 'must have the power of religion behind him as well as the power of the sword. It is more important to command the souls than the bodies of men. The Sultan, for example, is the head of the faith as well as of the army. So were some of the Roman Emperors. My position must be incomplete until this is accomplished. At the present instant there are thirty departments in France where the Pope is more powerful than I am. It is only by universal dominion that peace can be assured in the world. When there is only one authority in Europe, seated at Paris, and when all the kings are so many lieutenants who hold their crowns from the central power of France, it is then that the reign of peace will be established. Many powers of equal strength must always lead to struggles until one becomes predominant. Her central position, her wealth and her history, all mark France out as being the power which will control and regulate the others. Germany is divided. Russia is barbarous. England is insular. France only remains.'

I began to understand as I listened to him that my friends in England had not been so far wrong when they had declared that so long as he lived—this little thirty-six year old artilleryman—there could not possibly be any peace in the world. He drank some coffee which Constant had placed upon the small round table at his elbow. Then he leaned back in his chair once more, still staring moodily at the red glow of the fire, with his chin sunk upon his chest.

'In those days,' said he, 'the kings of Europe will walk

behind the Emperor of France in order to hold up his train at his coronation. Each of them will have to maintain a palace in Paris, and the city will stretch as far as Versailles. These are the plans which I have made for Paris if she will show herself to be worthy of them. But I have no love for them, these Parisians, and they have none for me, for they cannot forget that I turned my guns upon them once before, and they know that I am ready to do so again. I have made them admire me and fear me, but I have never made them like me. Look what I have done for them. Where are the treasures of Genoa, the pictures and statues of Venice and of the Vatican? They are in the Louvre. The spoils of my victories have gone to decorate her. But they must always be changing, always chattering. They wave their hats at me now, but they would soon be waving their fists if I did not give them something to talk over and to wonder at. When other things are quiet, I have the dome of the Invalides regilded to keep their thoughts from mischief. Louis XIV gave them wars. Louis XV gave them gallantries and scandals of his Court. Louis XVI gave them nothing, so they cut off his head. It was you who helped to bring him to the scaffold, Talleyrand.'

'No, Sire, I was always a moderate.'

'At least, you did not regret his death.'

'The less so, since it has made room for you, Sire.'

'Nothing could have held me down, Talleyrand. I was born to reach the highest. It has always been the same with me. I remember when we were arranging the Treaty of Campo Formio—I a young general under thirty— there was a high vacant throne with the Imperial arms in the Commissioner's tent. I instantly sprang up the steps, and threw myself down upon it. I could not endure to think that there was anything above myself. And all the time I knew in my heart all that was going to happen to me. Even in the days when my brother Lucien and I lived in a little room upon a few francs a week, I knew perfectly well that the day would come when I should stand where I am now. And yet I had no prospects and no reason for any great hopes. I was not clever at school. I was only the forty-second out of fifty-eight. At mathematics I had perhaps some ability, but at nothing else. The truth is that I was always dreaming when the others were working. There was nothing to encourage my ambition, for the only thing which I inherited from my father was a weak stomach. Once, when I was very young, I went up to Paris with my father and my sister Caroline. We were in the Rue Richelieu, and we saw the king pass in his carriage. Who would have thought that the little boy from Corsica, who took his hat off and stared, was destined to be the next monarch of France? And yet even then I felt as if that carriage ought to belong to me. What is it, Constant?'

The discreet valet bent down and whispered something to the Emperor.

'Ah, of course,' said he. 'It was an appointment. I had forgotten it. Is she there?'

'Yes, Sire.'

'In the side room?'

'Yes, Sire.'

Talleyrand and Berthier exchanged glances, and the minister began to move towards the door.

'No, no, you can remain here,' said the Emperor. 'Light the lamps, Constant, and have the carriages ready in half-an-hour. Look over this draft of a letter to the Emperor of Austria, and let me have your observations upon it, Talleyrand. De Meneval, there is a lengthy report here as to the new dockyard at Brest. Extract what is essential from it, and leave it upon my desk at five o'clock to-morrow morning. Berthier, I will have the whole army into the boats at seven. We will see if they can embark within three hours. Monsieur de Laval, you shall wait here until we start for Pont de Briques.' So with a crisp order to each of us, he walked with little swift steps across the room, and I saw his square green back and white legs framed for an instant in the doorway. There was the flutter of a pink skirt beyond, and then the curtains closed behind him.

Berthier stood biting his nails, while Talleyrand looked at him with a slight raising of his bushy eyebrows. De Meneval with a rueful face was turning over the great bundle of papers which had to be copied by morning. Constant, with a noiseless tread, was lighting the candles upon the sconces round the room.

'Which is it?' I heard the minister whisper.

'The girl from the Imperial Opera,' said Berthier.

'Is the little Spanish lady out of favour then?'

'No, I think not. She was here yesterday.'

'And the other, the Countess?'

'She has a cottage at Ambleteuse.'

'But we must have no scandal about the Court,' said Talleyrand, with a sour smile, recalling the moral sentiments with which the Emperor had reproved him. 'And now, Monsieur de Laval,' he added, drawing me aside, 'I very much wish to hear from you about the Bourbon party in England. You must have heard their views. Do they imagine that they have any chance of success?'

And so for ten minutes he plied me with questions, which showed me clearly that the Emperor had read him aright, and that he was determined, come what might, to be upon the side which won. We were still talking when Constant entered hurriedly, with a look of anxiety and perplexity which I could not have imagined upon so smooth and imperturbable a face.

'Good Heavens, Monsieur Talleyrand,' he cried, clasping and unclasping his hands. 'Such a misfortune! Who could have expected it?'

'What is it, then, Constant?'

'Oh, Monsieur, I dare not intrude upon the Emperor. And yet . . . And yet . . . The Empress is outside, and she is coming in.'

XIV. Josephine

AT this unexpected announcement Talleyrand and
Berthier looked at each other in silence, and for once
the trained features of the great diplomatist, who lived
behind a mask, betrayed the fact that he was still capable
of emotion. The spasm which passed over them was
caused, however, rather by mischievous amusement than
by consternation, while Berthier—who had an honest
affection for both Napoleon and Josephine—ran frantically to the door as if to bar the Empress from entering.
Constant rushed towards the curtains which screened the
Emperor's room, and then, losing courage, although he
was known to be a stout-hearted man, he came running
back to Talleyrand for advice. It was too late now, however, for Roustem the Mameluke had opened the door,
and two ladies had entered the room. The first was tall
and graceful, with a smiling face, and an affable though
dignified manner. She was dressed in a black velvet cloak
with white lace at the neck and sleeves, and she wore a
black hat with a curling white feather. Her companion
was shorter, with a countenance which would have been
plain had it not been for the alert expression and large
dark eyes, which gave it charm and character. A small
black terrier dog had followed them in, but the first lady
turned and handed the thin steel chain with which she
led it to the Mameluke attendant.

'You had better keep Fortuné outside, Roustem,' said
she, in a peculiarly sweet musical voice. 'The Emperor
is not very fond of dogs, and if we intrude upon his
quarters we cannot do less than consult his tastes. Good
evening, Monsieur de Talleyrand! Madame de Rémusat
and I have driven all along the cliffs, and we have
stopped as we passed to know if the Emperor is coming
to Pont de Briques. But perhaps he has already started.
I had expected to find him here.'

'His Imperial Majesty was here a short time ago,' said Talleyrand, bowing and rubbing his hands.

'I hold my *salon*—such a *salon* as Pont de Briques is capable of—this evening, and the Emperor promised me that he would set his work aside for once, and favour us with his presence. I wish we could persuade him to work less, Monsieur de Talleyrand. He has a frame of iron, but he cannot continue in this way. These nervous attacks come more frequently upon him. He will insist upon doing everything, everything himself. It is noble, but it is to be a martyr. I have no doubt that at the present moment—but you have not yet told me where he is, Monsieur de Talleyrand.'

'We expect him every instant, your Majesty.'

'In that case we shall sit down and await his return. Ah, Monsieur de Meneval, how I pity you when I see you among all those papers! I was desolate when Monsieur de Bourrienne deserted the Emperor, but you have more than taken his place. Come up to the fire, Madame de Rémusat! Yes, yes, I insist upon it, for I know that you must be cold. Constant, come and put the rug under Madame de Rémusat's feet.'

It was by little acts of thoughtfulness and kindness like this that the Empress so endeared herself that she had really no enemies in France, even among those who were most bitterly opposed to her husband. Whether as the consort of the first man in Europe, or as the lonely divorced woman eating her heart out at Malmaison, she was always praised and beloved by those who knew her. Of all the sacrifices which the Emperor ever made to his ambition that of his wife was the one which cost him the greatest struggle and the keenest regret.

Now as she sat before the fire in the same chair which had so recently been occupied by the Emperor, I had an opportunity of studying this person, whose strange fate had raised her from being the daughter of a lieutenant of artillery to the first position among the women of Europe. She was six years older than Napoleon, and on this occasion, when I saw her first, she was in her forty-second year; but at a little distance or in a discreet light, it was no courtier's flattery to say that she might very well have passed for thirty. Her tall, elegant figure was girlish in its supple slimness, and she had an easy and natural grace in every movement, which she inherited with her tropical West Indian blood. Her features were delicate, and I have heard that in her youth she was strikingly beautiful; but, like most Creole women, she had become *passée* in early middle age. She had made a brave fight, however—with art as her ally—against the attacks of time, and her success had been such that when she sat aloof upon a dais or drove past in a procession, she might still pass as a lovely woman. In a small room, however, or in a good light, the crude pinks and whites with which she had concealed her sallow cheeks became painfully harsh and artificial. Her own natural beauty, however, still lingered in that last refuge of beauty—the eyes, which were large, dark, and sympathetic. Her mouth, too, was small and amiable, and her most frequent expression was a smile, which seldom broadened into a laugh, as she had her own reasons for preferring that her teeth should not be seen. As to her bearing, it was so dignified, that if this little West Indian had come straight from the loins of Charlemagne, it could not have been improved upon. Her walk, her glance, the sweep of her dress, the wave of her hand—they had all the happiest mixture of the sweetness of a woman and the condescension of a queen. I watched her with admiration as she leaned forward, picking little pieces of aromatic aloes wood out of the basket and throwing them on to the fire.

'Napoleon likes the smell of burning aloes,' said she. 'There was never anyone who had such a nose as he, for he can detect things which are quite hidden from me.'

'The Emperor has an excellent nose for many things,' said Talleyrand. 'The State contractors have found that out to their cost.'

'Oh, it is dreadful when he comes to examine accounts

—dreadful, Monsieur de Talleyrand! Nothing escapes him. He will make no allowances. Everything must be exact. But who is this young gentleman, Monsieur de Talleyrand? I do not think that he has been presented to me.'

The minister explained in a few words that I had been received into the Emperor's personal service, and Josephine congratulated me upon it with the most kindly sympathy.

'It eases my mind so to know that he has brave and loyal men round him. Ever since that dreadful affair of the infernal machine I have always been uneasy if he is away from me. He is really safest in time of war, for it is only then that he is away from the assassins who hate him. And now I understand that a new Jacobin plot has only just been discovered.'

'This is the same Monsieur de Laval who was there when the conspirator was taken,' said Talleyrand.

The Empress overwhelmed me with questions, hardly waiting for the answers in her anxiety.

'But this dreadful man Toussac has not been taken yet,' she cried. 'Have I not heard that a young lady is endeavouring to do what has baffled the secret police, and that the freedom of her lover is to be the reward of her success?'

'She is my cousin, your Imperial Majesty. Mademoiselle Sybille Bernac is her name.'

'You have only been in France a few days, Monsieur de Laval,' said Josephine, smiling, 'but it seems to me that all the affairs of the Empire are already revolving around you. You must bring this pretty cousin of yours—the Emperor said that she is pretty—to Court with you, and present her to me. Madame de Rémusat, you will take a note of the name.'

The Empress had stooped again to the basket of aloes wood which stood beside the fireplace. Suddenly I saw her stare hard at something, and then, with a little cry of surprise, she stooped and lifted an object from the carpet.

It was the Emperor's soft flat beaver with the little tri-colour cockade. Josephine sprang up, and looked from the hat in her hand to the imperturbable face of the minister.

'How is this, Monsieur de Talleyrand,' she cried, and the dark eyes began to shine with anger and suspicion. 'You said to me that the Emperor was out, and here is his hat!'

'Pardon me, your Imperial Majesty, I did not say that he was out.'

'What did you say then?'

'I said that he left the room a short time before.'

'You are endeavouring to conceal something from me,' she cried, with the quick instinct of a woman.

'I assure you that I tell you all I know.'

The Empress's eyes darted from face to face.

'Marshal Berthier,' she cried, 'I insist upon your telling me this instant where the Emperor is, and what he is doing.'

The slow-witted soldier stammered and twisted his cocked hat about.

'I know no more than Monsieur de Talleyrand does,' said he; 'the Emperor left us some time ago.'

'By which door?'

Poor Berthier was more confused than ever.

'Really, your Imperial Majesty, I cannot undertake to say by which door it was that the Emperor quitted the apartment.'

Josephine's eyes flashed round at me, and my heart shrank within me as I thought that she was about to ask me that same dreadful question. But I had just time to breathe one prayer to the good Saint Ignatius, who has always been gracious to our family, and the danger passed.

'Come, Madame de Rémusat,' said she. 'If these gentle-men will not tell us we shall very soon find out for ourselves.'

She swept with great dignity towards the curtained

door, followed at the distance of a few yards by her waiting lady, whose frightened face and lagging, unwilling
steps showed that she perfectly appreciated the situation.
Indeed, the Emperor's open infidelities, and the public
scenes to which they gave rise, were so notorious, that
even in Ashford they had reached our ears. Napoleon's
self-confidence and his contempt of the world had the
effect of making him careless as to what was thought or
said of him, while Josephine, when she was carried away
by jealousy, lost all the dignity and restraint which
usually marked her conduct; so between them they gave
some embarrassing moments to those who were about
them. Talleyrand turned away with his fingers over his
lips, while Berthier, in an agony of apprehension, continued to double up and to twist the cocked hat which
he held between his hands. Only Constant, the faithful
valet, ventured to intervene between his mistress and the
fatal door.

'If your Majesty will resume your seat I shall inform
the Emperor that you are here,' said he, with two depre-
cating hands outstretched.

'Ah, then he *is* there!' she cried furiously. 'I see it all! I
understand it all! But I will expose him—I will reproach
him with his perfidy! Let me pass, Constant! How dare
you stand in my way?'

'Allow me to announce you, your Majesty.'

'I shall announce myself.' With swift undulations of
her beautiful figure she darted past the protesting valet,
parted the curtains, threw open the door, and vanished
into the next room.

She had seemed a creature full of fire and of spirit as,
with a flush which broke through the paint upon her
cheeks, and with eyes which gleamed with the just anger
of an outraged wife, she forced her way into her husband's presence. But she was a woman of change and
impulse, full of little squirts of courage and corresponding reactions into cowardice. She had hardly vanished
from our sight when there was a harsh roar, like an angry

beast, and next instant Josephine came flying into the room again, with the Emperor, inarticulate with passion, raving at her heels. So frightened was she, that she began to run towards the fireplace, upon which Madame de Rémusat, who had no wish to form a rearguard upon such an occasion, began running also, and the two of them, like a pair of startled hens, came rustling and fluttering back to the seats which they had left. There they cowered whilst the Emperor, with a convulsed face and a torrent of camp-fire oaths, stamped and raged about the room.

'You, Constant, you!' he shouted; 'is this the way in which you serve me? Have you no sense then—no discretion? Am I never to have any privacy? Must I eternally submit to be spied upon by women? Is everyone else to have liberty, and I only to have none? As to you, Josephine, this finishes it all. I had hesitations before, but now I have none. This brings everything to an end between us.'

We would all, I am sure, have given a good deal to slip from the room—at least, my own embarrassment far exceeded my interest—but the Emperor from his lofty standpoint cared as little about our presence as if we had been so many articles of furniture. In fact, it was one of this strange man's peculiarities that it was just those delicate and personal scenes with which privacy is usually associated that he preferred to have in public, for he knew that his reproaches had an additional sting when they fell upon other ears besides those of his victim. From his wife to his groom there was not one of those who were about him who did not live in dread of being held up to ridicule and infamy before a smiling crowd, whose amusement was only tempered by the reflection that each of them might be the next to endure the same exposure.

As to Josephine, she had taken refuge in a woman's last resource, and was crying bitterly, with her graceful neck stooping towards her knees and her two hands over her face. Madame de Rémusat was weeping also, and in every pause of his hoarse scolding—for his voice was very hoarse and raucous when he was angry—there came the soft hissing and clicking of their sobs. Sometimes his fierce taunts would bring some reply from the Empress, some gentle reproof to him for his gallantries, but each remonstrance only excited him to a fresh rush of vituperation. In one of his outbursts he threw his snuff-box with a crash upon the floor as a spoiled child would hurl down its toys.

'Morality!' he cried, 'morality was not made for me, and I was not made for morality. I am a man apart, and I accept nobody's conditions. I tell you always, Josephine, that these are the foolish phrases of mediocre people who wish to fetter the great. They do not apply to me. I will never consent to frame my conduct by the puerile arrangements of society.'

'Have you no feeling then?' sobbed the Empress.

'A great man is not made for feeling. It is for him to decide what he shall do, and then to do it without interference from anyone. It is your place, Josephine, to submit to all my fancies, and you should think it quite natural that I should allow myself some latitude.'

It was a favourite device of the Emperor's when he was in the wrong upon one point, to turn the conversation round so as to get upon some other one on which he was in the right. Having worked off the first explosion of his passion he now assumed the offensive, for in argument, as in war, his instinct was always to attack.

'I have been looking over Lenormand's accounts, Josephine,' said he. 'Are you aware how many dresses you have had last year? You have had a hundred and forty—no less—and many of them cost as much as twenty-five thousand livres. I am told that you have six hundred dresses in your wardrobe, many of which have hardly ever been used. Madame de Rémusat knows that what I say is true. She cannot deny it.'

'You like me to dress well, Napoleon.'

'I will not have such monstrous extravagance. I could have two regiments of cuirassiers, or a fleet of frigates, with the money which you squander upon foolish silks and furs. It might turn the fortunes of a campaign. Then again, Josephine, who gave you permission to order that parure of diamonds and sapphires from Lefebvre? The bill has been sent to me and I have refused to pay for it. If he applies again, I shall have him marched to prison between a file of grenadiers, and your milliner shall accompany him there.'

The Emperor's fits of anger, although tempestuous, were never very prolonged. The curious convulsive wriggle of one of his arms, which always showed when he was excited, gradually died away, and after looking for some time at the papers of de Meneval—who had written away like an automaton during all this uproar—he came across to the fire with a smile upon his lips, and a brow from which the shadow had departed.

'You have no excuse for extravagance, Josephine,' said he, laying his hand upon her shoulder. 'Diamonds and fine dresses are very necessary to an ugly woman in order to make her attractive, but *you* cannot need them for such a purpose. You had no fine dresses when first I saw you in the Rue Chautereine, and yet there was no woman in the world who ever attracted me so. Why will you vex me, Josephine, and make me say things which seem unkind? Drive back, little one, to Pont de Briques, and see that you do not catch cold.'

'You will come to the salon, Napoleon?' asked the Empress, whose bitterest resentment seemed to vanish in an instant at the first kindly touch from his hand. She still held her handkerchief before her eyes, but it was chiefly, I think, to conceal the effect which her tears had had upon her cheeks.

'Yes, yes, I will come. Our carriages will follow yours. See the ladies into the berline, Constant. Have you ordered the embarkation of the troops, Berthier? Come here, Talleyrand, for I wish to describe my views about the future of Spain and Portugal. Monsieur de Laval, you may escort the Empress to Pont de Briques, where I shall see you at the reception.'

XV. The Reception of the Empress

PONT DE BRIQUES is but a small village, and this sudden arrival of the Court, which was to remain for some weeks, had crammed it with visitors. It would have been very much simpler to have come to Boulogne, where there were more suitable buildings and better accommodation, but Napoleon had named Pont de Briques, so Pont de Briques it had to be. The word impossible was not permitted amongst those who had to carry out his wishes. So an army of cooks and footmen settled upon the little place, and then there arrived the dignitaries of the new Empire, and then the ladies of the Court, and then their admirers from the camp. The Empress had a château for her accommodation. The rest quartered themselves in cottages or where they best might, and waited ardently for the moment which was to take them back to the comforts of Versailles or Fontainebleau.

The Empress had graciously offered me a seat in her berline, and all the way to the village, entirely forgetful apparently of the scene through which she passed, she chatted away, asking me a thousand personal questions about myself and my affairs, for a kindly curiosity in the doings of everyone around her was one of her most marked characteristics. Especially was she interested in Eugénie, and as the subject was one upon which I was equally interested in talking it ended in a rhapsody upon my part, amid little sympathetic ejaculations from the Empress and titterings from Madame de Rémusat.

'But you must certainly bring her over to the Court!' cried the kindly woman. 'Such a paragon of beauty and of virtue must not be allowed to waste herself in this

English village. Have you spoken about her to the Emperor?'

'I found that he knew all about her, your Majesty.'

'He knows all about everything. Oh, what a man he is! You heard him about those diamonds and sapphires. Lefebvre gave me his word that no one should know of it but ourselves, and that I should pay at my leisure, and yet you see that the Emperor knew. But what did he say, Monsieur de Laval?'

'He said that my marriage should be his affair.'

Josephine shook her head and groaned.

'But this is serious, Monsieur de Laval. He is capable of singling out any one of the ladies of the Court and marrying you to her within a week. It is a subject upon which he will not listen to argument. He has brought about some extraordinary matches in this way. But I will speak to the Emperor before I return to Paris, and I will see what I can arrange for you.'

I was still endeavouring to thank her for her sympathy and kindness when the berline rattled up the drive and pulled up at the entrance to the château, where the knot of scarlet footmen and the bearskins of two sentries from the Guards announced the Imperial quarters. The Empress and her lady hurried away to prepare their toilets for the evening, and I was shown at once into the salon, in which the guests had already begun to assemble.

This was a large square room furnished as modestly as the sitting-room of a provincial gentleman would be likely to be. The wall-paper was gloomy, and the furniture was of dark mahogany upholstered in faded blue nankeen, but there were numerous candles in candelabra upon the tables and in sconces upon the walls which gave an air of festivity even to these sombre surroundings. Out of the large central room were several smaller ones in which card-tables had been laid out, and the doorways between had been draped with Oriental chintz. A number of ladies and gentlemen were standing about, the former in the high evening dresses to which the Emperor had given his sanction, the latter about equally divided between the civilians in black court costumes and the soldiers in their uniforms. Bright colours and graceful draperies predominated, for in spite of his lectures about economy the Emperor was very harsh to any lady who did not dress in a manner which would sustain the brilliancy of his Court. The prevailing fashions gave an opening to taste and to display, for the simple classical costumes had died out with the Republic, and Oriental dresses had taken their place as a compliment to the Conqueror of Egypt. Lucretia had changed to Zuleika, and the salons which had reflected the austerity of old Rome had turned suddenly into so many Eastern harems.

On entering the room I had retired into a corner, fearing that I should find none there whom I knew; but someone plucked at my arm, and turning round I found myself looking into the yellow inscrutable face of my Uncle Bernac. He seized my unresponsive hand and wrung it with a false cordiality.

'My dear Louis,' said he, 'it was really the hope of meeting you here which brought me over from Grosbois —although you can understand that living so far from Paris I cannot afford to miss such an opportunity of showing myself at Court. Nevertheless I can assure you that it was of you principally that I was thinking. I hear that you have had a splendid reception from the Emperor, and that you have been taken into his personal service. I had spoken to him about you, and I made him fully realise that if he treats you well he is likely to coax some of the other young émigrés into his service.'

I was convinced that he was lying, but none the less I had to bow and utter a few words of cold thanks.

'I see that you still bear me some grudge for what passed between us the other day,' said he, 'but really, my dear Louis, you have no occasion to do so. It was your own good which I had chiefly at heart. I am neither a young nor a strong man, Louis, and my profession, as you have seen, is a dangerous one. There is my child, and there is my estate. Who takes one, takes both. Sibylle is a charming girl, and you must not allow yourself to be prejudiced against her by any ill temper which she may have shown towards me. I will confess that she had some reason to be annoyed at the turn which things had taken. But I hope to hear that you have now thought better upon this matter.'

'I have never thought about it at all, and I beg that you will not discuss it,' said I curtly.

He stood in deep thought for a few moments, and then he raised his evil face and his cruel grey eyes to mine.

'Well, well, that is settled then,' said he. 'But you cannot bear me a grudge for having wished you to be my successor. Be reasonable, Louis. You must acknowledge that you would now be six feet deep in the salt-marsh with your neck broken if I had not stood your friend, at some risk to myself. Is that not true?'

'You had your own motive for that,' said I.

'Very likely. But none the less I saved you. Why should you bear me ill will? It is no fault of mine if I hold your estate.'

'It is not on account of that.'

'Why is it then?'

I could have explained that it was because he had betrayed his comrades, because his daughter hated him, because he had ill-used his wife, because my father regarded him as the source of all his troubles—but the salon of the Empress was no place for a family quarrel, so I merely shrugged my shoulders, and was silent.

'Well, I am very sorry,' said he, 'for I had the best of intentions towards you. I could have advanced you, for there are few men in France who exercise more influence. But I have one request to make to you.'

'What is that, sir?'

'I have a number of personal articles, belonging to your father—his sword, his seals, a deskful of letters, some silver plate—such things in short as you would wish to keep in memory of him. I should be glad if you will come to Grosbois—if it is only for one night—and look over these things, choosing what you wish to take away. My conscience will then be clear about them.'

I promised readily that I would do so.

'And when would you come?' he asked eagerly. Something in the tone of his voice aroused my suspicions, and glancing at him I saw exultation in his eyes. I remembered the warning of Sibylle.

'I cannot come until I have learned what my duties with the Emperor are to be. When that is settled I shall come.'

'Very good. Next week perhaps, or the week afterward. I shall expect you eagerly, Louis. I rely upon your promise, for a Laval was never known to break one.' With another unanswered squeeze of my hand, he slipped off among the crowd, which was growing denser every instant in the salon.

I was standing in silence thinking over this sinister invitation of my uncle's, when I heard my own name, and, looking up, I saw de Caulaincourt, with his brown handsome face and tall elegant figure, making his way towards me.

'It is your first entrance at Court, is it not, Monsieur de Laval,' said he, in his high-bred cordial manner; 'you should not feel lonely, for there are certainly many friends of your father here who will be overjoyed to make the acquaintance of your father's son. From what de Meneval told me I gather that you know hardly anyone —even by sight.'

'I know the Marshals,' said I; 'I saw them all at the council in the Emperor's tent. There is Ney with the red head. And there is Lefebvre with his singular mouth, and Bernadotte with the beak of a bird of prey.'

'Precisely. And that is Rapp, with the round, bullet head. He is talking to Junot, the handsome dark man with the whiskers. These poor soldiers are very unhappy.'

'Why so?' I asked.

'Because they are all men who have risen from nothing.

This society and etiquette terrifies them much more than all the dangers of war. When they can hear their sabres clashing against their big boots they feel at home, but when they have to stand about with their cocked hats under their arms, and have to pick their spurs out of the ladies' trains, and talk about David's picture or Paisiello's opera, it prostrates them. The Emperor will not even permit them to swear, although he has no scruples upon his own account. He tells them to be soldiers with the army, and courtiers with the Court, but the poor fellows cannot help being soldiers all the time. Look at Rapp with his twenty wounds, endeavouring to exchange little delicate drolleries with that young lady. There, you see, he has said something which would have passed very well with a vivandière, but it has made her fly to her mamma, and he is scratching his head, for he cannot imagine how he has offended her.'

'Who is the beautiful woman with the white dress and the tiara of diamonds?' I asked.

'That is Madame Murat, who is the sister of the Emperor. Caroline is beautiful, but she is not as pretty as her sister Marie, whom you see over yonder in the corner. Do you see the tall stately dark-eyed old lady with whom she is talking? That is Napoleon's mother—a wonderful woman, the source of all their strength, shrewd, brave, vigorous, forcing respect from everyone who knows her. She is as careful and as saving as when she was the wife of a small country gentleman in Corsica, and it is no secret that she has little confidence in the permanence of the present state of things, and that she is always laying by for an evil day. The Emperor does not know whether to be amused or exasperated by her precautions. Well, Murat, I suppose we shall see you riding across the Kentish hop-fields before long.'

The famous soldier had paused opposite to us, and shook hands with my companion. His elegant well-knit figure, large fiery eyes, and noble bearing made this inn-keeper's boy a man who would have drawn attention and admiration to himself in any assembly in Europe. His mop of curly hair and thick red lips gave that touch of character and individuality to his appearance which redeem a handsome face from insipidity.

'I am told that it is devilish bad country for cavalry— all cut up into hedges and ditches,' said he. 'The roads are good, but the fields are impossible. I hope that we are going soon, Monsieur de Caulaincourt, for our men will all settle down as gardeners if this continues. They are learning more about watering-pots and spuds than about horses and sabres.'

'The army, I hear, is to embark to-morrow.'

'Yes, yes, but you know very well that they will disembark again upon the wrong side of the Channel. Unless Villeneuve scatters the English fleet, nothing can be attempted.'

'Constant tells me that the Emperor was whistling "Malbrook" all the time that he was dressing this morning, and that usually comes before a move.'

'It was very clever of Constant to tell what tune it was which the Emperor was whistling,' said Murat, laughing. 'For my part I do not think that he knows the difference between the "Malbrook" and the "Marseillaise." Ah, here is the Empress—and how charming she is looking!'

Josephine had entered, with several of her ladies in her train, and the whole assembly rose to do her honour. The Empress was dressed in an evening gown of rose-coloured tulle, spangled with silver stars—an effect which might have seemed meretricious and theatrical in another woman, but which she carried off with great grace and dignity. A little sheaf of diamond wheat-ears rose above her head, and swayed gently as she walked. No one could entertain more charmingly than she, for she moved about among the people with her amiable smile, setting everybody at their ease by her kindly natural manner, and by the conviction which she gave them that she was thoroughly at her ease herself.

'How amiable she is!' I exclaimed. 'Who could help loving her?'

'There is only one family which can resist her,' said de Caulaincourt, glancing round to see that Murat was out of hearing. 'Look at the faces of the Emperor's sisters.'

I was shocked when I followed his direction to see the malignant glances with which these two beautiful women were following the Empress as she walked about the room. They whispered together and tittered maliciously. Then Madame Murat turned to her mother behind her, and the stern old lady tossed her haughty head in derision and contempt.

'They feel that Napoleon is theirs and that they ought to have everything. They cannot bear to think that she is Her Imperial Majesty, and they are only Her Highness. They all hate her, Joseph, Lucien—all of them. When they had to carry her train at the coronation they tried to trip her up, and the Emperor had to interfere. Oh yes, they have the real Corsican blood, and they are not very comfortable people to get along with.'

But in spite of the evident hatred of her husband's family, the Empress appeared to be entirely unconcerned and at her ease as she strolled about among the groups of her guests with a kindly glance and a pleasant word for each of them. A tall, soldierly man, brown-faced and moustached, walked beside her, and she occasionally laid her hand with a caressing motion upon his arm.

'That is her son, Eugène de Beauharnais,' said my companion.

'Her son!' I exclaimed, for he seemed to me to be the older of the two.

De Caulaincourt smiled at my surprise.

'You know she married Beauharnais when she was very young—in fact she was hardly sixteen. She has been sitting in her boudoir while her son has been baking in Egypt and Syria, so that they have pretty well bridged over the gap between them. Do you see the tall, handsome, clean-shaven man who has just kissed Josephine's hand? That is Talma the famous actor. He once helped Napoleon at a critical moment of his career, and the Emperor has never forgotten the debt which the Consul contracted. That is really the secret of Talleyrand's power. He lent Napoleon a hundred thousand francs before he set out for Egypt, and now, however much he distrusts him, the Emperor cannot forget that old kindness. I have never known him to abandon a friend or to forgive an enemy. If you have once served him well you may do what you like afterward. There is one of his coachmen who is drunk from morning to night. But he gained the cross at Marengo, and so he is safe.'

De Caulaincourt had moved on to speak with some lady, and I was again left to my own thoughts, which turned upon this extraordinary man, who presented himself at one moment as a hero and at another as a spoiled child, with his nobler and his worse side alternating so rapidly that I had no sooner made up my mind about him than some new revelation would destroy my views and drive me to some fresh conclusion. That he was necessary to France was evident, and that in serving him one was serving one's country. But was it an honour or a penance to serve him? Was he worthy merely of obedience, or might love and esteem be added to it? These were the questions which we found it difficult to answer—and some of us will never have answered them up to the end of time.

The company had now lost all appearance of formality, and even the soldiers seemed to be at their ease. Many had gone into the side rooms, where they had formed tables for whist and for vingt-et-un. For my own part I was quite entertained by watching the people, the beautiful women, the handsome men, the bearers of names which had been heard of in no previous generation, but which now rung round the world. Immediately in front of me were Ney, Lannes, and Murat chatting together and laughing with the freedom of the camp. Of the three, two were destined to be executed in cold blood,

140

and the third to die upon the battle-field, but no coming shadow ever cast a gloom upon their cheery, full-blooded lives.

A small, silent, middle-aged man, who looked unhappy and ill at ease, had been leaning against the wall beside me. Seeing that he was as great a stranger as myself, I addressed some observation to him, to which be replied with great good-will, but in the most execrable French.

'You don't happen to understand English?' he asked. 'I've never met one living soul in this country who did.'

'Oh yes, I understand it very well, for I have lived most of my life over yonder. But surely you are not English, sir? I understood that every Englishman in France was under lock and key ever since the breach of the treaty of Amiens.'

'No, I am not English,' he answered, 'I am an American. My name is Robert Fulton, and I have to come to these receptions because it is the only way in which I can keep myself in the memory of the Emperor, who is examining some inventions of mine which will make great changes in naval warfare.'

Having nothing else to do I asked this curious American what his inventions might be, and his replies very soon convinced me that I had to do with a madman. He had some idea of making a ship go against the wind and against the current by means of coal or wood which was to be burned inside of her. There was some other nonsense about floating barrels full of gunpowder which would blow a ship to pieces if she struck against them. I listened to him at the time with an indulgent smile, but now looking back from the point of vantage of my old age I can see that not all the warriors and statesmen in that room—no, not even the Emperor himself—have had as great an effect upon the history of the world as that silent American who looked so drab and so commonplace among the gold-slashed uniforms and the Oriental dresses.

But suddenly our conversation was interrupted by a

hush in the room—such a cold, uncomfortable hush as comes over a roomful of happy, romping children when a grave-faced elder comes amongst them. The chatting and the laughter died away. The sound of the rustling cards and of the clicking counters had ceased in the other rooms. Everyone, men and women, had risen to their feet with a constrained expectant expression upon their faces. And there in the doorway were the pale face and the green coat with the red cordon across the white waistcoat.

There was no saying how he might behave upon these occasions. Sometimes he was capable of being the merriest and most talkative of the company, but this was rather in his consular than in his imperial days. On the other hand he might be absolutely ferocious, with an insulting observation for everyone with whom he came in contact. As a rule he was between these two extremes, silent, morose, ill at ease, shooting out curt little remarks which made everyone uncomfortable. There was a sigh of relief when he would pass from one room into the next.

On this occasion he seemed to have not wholly recovered from the storm of the afternoon, and he looked about him with a brooding eye and a lowering brow. It chanced that I was not very far from the door, and that his glance fell upon me.

'Come here, Monsieur de Laval,' said he. He laid his hand upon my shoulder and turned to a big, gaunt man who had accompanied him into the room. 'Look here, Cambacérès, you simpleton,' said he. 'You always said that the old families would never come back, and that they would settle in England as the Huguenots have done. You see that, as usual, you have miscalculated, for here is the heir of the de Lavals come to offer his services. Monsieur de Laval, you are now my aide-de-camp, and I beg you to keep with me wherever I go.'

This was promotion indeed, and yet I had sense enough to know that it was not for my own sweet sake that the Emperor had done it, but in order to encourage others to follow me. My conscience approved what I had done, for no sordid motive and nothing but the love of my country had prompted me; but now, as I walked round behind Napoleon, I felt humiliated and ashamed, like a prisoner led behind the car of his captor.

And soon there was something else to make me ashamed, and that was the conduct of him whose servant I had become. His manners were outrageous. As he had himself said, it was his nature to be always first, and this being so he resented those courtesies and gallantries by which men are accustomed to disguise from the women the fact that they are the weaker sex. The Emperor, unlike Louis XIV, felt that even a temporary and conventional attitude of humility towards a woman was too great a condescension from his own absolute supremacy. Chivalry was among those conditions of society which he refused to accept.

To the soldiers he was amiable enough, with a nod and a joke for each of them. To his sisters also he said a few words, though rather in the tone of a drill sergeant to a pair of recruits. It was only when the Empress had joined him that his ill-humour came to a head.

'I wish you would not wear those wisps of pink about your head, Josephine,' said he, pettishly. 'All that women have to think about is how to dress themselves, and yet they cannot even do that with moderation or taste. If I see you again in such a thing I will thrust it in the fire as I did your shawl the other day.'

'You are so hard to please, Napoleon. You like one day what you cannot abide the next. But I will certainly change it if it offends you,' said Josephine, with admirable patience.

The Emperor took a few steps between the people, who had formed a lane for us to pass through. Then he stopped and looked over his shoulder at the Empress.

'How often have I told you, Josephine, that I cannot tolerate fat women.'

'I always bear it in mind, Napoleon.'

'Then why is Madame de Chevreux present?'

'But surely, Napoleon, madame is not very fat.'

'She is fatter than she should be. I should prefer not to see her. Who is this?' He had paused before a young lady in a blue dress, whose knees seemed to be giving way under her as the terrible Emperor transfixed her with his searching eyes.

'This is Mademoiselle de Bergerot.'

'How old are you?'

'Twenty-three, Sire.'

'It is time that you were married. Every woman should be married at twenty-three. How is it that you are not married?'

The poor girl appeared to be incapable of answering, so the Empress gently remarked that it was to the young men that that question should be addressed.

'Oh, that is the difficulty, is it?' said the Emperor. 'We must look about and find a husband for you.' He turned, and to my horror I found his eyes fixed with a questioning gaze upon my face.

'We have to find you a wife also, Monsieur de Laval,' said he. 'Well, well, we shall see—we shall see. What is your name?' to a quiet refined man in black.

'I am Grétry, the musician.'

'Yes, yes, I remember you. I have seen you a hundred times, but I can never recall your name. Who are you?'

'I am Joseph de Chenier.'

'Of course. I have seen your tragedy. I have forgotten the name of it, but it was not good. You have written some other poetry, have you not?'

'Yes, Sire. I had your permission to dedicate my last volume to you.'

'Very likely, but I have not had time to read it. It is a pity that we have no poets now in France, for the deeds of the last few years would have given a subject for a Homer or a Virgil. It seems that I can create kingdoms but not poets. Whom do you consider to be the greatest French writer?'

144

'Racine, Sire.'

'Then you are a blockhead, for Corneille was infinitely greater. I have no ear for metre or trivialities of the kind, but I can sympathise with the spirit of poetry, and I am conscious that Corneille is far the greatest of poets. I would have made him my prime minister had he had the good fortune to live in my epoch. It is his intellect which I admire, his knowledge of the human heart, and his profound feeling. Are you writing anything at present?'

'I am writing a tragedy upon Henry IV, Sire.'

'It will not do, sir. It is too near the present day, and I will not have politics upon the stage. Write a play about Alexander. What is your name?'

He had pitched upon the same person whom he had already addressed.

'I am still Grétry, the musician,' said he meekly.

The Emperor flushed for an instant at the implied rebuke. He said nothing, however, but passed on to where several ladies were standing together near the door of the card-room.

'Well, madame,' said he to the nearest of them, 'I hope you are behaving rather better. When last I heard from Paris your doings were furnishing the Quartier St. Germain with a good deal of amusement and gossip.'

'I beg that your Majesty will explain what you mean,' said she with spirit.

'They had coupled your name with that of Colonel Lasalle.'

'It is a foul calumny, Sire.'

'Very possibly, but it is awkward when so many calumnies cluster round one person. You are certainly a most unfortunate lady in that respect. You had a scandal once before with General Rapp's aide-de-camp. This must come to an end. What is your name?' he continued, turning to another.

'Mademoiselle de Périgord.'

'Your age?'

'Twenty.'

'You are very thin and your elbows are red. My God, Madame Boismaison, are we never to see anything but this same grey gown and the red turban with the diamond crescent?'

'I have never worn it before, Sire.'

'Then you had another the same, for I am weary of the sight of it. Let me never see you in it again. Monsieur de Rémusat, I make you a good allowance. Why do you not spend it?'

'I do, Sire.'

'I hear that you have been putting down your carriage. I do not give you money to hoard in a bank, but I give it to you that you may keep up a fitting appearance with it. Let me hear that your carriage is back in the coach-house when I return to Paris. Junot, you rascal, I hear that you have been gambling and losing.'

'The most infernal run of luck, Sire,' said the soldier. 'I give you my word that the ace fell four times running.'

'Ta, ta, you are a child, with no sense of the value of money. How much do you owe?'

'Forty thousand, Sire.'

'Well, well, go to Lebrun and see what he can do for you. After all, we were together at Toulon.'

'A thousand thanks, Sire.'

'Tut! You and Rapp and Lasalle are the spoiled children of the army. But no more cards, you rascal! I do not like low dresses, Madame Picard. They spoil even pretty women, but in you they are inexcusable. Now, Josephine, I am going to my room, and you can come in half an hour and read me to sleep. I am tired tonight, but I came to your salon, since you desired that I should help you in welcoming and entertaining your guests. You can remain here, Monsieur de Laval, for your presence will not be necessary until I send you my orders.'

And so the door closed behind him, and with a long sigh of relief from everyone, from the Empress to the waiter with the negus, the friendly chatter began once more, with the click of the counters and the rustle of the cards just as they had been before he came to help in the entertainment.

XVI. *The Library of Grosbois*

AND now, my friends, I am coming to the end of those singular adventures which I encountered upon my arrival in France, adventures which might have been of some interest in themselves had I not introduced the figure of the Emperor, who has eclipsed them all as completely as the sun eclipses the stars. Even now, you see, after all these years, in an old man's memoirs, the Emperor is still true to his traditions, and will not brook any opposition. As I draw his words and his deeds I feel that my own poor story withers before them. And yet if it had not been for that story I should not have had an excuse for describing to you my first and most vivid impressions of him, and so it has served a purpose after all. You must bear with me now while I tell you of our expedition to the Red Mill and of what befell in the library of Grosbois.

Two days had passed away since the reception of the Empress Josephine, and only one remained of the time which had been allowed to my cousin Sibylle in which she might save her lover, and capture the terrible Toussac. For my own part I was not so very anxious that she should save this craven lover of hers, whose handsome face belied the poor spirit within him. And yet this lonely beautiful woman, with the strong will and the loyal heart, had touched my feelings, and I felt that I would help her to anything—even against my own better judgment, if she should desire it. It was then with a mixture of feelings that late in the afternoon I saw her and General Savary enter the little room in which I lodged at Boulogne. One glance at her flushed cheeks and triumphant eyes told me that she was confident in her own success.

'I told you that I would find him, Cousin Louis!' she cried: 'I have come straight to you, because you said that you would help in the taking of him.'

'Mademoiselle insists upon it that I should not use soldiers,' said Savary, shrugging his shoulders.

'No, no, no,' she cried with vehemence. 'It has to be done with discretion, and at the sight of a soldier he would fly to some hiding-place, where you would never be able to follow him. I cannot afford to run a risk. There is too much already at stake.'

'In such an affair three men are as useful as thirty,' said Savary. 'I should not in any case have employed more. You say that you have another friend, Lieutenant——?'

'Lieutenant Gerard of the Hussars of Berchény.'

'Quite so. There is not a more gallant officer in the Grand Army than Etienne Gerard. The three of us, Monsieur de Laval, should be equal to any adventure.'

'I am at your disposal.'

'Tell us then, mademoiselle, where Toussac is hiding.'

'He is hiding at the Red Mill.'

'But we have searched it, I assure you that he is not there.'

'When did you search it?'

'Two days ago.'

'Then he has come there since. I knew that Jeanne Portal loved him. I have watched her for six days. Last night she stole down to the Red Mill with a basket of wine and fruit. All the morning I have seen her eyes sweeping the countryside, and I have read the terror in them whenever she has seen the twinkle of a bayonet. I am as sure that Toussac is in the mill as if I had seen him with my own eyes.'

'In that case there is not an instant to be lost,' cried Savary. 'If he knows of a boat upon the coast he is as likely as not to slip away after dark and make his escape for England. From the Red Mill one can see all the

148

surrounding country, and mademoiselle is right in thinking that a large body of soldiers would only warn him to
escape.'

'What do you propose then?' I asked.

'That you meet us at the south gate of the camp in an
hour's time dressed as you are. You might be any gentleman travelling upon the high road. I shall see Gerard,
and we shall adopt some suitable disguise. Bring your
pistols, for it is with the most desperate man in France
we have to do. We shall have a horse at your disposal.'

The setting sun lay dull and red upon the western
horizon, and the white chalk cliffs of the French coast
had all flushed into pink when I found myself once more
at the gate of the Boulogne Camp. There was no sign
of my companions, but a tall man dressed in a blue
coat with brass buttons like a small country farmer, was
tightening the girth of a magnificent black horse, whilst a
little further on a slim young ostler was waiting by the
roadside, holding the bridles of two others. It was only
when I recognised one of the pair as the horse which I
had ridden on my first coming to camp that I answered
the smile upon the keen handsome face of the ostler, and
saw the swarthy features of Savary under the broad-
brimmed hat of the farmer.

'I think that we may travel without fearing to excite
suspicion,' said he. 'Crook that straight back of yours a
little, Gerard! And now we shall push upon our way, or
we may find that we are too late.'

My life has had its share of adventures, and yet, somehow, this ride stands out above the others. There over the
waters I could dimly see the loom of the English coast,
with its suggestions of dreamy villages, humming bees,
and the pealing of Sunday bells. I thought of the long,
white High Street of Ashford, with its red brick houses,
and the inn with the great swinging sign. All my life had
been spent in these peaceful surroundings, and now, here
I was with a spirited horse between my knees, two pistols
peeping out of my holsters, and a commission upon

which my whole future might depend, to arrest the most redoubtable conspirator in France. No wonder that, looking back over many dangers and many vicissitudes, it is still that evening ride over the short crisp turf of the downs which stands out most clearly in my memory. One becomes blasé to adventure, as one becomes blasé to all else which the world can give, save only the simple joys of home, and to taste the full relish of such an expedition one must approach it with the hot blood of youth still throbbing in one's veins.

Our route, when we had left the uplands of Boulogne behind us, lay along the skirts of that desolate marsh in which I had wandered, and so inland, through plains of fern and bramble, until the familiar black keep of the Castle of Grosbois rose upon the left. Then, under the guidance of Savary, we struck to the right down a sunken road, and so over the shoulder of a hill until, on a further slope beyond, we saw the old windmill black against the evening sky. Its upper window burned red like a spot of blood in the last rays of the setting sun. Close by the door stood a cart full of grain sacks, with the shafts pointing downward and the horse grazing at some distance. As we gazed, a woman appeared upon the downs and stared round, with her hand over her eyes.

'See that!' said Savary eagerly. 'He is there sure enough, or why should they be on their guard? Let us take this road which winds round the hill, and they will not see us until we are at the very door.'

'Should we not gallop forward?' I suggested.

'The ground is too cut up. The longer way is the safer. As long as we are upon the road they cannot tell us from any other travellers.'

We walked our horses along the path, therefore, with as unconcerned an air as we could assume; but a sharp exclamation made us glance suddenly round, and there was the woman standing on a hillock by the roadside and gazing down at us with a face that was rigid with suspicion. The sight of the military bearing of my companions changed all her fear into certainties. In an instant she had whipped the shawl from her shoulders, and was waving it frantically over her head. With a hearty curse Savary spurred his horse up the bank and galloped straight for the mill, with Gerard and myself at his heels.

It was only just in time. We were still a hundred paces from the door when a man sprang out from it, and gazed about him, his head whisking this way and that. There could be no mistaking the huge bristling beard, the broad chest, and the rounded shoulders of Toussac. A glance showed him that we would ride him down before he could get away, and he sprang back into the mill, closing the heavy door with a clang behind him.

'The window, Gerard, the window!' cried Savary.

There was a small, square window opening into the basement room of the mill. The young hussar disengaged himself from the saddle and flew through it as the clown goes through the hoops at Franconi's. An instant later he had opened the door for us, with the blood streaming from his face and hands.

'He has fled up the stair,' said he.

'Then we need be in no hurry, since he cannot pass us,' said Savary, as we sprang from our horses. 'You have carried his first line of intrenchments most gallantly, Lieutenant Gerard. I hope you are not hurt?'

'A few scratches, General, nothing more.'

'Get your pistols, then. Where is the miller?'

'Here I am,' said a squat, rough little fellow, appearing in the open doorway. 'What do you mean, you brigands, by entering my mill in this fashion? I am sitting reading my paper and smoking my pipe of coltsfoot, as my custom is about this time of the evening, and suddenly, without a word, a man comes flying through my window, covers me with glass, and opens my door to his friends outside. I've had trouble enough with my one lodger all day without three more of you turning up.'

'You have the conspirator Toussac in your house.'

'Toussac!' cried the miller. 'Nothing of the kind. His name is Maurice, and he is a merchant in silks.'

'He is the man we want. We come in the Emperor's name.'

The miller's jaw dropped as he listened.

'I don't know who he is, but he offered a good price for a bed and I asked no more questions. In these days one cannot expect a certificate of character from every lodger. But, of course, if it is a matter of State, why, it is not for me to interfere. But, to do him justice, he was a quiet gentleman enough until he had that letter just now.'

'What letter? Be careful what you say, you rascal, for your own head may find its way into the sawdust basket.'

'It was a woman who brought it. I can only tell you what I know. He has been talking like a madman ever since. It made my blood run cold to hear him. There's someone whom he swears he will murder. I shall be very glad to see the last of him.'

'Now, gentlemen,' said Savary, drawing his sword, 'we may leave our horses here. There is no window for forty feet, so he cannot escape from us. If you will see that your pistols are primed, we shall soon bring the fellow to terms.'

The stair was a narrow winding one made of wood, which led to a small loft lighted from a slit in the wall.

Some remains of wood and a litter of straw showed that this was where Toussac had spent his day. There was, however, no sign of him now, and it was evident that he had ascended the next flight of steps. We climbed them, only to find our way barred by a heavy door.

'Surrender, Toussac!' cried Savary. 'It is useless to attempt to escape us.'

A hoarse laugh sounded from behind the door.

'I am not a man who surrenders. But I will make a bargain with you. I have a small matter of business to do to-night. If you will leave me alone, I will give you my solemn pledge to surrender at the camp to-morrow. I have a little debt that I wish to pay. It is only to-day that I understood to whom I owed it.'

'What you ask is impossible.'

'It would save you a great deal of trouble.'

'We cannot grant such a request. You must surrender.'

'You'll have some work first.'

'Come, come, you cannot escape us. Put your shoulders against the door! Now, all together!'

There was the hot flash of a pistol from the keyhole, and a bullet smacked against the wall between us. We hurled ourselves against the door. It was massive, but rotten with age. With a splintering and rending it gave way before us. We rushed in, weapons in hand, to find ourselves in an empty room.

'Where the devil has he got to?' cried Savary, glaring round him. 'This is the top room of all. There is nothing above it.'

It was a square empty space with a few corn-bags littered about. At the further side was an open window, and beside it lay a pistol, still smoking from the discharge. We all rushed across, and, as we craned our heads over, a simultaneous cry of astonishment escaped from us.

The distance to the ground was so great that no one could have survived the fall, but Toussac had taken advantage of the presence of that cart full of grain sacks, which I have described as having lain close to the mill. This had both shortened the distance and given him an excellent means of breaking the fall. Even so, however, the shock had been tremendous, and as we looked out he was lying panting heavily upon the top of the bags. Hearing our cry, however, he looked up, shook his fist defiantly, and, rolling from the cart, he sprang on to the back of Savary's black horse, and galloped off across the downs, his great beard flying in the wind, untouched by the pistol bullets with which we tried to bring him down.

How we flew down those creaking wooden stairs and out through the open door of the mill! Quick as we were, he had a good start, and by the time Gerard and I were in the saddle he had become a tiny man upon a small horse galloping up the green slope of the opposite hill. The shades of evening, too, were drawing in, and upon his left was the huge salt-marsh, where we should have found it difficult to follow him. The chances were certainly in his favour. And yet he never swerved from his course, but kept straight on across the downs on a line which took him farther and farther from the sea. Every instant we feared to see him dart away in the morass, but still he held his horse's head against the hillside. What could he be making for? He never pulled rein and never glanced round, but flew onward, like a man with a definite goal in view.

Lieutenant Gerard and I were lighter men, and our mounts were as good as his, so that it was not long before we began to gain upon him. If we could only keep him in sight it was certain that we should ride him down; but there was always the danger that he might use his knowledge of the country to throw us off his track. As we sank beneath each hill my heart sank also, to rise again with renewed hope as we caught sight of him once more galloping in front of us.

But at last that which I had feared befell us. We were not more than a couple of hundred paces behind him when we lost all trace of him. He had vanished behind some rolling ground, and we could see nothing of him when we reached the summit.

'There is a road there to the left,' cried Gerard, whose Gascon blood was aflame with excitement. 'On, my friend, on, let us keep to the left!'

'Wait a moment!' I cried. 'There is a bridle-path upon the right, and it is as likely that he took that.'

'Then do you take one and I the other.'

'One moment, I hear the sound of hoofs!'

'Yes, yes, it is his horse!'

A great black horse, which was certainly that of General Savary, had broken out suddenly through a dense tangle of brambles in front of us. The saddle was empty.

'He has found some hiding-place here amongst the brambles,' I cried.

Gerard had already sprung from his horse, and was leading him through the bushes. I followed his example, and in a minute or two we made our way down a winding path into a deep chalk quarry.

'There is no sign of him!' cried Gerard. 'He has escaped us.'

But suddenly I had understood it all. His furious rage which the miller had described to us was caused no doubt by his learning how he came to be betrayed upon the night of his arrival. This sweetheart of his had in some way discovered it, and had let him know. His promise to deliver himself up to-morrow was in order to give him time to have his revenge upon my uncle. And now with one idea in his head he had ridden to this chalk quarry. Of course, it must be the same chalk quarry into which the underground passage of Grosbois opened, and no doubt during his treasonable meetings with my uncle he had learned the secret. Twice I hit upon the wrong spot, but at the third trial I gained the face of the cliff, made my way between it and the bushes, and found the narrow opening, which was hardly visible in the gathering darkness. During our search Savary had overtaken us on foot, so now, leaving our horses in the chalk-pit, my two companions followed me through the narrow entrance tunnel, and on into the larger and older passage beyond. We had no lights, and it was as black as pitch within, so I stumbled forward as best I might, feeling my way by keeping one hand upon the side wall, and tripping occasionally over the stones which were scattered along the path. It had seemed no very great distance when my uncle had led the way with the light, but now, what with the darkness, and what with the uncertainty and the tension of our feelings, it appeared to be a long journey, and Savary's deep voice at my elbow growled out questions as to how many more miles we were to travel in this moleheap.

'Hush!' whispered Gerard. 'I hear someone in front of us.'

We stood listening in breathless silence. Then far away through the darkness I heard the sound of a door creaking upon its hinges.

'On, on!' cried Savary, eagerly. 'The rascal is there, sure enough. This time at least we have got him!'

But for my part I had my fears. I remembered that my uncle had opened the door which led into the castle by some secret catch. This sound which we had heard seemed to show that Toussac had also known how to open it. But suppose that he had closed it behind him. I remembered its size and the iron clampings which bound it together. It was possible that even at the last moment we might find ourselves face to face with an insuperable obstacle. On and on we hurried in the dark, and then suddenly I could have raised a shout of joy, for there in the distance was a yellow glimmer of light, only visible in contrast with the black darkness which lay between. The door was open. In his mad thirst for vengeance Toussac had never given a thought to the pursuers at his heels.

And now we need no longer grope. It was a race along the passage and up the winding stair, through the second door, and into the stone-flagged corridor of the Castle of Grosbois, with the oil-lamp still burning at the end of it. A frightful cry—a long-drawn scream of terror and of pain—rang through it as we entered.

'He is killing him! He is killing him!' cried a voice, and a woman servant rushed madly out into the passage. 'Help, help; he is killing Monsieur Bernac!'

'Where is he?' shouted Savary.

'There! The library! The door with the green curtain!' Again that horrible cry rang out, dying down to a harsh croaking. It ended in a loud, sharp snick, as when one cracks one's joint, but many times louder. I knew only too well what that dreadful sound portended. We rushed together into the room, but the hardened Savary and the dare-devil hussar both recoiled in horror from the sight which met our gaze.

My uncle had been seated writing at his desk, with his back to the door, when his murderer had entered. No doubt it was at the first glance over his shoulder that he had raised the scream when he saw that terrible hairy face coming in upon him, while the second cry may have been when those great hands clutched at his head. He had never risen from his chair—perhaps he had been too paralysed by fear—and he still sat with his back to the door. But what struck the colour from our cheeks was that his head had been turned completely round, so that his horribly distorted purple face looked squarely at us from between his shoulders. Often in my dreams that thin face, with the bulging grey eyes, and the shockingly open mouth, comes to disturb me. Beside him stood Toussac, his face flushed with triumph, and his great arms folded across his chest.

'Well, my friends,' said he, 'you are too late, you see. I have paid my debts after all.'

'Surrender!' cried Savary.

'Shoot away! Shoot away!' he cried, drumming his hands upon his breast. 'You don't suppose I fear your miserable pellets, do you? Oh, you imagine you will take me alive! I'll soon knock that idea out of your heads.'

In an instant he had swung a heavy chair over his head, and was rushing furiously at us. We all fired our pistols into him together, but nothing could stop that thunderbolt of a man. With the blood spurting from his wounds, he lashed madly out with his chair, but his eye-sight happily failed him, and his swashing blow came down upon the corner of the table with a crash which broke it into fragments. Then with a mad bellow of rage he sprang upon Savary, tore him down to the ground, and had his hand upon his chin before Gerard and I could seize him by the arms. We were three strong men, but he was as strong as all of us put together, for again and again he shook himself free, and again and again we got our grip upon him once more. But he was losing blood fast. Every instant his huge strength ebbed away. With a supreme effort he staggered to his feet, the three of us hanging on to him like hounds on to a bear. Then, with a shout of rage and despair which thundered through the whole castle, his knees gave way under him, and he fell in a huge inert heap upon the floor, his black beard bristling up towards the ceiling. We all stood panting round, ready to spring upon him if he should move; but it was over. He was dead.

Savary, deadly pale, was leaning with his hand to his side against the table. It was not for nothing that those mighty arms had been thrown round him.

'I feel as if I had been hugged by a bear,' said he. 'Well, there is one dangerous man the less in France, and the Emperor has lost one of his enemies. And yet he was a brave man too!'

'What a soldier he would have made!' said Gerard thoughtfully. 'What a quartermaster for the Hussars of Berchény! He must have been a very foolish person to set his will against that of the Emperor.'

I had seated myself, sick and dazed, upon the settee, for scenes of bloodshed were new to me then, and this one had been enough to shock the most hardened. Savary gave us all a little cognac from his flask, and then tearing down one of the curtains he laid it over the terrible figure of my Uncle Bernac.

'We can do nothing here,' said he. 'I must get back and report to the Emperor as soon as possible. But all these papers of Bernac's must be seized, for many of them bear upon this and other conspiracies.' As he spoke he gathered together a number of documents which were scattered about the table—among the others a letter which lay before him upon the desk, and which he had apparently just finished at the time of Toussac's irruption.

'Hullo, what's this?' said Savary, glancing over it. 'I fancy that our friend Bernac was a dangerous man also.

"My dear Catulle—I beg of you to send me by the very first mail another phial of the same tasteless essence which you sent three years ago. I mean the almond decoction which leaves no traces. I have particular reasons for wanting it in the course of next week, so I implore you not to delay. You may rely upon my interest with the Emperor whenever you have occasion to demand it." '

'Addressed to a chemist in Amiens,' said Savary, turning over the letter. 'A poisoner then, on the top of his other virtues. I wonder for whom this essence of almonds which leaves no trace was intended?'

'I wonder,' said I.

After all, he was my uncle, and he was dead, so why should I say further?

XVII. The End

GENERAL SAVARY rode straight to Pont de Briques to report to the Emperor, while Gerard returned with me to my lodgings to share a bottle of wine. I had expected to find my cousin Sibylle there, but to my surprise there was no sign of her, nor had she left any word to tell us whither she had gone.

It was just after daybreak in the morning when I woke to find an equerry of the Emperor with his hand upon my shoulder.

'The Emperor desires to see you, Monsieur de Laval,' said he.

'Where?'

'At the Pont de Briques.'

I knew that promptitude was the first requisite for those who hoped to advance themselves in his service. In ten minutes I was in the saddle, and in half an hour I was at the château. I was conducted upstairs to a room in which were the Emperor and Josephine, she reclining upon a sofa in a charming dressing-gown of pink and lace, he striding about in his energetic fashion, dressed in the curious costume which he assumed before his official hours had begun—a white sleeping suit, red Turkish slippers, and a white bandanna handkerchief tied round his head, the whole giving him the appearance of a West Indian planter. From the strong smell of eau-de-Cologne I judged that he had just come from his bath. He was in the best of humours, and she, as usual, reflected him, so that they were two smiling faces which were turned upon me as I was announced. It was hard to believe that it was this man with the kindly expression and the genial eye who had come like an east wind into the reception-room the other night, and left a trail of wet cheeks and downcast faces wherever he had passed.

'You have made an excellent début as aide-de-camp,' said he; 'Savary has told me all that has occurred, and nothing could have been better arranged. I have not time to think of such things myself, but my wife will sleep more soundly now that she knows that this Toussac is out of the way.'

'Yes, yes, he was a terrible man,' cried the Empress. 'So was that Georges Cadoudal. They were both terrible men.'

'I have my star, Josephine,' said Napoleon, patting her upon the head. 'I see my own career lying before me and I know exactly what I am destined to do. Nothing can harm me until my work is accomplished. The Arabs are believers in Fate, and the Arabs are in the right.'

'Then why should you plan, Napoleon, if everything is to be decided by Fate?'

'Because it is fated that I should plan, you little stupid. Don't you see that that is part of Fate also, that I should have a brain which is capable of planning? I am always building behind a scaffolding, and no one can see what I am building until I have finished. I never look forward for less than two years, and I have been busy all morning, Monsieur de Laval, in planning out the events which will occur in the autumn and winter of 1807. By the way, that good-looking cousin of yours appears to have managed this affair very cleverly. She is a very fine girl to be wasted upon such a creature as the Lucien Lesage who has been screaming for mercy for a week past. Do you not think that it is a great pity?'

I acknowledged that I did.

'It is always so with women—ideologists, dreamers, carried away by whims and imaginings. They are like the Easterns, who cannot conceive that a man is a fine soldier unless he has a formidable presence. I could not get the Egyptians to believe that I was a greater general than Kléber, because he had the body of a porter and the head of a hairdresser. So it is with this poor creature Lesage, who will be made a hero by women because he has an oval face and the eyes of a calf. Do you imagine that if she were to see him in his true colours it would turn her against him?'

'I am convinced of it, Sire. From the little that I have seen of my cousin I am sure that no one could have a greater contempt for cowardice or for meanness.'

'You speak warmly, sir. You are not by chance just a little touched yourself by this fair cousin of yours?'

'Sire, I have already told you——'

'Ta, ta, ta, but she is across the water, and many things have happened since then.'

Constant had entered the room.

'He has been admitted, Sire.'

'Very good. We shall move into the next room. Josephine, you shall come too, for it is your business rather than mine.'

The room into which we passed was a long, narrow one. There were two windows at one side, but the curtains had been drawn almost across, so that the light was not very good. At the further door was Roustem the Mameluke, and beside him, with arms folded and his face sunk downwards in an attitude of shame and contrition, there was standing the very man of whom we had

161

been talking. He looked up with scared eyes, and started with fear when he saw the Emperor approaching him. Napoleon stood with legs apart and his hands behind his back, and looked at him long and searchingly.

'Well, my fine fellow,' said he at last, 'you have burned your fingers, and I do not fancy that you will come near the fire again. Or do you perhaps think of continuing with politics as a profession?'

'If your Majesty will overlook what I have done,' Lesage stammered, 'I shall faithfully promise you that I will be your most loyal servant until the day of my death.'

'Hum!' said the Emperor, spilling a pinch of snuff over the front of his white jacket. 'There is some sense in what you say, for no one makes so good a servant as the man who has had a thorough fright. But I am a very exacting master.'

'I do not care what you require of me. Everything will be welcome, if you will only give me your forgiveness.'

'For example,' said the Emperor. 'It is one of my whims that when a man enters my service I shall marry him to whom I like. Do you agree to that?'

There was a struggle upon the poet's face, and he clasped and unclasped his hands.

'May I ask, Sire——?'

'You may ask nothing.'

'But there are circumstances, Sire——'

'There, there, that is enough!' cried the Emperor harshly, turning upon his heel. 'I do not argue, I order. There is a young lady, Mademoiselle de Bergerot, for whom I desire a husband. Will you marry her, or will you return to prison?'

Again there was the struggle in the man's face, and he was silent, twitching and writhing in his indecision.

'It is enough!' cried the Emperor. 'Roustem, call the guard!'

'No, no, Sire, do not send me back to prison.'

'The guard, Roustem!'

'I will do it, Sire! I will do it! I will marry whomever you please!'

'You villain!' cried a voice, and there was Sibylle standing in the opening of the curtains at one of the windows. Her face was pale with anger and her eyes shining with scorn; the parting curtains framed her tall, slim figure, which leaned forward in her fury of passion. She had forgotten the Emperor, the Empress, everything, in her revulsion of feeling against this craven whom she had loved.

'They told me what you were,' she cried. 'I would not believe them, I *could* not believe them—for I did not know that there was upon this earth a thing so contemptible. They said that they would prove it, and I defied them to do so, and now I see you as you are. Thank God that I have found you out in time! And to think that for your sake I have brought about the death of a man who was worth a hundred of you! Oh, I am rightly punished for an unwomanly act. Toussac has had his revenge.'

'Enough!' said the Emperor sternly. 'Constant, lead Mademoiselle Bernac into the next room. As to you, sir, I do not think that I can condemn any lady of my Court to take such a man as a husband. Suffice it that you have been shown in your true colours, and that Mademoiselle Bernac has been cured of a foolish infatuation. Roustem, remove the prisoner!'

'There, Monsieur de Laval,' said the Emperor, when the wretched Lesage had been conducted from the room. 'We have not done such a bad piece of work between the coffee and the breakfast. It was your idea, Josephine, and I give you credit for it. But now, de Laval, I feel that we owe you some recompense for having set the young aristocrats a good example, and for having had a share in this Toussac business. You have certainly acted very well.'

'I ask no recompense, Sire,' said I, with an uneasy sense of what was coming.

'It is your modesty that speaks. But I have already

163

decided upon your reward. You shall have such an allowance as will permit you to keep up a proper appearance as my aide-de-camp, and I have determined to marry you suitably to one of the ladies-in-waiting of the Empress.'

My heart turned to lead within me.

'But, Sire,' I stammered, 'this is impossible.'

'Oh, you have no occasion to hesitate. The lady is of excellent family and she is not wanting in personal charm. In a word, the affair is settled, and the marriage takes place upon Thursday.'

'But it is impossible, Sire,' I repeated.

'Impossible! When you have been longer in my service, sir, you will understand that that is a word which I do not tolerate. I tell you that it is settled.'

'My love is given to another, Sire. It is not possible for me to change.'

'Indeed!' said the Emperor coldly. 'If you persist in such a resolution you cannot expect to retain your place in my household.'

Here was the whole structure which my ambition had planned out crumbling hopelessly about my ears. And yet what was there for me to do?

'It is the bitterest moment of my life, Sire,' said I, 'and yet I must be true to the promise which I have given. If I have to be a beggar by the roadside, I shall none the less marry Eugénie de Choiseul or no one.'

The Empress had risen and had approached the window.

'Well, at least, before you make up your mind, Monsieur de Laval,' said she, 'I should certainly take a look at this lady-in-waiting of mine, whom you refuse with such indignation.'

With a quick rasping of rings she drew back the curtain of the second window. A woman was standing in the recess. She took a step forward into the room, and then —and then with a cry and a spring my arms were round her, and hers round me, and I was standing like a man in a dream, looking down into the sweet laughing eyes of my Eugénie. It was not until I had kissed her and kissed her again upon her lips, her cheeks, her hair, that I could persuade myself that she was indeed really there.

'Let us leave them,' said the voice of the Empress behind me. 'Come, Napoleon. It makes me sad! It reminds me too much of the old days in the Rue Chautereine.'

So there is an end of my little romance, for the Emperor's plans were, as usual, carried out, and we were married upon the Thursday, as he had said. That long and all-powerful arm had plucked her out from the Kentish town, and had brought her across the Channel, in order to make sure of my allegiance, and to strengthen the Court by the presence of a de Choiseul. As to my Cousin Sibylle, it shall be written some day how she married the gallant Lieutenant Gerard many years afterward, when he had become the chief of a brigade, and one of the most noted cavalry leaders in all the armies of France. Some day also I may tell how I came back into my rightful inheritance of Grosbois, which is still darkened to me by the thought of that terrible uncle of mine, and of what happened that night when Toussac stood at bay in the library. But enough of me and of my small fortunes. You have already heard more of them, perhaps, than you care for.

As to the Emperor, some faint shadow of whom I have tried in these pages to raise before you, you have heard from history how, despairing of gaining command of the Channel, and fearing to attempt an invasion which might be cut off from behind, he abandoned the camp of Boulogne. You have heard also how, with this very army which was meant for England, he struck down Austria and Russia in one year, and Prussia in the next. From the day that I entered his service until that on which he sailed forth over the Atlantic, never to return, I have faithfully shared his fortunes, rising with his star and sinking with it also. And yet, as I look back at my old master, I find it very difficult to say if he was a very good man or a very bad one. I only know that he was a very great one, and that the things in which he dealt were also so great that it is impossible to judge him by any ordinary standard. Let him rest silently, then, in his great red tomb at the Invalides, for the workman's work is done, and the mighty hand which moulded France and traced the lines of modern Europe has crumbled into dust. The Fates have used him, and the Fates have thrown him away, but still it lives, the memory of the little man in the grey coat, and still it moves the thoughts and actions of men. Some have written to praise and some to blame, but for my own part I have tried to do neither one nor the other, but only to tell the impression which he made upon me in those far-off days when the Army of England lay at Boulogne, and I came back once more to my Castle of Grosbois.

EXPLOITS OF BRIGADIER GERARD

I. How the Brigadier Came to the Castle of Gloom [1]

You do very well, my friends, to treat me with some little reverence, for in honouring me you are honouring both France and yourselves. It is not merely an old, grey-moustached officer whom you see eating his omelette or draining his glass, but it is a fragment of history. In me you see one of the last of those wonderful men, the men who were veterans when they were yet boys, who learned to use a sword earlier than a razor, and who during a hundred battles had never once let the enemy see the colour of their knapsacks. For twenty years we were teaching Europe how to fight, and even when they had learned their lesson it was only the thermometer, and never the bayonet, which could break the Grand Army down. Berlin, Naples, Vienna, Madrid, Lisbon, Moscow —we stabled our horses in them all. Yes, my friends, I say again that you do well to send your children to me with flowers, for these ears have heard the trumpet calls of France, and these eyes have seen her standards in lands where they may never be seen again.

Even now, when I doze in my arm-chair, I can see those great warriors stream before me—the green-jacketed chasseurs, the giant cuirassiers, Poniatowski's lancers, the white-mantled dragoons, the nodding bearskins of the horse grenadiers. And then there comes the thick, low rattle of the drums, and through wreaths of dust and smoke I see the line of high bonnets, the row of brown faces, the swing and toss of the long, red plumes amid the sloping lines of steel. And there rides Ney with his red head, and Lefebvre with his bulldog jaw, and Lannes with his Gascon swagger; and then amidst the gleam of brass and the flaunting feathers I catch a glimpse of *him*, the man with the pale smile, the rounded shoulders, and

[1] The term Brigadier is used throughout in its English and not in its French sense.

169

the far-off eyes. There is an end of my sleep, my friends, for up I spring from my chair, with a cracked voice calling and a silly hand outstretched, so that Madame Titaux has one more laugh at the old fellow who lives among the shadows.

Although I was a full Chief of Brigade when the wars came to an end, and had every hope of soon being made a General of Division, it is still rather to my earlier days that I turn when I wish to talk of the glories and the trials of a soldier's life. For you will understand that when an officer has so many men and horses under him, he has his mind full of recruits and remounts, fodder and farriers, and quarters, so that even when he is not in the face of the enemy, life is a very serious matter for him. But when he is only a lieutenant or a captain, he has nothing heavier than his epaulettes upon his shoulders, so that he can clink his spurs and swing his dolman, drain his glass and kiss his girl, thinking of nothing save enjoying a gallant life. That is the time when he is likely to have adventures, and it is often to that time that I shall turn in the stories which I may have for you. So it will be to-night when I tell you of my visit to the Castle of Gloom; of the strange mission of Sub-Lieutenant Duroc, and of the horrible affair of the man who was once known as Jean Carabin, and afterwards as the Baron Straubenthal.

You must know, then, that in the February of 1807, immediately after the taking of Danzig, Major Legendre and I were commissioned to bring four hundred remounts from Prussia into Eastern Poland.

The hard weather, and especially the great battle at Eylau, had killed so many of the horses that there was some danger of our beautiful Tenth of Hussars becoming a battalion of light infantry. We knew, therefore, both the Major and I, that we should be very welcome at the front. We did not advance very rapidly, however, for the snow was deep, the roads detestable, and we had but twenty returning invalids to assist us. Besides, it is impossible, when you have a daily change of forage, and sometimes none at all, to move horses faster than a walk. I am aware that in the story-books the cavalry whirls past at the maddest of gallops; but for my own part, after twelve campaigns, I should be very satisfied to know that my brigade could always walk upon the march and trot in the presence of the enemy. This I say of the hussars and chasseurs, mark you, so that it is far more the case with cuirassiers or dragoons.

For myself I am fond of horses, and to have four hundred of them, of every age and shade and character, all under my own hands, was a very great pleasure to me. They were from Pomerania for the most part, though some were from Normandy and some from Alsace, and it amused us to notice that they differed in character as much as the people of those provinces. We observed also, what I have often proved since, that the nature of a horse can be told by his colour, from the coquettish light bay, full of fancies and nerves, to the hardy chestnut, and from the docile roan to the pig-headed rusty-black. All this has nothing in the world to do with my story, but how is an officer of cavalry to get on with his tale when he finds four hundred horses waiting for him at the outset? It is my habit, you see, to talk of that which interests myself and so I hope that I may interest you.

We crossed the Vistula opposite Marienwerder, and had got as far as Riesenberg, when Major Legendre came into my room in the post-house with an open paper in his hand.

'You are to leave me,' said he, with despair upon his face.

It was no very great grief to me to do that, for he was, if I may say so, hardly worthy to have such a subaltern. I saluted, however, in silence.

'It is an order from General Lasalle,' he continued; 'you are to proceed to Rossel instantly, and to report yourself at the headquarters of the regiment.'

No message could have pleased me better. I was already very well thought of by my superior officers. It was evident to me, therefore, that this sudden order meant that the regiment was about to see service once more, and that Lasalle understood how incomplete my squadron would be without me. It is true that it came at an inconvenient moment, for the keeper of the post-house had a daughter—one of those ivory-skinned, black-haired Polish girls—with whom I had hoped to have some further talk. Still, it is not for the pawn to argue when the fingers of the player move him from the square; so down I went, saddled my big black charger, Rataplan, and set off instantly upon my lonely journey.

My word, it was a treat for those poor Poles and Jews, who have so little to brighten their dull lives, to see such a picture as that before their doors! The frosty morning air made Rataplan's great black limbs and the beautiful curves of his back and sides gleam and shimmer with every gambade. As for me, the rattle of hoofs upon a road, and the jingle of bridle chains which comes with every toss of a saucy head, would even now set my blood dancing through my veins. You may think, then, how I carried myself in my five-and-twentieth year—I, Etienne Gerard, the picked horseman and surest blade in the ten regiments of hussars. Blue was our colour in the Tenth —a sky-blue dolman and pelisse with a scarlet front—and it was said of us in the army that we could set a whole population running, the women towards us, and the men away. There were bright eyes in the Riesenberg windows that morning which seemed to beg me to tarry; but what can a soldier do, save to kiss his hand and shake his bridle as he rides upon his way?

It was a bleak season to ride through the poorest and ugliest country in Europe, but there was a cloudless sky above, and a bright, cold sun, which shimmered on the huge snow-fields. My breath reeked into the frosty air, and Rataplan sent up two feathers of steam from his nostrils, while the icicles drooped from the side-irons of his bit. I let him trot to warm his limbs, while for my own part I had too much to think of to give much heed to the cold. To north and south stretched the great plains, mottled over with dark clumps of fir and lighter patches of larch. A few cottages peeped out here and there, but it was only three months since the Grand Army had passed that way, and you know what that meant to a country. The Poles were our friends, it was true, but out of a hundred thousand men, only the Guard had waggons, and the rest had to live as best they might. It did not surprise me, therefore, to see no signs of cattle and no smoke from the silent houses. A weal had been left across the country where the great host had passed, and it was said that even the rats were starved wherever the Emperor had led his men.

By midday I had got as far as the village of Saalfeldt, but as I was on the direct road for Osterode, where the Emperor was wintering, and also for the main camp of the seven divisions of infantry, the highway was choked with carriages and carts. What with artillery caissons and waggons and couriers, and the ever-thickening stream of recruits and stragglers, it seemed to me that it would be a very long time before I should join my comrades. The plains, however, were five feet deep in snow, so there was nothing for it but to plod upon our way. It was with joy, therefore, that I found a second road which branched away from the other, trending through a fir-wood towards the north. There was a small auberge at the cross-roads, and a patrol of the Third Hussars of Conflans—the very regiment of which I was afterwards colonel—were mounting their horses at the door. On the steps stood their officer, a slight, pale young man, who looked more like a young priest from a seminary than a leader of the devil-may-care rascals before him.

'Good-day, sir,' said he, seeing that I pulled up my horse.

'Good-day,' I answered. 'I am Lieutenant Etienne Gerard, of the Tenth.'

173

I could see by his face that he had heard of me. Everybody had heard of me since my duel with the six fencing-masters. My manner, however, served to put him at his ease with me.

'I am Sub-Lieutenant Duroc, of the Third,' said he.

'Newly joined?' I asked.

'Last week.'

I had thought as much, from his white face and from the way in which he let his men lounge upon their horses. It was not so long, however, since I had learned myself what it was like when a schoolboy has to give orders to veteran troopers. It made me blush, I remember, to shout abrupt commands to men who had seen more battles than I had years, and it would have come more natural for me to say, 'With your permission, we shall now wheel into line,' or, 'If you think it best, we shall trot.' I did not think the less of the lad, therefore, when I observed that his men were somewhat out of hand, but I gave them a glance which stiffened them in their saddles.

'May I ask, monsieur, whether you are going by this northern road?' I asked.

'My orders are to patrol it as far as Arensdorf,' said he.

'Then I will, with your permission, ride so far with you,' said I. 'It is very clear that the longer way will be the faster.'

So it proved, for this road led away from the army into a country which was given over to Cossacks and marauders, and it was as bare as the other was crowded. Duroc and I rode in front, with our six troopers clattering in the rear. He was a good boy, this Duroc, with his head full of the nonsense that they teach at St. Cyr, knowing more about Alexander and Pompey than how to mix a horse's fodder or care for a horse's feet. Still, he was, as I have said, a good boy, unspoiled as yet by the camp. It pleased me to hear him prattle away about his sister Marie and about his mother in Amiens. Presently we found ourselves at the village of Hayenau. Duroc rode up to the post-house and asked to see the master.

'Can you tell me,' said he, 'whether the man who calls himself the Baron Straubenthal lives in these parts?'

The postmaster shook his head, and we rode upon our way. I took no notice of this, but when, at the next village, my comrade repeated the same question, with the same result, I could not help asking him who this Baron Straubenthal might be.

'He is a man,' said Duroc, with a sudden flush upon his boyish face, 'to whom I have a very important message to convey.'

Well, this was not satisfactory, but there was something in my companion's manner which told me that any further questioning would be distasteful to him. I said nothing more, therefore, but Duroc would still ask every peasant whom we met whether he could give him any news of the Baron Straubenthal.

For my own part I was endeavouring, as an officer of light cavalry should, to form an idea of the lay of the country, to note the course of the streams, and to mark the places where there should be fords. Every step was taking us farther from the camp round the flanks of which we were travelling. Far to the south a few plumes of grey smoke in the frosty air marked the position of some of our outposts. To the north, however, there was nothing between ourselves and the Russian winter quarters. Twice on the extreme horizon I caught a glimpse of the glitter of steel, and pointed it out to my companion. It was too distant for us to tell whence it came, but we had little doubt that it was from the lance-heads of marauding Cossacks.

The sun was just setting when we rode over a low hill and saw a small village upon our right, and on our left a high black castle, which jutted out from amongst the pine-woods. A farmer with his cart was approaching us— a matted-haired, downcast fellow, in a sheepskin jacket.

'What village is this?' asked Duroc.

'It is Arensdorf,' he answered, in his barbarous German dialect.

'Then here I am to stay the night,' said my young companion. Then, turning to the farmer, he asked his eternal question, 'Can you tell me where the Baron Straubenthal lives?'

'Why, it is he who owns the Castle of Gloom,' said the farmer, pointing to the dark turrets over the distant fir forest.

Duroc gave a shout like the sportsman who sees his game rising in front of him. The lad seemed to have gone off his head—his eyes shining, his face deathly white, and such a grim set about his mouth as made the farmer shrink away from him. I can see him now, leaning forward on his brown horse, with his eager gaze fixed upon the great black tower.

'Why do you call it the Castle of Gloom?' I asked.

'Well, it's the name it bears upon the country-side,' said the farmer. 'By all accounts there have been some black doings up yonder. It's not for nothing that the wickedest man in Poland has been living there these fourteen years past.'

'A Polish nobleman?' I asked.

'Nay, we breed no such men in Poland,' he answered.

'A Frenchman, then?' cried Duroc.

'They say that he came from France.'

'And with red hair?'

'As red as a fox.'

'Yes, yes, it is my man,' cried my companion, quivering all over in his excitement. 'It is the hand of Providence which has led me here. Who can say that there is not justice in this world? Come, Monsieur Gerard, for I must see the men safely quartered before I can attend to this private matter.'

He spurred on his horse, and ten minutes later we were at the door of the inn of Arensdorf, where his men were to find their quarters for the night.

Well, all this was no affair of mine, and I could not imagine what the meaning of it might be. Rossel was still far off, but I determined to ride on for a few hours and take my chance of some wayside barn in which I could find shelter for Rataplan and myself. I had mounted my horse, therefore, after tossing off a cup of wine, when young Duroc came running out of the door and laid his hand upon my knee.

'Monsieur Gerard,' he panted, 'I beg of you not to abandon me like this!'

'My good sir,' said I, 'if you would tell me what is the matter and what you would wish me to do, I should be better able to tell you if I could be of any assistance to you.'

'You can be of the very greatest,' he cried. 'Indeed, from all that I have heard of you, Monsieur Gerard, you are the one man whom I should wish to have by my side to-night.'

'You forget that I am riding to join my regiment.'

'You cannot, in any case, reach it to-night. To-morrow will bring you to Rossel. By staying with me you will confer the very greatest kindness upon me, and you will aid me in a matter which concerns my own honour and the honour of my family. I am compelled, however, to confess to you that some personal danger may possibly be involved.'

It was a crafty thing for him to say. Of course, I sprang from Rataplan's back and ordered the groom to lead him back into the stables.

'Come into the inn,' said I, 'and let me know exactly what it is that you wish me to do.'

He led the way into a sitting-room, and fastened the door lest we should be interrupted. He was a well-grown lad, and as he stood in the glare of the lamp, with the light beating upon his earnest face and upon his uniform of silver grey, which suited him to a marvel, I felt my heart warm towards him. Without going so far as to say that he carried himself as I had done at his age, there was at least similarity enough to make me feel in sympathy with him.

'I can explain it all in a few words,' said he. 'If I have not already satisfied your very natural curiosity, it is because the subject is so painful a one to me that I can hardly bring myself to allude to it. I cannot, however, ask for your assistance without explaining to you exactly how the matter lies.

'You must know, then, that my father was the well-known banker, Christophe Duroc, who was murdered by the people during the September massacres. As you are aware, the mob took possession of the prisons, chose three so-called judges to pass sentence upon the unhappy aristocrats, and then tore them to pieces when they were passed out into the street. My father had been a benefactor of the poor all his life. There were many to plead for him. He had the fever, too, and was carried in, half-dead, upon a blanket. Two of the judges were in favour of acquitting him; the third, a young Jacobin, whose huge body and brutal mind had made him a leader among these wretches, dragged him, with his own hands, from the litter, kicked him again and again with his heavy boots, and hurled him out of the door, where in an instant he was torn limb from limb under circumstances which are too horrible for me to describe. This, as you perceive, was murder, even under their own unlawful laws, for two of their own judges had pronounced in my father's favour.

'Well, when the days of order came back again, my elder brother began to make inquiries about this man. I was only a child then, but it was a family matter, and it was discussed in my presence. The fellow's name was Carabin. He was one of Sansterre's Guard, and a noted duellist. A foreign lady named the Baroness Straubenthal having been dragged before the Jacobins, he had gained her liberty for her on the promise that she with her money and estates should be his. He had married her, taken her name and title, and escaped out of France at the time of the fall of Robespierre. What had become of him we had no means of learning.

'You will think, doubtless, that it would be easy for us to find him, since we had both his name and his title. You must remember, however, that the Revolution left us without money, and that without money such a search is very difficult. Then came the Empire, and it became more difficult still, for, as you are aware, the Emperor considered that the 18th Brumaire brought all accounts to a settlement, and that on that day a veil had been drawn across the past. None the less, we kept our own family story and our own family plans.

'My brother joined the army, and passed with it through all Southern Europe, asking everywhere for the Baron Straubenthal. Last October he was killed at Jena, with his mission still unfulfilled. Then it became my turn, and I have the good fortune to hear of the very man of whom I am in search at one of the first Polish villages which I have to visit, and within a fortnight of joining my regiment. And then, to make the matter even better, I find myself in the company of one whose name is never mentioned throughout the army save in connection with some daring and generous deed.'

This was all very well, and I listened to it with the greatest interest, but I was none the clearer as to what young Duroc wished me to do.

'How can I be of service to you?' I asked.

'By coming up with me.'

'To the Castle?'

'Precisely.'

'When?'

'At once.'

'But what do you intend to do?'

'I shall know what to do. But I wish you to be with me, all the same.'

Well, it was never in my nature to refuse an adventure, and, besides, I had every sympathy with the lad's feelings. It is very well to forgive one's enemies, but one wishes to give them something to forgive also. I held out my hand to him, therefore.

'I must be on my way for Rossel to-morrow morning, but to-night I am yours,' said I.

We left our troopers in snug quarters, and, as it was but a mile to the Castle, we did not disturb our horses. To tell the truth, I hate to see a cavalry man walk, and I hold that just as he is the most gallant thing upon earth when he has his saddle-flaps between his knees, so he is the most clumsy when he has to loop up his sabre and his sabre-tasche in one hand and turn in his toes for fear of catching the rowels of his spurs. Still, Duroc and I were of the age when one can carry things off, and I dare swear that no woman at least would have quarrelled with the appearance of the two young hussars, one in blue and one in grey, who set out that night from the Arensdorf post-house. We both carried our swords, and for my own part I slipped a pistol from my holster into the inside of my pelisse, for it seemed to me that there might be some wild work before us.

The track which led to the Castle wound through a pitch-black fir-wood, where we could see nothing save the ragged patch of stars above our head. Presently, however, it opened up, and there was the Castle right in front of us, about as far as a carbine would carry. It was a huge, uncouth place, and bore every mark of being exceedingly old, with turrets at every corner, and a square keep on the side which was nearest to us. In all its great shadow there was no sign of light save from a single window, and no sound came from it. To me there was something awful in its size and its silence, which corresponded so well with its sinister name. My companion pressed on eagerly, and I followed him along the ill-kept path which led to the gate.

There was no bell or knocker upon the great iron-studded door, and it was only by pounding with the hilts of our sabres that we could attract attention. A thin, hawk-faced man, with a beard up to his temples, opened it at last. He carried a lantern in one hand, and in the other a chain which held an enormous black hound. His manner at the first moment was threatening, but the sight of our uniforms and of our faces turned it into one of sulky reserve.

'The Baron Straubenthal does not receive visitors at so late an hour,' said he, speaking in very excellent French.

'You can inform Baron Straubenthal that I have come eight hundred leagues to see him, and that I will not leave until I have done so,' said my companion. I could not myself have said it with a better voice and manner.

The fellow took a sidelong look at us, and tugged at his black beard in his perplexity.

'To tell the truth, gentlemen,' said he, 'the Baron has a cup or two of wine in him at this hour, and you would certainly find him a more entertaining companion if you were to come again in the morning.'

He had opened the door a little wider as he spoke, and I saw by the light of the lamp in the hall behind him that three other rough fellows were standing there, one of whom held another of these monstrous hounds. Duroc must have seen it also, but it made no difference to his resolution.

'Enough talk,' said he, pushing the man to one side. 'It is with your master that I have to deal.'

The fellows in the hall made way for him as he strode in among them, so great is the power of one man who knows what he wants over several who are not sure of themselves. My companion tapped one of them upon the shoulder with as much assurance as though he owned him.

'Show me to the Baron,' said he.

The man shrugged his shoulders, and answered something in Polish. The fellow with the beard, who had shut and barred the front door, appeared to be the only one among them who could speak French.

'Well, you shall have your way,' said he, with a sinister smile. 'You shall see the Baron. And perhaps, before you have finished, you will wish that you had taken my advice.'

We followed him down the hall, which was stone-flagged and very spacious, with skins scattered upon the floor, and the heads of wild beasts upon the walls. At the farther end he threw open a door, and we entered.

It was a small room, scantily furnished, with the same marks of neglect and decay which met us at every turn. The walls were hung with discoloured tapestry, which had come loose at one corner, so as to expose the rough stonework behind. A second door, hung with a curtain, faced us upon the other side. Between lay a square table, strewn with dirty dishes and the sordid remains of a meal. Several bottles were scattered over it. At the head of it, and facing us, there sat a huge man with a lion-like head and a great shock of orange-coloured hair. His beard was of the same glaring hue; matted and tangled and coarse as a horse's mane. I have seen some strange faces in my time, but never one more brutal than that, with its small, vicious, blue eyes, its white, crumpled cheeks, and the thick, hanging lip which protruded over his monstrous beard. His head swayed about on his shoulders, and he looked at us with the vague, dim gaze of a drunken man. Yet he was not so drunk but that our uniforms carried their message to him.

'Well, my brave boys,' he hiccoughed. 'What is the latest news from Paris, eh? You're going to free Poland, I hear, and have meantime all become slaves yourselves—slaves to a little aristocrat with his grey coat and his three-cornered hat. No more citizens either, I am told, and nothing but monsieur and madame. My faith, some more heads will have to roll into the sawdust basket some of these mornings.'

Duroc advanced in silence, and stood by the ruffian's side.

'Jean Carabin,' said he.

The Baron started, and the film of drunkenness seemed to be clearing from his eyes.

'Jean Carabin,' said Duroc, once more.

He sat up and grasped the arms of his chair.

'What do you mean by repeating that name, young man?' he asked.

'Jean Carabin, you are a man whom I have long wished to meet.'

'Supposing that I once had such a name, how can it concern you, since you must have been a child when I bore it?'

'My name is Duroc.'

'Not the son of——?'

'The son of the man you murdered.'

The Baron tried to laugh, but there was terror in his eyes.

'We must let bygones be bygones, young man,' he cried. 'It was our life or theirs in those days: the aristocrats or the people. Your father was of the Gironde. He fell. I was of the mountain. Most of my comrades fell. It was all the fortune of war. We must forget all this and learn to know each other better, you and I.' He held out a red, twitching hand as he spoke.

'Enough,' said young Duroc. 'If I were to pass my sabre through you as you sit in that chair, I should do what is just and right. I dishonour my blade by crossing it with yours. And yet you are a Frenchman, and have even held a commission under the same flag as myself. Rise, then, and defend yourself!'

'Tut, tut!' cried the Baron. 'It is all very well for you young bloods——'

Duroc's patience could stand no more. He swung his open hand into the centre of the great orange beard. I saw a lip fringed with blood, and two glaring blue eyes above it.

'You shall die for that blow.'

'That is better,' said Duroc.

'My sabre!' cried the other. 'I will not keep you waiting, I promise you!' and he hurried from the room.

I have said that there was a second door covered with a curtain. Hardly had the Baron vanished when there ran from behind it a woman, young and beautiful. So swiftly and noiselessly did she move that she was between us in an instant, and it was only the shaking curtains which told us whence she had come.

'I have seen it all,' she cried. 'Oh, sir, you have carried yourself splendidly.' She stooped to my companion's hand, and kissed it again and again ere he could disengage it from her grasp.

'Nay, madame, why should you kiss my hand?' he cried.

'Because it is the hand which struck him on his vile, lying mouth. Because it may be the hand which will avenge my mother. I am his step-daughter. The woman whose heart he broke was my mother. I loathe him, I fear him. Ah, there is his step!' In an instant she had vanished as suddenly as she had come. A moment later, the Baron entered with a drawn sword in his hand, and the fellow who had admitted us at his heels.

'This is my secretary,' said he. 'He will be my friend in this affair. But we shall need more elbow-room than we can find here. Perhaps you will kindly come with me to a more spacious apartment.'

It was evidently impossible to fight in a chamber which was blocked by a great table. We followed him out, therefore, into the dimly-lit hall. At the farther end a light was shining through an open door.

'We shall find what we want in here,' said the man with the dark beard. It was a large, empty room, with rows of barrels and cases round the walls. A strong lamp stood upon a shelf in the corner. The floor was level and true, so that no swordsman could ask for more. Duroc drew his sabre and sprang into it. The Baron stood back with a bow and motioned me to follow my companion. Hardly were my heels over the threshold when the heavy door crashed behind us and the key screamed in the lock. We were taken in a trap.

For a moment we could not realise it. Such incredible baseness was outside all our experiences. Then, as we understood how foolish we had been to trust for an instant a man with such a history, a flush of rage came over us, rage against his villainy and against our own stupidity. We rushed at the door together, beating it with our fists and kicking with our heavy boots. The sound of our blows and of our execrations must have resounded through the Castle. We called to this villain, hurling at him every name which might pierce even into his hardened soul. But the door was enormous—such a door as one finds in mediæval castles—made of huge beams clamped together with iron. It was as easy to break as a square of the Old Guard. And our cries appeared to be of as little avail as our blows, for they only brought for answer the clattering echoes from the high roof above us. When you have done some soldiering, you soon learn to put up with what cannot be altered. It was I, then, who first recovered my calmness, and prevailed upon Duroc to join with me in examining the apartment which had become our dungeon.

There was only one window, which had no glass in it, and was so narrow that one could not so much as get one's head through. It was high up, and Duroc had to stand upon a barrel in order to see from it.

'What can you see?' I asked.

'Fir-woods and an avenue of snow between them,' said he. 'Ah!' he gave a cry of surprise.

I sprang upon the barrel beside him. There was, as he said, a long, clear strip of snow in front. A man was riding down it, flogging his horse and galloping like a madman. As we watched, he grew smaller and smaller, until he was swallowed up by the black shadows of the forest.

'What does that mean?' asked Duroc.

'No good for us,' said I. 'He may have gone for some brigands to cut our throats. Let us see if we cannot find a way out of this mouse-trap before the cat can arrive.'

The one piece of good fortune in our favour was that beautiful lamp. It was nearly full of oil, and would last us until morning. In the dark our situation would have been far more difficult. By its light we proceeded to examine the packages and cases which lined the walls. In some places there was only a single line of them, while in one corner they were piled nearly to the ceiling. It seemed that we were in the storehouse of the Castle, for there were a great number of cheeses, vegetables of various kinds, bins full of dried fruits, and a line of wine barrels. One of these had a spigot in it, and as I had eaten little during the day, I was glad of a cup of claret and some food. As to Duroc, he would take nothing, but paced up and down the room in a fever of anger and impatience. 'I'll have him yet!' he cried, every now and then. 'The rascal shall not escape me!'

This was all very well, but it seemed to me, as I sat on a great round cheese eating my supper, that this young-ster was thinking rather too much of his own family affairs and too little of the fine scrape into which he had got me. After all, his father had been dead fourteen years, and nothing could set that right; but here was Etienne Gerard, the most dashing lieutenant in the whole Grand Army, in imminent danger of being cut off at the very outset of his brilliant career. Who was ever to know the heights to which I might have risen if I were knocked on the head in this hole-and-corner business, which had nothing whatever to do with France or the Emperor? I could not help thinking what a fool I had been, when I had a fine war before me and everything which a man could desire, to go off on a hare-brained expedition of this sort, as if it were not enough to have a quarter of a million Russians to fight against, without plunging into all sorts of private quarrels as well.

'That is all very well,' I said at last, as I heard Duroc muttering his threats. 'You may do what you like to him when you get the upper hand. At present the question rather is, what is *he* going to do to us?'

'Let him do his worst!' cried the boy. 'I owe a duty to my father.'

'That is mere foolishness,' said I. 'If you owe a duty to your father, I owe one to my mother, which is to get out of this business safe and sound.'

My remark brought him to his senses.

'I have thought too much of myself!' he cried. 'Forgive me, Monsieur Gerard. Give me your advice as to what I should do.'

'Well,' said I, 'it is not for our health that they have shut us up here among the cheeses. They mean to make an end of us if they can. That is certain. They hope that no one knows that we have come here, and that none will trace us if we remain. Do your hussars know where you have gone to?'

'I said nothing.'

'Hum! It is clear that we cannot be starved here. They must come to us if they are to kill us. Behind a barricade of barrels we could hold our own against the five rascals whom we have seen. That is, probably, why they have sent that messenger for assistance.'

'We must get out before he returns.'

'Precisely, if we are to get out at all.'

'Could we not burn down this door?' he cried.

'Nothing could be easier,' said I. 'There are several casks of oil in the corner. My only objection is that we should ourselves be nicely toasted, like two little oyster *pâtés*.'

'Can you not suggest something?' he cried, in despair. 'Ah, what is that?'

There had been a low sound at our little window, and a shadow came between the stars and ourselves. A small, white hand was stretched into the lamplight. Something glittered between the fingers.

'Quick! quick!' cried a woman's voice.

We were on the barrel in an instant.

'They have sent for the Cossacks. Your lives are at stake. Ah, I am lost! I am lost!'

There was the sound of rushing steps, a hoarse oath, a blow, and the stars were once more twinkling through the window. We stood helpless upon the barrel with our blood cold with horror. Half a minute afterwards we heard a smothered scream, ending in a choke. A great door slammed somewhere in the silent night.

'Those ruffians have seized her. They will kill her,' I cried.

Duroc sprang down with the inarticulate shouts of one whose reason has left him. He struck the door so frantically with his naked hands that he left a blotch of blood with every blow.

'Here is the key!' I shouted, picking one from the floor. 'She must have thrown it in at the instant that she was torn away.'

My companion snatched it from me with a shriek of joy. A moment later he dashed it down upon the boards. It was so small that it was lost in the enormous lock. Duroc sank upon one of the boxes with his head between his hands. He sobbed in his despair. I could have sobbed, too, when I thought of the woman and how helpless we were to save her.

But I am not easily baffled. After all, this key must have been sent to us for a purpose. The lady could not bring us that of the door, because this murderous step-father of hers would most certainly have it in his pocket. Yet this other must have a meaning, or why should she risk her life to place it in our hands? It would say little for our wits if we could not find out what that meaning might be.

I set to work moving all the cases out from the wall, and Duroc, gaining new hope from my courage, helped me with all his strength. It was no light task, for many of them were large and heavy. On we went, working like maniacs, slinging barrels, cheeses, and boxes pell-mell into the middle of the room. At last there only remained one huge barrel of vodki, which stood in the corner. With our united strength we rolled it out, and there was a little low wooden door in the wainscot behind it. The key fitted, and with a cry of delight we saw it swing open before us. With the lamp in my hand, I squeezed my way in, followed by my companion.

We were in the powder-magazine of the Castle—a rough, walled cellar, with barrels all round it, and one with the top staved in in the centre. The powder from it lay in a black heap upon the floor. Beyond there was another door, but it was locked.

'We are no better off than before,' cried Duroc. 'We have no key.'

'We have a dozen!' I cried.

'Where?'

I pointed to the line of powder barrels.

'You would blow this door open?'

'Precisely.'

'But you would explode the magazine.'

It was true, but I was not at the end of my resources.

'We will blow open the store-room door,' I cried.

I ran back and seized a tin box which had been filled with candles. It was about the size of my busby—large enough to hold several pounds of powder. Duroc filled it while I cut off the end of a candle. When we had finished it, it would have puzzled a colonel of engineers to make a better petard. I put three cheeses on the top of each other and placed it above them, so as to lean against the lock. Then we lit our candle-end and ran for shelter, shutting the door of the magazine behind us.

It is no joke, my friends, to be among all those tons of powder, with the knowledge that if the flame of the explosion should penetrate through one thin door our blackened limbs would be shot higher than the Castle keep. Who could have believed that a half-inch of candle could take so long to burn? My ears were straining all the time for the thudding of the hoofs of the Cossacks who were coming to destroy us. I had almost made up my mind that the candle must have gone out when there was a smack like a bursting bomb, our door flew to bits, and pieces of cheese, with a shower of turnips, apples, and splinters of cases, were shot in among us. As we rushed out we had to stagger through an impenetrable smoke, with all sorts of débris beneath our feet, but there was a glimmering square where the dark door had been. The petard had done its work.

In fact, it had done more for us than we had even ventured to hope. It had shattered gaolers as well as gaol. The first thing that I saw as I came out into the hall was a man with a butcher's axe in his hand, lying flat upon his back, with a gaping wound across his forehead. The second was a huge dog, with two of its legs broken, twisting in agony upon the floor. As it raised itself up I saw the two broken ends flapping like flails. At the same instant I heard a cry, and there was Duroc, thrown against the wall, with the other hound's teeth in his throat. He pushed it off with his left hand, while again and again he passed his sabre through its body, but it was not until I blew out its brains with my pistol that the iron jaws relaxed, and the fierce, bloodshot eyes were glazed in death.

There was no time for us to pause. A woman's scream from in front—a scream of mortal terror—told us that even now we might be too late. There were two other men in the hall, but they cowered away from our drawn swords and furious faces. The blood was streaming from Duroc's neck and dyeing the grey fur of his pelisse. Such was the lad's fire, however, that he shot in front of me, and it was only over his shoulder that I caught a glimpse of the scene as we rushed into the chamber in which we had first seen the master of the Castle of Gloom.

The Baron was standing in the middle of the room, with his tangled mane bristling like an angry lion. He was, as I have said, a huge man with enormous shoulders; and as he stood there, with his face flushed with rage and his sword advanced, I could not but think that, in spite of all his villainies, he had a proper figure for a grenadier. The lady lay cowering in a chair behind him. A weal across one of her white arms and a dog-whip upon the floor were enough to show that our escape had hardly been in time to save her from his brutality. He gave a howl like a wolf as we broke in, and was upon us in an instant, hacking and driving, with a curse at every blow.

I have already said that the room gave no space for

swordsmanship. My young companion was in front of me in the narrow passage between the table and the wall, so that I could only look on without being able to aid him. The lad knew something of his weapon, and was as fierce and active as a wild cat, but in so narrow a space the weight and strength of the giant gave him the advantage. Besides, he was an admirable swordsman. His parade and riposte were as quick as lightning. Twice he touched Duroc upon the shoulder, and then, as the lad slipped on a lunge, he whirled up his sword to finish him before he could recover his feet. I was quicker than he, however, and took the cut upon the pommel of my sabre.

'Excuse me,' said I, 'but you have still to deal with Etienne Gerard.'

He drew back and leaned against the tapestry-covered wall, breathing in little, hoarse gasps, for his foul living was against him.

'Take your breath,' said I. 'I will await your convenience.'

'You have no cause of quarrel against me,' he panted.

'I owe you some little attention,' said I, 'for having shut me up in your store-room. Besides, if all other were wanting, I see cause enough upon that lady's arm.'

'Have your way, then!' he snarled, and leaped at me like a madman. For a minute I saw only the blazing blue eyes, and the red glazed point which stabbed and stabbed, rasping off to right or to left, and yet ever back at my throat and my breast. I had never thought that such good sword-play was to be found at Paris in the days of the Revolution. I do not suppose that in all my little affairs I have met six men who had a better knowledge of their weapon. But he knew that I was his master. He read death in my eyes, and I could see that he read it. The flush died from his face. His breath came in shorter and in thicker gasps. Yet he fought on, even after the final thrust had come, and died still hacking and cursing, with foul cries upon his lips, and his blood clotting upon his orange beard. I who speak to you have seen so many battles, that my old memory can scarce contain their names, and yet of all the terrible sights which these eyes have rested upon, there is none which I care to think of less than of that orange beard with the crimson stain in the centre, from which I had drawn my sword-point.

It was only afterwards that I had time to think of all this. His monstrous body had hardly crashed down upon the floor before the woman in the corner sprang to her feet, clapping her hands together and screaming out in her delight. For my part I was disgusted to see a woman take such delight in a deed of blood, and I gave no thought as to the terrible wrongs which must have befallen her before she could so far forget the gentleness of her sex. It was on my tongue to tell her sharply to be silent, when a strange, choking smell took the breath from my nostrils, and a sudden yellow glare brought out the figures upon the faded hangings.

'Duroc, Duroc!' I shouted, tugging at his shoulder. 'The Castle is on fire!'

The boy lay senseless upon the ground, exhausted by his wounds. I rushed out into the hall to see whence the danger came. It was our explosion which had set alight to the dry framework of the door. Inside the store-room some of the boxes were already blazing. I glanced in, and as I did so my blood was turned to water by the sight of the powder barrels beyond, and of the loose heap upon the floor. It might be seconds, it could not be more than minutes, before the flames would be at the edge of it. These eyes will be closed in death, my friends, before they cease to see those crawling lines of fire and the black heap beyond.

How little I can remember what followed. Vaguely I can recall how I rushed into the chamber of death, how I seized Duroc by one limp hand and dragged him down the hall, the woman keeping pace with me and pulling at the other arm. Out of the gateway we rushed, and on down the snow-covered path until we were on the fringe of the fir forest. It was at that moment that I heard a crash behind me, and, glancing round, saw a great spout of fire shoot up into the wintry sky. An instant later there seemed to come a second crash, far louder than the first. I saw the fir trees and the stars whirling round me, and I fell unconscious across the body of my comrade.

It was some weeks before I came to myself in the post-house of Arensdorf, and longer still before I could be told all that had befallen me. It was Duroc, already able to go soldiering, who came to my bedside and gave me an account of it. He it was who told me how a piece of timber had struck me on the head and laid me almost dead upon the ground. From him, too, I learned how the Polish girl had run to Arensdorf, how she had roused our hussars, and how she had only just brought them back in time to save us from the spears of the Cossacks who had been summoned from their bivouac by that same black-bearded secretary whom we had seen galloping so swiftly over the snow. As to the brave lady who had twice saved our lives, I could not learn very much about her at that moment from Duroc, but when I chanced to meet him in Paris two years later, after the campaign of Wagram, I was not very much surprised to find that I needed no introduction to his bride, and that by the queer turns of fortune he had himself, had he chosen to use it, that very name and title of the Baron Straubenthal, which showed him to be the owner of the blackened ruins of the Castle of Gloom.

II. How the Brigadier Slew the Brothers of Ajaccio

WHEN the Emperor needed an agent he was always very ready to do me the honour of recalling the name of Etienne Gerard, though it occasionally escaped him when rewards were to be distributed. Still, I was a colonel at twenty-eight, and the chief of a brigade at thirty-one, so that I have no reason to be dissatisfied with my career. Had the wars lasted another two or three years I might have grasped my baton, and the man who had his hand upon that was only one stride from a throne. Murat had changed his hussar's cap for a crown, and another light cavalry man might have done as much. However, all those dreams were driven away by Waterloo, and, although I was not able to write my name upon history, it is sufficiently well known by all who served with me in the great wars of the Empire.

What I want to tell you to-night is about the very singular affair which first started me upon my rapid upward course, and which had the effect of establishing a secret bond between the Emperor and myself.

There is just one little word of warning which I must give you before I begin. When you hear me speak, you must always bear in mind that you are listening to one who has seen history from the inside. I am talking about what my ears have heard and my eyes have seen, so you must not try to confute me by quoting the opinions of some student or man of the pen, who has written a book of history or memoirs. There is much which is unknown by such people, and much which never will be known by the world. For my own part, I could tell you some very surprising things were it discreet to do so. The facts which I am about to relate to you to-night were kept secret by me during the Emperor's lifetime, because I gave him my promise that it should be so, but I do not think that there can be any harm now in my telling the remarkable part which I played.

You must know, then, that at the time of the Treaty of Tilsit I was a simple lieutenant in the 10th Hussars, without money or interest. It is true that my appearance and my gallantry were in my favour, and that I had already won a reputation as being one of the best swordsmen in the army; but among the host of brave men who surrounded the Emperor it needed more than this to insure a rapid career. I was confident, however, that my chance would come, though I never dreamed that it would take so remarkable a form.

When the Emperor returned to Paris, after the declaration of peace in the year 1807, he spent much of his time with the Empress and the Court at Fontainebleau. It was the time when he was at the pinnacle of his career. He had in three successive campaigns humbled Austria, crushed Prussia, and made the Russians very glad to get upon the right side of the Niemen. The old Bulldog over the Channel was still growling, but he could not get very far from his kennel. If we could have made a perpetual peace at that moment, France would have taken a higher place than any nation since the days of the Romans. So I have heard the wise folk say, though for my part I had other things to think of. All the girls were glad to see the army back after its long absence, and you may be sure that I had my share of any favours that were going. You may judge how far I was a favourite in those days when I say that even now, in my sixtieth year—but why should I dwell upon that which is already sufficiently well known?

Our regiment of hussars was quartered with the horse chasseurs of the guard at Fontainebleau. It is, as you know, but a little place, buried in the heart of the forest, and it was wonderful at this time to see it crowded with Grand Dukes and Electors and Princes, who thronged round Napoleon like puppies round their master, each hoping that some bone might be thrown to him. There was more German than French to be heard in the street, for those who had helped us in the late war had come to beg for a reward, and those who had opposed us had come to try and escape their punishment.

And all the time our little man, with his pale face and his cold, grey eyes, was riding to the hunt every morning, silent and brooding, all of them following in his train, in the hope that some word would escape him. And then, when the humour seized him, he would throw a hundred square miles to that man, or tear as much off the other, round off one kingdom by a river, or cut off another by a chain of mountains. That was how he used to do business, this little artilleryman, whom we had raised so high with our sabres and our bayonets. He was very civil to us always, for he knew where his power came from. We knew also, and showed it by the way in which we carried ourselves. We were agreed, you understand, that he was the finest leader in the world, but we did not forget that he had the finest men to lead.

Well, one day I was seated in my quarters playing cards with young Morat, of the horse chasseurs, when the door opened and in walked Lasalle, who was our Colonel. You know what a fine, swaggering fellow he was, and the sky-blue uniform of the Tenth suited him to a marvel. My faith, we youngsters were so taken by him that we all swore and diced and drank and played the deuce whether we liked it or no, just that we might resemble our Colonel! We forgot that it was not because he drank or gambled that the Emperor was going to make him the head of the light cavalry, but because he had the surest eye for the nature of a position or for the strength of a column, and the best judgment as to when infantry could be broken, or whether guns were exposed, of any man in the army. We were too young to understand all that, however, so we waxed our moustaches and clinked our spurs and let the ferrules of our scabbards wear out by trailing them along the pavement in the hope that we should all become Lasalles. When he came clanking into my quarters, both Morat and I sprang to our feet.

'My boy,' said he, clapping me on the shoulder, 'the Emperor wants to see you at four o'clock.'

The room whirled round me at the words, and I had to lean my hands upon the edge of the card-table.

'What?' I cried. 'The Emperor!'

'Precisely,' said he, smiling at my astonishment.

'But the Emperor does not know of my existence, Colonel,' I protested. 'Why should he send for me?'

'Well, that's just what puzzles me,' cried Lasalle, twirling his moustache. 'If he wanted the help of a good sabre, why should he descend to one of my lieutenants when he might have found all that he needed at the head of the regiment? However,' he added, clapping me on the shoulder again in his hearty fashion, 'every man has his chance. I have had mine, otherwise I should not be Colonel of the Tenth. I must not grudge you yours. Forward, my boy, and may it be the first step towards changing your busby for a cocked hat.'

It was but two o'clock, so he left me, promising to come back and to accompany me to the palace. My faith, what a time I passed, and how many conjectures did I make as to what it was that the Emperor could want of me! I paced up and down my little room in a fever of anticipation. Sometimes I thought that perhaps he had heard of the guns which we had taken at Austerlitz; but, then, there were so many who had taken guns at Austerlitz, and two years had passed since the battle. Or it might be that he wished to reward me for my affair with the aide-de-camp of the Russian Emperor. But then again a cold fit would seize me, and I would fancy that he had sent for me to reprimand me. There were a few duels which he might have taken in ill part, and there were one or two little jokes in Paris since the peace.

But, no! I considered the words of Lasalle. 'If he had need of a brave man,' said Lasalle.

It was obvious that my Colonel had some idea of what was in the wind. If he had not known that it was to my advantage, he would not have been so cruel as to congratulate me. My heart glowed with joy as this conviction grew upon me, and I sat down to write to my mother and to tell her that the Emperor was waiting, at that very moment, to have my opinion upon a matter of importance. It made me smile as I wrote it to think that, wonderful as it appeared to me, it would probably only confirm my mother in her opinion of the Emperor's good sense.

At half-past three I heard a sabre come clanking

against every step of my wooden stair. It was Lasalle, and with him was a lame gentleman, very neatly dressed in black with dapper ruffles and cuffs. We did not know many civilians, we of the army, but, my word, this was one whom we could not afford to ignore! I had only to glance at those twinkling eyes, the comical, upturned nose, and the straight, precise mouth, to know that I was in the presence of the one man in France whom even the Emperor had to consider.

'This is Monsieur Etienne Gerard, Monsieur de Talleyrand,' said Lasalle.

I saluted, and the statesman took me in from the top of my panache to the rowel of my spur, with a glance that played over me like a rapier point.

'Have you explained to the lieutenant the circumstances under which he is summoned to the Emperor's presence?' he asked, in his dry, creaking voice.

They were such a contrast, these two men, that I could not help glancing from one to the other of them: the black, sly politician, and the big, sky-blue hussar with one fist on his hip and the other on the hilt of his sabre. They both took their seats as I looked, Talleyrand without a sound, and Lasalle with a clash and a jingle like a prancing charger.

'It's this way, youngster,' said he, in his brusque fashion; 'I was with the Emperor in his private cabinet this morning when a note was brought in to him. He opened it, and as he did so he gave such a start that it fluttered down on to the floor. I handed it up to him again, but he was staring at the wall in front of him as if he had seen a ghost. "Fratelli dell' Ajaccio," he muttered; and then again, "Fratelli dell' Ajaccio." I don't pretend to know more Italian than a man can pick up in two campaigns, and I could make nothing of this. It seemed to me that he had gone out of his mind; and you would have said so also, Monsieur de Talleyrand, if you had seen the look in his eyes. He read the note, and then he sat for half an hour or more without moving.'

'And you?' asked Talleyrand.

'Why, I stood there not knowing what I ought to do. Presently he seemed to come back to his senses.

' "I suppose, Lasalle," said he, "that you have some gallant young officers in the Tenth?"

' "They are all that, sire," I answered.

' "If you had to pick one who was to be depended upon for action, but who would not think too much—you understand me, Lasalle—which would you select?" he asked.

' "I have one," said I, "who is all spurs and moustaches, with never a thought beyond women and horses."

' "That is the man I want," said Napoleon. "Bring him to my private cabinet at four o'clock."

'So, youngster, I came straight away to you at once, and mind that you do credit to the 10th Hussars.'

I was by no means flattered by the reasons which had led to my Colonel's choice, and I must have shown as much in my face, for he roared with laughter and Talleyrand gave a dry chuckle also.

'Just one word of advice before you go, Monsieur Gerard,' said he: 'you are now coming into troubled waters, and you might find a worse pilot than myself. We have none of us any idea as to what this little affair means, and, between ourselves, it is very important for us, who have the destinies of France upon our shoulders, to keep ourselves in touch with all that goes on. You understand me, Monsieur Gerard?'

I had not the least idea what he was driving at, but I bowed and tried to look as if it was clear to me.

'Act very guardedly, then, and say nothing to anybody,' said Talleyrand. 'Colonel de Lasalle and I will not show ourselves in public with you, but we will await you here, and we will give you our advice when you have told us what has passed between the Emperor and yourself. It is time that you started now, for the Emperor never forgives unpunctuality.'

Off I went on foot to the palace, which was only a

hundred paces off. I made my way to the antechamber, where Duroc, with his grand new scarlet and gold coat, was fussing about among the crowd of people who were waiting. I heard him whisper to Monsieur de Caulain-court that half of them were German Dukes who expected to be made Kings, and the other half German Dukes who expected to be made paupers. Duroc, when he heard my name, showed me straight in, and I found myself in the Emperor's presence.

I had, of course, seen him in camp a hundred times, but I had never been face to face with him before. I have no doubt that if you had met him without knowing in the least who he was, you would simply have said that he was a sallow little fellow with a good forehead and fairly well-turned calves. His tight white cashmere breeches and white stockings showed off his legs to advantage. But even a stranger must have been struck by the singular look of his eyes, which could harden into an expression which would frighten a grenadier. It is said that even Augereau, who was a man who had never known what fear was, quailed before Napoleon's gaze, at a time, too, when the Emperor was but an unknown soldier. He looked mildly enough at me, however, and motioned me to remain by the door. De Meneval was writing to his dictation, looking up at him between each sentence with his spaniel eyes.

'That will do. You can go,' said the Emperor, abruptly. Then, when the secretary had left the room, he strode across with his hands behind his back, and he looked me up and down without a word. Though he was a small man himself, he was very fond of having fine-looking fellows about him, and so I think that my appearance gave him pleasure. For my own part, I raised one hand to the salute and held the other upon the hilt of my sabre, looking straight ahead of me, as a soldier should.

'Well, Monsieur Gerard,' said he, at last, tapping his forefinger upon one of the Brandenburgs of gold braid upon the front of my pelisse, 'I am informed that you are a very deserving young officer. Your Colonel gives me an excellent account of you.'

I wished to make a brilliant reply, but I could think of nothing save Lasalle's phrase that I was all spurs and moustaches, so it ended in my saying nothing at all. The Emperor watched the struggle which must have shown itself upon my features, and when, finally, no answer came he did not appear to be displeased.

'I believe that you are the very man that I want,' said he. 'Brave and clever men surround me upon every side. But a brave man who——' He did not finish his sentence, and for my own part I could not understand what he was driving at. I contented myself with assuring him that he could count upon me to the death.

'You are, as I understand, a good swordsman?' said he.

'Tolerable, sire,' I answered.

'You were chosen by your regiment to fight the champion of the Hussars of Chambarant?' said he.

I was not sorry to find that he knew so much of my exploits.

'My comrades, sire, did me that honour,' said I.

'And for the sake of practice you insulted six fencing masters in the week before your duel?'

'I had the privilege of being out seven times in as many days, sire,' said I.

'And escaped without a scratch?'

'The fencing master of the 23rd Light Infantry touched me on the left elbow, sire.'

'Let us have no more child's play of the sort, monsieur,' he cried, turning suddenly to that cold rage of his which was so appalling. 'Do you imagine that I place veteran soldiers in these positions that you may practise quarte and tierce upon them? How am I to face Europe if my soldiers turn their points upon each other? Another word of your duelling, and I break you between these fingers.'

I saw his plump white hands flash before my eyes as he spoke, and his voice had turned to the most discordant hissing and growling. My word, my skin pringled all over as I listened to him, and I would gladly have changed my position for that of the first man in the steepest and narrowest breach that ever swallowed up a storming party. He turned to the table, drank off a cup of coffee, and then when he faced me again every trace of this storm had vanished, and he wore that singular smile which came from his lips but never from his eyes.

'I have need of your services, Monsieur Gerard,' said he. 'I may be safer with a good sword at my side, and there are reasons why yours should be the one which I select. But first of all I must bind you to secrecy. Whilst I live what passes between us to-day must be known to none but ourselves.'

I thought of Talleyrand and of Lasalle, but I promised.

'In the next place, I do not want your opinions or conjectures, and I wish you to do exactly what you are told.'

I bowed.

'It is your sword that I need, and not your brains. I will do the thinking. Is that clear to you?'

'Yes, sire.'

'You know the Chancellor's Grove, in the forest?'

I bowed.

'You know also the large double fir-tree where the hounds assembled on Tuesday?'

Had he known that I met a girl under it three times a week, he would not have asked me. I bowed once more without remark.

'Very good. You will meet me there at ten o'clock to-night.'

I had got past being surprised at anything which might happen. If he had asked me to take his place upon the Imperial throne I could only have nodded my busby.

'We shall then proceed into the wood together,' said the Emperor. 'You will be armed with a sword, but not with pistols. You must address no remark to me, and I shall say nothing to you. We will advance in silence. You understand?'

'I understand, sire.'

'After a time we shall see a man, or more probably two men, under a certain tree. We shall approach them together. If I signal to you to defend me, you will have your sword ready. If, on the other hand, I speak to these men, you will wait and see what happens. If you are called upon to draw, you must see that neither of them, in the event of there being two, escapes from us. I shall myself assist you.'

'Sire,' I cried, 'I have no doubt that two would not be too many for my sword; but would it not be better that I should bring a comrade than that you should be forced to join in such a struggle?'

'Ta, ta, ta,' said he. 'I was a soldier before I was an Emperor. Do you think, then, that artillerymen have not swords as well as the hussars? But I ordered you not to argue with me. You will do exactly what I tell you. If swords are once out, neither of these men is to get away alive.'

'They shall not, sire,' said I.

'Very good. I have no more instructions for you. You can go.'

I turned to the door, and then an idea occurring to me I turned.

'I have been thinking, sire——' said I.

He sprang at me with the ferocity of a wild beast. I really thought he would have struck me.

'Thinking!' he cried. 'You, *you!* Do you imagine I chose you out because you could think? Let me hear of your doing such a thing again! You, the one man—but, there! You meet me at the fir-tree at ten o'clock.'

My faith, I was right glad to get out of the room. If I have a good horse under me, and a sword clanking against my stirrup-iron, I know where I am. And in all that relates to green fodder or dry, barley and oats and rye, and the handling of squadrons upon the march, there is no one who can teach me very much. But when I meet a Chamberlain and a Marshal of the Palace, and have to pick my words with an Emperor, and find that everybody hints instead of talking straight out, I feel like a troop-horse who has been put in a lady's *calèche*. It is not my trade, all this mincing and pretending. I have learned the manners of a gentleman, but never those of a courtier. I was right glad then to get into the fresh air again, and I ran away up to my quarters like a schoolboy who has just escaped from the seminary master.

But as I opened the door, the very first thing that my eye rested upon was a long pair of sky-blue legs with hussar boots, and a short pair of black ones with knee breeches and buckles. They both sprang up together to greet me.

'Well, what news?' they cried, the two of them.

'None,' I answered.

'The Emperor refused to see you?'

'No, I have seen him.'

'And what did he say?'

'Monsieur de Talleyrand,' I answered, 'I regret to say that it is quite impossible for me to tell you anything about it. I have promised the Emperor.'

'Pooh, pooh, my dear young man,' said he, sidling up to me, as a cat does when it is about to rub itself against you. 'This is all among friends, you understand, and goes no farther than these four walls. Besides, the Emperor never meant to include me in this promise.'

'It is but a minute's walk to the palace. Monsieur de Talleyrand,' I answered; 'if it would not be troubling you too much to ask you to step up to it and bring back the Emperor's written statement that he did not mean to include you in this promise, I shall be happy to tell you every word that passed.'

He showed his teeth to me then like the old fox that he was.

'Monsieur Gerard appears to be a little puffed up,' said he. 'He is too young to see things in their just proportion. As he grows older he may understand that it is not always very discreet for a subaltern of cavalry to give such very abrupt refusals.'

I did not know what to say to this, but Lasalle came to my aid in his downright fashion.

'The lad is quite right,' said he. 'If I had known that there was a promise I should not have questioned him. You know very well, Monsieur de Talleyrand, that if he had answered you, you would have laughed in your sleeve and thought as much about him as I think of the bottle when the burgundy is gone. As for me, I promise you that the Tenth would have had no room for him, and that we should have lost our best swordsman if I had heard him give up the Emperor's secret.'

But the statesman became only the more bitter when he saw that I had the support of my Colonel.

'I have heard, Colonel de Lasalle,' said he, with an icy dignity, 'that your opinion is of great weight upon the subject of light cavalry. Should I have occasion to seek information about that branch of the army, I shall be very happy to apply to you. At present, however, the matter concerns diplomacy, and you will permit me to form my own views upon that question. As long as the welfare of France and the safety of the Emperor's person are largely committed to my care, I will use every means in my power to secure them, even if it should be against the Emperor's own temporary wishes. I have the honour, Colonel de Lasalle, to wish you a very good-day!'

He shot a most unamiable glance in my direction, and, turning upon his heel, he walked with little, quick, noiseless steps out of the room.

I could see from Lasalle's face that he did not at all relish finding himself at enmity with the powerful Minister. He rapped out an oath or two, and then, catching up his sabre and his cap, he clattered away down the stairs. As I looked out of the window I saw the two of them, the big blue man and the limping black one, going up the street together. Talleyrand was walking very rigidly, and Lasalle was waving his hands and talking, so I suppose he was trying to make his peace.

The Emperor had told me not to think, and I endeavoured to obey him. I took up the cards from the table where Morat had left them, and I tried to work out a few combinations at écarté. But I could not remember which were trumps, and I threw them under the table in despair. Then I drew my sabre and practised giving point until I was weary, but it was all of no use at all. My mind *would* work, in spite of myself. At ten o'clock I was to meet the Emperor in the forest. Of all extra-ordinary combinations of events in the whole world, surely this was the last which would have occurred to me when I rose from my couch that morning. But the responsibility—the dreadful responsibility! It was all upon my shoulders. There was no one to halve it with me. It made me cold all over. Often as I have faced death upon the battle-field, I have never known what real fear was until that moment. But then I considered that after all I could but do my best like a brave and honourable gentleman, and above all obey the orders which I had received, to the very letter. And, if all went well, this would surely be the foundation of my fortunes. Thus, swaying between my fears and my hopes, I spent the long, long evening until it was time to keep my appointment.

I put on my military overcoat, as I did not know how much of the night I might have to spend in the woods, and I fastened my sword outside it. I pulled off my hussar boots also, and wore a pair of shoes and gaiters, that I might be lighter upon my feet. Then I stole out of my quarters and made for the forest, feeling very much easier in my mind, for I am always at my best when the time of thought has passed and the moment for action arrived.

I passed the barracks of the Chasseurs of the Guards, and the line of cafés all filled with uniforms. I caught a glimpse as I went by of the blue and gold of some of my comrades, amid the swarm of dark infantry coats and the light green of the Guides. There they sat, sipping their wine and smoking their cigars, little dreaming what their comrade had on hand. One of them, the chief of my squadron, caught sight of me in the lamplight, and came shouting after me into the street. I hurried on, however, pretending not to hear him, so he, with a curse at my deafness, went back at last to his wine bottle.

It is not very hard to get into the forest at Fontainebleau. The scattered trees steal their way into the very streets, like the tirailleurs in front of a column. I turned into a path, which led to the edge of the woods, and then I pushed rapidly forward towards the old fir-tree. It was a place which, as I have hinted, I had my own reasons for knowing well, and I could only thank the Fates that it was not one of the nights upon which Léonie would be waiting for me. The poor child would have died of terror at sight of the Emperor. He might have been too harsh with her—and worse still, he might have been too kind.

There was a half moon shining, and, as I came up to our trysting-place, I saw that I was not the first to arrive. The Emperor was pacing up and down, his hands behind him and his face sunk somewhat forward upon his breast. He wore a grey great-coat with a capote over his head. I had seen him in such a dress in our winter campaign in Poland, and it was said that he used it because the hood was such an excellent disguise. He was always fond, whether in the camp or in Paris, of walking round at night, and overhearing the talk in the cabarets or round the fires. His figure, however, and his way of carrying his head and his hands were so well known that he was always recognised, and then the talkers would say whatever they thought would please him best.

My first thought was that he would be angry with me for having kept him waiting, but as I approached him, we heard the big church clock of Fontainebleau clang out the hour of ten. It was evident, therefore, that it was he who was too soon, and not I too late. I remembered his order that I should make no remark, so contented myself with halting within four paces of him, clicking my spurs together, grounding my sabre, and saluting. He glanced at me, and then without a word he turned and walked slowly through the forest, I keeping always about the same distance behind him. Once or twice he seemed to me to look apprehensively to right and to left, as if he feared that someone was observing us. I looked also, but although I have the keenest sight, it was quite impossible to see anything except the ragged patches of moonshine between the great black shadows of the trees. My ears are as quick as my eyes, and once or twice I thought that I heard a twig crack; but you know how many sounds there are in a forest at night, and how difficult it is even to say what direction they come from.

We walked for rather more than a mile, and I knew exactly what our destination was, long before we got there. In the centre of one of the glades, there is the shattered stump of what must at some time have been a most gigantic tree. It is called the Abbot's Beech, and there are so many ghostly stories about it that I know many a brave soldier who would not care about mounting sentinel over it. However, I cared as little for such folly as the Emperor did, so we crossed the glade and made straight for the old broken trunk. As we approached, I saw that two men were waiting for us beneath it.

When I first caught sight of them they were standing rather behind it, as if they were not anxious to be seen, but as we came nearer they emerged from its shadow and walked forward to meet us. The Emperor glanced back at me, and slackened his pace a little so that I came within arm's length of him. You may think that I had my hilt well to the front, and that I had a very good look at these two people who were approaching us.

The one was tall, remarkably so, and of very spare frame, while the other was rather below the usual height, and had a brisk, determined way of walking. They each wore black cloaks, which were slung right across their figures, and hung down upon one side, like the mantles of Murat's dragoons. They had flat black caps, like those I have since seen in Spain, which threw their faces into darkness, though I could see the gleam of their eyes from beneath them. With the moon behind them and their long black shadows walking in front, they were such figures as one might expect to meet at night near the Abbot's Beech. I can remember that they had a stealthy way of moving, and that as they approached, the moon-shine formed two white diamonds between their legs and the legs of their shadows.

The Emperor had paused, and these two strangers came to a stand also within a few paces of us. I had drawn up close to my companion's elbow, so that the four of us were facing each other without a word spoken. My eyes were particularly fixed upon the taller one, because he was slightly the nearer to me, and I became certain as I watched him that he was in the last state of nervousness. His lean figure was quivering all over, and I heard a quick, thin panting like that of a tired dog. Suddenly one of them gave a short, hissing signal. The tall man bent his back and his knees like a diver about to spring, but before he could move, I had jumped with drawn sabre in front of him. At the same instant the smaller man bounded past me, and buried a long poniard in the Emperor's heart.

My God! the horror of that moment! It is a marvel that I did not drop dead myself. As in a dream, I saw the grey coat whirl convulsively round, and caught a glimpse in the moonlight of three inches of red point which jutted out from between the shoulders. Then down he fell with a dead man's gasp upon the grass, and the assassin, leaving his weapon buried in his victim, threw up both his hands and shrieked with joy. But I—I drove my sword through his midriff with such frantic force, that the mere blow of the hilt against the end of his breast-bone sent him six paces before he fell, and left my reeking blade ready for the other. I sprang round upon him with such a lust for blood upon me as I had never felt, and never have felt, in all my days. As I turned, a dagger flashed before my eyes, and I felt the cold wind of it pass my neck and the villain's wrist jar upon my shoulder. I shortened my sword, but he winced away from me, and an instant afterwards was in full flight, bounding like a deer across the glade in the moonlight.

But he was not to escape me thus. I knew that the murderer's poniard had done its work. Young as I was, I had seen enough of war to know a mortal blow. I paused but for an instant to touch the cold hand.

'Sire! Sire!' I cried, in an agony; and then as no sound came back and nothing moved, save an ever-widening dark circle in the moonlight, I knew that all was indeed over. I sprang madly to my feet, threw off my great-coat, and ran at the top of my speed after the remaining assassin.

Ah, how I blessed the wisdom which had caused me to come in shoes and gaiters! And the happy thought which had thrown off my coat. He could not get rid of his mantle, this wretch, or else he was too frightened to think of it. So it was that I gained upon him from the beginning. He must have been out of his wits, for he never tried to bury himself in the darker parts of the woods, but he flew on from glade to glade, until he came to the heath-land which leads up to the great Fontainebleau quarry. There I had him in full sight, and knew that he could not escape me. He ran well, it is true—ran as a coward runs when his life is the stake. But I ran as Destiny runs when it gets behind a man's heels. Yard by yard I drew in upon him. He was rolling and staggering. I could hear the rasping and crackling of his breath. The great gulf of the quarry suddenly yawned in front of his path, and glancing at me over his shoulder, he gave a shriek of despair. The next instant he had vanished from my sight.

Vanished utterly, you understand. I rushed to the spot, and gazed down into the black abyss. Had he hurled himself over? I had almost made up my mind that he had done so, when a gentle sound rising and falling came out of the darkness beneath me. It was his breathing once more, and it showed me where he must be. He was hiding in the tool-house.

At the edge of the quarry and beneath the summit there is a small platform upon which stands a wooden hut for the use of the labourers. It was into this, then, that he had darted. Perhaps he had thought, the fool, that, in the darkness, I would not venture to follow him. He little knew Etienne Gerard. With a spring I was on the platform, with another I was through the doorway, and then, hearing him in the corner, I hurled myself down upon the top of him.

He fought like a wild cat, but he never had a chance with his shorter weapon. I think that I must have transfixed him with that first mad lunge, for, though he struck and struck, his blows had no power in them, and presently his dagger tinkled down upon the floor. When I was sure that he was dead, I rose up and passed out into the moonlight. I climbed on to the heath again, and wandered across it as nearly out of my mind as a man could be.

With the blood singing in my ears, and my naked sword still clutched in my hand, I walked aimlessly on until, looking round me, I found that I had come as far as the glade of the Abbot's Beech, and saw in the distance that gnarled stump which must ever be associated with the most terrible moment of my life. I sat down upon a fallen trunk with my sword across my knees and my head between my hands, and I tried to think about what had happened and what would happen in the future.

The Emperor had committed himself to my care. The Emperor was dead. Those were the two thoughts which clanged in my head, until I had no room for any other ones. He had come with me and he was dead. I had done what he had ordered when living. I had revenged him when dead. But what of all that? The world would look upon me as responsible. They might even look upon me as the assassin. What could I prove? What witnesses had I? Might I not have been the accomplice of these wretches? Yes, yes, I was eternally dishonoured—the lowest, most despicable creature in all France. This, then, was the end of my fine military ambitions—of the hopes of my mother. I laughed bitterly at the thought. And what was I to do now? Was I to go into Fontainebleau, to wake up the palace, and to inform them that the great Emperor had been murdered within a pace of me? I could not do it—no, I could not do it! There was but one course for an honourable gentleman whom Fate had placed in so cruel a position. I would fall upon my dishonoured sword, and so share, since I could not avert, the Emperor's fate. I rose with my nerves strung to this last piteous deed, and as I did so, my eyes fell upon something which struck the breath from my lips. The Emperor was standing before me!

He was not more than ten yards off, with the moon shining straight upon his cold, pale face. He wore his grey overcoat, but the hood was turned back, and the front open, so that I could see the green coat of the Guides and the white breeches. His hands were clasped behind his back, and his chin sunk forward upon his breast, in the way that was usual with him.

'Well,' said he, in his hardest and most abrupt voice, 'what account do you give of yourself?'

I believe that, if he had stood in silence for another minute, my brain would have given way. But those sharp military accents were exactly what I needed to bring me to myself. Living or dead, here was the Emperor standing before me and asking me questions. I sprang to the salute.

'You have killed one, I see,' said he, jerking his head towards the beech.

'Yes, sire.'

'And the other escaped?'

'No, sire, I killed him also.'

'What!' he cried. 'Do I understand that you have killed them both?' He approached me as he spoke with a smile which set his teeth gleaming in the moonlight.

'One body lies there, sire,' I answered. 'The other is in the tool-house at the quarry.'

'Then the Brothers of Ajaccio are no more,' he cried, and after a pause, as if speaking to himself: 'The shadow has passed me for ever.' Then he bent forward and laid his hand upon my shoulder.

'You have done very well, my young friend,' said he. 'You have lived up to your reputation.'

He was flesh and blood, then, this Emperor. I could feel the little, plump palm that rested upon me. And yet I could not get over what I had seen with my own eyes, and so I stared at him in such bewilderment that he broke once more into one of his smiles.

'No, no, Monsieur Gerard,' said he, 'I am not a ghost, and you have not seen me killed. You will come here, and all will be clear to you.'

He turned as he spoke, and led the way towards the great beech stump.

The bodies were still lying upon the ground, and two men were standing beside them. As we approached I saw from the turbans that they were Roustem and Mustafa, the two Mameluke servants. The Emperor paused when he came to the grey figure upon the ground, and turning back the hood which shrouded the features, he showed a face which was very different from his own.

'Here lies a faithful servant who has given up his life for his master,' said he. 'Monsieur de Goudin resembles me in figure and in manner, as you must admit.'

What a delirium of joy came upon me when these few words made everything clear to me. He smiled again as he saw the delight which urged me to throw my arms round him and to embrace him, but he moved a step away, as if he had divined my impulse.

'You are unhurt?' he asked.

'I am unhurt, sire. But in another minute I should in my despair——'

'Tut, tut!' he interrupted. 'You did very well. He should himself have been more on his guard. I saw everything which passed.'

'You saw it, sire!'

'You did not hear me follow you through the wood, then? I hardly lost sight of you from the moment that you left your quarters until poor De Goudin fell. The counterfeit Emperor was in front of you and the real one behind. You will now escort me back to the palace.'

He whispered an order to his Mamelukes, who saluted in silence and remained where they were standing. For my part, I followed the Emperor with my pelisse bursting with pride. My word, I have always carried myself as a hussar should, but Lasalle himself never strutted and swung his dolman as I did that night. Who should clink his spurs and clatter his sabre if it were not I—I, Etienne Gerard—the confidant of the Emperor, the chosen swordsman of the light cavalry, the man who slew the would-be assassins of Napoleon? But he noticed my bearing and turned upon me like a blight.

'Is that the way you carry yourself on a secret mission?' he hissed, with that cold glare in his eyes. 'Is it thus that you will make your comrades believe that nothing remarkable has occurred? Have done with this nonsense, monsieur, or you will find yourself transferred to the sappers, where you would have harder work and duller plumage.'

That was the way with the Emperor. If ever he thought that anyone might have a claim upon him, he took the first opportunity to show him the gulf that lay between. I saluted and was silent, but I must confess to you that it hurt me after all that had passed between us. He led on to the palace, where we passed through the side door and up into his own cabinet. There were a couple of grenadiers at the staircase, and their eyes started out from under their fur caps, I promise you, when they saw a young lieutenant of hussars going up to the Emperor's room at midnight. I stood by the door, as I had done in the afternoon, while he flung himself down in an arm-chair, and remained silent so long that it seemed to me that he had forgotten all about me. I ventured at last upon a slight cough to remind him.

'Ah, Monsieur Gerard,' said he, 'you are very curious, no doubt, as to the meaning of all this?'

'I am quite content, sire, if it is your pleasure not to tell me,' I answered.

'Ta, ta, ta,' said he, impatiently. 'These are only words. The moment that you were outside that door you would begin making inquiries about what it means. In two days your brother officers would know about it, in three days it would be all over Fontainebleau, and it would be in Paris on the fourth. Now, if I tell you enough to appease your curiosity, there is some reasonable hope that you may be able to keep the matter to yourself.'

He did not understand me, this Emperor, and yet I could only bow and be silent.

'A few words will make it clear to you,' said he, speaking very swiftly and pacing up and down the room. 'They were Corsicans, these two men. I had known them in my youth. We had belonged to the same society— Brothers of Ajaccio, as we called ourselves. It was founded in the old Paoli days, you understand, and we had some strict rules of our own, which were not infringed with impunity.'

A very grim look came over his face as he spoke, and it seemed to me that all that was French had gone out of him, and that it was the pure Corsican, the man of strong passions and of strange revenges, who stood before me. His memory had gone back to those early days of his, and for five minutes, wrapped in thought, he paced up and down the room with his quick little tiger steps. Then with an impatient wave of his hands he came back to his palace and to me.

'The rules of such a society,' he continued, 'are all very

well for a private citizen. In the old days there was no more loyal brother than I. But circumstances change, and it would be neither for my welfare nor for that of France that I should now submit myself to them. They wanted to hold me to it, and so brought their fate upon their own heads. These were the two chiefs of the order, and they had come from Corsica to summon me to meet them at the spot which they named. I knew what such a summons meant. No man had ever returned from obeying one. On the other hand, if I did not go, I was sure that disaster would follow. I am a brother myself, you remember, and I know their ways.'

Again there came that hardening of his mouth and cold glitter of his eyes.

'You perceive my dilemma, Monsieur Gerard,' said he. 'How would you have acted yourself, under such circumstances?'

'Given the word to the 10th Hussars, sire,' I cried. 'Patrols could have swept the woods from end to end, and brought these two rascals to your feet.'

He smiled, but he shook his head.

'I had very excellent reasons why I did not wish them taken alive,' said he. 'You can understand that an assassin's tongue might be as dangerous a weapon as an assassin's dagger. I will not disguise from you that I wished to avoid scandal at all cost. That was why I ordered you to take no pistols with you. That also is why my Mamelukes will remove all traces of the affair, and nothing more will be heard about it. I thought of all possible plans, and I am convinced that I selected the best one. Had I sent more than one guard with De Goudin into the woods, then the brothers would not have appeared. They would not change their plans nor miss their chance for the sake of a single man. It was Colonel Lasalle's accidental presence at the moment when I received the summons which led to my choosing one of his hussars for the mission. I selected you, Monsieur Gerard, because I wanted a man who could handle a sword, and who would not pry more deeply into the affair than I desired. I trust that, in this respect, you will justify my choice as well as you have done in your bravery and skill.'

'Sire,' I answered, 'you may rely upon it.'

'As long as I live,' said he, 'you never open your lips upon this subject.'

'I dismiss it entirely from my mind, sire. I will efface it from my recollection as if it had never been. I will promise you to go out of your cabinet at this moment exactly as I was when I entered it at four o'clock.'

'You cannot do that,' said the Emperor, smiling. 'You were a lieutenant at that time. You will permit me, Captain, to wish you a very good-night.'

III. How the Brigadier Held the King

HERE, upon the lapel of my coat, you may see the ribbon of my decoration, but the medal itself I keep in a leathern pouch at home, and I never venture to take it out unless one of the modern peace generals, or some foreigner of distinction who finds himself in our little town, takes advantage of the opportunity to pay his respects to the well-known Brigadier Gerard. Then I place it upon my breast, and I give my moustache the old Marengo twist which brings a grey point into either eye. Yet with it all I fear that neither they, nor you either, my friends, will ever realize the man that I was. You know me only as a civilian—with an air and a manner, it is true—but still merely as a civilian. Had you seen me as I stood in the doorway of the inn at Alamo, on the 1st of July, in the year 1810, you would then have known what the hussar may attain to.

For a month I had lingered in that accursed village, and all on account of a lance-thrust in my ankle, which made it impossible for me to put my foot to the ground.

There were three besides myself at first: old Bouvet, of the Hussars of Berchény, Jacques Regnier, of the Cuirassiers, and a funny little voltigeur captain whose name I forget; but they all got well and hurried on to the front, while I sat gnawing my fingers and tearing my hair, and even, I must confess, weeping from time to time as I thought of my Hussars of Conflans, and the deplorable condition in which they must find themselves when deprived of their colonel. I was not a chief of brigade yet, you understand, although I already carried myself like one, but I was the youngest colonel in the whole service, and my regiment was wife and children to me. It went to my heart that they should be so bereaved. It is true that Villaret, the senior major, was an excellent soldier; but still, even among the best there are degrees of merit.

Ah, that happy July day of which I speak, when first I limped to the door and stood in the golden Spanish sunshine! It was but the evening before that I had heard from the regiment. They were at Pastores, on the other side of the mountains, face to face with the English—not forty miles from me by road. But how was I to get to them? The same thrust which had pierced my ankle had slain my charger. I took advice both from Gomez, the landlord, and from an old priest who had slept that night in the inn, but neither of them could do more than assure me that there was not so much as a colt left upon the whole country-side.

The landlord would not hear of my crossing the mountains without an escort, for he assured me that El Cuchillo, the Spanish guerilla chief, was out that way with his band, and that it meant a death by torture to fall into his hands. The old priest observed, however, that he did not think a French hussar would be deterred by that, and if I had had any doubts, they would of course have been decided by his remark.

But a horse! How was I to get one? I was standing in the doorway, plotting and planning, when I heard the clink of shoes, and, looking up, I saw a great bearded man, with a blue cloak frogged across in military fashion, coming towards me. He was riding a big black horse with one white stocking on his near fore-leg.

'Halloa, comrade!' said I, as he came up to me.

'Halloa!' said he.

'I am Colonel Gerard of the Hussars,' said I. 'I have lain here wounded for a month, and I am now ready to rejoin my regiment at Pastores.'

'I am Monsieur Vidal, of the Commissariat,' he answered, 'and I am myself upon my way to Pastores. I should be glad to have your company, Colonel, for I hear that the mountains are far from safe.'

'Alas,' said I, 'I have no horse. But if you will sell me yours, I will promise that an escort of hussars shall be sent back for you.'

He would not hear of it, and it was in vain that the landlord told him dreadful stories of the doings of El Cuchillo, and that I pointed out the duty which he owed to the army and to the country. He would not even argue, but called loudly for a cup of wine. I craftily asked him to dismount and to drink with me, but he must have seen something in my face, for he shook his head; and then, as I approached him with some thought of seizing him by the leg, he jerked his heels into his horse's flanks, and was off in a cloud of dust.

My faith! it was enough to make a man mad to see this fellow riding away so gaily to join his beef-barrels, and his brandy-casks, and then to think of my five hundred beautiful hussars without their leader. I was gazing after him with bitter thoughts in my mind, when who should touch me on the elbow but the little priest whom I have mentioned.

'It is I who can help you,' he said. 'I am myself travelling south.'

I put my arms about him and, as my ankle gave way at the same moment, we nearly rolled upon the ground together.

'Get me to Pastores,' I cried, 'and you shall have a

rosary of golden beads.' I had taken one from the Convent of Spiritu Santo. It shows how necessary it is to take what you can when you are upon a campaign, and how the most unlikely things may become useful.

'I will take you,' he said, in very excellent French, 'not because I hope for any reward, but because it is my way always to do what I can to serve my fellow-man, and that is why I am so beloved wherever I go.'

With that he led me down the village to an old cowhouse, in which we found a tumble-down sort of diligence, such as they used to run early in this century, between some of our remote villages. There were three old mules, too, none of which were strong enough to carry a man, but together they might draw the coach. The sight of their gaunt ribs and spavined legs gave me more delight than the whole two hundred and twenty hunters of the Emperor which I have seen in their stalls at Fontainebleau. In ten minutes the owner was harnessing them into the coach, with no very good will, however, for he was in mortal dread of this terrible Cuchillo. It was only by promising him riches in this world, while the priest threatened him with perdition in the next, that we at last got him safely upon the box with the reins between his fingers. Then he was in such a hurry to get off, out of fear lest we should find ourselves in the dark in the passes, that he hardly gave me time to renew my vows to the innkeeper's daughter. I cannot at this moment recall her name, but we wept together as we parted, and I can remember that she was a very beautiful woman. You will understand, my friends, that when a man like me, who has fought the men and kissed the women in fourteen separate kingdoms, gives a word of praise to the one or the other, it has a little meaning of its own.

The little priest had seemed a trifle grave when we kissed good-bye, but he soon proved himself the best of companions in the diligence. All the way he amused me with tales of his little parish up in the mountains, and I in my turn told him stories about the camp; but, my faith, I had to pick my steps, for when I said a word too much he would fidget in his seat and his face would show the pain that I had given him. And of course it is not the act of a gentleman to talk in anything but a proper manner to a religious man, though, with all the care in the world, one's words may get out of hand sometimes.

He had come from the north of Spain, as he told me, and was going to see his mother in a village of Estremadura, and as he spoke about her little peasant home, and her joy in seeing him, it brought my own mother so vividly to my thoughts that the tears started to my eyes. In his simplicity he showed me the little gifts which he was taking to her, and so kindly was his manner that I could readily believe him when he said he was loved wherever he went. He examined my own uniform with as much curiosity as a child, admiring the plume of my busby, and passing his fingers through the sable with which my dolman was trimmed. He drew my sword, too, and then when I told him how many men I had cut down with it, and set my finger on the notch made by the shoulder-bone of the Russian Emperor's aide-de-camp, he shuddered and placed the weapon under the leathern cushion, declaring that it made him sick to look at it.

Well, we had been rolling and creaking on our way whilst this talk had been going forward, and as we reached the base of the mountains we could hear the rumbling of cannon far away upon the right. This came from Massena, who was, as I knew, besieging Ciudad Rodrigo. There was nothing I should have wished better than to have gone straight to him, for if, as some said, he had Jewish blood in his veins, he was the best Jew that I have heard of since Joshua's time. If you were in sight of his beaky nose and bold, black eyes, you were not likely to miss much of what was going on. Still, a siege is always a poor sort of a pick-and-shovel business, and there were better prospects with my hussars in front of the English. Every mile that I passed, my heart grew lighter and lighter, until I found myself shouting and singing like a young ensign fresh from St. Cyr, just to think of seeing all my fine horses and my gallant fellows once more.

As we penetrated the mountains the road grew rougher and the pass more savage. At first we had met a few muleteers, but now the whole country seemed deserted, which is not to be wondered at when you think that the French, the English, and the guerillas had each in turn had command over it. So bleak and wild was it, one great brown wrinkled cliff succeeding another, and the pass growing narrower and narrower, that I ceased to look out, but sat in silence, thinking of this and that, of women whom I had loved and of horses which I had handled. I was suddenly brought back from my dreams, however, by observing the difficulties of my companion, who was trying with a sort of brad-awl, which he had drawn out, to bore a hole through the leathern strap which held up his water-flask. As he worked with twitching fingers the strap escaped his grasp, and the wooden bottle fell at my feet. I stooped to pick it up, and as I did so the priest silently leaped upon my shoulders and drove his brad-awl into my eye!

My friends, I am, as you know, a man steeled to face every danger. When one has served from the affair of Zurich to that last fatal day of Waterloo, and has had the special medal, which I keep at home in a leathern pouch, one can afford to confess when one is frightened. It may console some of you, when your own nerves play you tricks, to remember that you have heard even me, Brigadier Gerard, say that I have been scared. And besides my terror at this horrible attack, and the maddening pain of my wound, there was a sudden feeling of loathing such as you might feel were some filthy tarantula to strike its fangs into you.

I clutched the creature in both hands, and, hurling him on to the door of the coach, I stamped on him with my heavy boots. He had drawn a pistol from the front of his soutane, but I kicked it out of his hand, and again I fell with my knees upon his chest. Then, for the first time, he screamed horribly, while I, half blinded, felt about for the sword which he had so cunningly concealed. My hand had just lighted upon it, and I was dashing the blood from my face to see where he lay that I might transfix him, when the whole coach turned partly over upon its side, and my weapon was jerked out of my grasp by the shock.

Before I could recover myself the door was burst open, and I was dragged by the heels on to the road. But even as I was torn out on to the flint stones, and realized that thirty ruffians were standing around me, I was filled with joy, for my pelisse had been pulled over my head in the struggle and was covering one of my eyes, and it was with my wounded eye that I was seeing this gang of brigands. You see for yourself by this pucker and scar how the thin blade passed between socket and ball, but it was only at that moment, when I was dragged from the coach, that I understood that my sight was not gone for ever. The creature's intention, doubtless, was to drive it through into my brain, and indeed he loosened some portion of the inner bone of my head, so that I afterwards had more trouble from that wound than from any one of the seventeen which I have received.

They dragged me out, these sons of dogs, with curses and execrations, beating me with their fists and kicking me as I lay upon the ground. I had frequently observed that the mountaineers wore cloth swathed round their feet, but never did I imagine that I should have so much cause to be thankful for it. Presently, seeing the blood upon my head, and that I lay quiet, they thought that I was unconscious, whereas I was storing every ugly face among them into my memory, so that I might see them all safely hanged if ever my chance came round. Brawny rascals they were, with yellow handkerchiefs round their heads, and great red sashes stuffed with weapons. They had rolled two rocks across the path, where it took a sharp turn, and it was these which had torn off one of the wheels of the coach and upset us. As to this reptile, who had acted the priest so cleverly and had told me so much of his parish and his mother, he, of course, had known where the ambuscade was laid, and had attempted to put me beyond all resistance at the moment when we reached it.

I cannot tell you how frantic their rage was when they drew him out of the coach and saw the state to which I had reduced him. If he had not got all his deserts, he had, at least, something as a souvenir of his meeting with Etienne Gerard, for his legs dangled aimlessly about, and though the upper part of his body was convulsed with rage and pain, he sat straight down upon his feet when they tried to set him upright. But all the time his two little black eyes, which had seemed so kindly and so inno-cent in the coach, were glaring at me like a wounded cat, and he spat, and spat, and spat in my direction. My faith! when the wretches jerked me on to my feet again, and when I was dragged off up one of the mountain paths, I understood that a time was coming when I was to need all my courage and resource. My enemy was carried upon the shoulders of two men behind me, and I could hear his hissing and his reviling, first in one ear and then in the other, as I was hurried up the winding track.

I suppose that it must have been for an hour that we ascended, and what with my wounded ankle and the pain from my eye, and the fear lest this wound should have spoiled my appearance, I have made no journey to which I look back with less pleasure. I have never been a good climber at any time, but it is astonishing what you can do, even with a stiff ankle, when you have a copper-coloured brigand at each elbow and a nine-inch blade within touch of your whiskers.

We came at last to a place where the path wound over a ridge, and descended upon the other side through thick pine-trees into a valley which opened to the south. In time of peace I had little doubt that the villains were all smugglers, and that these were the secret paths by which they crossed the Portuguese frontier. There were many mule-tracks, and once I was surprised to see the marks of a large horse where a stream had softened the track. These were explained when, on reaching a place where there was a clearing in the fir wood, I saw the animal itself haltered to a fallen tree. My eyes had hardly rested upon it, when I recognised the great black limbs and the white near fore-leg. It was the very horse which I had begged for in the morning.

What, then, had become of Commissariat Vidal? Was it possible that there was another Frenchman in as perilous a plight as myself? The thought had hardly entered my head when our party stopped and one of them uttered a peculiar cry. It was answered from among the brambles which lined the base of a cliff at one side of a clearing, and an instant later ten or a dozen more brigands came out from amongst them, and the two parties greeted each other. The new-comers surrounded my friend of the brad-awl with cries of grief and sympathy, and then, turning upon me, they brandished their knives and howled at me like the gang of assassins that they were. So frantic were their gestures that I was convinced that my end had come, and was just bracing myself to meet it in a manner which should be worthy of my past reputation, when one of them gave an order and I was dragged roughly across the little glade to the brambles from which this new band had emerged.

A narrow pathway led through them to a deep grotto in the side of a cliff. The sun was already setting outside, and in the cave itself it would have been quite dark but for a pair of torches which blazed from a socket on either side. Between them there was sitting at a rude table a very singular-looking person, whom I saw instantly, from the respect with which the others addressed him, could be none other than the brigand chief who had received, on account of his dreadful character, the sinister name of El Cuchillo.

The man whom I had injured had been carried in and

placed upon the top of a barrel, his helpless legs dangling about in front of him, and his cat's eyes still darting glances of hatred at me. I understood, from the snatches of talk which I could follow between the chief and him, that he was the lieutenant of the band, and that part of his duties was to lie in wait with his smooth tongue and his peaceful garb for travellers like myself. When I thought of how many gallant officers may have been lured to their death by this monster of hypocrisy, it gave me a glow of pleasure to think that I had brought his villainies to an end—though I feared it would be at the price of a life which neither the Emperor nor the army could well spare.

As the injured man, still supported upon the barrel by two comrades, was explaining in Spanish all that had befallen him, I was held by several of the villains in front of the table at which the chief was seated, and had an excellent opportunity of observing him. I have seldom seen any man who was less like my idea of a brigand, and especially of a brigand with such a reputation that in a land of cruelty he had earned so dark a nickname. His face was bluff and broad and bland, with ruddy cheeks and comfortable little tufts of side-whiskers, which gave him the appearance of a well-to-do grocer of the Rue St. Antoine. He had not any of those flaring sashes or gleaming weapons which distinguished his followers, but on the contrary he wore a good broadcloth coat like a respectable father of a family, and save for his brown leggings there was nothing to indicate a life among the mountains. His surroundings, too, corresponded with himself, and beside his snuff-box upon the table there stood a great brown book, which looked like a commercial ledger. Many other books were ranged along a plank between two powder-casks, and there was a great litter of papers, some of which had verses scribbled upon them. All this I took in while he, leaning indolently back in his chair, was listening to the report of his lieutenant. Having heard everything, he ordered the cripple to be carried out again, and I was left with my three guards, waiting to hear my fate. He took up his pen, and tapping his forehead with the handle of it, he pursed up his lips and looked out of the corner of his eyes at the roof of the grotto.

'I suppose,' said he at last, speaking very excellent French, 'that you are not able to suggest a rhyme for the word Covilha.'

I answered him that my acquaintance with the Spanish language was so limited that I was unable to oblige him.

'It is a rich language,' said he, 'but less prolific in rhymes than either the German or the English. That is why our best work has been done in blank verse, a form of composition which is capable of reaching great heights. But I fear that such subjects are somewhat outside the range of a hussar.'

I was about to answer that if they were good enough for a guerilla, they could not be too much for the light cavalry, but he was already stooping over his half-finished verse. Presently he threw down the pen with an exclamation of satisfaction, and declaimed a few lines which drew a cry of approval from the three ruffians who held me. His broad face blushed like a young girl who receives her first compliment.

'The critics are in my favour, it appears,' said he; 'we amuse ourselves in our long evenings by singing our own ballads, you understand. I have some little facility in that direction, and I do not at all despair of seeing some of my poor efforts in print before long, and with "Madrid" upon the title-page, too. But we must get back to business. May I ask what your name is?'

'Etienne Gerard.'

'Rank?'

'Colonel.'

'Corps?'

'The Third Hussars of Conflans.'

'You are young for a colonel.'

'My career has been an eventful one.'

'Tut, that makes it the sadder,' said he, with his bland smile.

I made no answer to that, but I tried to show him by my bearing that I was ready for the worst which could befall me.

'By the way, I rather fancy that we have had some of your corps here,' said he, turning over the pages of his big brown register. 'We endeavour to keep a record of our operations. Here is a heading under June 24th. Have you not a young officer named Soubiron, a tall, slight youth with light hair?'

'Certainly.'

'I see that we buried him upon that date.'

'Poor lad!' I cried. 'And how did he die?'

'We buried him.'

'But before you buried him?'

'You misunderstand me, Colonel. He was not dead before we buried him.'

'You buried him alive!'

For a moment I was too stunned to act. Then I hurled myself upon the man, as he sat with that placid smile of his upon his lips, and I would have torn his throat out had the three wretches not dragged me away from him. Again and again I made for him, panting and cursing, shaking off this man and that, straining and wrenching, but never quite free. At last, with my jacket torn nearly off my back and blood dripping from my wrists, I was hauled backwards in the bight of a rope and cords passed round my ankles and my arms.

'You sleek hound!' I cried. 'If ever I have you at my sword's point, I will teach you to maltreat one of my lads. You will find, you bloodthirsty beast, that my Emperor has long arms, and though you lie here like a rat in its hole, the time will come when he will tear you out of it, and you and your vermin will perish together.'

My faith, I have a rough side to my tongue, and there was not a hard word that I had learned in fourteen campaigns which I did not let fly at him; but he sat with the handle of his pen tapping against his forehead and his eyes squinting up at the roof as if he had conceived the idea of some new stanza. It was this occupation of his which showed me how I might get my point into him.

'You spawn!' said I; 'you think that you are safe here, but your life may be as short as that of your absurd verses, and God knows that it could not be shorter than that.'

Ah, you should have seen him bound from his chair when I said the words. This vile monster, who dispensed death and torture as a grocer serves out his figs, had one raw nerve then which I could prod at pleasure. His face grew livid, and those little bourgeois side-whiskers quivered and thrilled with passion.

'Very good, Colonel. You have said enough,' he cried, in a choking voice. 'You say that you have had a very distinguished career. I promise you also a very distinguished ending. Colonel Etienne Gerard of the Third Hussars shall have a death of his own.'

'And I only beg,' said I, 'that you will not commemorate it in verse.' I had one or two little ironies to utter, but he cut me short by a furious gesture which caused my three guards to drag me from the cave.

Our interview, which I have told you as nearly as I can remember it, must have lasted some time, for it was quite dark when we came out, and the moon was shining very clearly in the heavens. The brigands had lighted a great fire of the dried branches of the fir-trees; not, of course, for warmth, since the night was already very sultry, but to cook their evening meal. A huge copper pot hung over the blaze, and the rascals were lying all round in the yellow glare, so that the scene looked like one of those pictures which Junot stole out of Madrid. There are some soldiers who profess to care nothing for art and the like, but I have always been drawn towards it myself, in which respect I show my good taste and my breeding. I remember, for example, that when Lefebvre was selling the plunder after the fall of Danzig, I bought a very fine picture, called 'Nymphs Surprised in a Wood,' and I carried it with me through two compaigns, until my charger had the misfortune to put his hoof through it.

I only tell you this, however, to show you that I was never a mere rough soldier like Rapp or Ney. As I lay in that brigands' camp, I had little time or inclination to think about such matters. They had thrown me down under a tree, the three villains squatting round and smoking their cigarettes within hands' touch of me. What to do I could not imagine. In my whole career I do not suppose that I have ten times been in as hopeless a situation. 'But courage,' thought I. 'Courage, my brave boy! You were not made a Colonel of Hussars at twenty-eight because you could dance a cotillon. You are a picked man, Etienne; a man who has come through more than two hundred affairs, and this little one is surely not going to be the last.' I began eagerly to glance about for some chance of escape, and as I did so I saw something which filled me with great astonishment.

I have already told you that a large fire was burning in the centre of the glade. What with its glare, and what with the moonlight, everything was as clear as possible. On the other side of the glade there was a single fir-tree which attracted my attention because its trunk and lower branches were discoloured, as if a large fire had recently been lit underneath it. A clump of bushes grew in front of it which concealed the base. Well, as I looked towards it, I was surprised to see projecting above the bush, and fastened apparently to the tree, a pair of fine riding boots with the toes upwards. At first I thought that they were tied there, but as I looked harder I saw that they were secured by a great nail which was hammered through the foot of each. And then, suddenly, with a thrill of horror, I understood that these were not empty boots; and moving my head a little to the right, I was able to see who it was that had been fastened there, and why a fire had been lit beneath the tree. It is not pleasant to speak or to think of horrors, my friends, and I do not wish to give any of you bad dreams to-night—but I cannot take you among the Spanish guerillas without showing you what kind of men they were, and the sort of warfare that they waged. I will only say that I understood why Monsieur Vidal's horse was waiting masterless in the grove, and that I hoped he had met this terrible fate with sprightliness and courage, as a good Frenchman ought.

It was not a very cheering sight for me, as you can imagine. When I had been with their chief in the grotto I had been so carried away by my rage at the cruel death of young Soubiron, who was one of the brightest lads who ever threw his thigh over a charger, that I had never given a thought to my own position. Perhaps it would have been more politic had I spoken the ruffian fair, but it was too late now. The cork was drawn and I must drain the wine. Besides, if the harmless commissariat man were put to such a death, what hope was there for me, who had snapped the spine of their lieutenant? No, I was doomed in any case, and it was as well perhaps that I should have put the best face on the matter. This beast could bear witness that Etienne Gerard had died as he had lived, and that one prisoner at least had not quailed before him. I lay there thinking of the various girls who would mourn for me, and of my dear old mother, and of the deplorable loss which I should be, both to my regiment and to the Emperor, and I am not ashamed to confess to you that I shed tears as I thought of the general consternation which my premature end would give rise to.

But all the time I was taking the very keenest notice of everything which might possibly help me. I am not a man who would lie like a sick horse waiting for the farrier sergeant and the pole-axe. First I would give a little tug at my ankle cords, and then another at those which were round my wrists, and all the time that I was trying to loosen them I was peering round to see if I could find something which was in my favour. There was one thing which was very evident. A hussar is but half

formed without a horse, and there was my other half
quietly grazing within thirty yards of me. Then I observed yet another thing. The path by which we had
come over the mountains was so steep that a horse could
only be led across it slowly and with difficulty, but in the
other direction the ground appeared to be more open,
and to lead straight down into a gently-sloping valley.
Had I but my feet in yonder stirrups and my sabre in my
hand, a single bold dash might take me out of the power
of these vermin of the rocks.

I was still thinking it over and straining with my wrists
and my ankles, when their chief came out from his
grotto, and after some talk with his lieutenant, who lay
groaning near the fire, they both nodded their heads and
looked across at me. He then said some few words to
the band, who clapped their hands and laughed up-
roariously. Things looked ominous, and I was delighted
to feel that my hands were so far free that I could easily
slip them through the cords if I wished. But with my
ankles I feared that I could do nothing, for when I
strained it brought such pain into my lance-wound that
I had to gnaw my moustache to keep from crying out. I
could only lie still, half-free and half-bound, and see
what turn things were likely to take.

For a little I could not make out what they were after.
One of the rascals climbed up a well-grown fir-tree upon
one side of the glade, and tied a rope round the top of the
trunk. He then fastened another rope in the same fashion
to a similar tree upon the other side. The two loose
ends were now dangling down, and I waited with some
curiosity, and just a little trepidation also, to see what
they would do next. The whole band pulled upon one of
the ropes until they had bent the strong young tree down
into a semi-circle, and they then fastened it to a stump, so
as to hold it so. When they had bent the other tree down
in similar fashion, the two summits were within a few
feet of each other, though, as you understand, they would
each spring back into their original position the instant

that they were released. I already saw the diabolical plan which these miscreants had formed.

'I presume that you are a strong man, Colonel,' said the chief, coming towards me with his hateful smile.

'If you will have the kindness to loosen these cords,' I answered, 'I will show you how strong I am.'

'We were all interested to see whether you were as strong as these two young saplings,' said he. 'It is our intention, you see, to tie one end of each rope round your ankles and then let the trees go. If you are stronger than the trees, then, of course, no harm would be done; if, on the other hand, the trees are stronger than you, why, in that case, Colonel, we may have a souvenir of you upon each side of our little glade.'

He laughed as he spoke, and at the sight of it the whole forty of them laughed also. Even now if I am in my darker humour, or if I have a touch of my old Lithuanian ague, I see in my sleep that ring of dark, savage faces, with their cruel eyes, and the firelight flashing upon their strong white teeth.

It is astonishing—and I have heard many make the same remark—how acute one's senses become at such a crisis as this. I am convinced that at no moment is one living so vividly, so acutely, as at the instant when a violent and foreseen death overtakes one. I could smell the resinous fagots, I could see every twig upon the ground, I could hear every rustle of the branches, as I have never smelled or seen or heard save at such times of danger. And so it was that long before anyone else, before even the time when the chief had addressed me, I had heard a low, monotonous sound, far away indeed, and yet coming nearer at every instant. At first it was but a murmur, a rumble, but by the time he had finished speaking, while the assassins were untying my ankles in order to lead me to the scene of my murder, I heard, as plainly as ever I heard anything in my life, the clinking of horseshoes and the jingling of bridle-chains, with the clank of sabres against stirrup-irons. Is it likely that I, who had lived with the light cavalry since the first hair shaded my lip, would mistake the sound of troopers on the march?

'Help, comrades, help!' I shrieked, and though they struck me across the mouth and tried to drag me up to the trees, I kept on yelling, 'Help me, my brave boys! Help me, my children! They are murdering your colonel!'

For the moment my wounds and my troubles had brought on a delirium, and I looked for nothing less than my five hundred hussars, kettle-drums and all, to appear at the opening of the glade.

But that which really appeared was very different to anything which I had conceived. Into the clear space there came galloping a fine young man upon a most beautiful roan horse. He was fresh-faced and pleasant-looking, with the most debonair bearing in the world and the most gallant way of carrying himself—a way which reminded me somewhat of my own. He wore a singular coat which had once been red all over, but which was now stained to the colour of a withered oak-leaf wherever the weather could reach it. His shoulder-straps, however, were of golden lace, and he had a bright metal helmet upon his head, with a coquettish white plume upon one side of its crest. He trotted his horse up the glade, while behind him rode four cavaliers in the same dress—all clean-shaven, with round, comely faces, looking to me more like monks than dragoons. At a short, gruff order they halted with a rattle of arms, while their leader cantered forward, the fire beating upon his eager face and the beautiful head of his charger. I knew, of course, by the strange coats that they were English. It was the first sight that I had ever had of them, but from their stout bearing and their masterful way I could see at a glance that what I had always been told was true, and that they were excellent people to fight against.

'Well, well, well!' cried the young officer in sufficiently bad French, 'what game are you up to here? Who was that who was yelling for help, and what are you trying to do to him?'

It was at that moment that I learned to bless those months which Obriant, the descendant of the Irish kings, had spent in teaching me the tongue of the English. My ankles had just been freed, so that I had only to slip my hands out of the cords, and with a single rush I had flown across, picked up my sabre where it lay by the fire, and hurled myself on to the saddle of poor Vidal's horse. Yes, for all my wounded ankle, I never put foot to stirrup, but was in the seat in a single bound. I tore the halter from the tree, and before these villains could so much as snap a pistol at me I was beside the English officer.

'I surrender to you, sir,' I cried; though I daresay my English was not very much better than his French. 'If you will look at that tree to the left you will see what these villains do to the honourable gentlemen who fall into their hands.'

The fire had flared up at that moment, and there was poor Vidal exposed before them, as horrible an object as one could see in a nightmare. 'Godam!' cried the officer, and 'Godam!' cried each of the four troopers, which is the same as with us when we cry *Mon Dieu!* Out rasped the five swords, and the four men closed up. One, who wore a sergeant's chevrons, laughed and clapped me on the shoulder.

'Fight for your skin, froggy,' said he.

Ah, it was so fine to have a horse between my thighs and a weapon in my grip. I waved it above my head and shouted in my exultation. The chief had come forward with that odious smiling face of his.

'Your excellency will observe that this Frenchman is our prisoner,' said he.

'You are a rascally robber,' said the Englishman, shaking his sword at him. 'It is a disgrace to us to have such allies. By my faith, if Lord Wellington were of my mind we would swing you up on the nearest tree.'

'But my prisoner?' said the brigand, in his suave voice.

'He shall come with us to the British camp.'

'Just a word in your ear before you take him.'

He approached the young officer, and then turning as quick as a flash, he fired his pistol in my face. The bullet scored its way through my hair and burst a hole on each side of my busby. Seeing that he had missed me, he raised the pistol and was about to hurl it at me when the English sergeant, with a single back-handed cut, nearly severed his head from his body. His blood had not reached the ground, nor the last curse died on his lips, before the whole horde was upon us, but with a dozen bounds and as many slashes we were all safely out of the glade, and galloping down the winding track which led to the valley.

It was not until we had left the ravine far behind us and were right out in the open fields that we ventured to halt, and to see what injuries we had sustained. For me, wounded and weary as I was, my heart was beating proudly, and my chest was nearly bursting my tunic to think that I, Etienne Gerard, had left this gang of murderers so much by which to remember me. My faith, they would think twice before they ventured again to lay hands upon one of the Third Hussars. So carried away was I that I made a small oration to these brave Englishmen, and told them who it was that they had helped to rescue. I would have spoken of glory also, and of the sympathies of brave men, but the officer cut me short.

'That's all right,' said he. 'Any injuries, Sergeant?'

'Trooper Jones's horse hit with a pistol bullet on the fetlock.'

'Trooper Jones to go with us. Sergeant Halliday, with troopers Harvey and Smith, to keep to the right until they touch the vedettes of the German Hussars.'

So these three jingled away together, while the officer and I, followed at some distance by the trooper whose horse had been wounded, rode straight down in the direction of the English camp. Very soon we had opened our hearts, for we each liked the other from the beginning. He was of the nobility, this brave lad, and he had been sent out scouting by Lord Wellington to see if there were any signs of our advancing through the mountains. It is one advantage of a wandering life like mine, that you learn to pick up those bits of knowledge which distinguish the man of the world. I have, for example, hardly ever met a Frenchman who could repeat an English title correctly. If I had not travelled I should not be able to say with confidence that this young man's real name was Milor the Hon. Sir Russell, Bart., this last being an honourable distinction, so that it was as the Bart that I usually addressed him, just as in Spanish one might say 'the Don'.

As we rode beneath the moonlight in the lovely Spanish night, we spoke our minds to each other, as if we were brothers. We were both of an age, you see, both of the light cavalry also (the Sixteenth Light Dragoons were his regiment), and both with the same hopes and ambitions. Never have I learned to know a man so quickly as I did the Bart. He gave me the name of a girl whom he had loved at a garden called Vauxhall, and, for my own part, I spoke to him of little Coralie, of the Opera. He took a lock of hair from his bosom, and I a garter. Then we nearly quarrelled over hussar and dragoon, for he was absurdly proud of his regiment, and you should have seen him curl his lip and clap his hand to his hilt when I said that I hoped it might never be its misfortune to come in the way of the Third. Finally, he began to speak about what the English call sport, and he told such stories of the money which he had lost over which of two cocks could kill the other, or which of two men could strike the other the most in a fight for a prize, that I was filled with astonishment. He was ready to bet upon anything in the most wonderful manner, and when I chanced to see a shooting star he was anxious to bet that he would see more than me, twenty-five francs a star, and it was only when I explained that my purse was in the hands of the brigands that he would give over the idea.

Well, we chatted away in this very amiable fashion until the day began to break, when suddenly we heard a great volley of musketry from somewhere in front of us. It was very rocky and broken ground, and I thought, although I could see nothing, that a general engagement had broken out. The Bart laughed at my idea, however, and explained that the sound came from the English camp, where every man emptied his piece each morning so as to make sure of having a dry priming.

'In another mile we shall be up with the outposts,' said he.

I glanced round at this, and I perceived that we had trotted along at so good a pace during the time that we were keeping up our pleasant chat, that the dragoon with the lame horse was altogether out of sight. I looked on every side, but in the whole of that vast rocky valley there was no one save only the Bart and I—both of us armed, you understand, and both of us well mounted. I began to ask myself whether after all it was quite necessary that I should ride that mile which would bring me to the British outposts.

Now, I wish to be very clear with you on this point, my friends, for I would not have you think that I was acting dishonourably or ungratefully to the man who had helped me away from the brigands. You must remember that of all duties the strongest is that which a commanding officer owes to his men. You must also bear in mind that war is a game which is played under fixed rules, and when these rules are broken one must at once claim the forfeit. If, for example, I had given a parole, then I should have been an infamous wretch had I dreamed of escaping. But no parole had been asked of me. Out of over-confidence, and the chance of the lame horse dropping behind, the Bart had permitted me to get upon equal terms with him. Had it been I who had taken him, I should have used him as courteously as he had me, but, at the same time, I should have respected his enterprise so far as to have deprived him of his sword, and seen that

I had at least one guard beside myself. I reined up my horse and explained this to him, asking him at the same time whether he saw any breach of honour in my leaving him.

He thought about it, and several times repeated that which the English say when they mean '*Mon Dieu.*'

'You would give me the slip, would you?' said he.

'If you can give no reason against it.'

'The only reason that I can think of,' said the Bart, 'is that I should instantly cut your head off if you were to attempt it.'

'Two can play at that game, my dear Bart,' said I.

'Then we'll see who can play at it best,' he cried, pulling out his sword.

I had drawn mine also, but I was quite determined not to hurt this admirable young man who had been my benefactor.

'Consider,' said I, 'you say that I am your prisoner. I might with equal reason say that you are mine. We are alone here, and though I have no doubt that you are an excellent swordsman, you can hardly hope to hold your own against the best blade in the six light cavalry brigades.'

His answer was a cut at my head. I parried and shore off half of his white plume. He thrust at my breast. I turned his point and cut away the other half of his cockade.

'Curse your monkey-tricks!' he cried, as I wheeled my horse away from him.

'Why should you strike at me?' said I. 'You see that I will not strike back.'

'That's all very well,' said he; 'but you've got to come along with me to the camp.'

'I shall never see the camp,' said I.

'I'll lay you nine to four you do,' he cried, as he made at me, sword in hand.

But those words of his put something new into my head. Could we not decide the matter in some better

239

way than fighting? The Bart was placing me in such a position that I should have to hurt him, or he would certainly hurt me. I avoided his rush, though his sword-point was within an inch of my neck.

'I have a proposal,' I cried. 'We shall throw dice as to which is the prisoner of the other.'

He smiled at this. It appealed to his love of sport.

'Where are your dice?' he cried.

'I have none.'

'Nor I. But I have cards.'

'Cards let it be,' said I.

'And the game?'

'I leave it to you.'

'Ecarté, then—the best of three.'

I could not help smiling as I agreed, for I do not suppose that there were three men in France who were my masters at the game. I told the Bart as much as we dismounted. He smiled also as he listened.

'I was counted the best player at Watier's,' said he. 'With even luck you deserve to get off if you beat me.'

So we tethered our two horses and sat down one on either side of a great flat rock. The Bart took a pack of cards out of his tunic, and I had only to see him shuffle to convince me that I had no novice to deal with. We cut, and the deal fell to him.

My faith, it was a stake worth playing for. He wished to add a hundred gold pieces a game, but what was money when the fate of Colonel Etienne Gerard hung upon the cards? I felt as though all those who had reason to be interested in the game—my mother, my hussars, the Sixth Corps d'Armée, Ney, Massena, even the Emperor himself—were forming a ring round us in that desolate valley. Heavens, what a blow to one and all of them should the cards go against me! But I was confident, for my écarté play was as famous as my swordsmanship, and save old Bouvet of the Hussars of Berchény, who won seventy-six out of one hundred and fifty games off me, I have always had the best of a series.

The first game I won right off, though I must confess that the cards were with me, and that my adversary could have done no more. In the second, I never played better and saved a trick by a finesse, but the Bart voled me once, marked the king, and ran out in the second hand. My faith, we were so excited that he laid his helmet down beside him and I my busby.

'I'll lay my roan mare against your black horse,' said he.

'Done!' said I.

'Sword against sword.'

'Done!' said I.

'Saddle, bridle, and stirrups!' he cried.

'Done!' I shouted.

I had caught this spirit of sport from him. I would have laid my hussars against his dragoons had they been ours to pledge.

And then began the game of games. Oh, he played, this Englishman—he played in a way that was worthy of such a stake. But I, my friends, I was superb! Of the five which I had to make to win, I gained three on the first hand. The Bart bit his moustache and drummed his hands, while I already felt myself at the head of my dear little rascals. On the second, I turned the king, but lost two tricks—and my score was four to his two. When I saw my next hand I could not but give a cry of delight. 'If I cannot gain my freedom on this,' thought I, 'I deserve to remain for ever in chains.'

Give me the cards, landlord, and I will lay them out on the table for you.

Here was my hand: knave and ace of clubs, queen and knave of diamonds, and king of hearts. Clubs were trumps, mark you, and I had but one point between me and freedom. He knew it was the crisis, and he undid his tunic. I threw my dolman on the ground. He led the ten of spades. I took it with my ace of trumps. One point in my favour. The correct play was to clear the trumps, and I led the knave. Down came the queen upon it, and the game was equal. He led the eight of spades, and I could only discard my queen of diamonds. Then came the seven of spades, and the hair stood straight up on my head. We each threw down a king at the final. He had won two points, and my beautiful hand had been mastered by his inferior one. I could have rolled on the ground as I thought of it. They used to play very good écarté at Watier's in the year '10. I say it—I, Brigadier Gerard.

The last game was now four all. This next hand must settle it one way or the other. He undid his sash, and I put away my sword-belt. He was cool, this Englishman, and I tried to be also, but the perspiration would trickle into my eyes. The deal lay with him, and I may confess to you, my friends, that my hands shook so that I could hardly pick my cards from the rock. But when I raised them, what was the first thing that my eyes rested upon? It was the king, the king, the glorious king of trumps! My mouth was open to declare it when the words were frozen upon my lips by the appearance of my comrade.

He held his cards in his hand, but his jaw had fallen, and his eyes were staring over my shoulder with the most dreadful expression of consternation and surprise. I whisked round, and I was myself amazed at what I saw.

Three men were standing quite close to us—fifteen metres at the farthest. The middle one was of a good height, and yet not too tall—about the same height, in fact, that I am myself. He was clad in a dark uniform with a small cocked hat, and some sort of white plume upon the side. But I had little thought of his dress. It was his face, his gaunt cheeks, his beak-like nose, his masterful blue eyes, his thin, firm slit of a mouth which made one feel that this was a wonderful man, a man of a million. His brows were tied into a knot, and he cast such a glance at my poor Bart from under them that one by one the cards came fluttering down from his nerveless fingers. Of the two other men, one, who had a face as brown and hard as though it had been carved out of old oak, wore a bright red coat, while the other, a fine portly man with bushy side-whiskers, was in a blue jacket with gold facings. Some little distance behind, three orderlies were holding as many horses, and an escort of dragoons was waiting in the rear.

'Heh, Crauford, what the deuce is this?' asked the thin man.

'D'you hear, sir?' cried the man with the red coat. 'Lord Wellington wants to know what this means.'

My poor Bart broke into an account of all that had occurred, but that rock-face never softened for an instant.

'Pretty fine, 'pon my word, General Crauford,' he broke in. 'The discipline of this force must be maintained, sir. Report yourself at headquarters as a prisoner.'

It was dreadful for me to see the Bart mount his horse and ride off with hanging head. I could not endure it. I threw myself before this English General. I pleaded with him for my friend. I told him how I, Colonel Gerard, would witness what a dashing young officer he was. Ah, my eloquence might have melted the hardest heart; I brought tears to my own eyes, but none to his. My voice broke, and I could say no more.

'What weight do you put on your mules, sir, in the French service?' he asked. Yes, that was all this phlegmatic Englishman had to answer to these burning words of mine. That was his reply to what would have made a Frenchman weep upon my shoulder.

'What weight on a mule?' asked the man with the red coat.

'Two hundred and ten pounds,' said I.

'Then you load them deucedly badly,' said Lord Wellington. 'Remove the prisoner to the rear.'

His dragoons closed in upon me, and I—I was driven mad, as I thought that the game had been in my hands, and that I ought at that moment to be a free man. I held the cards up in front of the General.

'See, my lord!' I cried; 'I played for my freedom and I won, for, as you perceive, I hold the king.'

For the first time a slight smile softened his gaunt face.

'On the contrary,' said he, as he mounted his horse, 'it is I who won, for, as you perceive, my King holds you.'

IV. How the King Held the Brigadier

MURAT was undoubtedly an excellent cavalry officer, but he had too much swagger, which spoils many a good soldier. Lasalle, too, was a very dashing leader, but he ruined himself with wine and folly. Now I, Etienne Gerard, was always totally devoid of swagger, and at the same time I was very abstemious, except, maybe, at the end of a campaign, or when I met an old comrade-in-arms. For these reasons I might, perhaps, had it not been for a certain diffidence, have claimed to be the most valuable officer in my own branch of the Service. It is true that I never rose to be more than a chief of brigade, but then, as everyone knows, no one had a chance of rising to the top unless he had the good fortune to be with the Emperor in his early campaigns. Except Lasalle, and Labau, and Drouet, I can hardly remember any one of the generals who had not already made his name before the Egyptian business. Even I, with all my brilliant qualities, could only attain the head of my brigade, and also the special medal of honour, which I received from the Emperor himself, and which I keep at home in a leathern pouch.

But though I never rose higher than this, my qualities were very well known to those who had served with me, and also to the English. After they had captured me in the way which I described to you the other night, they kept a very good guard over me at Oporto, and I promise you that they did not give such a formidable opponent a chance of slipping through their fingers. It was on the 10th of August that I was escorted on board the transport which was to take us to England, and behold me before the end of the month in the great prison which had been built for us at Dartmoor! 'L'hôtel Français, et Pension,' we used to call it, for you understand that we were all brave men there, and that we did not lose our spirits because we were in adversity.

It was only those officers who refused to give their parole who were confined at Dartmoor, and most of the prisoners were seamen, or from the ranks. You ask me, perhaps, why it was that I did not give this parole, and so enjoy the same good treatment as most of my brother officers. Well, I had two reasons, and both of them were sufficiently strong.

In the first place, I had so much confidence in myself, that I was quite convinced that I could escape. In the second, my family, though of good repute, has never been wealthy, and I could not bring myself to take anything from the small income of my mother. On the other hand, it would never do for a man like me to be outshone by the bourgeois society of an English country town, or to be without the means of showing courtesies and attentions to those ladies whom I should attract. It was for these reasons that I preferred to be buried in the dreadful prison of Dartmoor. I wish now to tell you of my adventures in England, and how far Milor Wellington's words were true when he said that his King would hold me.

And first of all I may say that if it were not that I have set off to tell you about what befell myself, I could keep you here until morning with my stories about Dartmoor itself, and about the singular things which occurred there. It was one of the very strangest places in the whole world, for there, in the middle of that great desolate waste were herded together seven or eight thousand men—warriors, you understand, men of experience and courage. Around there were a double wall and a ditch, and warders and soldiers; but, my faith! you could not coop men like that up like rabbits in a hutch! They would escape by twos and tens and twenties, and then the cannon would boom, and the search parties run, and we, who were left behind, would laugh and dance and shout 'Vive l'Empereur' until the warders would turn their muskets upon us in their passion. And then we would have our little mutinies, too, and up would come the infantry and guns from Plymouth, and that would set us yelling 'Vive l'Empereur' once more, as though we wished them to hear us in Paris. We had lively moments at Dartmoor, and we contrived that those who were about us should be lively also.

You must know that the prisoners there had their own Courts of Justice, in which they tried their own cases, and inflicted their own punishments. Stealing and quarrelling were punished—but most of all treachery. When I came there first there was a man, Meunier, from Rheims, who had given information of some plot to escape. Well, that night, owing to some form or other which had to be gone through, they did not take him out from among the other prisoners, and though he wept and screamed, and grovelled upon the ground, they left him there amongst the comrades whom he had betrayed. That night there was a trial and a whispered accusation and a whispered defence, a gagged prisoner, and a judge whom none could see. In the morning, when they came for their man with papers for his release, there was not as much of him left as you could put upon your thumbnail. They were ingenious people, these prisoners, and they had their own way of managing.

We officers, however, lived in a separate wing, and a very singular group of people we were. They had left us our uniforms, so that there was hardly a corps which had served under Victor, or Massena, or Ney, which was not represented there, and some had been there from the time when Junot was beaten at Vimiera. We had chasseurs in their green tunics, and hussars, like myself, and blue-coated dragoons, and white-fronted lancers, and voltigeurs, and grenadiers, and men of the artillery and engineers. But the greater part were naval officers, for the English had had the better of us upon the seas. I could never understand this until I journeyed myself from Oporto to Plymouth, when I lay for seven days upon my back, and could not have stirred had I seen the eagle of the regiment carried off before my eyes. It was in perfidious weather like this that Nelson took advantage of us.

I had no sooner got into Dartmoor than I began to plan to get out again, and you can readily believe that, with wits sharpened by twelve years of warfare, it was not very long before I saw my way.

You must know, in the first place, that I had a very great advantage in having some knowledge of the English language. I learned it during the months that I spent before Danzig, from Adjutant Obriant, of the Regiment Irlandais, who was sprung from the ancient kings of the country. I was quickly able to speak it with some facility, for I do not take long to master anything to which I set my mind. In three months I could not only express my meaning, but I could use the idioms of the people. It was Obriant who taught me to say 'Be jabers', just as we might say *Ma foi*'; and also 'The curse of Crummle!' which means *Ventre bleu!* Many a time I have seen the English smile with pleasure when they have heard me speak so much like one of themselves.

We officers were put two in a cell, which was very little to my taste, for my room-mate was a tall, silent man named Beaumont, of the Flying Artillery, who had been taken by the English cavalry at Astorga.

It is seldom I meet a man of whom I cannot make a friend, for my disposition and manners are—as you know them. But this fellow had never a smile for my jests, nor an ear for my sorrows, but would sit looking at me with his sullen eyes, until sometimes I thought that his two years of captivity had driven him crazy. Ah, how I longed that old Bouvet, or any of my comrades of the hussars, was there, instead of this mummy of a man. But such as he was I had to make the best of him, and it was very evident that no escape could be made unless he were my partner in it, for what could I possibly do without him

247

observing me? I hinted at it, therefore, and then by degrees I spoke more plainly, until it seemed to me that I had prevailed upon him to share my lot.

I tried the walls, and I tried the floor, and I tried the ceiling, but though I tapped and probed, they all appeared to be very thick and solid. The door was of iron, shutting with a spring lock, and provided with a small grating, through which a warder looked twice in every night. Within there were two beds, two stools, two washstands—nothing more. It was enough for my wants, for when had I had as much during those twelve years spent in camps? But how was I to get out? Night after night I thought of my five hundred hussars, and had dreadful nightmares, in which I fancied that the whole regiment needed shoeing, or that my horses were all bloated with green fodder, or that they were foundered from bogland, or that six squadrons were clubbed in the presence of the Emperor. Then I would awake in a cold sweat, and set to work picking and tapping at the walls once more; for I knew very well that there is no difficulty which cannot be overcome by a ready brain and a pair of cunning hands.

There was a single window in our cell, which was too small to admit a child. It was further defended by a thick iron bar in the centre. It was not a very promising point of escape, as you will allow, but I became more and more convinced that our efforts must be directed towards it. To make matters worse, it only led out into the exercise yard, which was surrounded by two high walls. Still, as I said to my sullen comrade, it is time to talk of the Vistula when you are over the Rhine. I got a small piece of iron, therefore, from the fittings of my bed, and I set to work to loosen the plaster at the top and the bottom of the bar. Three hours I would work, and then leap into my bed upon the sound of the warder's step. Then another three hours, and then very often another yet, for I found that Beaumont was so slow and clumsy at it that it was on myself only that I could rely.

I pictured to myself my Third of Hussars waiting just outside that window, with kettle-drums and standards and leopard-skin schabraques all complete. Then I would work like a madman, until my iron was crusted with blood, as if with rust. And so, night by night, I loosened that stony plaster, and hid it away in the stuffing of my pillow, until the hour came when the iron shook; and then with one good wrench it came off in my hand, and my first step had been made towards freedom.

You will ask me what better off I was, since, as I have said, a child could not have fitted through the opening. I will tell you. I had gained two things—a tool and a weapon. With the one I might loosen the stone which flanked the window. With the other I might defend myself when I had scrambled through. So now I turned my attention to that stone, and I picked and picked with the sharpened end of my bar until I had worked out the mortar all round. You understand, of course, that during the day I replaced everything in its position, and that the warder was never permitted to see a speck upon the floor. At the end of three weeks I had separated the stone, and had the rapture of drawing it through, and seeing a hole left with ten stars shining through it, where there had been but four before. All was ready for us now, and I replaced the stone, smearing the edges of it round with a little fat and soot, so as to hide the cracks where the mortar should have been. In three nights the moon would be gone, and that seemed the best time for our attempt.

I had now no doubt at all about getting into the yard, but I had very considerable misgivings as to how I was to get out again. It would be too humiliating, after trying there, to have to go back to my hole again in despair, or to be arrested by the guards outside, and thrown into those damp underground cells which are reserved for prisoners who are caught in escaping. I set to work, therefore, to plan what I should do. I have never, as you know, had the chance of showing what I could do as a general. Sometimes, after a glass or two of wine, I have found myself capable of thinking out surprising combinations, and have felt that if Napoleon had intrusted me with an army corps, things might have gone differently with him. But however that may be, there is no doubt that in the small stratagems of war, and in that quickness of invention which is so necessary for an officer of light cavalry, I could hold my own against anyone. It was now that I had need of it, and I felt sure that it would not fail me.

The inner wall which I had to scale was built of bricks, 12 ft. high, with a row of iron spikes, 3 in. apart, upon the top. The outer I had only caught a glimpse of once or twice, when the gate of the exercise yard was open. It appeared to be about the same height, and was also spiked at the top. The space between the walls was over twenty feet, and I had reason to believe that there were no sentries there, except at the gates. On the other hand, I knew that there was a line of soldiers outside. Behold the little nut, my friends, which I had to open with no crackers, save these two hands.

One thing upon which I relied was the height of my comrade Beaumont. I have already said that he was a very tall man, six feet at least, and it seemed to me that if I could mount upon his shoulders, and get my hands upon the spikes, I could easily scale the wall. Could I pull my big companion up after me? That was the question, for when I set forth with a comrade, even though it be one for whom I bear no affection, nothing on earth would make me abandon him. If I climbed the wall and he could not follow me, I should be compelled to return to him. He did not seem to concern himself much about it, however, so I hoped that he had confidence in his own activity.

Then another very important matter was the choice of the sentry who should be on duty in front of my window at the time of our attempt. They were changed every two hours to insure their vigilance, but I, who watched them closely each night out of my window, knew that there was a great difference between them. There were some who were so keen that a rat could not cross the yard unseen, while others thought only of their own ease, and could sleep as soundly leaning upon a musket as if they were at home upon a feather bed. There was one especially, a fat, heavy man, who would retire into the shadow of the wall and doze so comfortably during his two hours, that I have dropped pieces of plaster from my window at his very feet, without his observing it. By good luck, this fellow's watch was due from twelve to two upon the night which we had fixed upon for our enterprise.

As the last day passed, I was so filled with nervous agitation that I could not control myself, but ran ceaselessly about my cell, like a mouse in a cage. Every moment I thought that the warder would detect the looseness of the bar, or that the sentry would observe the unmortared stone, which I could not conceal outside, as I did within. As for my companion, he sat brooding upon the end of his bed, looking at me in a sidelong fashion from time to time, and biting his nails like one who is deep in thought.

'Courage, my friend!' I cried, slapping him upon the shoulder. 'You will see your guns before another month be past.'

'That is very well,' said he. 'But whither will you fly when you get free?'

'To the coast,' I answered. 'All comes right for a brave man, and I shall make straight for my regiment.'

'You are more likely to make straight for the underground cells, or for the Portsmouth hulks,' said he.

'A soldier takes his chances,' I remarked. 'It is only the poltroon who reckons always upon the worst.'

I raised a flush in each of his sallow cheeks at that, and I was glad of it, for it was the first sign of spirit which I had ever observed in him. For a moment he put his hand out towards his water-jug, as though he would have hurled it at me, but then he shrugged his shoulders and sat in silence once more, biting his nails, and scowling down at the floor. I could not but think, as I looked at him, that perhaps I was doing the Flying Artillery a very bad service by bringing him back to them.

I never in my life have known an evening pass as slowly as that one. Towards nightfall a wind sprang up, and as the darkness deepened it blew harder and harder, until a terrible gale was whistling over the moor. As I looked out of my window I could not catch a glimpse of a star, and the black clouds were flying low across the heavens. The rain was pouring down, and what with its hissing and splashing, and the howling and screaming of the wind, it was impossible for me to hear the steps of the sentinels. 'If I cannot hear them,' thought I, 'then it is unlikely that they can hear me'; and I waited with the utmost impatience until the time when the inspector should have come round for his nightly peep through our grating. Then having peered through the darkness, and seen nothing of the sentry, who was doubtless crouching in some corner out of the rain, I felt that the moment was come. I removed the bar, pulled out the stone, and motioned to my companion to pass through.

'After you, Colonel,' said he.

'Will you not go first?' I asked.

'I had rather you showed me the way.'

'Come after me, then, but come silently, as you value your life.'

In the darkness I could hear the fellow's teeth chattering, and I wondered whether a man ever had such a partner in a desperate enterprise. I seized the bar, however, and mounting upon my stool, I thrust my head and shoulders into the hole. I had wriggled through as far as my waist, when my companion seized me suddenly by the knees, and yelled at the top of his voice: 'Help! Help! A prisoner is escaping!'

Ah, my friends, what did I not feel at that moment! Of course, I saw in an instant the game of this vile creature. Why should he risk his skin in climbing walls when he might be sure of a free pardon from the English for having prevented the escape of one so much more distinguished than himself? I had recognised him as a poltroon and a sneak, but I had not understood the depth of baseness to which he could descend. One who has spent his life among gentlemen and men of honour does not think of such things until they happen.

The blockhead did not seem to understand that he was lost more certainly than I. I writhed back in the darkness, and seizing him by the throat, I struck him twice with my iron bar. At the first blow he yelped as a little cur does when you tread upon its paw. At the second, down he fell with a groan upon the floor. Then I seated myself upon my bed, and waited resignedly for whatever punishment my gaolers might inflict upon me.

But a minute passed and yet another, with no sound save the heavy, snoring breathing of the senseless wretch upon the floor. Was it possible, then, that amid the fury of the storm his warning cries had passed unheeded? At first it was but a tiny hope, another minute and it was probable, another and it was certain. There was no sound in the corridor, none in the courtyard. I wiped the cold sweat from my brow, and asked myself what I should do next.

One thing seemed certain. The man on the floor must die. If I left him I could not tell how short a time it might be before he gave the alarm. I dare not strike a light, so I felt about in the darkness until my hand came upon something wet, which I knew to be his head. I raised my iron bar, but there was something, my friends, which prevented me from bringing it down. In the heat of fight I have slain many men—men of honour, too, who had done me no injury. Yet here was this wretch, a creature too foul to live, who had tried to work me so great a mischief, and yet I could not bring myself to crush his skull in. Such deeds are very well for a Spanish partida—or for that matter a sansculotte of the Faubourg St. Antoine—but not for a soldier and a gentleman like me.

However, the heavy breathing of the fellow made me hope that it might be a very long time before he recovered his senses. I gagged him, therefore, and bound him with strips of blanket to the bed, so that in his weakened condition there was good reason to think that, in any case, he might not get free before the next visit of the warder. But now again I was faced with new difficulties, for you will remember that I had relied upon his height to help me over the walls. I could have sat down and shed tears of despair had not the thought of my mother and of the Emperor come to sustain me. 'Courage!' said I. 'If it were anyone but Etienne Gerard he would be in a bad fix now; that is a young man who is not easily caught.'

I set to work therefore upon Beaumont's sheet as well as my own, and by tearing them into strips and then plaiting them together, I made a very excellent rope. This I tied securely to the centre of my iron bar, which was a little over a foot in length. Then I slipped out into the yard, where the rain was pouring and the wind screaming louder than ever. I kept in the shadow of the prison wall, but it was as black as the ace of spades, and I could not see my own hand in front of me. Unless I walked into the sentinel I felt that I had nothing to fear from him. When I had come under the wall I threw up my bar, and to my joy it stuck the very first time between the spikes at the top. I climbed up my rope, pulled it after me, and dropped down on the other side. Then I scaled the second wall, and was sitting astride among the spikes upon the top, when I saw something twinkle in the darkness beneath me. It was the bayonet of the sentinel below, and so close was it (the second wall being rather lower than the first) that I could easily, by leaning over, have unscrewed it from its socket. There he was, humming a tune to himself, and cuddling up against the wall to keep himself warm, little thinking that a desperate man within a few feet of him was within an ace of stabbing him to the heart with his own weapon. I was already bracing myself for the spring when the fellow, with an oath, shouldered his musket, and I heard his steps squelching through the mud as he resumed his beat. I slipped down my rope, and, leaving it hanging, I ran at the top of my speed across the moor.

Heavens, how I ran! The wind buffeted my face and buzzed in my nostrils. The rain pringled upon my skin and hissed past my ears. I stumbled into holes. I tripped over bushes. I fell among brambles. I was torn and breathless and bleeding. My tongue was like leather, my feet like lead, and my heart beating like a kettle-drum. Still I ran, and I ran, and I ran.

But I had not lost my head, my friends. Everything was done with a purpose. Our fugitives always made for the coast. I was determined to go inland, and the more so as I had told Beaumont the opposite. I would fly to the north, and they would seek me in the south. Perhaps you will ask me how I could tell which was which on such a night. I answer that it was by the wind. I had observed in the prison that it came from the north, and so, as long as I kept my face to it, I was going in the right direction.

Well, I was rushing along in this fashion when, suddenly, I saw two yellow lights shining out of the darkness in front of me. I paused for a moment, uncertain what I should do. I was still in my hussar uniform, you understand, and it seemed to me that the very first thing that I should aim at was to get some dress which should not betray me. If these lights came from a cottage, it was probable enough that I might find what I wanted there. I approached, therefore, feeling very sorry that I had left my iron bar behind; for I was determined to fight to the death before I should be retaken.

But very soon I found that there was no cottage there. The lights were two lamps hung upon each side of a carriage, and by their glare I saw that a broad road lay in front of me. Crouching among the bushes, I observed that there were two horses to the equipage, that a small post-boy was standing at their heads, and that one of the wheels was lying in the road beside him. I can see them now, my friends: the steaming creatures, the stunted lad with his hands to their bits, and the big, black coach, all shining with the rain, and balanced upon its three wheels. As I looked, the window was lowered, and a pretty little face under a bonnet peeped out from it.

'What shall I do?' the lady cried to the post-boy, in a voice of despair. 'Sir Charles is certainly lost, and I shall have to spend the night upon the moor.'

'Perhaps I can be of some assistance to madame,' said I, scrambling out from among the bushes into the glare of the lamps. A woman in distress is a sacred thing to me, and this one was beautiful. You must not forget that, although I was a colonel, I was only eighty-and-twenty years of age.

My word, how she screamed, and how the post-boy stared! You will understand that after that long race in the darkness, with my shako broken in, my face smeared with dirt, and my uniform all stained and torn with brambles, I was not entirely the sort of gentleman whom one would choose to meet in the middle of a lonely moor. Still, after the first surprise, she soon understood that I was her very humble servant, and I could even read in her pretty eyes that my manner and bearing had not failed to produce an impression upon her.

'I am sorry to have startled you, madame,' said I. 'I chanced to overhear your remark, and I could not refrain from offering you my assistance.' I bowed as I spoke. You know my bow, and can realise what its effect was upon the lady.

'I am much indebted to you, sir,' said she. 'We have had a terrible journey since we left Tavistock. Finally, one of our wheels came off, and here we are helpless in the middle of the moor. My husband, Sir Charles, has gone on to get help, and I much fear that he must have lost his way.'

I was about to attempt some consolation, when I saw beside the lady a black travelling coat, faced with astrakhan, which her companion must have left behind him. It was exactly what I needed to conceal my uniform. It is true that I felt very much like a highway robber, but then, what would you have? Necessity has no law, and I was in an enemy's country.

'I presume, madame, that this is your husband's coat,' I remarked. 'You will, I am sure, forgive me, if I am compelled to——' I pulled it through the window as I spoke.

I could not bear to see the look of surprise and fear and disgust which came over her face.

'Oh, I have been mistaken in you!' she cried. 'You came to rob me, then, and not to help me. You have the bearing of a gentleman, and yet you steal my husband's coat.'

'Madame,' said I, 'I beg that you will not condemn me until you know everything. It is quite necessary that I should take this coat, but if you will have the goodness to tell me who it is who is fortunate enough to be your husband, I shall see that the coat is sent back to him.'

Her face softened a little, though she still tried to look severe. 'My husband,' she answered, 'is Sir Charles Meredith, and he is travelling to Dartmoor Prison, upon important Government business. I only ask you, sir, to go upon your way, and to take nothing which belongs to him.'

'There is only one thing which belongs to him that I covet,' said I.

'And you have taken it from the carriage,' she cried.

'No,' I answered. 'It still remains there.'

She laughed in her frank English way.

'If, instead of paying me compliments, you were to return my husband's coat——' she began.

'Madame,' I answered, 'what you ask is quite impossible. If you will allow me to come into the carriage, I will explain to you how necessary this coat is to me.'

Heaven knows into what foolishness I might have plunged myself had we not, at this instant, heard a faint halloa in the distance, which was answered by a shout from the little post-boy. In the rain and the darkness, I saw a lantern some distance from us, but approaching rapidly.

'I am sorry, madame, that I am forced to leave you,' said I. 'You can assure your husband that I shall take every care of his coat.' Hurried as I was, I ventured to pause a moment to salute the lady's hand, which she snatched through the window with an admirable pretence of being offended at my presumption. Then, as the lantern was quite close to me, and the post-boy seemed inclined to interfere with my flight, I tucked my precious overcoat under my arm, and dashed off into the darkness.

And now I set myself to the task of putting as broad a stretch of moor between the prison and myself as the remaining hours of darkness would allow. Setting my face to the wind once more, I ran until I fell from exhaustion. Then, after five minutes of panting among the heather, I made another start, until again my knees gave way beneath me. I was young and hard, with muscles of steel, and a frame which had been toughened by twelve years of camp and field. Thus I was able to keep up this wild flight for another three hours, during which I still guided myself, you understand, by keeping the wind in my face. At the end of that time I calculated that I had put nearly twenty miles between the prison and myself. Day was about to break, so I crouched down among the heather upon the top of one of those small hills which abound in that country, with the intention of hiding myself until nightfall. It was no new thing for me to sleep in the wind and the rain, so, wrapping myself up in my thick warm cloak, I soon sank into a doze.

But it was not a refreshing slumber. I tossed and tumbled amid a series of vile dreams, in which everything seemed to go wrong with me. At last, I remember, I was charging an unshaken square of Hungarian Grenadiers, with a single squadron upon spent horses, just as I did at Elchingen. I stood in my stirrups to shout 'Vive l'Empereur!' and as I did so, there came the answering roar from my hussars, 'Vive l'Empereur!' I sprang from my rough bed, with the words still ringing in my ears, and then, as I rubbed my eyes, and wondered if I were mad, the same cry came again, five thousand voices in one long-drawn yell. I looked out from my screen of brambles, and saw in the clear light of morning the very last thing that I should either have expected or chosen.

It was Dartmoor Prison! There it stretched, grim and hideous, within a furlong of me. Had I run on for a few more minutes in the dark, I should have butted my shako against the wall. I was so taken aback at the sight, that I could scarcely realise what had happened. Then it all became clear to me, and I struck my head with my hands in my despair. The wind had veered from north to south during the night, and I, keeping my face always towards it, had run ten miles out and ten miles in, winding up where I had started. When I thought of my hurry, my falls, my mad rushing and jumping, all ending in this, it seemed so absurd, that my grief changed suddenly to amusement, and I fell among the brambles, and laughed, and laughed, until my sides were sore. Then I rolled myself up in my cloak and considered seriously what I should do.

One lesson which I have learned in my roaming life, my friends, is never to call anything a misfortune until you have seen the end of it. Is not every hour a fresh point of view? In this case I soon perceived that accident had done for me as much as the most profound cunning. My guards naturally commenced their search from the place where I had taken Sir Charles Meredith's coat, and from my hiding-place I could see them hurrying along the road to that point. Not one of them ever dreamed that I could have doubled back from there, and I lay quite undisturbed in the little bush-covered cup at the summit of my knoll. The prisoners had, of course, learned of my escape, and all the day exultant yells, like that which had aroused me in the morning, resounded over the moor, bearing a welcome message of sympathy and companionship to my ears. How little did they dream that on the top of that very mound, which they could see from their windows, was lying the comrade whose escape they were celebrating? As for me—I could look down upon this poor herd of idle warriors, as they paced about the great exercise yard, or gathered in little groups, gesticulating joyfully over my success. Once I heard a howl of execration, and I saw Beaumont, his head all covered with bandages, being led across the yard by two of the warders. I cannot tell you the pleasure which this sight gave me, for it proved that I had not killed him, and also that the others knew the true story of what had passed. They had all known me too well to think I could have abandoned him.

All that long day I lay behind my screen of bushes, listening to the bells which struck the hours below.

My pockets were filled with bread which I had saved out of my allowance, and on searching my borrowed overcoat I came upon a silver flask, full of excellent brandy and water, so that I was able to get through the day without hardship. The only other things in the pockets were a red silk handkerchief, a tortoise-shell snuff-box, and a blue envelope, with a red seal, addressed to the Governor of Dartmoor Prison. As to the first two, I determined to send them back when I should return the coat itself.

The letter caused me more perplexity, for the Governor had always shown me every courtesy, and it offended my sense of honour that I should interfere with his correspondence. I had almost made up my mind to leave it under a stone upon the roadway within musket-shot of the gate. This would guide them in their search for me, however, and so, on the whole, I saw no better way than just to carry the letter with me in the hope that I might find some means of sending it back to him. Meanwhile I packed it safely away in my innermost pocket.

There was a warm sun to dry my clothes, and when night fell I was ready for my journey. I promise you that there were no mistakes this time. I took the stars for my guides, as every hussar should be taught to do, and I put eight good leagues between myself and the prison. My plan was now to obtain a complete suit of clothes from the first person whom I could waylay, and I should then find my way to the north coast, where there were many smugglers and fishermen who would be ready to earn the reward which was paid by the Emperor to those who brought escaping prisoners across the Channel. I had taken the panache from my shako so that it might escape notice, but even with my fine overcoat I feared that sooner or later my uniform would betray me. My first care must be to provide myself with a complete disguise.

When day broke, I saw a river upon my right and a small town upon my left—the blue smoke reeking up above the moor. I should have liked well to have entered it, because it would have interested me to see something of the customs of the English, which differ very much from those of other nations. Much as I should have wished, however, to have seen them eat their raw meat and sell their wives, it would have been dangerous until I had got rid of my uniform. My cap, my moustache, and my speech would all help to betray me. I continued to travel towards the north therefore, looking about me continually, but never catching a glimpse of my pursuers.

About mid-day I came to where, in a secluded valley, there stood a single small cottage without any other building in sight. It was a neat little house, with a rustic porch and a small garden in front of it, with a swarm of cocks and hens. I lay down among the ferns and watched it, for it seemed to be exactly the kind of place where I might obtain what I wanted. My bread was finished, and I was exceedingly hungry after my long journey; I determined, therefore, to make a short reconnaissance, and then to march up to this cottage, summon it to surrender, and help myself to all that I needed. It could at least provide me with a chicken and with an omelette. My mouth watered at the thought.

As I lay there, wondering who could live in this lonely place, a brisk little fellow came out through the porch, accompanied by another older man, who carried two large clubs in his hands.. These he handed to his young companion, who swung them up and down, and round and round, with extraordinary swiftness. The other, standing beside him, appeared to watch him with great attention, and occasionally to advise him. Finally he took a rope, and began skipping like a girl, the other still gravely observing him. As you may think, I was utterly puzzled as to what these people could be, and could only surmise that one was a doctor, and the other a patient who had submitted himself to some singular method of treatment.

Well, as I lay watching and wondering, the older man brought out a great-coat, and held it while the other put it on and buttoned it to his chin. The day was a warmish one, so that this proceeding amazed me even more than the other. 'At least,' thought I, 'it is evident that his exercise is over'; but, far from this being so, the man began to run, in spite of his heavy coat, and as it chanced, he came right over the moor in my direction. His companion had re-entered the house, so that this arrangement suited me admirably. I would take the small man's clothing, and hurry on to some village where I could buy provisions. The chickens were certainly tempting, but still there were at least two men in the house, so perhaps it would be wiser for me, since I had no arms, to keep away from it.

I lay quietly then among the ferns. Presently I heard the steps of the runner, and there he was quite close to me, with his huge coat, and the perspiration running down his face. He seemed to be a very solid man—but small— so small that I feared that his clothes might be of little use to me. When I jumped out upon him he stopped running, and looked at me in the greatest astonishment.

'Blow my dickey,' said he, 'give it a name, guv'nor! Is it a circus, or what?'

That was how he talked, though I cannot pretend to tell you what he meant by it.

'You will excuse me, sir,' said I, 'but I am under the necessity of asking you to give me your clothes.'

'Give you what?' he cried.

'Your clothes.'

'Well, if this don't lick cock-fighting!' said he. 'What am I to give you my clothes for?'

'Because I need them.'

'And suppose I won't?'

'Be jabers,' said I, 'I shall have no choice but to take them.'

He stood with his hands in the pockets of his great-coat, and a most amused smile upon his square-jawed, clean-shaven face.

'You'll take them, will you?' said he. 'You're a very leery cove, by the look of you, but I can tell you that you've got the wrong sow by the ear this time. I know who you are. You're a runaway Frenchy, from the prison yonder, as anyone could tell with half an eye. But you don't know who I am, else you wouldn't try such a plant as that. Why, man, I'm the Bristol Bustler, nine stone champion, and them's my training quarters down yonder.'

He stared at me as if this announcement of his would have crushed me to the earth, but I smiled at him in my turn, and looked him up and down, with a twirl of my moustache.

'You may be a very brave man, sir,' said I, 'but when I tell you that you are opposed to Colonel Etienne Gerard, of the Hussars of Conflans, you will see the necessity of giving up your clothes without further parley.'

'Look here, mounseer, drop it!' he cried; 'this'll end by your getting pepper.'

'Your clothes, sir, this instant!' I shouted, advancing fiercely upon him.

For answer he threw off his heavy great-coat, and stood in a singular attitude, with one arm out, and the other across his chest, looking at me with a curious smile. For myself, I knew nothing of the methods of fighting which these people have, but on horse or on foot, with arms or without them, I am always ready to take my own part. You understand that a soldier cannot always choose his own methods, and that it is time to howl when you are living among wolves. I rushed at him, therefore, with a warlike shout, and kicked him with both my feet. At the same moment my heels flew into the air, I saw as many flashes as at Austerlitz, and the back of my head came down with a crash upon a stone. After that I can remember nothing more.

When I came to myself I was lying upon a truckle-bed, in a bare, half-furnished room. My head was ringing like a bell, and when I put up my hand, there was a lump like a walnut over one of my eyes. My nose was full of a pungent smell, and I soon found that a strip of paper soaked in vinegar was fastened across my brow. At the other end of the room this terrible little man was sitting with his knee bare, and his elderly companion was rubbing it with some liniment. The latter seemed to be in the worst of tempers, and he kept up a continual scolding, which the other listened to with a gloomy face.

'Never heard tell of such a thing in my life,' he was saying. 'In training for a month with all the weight of it on my shoulders, and then when I get you as fit as a trout, and within two days of fighting the likeliest man on the list, you let yourself into a by-battle with a foreigner.'

'There, there! Stow your gab!' said the other, sulkily. 'You're a very good trainer, Jim, but you'd be better with less jaw.'

'I should think it was time to jaw,' the elderly man answered. 'If this knee don't get well before next Wednesday, they'll have it that you fought a cross, and a pretty job you'll have next time you look for a backer.'

'Fought a cross!' growled the other. 'I've won nineteen battles, and no man ever so much as dared to say the word "cross" in my hearin'. How the deuce was I to get out of it when the cove wanted the very clothes off my back?'

'Tut, man; you knew that the beak and the guards were within a mile of you. You could have set them on to him as well then as now. You'd have got your clothes back again all right.'

'Well, strike me!' said the Bustler. 'I don't often break my trainin', but when it comes to givin' up my clothes to a Frenchy who couldn't hit a dint in a pat o' butter, why, it's more than I can swaller.'

'Pooh, man, what are the clothes worth? D'you know that Lord Rufton alone has five thousand pounds on you? When you jump the ropes on Wednesday, you'll carry every penny of fifty thousand into the ring. A pretty thing to turn up with a swollen knee and a story about a Frenchman!'

'I never thought he'd ha' kicked,' said the Bustler.

'I suppose you expected he'd fight Broughton's rules, and strict P.R.? Why, you silly, they don't know what fighting is in France.'

'My friends,' said I, sitting up on my bed, 'I do not understand very much of what you say, but when you speak like that it is foolishness. We know so much about fighting in France, that we have paid our little visit to nearly every capital in Europe, and very soon we are coming to London. But we fight like soldiers, you understand, and not like gamins in the gutter. You strike me on the head. I kick you on the knee. It is child's play. But if you will give me a sword, and take another one, I will show you how we fight over the water.'

They both stared at me in their solid, English way.

'Well, I'm glad you're not dead, mounseer,' said the elder one at last. 'There wasn't much sign of life in you when the Bustler and me carried you down. That head of yours ain't thick enough to stop the crook of the hardest hitter in Bristol.'

'He's a game cove, too, and he came for me like a

bantam,' said the other, still rubbing his knee. 'I got my old left-right in, and he went over as if he had been pole-axed. It wasn't my fault, mounseer. I told you you'd get pepper if you went on.'

'Well, it's something to say all your life, that you've been handled by the finest lightweight in England,' said the older man, looking at me with an expression of congratulation upon his face. 'You've had him at his best, too—in the pink of condition, and trained by Jim Hunter.'

'I am used to hard knocks,' said I, unbuttoning my tunic, and showing my two musket wounds. Then I bared my ankle also, and showed the place in my eye where the guerilla had stabbed me.

'He can take his gruel,' said the Bustler.

'What a glutton he'd have made for the middle-weights,' remarked the trainer; 'with six months' coaching he'd astonish the fancy. It's a pity he's got to go back to prison.'

I did not like that last remark at all. I buttoned up my coat and rose from the bed.

'I must ask you to let me continue my journey,' said I.

'There's no help for it, mounseer,' the trainer answered. 'It's a hard thing to send such a man as you back to such a place, but business is business, and there's a twenty pound reward. They were here this morning, looking for you, and I expect they'll be round again.'

His words turned my heart to lead.

'Surely, you would not betray me!' I cried. 'I will send you twice twenty pounds on the day that I set foot upon France. I swear it upon the honour of a French gentleman.'

But I only got head-shakes for a reply. I pleaded, I argued, I spoke of the English hospitality and the fellow-ship of brave men, but I might as well have been addressing the two great wooden clubs which stood balanced upon the floor in front of me. There was no sign of sympathy upon their bull-faces.

'Business is business, mounseer,' the old trainer repeated. 'Besides, how am I to put the Bustler into the ring on Wednesday if he's jugged by the beak for aidin' and abettin' a prisoner of war? I've got to look after the Bustler, and I take no risks.'

This, then, was the end of all my struggles and strivings. I was to be led back again like a poor silly sheep who has broken through the hurdles. They little knew me who could fancy that I should submit to such a fate. I had heard enough to tell me where the weak point of these two men was, and I showed, as I have often showed before, that Etienne Gerard is never so terrible as when all hope seems to have deserted him. With a single spring I seized one of the clubs and swung it over the head of the Bustler.

'Come what may,' I cried, '*you* shall be spoiled for Wednesday.'

The fellow growled out an oath, and would have sprung at me, but the other flung his arms round him and pinned him to the chair.

'Not if I know it, Bustler,' he screamed. 'None of your games while I am by. Get away out of this, Frenchy. We only want to see your back. Run away, run away, or he'll get loose!'

It was good advice, I thought, and I ran to the door, but as I came out into the open air my head swam round and I had to lean against the porch to save myself from falling. Consider all that I had been through, the anxiety of my escape, the long, useless flight in the storm, the day spent amid wet ferns, with only bread for food, the second journey by night, and now the injuries which I had received in attempting to deprive the little man of his clothes. Was it wonderful that even I should reach the limits of my endurance?

I stood there in my heavy coat and my poor battered shako, my chin upon my chest, and my eyelids over my eyes. I had done my best, and I could do no more. It was the sound of horses' hoofs which made me at last raise my head, and there was the grey-moustached Governor of Dartmoor Prison not ten paces in front of me, with six mounted warders behind him!

'So, Colonel,' said he, with a bitter smile, 'we have found you once more.'

When a brave man has done his utmost, and has failed, he shows his breeding by the manner in which he accepts his defeat. For me, I took the letter which I had in my pocket, and stepping forward, I handed it with such grace of manner as I could summon to the Governor.

'It has been my misfortune, sir, to detain one of your letters,' said I.

He looked at me in amazement, and beckoned to the warders to arrest me. Then he broke the seal of the letter. I saw a curious expression come over his face as he read it.

'This must be the letter which Sir Charles Meredith lost,' said he.

'It was in the pocket of his coat.'

'You have carried it for two days?'

'Since the night before last.'

'And never looked at the contents?'

I showed him by my manner that he had committed an indiscretion in asking a question which one gentleman should not have put to another.

To my surprise he burst out into a roar of laughter.

'Colonel,' said he, wiping the tears from his eyes, 'you have really given both yourself and us a great deal of unnecessary trouble. Allow me to read the letter which you carried with you in your flight.'

And this was what I heard:—

'On receipt of this you are directed to release Colonel Etienne Gerard, of the 3rd Hussars, who has been exchanged against Colonel Mason, of the Horse Artillery, now in Verdun.'

And as he read it, he laughed again, and the warders laughed, and the two men from the cottage laughed, and then, as I heard this universal merriment, and thought of all my hopes and fears, and my struggles and dangers, what could a debonair soldier do but lean against the porch once more, and laugh as heartily as any of them? And of them all was it not I who had the best reason to laugh, since in front of me I could see my dear France, and my mother, and the Emperor, and my horsemen; while behind lay the gloomy prison, and the heavy hand of the English King?

V. How the Brigadier Took the Field
Against the Marshal Millefleurs

MASSENA was a thin, sour little fellow, and after his hunting accident he had only one eye, but when it looked out from under his cocked hat there was not much upon a field of battle which escaped it. He could stand in front of a battalion, and with a single sweep tell you if a buckle or a gaiter button were out of place. Neither the officers nor the men were very fond of him, for he was, as you know, a miser, and soldiers love that their leaders should be free-handed. At the same time, when it came to work they had a very high respect for him, and they would rather fight under him than under anyone except the Emperor himself, and Lannes, when he was alive. After all, if he had a tight grasp upon his money-bags, there was a day also, you must remember, when that same grip was upon Zurich and Genoa. He clutched on to his positions as he did to his strong box, and it took a very clever man to loosen him from either.

When I received his summons I went gladly to his head-quarters, for I was always a great favourite of his, and there was no officer of whom he thought more highly. That was the best of serving with those good old generals, that they knew enough to be able to pick out a fine soldier when they saw one. He was seated alone in his tent, with his chin upon his hand, and his brow as wrinkled as if he had been asked for a subscription. He smiled, however, when he saw me before him.

'Good-day, Colonel Gerard.'

'Good-day, Marshal.'

'How is the Third of Hussars?'

'Seven hundred incomparable men upon seven hundred excellent horses.'

'And your wounds—are they healed?'

'My wounds never heal, Marshal,' I answered.

'And why?'

'Because I have always new ones.'

'General Rapp must look to his laurels,' said he, his face all breaking into wrinkles as he laughed. 'He has had twenty-one from the enemy's bullets, and as many from Larrey's knives and probes. Knowing that you were hurt, Colonel, I have spared you of late.'

'Which hurt me most of all.'

'Tut, tut! Since the English got behind these accursed lines of Torres Vedras, there has been little for us to do. You did not miss much during your imprisonment at Dartmoor. But now we are on the eve of action.'

'We advance?'

'No, retire.'

My face must have shown my dismay. What, retire before this sacred dog of a Wellington—he who had listened unmoved to my words, and had sent me to his land of fogs? I could have sobbed as I thought of it.

'What would you have?' cried Massena, impatiently. 'When one is in check, it is necessary to move the king.'

'Forwards,' I suggested.

He shook his grizzled head.

'The lines are not to be forced,' said he. 'I have already lost General St. Croix and more men than I can replace. On the other hand, we have been here at Santarem for nearly six months. There is not a pound of flour nor a jug of wine on the country-side. We must retire.'

'There are flour and wine in Lisbon,' I persisted.

'Tut, you speak as if an army could charge in and

charge out again like your regiment of hussars. If Soult were here with thirty thousand men—but he will not come. I sent for you, however, Colonel Gerard, to say that I have a very singular and important expedition which I intend to place under your direction.'

I pricked up my ears, as you can imagine. The Marshal unrolled a great map of the country and spread it upon the table. He flattened it out with his little, hairy hands.

'This is Santarem,' he said, pointing.

I nodded.

'And here, twenty-five miles to the east, is Almeixal, celebrated for its vintages and for its enormous Abbey.'

Again I nodded; I could not think what was coming.

'Have you heard of the Marshal Millefleurs?' asked Massena.

'I have served with all the Marshals,' said I, 'but there is none of that name.'

'It is but the nickname which the soldiers have given him,' said Massena. 'If you had not been away from us for some month's, it would not be necessary for me to tell you about him. He is an Englishman, and a man of good breeding. It is on account of his manners that they have given him his title. I wish you to go to this polite English-man at Almeixal.'

'Yes, Marshal.'

'And to hang him to the nearest tree.'

'Certainly, Marshal.'

I turned briskly upon my heels, but Massena recalled me before I could reach the opening of his tent.

'One moment, Colonel,' said he; 'you had best learn how matters stand before you start. You must know, then, that this Marshal Millefleurs, whose real name is Alexis Morgan, is a man of very great ingenuity and bravery. He was an officer in the English Guards, but having been broken for cheating at cards, he left the army. In some manner he gathered a number of English deserters round him and took to the mountains. French stragglers and Portuguese brigands joined him, and he found himself at the head of five hundred men. With these he took possession of the Abbey of Almeixal, sent the monks about their business, fortified the place, and gathered in the plunder of all the country round.'

'For which it is high time he was hanged,' said I, making once more for the door.

'One instant!' cried the Marshal, smiling at my impatience. 'The worst remains behind. Only last week the Dowager Countess of La Ronda, the richest woman in Spain, was taken by these ruffians in the passes as she was journeying from King Joseph's Court to visit her grandson. She is now a prisoner in the Abbey, and is only protected by her——'

'Grandmotherhood,' I suggested.

'Her power of paying a ransom,' said Massena. 'You have three missions, then: To rescue this unfortunate lady; to punish this villain; and, if possible, to break up this nest of brigands. It will be a proof of the confidence which I have in you when I say that I can only spare you half a squadron with which to accomplish all this.'

My word, I could hardly believe my ears! I thought that I should have had my regiment at the least.

'I would give you more,' said he, 'but I commence my retreat to-day, and Wellington is so strong in horse that every trooper becomes of importance. I cannot spare you another man. You will see what you can do, and you will report yourself to me at Abrantes not later than to-morrow night.'

It was very complimentary that he should rate my powers so high, but it was also a little embarrassing. I was to rescue an old lady, to hang an Englishman, and to break up a band of five hundred assassins—all with fifty men. But after all, the fifty men were Hussars of Conflans, and they had an Etienne Gerard to lead them. As I came out into the warm Portuguese sunshine my confidence had returned to me, and I had already begun to wonder whether the medal which I had so often deserved might not be waiting for me at Almeixal.

You may be sure that I did not take my fifty men at haphazard. They were all old soldiers of the German wars, some of them with three stripes, and most of them with two. Oudet and Papilette, two of the best sub-officers in the regiment, were at their head. When I had them formed up in fours, all in silver grey and upon chestnut horses, with their leopard skin shabracks and their little red panaches, my heart beat high at the sight. I could not look at their weather-stained faces, with the great moustaches which bristled over their chin-straps, without feeling a glow of confidence, and, between ourselves, I have no doubt that that was exactly how they felt when they saw their young Colonel on his great black war-horse riding at their head.

Well, when we got free of the camp and over the Tagus, I threw out my advance and my flankers, keeping my own place at the head of the main body. Looking back from the hills above Santarem, we could see the dark lines of Massena's army, with the flash and twinkle of the sabres and bayonets as he moved his regiments into position for their retreat. To the south lay the scattered red patches of the English outposts, and behind the grey smoke-cloud which rose from Wellington's camp—thick, oily smoke, which seemed to our poor starving fellows to bear with it the rich smell of seething camp-kettles. Away to the west lay a curve of blue sea flecked with the white sails of the English ships.

You will understand that as we were riding to the east, our road lay away from both armies. Our own marauders, however, and the scouting parties of the English, covered the country, and it was necessary with my small troop that I should take every precaution. During the whole day we rode over desolate hill-sides, the lower portions covered by the budding vines, but the upper turning from green to grey, and jagged along the sky-line like the back of a starved horse. Mountain streams crossed our path, running west to the Tagus, and once we came to a deep, strong river, which might have checked us had I not found the ford by observing where houses had been built opposite each other upon either bank. Between them, as every scout should know, you will find your ford. There was none to give us information, for neither man nor beast, nor any living thing except great clouds of crows, was to be seen during our journey.

The sun was beginning to sink when we came to a valley clear in the centre, but shrouded by huge oak trees upon either side. We could not be more than a few miles from Almeixal, so it seemed to me to be best to keep among the groves, for the spring had been an early one and the leaves were already thick enough to conceal us. We were riding then in open order among the great trunks, when one of my flankers came galloping up.

'There are English across the valley, Colonel,' he cried, as he saluted.

'Cavalry or infantry?'

'Dragoons, Colonel,' said he; 'I saw the gleam of their helmets, and heard the neigh of a horse.'

Halting my men I hastened to the edge of the wood. There could be no doubt about it. A party of English cavalry was travelling in a line with us, and in the same direction. I caught a glimpse of their red coats and of their flashing arms glowing and twinkling among the tree-trunks. Once, as they passed through a small clearing, I could see their whole force, and I judged that they were of about the same strength as my own—a half squadron at the most.

You who have heard some of my little adventures will give me credit for being quick in my decisions, and prompt in carrying them out. But here I must confess that I was in two minds. On the one hand there was the chance of a fine cavalry skirmish with the English. On the other hand, there was my mission at the Abbey of Almeixal, which seemed already to be so much above my power. If I were to lose any of my men, it was certain that I should be unable to carry out my orders. I was sitting my horse, with my chin in my gauntlet, looking across at the rippling gleams of light from the further wood, when suddenly one of these red-coated Englishmen rode out from the cover, pointing at me and breaking into a shrill whoop and halloa as if I had been a fox. Three others joined him, and one who was a bugler sounded a call, which brought the whole of them into the open. They were, as I had thought, a half squadron, and they formed a double line with a front of twenty-five, their officer—the one who had whooped at me—at their head.

For my own part, I had instantly brought my own troopers into the same formation, so that there we were, hussars and dragoons, with only two hundred yards of grassy sward between us. They carried themselves well, those red-coated troopers, with their silver helmets, their high white plumes, and their long, gleaming swords; while, on the other hand, I am sure they would acknowledge that they had never looked upon finer light horsemen than the fifty hussars of Conflans who were facing them. They were heavier, it is true, and they may have seemed the smarter, for Wellington used to make them burnish their metal work, which was not usual among us. On the other hand, it is well known that the English tunics were too tight for the sword-arm, which gave our men an advantage. As to bravery, foolish, inexperienced people of every nation always think that their own soldiers are braver than any others. There is no nation in the world which does not entertain this idea. But when one has seen as much as I have done, one understands that there is no very marked difference, and that although nations differ very much in discipline, they are all equally brave—except that the French have rather more courage than the rest.

Well, the cork was drawn and the glasses ready, when suddenly the English officer raised his sword to me as if in a challenge, and cantered his horse across the grassland. My word, there is no finer sight upon earth than that of a gallant man upon a gallant steed! I could have halted there just to watch him as he came with such careless grace, his sabre down by his horse's shoulder, his head thrown back, his white plume tossing—youth and strength and courage, with the violet evening sky above and the oak trees behind. But it was not for me to stand and stare. Etienne Gerard may have his faults, but, my faith, he was never accused of being backward in taking his own part. The old horse, Rataplan, knew me so well that he had started off before ever I gave the first shake to the bridle.

There are two things in this world that I am very slow to forget: the face of a pretty woman, and the legs of a fine horse. Well, as we drew together, I kept on saying, 'Where have I seen those great roan shoulders? Where have I seen that dainty fetlock?' Then suddenly I remembered, and as I looked up at the reckless eyes and the challenging smile, whom should I recognise but the man who had saved me from the brigands and played me for my freedom—he whose correct title was Milor the Hon. Sir Russell Bart!

'Bart!' I shouted.

He had his arm raised for a cut, and three parts of his body open to my point, for he did not know very much about the use of the sword. As I brought my hilt to the salute he dropped his hand and stared at me.

'Halloa!' said he. 'It's Gerard!' You would have thought by his manner that I had met him by appointment. For my own part, I would have embraced him had he but come an inch of the way to meet me.

'I thought we were in for some sport,' said he. 'I never dreamed that it was you.'

I found this tone of disappointment somewhat irritating. Instead of being glad at having met a friend, he was sorry at having missed an enemy.

'I should have been happy to join in your sport, my dear Bart,' said I. 'But I really cannot turn my sword upon a man who saved my life.'

'Tut, never mind about that.'

'No, it is impossible. I should never forgive myself.'

'You make too much of a trifle.'

'My mother's one desire is to embrace you. If ever you should be in Gascony——'

'Lord Wellington is coming there with sixty thousand men.'

'Then one of them will have a chance of surviving,' said I, laughing. 'In the meantime, put your sword in your sheath!'

Our horses were standing head to tail, and the Bart put out his hand and patted me on the thigh.

'You're a good chap, Gerard,' said he. 'I only wish you had been born on the right side of the Channel.'

'I was,' said I.

'Poor devil!' he cried, with such an earnestness of pity that he set me laughing again. 'But look here, Gerard,' he continued; 'this is all very well, but it is not business, you know. I don't know what Massena would say to it, but our Chief would jump out of his riding-boots if he saw us. We weren't sent out here for a picnic—either of us.'

'What would you have?'

'Well, we had a little argument about our hussars and dragoons, if you remember. I've got fifty of the Sixteenth all chewing their carbine bullets behind me. You've got as many fine-looking boys over yonder, who seem to be fidgeting in their saddles. If you and I took the right flanks we should not spoil each other's beauty—though a little blood-letting is a friendly thing in this climate.'

There seemed to me to be a good deal of sense in what he said. For the moment Mr. Alexis Morgan and the Countess of La Ronda and the Abbey of Almeixal went right out of my head, and I could only think of the fine level turf and of the beautiful skirmish which we might have.

'Very good, Bart,' said I. 'We have seen the front of your dragoons. We shall now have a look at their backs.'

'Any betting?' he asked.

'The stake,' said I, 'is nothing less than the honour of the Hussars of Conflans.'

'Well, come on!' he answered. 'If we break you, well and good—if you break us, it will be all the better for Marshal Millefleurs.'

When he said that I could only stare at him in astonishment.

'Why for Marshal Millefleurs?' I asked.

'It is the name of a rascal who lives out this way. My dragoons have been sent by Lord Wellington to see him safely hanged.'

'Name of a name!' I cried. 'Why, my hussars have been sent by Massena for that very object."

We burst out laughing at that, and sheathed our swords. There was a whirr of steel from behind us as our troopers followed our example.

'We are allies!' he cried.

'For a day.'

'We must join forces.'

'There is no doubt of it.'

And so, instead of fighting, we wheeled our half squadrons round and moved in two little columns down the valley, the shakos and the helmets turned inwards, and the men looking their neighbours up and down, like old fighting dogs with tattered ears who have learned to respect each other's teeth. The most were on the broad grin, but there were some on either side who looked black and challenging, especially the English sergeant and my own sub-officer Papilette. They were men of habit, you see, who could not change all their ways of thinking in a moment. Besides, Papilette had lost his only brother at Busaco. As for the Bart and me, we rode together at the head and chatted about all that had occurred to us since that famous game of écarté of which I have told you.

For my own part, I spoke to him of my adventures in England. They are a very singular people, these English. Although he knew that I had been engaged in twelve campaigns, yet I am sure that the Bart thought more highly of me because I had had an affair with the Bristol Bustler. He told me, too, that the Colonel who presided over his court-martial for playing cards with a prisoner acquitted him of neglect of duty, but nearly broke him because he thought that he had not cleared his trumps before leading his suit. Yes, indeed, they are a singular people.

At the end of the valley the road curved over some rising ground before winding down into another wider valley beyond. We called a halt when we came to the top; for there, right in front of us, at the distance of about three miles, was a scattered, grey town, with a single enormous building upon the flank of the mountain which overlooked it. We could not doubt that we were at last in sight of the Abbey that held the gang of rascals whom we had come to disperse. It was only now, I think, that we fully understood what a task lay in front of us, for the place was a veritable fortress, and it was evident that cavalry should never have been sent out upon such an errand.

'That's got nothing to do with us,' said the Bart; 'Wellington and Massena can settle that between them.'

'Courage!' I answered. 'Piré took Leipzig with fifty hussars.'

'Had they been dragoons,' said the Bart, laughing, 'he would have had Berlin. But you are senior officer; give us a lead, and we'll see who will be the first to flinch.'

'Well,' said I, 'whatever we do must be done at once, for my orders are to be on my way to Abrantes by to-morrow night. But we must have some information first, and here is someone who should be able to give it to us.'

There was a square, whitewashed house standing by the roadside, which appeared, from the bush hanging over the door, to be one of those wayside tabernas which are provided for the muleteers. A lantern was hung in the porch, and by its light we saw two men, the one in the brown habit of a Capuchin monk, and the other girt with an apron, which showed him to be the landlord. They were conversing together so earnestly that we were upon

them before they were aware of us. The innkeeper turned
to fly, but one of the Englishmen seized him by the hair,
and held him tight.

'For mercy's sake, spare me,' he yelled. 'My house has
been gutted by the French and harried by the English,
and my feet have been burned by the brigands. I swear
by the Virgin that I have neither money nor food in my
inn, and the good Father Abbot, who is starving upon
my doorstep, will be witness to it.'

'Indeed, sir,' said the Capuchin, in excellent French,
'what this worthy man says is very true. He is one of the
many victims to these cruel wars, although his loss is but
a feather-weight compared to mine. Let him go,' he
added, in English, to the trooper, 'he is too weak to fly,
even if he desired to.'

In the light of the lantern I saw that this monk was a
magnificent man, dark and bearded, with the eyes of a
hawk, and so tall that his cowl came up to Rataplan's
ears. He wore the look of one who had been through
much suffering, but he carried himself like a king, and
we could form some opinion of his learning when we
each heard him talk our own language as fluently as if
he were born to it.

'You have nothing to fear,' said I, to the trembling
innkeeper. 'As to you, father, you are, if I am not mistaken, the very man who can give us the information
which we require.'

'All that I have is at your service, my son. But,' he
added, with a wan smile, 'my Lenten fare is always somewhat meagre, and this year it has been such that I must
ask you for a crust of bread if I am to have the strength
to answer your questions.'

We bore two days' rations in our haversacks, so that
he soon had the little he asked for. It was dreadful to see
the wolfish way in which he seized the piece of dried
goat's flesh which I was able to offer him.

'Time presses, and we must come to the point,' said I.
'We want your advice as to the weak points of yonder

Abbey, and concerning the habits of the rascals who infest it.'

He cried out something which I took to be Latin, with his hands clasped and his eyes upturned. 'The prayer of the just availeth much,' said he, 'and yet I had not dared to hope that mine would have been so speedily answered. In me you see the unfortunate Abbot of Almeixal, who has been cast out by this rabble of three armies with their heretical leader. Oh! to think of what I have lost!' his voice broke, and the tears hung upon his lashes.

'Cheer up, sir,' said the Bart. 'I'll lay nine to four that we have you back again by to-morrow night.'

'It is not of my own welfare that I think,' said he, 'nor even of that of my poor, scattered flock. But it is of the holy relics which are left in the sacrilegious hands of these robbers.'

'It's even betting whether they would ever bother their heads about them,' said the Bart. 'But show us the way inside the gates, and we'll soon clear the place out for you.'

In a few short words the good Abbot gave us the very points that we wished to know. But all that he said only made our task more formidable. The walls of the Abbey were forty feet high. The lower windows were barricaded, and the whole building loopholed for musketry fire. The gang preserved military discipline, and their sentries were too numerous for us to hope to take them by surprise. It was more than ever evident that a battalion of grenadiers and a couple of breaching pieces were what was needed. I raised my eyebrows, and the Bart began to whistle.

'We must have a shot at it, come what may,' said he.

The men had already dismounted, and, having watered their horses, were eating their suppers. For my own part I went into the sitting-room of the inn with the Abbot and the Bart, that we might talk about our plans.

I had a little cognac in my *sauve vie*, and I divided it among us—just enough to wet our moustaches.

'It is unlikely,' said I, 'that those rascals know anything about our coming. I have seen no signs of scouts along the road. My own plan is that we should conceal ourselves in some neighbouring wood, and then, when they open their gates, charge down upon them and take them by surprise.'

The Bart was of opinion that this was the best that we could do, but, when we came to talk it over, the Abbot made us see that there were difficulties in the way.

'Save on the side of the town, there is no place within a mile of the Abbey where you could shelter man or horse,' said he. 'As to the townsfolk, they are not to be trusted. I fear, my son, that your excellent plan would have little chance of success in the face of the vigilant guard which these men keep.'

'I see no other way,' answered I. 'Hussars of Conflans are not so plentiful that I can afford to run half a squadron of them against a forty-foot wall with five hundred infantry behind it.'

'I am a man of peace,' said the Abbot, 'and yet I may, perhaps, give a word of counsel. I know these villains and their ways. Who should do so better, seeing that I have stayed for a month in this lonely spot, looking down in weariness of heart at the Abbey which was my own? I will tell you now what I should myself do if I were in your place.'

'Pray tell us, father,' we cried, both together.

'You must know that bodies of deserters, both French and English, are continually coming in to them, carrying their weapons with them. Now, what is there to prevent you and your men from pretending to be such a body, and so making your way into the Abbey?'

I was amazed at the simplicity of the thing, and I embraced the good Abbot. The Bart, however, had some objections to offer.

'That is all very well,' said he, 'but if these fellows are as sharp as you say, it is not very likely that they are going to let a hundred armed strangers into their crib.

From all I have heard of Mr. Morgan, or Marshal Mille-fleurs, or whatever the rascal's name is, I give him credit for more sense than that.'

'Well, then,' I cried, 'let us send fifty in, and let them at daybreak throw open the gates to the other fifty, who will be waiting outside.'

We discussed the question at great length and with much foresight and discretion. If it had been Massena and Wellington instead of two young officers of light cavalry, we could not have weighed it all with more judgment. At last we agreed, the Bart and I, that one of us should indeed go with fifty men, under pretence of being deserters, and that in the early morning he should gain command of the gate and admit the others. The Abbot, it is true, was still of opinion that it was dangerous to divide our force, but finding that we were both of the same mind, he shrugged his shoulders and gave in.

'There is only one thing that I would ask,' said he. 'If you lay hands upon this Marshal Millefleurs—this dog of a brigand—what will you do with him?'

'Hang him,' I answered.

'It is too easy a death,' cried the Capuchin, with a vindictive glow in his dark eyes. 'Had I my way with him—but oh, what thoughts are these for a servant of God to harbour!' He clapped his hands to his forehead like one who is half demented by his troubles, and rushed out of the room.

There was an important point which we had still to settle, and that was whether the French or the English party should have the honour of entering the Abbey first. My faith, it was asking a great deal of Etienne Gerard that he should give place to any man at such a time! But the poor Bart pleaded so hard, urging the few skirmishes which he had seen against my four-and-seventy engagements, that at last I consented that he should go. We had just clasped hands over the matter when there broke out such a shouting and cursing and yelling from the front of the inn, that out we rushed with our drawn sabres in our hands, convinced that the brigands were upon us.

You may imagine our feelings when, by the light of the lantern which hung from the porch, we saw a score of our hussars and dragoons all mixed in one wild heap, red coats and blue, helmets and busbies, pommelling each other to their hearts' content. We flung ourselves upon them, imploring, threatening, tugging at a lace collar, or at a spurred heel, until, at last, we had dragged them all apart. There they stood, flushed and bleeding, glaring at each other, and all panting together like a line of troop horses after a ten-mile chase. It was only with our drawn swords that we could keep them from each other's throats. The poor Capuchin stood in the porch in his long brown habit, wringing his hands and calling upon all the saints for mercy.

He was, indeed, as I found upon inquiry, the innocent cause of all the turmoil, for, not understanding how soldiers look upon such things, he had made some remark to the English sergeant that it was a pity that his squadron was not as good as the French. The words were not out of his mouth before a dragoon knocked down the nearest hussar, and then, in a moment, they all flew at each other like tigers. We would trust them no more after that, but the Bart moved his men to the front of the inn, and I mine to the back, the English all scowling and silent, and our fellows shaking their fists and chattering, each after the fashion of their own people.

Well, as our plans were made, we thought it best to carry them out at once, lest some fresh cause of quarrel should break out between our followers. The Bart and his men rode off, therefore, he having first torn the lace from his sleeves, and the gorget and sash from his uniform, so that he might pass as a simple trooper. He explained to his men what it was that was expected of them, and though they did not raise a cry or wave their weapons as mine might have done, there was an expression upon their stolid and clean-shaven faces which filled me with confidence. Their tunics were left unbuttoned, their scabbards and helmets stained with dirt, and their harness badly fastened, so that they might look the part of deserters, without order or discipline. At six o'clock next morning they were to gain command of the main gate of the Abbey, while at that same hour my hussars were to gallop up to it from outside. The Bart and I pledged our words to it before he trotted off with his detachment. My sergeant, Papilette, with two troopers, followed the English at a distance, and returned in half an hour to say that, after some parley, and the flashing of lanterns upon them from the grille, they had been admitted into the Abbey.

So far, then, all had gone well. It was a cloudy night with a sprinkling of rain, which was in our favour, as there was the less chance of our presence being discovered. My vedettes I placed two hundred yards in every direction, to guard against a surprise, and also to prevent any peasant who might stumble upon us from carrying the news to the Abbey. Oudin and Papilette were to take turns of duty, while the others with their horses had snug quarters in a great wooden granary. Having walked round and seen that all was as it should be, I flung myself upon the bed which the innkeeper had set apart for me, and fell into a dreamless sleep.

No doubt you have heard my name mentioned as being the beau-ideal of a soldier, and that not only by friends and admirers like our fellow-townsfolk, but also by old officers of the great wars who have shared the fortunes of those famous campaigns with me. Truth and modesty compel me to say, however, that this is not so. There are some gifts which I lack—very few, no doubt— but, still, amid the vast armies of the Emperor there may have been some who were free from those blemishes which stood between me and perfection. Of bravery I say nothing. Those who have seen me in the field are best fitted to speak about that. I have often heard the soldiers discussing round the camp-fires as to who was the bravest man in the Grand Army. Some said Murat, and some said Lasalle, and some Ney; but for my own part, when they asked me, I merely shrugged my shoulders and smiled. It would have seemed mere conceit if I had answered that there was no man braver than Brigadier Gerard. At the same time, facts are facts, and a man knows best what his own feelings are. But there are other gifts besides bravery which are necessary for a soldier, and one of them is that he should be a light sleeper. Now, from my boyhood onwards, I have been hard to wake, and it was this which brought me to ruin upon that night.

It may have been about two o'clock in the morning that I was suddenly conscious of a feeling of suffocation. I tried to call out, but there was something which prevented me from uttering a sound. I struggled to rise, but I could only flounder like a hamstrung horse. I was strapped at the ankles, strapped at the knees, and strapped again at the wrists. Only my eyes were free to move, and there at the foot of my couch, by the light of a Portuguese lamp, whom should I see but the Abbot and the innkeeper!

The latter's heavy, white face had appeared to me when I looked upon it the evening before to express nothing but stupidity and terror. Now, on the contrary, every feature bespoke brutality and ferocity. Never have I seen a more dreadful-looking villain. In his hand he held a long, dull-coloured knife. The Abbot, on the other hand, was as polished and as dignified as ever. His Capuchin gown had been thrown open, however, and I saw beneath it a black, frogged coat, such as I have seen among the English officers. As our eyes met he leaned over the wooden end of the bed and laughed silently until it creaked again.

'You will, I am sure, excuse my mirth, my dear Colonel Gerard,' said he. 'The fact is, that the expression upon your face when you grasped the situation was just a little funny. I have no doubt that you are an excellent soldier, but I hardly think that you are fit to measure wits with the Marshal Millefleurs, as your fellows have been good enough to call me. You appear to have given me credit for singularly little intelligence, which argues, if I may be allowed to say so, a want of acuteness upon your own part. Indeed, with the single exception of my thick-headed compatriot the British dragoon, I have never met anyone who was less competent to carry out such a mission.'

You can imagine how I felt and how I looked, as I listened to this insolent harangue, which was all delivered in that flowery and condescending manner which had gained this rascal his nickname. I could say nothing, but they must have read my threat in my eyes, for the fellow who had played the part of the innkeeper whispered something to his companion.

'No, no, my dear Chenier, he will be infinitely more valuable alive,' said he. 'By the way, Colonel, it is just as well that you are a sound sleeper, for my friend here, who is a little rough in his ways, would certainly have cut your throat if you had raised any alarm. I should recommend you to keep in his good graces, for Sergeant Chenier, late of the 7th Imperial Light Infantry, is a much more dangerous person than Captain Alexis Morgan, of His Majesty's foot-guards.'

Chenier grinned and shook his knife at me, while I tried to look the loathing which I felt at the thought that a soldier of the Emperor could fall so low.

'It may amuse you to know,' said the Marshal, in that soft, suave voice of his, 'that both your expeditions were watched from the time that you left your respective camps. I think that you will allow that Chenier and I played our parts with some subtlety. We had made every arrangement for your reception at the Abbey, though we had hoped to receive the whole squadron instead of half. When the gates are secured behind them, our visitors find themselves in a very charming mediæval quadrangle, with no possible exit, commanded by musketry fire from a hundred windows. They may choose to be shot down;

or they may choose to surrender. Between ourselves, I have not the slightest doubt that they have been wise enough to do the latter. But since you are naturally interested in the matter, we thought that you would care to come with us and to see for yourself. I think I can promise you that you will find your titled friend waiting for you at the Abbey with a face as long as your own.'

The two villains began whispering together, debating, as far as I could hear, which was the best way of avoiding my vedettes.

'I will make sure that it is all clear upon the other side of the barn,' said the Marshal at last. 'You will stay here, my good Chenier, and if the prisoner gives any trouble you will know what to do.'

So we were left together, this murderous renegade and I—he sitting at the end of the bed, sharpening his knife upon his boot in the light of the single smoky little oil-lamp. As to me, I only wonder now, as I look back upon it, that I did not go mad with vexation and self-reproach as I lay helplessly upon the couch, unable to utter a word or move a finger, with the knowledge that my fifty gallant lads were so close to me, and yet with no means of letting them know the straits to which I was reduced. It was no new thing for me to be a prisoner; but to be taken by these renegades, and to be led into their Abbey in the midst of their jeers, befooled and outwitted by their insolent leaders—that was indeed more than I could endure. The knife of the butcher beside me would cut less deeply than that.

I twitched softly at my wrists, and then at my ankles, but whichever of the two had secured me was no bungler at his work. I could not move either of them an inch. Then I tried to work the handkerchief down over my mouth, but the ruffian beside me raised his knife with such a threatening snarl that I had to desist. I was lying still looking at his bull neck, and wondering whether it would ever be my good fortune to fit it for a cravat, when I heard returning steps coming down the inn passage and up the stair. What word would the villain bring back? If he found it impossible to kidnap me, he would probably murder me where I lay. For my own part, I was indifferent which it might be, and I looked at the doorway with the contempt and defiance which I longed to put into words But you can imagine my feelings, my dear friends, when, instead of the tall figure and dark, sneering face of the Capuchin, my eyes fell upon the grey pelisse and huge moustaches of my good little sub-officer, Papilette!

The French soldier of those days had seen too much to be ever taken by surprise. His eyes had hardly rested upon my bound figure and the sinister face beside me before he had seen how the matter lay.

'Sacred name of a dog!' he growled, and out flashed his great sabre. Chenier sprang forward at him with his knife, and then, thinking better of it, he darted back and stabbed frantically at my heart. For my own part, I had hurled myself off the bed on the side opposite to him, and the blade grazed my side before ripping its way through blanket and sheet. An instant later I heard the thud of a heavy fall, and then almost simultaneously a second object struck the floor—something lighter but harder, which rolled under the bed. I will not horrify you with details, my friends. Suffice it that Papilette was one of the strongest swordsmen in the regiment, and that his sabre was heavy and sharp. It left a red blotch upon my wrists and my ankles, as it cut the thongs which bound me.

When I had thrown off my gag, the first use which I made of my lips was to kiss the sergeant's scarred cheeks. The next was to ask him if all was well with the command. Yes, they had had no alarms. Oudin had just relieved him, and he had come to report. Had he seen the Abbot? No, he had seen nothing of him. Then we must form a cordon and prevent his escape. I was hurrying out to give the orders, when I heard a slow and measured step enter the door below, and come creaking up the stairs.

Papilette understood it all in an instant. 'You are not to kill him,' I whispered, and thrust him into the shadow on one side of the door; I crouched on the other. Up he came, up and up, and every footfall seemed to be upon my heart. The brown skirt of his gown was not over the threshold before we were both on him, like two wolves on a buck. Down we crashed, the three of us, he fighting like a tiger, and with such amazing strength that he might have broken away from the two of us. Thrice he got to his feet, and thrice we had him over again, until Papilette made him feel that there was a point to his sabre. He had sense enough then to know that the game was up, and to lie still while I lashed him with the very cords which had been round my own limbs.

'There has been a fresh deal, my fine fellow,' said I, 'and you will find that I have some of the trumps in *my* hand this time.'

'Luck always comes to the aid of a fool,' he answered. 'Perhaps it is as well, otherwise the world would fall too completely into the power of the astute. So, you have killed Chenier, I see. He was an insubordinate dog, and always smelt abominably of garlic. Might I trouble you to lay me upon the bed? The floor of these Portuguese tabernas is hardly a fitting couch for anyone who has prejudices in favour of cleanliness.'

I could not but admire the coolness of the man, and the way in which he preserved the same insolent air of condescension in spite of this sudden turning of the tables. I dispatched Papilette to summon a guard, whilst I stood over our prisoner with my drawn sword, never taking my eyes off him for an instant, for I must confess that I had conceived a great respect for his audacity and resource.

'I trust,' said he, 'that your men will treat me in a becoming manner.'

'You will get your deserts—you may depend upon that.'

'I ask nothing more. You may not be aware of my

exalted birth, but I am so placed that I cannot name my
father without treason, nor my mother without a scandal.
I cannot *claim* Royal honours, but these things are so
much more graceful when they are conceded without a
claim. The thongs are cutting my skin. Might I beg you
to loosen them?'

'You do not give me credit for much intelligence,' I
remarked, repeating his own words.

'*Touché*,' he cried, like a pinked fencer. 'But here come
your men, so it matters little whether you loosen them
or not.'

I ordered the gown to be stripped from him and
placed him under a strong guard. Then, as morning was
already breaking, I had to consider what my next step
was to be. The poor Bart and his Englishmen had fallen
victims of the deep scheme which might, had we adopted
all the crafty suggestions of our adviser, have ended in
the capture of the whole instead of the half of our force.
I must extricate them if it were still possible. Then there
was the old lady, the Countess of La Ronda, to be
thought of. As to the Abbey, since its garrison was on
the alert it was hopeless to think of capturing that. All
turned now upon the value which they placed upon
their leader. The game depended upon my playing that
one card. I will tell you how boldly and how skilfully I
played it.

It was hardly light before my bugler blew the assembly,
and out we trotted on to the plain. My prisoner was
placed on horseback in the very centre of the troops. It
chanced that there was a large tree just out of musket-
shot from the main gate of the Abbey, and under this we
halted. Had they opened the great doors in order to
attack us, I should have charged home upon them; but,
as I had expected, they stood upon the defensive, lining
the long wall and pouring down a torrent of hootings
and taunts and derisive laughter upon us. A few fired
their muskets, but finding that we were out of reach they
soon ceased to waste their powder. It was the strangest

sight to see that mixture of uniforms, French, English, and Portuguese, cavalry, infantry, and artillery, all wagging their heads and shaking their fists at us.

My word, their hubbub soon died away when we opened our ranks, and showed whom we had got in the midst of us! There was silence for a few seconds, and then such a howl of rage and grief! I could see some of them dancing like madmen upon the wall. He must have been a singular person, this prisoner of ours, to have gained the affection of such a gang.

I had brought a rope from the inn, and we slung it over the lower bough of the tree.

'You will permit me, monsieur, to undo your collar,' said Papilette, with mock politeness.

'If your hands are perfectly clean,' answered our prisoner, and set the whole half-squadron laughing.

There was another yell from the wall, followed by a profound hush as the noose was tightened round Marshal Millefleurs' neck. Then came a shriek from a bugle, the Abbey gates flew open, and three men rushed out waving white cloths in their hands. Ah, how my heart bounded with joy at the sight of them. And yet I would not advance an inch to meet them, so that all the eagerness might seem to be upon their side. I allowed my trumpeter, however, to wave a handkerchief in reply, upon which the three envoys came running towards us. The Marshal, still pinioned, and with the rope round his neck, sat his horse with a half smile, as one who is slightly bored and yet strives out of courtesy not to show it. If I were in such a situation I could not wish to carry myself better, and surely I can say no more than that.

They were a singular trio, these ambassadors. The one was a Portuguese caçadore in his dark uniform, the second a French chasseur in the lightest green, and the third a big English artilleryman in blue and gold. They saluted, all three, and the Frenchman did the talking.

'We have thirty-seven English dragoons in our hands,' said he. 'We give you our most solemn oath that they shall all hang from the Abbey wall within five minutes of the death of our Marshal.'

'Thirty-seven!' I cried. 'You have fifty-one.'

'Fourteen were cut down before they could be secured.'

'And the officer?'

'He would not surrender his sword save with his life. It was not our fault. We would have saved him if we could.'

Alas for my poor Bart! I had met him but twice, and yet he was a man very much after my heart. I have always had a regard for the English for the sake of that one friend. A braver man and a worse swordsman I have never met.

I did not, as you may think, take these rascals' word for anything. Papilette was dispatched with one of them, and returned to say that it was too true. I had now to think of the living.

'You will release the thirty-seven dragoons if I free your leader?'

'We will give you ten of them.'

'Up with him!' I cried.

'Twenty,' shouted the chasseur.

'No more words,' said I. 'Pull on the rope!'

'All of them,' cried the envoy, as the cord tightened round the Marshal's neck.

'With horses and arms?'

They could see that I was not a man to jest with.

'All complete,' said the chasseur, sulkily.

'And the Countess of La Ronda as well?' said I.

But here I met with firmer opposition. No threats of mine could induce them to give up the Countess. We tightened the cord. We moved the horse. We did all but leave the Marshal suspended. If once I broke his neck the dragoons were dead men. It was as precious to me as to them.

'Allow me to remark,' said the Marshal, blandly, 'that you are exposing me to a risk of a quinsy. Do you not think, since there is a difference of opinion upon this point, that it would be an excellent idea to consult the lady herself? We would neither of us, I am sure, wish to override her own inclinations.'

Nothing could be more satisfactory. You can imagine how quickly I grasped at so simple a solution. In ten minutes she was before us, a most stately dame, with her grey curls peeping out from under her mantilla. Her face was as yellow as though it reflected the countless doubloons of her treasury.

'This gentleman,' said the Marshal, 'is exceedingly anxious to convey you to a place where you will never see us more. It is for you to decide whether you would wish to go with him, or whether you prefer to remain with me.'

She was at his horse's side in an instant. 'My own Alexis,' she cried, 'nothing can ever part us.'

He looked at me with a sneer upon his handsome face.

'By the way, you made a small slip of the tongue, my dear Colonel,' said he. 'Except by courtesy, no such person exists as the Dowager Countess of La Ronda. The lady whom I have the honour to present to you is my very dear wife, Mrs. Alexis Morgan—or shall I say Madame la Marèchale Millefleurs?'

It was at this moment that I came to the conclusion that I was dealing with the cleverest, and also the most unscrupulous, man whom I had ever met. As I looked upon this unfortunate old woman my soul was filled with wonder and disgust. As for her, her eyes were raised to his face with such a look as a young recruit might give to the Emperor.

'So be it,' said I at last; 'give me the dragoons and let me go.'

They were brought out with their horses and weapons, and the rope was taken from the Marshal's neck.

'Good-bye, my dear Colonel,' said he. 'I am afraid that you will have rather a lame account to give of your mission, when you find your way back to Massena, though, from all I hear, he will probably be too busy to think of you. I am free to confess that you have extricated yourself from your difficulties with greater ability than I had given you credit for. I presume that there is nothing which I can do for you before you go?'

'There is one thing.'

'And that is?'

'To give fitting burial to this young officer and his men.'

'I pledge my word to it.'

'And there is one other.'

'Name it.'

'To give me five minutes in the open with a sword in your hand and a horse between your legs.'

'Tut, tut!' said he. 'I should either have to cut short your promising career, or else to bid adieu to my own bonny bride. It is unreasonable to ask such a request of a man in the first joys of matrimony.'

I gathered my horsemen together and wheeled them into column.

'Au revoir,' I cried, shaking my sword at him. 'The next time you may not escape so easily.'

'Au revoir,' he answered. 'When you are weary of the Emperor, you will always find a commission waiting for you in the service of the Marshal Millefleurs.'

VI. How the Brigadier Played for a Kingdom

IT has sometimes struck me that some of you, when you have heard me tell these little adventures of mine, may have gone away with the impression that I was conceited. There could not be a greater mistake than this, for I have always observed that really fine soldiers are free from this failing. It is true that I have had to depict myself sometimes as brave, sometimes as full of resource, always as interesting; but then, it really was so, and I had to take the facts as I found them. It would be an unworthy affectation if I were to pretend that my career has been anything but a fine one. The incident which I will tell you to-night, however, is one which you will understand that only a modest man would describe. After all, when one has attained such a position as mine, one can afford to speak of what an ordinary man might be tempted to conceal.

You must know, then, that after the Russian campaign the remains of our poor army were quartered along the western bank of the Elbe, where they might thaw their frozen blood and try, with the help of the good German beer, to put a little between their skin and their bones. There were some things which we could not hope to regain, for I daresay that three large commissariat four-gons would not have sufficed to carry the fingers and toes which the army had shed during that retreat. Still, lean and crippled as we were, we had much to be thankful for when we thought of our poor comrades whom we had left behind, and of the snowfields—the horrible, horrible snowfields. To this day, my friends, I do not care to see red and white together. Even my red cap thrown down upon my white counterpane has given me dreams in which I have seen those monstrous plains, the reeling, tortured army, and the crimson smears which glared upon the snow behind them. You will coax no story out of me about that business, for the thought of it is enough to turn my wine to vinegar and my tobacco to straw.

Of the half-million who crossed the Elbe in the autumn of the year '12, about forty thousand infantry were left in the spring of '13. But they were terrible men, these forty thousand: men of iron, eaters of horses, and sleepers in the snow; filled, too, with rage and bitterness against the Russians. They would hold the Elbe until the great army of conscripts, which the Emperor was raising in France, should be ready to help them to cross it once more.

But the cavalry was in a deplorable condition. My own hussars were at Borna, and when I paraded them first, I burst into tears at the sight of them. My fine men and my beautiful horses—it broke my heart to see the state to which they were reduced. 'But, courage,' I thought, 'they have lost much, but their Colonel is still left to them.' I set to work, therefore, to repair their disasters, and had already constructed two good squadrons, when an order came that all colonels of cavalry should repair instantly to the depôts of the regiments in France to organise the recruits and the remounts for the coming campaign.

You will think, doubtless, that I was over-joyed at this chance of visiting home once more. I will not deny that it was a pleasure to me to know that I should see my mother again, and there were a few girls who would be very glad at the news; but there were others in the army who had a stronger claim. I would have given my place to any who had wives and children whom they might not see again. However, there is no arguing when the blue papers with the little red seal arrives, so within an hour I was off upon my great ride from the Elbe to the Vosges. At last I was to have a period of quiet. War lay behind my mare's tail and peace in front of her nostrils. So I thought, as the sound of the bugles died in the distance, and the long, white road curled away in front of me through plain and forest and mountain, with France somewhere beyond the blue haze which lay upon the horizon.

It is interesting, but it is also fatiguing, to ride in the rear of an army. In the harvest time our soldiers could do without supplies, for they had been trained to pluck the grain in the fields as they passed, and to grind it for themselves in their bivouacs. It was at that time of year, therefore, that those swift marches were performed which were the wonder and the despair of Europe. But now the starving men had to be made robust once more, and I was forced to draw into the ditch continually as the Coburg sheep and the Bavarian bullocks came streaming past with waggon loads of Berlin beer and good French cognac. Sometimes, too, I would hear the dry rattle of the drums and the shrill whistle of the fifes, and long columns of our good little infantry men would swing past me with the white dust lying thick upon their blue tunics. These were old soldiers drawn from the garrisons of our German fortresses, for it was not until May that the new conscripts began to arrive from France.

Well, I was rather tired of this eternal stopping and dodging, so that I was not sorry when I came to Altenburg to find that the road divided, and that I could take the southern and quieter branch. There were few wayfarers between there and Greiz, and the road wound through groves of oaks and beeches, which shot their branches across the path. You will think it strange that a Colonel of hussars should again and again pull up his horse in order to admire the beauty of the feathery branches and the little, green, new-budded leaves, but if you had spent six months among the fir trees of Russia you would be able to understand me.

There was something, however, which pleased me very much less than the beauty of the forests, and that was the words and looks of the folk who lived in the woodland villages. We had always been excellent friends with the Germans, and during the last six years they had never seemed to bear us any malice for having made a little free with their country. We had shown kindnesses to the men and received them from the women, so that good, comfortable Germany was a second home to all of us. But now there was something which I could not understand in the behaviour of the people. The travellers made no answer to my salute; the foresters turned their heads away to avoid seeing me; and in the villages the folk would gather into knots in the roadway and would scowl at me as I passed. Even women would do this, and it was something new for me in those days to see anything but a smile in a woman's eyes when they were turned upon me.

It was in the hamlet of Schmolin, just ten miles out of Altenburg, that the thing became most marked. I had

298

stopped at the little inn there just to damp my moustache and to wash the dust out of poor Violette's throat. It was my way to give some little compliment, or possibly a kiss, to the maid who served me; but this one would have neither the one nor the other, but darted a glance at me like a bayonet-thrust. Then when I raised my glass to the folk who drank their beer by the door they turned their backs on me, save only one fellow, who cried, 'Here's a toast for you, boys! Here's to the letter T!' At that they all emptied their beer mugs and laughed; but it was not a laugh that had good fellowship in it.

I was turning this over in my head and wondering what their boorish conduct could mean, when I saw, as I rode from the village, a great T new carved upon a tree. I had already seen more than one in my morning's ride, but I had given no thought to them until the words of the beer-drinker gave them an importance. It chanced that a respectable-looking person was riding past me at the moment, so I turned to him for information.

'Can you tell me, sir,' said I, 'what this letter T is?'

He looked at it and then at me in the most singular fashion. 'Young man,' said he, 'it is not the letter N.' Then before I could ask further he clapped his spurs into his horse's ribs and rode, stomach to earth, upon his way.

At first his words had no particular significance in my mind, but as I trotted onwards Violette chanced to half turn her dainty head, and my eyes were caught by the gleam of the brazen N's at the end of the bridle-chain. It was the Emperor's mark. And those T's meant something which was opposite to it. Things had been happening in Germany, then, during our absence, and the giant sleeper had begun to stir. I thought of the mutinous faces that I had seen, and I felt that if I could only have looked into the hearts of these people I might have had some strange news to bring into France with me. It made me the more eager to get my remounts, and to see ten strong squadrons behind my kettle-drums once more.

While these thoughts were passing through my head

I had been alternately walking and trotting, as a man should who has a long journey before, and a willing horse beneath, him. The woods were very open at this point, and beside the road there lay a great heap of fagots. As I passed there came a sharp sound from among them, and, glancing round, I saw a face looking out at me—a hot, red face, like that of a man who is beside himself with excitement and anxiety. A second glance told me that it was the very person with whom I had talked an hour before in the village.

'Come nearer!' he hissed. 'Nearer still! Now dismount and pretend to be mending the stirrup leather. Spies may be watching us, and it means death to me if I am seen helping you.'

'Death!' I whispered. 'From whom?'

'From the Tugendbund. From Lutzow's night-riders. You Frenchmen are living on a powder magazine, and the match has been struck that will fire it.'

'But this is all strange to me,' said I, still fumbling at the leathers of my horse. 'What is this Tugendbund?'

'It is the secret society which has planned the great rising which is to drive you out of Germany, just as you have been driven out of Russia.'

'And these T's stand for it?'

'They are the signal. I should have told you all this in the village, but I dared not be seen speaking with you. I galloped through the woods to cut you off, and concealed both my horse and myself.'

'I am very much indebted to you,' said I, 'and the more so as you are the only German that I have met to-day from whom I have had common civility.'

'All that I possess I have gained through contracting for the French armies,' said he. 'Your Emperor has been a good friend to me. But I beg that you will ride on now, for we have talked long enough. Beware only of Lutzow's night-riders!'

'Banditti?' I asked.

'All that is best in Germany,' said he. 'But for God's

sake ride forwards, for I have risked my life and exposed my good name in order to carry you this warning.'

Well, if I had been heavy with thought before, you can think how I felt after my strange talk with the man among the fagots. What came home to me even more than his words was his shivering, broken voice, his twitching face, and his eyes glancing swiftly to right and left, and opening in horror whenever a branch cracked upon a tree. It was clear that he was in the last extremity of terror, and it is possible that he had cause, for shortly after I had left him I heard a distant gunshot and a shouting from somewhere behind me. It may have been some sportsman halloaing to his dogs, but I never again heard of or saw the man who had given me my warning.

I kept a good look-out after this, riding swiftly where the country was open, and slowly where there might be an ambuscade. It was serious for me, since five hundred good miles of German soil lay in front of me; but somehow I did not take it very much to heart, for the Germans had always seemed to me to be a kindly, gentle people, whose hands closed more readily round a pipe-stem than a sword-hilt—not out of want of valour, you understand, but because they are genial, open souls, who would rather be on good terms with all men. I did not know then that beneath that homely surface there lurks a devilry as fierce as, and far more persistent than, that of the Castilian or the Italian.

And it was not long before I had shown to me that there was something more serious abroad than rough words and hard looks. I had come to a spot where the road runs upwards through a wild tract of heathland and vanishes into an oak wood. I may have been half-way up the hill when, looking forward, I saw something gleaming under the shadow of the tree-trunks, and a man came out with a coat which was so slashed and spangled with gold that he blazed like fire in the sunlight. He appeared to be very drunk, for he reeled and staggered as he came towards me. One of his hands was held up to his ear and clutched a great red handkerchief, which was fixed to his neck.

I had reined up the mare and was looking at him with some disgust, for it seemed strange to me that one who wore so gorgeous a uniform should show himself in such a state in broad daylight. For his part, he looked hard in my direction and came slowly onwards, stopping from time to time and swaying about as he gazed at me. Suddenly, as I again advanced, he screamed out his thanks to Christ, and, lurching forwards, he fell with a crash upon the dusty road. His hands flew forward with the fall, and I saw that what I had taken for a red cloth was a monstrous wound, which had left a great gap in his neck, from which a dark blood-clot hung, like an epaulette upon his shoulder.

'My God!' I cried, as I sprang to his aid. 'And I thought that you were drunk!'

'Not drunk, but dying,' said he. 'But thank Heaven that I have seen a French officer while I have still strength to speak.'

I laid him among the heather and poured some brandy down his throat. All round us was the vast country-side, green and peaceful, with nothing living in sight save only the mutilated man beside me.

'Who has done this?' I asked, 'and what are you? You are French, and yet the uniform is strange to me.'

'It is that of the Emperor's new guard of honour. I am the Marquis of Château St. Arnaud, and I am the ninth of my blood who has died in the service of France. I have been pursued and wounded by the night-riders of Lutzow, but I hid among the brushwood yonder, and waited in the hope that a Frenchman might pass. I could not be sure at first if you were friend or foe, but I felt that death was very near, and that I must take the chance.'

'Keep your heart up, comrade,' said I; 'I have seen a man with a worse wound who has lived to boast of it.'

'No, no,' he whispered; 'I am going fast.' He laid his

hand upon mine as he spoke, and I saw that his finger-nails were already blue. 'But I have papers here in my tunic which you must carry at once to the Prince of Saxe-Felstein, at his Castle of Hof. He is still true to us, but the Princess is our deadly enemy. She is striving to make him declare against us. If he does so, it will determine all those who are wavering, for the King of Prussia is his uncle and the King of Bavaria his cousin. These papers will hold him to us if they can only reach him before he takes the last step. Place them in his hands to-night, and, perhaps, you will have saved all Germany for the Em-peror. Had my horse not been shot, I might, wounded as I am——' he choked, and the cold hand tightened into a grip, which left mine as bloodless as itself. Then, with a groan, his head jerked back, and it was all over with him.

Here was a fine start for my journey home. I was left with a commission of which I knew little, which would lead me to delay the pressing needs of my hussars, and which at the same time was of such importance that it was impossible for me to avoid it. I opened the Marquis's tunic, the brilliance of which had been devised by the Emperor in order to attract those young aristocrats from whom he hoped to raise these new regiments of his Guard. It was a small packet of papers which I drew out, tied up with silk, and addressed to the Prince of Saxe-Felstein. In the corner, in a sprawling, untidy hand, which I knew to be the Emperor's own, was written: 'Pressing and most important.' It was an order to me, those four words—an order as clear as if it had come straight from the firm lips with the cold grey eyes looking into mine. My troopers might wait for their horses, the dead Marquis might lie where I had laid him amongst the heather, but if the mare and her rider had a breath left in them the papers should reach the Prince that night.

I should not have feared to ride by the road through the wood, for I have learned in Spain that the safest time to pass through a guerilla country is after an outrage, and that the moment of danger is when all is peaceful. When I came to look upon my map, however, I saw that Hof lay further to the south of me, and that I might reach it more directly by keeping to the moors. Off I set, therefore, and had not gone fifty yards before two carbine shots rang out of the brushwood and a bullet hummed past me like a bee. It was clear that the night-riders were bolder in their ways than the brigands of Spain, and that my mission would have ended where it had begun if I had kept to the road.

It was a mad ride, that—a ride with a loose rein, girth-deep in heather and in gorse, plunging through bushes, flying down hill-sides, with my neck at the mercy of my dear little Violette. But she—she never slipped, she never faltered, as swift and as surefooted as if she knew that her rider carried the fate of all Germany beneath the buttons of his pelisse. And I—I had long borne the name of being the best horseman in the six brigades of light cavalry, but I never rode as I rode then. My friend the Bart has told me of how they hunt the fox in England, but the swiftest fox would have been captured by me that day. The wild pigeons which flew overhead did not take a straighter course than Violette and I below. As an officer, I have always been ready to sacrifice myself for my men, though the Emperor would not have thanked me for it, for he had many men, but only one—well, cavalry leaders of the first class are rare.

But here I had an object which was indeed worth a sacrifice, and I thought no more of my life than of the clods of earth that flew from my darling's heels.

We struck the road once more as the light was failing, and galloped into the little village of Lobenstein. But we had hardly got upon the cobble-stones when off came one of the mare's shoes, and I had to lead her to the village smithy. His fire was low, and his day's work done, so that it would be an hour at the least before I could hope to push on to Hof. Cursing at the delay, I strode into the village inn and ordered a cold chicken and some wine to be served for my dinner. It was but a few miles to Hof, and I had every hope that I might deliver my papers to the Prince on that very night, and be on my way for France next morning with despatches for the Emperor in my bosom. I will tell you now what befell me in the inn of Lobenstein.

The chicken had been served and the wine drawn, and I had turned upon both as a man may who has ridden such a ride, when I was aware of a murmur and a scuffling in the hall outside my door. At first I thought that it was some brawl between peasants in their cups, and I left them to settle their own affairs. But of a sudden there broke from among the low, sullen growl of the voices such a sound as would send Etienne Gerard leaping from his death-bed. It was the whimpering cry of a woman in pain. Down clattered my knife and my fork, and in an instant I was in the thick of the crowd which had gathered outside my door.

The heavy-cheeked landlord was there and his flaxen-haired wife, the two men from the stables, a chamber-maid, and two or three villagers. All of them, women and men, were flushed and angry, while there in the centre of them, with pale cheeks and terror in her eyes, stood the loveliest woman that ever a soldier would wish to look upon. With her queenly head thrown back, and a touch of defiance mingled with her fear, she looked as she gazed round her like a creature of a different race from the vile, coarse-featured crew who surrounded her. I had not taken two steps from my door before she sprang to meet me, her hand resting upon my arm and her blue eyes sparkling with joy and triumph.

'A French soldier and gentleman!' she cried. 'Now at last I am safe.'

'Yes, madame, you are safe,' said I, and I could not resist taking her hand in mine in order than I might reassure her. 'You have only to command me,' I added, kissing the hand as a sign that I meant what I was saying.

'I am Polish,' she cried; 'the Countess Palotta is my

name. They abuse me because I love the French. I do not know what they might have done to me had Heaven not sent you to my help.'

I kissed her hand again lest she should doubt my intentions. Then I turned upon the crew with such an expression as I know how to assume. In an instant the hall was empty.

'Countess,' said I, 'you are now under my protection. You are faint, and a glass of wine is necessary to restore you.' I offered her my arm and escorted her into my room, where she sat by my side at the table and took the refreshment which I offered her.

How she blossomed out in my presence, this woman, like a flower before the sun! She lit up the room with her beauty. She must have read my admiration in my eyes, and it seemed to me that I also could see something of the sort in her own. Ah! my friends, I was no ordinary-looking man when I was in my thirtieth year. In the whole light cavalry it would have been hard to find a finer pair of whiskers. Murat's may have been a shade longer, but the best judges are agreed that Murat's were a shade too long. And then I had a manner. Some women are to be approached in one way and some in another, just as a siege is an affair of fascines and gabions in hard weather and of trenches in soft. But the man who can mix daring with timidity, who can be outrageous with an air of humility, and presumptuous with a tone of deference, that is the man whom mothers have to fear. For myself, I felt that I was the guardian of this lonely lady, and knowing what a dangerous man I had to deal with, I kept strict watch upon myself. Still, even a guardian has his privileges, and I did not neglect them.

But her talk was as charming as her face. In a few words she explained that she was travelling to Poland, and that her brother who had been her escort had fallen ill upon the way. She had more than once met with ill-treatment from the country folk because she could not conceal her good-will towards the French. Then turning from her own affairs she questioned me about the army, and so came round to myself and my own exploits. They were familiar to her, she said, for she knew several of Poniatowski's officers, and they had spoken of my doings. Yet she would be glad to hear them from my own lips. Never have I had so delightful a conversation. Most women make the mistake of talking rather too much about their own affairs, but this one listened to my tales just as you are listening now, ever asking for more and more and more. The hours slipped rapidly by, and it was with horror that I heard the village clock strike eleven, and so learned that for four hours I had forgotten the Emperor's business.

'Pardon me, my dear lady,' I cried, springing to my feet, 'but I must on instantly to Hof.'

She rose also, and looked at me with a pale, reproachful face. 'And me?' she said. 'What is to become of me?'

'It is the Emperor's affair. I have already stayed far too long. My duty calls me, and I must go.'

'You must go? And I must be abandoned alone to these savages? Oh, why did I ever meet you? Why did you ever teach me to rely upon your strength?' Her eyes glazed over, and in an instant she was sobbing upon my bosom.

Here was a trying moment for a guardian! Here was a time when he had to keep a watch upon a forward young officer. But I was equal to it. I smoothed her rich brown hair and whispered such consolations as I could think of in her ear, with one arm round her, it is true, but that was to hold her lest she should faint. She turned her tear-stained face to mine. 'Water,' she whispered. 'For God's sake, water!'

I saw that in another moment she would be senseless. I laid the drooping head upon the sofa, and then rushed furiously from the room, hunting from chamber to chamber for a carafe. It was some minutes before I could get one and hurry back with it. You can imagine my feelings to find the room empty and the lady gone.

Not only was she gone, but her cap and silver-mounted

riding switch which had lain upon the table were gone also. I rushed out and roared for the landlord. He knew nothing of the matter, had never seen the woman before, and did not care if he never saw her again. Had the peasants at the door seen anyone ride away? No, they had seen nobody. I searched here and searched there, until at last I chanced to find myself in front of a mirror, where I stood with my eyes staring and my jaw as far dropped as the chin-strap of my shako would allow.

Four buttons of my pelisse were open, and it did not need me to put my hand up to know that my precious papers were gone. Oh! the depth of cunning that lurks in a woman's heart. She had robbed me, this creature, robbed me as she clung to my breast. Even while I smoothed her hair, and whispered kind words into her ear, her hands had been at work beneath my dolman. And here I was, at the very last step of my journey, without the power of carrying out this mission which had already deprived one good man of his life, and was likely to rob another one of his credit. What would the Emperor say when he heard that I had lost his despatches? Would the army believe it of Etienne Gerard? And when they heard that a woman's hand had coaxed them from me, what laughter there would be at mess-table and at camp-fire! I could have rolled upon the ground in my despair.

But one thing was certain—all this affair of the fracas in the hall and the persecution of the so-called Countess was a piece of acting from the beginning. This villainous innkeeper must be in the plot. From him I might learn who she was and where my papers had gone. I snatched my sabre from the table and rushed out in search of him. But the scoundrel had guessed what I would do, and had made his preparations for me. It was in the corner of the yard that I found him, a blunderbuss in his hands and a mastiff held upon a leash by his son. The two stable-hands, with pitchforks, stood upon either side, and the wife held a great lantern behind him, so as to guide his aim.

'Ride away, sir, ride away!' he cried, with a crackling voice. 'Your horse is at the door, and no one will meddle with you if you go your way; but if you come against us, you are alone against three brave men.'

I had only the dog to fear, for the two forks and the blunderbuss were shaking about like inches in a wind. Still, I considered that, though I might force an answer with my sword-point at the throat of this fat rascal, still I should have no means of knowing whether that answer was the truth. It would be a struggle, then, with much to lose and nothing certain to gain. I looked them up and down, therefore, in a way that set their foolish weapons shaking worse than ever, and then, throwing myself upon my mare, I galloped away with the shrill laughter of the landlady jarring upon my ears.

I had already formed my resolution. Although I had lost my papers, I could make a very good guess as to what their contents would be, and this I would say from my own lips to the Prince of Saxe-Felstein, as though the Emperor had commissioned me to convey it that way. It was a bold stroke and a dangerous one, but if I went too far I could afterwards be disavowed. It was that or nothing, and when all Germany hung on the balance the game should not be lost if the nerve of one man could save it.

It was midnight when I rode into Hof, but every window was blazing, which was enough in itself, in that sleepy country, to tell the ferment of excitement in which the people were. There was hooting and jeering as I rode through the crowded streets, and once a stone sang past my head, but I kept upon my way, neither slowing nor quickening my pace, until I came to the palace. It was lit from base to battlement, and the dark shadows, coming and going against the yellow glare, spoke of the turmoil within. For my part, I handed my mare to a groom at the gate, and striding in I demanded, in such a voice as an ambassador should have, to see the Prince instantly, upon business which would brook no delay.

The hall was dark, but I was conscious as I entered of a buzz of innumerable voices, which hushed into silence as I loudly proclaimed my mission. Some great meeting was being held then—a meeting which, as my instincts told me, was to decide this very question of war and peace. It was possible that I might still be in time to turn the scale for the Emperor and for France. As to the major-domo, he looked blackly at me, and showing me into a small ante-chamber he left me. A minute later he returned to say that the Prince could not be disturbed at present, but that the Princess would take my message.

The Princess! What use was there in giving it to her? Had I not been warned that she was German in heart and soul, and that it was she who was turning her husband and her State against us?

'It is the Prince that I must see,' said I.

'Nay, it is the Princess,' said a voice at the door, and a woman swept into the chamber. 'Von Rosen, you had best stay with us. Now, sir, what is it that you have to say to either Prince or Princess of Saxe-Felstein?'

At the first sound of the voice I had sprung to my feet. At the first glance I had thrilled with anger. Not twice in a lifetime does one meet that noble figure, that queenly head, and those eyes as blue as the Garonne, and as chilling as her winter waters.

'Time presses, sir!' she cried, with an impatient tap of her foot. 'What have you to say to me?'

'What have I to say to you?' I cried. 'What can I say, save that you have taught me never to trust a woman more? You have ruined and dishonoured me for ever.'

She looked with arched brows at her attendant.

'Is this the raving of fever, or does it come from some less innocent cause?' said she. 'Perhaps a little blood-letting——'

'Ah, you can act!' I cried. 'You have shown me that already.'

'Do you mean that we have met before?'

'I mean that you have robbed me within the last two hours.'

'This is past all bearing,' she cried, with an admirable affectation of anger. 'You claim, as I understand, to be an ambassador, but there are limits to the privileges which such an office brings with it.'

'You brazen it admirably,' said I. 'Your Highness will not make a fool of me twice in one night.' I sprang forward and, stooping down, caught up the hem of her dress. 'You would have done well to change it after you had ridden so far and so fast,' said I.

It was like the dawn upon a snow-peak to see her ivory cheeks flush suddenly to crimson.

'Insolent!' she cried. 'Call the foresters and have him thrust from the palace!'

'I will see the Prince first.'

'You will never see the Prince. Ah! Hold him, Von Rosen, hold him!'

She had forgotten the man with whom she had to deal —was it likely that I would wait until they could bring their rascals? She had shown me her cards too soon. Her game was to stand between me and her husband. Mine was to speak face to face with him at any cost. One spring took me out of the chamber. In another I had crossed the hall. An instant later I had burst into the great room from which the murmur of the meeting had come. At the far end I saw a figure upon a high chair under a daïs. Beneath him was a line of high dignitaries, and then on every side I saw vaguely the heads of a vast assembly. Into the centre of the room I strode, my sabre clanking, my shako under my arm.

'I am the messenger of the Emperor,' I shouted. 'I bear his message to His Highness the Prince of Saxe-Felstein.'

The man beneath the daïs raised his head, and I saw that his face was thin and wan, and that his back was bowed as though some huge burden was balanced between his shoulders.

'Your name, sir?' he asked.

'Colonel Etienne Gerard, of the 3rd Hussars.'

Every face in the gathering was turned upon me, and I heard the rustle of the innumerable necks and saw count-less eyes without meeting one friendly one amongst them. The woman had swept past me, and was whispering, with many shakes of her head and dartings of her hands, into the Prince's ear. For my own part I threw out my chest and curled my moustache, glancing round in my own debonair fashion at the assembly. They were men, all of them, professors from the college, a sprinkling of their students, soldiers, gentlemen, artisans, all very silent and serious. In one corner there sat a group of men in black, with riding-coats drawn over their shoulders. They leaned their heads to each other, whispering under their breath, and with every movement I caught the clank of their sabres or the clink of their spurs.

'The Emperor's private letter to me informs me that it is the Marquis Château St. Arnaud who is bearing his despatches,' said the Prince.

'The Marquis has been foully murdered,' I answered, and a buzz rose up from the people as I spoke. Many heads were turned, I noticed, towards the dark men in the cloaks.

'Where are your papers?' asked the Prince.

'I have none.'

A fierce clamour rose instantly around me. 'He is a spy! He plays a part!' they cried. 'Hang him!' roared a deep voice from the corner, and a dozen others took up the shout. For my part, I drew out my handkerchief and flicked the dust from the fur of my pelisse. The Prince held out his thin hands, and the tumult died away.

'Where, then, are your credentials, and what is your message?'

'My uniform is my credential, and my message is for your private ear.'

He passed his hand over his forehead with the gesture of a weak man who is at his wits' end what to do. The

Princess stood beside him with her hand upon his throne, and again whispered in his ear.

'We are here in council together, some of my trusty subjects and myself,' said he. 'I have no secrets from them, and whatever message the Emperor may send to me at such a time concerns their interests no less than mine.'

There was a hum of applause at this, and every eye was turned once more upon me. My faith, it was an awkward position in which I found myself, for it is one thing to address eight hundred hussars, and another to speak to such an audience on such a subject. But I fixed my eyes upon the Prince, and tried to say just what I should have said if we had been alone, shouting it out, too, as though I had my regiment on parade.

'You have often expressed friendship for the Emperor,' I cried. 'It is now at last that this friendship is about to be tried. If you will stand firm, he will reward you as only he can reward. It is an easy thing for him to turn a Prince into a King and a province into a power. His eyes are fixed upon you, and though you can do little to harm him, you can ruin yourself. At this moment he is crossing the Rhine with two hundred thousand men. Every fortress in the country is in his hands. He will be upon you in a week, and if you have played him false, God help both you and your people. You think that he is weakened because a few of us got the chilblains last winter. Look there!' I cried, pointing to a great star which blazed through the window above the Prince's head. 'That is the Emperor's star. When it wanes, he will wane—but not before.'

You would have been proud of me, my friends, if you could have seen and heard me, for I clashed my sabre as I spoke, and swung my dolman as though my regiment was picketed outside in the courtyard. They listened to me in silence, but the back of the Prince bowed more and more as though the burden which weighed upon it was greater than his strength. He looked round with haggard eyes.

'We have heard a Frenchman speak for France,' said he. 'Let us have a German speak for Germany.'

The folk glanced at each other, and whispered to their neighbours. My speech, as I think, had its effect, and no man wished to be the first to commit himself in the eyes of the Emperor. The Princess looked round her with blazing eyes, and her clear voice broke the silence.

'Is a woman to give this Frenchman his answer?' she cried. 'Is it possible, then, that among the night-riders of Lutzow there is none who can use his tongue as well as his sabre?'

Over went a table with a crash, and a young man had bounded upon one of the chairs. He had the face of one inspired—pale, eager, with wild hawk eyes, and tangled hair. His sword hung straight from his side, and his riding-boots were brown with mire.

'It is Korner!' the people cried. 'It is young Korner, the poet! Ah, he will sing, he will sing.'

And he sang! It was soft, at first, and dreamy, telling of old Germany, the mother of nations, of the rich, warm plains, and the grey cities, and the fame of dead heroes. But then verse after verse rang like a trumpet-call. It was of the Germany of now, the Germany which had been taken unawares and overthrown, but which was up again, and snapping the bonds upon her giant limbs. What was life that one should covet it? What was glorious death that one should shun it? The mother, the great mother, was calling. Her sigh was in the night wind. She was crying to her own children for help. Would they come? Would they come? Would they come?

Ah, that terrible song, the spirit face and the ringing voice! Where were I, and France, and the Emperor? They did not shout, these people—they howled. They were up on the chairs and the tables. They were raving, sobbing, the tears running down their faces. Korner had sprung from the chair, and his comrades were round him with their sabres in the air. A flush had come into the pale face of the Prince, and he rose from his throne.

Colonel Gerard,' said he, 'you have heard the answer

314

which you are to carry to your Emperor. The die is cast, my children. Your Prince and you must stand or fall together.'

He bowed to show that all was over, and the people with a shout made for the door to carry the tidings into the town. For my own part, I had done all that a brave man might, and so I was not sorry to be carried out amid the stream. Why should I linger in the palace? I had had my answer and must carry it, such as it was. I wished neither to see Hof nor its people again until I entered it at the head of a vanguard. I turned from the throng, then, and walked silently and sadly in the direction in which they had led the mare.

It was dark down there by the stables, and I was peering round for the hostler, when suddenly my two arms were seized from behind. There were hands at my wrists and at my throat, and I felt the cold muzzle of a pistol under my ear.

'Keep your lips closed, you French dog,' whispered a fierce voice. 'We have him, captain.'

'Have you the bridle?'

'Here it is.'

'Sling it over his head.'

I felt the cold coil of leather tighten round my neck. An hostler with a stable lantern had come out and was gazing upon the scene. In its dim light I saw stern faces breaking everywhere through the gloom, with the black caps and dark cloaks of the night-riders.

'What would you do with him, captain?' cried a voice.

'Hang him at the palace gate.'

'An ambassador?'

'An ambassador without papers.'

'But the Prince?'

'Tut, man, do you not see that the Prince will then be committed to our side? He will be beyond all hope of forgiveness. At present he may swing round to-morrow as he has done before. He may eat his words, but a dead hussar is more than he can explain.'

'No, no, Von Strelitz, we cannot do it,' said another voice.

'Can we not? I shall show you that!' and there came a jerk on the bridle which nearly pulled me to the ground. At the same instant a sword flashed and the leather was cut through within two inches of my neck.

'By Heaven, Korner, this is rank mutiny,' cried the captain. 'You may hang yourself before you are through with it.'

'I have drawn my sword as a soldier and not as a brigand,' said the young poet. 'Blood may dim its blade, but never dishonour. Comrades, will you stand by and see this gentleman mishandled?'

A dozen sabres flew from their sheaths, and it was evident that my friends and my foes were about equally balanced. But the angry voices and the gleam of steel had brought the folk running from all parts.

'The Princess!' they cried. 'The Princess is coming!'

And even as they spoke I saw her in front of us, her sweet face framed in the darkness. I had cause to hate her, for she had cheated and befooled me, and yet it thrilled me then and thrills me now to think that my arms have embraced her, and that I have felt the scent of her hair in my nostrils. I know not whether she lies under her German earth, or whether she still lingers, a grey-haired woman in her Castle of Hof, but she lives ever, young and lovely, in the heart and memory of Etienne Gerard.

'For shame!' she cried, sweeping up to me, and tearing with her own hands the noose from my neck. 'You are fighting in God's own quarrel, and yet you would begin with such a devil's deed as this. This man is mine, and he who touches a hair of his head will answer for it to me.'

They were glad enough to slink off into the darkness before those scornful eyes. Then she turned once more to me.

'You can follow me, Colonel Gerard,' she said. 'I have a word that I would speak to you.'

I walked behind her to the chamber into which I had originally been shown. She closed the door, and then looked at me with the archest twinkle in her eyes.

'Is it not confiding of me to trust myself with you?' said she. 'You will remember that it is the Princess of Saxe-Felstein and not the poor Countess Palotta of Poland.'

'Be the name what it might,' I answered, 'I helped a lady whom I believed to be in distress, and I have been robbed of my papers and almost of my honour as a reward.'

'Colonel Gerard,' said she, 'we have been playing a game, you and I, and the stake was a heavy one. You have shown by delivering a message which was never given to you that you would stand at nothing in the cause of your country. My heart is German and yours is French, and I also would go all lengths, even to deceit and to theft, if at this crisis I could help my suffering fatherland. You see how frank I am.'

'You tell me nothing that I have not seen.'

'But now that the game is played and won, why should we bear malice? I will say this, that if ever I were in such a plight as that which I pretended in the inn of Loben-stein, I should never wish to meet a more gallant protec-tor or a truer-hearted gentleman than Colonel Etienne Gerard. I had never thought that I could feel for a Frenchman as I felt for you when I slipped the papers from your breast.'

'But you took them, none the less.'

'They were necessary to me and to Germany. I knew the arguments which they contained and the effect which they would have upon the Prince. If they had reached him all would have been lost.'

'Why should your Highness descend to such expedients when a score of these brigands, who wished to hang me at your castle gate, would have done the work as well?'

'They are not brigands, but the best blood of Ger-many,' she cried, hotly. 'If you have been roughly used, you will remember the indignities to which every German

317

has been subjected, from the Queen of Prussia downwards. As to why I did not have you waylaid upon the road, I may say that I had parties out on all sides, and that I was waiting at Lobenstein to hear of their success. When instead of their news you yourself arrived I was in despair, for there was only the one weak woman betwixt you and my husband. You see the straits to which I was driven before I used the weapon of my sex.'

'I confess that you have conquered me, your Highness, and it only remains for me to leave you in possession of the field.'

'But you will take your papers with you.' She held them out to me as she spoke. 'The Prince has crossed the Rubicon now, and nothing can bring him back. You can return these to the Emperor, and tell him that we refused to receive them. No one can accuse you then of having lost your despatches. Good-bye, Colonel Gerard, and the best I can wish you is that when you reach France you may remain there. In a year's time there will be no place for a Frenchman upon this side of the Rhine.'

And thus it was that I played the Princess of Saxe-Felstein with all Germany for a stake, and lost my game to her. I had much to think of as I walked my poor, tired Violette along the highway which leads westward from Hof. But amid all the thoughts there came back to me always the proud, beautiful face of the German woman, and the voice of the soldier-poet as he sang from the chair. And I understood then that there was something terrible in this strong, patient Germany—this mother root of nations—and I saw that such a land, so old and so beloved, never could be conquered. And as I rode I saw that the dawn was breaking, and that the great star at which I had pointed through the palace window was dim and pale in the western sky.

VII. How the Brigadier Won his Medal

THE Duke of Tarentum, or Macdonald, as his old comrades prefer to call him, was, as I could perceive, in the vilest of tempers. His grim, Scotch face was like one of those grotesque door-knockers which one sees in the Faubourg St. Germain. We heard afterwards that the Emperor had said in jest that he would have sent him against Wellington in the South, but that he was afraid to trust him within the sound of the pipes. Major Charpentier and I could plainly see that he was smouldering with anger.

'Brigadier Gerard of the Hussars,' said he, with the air of the corporal with the recruit.

I saluted.

'Major Charpentier of the Horse Grenadiers.'

My companion answered to his name.

'The Emperor has a mission for you.'

Without more ado he flung open the door and announced us.

I have seen Napoleon ten times on horseback to one on foot, and I think that he does wisely to show himself to the troops in this fashion, for he cuts a very good figure in the saddle. As we saw him now he was the shortest man out of six by a good hand's breadth, and yet I am no very big man myself, though I ride quite heavy enough for a hussar. It is evident, too, that his body is too long for his legs. With his big, round head, his curved shoulders, and his clean-shaven face, he is more like a Professor at the Sorbonne than the first soldier in France. Every man to his taste, but it seems to me that, if I could clap a pair of fine light cavalry whiskers, like my own, on to him, it would do him no harm. He has a firm mouth, however, and his eyes are remarkable. I have seen them once turned on me in anger, and I had rather ride at a square on a spent horse than face them again. I am not a man who is easily daunted, either.

He was standing at the side of the room, away from the window, looking up at a great map of the country which was hung upon the wall. Berthier stood beside him, trying to look wise, and just as we entered, Napoleon snatched his sword impatiently from him and pointed with it on the map. He was talking fast and low, but I heard him say, 'The valley of the Meuse,' and twice he repeated 'Berlin'. As we entered, his aide-de-camp advanced to us, but the Emperor stopped him and beckoned us to his side.

'You have not yet received the cross of honour, Brigadier Gerard?' he asked.

I replied that I had not, and was about to add that it was not for want of having deserved it, when he cut me short in his decided fashion.

'And you, Major?' he asked.

'No, sire.'

'Then you shall both have your opportunity now.'

He led us to the great map upon the wall and placed the tip of Berthier's sword on Rheims.

'I will be frank with you, gentlemen, as with two comrades. You have both been with me since Marengo, I believe?' He had a strangely pleasant smile, which used to light up his pale face with a kind of cold sunshine. 'Here at Rheims are our present head-quarters on this the 14th of March. Very good. Here is Paris, distant by road a good twenty-five leagues. Blucher lies to the north, Schwarzenburg to the south.' He prodded at the map with the sword as he spoke.

'Now,' said he, 'the further into the country these people march, the more completely I shall crush them. They are about to advance upon Paris. Very good. Let them do so. My brother, the King of Spain, will be there with a hundred thousand men. It is to him that I send you. You will hand him this letter, a copy of which I confide to each of you. It is to tell him that I am coming at once, in two days' time, with every man and horse and gun to his relief. I must give them forty-eight hours to recover. Then straight to Paris! You understand me, gentlemen?'

Ah, if I could tell you the glow of pride which it gave me to be taken into the great man's confidence in this way. As he handed our letters to us I clicked my spurs and threw out my chest, smiling and nodding to let him know that I saw what he would be after. He smiled also, and rested his hand for a moment upon the cape of my dolman. I would have given half my arrears of pay if my mother could have seen me at that instant.

'I will show you your route,' said he, turning back to the map. 'Your orders are to ride together as far as Bazoches. You will then separate, the one making for Paris by Oulchy and Neuilly, and the other to the north by Braine, Soissons, and Senlis. Have you anything to say, Brigadier Gerard?'

I am a rough soldier, but I have words and ideas. I had begun to speak about glory and the peril of France when he cut me short.

'And you, Major Charpentier?'

'If we find our route unsafe, are we at liberty to choose another?' said he.

'Soldiers do not choose, they obey.' He inclined his head to show that we were dismissed, and turned round to Berthier. I do not know what he said, but I heard them both laughing.

Well, as you may think, we lost little time in getting upon our way. In half an hour we were riding down the High Street of Rheims, and it struck twelve o'clock as we passed the Cathedral. I had my little grey mare, Violette, the one which Sebastiani had wished to buy after Dresden. It is the fastest horse in the six brigades of light cavalry, and was only beaten by the Duke of Rovigo's racer from England. As to Charpentier, he had the kind of horse which a horse grenadier or a cuirassier would be likely to ride: a back like a bedstead, you understand, and legs like the posts. He is a hulking fellow himself, so that they they looked a singular pair. And yet in his insane conceit he ogled the girls as they waved their hand-kerchiefs to me from the windows, and he twirled his ugly red moustache up into his eyes, just as if it were to him that their attention was addressed.

When we came out of the town we passed through the French camp, and then across the battle-field of yester-day, which was still covered both by our own poor fellows and by the Russians. But of the two the camp was the sadder sight. Our army was thawing away. The Guards were all right, though the young guard was full of con-scripts. The artillery and the heavy cavalry were also good if there were more of them, but the infantry privates with their under officers looked like schoolboys with their masters. And we had no reserves. When one considered that there were 80,000 Prussians to the north and 150,000 Russians and Austrians to the south, it might make even the bravest man grave.

For my own part, I confess that I shed a tear until the thought came that the Emperor was still with us, and that on that very morning he had placed his hand upon my dolman and had promised me a medal of honour. This set me singing, and I spurred Violette on, until Charpentier had to beg me to have mercy on his great, snorting, panting camel. The road was beaten into paste and rutted two feet deep by the artillery, so that he was right in saying that it was not the place for a gallop.

I have never been very friendly with this Charpentier; and now for twenty miles of the way I could not draw a word from him. He rode with his brows puckered and his chin upon his breast, like a man who is heavy with thought. More than once I asked him what was on his mind, thinking that, perhaps, with my quicker intelli-gence I might set the matter straight. His answer always was that it was his mission of which he was thinking, which surprised me, because, although I had never thought much of his intelligence, still it seemed to me to be impossible that anyone could be puzzled by so simple and soldierly a task.

Well, we came at last to Bazoches, where he was to take the southern road and I the northern. He half turned in his saddle before he left me, and he looked at me with a singular expression of inquiry in his face.

'What do you make of it, Brigadier?' he asked.

'Of what?'

'Of our mission.'

'Surely it is plain enough.'

'You think so? Why should the Emperor tell us his plans?'

'Because he recognised our intelligence.'

My companion laughed in a manner which I found annoying.

'May I ask what you intend to do if you find these villages full of Prussians?' he asked.

'I shall obey my orders.'

'But you will be killed.'

'Very possibly.'

He laughed again, and so offensively that I clapped my hand to my sword. But before I could tell him what I thought of his stupidity and rudeness he had wheeled his horse, and was lumbering away down the other road. I saw his big fur cap vanish over the brow of the hill, and then I rode upon my way, wondering at his conduct. From time to time I put my hand to the breast of my tunic, and felt the paper crackle beneath my fingers. Ah, my precious paper, which should be turned into the little silver medal for which I had yearned so long. All the way from Braine to Sermoise I was thinking of what my mother would say when she saw it.

I stopped to give Violette a meal at a wayside auberge on the side of a hill not far from Soissons—a place surrounded by old oaks, and with so many crows that one could scarce hear one's own voice. It was from the inn-keeper that I learned that Marmont had fallen back two days before, and that the Prussians were over the Aisne. An hour later, in the fading light, I saw two of their vedettes upon the hill to the right, and then, as darkness gathered, the heavens to the north were all glimmering from the lights of a bivouac.

When I heard that Blucher had been there for two days, I was much surprised that the Emperor should not have known that the country through which he had ordered me to carry my precious letter was already occupied by the enemy. Still, I thought of the tone of his voice when he said to Charpentier that a soldier must not choose, but must obey. I should follow the route he had laid down for me as long as Violette could move a hoof or I a finger upon her bridle. All the way from Sermoise to Soissons, where the road dips up and down, curving among fir woods, I kept my pistol ready and my sword-belt braced, pushing on swiftly where the path was straight, and then coming slowly round the corners in the way we learned in Spain.

When I came to the farmhouse which lies to the right of the road just after you cross the wooden bridge over the Crise, near where the great statue of the Virgin stands, a woman cried to me from the field, saying that the Prussians were in Soissons. A small party of their lancers, she said, had come in that very afternoon, and a whole division was expected before midnight. I did not wait to hear the end of her tale, but clapped spurs into Violette, and in five minutes was galloping her into the town.

Three Uhlans were at the mouth of the main street, their horses tethered, and they gossiping together, each with a pipe as long as my sabre. I saw them well in the light of an open door, but of me they could have seen only the flash of Violette's grey side and the black flutter of my cloak. A moment later I flew through a stream of them rushing from an open gateway. Violette's shoulder sent one of them reeling, and I stabbed at another but missed him. Pang, pang, went two carbines, but I had flown round the curve of the street, and never so much as heard the hiss of the balls. Ah, we were great, both Violette and I. She lay down to it like a coursed hare, the fire flying from her hoofs. I stood in my stirrups and brandished my sword. Someone sprang for my bridle. I sliced him through the arm, and I heard him howling behind me. Two horsemen closed upon me. I cut one down and outpaced the other. A minute later I was clear of the town, and flying down a broad white road with the black poplars on either side. For a time I heard the rattle of hoofs behind me, but they died and died until I could not tell them from the throbbing of my own heart. Soon I pulled up and listened, but all was silent. They had given up the chase.

Well, the first thing that I did was to dismount and to lead my mare into a small wood through which a stream ran. There I watered her and rubbed her down, giving her two pieces of sugar soaked in cognac from my flask. She was spent from the sharp chase, but it was wonderful to see how she came round with a half-hour's rest. When my thighs closed upon her again, I could tell by the spring and the swing of her that it would not be her fault if I did not win my way safe to Paris.

I must have been well within the enemy's lines now, for I heard a number of them shouting one of their rough drinking songs out of a house by the roadside, and I went round by the fields to avoid it. At another time two men came out into the moonlight (for by this time it was a cloudless night) and shouted something in German, but I galloped on without heeding them, and they were afraid to fire, for their own hussars are dressed exactly as I was. It is best to take no notice at these times, and then they put you down as a deaf man.

It was a lovely moon, and every tree threw a black bar across the road. I could see the country-side just as if it were daytime, and very peaceful it looked, save that there was a great fire raging somewhere in the north. In the silence of the night-time, and with the knowledge that danger was in front and behind me, the sight of that great distant fire was very striking and awesome. But I am not easily clouded, for I have seen too many singular things, so I hummed a tune between my teeth and thought of little Lisette, whom I might see in Paris. My mind was full of her when, trotting round a corner, I came straight upon half-a-dozen German dragoons, who were sitting round a brushwood fire by the roadside.

I am an excellent soldier. I do not say this because I am prejudiced in my own favour, but because I really am so. I can weigh every chance in a moment, and decide with as much certainty as though I had brooded for a week. Now I saw like a flash that, come what might, I should be chased, and on a horse which had already done a long twelve leagues. But it was better to be chased onwards than to be chased back. On this moonlit night, with fresh horses behind me, I must take my risk in either case; but if I were to shake them off, I preferred that it should be near Senlis than near Soissons.

All this flashed on me as if by instinct, you understand. My eyes had hardly rested on the bearded faces under the brass helmets before my rowels had touched Violette, and she off with a rattle like a *pas-de-charge*. Oh, the shouting and rushing and stamping from behind us! Three of them fired and three swung themselves on to their horses. A bullet rapped on the crupper of my saddle with a noise like a stick on a door. Violette sprang madly forward, and I thought she had been wounded, but it was only a graze above the near fore-fetlock. Ah, the dear little mare, how I loved her when I felt her settle down into that long, easy gallop of hers, her hoofs going like a Spanish girl's castanets. I could not hold myself. I turned on my saddle and shouted and raved, 'Vive l'Empereur!' I screamed and laughed at the gust of oaths that came back to me.

But it was not over yet. If she had been fresh she might have gained a mile in five. Now she could only hold her own with a very little over. There was one of them, a young boy of an officer, who was better mounted than the others. He drew ahead with every stride. Two hundred yards behind him were two troopers, but I saw every time that I glanced round that the distance between them was increasing. The other three who had waited to shoot were a long way in the rear.

The officer's mount was a bay—a fine horse, though not to be spoken of with Violette; yet it was a powerful brute, and it seemed to me that in a few miles its freshness might tell. I waited until the lad was a long way in front of his comrades, and then I eased my mare down a little —a very, very little, so that he might think he was really catching me. When he came within pistol-shot of me I drew and cocked my own pistol, and laid my chin upon my shoulder to see what he would do. He did not offer to fire, and I soon discerned the cause. The silly boy had taken his pistols from his holsters when he had camped for the night. He wagged his sword at me now and roared some threat or other. He did not seem to understand that he was at my mercy. I eased Violette down until there was not the length of a long lance between the grey tail and the bay muzzle.

'*Rendez-vous!*' he yelled.

'I must compliment monsieur upon his French,' said I, resting the barrel of my pistol upon my bridle-arm, which I have always found best when shooting from the saddle. I aimed at his face, and could see, even in the moonlight, how white he grew when he understood that it was all up with him. But even as my finger pressed the trigger I thought of his mother, and I put my ball through his horse's shoulder. I fear he hurt himself in the fall, for it was a fearful crash, but I had my letter to think of, so I stretched the mare into a gallop once more.

But they were not so easily shaken off, these brigands. The two troopers thought no more of their young officer than if he had been a recruit thrown in the riding-school. They left him to the others and thundered on after me. I had pulled up on the brow of a hill, thinking that I had heard the last of them; but, my faith, I soon saw there was no time for loitering, so away we went, the mare tossing her head and I my shako, to show what we

327

thought of two dragoons who tried to catch a hussar. But at this moment, even while I laughed at the thought, my heart stood still within me, for there at the end of the long white road was a black patch of cavalry waiting to receive me. To a young soldier it might have seemed the shadow of the trees, but to me it was a troop of hussars, and, turn where I could, death seemed to be waiting for me.

Well, I had the dragoons behind me, and the hussars in front. Never since Moscow have I seemed to be in such peril. But for the honour of the brigade I had rather be cut down by a light cavalryman than by a heavy. I never drew bridle, therefore, or hesitated for an instant, but I let Violette have her head. I remembered that I tried to pray as I rode, but I am a little out of practice at such things, and the only words I could remember were the prayer for fine weather which we used at the school on the evening before holidays. Even this seemed better than nothing, and I was pattering it out, when suddenly I heard French voices in front of me. Ah, *mon Dieu*, but the joy went through my heart like a musket-ball. They were ours—our own dear little rascals from the corps of Marmont. Round whisked my two dragoons and galloped for their lives, with the moon gleaming on their brass helmets, while I trotted up to my friends with no undue haste, for I would have them understand that though a hussar may fly, it is not in his nature to fly very fast. Yet I fear that Violette's heaving flanks and foam-spattered muzzle gave the lie to my careless bearing.

Who should be at the head of the troop but old Bouvet, whom I saved at Leipzig! When he saw me his little pink eyes filled with tears, and, indeed, I could not but shed a few myself at the sight of his joy. I told him of my mission, but he laughed when I said that I must pass through Senlis.

'The enemy is there,' said he. 'You cannot go.'

'I prefer to go where the enemy is,' I answered.

'But why not go straight to Paris with your despatch?

Why should you choose to pass through the one place where you are almost sure to be taken or killed?'

'A soldier does not choose—he obeys,' said I, just as I had heard Napoleon say it.

Old Bouvet laughed in his wheezy way, until I had to give my moustachios a twirl and look him up and down in a manner which brought him to reason.

'Well,' said he, 'you had best come along with us, for we are all bound for Senlis. Our orders are to reconnoitre the place. A squadron of Poniatowski's Polish Lancers are in front of us. If you must ride through it, it is possible that we may be able to go with you.'

So away we went, jingling and clanking through the quiet night until we came up with the Poles—fine old soldiers all of them, though a trifle heavy for their horses. It was a treat to see them, for they could not have carried themselves better if they had belonged to my own brigade. We rode together, until in the early morning we saw the lights of Senlis. A peasant was coming along with a cart, and from him we learned how things were going there.

His information was certain, for his brother was the Mayor's coachman, and he had spoken with him late the night before. There was a single squadron of Cossacks— or a polk, as they call it in their frightful language— quartered upon the Mayor's house, which stands at the corner of the market-place, and is the largest building in the town. A whole division of Prussian infantry was en- camped in the woods to the north, but only the Cossacks were in Senlis. Ah, what a chance to avenge ourselves upon these barbarians, whose cruelty to our poor country- folk was the talk at every camp fire.

We were into the town like a torrent, hacked down the vedettes, rode over the guard, and were smashing in the doors of the Mayor's house before they understood that there was a Frenchman within twenty miles of them. We saw horrid heads at the windows—heads bearded to the temples, with tangled hair and sheepskin caps, and silly, gaping mouths. 'Hourra! Hourra!' they shrieked, and fired with their carbines, but our fellows were into the house and at their throats before they had wiped the sleep out of their eyes. It was dreadful to see how the Poles flung themselves upon them, like starving wolves upon a herd of fat bucks—for, as you know, the Poles have a blood feud against the Cossacks. The most were killed in the upper rooms, whither they had fled for shelter, and the blood was pouring down into the hall like rain from a roof. They are terrible soldiers, these Poles, though I think they are a trifle heavy for their horses. Man for man, they are as big as Kellermann's cuirassiers. Their equipment is, of course, much lighter, since they are without the cuirass, back-plate, and helmet.

Well, it was at this point that I made an error—a very serious error it must be admitted. Up to this moment I had carried out my mission in a manner which only my modesty prevents me from describing as remarkable. But now I did that which an official would condemn and a soldier excuse.

There is no doubt that the mare was spent, but still it is true that I might have galloped on through Senlis and reached the country, where I should have had no enemy between me and Paris. But what hussar can ride past a fight and never draw rein? It is to ask too much of him. Besides, I thought that if Violette had an hour of rest I might have three hours the better at the other end. Then on top of it came those heads at the windows, with their sheepskin hats and their barbarous cries. I sprang from my saddle, threw Violette's bridle over a rail-post, and ran into the house with the rest. It is true that I was too late to be of service, and that I was nearly wounded by a lance-thrust from one of these dying savages. Still, it is a pity to miss even the smallest affair, for one never knows what opportunity for advancement may present itself. I have seen more soldierly work in outpost skirmishes and little gallop-and-hack affairs of the kind than in any of the Emperor's big battles.

When the house was cleared I took a bucket of water out for Violette, and our peasant guide showed me where the good Mayor kept his fodder. My faith, but the little sweetheart was ready for it. Then I sponged down her legs, and leaving her still tethered I went back into the house to find a mouthful for myself, so that I should not need to halt again until I was in Paris.

And now I come to the part of my story which may seem singular to you, although I could tell you at least ten things every bit as queer which have happened to me in my lifetime. You can understand that, to a man who spends his life in scouting and vedette duties on the bloody ground which lies between two great armies, there are many chances of strange experiences. I'll tell you, however, exactly what occurred.

Old Bouvet was waiting in the passage when I entered, and he asked me whether we might not crack a bottle of wine together. 'My faith, we must not be long,' said he. 'There are ten thousand of Theilmann's Prussians in the woods up yonder.'

'Where is the wine?' I asked.

'Ah, you may trust two hussars to find where the wine is,' said he, and taking a candle in his hand, he led the way down the stone stairs into the kitchen.

When we got there we found another door, which opened on to a winding stair with the cellar at the bottom. The Cossacks had been there before us, as was easily seen by the broken bottles littered all over it. However, the Mayor was a *bon-vivant*, and I do not wish to have a better set of bins to pick from. Chambertin, Graves, Alicant, white wine and red, sparkling and still, they lay in pyramids peeping coyly out of sawdust. Old Bouvet stood with his candle looking here and peeping there, purring in his throat like a cat before a milk-pail. He had picked upon a Burgundy at last, and had his hand outstretched to the bottle when there came a roar of musketry from above us, a rush of feet, and such a yelping and screaming as I have never listened to. The Prussians were upon us!

Bouvet is a brave man: I will say that for him. He flashed out his sword and away he clattered up the stone steps, his spurs clinking as he ran. I followed him, but just as we came out into the kitchen passage a tremendous shout told us that the house had been recaptured.

'It is all over,' I cried, grasping at Bouvet's sleeve.

'There is one more to die,' he shouted, and away he went like a madman up the second stair. In effect, I should have gone to my death also had I been in his place, for he had done very wrong in not throwing out his scouts to warn him if the Germans advanced upon him. For an instant I was about to rush up with him, and then I bethought myself that, after all, I had my own mission to think of, and that if I were taken the important letter of the Emperor would be sacrificed. I let Bouvet die alone, therefore, and I went down into the cellar again, closing the door behind me.

Well, it was not a very rosy prospect down there either. Bouvet had dropped the candle when the alarm came, and I, pawing about in the darkness, could find nothing but broken bottles. At last I came upon the candle, which had rolled under the curve of a cask, but, try as I would with my tinder-box, I could not light it. The reason was that the wick had been wet in a puddle of wine, so suspecting that this might be the case, I cut the end off with my sword. Then I found that it lighted easily enough. But what to do I could not imagine. The scoundrels upstairs were shouting themselves hoarse, several hundred of them from the sound, and it was clear that some of them would soon want to moisten their throats. There would be an end to a dashing soldier, and of the mission and of the medal. I thought of my mother and I thought of the Emperor. It made me weep to think that the one would lose so excellent a son and the other the best light cavalry officer he ever had since Lasalle's time. But presently I dashed the tears from my eyes. 'Courage!' I cried, striking myself upon the chest. 'Courage, my brave boy! Is it possible that one who has come safely from Moscow without so much as a frost-bite will die in a French wine-cellar?' At the thought I was up on my feet and clutching at the letter in my tunic, for the crackle of it gave me courage.

My first plan was to set fire to the house, in the hope of escaping in the confusion. My second to get into an empty wine-cask. I was looking round to see if I could find one, when suddenly, in the corner, I espied a little low door, painted of the same grey colour as the wall, so that it was only a man with quick sight who would have noticed it. I pushed against it, and at first I imagined that it was locked. Presently, however, it gave a little, and then I understood that it was held by the pressure of something on the other side. I put my feet against a hogshead of wine, and I gave such a push that the door flew open and I came down with a crash upon my back, the candle flying out of my hands, so that I found myself in darkness once more. I picked myself up and stared through the black archway into the gloom beyond.

There was a slight ray of light coming from some slit or grating. The dawn had broken outside, and I could dimly see the long, curving sides of several huge casks, which made me think that perhaps this was where the Mayor kept his reserves of wine while they were maturing. At any rate, it seemed to be a safer hiding-place than the outer cellar, so gathering up my candle, I was just closing the door behind me, when I suddenly saw something which filled me with amazement, and even, I confess, with the smallest little touch of fear.

I have said that at the further end of the cellar there was a dim grey fan of light striking downwards from somewhere near the roof. Well, as I peered through the darkness, I suddenly saw a great, tall man skip into this belt of daylight, and then out again into the darkness at the further end. My word, I gave such a start that my shako nearly broke its chin-strap! It was only a glance, but, none the less, I had time to see that the fellow had a hairy Cossack cap on his head, and that he was a great, long-legged, broad-shouldered brigand, with a sabre at his waist. My faith, even Etienne Gerard was a little staggered at being left alone with such a creature in the dark.

But only for a moment. 'Courage!' I thought. 'Am I not a hussar, a brigadier, too, at the age of thirty-one, and the chosen messenger of the Emperor?' After all, this skulker had more cause to be afraid of me than I of him. And then suddenly I understood that he was afraid— horribly afraid. I could read it from his quick step and his bent shoulders as he ran among the barrels, like a rat making for its hole. And, of course, it must have been he who had held the door against me, and not some packing-case or wine-cask as I had imagined. He was the pursued then, and I the pursuer. Aha, I felt my whiskers bristle as I advanced upon him through the darkness! He would find that he had no chicken to deal with, this robber from the North. For the moment I was magnificent.

At first I had feared to light my candle lest I should make a mark of myself, but now, after cracking my shin over a box, and catching my spurs in some canvas, I thought the bolder course the wiser. I lit it, therefore, and then I advanced with long strides, my sword in my hand. 'Come out, you rascal!' I cried. 'Nothing can save you. You will at last meet with your deserts.'

I held my candle high, and presently I caught a glimpse of the man's head staring at me over a barrel. He had a gold chevron on his black cap, and the expression of his face told me in an instant that he was an officer and a man of refinement.

'Monsieur,' he cried, in excellent French, 'I surrender myself on a promise of quarter. But if I do not have your promise, I will then sell my life as dearly as I can.'

'Sir,' said I, 'a Frenchman knows how to treat an unfortunate enemy. Your life is safe.' With that he handed his sword over the top of the barrel, and I bowed with the candle on my heart. 'Whom have I the honour of capturing?' I asked.

'I am the Count Boutkine, of the Emperor's own Don Cossacks,' said he. 'I came out with my troop to reconnoitre Senlis, and as we found no sign of your people we determined to spend the night here.'

'And would it be an indiscretion,' I asked, 'if I were to inquire how you came into the back cellar?'

'Nothing more simple,' said he. 'It was our intention to start at early dawn. Feeling chilled after dressing, I thought that a cup of wine would do me no harm, so I came down to see what I could find. As I was rummaging about, the house was suddenly carried by assault so rapidly that by the time I had climbed the stairs it was all over. It only remained for me to save myself, so I came down here and hid myself in the back cellar, where you have found me.'

I thought of how old Bouvet had behaved under the same conditions, and the tears sprang to my eyes as I contemplated the glory of France. Then I had to consider what I should do next. It was clear that this Russian Count, being in the back cellar while we were in the front one, had not heard the sounds which would have told him that the house was once again in the hands of his own allies. If he should once understand this the tables would be turned, and I should be his prisoner instead of he being mine. What was I to do? I was at my wits' end, when suddenly there came to me an idea so brilliant that I could not but be amazed at my own invention.

'Count Boutkine,' said I, 'I find myself in a most difficult position.'

'And why?' he asked.

'Because I have promised you your life.'

His jaw dropped a little.

'You would not withdraw your promise?' he cried.

'If the worst comes to the worst I can die in your defence,' said I; 'but the difficulties are great.'

'What is it, then?' he asked.

'I will be frank with you,' said I. 'You must know that our fellows, and especially the Poles, are so incensed against the Cossacks that the mere sight of the uniform drives them mad. They precipitate themselves instantly upon the wearer and tear him limb from limb. Even their officers cannot restrain them.'

The Russian grew pale at my words and the way in which I said them.

'But this is terrible,' said he.

'Horrible!' said I. 'If we were to go up together at this moment I cannot promise how far I could protect you.'

'I am in your hands,' he cried. 'What would you suggest that we should do? Would it not be best that I should remain here?'

'That worst of all.'

'And why?'

'Because our fellows will ransack the house presently, and then you would be cut to pieces. No, no, I must go and break it to them. But even then, when once they see that accursed uniform, I do not know what may happen.'

'Should I then take the uniform off?'

'Excellent!' I cried. 'Hold, we have it! You will take your uniform off and put on mine. That will make you sacred to every French soldier.'

'It is not the French I fear so much as the Poles.'

'But my uniform will be a safeguard against either.'

'How can I thank you?' he cried. 'But you—what are you to wear?'

'I will wear yours.'

'And perhaps fall a victim to your generosity?'

'It is my duty to take the risk,' I answered; 'but I have no fears. I will ascend in your uniform. A hundred swords will be turned upon me. "Hold!" I will shout, "I am the Brigadier Gerard!" Then they will see my face.

They will know me. And I will tell them about you. Under the shield of these clothes you will be sacred.'

His fingers trembled with eagerness as he tore off his tunic. His boots and breeches were much like my own, so there was no need to change them, but I gave him my hussar jacket, my dolman, my shako, my sword-belt, and my sabre-tasche, while I took in exchange his high sheepskin cap with the gold chevron, his fur-trimmed coat, and his crooked sword. Be it well understood that in changing the tunics I did not forget to change my thrice-precious letter also from my old one to my new.

'With your leave,' said I, 'I shall now bind you to a barrel.'

He made a great fuss over this, but I have learned in my soldiering never to throw away chances, and how could I tell that he might not, when my back was turned, see how the matter really stood, and break in upon my plans? He was leaning against a barrel at the time, so I ran six times round it with a rope, and then tied it with a big knot behind. If he wished to come upstairs he would, at least, have to carry a thousand litres of good French wine for a knapsack. I then shut the door of the back cellar behind me, so that he might not hear what was going forward, and tossing the candle away I ascended the kitchen stair.

There were only about twenty steps, and yet, while I came up them, I seemed to have time to think of everything that I had ever hoped to do. It was the same feeling that I had at Eylau when I lay with my broken leg and saw the horse artillery galloping down upon me. Of course, I knew that if I were taken I should be shot instantly as being disguised within the enemy's lines. Still, it was a glorious death—in the direct service of the Emperor—and I reflected that there could not be less than five lines, and perhaps seven, in the *Moniteur* about me. Palaret had eight lines, and I am sure that he had not so fine a career.

When I made my way out into the hall, with all the

nonchalance in my face and manner that I could assume, the very first thing that I saw was Bouvet's dead body, with his legs drawn up and a broken sword in his hand. I could see by the black smudge that he had been shot at close quarters. I should have wished to salute as I went by, for he was a gallant man, but I feared lest I should be seen, and so I passed on.

The front of the hall was full of Prussian infantry, who were knocking loopholes in the wall, as though they expected that there might be yet another attack. Their officer, a little man, was running about giving directions. They were all too busy to take much notice of me, but another officer, who was standing by the door with a long pipe in his mouth, strode across and clapped me on the shoulder, pointing to the dead bodies of our poor hussars, and saying something which was meant for a jest, for his long beard opened and showed every fang in his head. I laughed heartily also, and said the only Russian words that I knew. I learned them from little Sophie, at Wilna, and they meant: 'If the night is fine we shall meet under the oak tree, but if it rains we shall meet in the byre.' It was all the same to this German, however, and I have no doubt that he gave me credit for saying something very witty indeed, for he roared laughing, and slapped me on my shoulder again. I nodded to him and marched out of the hall-door as coolly if I were the commandant of the garrison.

There were a hundred horses tethered about outside, most of them belonging to the Poles and hussars. Good little Violette was waiting with the others, and she whinnied when she saw me coming towards her. But I would not mount her. No. I was much too cunning for that. On the contrary, I chose the most shaggy little Cossack horse that I could see, and I sprang upon it with as much assurance as though it had belonged to my father before me. It had a great bag of plunder slung over its neck, and this I laid upon Violette's back, and led her along beside me. Never have you seen such a picture of the Cossack returning from the foray. It was superb.

Well, the town was full of Prussians by this time. They lined the side-walks and pointed me out to each other, saying, as I could judge from their gestures, 'There goes one of those devils of Cossacks. They are the boys for foraging and plunder.'

One or two officers spoke to me with an air of authority, but I shook my head and smiled, and said, 'If the night is fine we shall meet under the oak tree, but if it rains we shall meet in the byre,' at which they shrugged their shoulders and gave the matter up. In this way I worked along until I was beyond the northern outskirt of the town. I could see in the roadway two lancer vedettes with their black and white pennons, and I knew that when I was once past these I should be a free man once more. I made my pony trot, therefore, Violette rubbing her nose against my knee all the time, and looking up at me to ask how she had deserved that this hairy doormat of a creature should be preferred to her. I was not more than a hundred yards from the Uhlans when, suddenly, you can imagine my feelings when I saw a real Cossack coming galloping along the road towards me.

Ah, my friend, you who read this, if you have any heart, you will feel for a man like me, who had gone through so many dangers and trials, only at this very last moment to be confronted with one which appeared to put an end to everything. I will confess that for a moment I lost heart, and was inclined to throw myself down in my despair, and to cry out that I had been betrayed. But, no; I was not beaten even now. I opened two buttons of my tunic so that I might get easily at the Emperor's message, for it was my fixed determination when all hope was gone to swallow the letter and then die sword in hand. Then I felt that my little, crooked sword was loose in its sheath, and I trotted on to where the vedettes were waiting. They seemed inclined to stop me, but I pointed to the other Cossack, who was still a couple of hundred yards off, and they, understanding that I merely wished to meet him, let me pass with a salute.

I dug my spurs into my pony then, for if I were only far enough from the lancers I thought I might manage the Cossack without much difficulty. He was an officer, a large, bearded man, with a gold chevron in his cap, just the same as mine. As I advanced he unconsciously aided me by pulling up his horse, so that I had a fine start of the vedettes. On I came for him, and I could see wonder changing to suspicion in his brown eyes as he looked at me and at my pony, and at my equipment. I do not know what it was that was wrong, but he saw something which was as it should not be. He shouted out a question, and then when I gave no answer he pulled out his sword. I was glad in my heart to see him do so, for I had always rather fight than cut down an unsuspecting enemy. Now I made at him full tilt, and, parrying his cut, I got my point in just under the fourth button of his tunic. Down he went, and the weight of him nearly took me off my horse before I could disengage. I never glanced at him to see if he were living or dead, for I sprang off my pony and on to Violette, with a shake of my bridle and a kiss of my hand to the two Uhlans behind me. They galloped after me, shouting, but Violette had had her rest, and was just as fresh as when she started. I took the first side road to the west and then the first to the south, which would take me away from the enemy's country. On we went and on, every stride taking me further from my foes and nearer to my friends. At last, when I reached the end of a long stretch of road, and looking back from it could see no sign of any pursuers, I understood that my troubles were over.

And it gave me a glow of happiness, as I rode, to think that I had done to the letter what the Emperor had ordered. What would he say when he saw me? What could he say which would do justice to the incredible way in which I had risen above every danger? He had ordered me to go through Sermoise, Soissons, and Senlis, little dreaming that they were all three occupied by the enemy. And yet I had done it. I had borne his letter in safety through each of these towns. Hussars, dragoons, lancers, Cossacks, and infantry—I had run the gauntlet of all of them, and had come out unharmed.

When I had got as far as Dammartin I caught a first glimpse of our own outposts. There was a troop of dragoons in a field, and of course I could see from the horsehair crests that they were French. I galloped towards them in order to ask them if all was safe between there and Paris, and as I rode I felt such a pride at having won my way back to my friends again, that I could not refrain from waving my sword in the air.

At this a young officer galloped out from among the dragoons, also brandishing his sword, and it warmed my heart to think that he should come riding with such ardour and enthusiasm to greet me. I made Violette caracole, and as we came together I brandished my sword more gallantly than ever, but you can imagine my feelings when he suddenly made a cut at me which would certainly have taken my head off if I had not fallen forward with my nose in Violette's mane. My faith, it whistled just over my cap like an east wind. Of course, it came from this accursed Cossack uniform which, in my excitement, I had forgotten all about, and this young dragoon had imagined that I was some Russian champion who was challenging the French cavalry. My word, he was a frightened man when he understood how near he had been to killing the celebrated Brigadier Gerard.

Well, the road was clear, and about three o'clock in the afternoon I was at St. Denis, though it took me a long two hours to get from there to Paris, for the road was blocked with commissariat waggons and guns of the artillery reserve, which was going north to Marmont and Mortier. You cannot conceive the excitement which my appearance in such a costume made in Paris, and when I came to the Rue de Rivoli I should think I had a quarter of a mile of folk riding or running behind me. Word had got about from the dragoons (two of whom had come with me), and everybody knew about my adventures and how I had come by my uniform. It was a triumph—men shouting and women waving their handkerchiefs and blowing kisses from the windows.

Although I am a man singularly free from conceit, still I must confess that, on this one occasion, I could not restrain myself from showing that this reception gratified me. The Russian's coat had hung very loose upon me, but now I threw out my chest until it was as tight as a sausage-skin. And my little sweetheart of a mare tossed her mane and pawed with her front hoofs, frisking her tail about as though she said, 'We've done it together this time. It is to us that commissions should be intrusted.' When I kissed her between the nostrils as I dismounted at the gate of the Tuileries, there was as much shouting as if a bulletin had been read from the Grand Army.

I was hardly in costume to visit a King; but, after all, if one has a soldierly figure one can do without all that. I was shown up straight away to Joseph, whom I had often seen in Spain. He seemed as stout, as quiet, and as amiable as ever. Talleyrand was in the room with him, or I suppose I should call him the Duke of Benevento, but I confess that I like old names best. He read my letter when Joseph Buonaparte handed it to him, and then he looked at me with the strangest expression in those funny little, twinkling eyes of his.

'Were you the only messenger?' he asked.

'There was one other, sir,' said I. 'Major Charpentier, of the Horse Grenadiers.'

'He has not yet arrived,' said the King of Spain.

'If you had seen the legs of his horse, sire, you would not wonder at it,' I remarked.

'There may be other reasons,' said Talleyrand, and he gave that singular smile of his.

Well, they paid me a compliment or two, though they

342

might have said a good deal more and yet have said too little. I bowed myself out, and very glad I was to get away, for I hate a Court as much as I love a camp. Away I went to my old friend Chaubert, in the Rue Miromesnil, and there I got his hussar uniform, which fitted me very well. He and Lisette and I supped together in his rooms, and all my dangers were forgotten. In the morning I found Violette ready for another twenty-league stretch. It was my intention to return instantly to the Emperor's head-quarters, for I was, as you may well imagine, impatient to hear his words of praise, and to receive my reward.

I need not say that I rode back by a safe route, for I had seen quite enough of Uhlans and Cossacks. I passed through Meaux and Château Thierry, and so in the evening I arrived at Rheims, where Napoleon was still lying. The bodies of our fellows and of St. Prest's Russians had all been buried, and I could see changes in the camp also. The soldiers looked better cared for; some of the cavalry had received remounts, and everything was in excellent order. It was wonderful what a good general can effect in a couple of days.

When I came to the head-quarters I was shown straight into the Emperor's room. He was drinking coffee at a writing-table, with a big plan drawn out on paper in front of him. Berthier and Macdonald were leaning, one over each shoulder, and he was talking so quickly that I don't believe that either of them could catch a half of what he was saying. But when his eyes fell upon me he dropped the pen on to the chart, and he sprang up with a look in his pale face which struck me cold.

'What the deuce are you doing here?' he shouted. When he was angry he had a voice like a peacock.

'I have the honour to report to you, sire,' said I, 'that I have delivered your despatch safely to the King of Spain.'

'What!' he yelled, and his two eyes transfixed me like bayonets. Oh, those dreadful eyes, shifting from grey to blue, like steel in the sunshine. I can see them now when I have a bad dream.

'What has become of Charpentier?' he asked.

'He is captured,' said Macdonald.

'By whom?'

'The Russians.'

'The Cossacks?'

'No, a single Cossack.'

'He gave himself up?'

'Without resistance.'

'He is an intelligent officer. You will see that the medal of honour is awarded to him.'

When I heard those words I had to rub my eyes to make sure that I was awake.

'As to you,' cried the Emperor, taking a step forward as if he would have struck me, 'you brain of a hare, what do you think that you were sent upon this mission for? Do you conceive that I would send a really important message by such a hand as yours, and through every village which the enemy holds? How you came through them passes my comprehension; but if your fellow-messenger had had but as little sense as you, my whole plan of campaign would have been ruined. Can you not see, *coglione*, that this message contained false news, and that it was intended to deceive the enemy whilst I put a very different scheme into execution?'

When I heard those cruel words and saw the angry, white face which glared at me, I had to hold the back of a chair, for my mind was failing me and my knees would hardly bear me up. But then I took courage as I reflected that I was an honourable gentleman, and that my whole life had been spent in toiling for this man and for my beloved country.

'Sire,' said I, and the tears would trickle down my cheeks whilst I spoke, 'when you are dealing with a man like me you would find it wiser to deal openly. Had I known that you had wished the despatch to fall into the hands of the enemy, I would have seen that it came there.

344

As I believed that I was to guard it, I was prepared to sacrifice my life for it. I do not believe, sire, that any man in the world ever met with more toils and perils than I have done in trying to carry out what I thought was your will.'

I dashed the tears from my eyes as I spoke, and with such fire and spirit as I could command I gave him an account of it all, of my dash through Soissons, my brush with the dragoons, my adventure in Senlis, my rencontre with Count Boutkine in the cellar, my disguise, my meeting with the Cossack officer, my flight, and how at the last moment I was nearly cut down by a French dragoon. The Emperor, Berthier, and Macdonald listened with astonishment on their faces. When I had finished Napoleon stepped forward and he pinched me by the ear.

'There, there!' said he. 'Forget anything which I may have said. I would have done better to trust you. You may go.'

I turned to the door, and my hand was upon the handle, when the Emperor called upon me to stop.

'You will see,' said he, turning to the Duke of Tarentum, 'that Brigadier Gerard has the special medal of honour, for I believe that if he has the thickest head he has also the stoutest heart in my army.'

VIII. How the Brigadier was Tempted by the Devil

THE spring is at hand, my friends. I can see the little green spear-heads breaking out once more upon the chestnut trees, and the café tables have all been moved into the sunshine. It is more pleasant to sit there, and yet I do not wish to tell my little stories to the whole town. You have heard my doings as a lieutenant, as a squadron officer, as a colonel, as the chief of a brigade. But now I suddenly become something higher and more important. I become history.

If you have read of those closing years of the life of the Emperor which were spent in the Island of St. Helena, you will remember that, again and again, he implored permission to send out one single letter which should be unopened by those who held him. Many times he made this request, and even went so far as to promise that he would provide for his own wants and cease to be an expense to the British Government if it were granted to him. But his guardians knew that he was a terrible man, this pale, fat gentleman in the straw hat, and they dared not grant him what he asked. Many have wondered who it was to whom he could have had anything so secret to say. Some have supposed that it was to his wife, and some that it was to his father-in-law; some that it was to the Emperor Alexander and some to Marshal Soult. What will you think of me, my friends, when I tell you it was to me—to me, the Brigadier Gerard—that the Emperor wished to write? Yes, humble as you see me, with only my hundred francs a month of half-pay between me and hunger, it is none the less true I was always in the Emperor's mind, and that he would have given his left hand for five minutes' talk with me. I will tell you to-night how this came about.

It was after the Battle of Fère-Champenoise, where the conscripts in their blouses and their sabots made such a fine stand, that we, the more long-headed of us, began to understand that it was all over with us. Our reserve ammunition had been taken in the battle, and we were left with silent guns and empty caissons. Our cavalry, too, was in a deplorable condition, and my own brigade had been destroyed in the charge at Craonne. Then came the news that the enemy had taken Paris, that the citizens had mounted the white cockade; and finally, most terrible of all, that Marmont and his corps had gone over to the Bourbons. We looked at each other and asked how many more of our generals were going to turn against us. Already there were Jourdan, Marmont, Murat, Bernadotte, and Jomini—though nobody minded much about

Jomini, for his pen was always sharper than his sword. We had been ready to fight Europe, but it looked now as though we were to fight Europe and half France as well.

We had come to Fontainebleau by a long, forced march, and there we were assembled, the poor remnants of us, the corps of Ney, the corps of my cousin Gerard, and the corps of Macdonald: twenty-five thousand in all, with seven thousand of the guard. But we had our prestige, which was worth fifty thousand, and our Emperor, who was worth fifty thousand more. He was always among us, serene, smiling, confident, taking his snuff and playing with his little riding-whip. Never in the days of his greatest victories have I admired him as much as I did during the Campaign of France.

One evening I was with a few of my officers, drinking a glass of wine of Suresnes. I mention that it was wine of Suresnes just to show you that times were not very good with us. Suddenly I was disturbed by a message from Berthier that he wished to see me. When I speak of my old comrades-in-arms, I will, with your permission, leave out all the fine foreign titles which they had picked up during the wars. They are excellent for a Court, but you never heard them in the camp, for we could not afford to do away with our Ney, our Rapp, or our Soult—names which were as stirring to our ears as the blare of our trumpets blowing the reveille. It was Berthier, then, who sent to say that he wished to see me.

He had a suite of rooms at the end of the gallery of Francis the First, not very far from those of the Emperor. In the ante-chamber were waiting two men whom I knew well: Colonel Despienne, of the 57th of the line, and Captain Tremeau, of the Voltigeurs. They were both old soldiers—Tremeau had carried a musket in Egypt—and they were also both famous in the army for their courage and their skill with weapons. Tremeau had become a little stiff in the wrist, but Despienne was capable at his best of making me exert myself. He was a tiny fellow, about three inches short of the proper height for a man

—he was exactly three inches shorter than myself—but both with the sabre and with the small-sword he had several times almost held his own against me when we used to exhibit at Verron's Hall of Arms in the Palais Royal. You may think that it made us sniff something in the wind when we found three such men called together into one room. You cannot see the lettuce and dressing without suspecting a salad.

'Name of a pipe!' said Tremeau, in his barrack-room fashion. 'Are we then expecting three champions of the Bourbons?'

To all of us the idea appeared not improbable. Certainly in the whole army we were the very three who might have been chosen to meet them.

'The Prince of Neufchâtel desires to speak with the Brigadier Gerard,' said a footman, appearing at the door.

In I went, leaving my two companions consumed with impatience behind me. It was a small room, but very gorgeously furnished. Berthier was seated opposite to me at a little table, with a pen in his hand and a note-book open before him. He was looking weary and slovenly—very different from that Berthier who used to give the fashion to the army, and who had so often set us poorer officers tearing our hair by trimming his pelisse with fur one campaign, and with grey astrakhan the next. On his clean-shaven, comely face there was an expression of trouble, and he looked at me as I entered his chamber in a way which had in it something furtive and displeasing.

'Chief of Brigade Gerard!' said he.

'At your service, your Highness!' I answered.

'I must ask you, before I go farther, to promise me, upon your honour as a gentleman and a soldier, that what is about to pass between us shall never be mentioned to any third person.'

My word, this was a fine beginning! I had no choice but to give the promise required.

'You must know, then, that it is all over with the Emperor,' said he, looking down at the table and speaking very slowly, as if he had a hard task in getting out the words. 'Jourdan at Rouen and Marmont at Paris have both mounted the white cockade, and it is rumoured that Talleyrand has talked Ney into doing the same. It is evident that further resistance is useless, and that it can only bring misery upon our country. I wish to ask you, therefore, whether you are prepared to join me in laying hands upon the Emperor's person, and bringing the war to a conclusion by delivering him over to the allies?'

I assure you that when I heard this infamous proposition put forward by the man who had been the earliest friend of the Emperor, and who had received greater favours from him than any of his followers, I could only stand and stare at him in amazement. For his part he tapped his pen-handle against his teeth, and looked at me with a slanting head.

'Well?' he asked.

'I am a little deaf on one side,' said I, coldly. There are some things which I cannot hear. I beg that you will permit me to return to my duties.'

'Nay, but you must not be headstrong,' rising up and laying his hand upon my shoulder. 'You are aware that the Senate has declared against Napoleon, and that the Emperor Alexander refuses to treat with him.'

'Sir,' I cried, with passion, 'I would have you know that I do not care the dregs of a wine-glass for the Senate or for the Emperor Alexander either.'

'Then for what do you care?'

'For my own honour and for the service of my glorious master, the Emperor Napoleon.'

'That is all very well,' said Berthier, peevishly, shrugging his shoulders. 'Facts are facts, and as men of the world, we must look them in the face. Are we to stand against the will of the nation? Are we to have civil war on the top of all our misfortunes? And, besides, we are thinning away. Every hour comes the news of fresh desertions. We have still time to make our peace, and, indeed, to earn the highest reward, by giving up the Emperor.'

I shook so with passion that my sabre clattered against my thigh.

'Sir,' I cried, 'I never thought to have seen the day when a Marshal of France would have so far degraded himself as to put forward such a proposal. I leave you to your own conscience; but as for me, until I have the Emperor's own order, there shall always be the sword of Etienne Gerard between his enemies and himself.'

I was so moved by my own words and by the fine position which I had taken up, that my voice broke, and I could hardly refrain from tears. I should have liked the whole army to have seen me as I stood with my head so proudly erect and my hand upon my heart proclaiming my devotion to the Emperor in his adversity. It was one of the supreme moments of my life.

'Very good,' said Berthier, ringing a bell for the lackey. 'You will show the Chief of Brigade Gerard into the salon.'

The footman led me into an inner room, where he desired me to be seated. For my own part, my only desire was to get away, and I could not understand why they should wish to detain me. When one has had no change of uniform during a whole winter's campaign, one does not feel at home in a palace.

I had been there about a quarter of an hour when the footman opened the door again, and in came Colonel Despienne. Good heavens, what a sight he was! His face was as white as a guardsman's gaiters, his eyes projecting, the veins swollen upon his forehead, and every hair of his moustache bristling like those of an angry cat. He was too angry to speak, and could only shake his hands at the ceiling and make a gurgling in his throat. 'Parricide! Viper!' those were the words that I could catch as he stamped up and down the room.

Of course it was evident to me that he had been subjected to the same infamous proposals as I had, and that

he had received them in the same spirit. His lips were
sealed to me, as mine were to him, by the promise which
we had taken, but I contented myself with muttering
'Atrocious! Unspeakable!'—so that he might know that I
was in agreement with him.

Well, we were still there, he striding furiously up and
down, and I seated in the corner, when suddenly a most
extraordinary uproar broke out in the room which we
had just quitted. There was a snarling, worrying growl,
like that of a fierce dog which has got his grip. Then
came a crash and a voice calling for help. In we rushed,
the two of us, and, my faith, we were none too soon.

Old Tremeau and Berthier were rolling together upon
the floor, with the table upon the top of them. The
Captain had one of his great, skinny yellow hands upon
the Marshal's throat, and already his face was lead-
coloured, and his eyes were starting from their sockets.
As to Tremeau, he was beside himself, with foam upon
the corners of his lips, and such a frantic expression upon
him that I am convinced, had we not loosened his iron
grip, finger by finger, that it would never have relaxed
while the Marshal lived. His nails were white with the
power of his grasp.

'I have been tempted by the devil!' he cried, as he
staggered to his feet. 'Yes, I have been tempted by the
devil!'

As to Berthier, he could only lean against the wall, and
pant for a couple of minutes, putting his hands up to his
throat and rolling his head about. Then, with an angry
gesture, he turned to the heavy blue curtain which hung
behind his chair.

The curtain was torn to one side and the Emperor
stepped out into the room. We sprang to the salute, we
three old soldiers, but it was all like a scene in a dream
to us, and our eyes were as far out as Berthier's had been.
Napoleon was dressed in his green-coated chasseur uniform, and he held his little, silver-headed switch in his
hand. He looked at us each in turn, with a smile upon his

face—that frightful smile in which neither eyes nor brow joined—and each in turn had, I believe, a pringling on his skin, for that was the effect which the Emperor's gaze had upon most of us. Then he walked across to Berthier and put his hand upon his shoulder.

'You must not quarrel with blows, my dear Prince,' said he; 'they are your title to nobility.' He spoke in that soft, caressing manner which he could assume. There was no one who could make the French tongue sound so pretty as the Emperor, and no one who could make it more harsh and terrible.

'I believe he would have killed me,' cried Berthier, still rolling his head about.

'Tut, tut! I should have come to your help had these officers not heard your cries. But I trust that you are not really hurt!' He spoke with earnestness, for he was in truth very fond of Berthier—more so than of any man, unless it were of poor Duroc.

Berthier laughed, though not with a very good grace.

'It is new for me to receive my injuries from French hands,' said he.

'And yet it was in the cause of France,' returned the Emperor. Then, turning to us, he took old Tremeau by the ear. 'Ah, old grumbler,' said he, 'you were one of my Egyptian grenadiers, were you not, and had your musket of honour at Marengo. I remember you very well, my good friend. So the old fires are not yet extinguished! They still burn up when you think that your Emperor is wronged. And you, Colonel Despienne, you would not even listen to the tempter. And you, Gerard, your faithful sword is ever to be between me and my enemies. Well, well, I have had some traitors about me, but now at last we are beginning to see who are the true men.'

You can fancy, my friends, the thrill of joy which it gave us when the greatest man in the whole world spoke to us in this fashion. Tremeau shook until I thought he would have fallen, and the tears ran down his gigantic moustache. If you had not seen it, you could never believe the influence which the Emperor had upon those coarse-grained, savage old veterans.

'Well, my faithful friends,' said he, 'if you will follow me into this room, I will explain to you the meaning of this little farce which we have been acting. I beg, Berthier, that you will remain in this chamber, and so make sure that no one interrupts us.'

It was new for us to be doing business, with a Marshal of France as sentry at the door. However, we followed the Emperor as we were ordered, and he led us into the recess of the window, gathering us around him and sinking his voice as he addressed us.

'I have picked you out of the whole army,' said he, 'as being not only the most formidable but also the most faithful of my soldiers. I was convinced that you were all three men who would never waver in your fidelity to me. If I have ventured to put that fidelity to the proof, and to watch you while attempts were at my orders made upon your honour, it was only because, in the days when I have found the blackest treason amongst my own flesh and blood, it is necessary that I should be doubly circumspect. Suffice it that I am well convinced now that I can rely upon your valour.'

'To the death, sire!' cried Tremeau, and we both repeated it after him.

Napoleon drew us all yet a little closer to him, and sank his voice still lower.

'What I say to you now I have said to no one—not to my wife or my brothers; only to you. It is all up with us, my friends. We have come to our last rally. The game is finished, and we must make provision accordingly.'

My heart seemed to have changed to a nine-pounder ball as I listened to him. We had hoped against hope, but now when he, the man who was always serene and who always had reserves—when he, in that quiet, impassive voice of his, said that everything was over, we realised that the clouds had shut for ever, and the last gleam gone. Tremeau snarled and gripped at his sabre, Despienne ground his teeth, and for my own part I threw out my chest and clicked my heels to show the Emperor that there were some spirits which could rise to adversity.

'My papers and my fortune must be secured,' whispered the Emperor. 'The whole course of the future may depend upon my having them safe. They are our base for the next attempt—for I am very sure that these poor Bourbons would find that my footstool is too large to make a throne for them. Where am I to keep these precious things? My belongings will be searched—so will the houses of my supporters. They must be secured and concealed by men whom I can trust with that which is more precious to me than my life. Out of the whole of France, you are those whom I have chosen for this sacred trust.

'In the first place, I will tell you what these papers are. You shall not say that I have made you blind agents in the matter. They are the official proof of my divorce from Josephine, of my legal marriage to Marie Louise, and of the birth of my son and heir, the King of Rome. If we cannot prove each of these, the future claim of my family to the throne of France falls to the ground. Then there are securities to the value of forty millions of francs—an immense sum, my friends, but of no more value than this riding-switch when compared to the other papers of which I have spoken. I tell you these things that you may realise the enormous importance of the task which I am committing to your care. Listen, now, while I inform you where you are to get these papers, and what you are to do with them.

'They were handed over to my trusty friend, the Countess Walewski, at Paris, this morning. At five o'clock she starts for Fontainebleau in her blue berline. She should reach here between half-past nine and ten. The papers will be concealed in the berline, in a hiding-place which none know but herself. She has been warned that her carriage will be stopped outside the town by three mounted officers, and she will hand the packet over to your care. You are the younger man, Gerard, but

354

you are of the senior grade. I confide to your care this amethyst ring, which you will show the lady as a token of your mission, and which you will leave with her as a receipt for her papers.

'Having received the packet, you will ride with it into the forest as far as the ruined dove-house—the Colombier. It is possible that I may meet you there—but if it seems to me to be dangerous, I will send my body-servant, Mustapha, whose directions you may take as being mine. There is no roof to the Colombier, and to-night will be a full moon. At the right of the entrance you will find three spades leaning against the wall. With these you will dig a hole three feet deep in the north-eastern corner— that is, in the corner to the left of the door, and nearest to Fontainebleau. Having buried the papers, you will replace the soil with great care, and you will then report to me at the palace.'

These were the Emperor's directions, but given with an accuracy and minuteness of detail such as no one but himself could put into an order. When he had finished, he made us swear to keep his secret as long as he lived, and as long as the papers should remain buried. Again and again he made us swear it before he dismissed us from his presence.

Colonel Despienne had quarters at the 'Sign of the Pheasant,' and it was there that we supped together. We were all three men who had been trained to take the strangest turns of fortune as part of our daily life and business, yet we were all flushed and moved by the extraordinary interview which we had had, and by the thought of the great adventure which lay before us. For my own part, it had been my fate three several times to take my orders from the lips of the Emperor himself, but neither the incident of the Ajaccio murderers nor the famous ride which I made to Paris appeared to offer such opportunities as this new and most intimate commission.

'If things go right with the Emperor,' said Despienne, 'we shall all live to be marshals yet.'

We drank with him to our future cocked hats and our batons.

It was agreed between us that we should make our way separately to our rendezvous, which was to be the first milestone upon the Paris road. In this way we should avoid the gossip which might get about if three men who were so well known were to be seen riding out together. My little Violette had cast a shoe that morning, and the farrier was at work upon her when I returned, so that my comrades were already there when I arrived at the trysting-place. I had taken with me not only my sabre, but also my new pair of English rifled pistols, with a mallet for knocking in the charges. They had cost me a hundred and fifty francs at Trouvel's, in the Rue de Rivoli, but they would carry far further and straighter than the others. It was with one of them that I had saved old Bouvet's life at Leipzig.

The night was cloudless, and there was a brilliant moon behind us, so that we always had three black horsemen riding down the white road in front of us. The country is so thickly wooded, however, that we could not see very far. The great palace clock had already struck ten, but there was no sign of the Countess. We began to fear that something might have prevented her from starting.

And then suddenly we heard her in the distance. Very faint at first were the birr of wheels and the tat-tat-tat of the horses' feet. Then they grew louder and clearer and louder yet, until a pair of yellow lanterns swung round the curve, and in their light we saw the two big brown horses tearing along with the high, blue carriage at the back of them. The postilion pulled them up panting and foaming within a few yards of us. In a moment we were at the window and had raised our hands in a salute to the beautiful pale face which looked out at us.

'We are the three officers of the Emperor, madame,' said I, in a low voice, leaning my face down to the open window. 'You have already been warned that we should wait upon you.'

The Countess had a very beautiful, cream-tinted complexion of a sort which I particularly admire, but she grew whiter and whiter as she looked up at me. Harsh lines deepened upon her face until she seemed, even as I looked at her, to turn from youth into age.

'It is evident to me,' she said, 'that you are three impostors.'

If she had struck me across the face with her delicate hand she could not have startled me more. It was not her words only, but the bitterness with which she hissed them out.

'Indeed, madame,' said I. 'You do us less than justice. These are the Colonel Despienne and Captain Tremeau. For myself, my name is Brigadier Gerard, and I have only to mention it to assure anyone who has heard of me that——'

'Oh, you villains!' she interrupted. 'You think that because I am only a woman I am very easily to be hoodwinked! You miserable impostors!'

I looked at Despienne, who had turned white with anger, and at Tremeau, who was tugging at his moustache.

'Madame,' said I, coldly, 'when the Emperor did us the honour to intrust us with this mission, he gave me this amethyst ring as a token. I had not thought that three honourable gentlemen would have needed such corroboration, but I can only confute your unworthy suspicions by placing it in your hands.'

She held it up in the light of the carriage lamp, and the most dreadful expression of grief and of horror contorted her face.

'It is his!' she screamed, and then, 'Oh, my God, what have I done? What have I done?'

I felt that something terrible had befallen. 'Quick, madame, quick!' I cried. 'Give us the papers!'

'I have already given them.'

'Given them! To whom?'

'To three officers.'

'When?'

'Within the half-hour.'

'Where are they?'

'God help me, I do not know. They stopped the ber-line, and I handed them over to them without hesitation, thinking that they had come from the Emperor.'

It was a thunder-clap. But those are the moments when I am at my finest.

'You remain here,' said I, to my comrades. 'If three horsemen pass you, stop them at any hazard. The lady will describe them to you. I will be with you presently.' One shake of the bridle, and I was flying into Fontaine-bleau as only Violette could have carried me. At the palace I flung myself off, rushed up the stairs, brushed aside the lackeys who would have stopped me, and pushed my way into the Emperor's own cabinet. He and Macdonald were busy with pencil and compasses over a chart. He looked up with an angry frown at my sudden entry, but his face changed colour when he saw that it was I.

'You can leave us, Marshal,' said he, and then, the instant the door was closed: 'What news about the papers?'

'They are gone!' said I, and in a few curt words I told him what had happened. His face was calm, but I saw the compasses quiver in his hand.

'You must recover them, Gerard!' he cried. 'The des-tinies of my dynasty are at stake. Not a moment is to be lost! To horse, sir, to horse!'

'Who are they, sire?'

'I cannot tell. I am surrounded with treason. But they will take them to Paris. To whom should they carry them but to the villain Talleyrand? Yes, yes, they are on the Paris road, and may yet be overtaken. With the three best mounts in my stables and——'

I did not wait to hear the end of the sentence. I was already clattering down the stair. I am sure that five minutes had not passed before I was galloping Violette out of the town with the bridle of one of the Emperor's own Arab chargers in either hand. They wished me to take three, but I should have never dared to look my Violette in the face again. I feel that the spectacle must have been superb when I dashed up to my comrades and pulled the horses on to their haunches in the moonlight.

'No one has passed?'

'No one.'

'Then they are on the Paris road. Quick! Up and after them!'

They did not take long, those good soldiers. In a flash they were upon the Emperor's horses, and their own left masterless by the roadside. Then away we went upon our long chase, I in the centre, Despienne upon my right, and Tremeau a little behind, for he was the heavier man. Heavens, how we galloped! The twelve flying hoofs roared and roared along the hard, smooth road. Poplars and moon, black bars and silver streaks, for mile after mile our course lay along the same chequered track, with our shadows in front and our dust behind. We could hear the rasping of bolts and the creaking of shutters from the cottages as we thundered past them, but we were only three dark blurs upon the road by the time that the folk could look after us. It was just striking midnight as we raced into Corbeil; but an hostler with a bucket in either hand was throwing his black shadow across the golden fan which was cast from the open door of the inn.

'Three riders!' I gasped. 'Have they passed?'

'I have just been watering their horses,' said he. 'I should think they——'

'On, my friends!' and away we flew, striking fire from the cobblestones of the little town. A gendarme tried to stop us, but his voice was drowned by our rattle and clatter. The houses slid past, and we were out on the country road again, with a clear twenty miles between ourselves and Paris. How could they escape us, with the finest horses in France behind them? Not one of the three had turned a hair, but Violette was always a head and shoulders to the front. She was going within herself too, and I knew by the spring of her that I had only to let her stretch herself, and the Emperor's horses would see the colour of her tail.

'There they are!' cried Despienne.

'We have them!' growled Tremeau.

'On, comrades, on!' I shouted, once more.

A long stretch of white road lay before us in the moonlight. Far away down it we could see three cavaliers, lying low upon their horses' necks. Every instant they grew larger and clearer as we gained upon them. I could see quite plainly that the two upon either side were wrapped in mantles and rode upon chestnut horses, whilst the man between them was dressed in a chasseur uniform and mounted upon a grey. They were keeping abreast, but it was easy enough to see from the way in which he gathered his legs for each spring that the centre horse was far the fresher of the three. And the rider appeared to be the leader of the party, for we continually saw the glint of his face in the moonshine as he looked back to measure the distance between us. At first it was only a glimmer, then it was cut across with a moustache, and at last when we began to feel their dust in our throats I could give a name to my man.

'Halt, Colonel de Montluc!' I shouted. 'Halt, in the Emperor's name!'

I had known him for years as a daring officer and an unprincipled rascal. Indeed, there was a score between us, for he had shot my friend, Treville, at Warsaw, pulling his trigger, as some said, a good second before the drop of the handkerchief.

Well, the words were hardly out of my mouth when his two comrades wheeled round and fired their pistols at us. I heard Despienne give a terrible cry, and at the same instant both Tremeau and I let drive at the same man. He fell forward with his hands swinging on each side of his horse's neck. His comrade spurred on to Tremeau, sabre in hand, and I heard the crash which comes when a strong cut is met by a stronger parry. For my own part I never turned my head, but I touched Violette with the spur for the first time and flew after the leader. That he should leave his comrades and fly was proof enough that I should leave mine and follow.

He had gained a couple of hundred paces, but the good little mare set that right before we could have passed two milestones. It was in vain that he spurred and thrashed like a gunner driver on a soft road. His hat flew off with his exertions, and his bald head gleamed in the moonshine. But do what he might, he still heard the rattle of the hoofs growing louder and louder behind him. I could not have been twenty yards from him, and the shadow head was touching the shadow haunch, when he turned with a curse in his saddle and emptied both his pistols, one after the other, into Violette.

I have been wounded myself so often that I have to stop and think before I can tell you the exact number of times. I have been hit by musket balls, by pistol bullets, and by bursting shells, besides being pierced by bayonet, lance, sabre, and finally by a brad-awl, which was the most painful of any. Yet out of all these injuries I have never known the same deadly sickness as came over me when I felt the poor, silent, patient creature, which I had come to love more than anything in the world except my mother and the Emperor, reel and stagger beneath me. I pulled my second pistol from my holster and fired point-blank between the fellow's broad shoulders. He slashed his horse across the flank with his whip, and for a moment I thought that I had missed him. But then on the green of his chasseur jacket I saw an ever-widening black smudge, and he began to sway in his saddle, very slightly at first, but more and more with every bound, until at last over he went, with his foot caught in the stirrup and his shoulders thud-thudding along the road, until the drag was too much for the tired horse, and I closed my hand upon the foam-spattered bridle-chain. As

I pulled him up it eased the stirrup leather, and the spurred heel clinked loudly as it fell.

'Your papers!' I cried, springing from my saddle. 'This instant!'

But even as I said it, the huddle of the green body and the fantastic sprawl of the limbs in the moonlight told me clearly enough that it was all over with him. My bullet had passed through his heart, and it was only his iron will which had held him so long in the saddle. He had lived hard, this Montluc, and I will do him justice to say that he died hard also.

But it was the papers—always the papers—of which I thought. I opened his tunic and I felt in his shirt. Then I searched his holsters and his sabre-tasche. Finally I dragged off his boots, and undid his horse's girth so as to hunt under the saddle. There was not a nook or crevice which I did not ransack. It was useless. They were not upon him.

When this stunning blow came upon me I could have sat down by the roadside and wept. Fate seemed to be fighting against me, and that is an enemy from whom even a gallant hussar might not be ashamed to flinch. I stood with my arm over the neck of my poor wounded Violette, and I tried to think it all out, that I might act in the wisest way. I was aware that the Emperor had no great respect for my wits, and I longed to show him that he had done me an injustice. Montluc had not the papers. And yet Montluc had sacrificed his companions in order to make his escape. I could make nothing of that. On the other hand, it was clear that, if he had not got them, one or other of his comrades had. One of them was certainly dead. The other I had left fighting with Tremeau, and if he escaped from the old swordsman he had still to pass me. Clearly, my work lay behind me.

I hammered fresh charges into my pistols after I had turned this over in my head. Then I put them back in the holsters, and I examined my little mare, she jerking her head and cocking her ears the while, as if to tell me that an old soldier like herself did not make a fuss about a scratch or two. The first shot had merely grazed her off-shoulder, leaving a skin-mark, as if she had brushed a wall. The second was more serious. It had passed through the muscle of her neck, but already it had ceased to bleed. I reflected that if she weakened I could mount Montluc's grey, and meanwhile I led him along beside us, for he was a fine horse, worth fifteen hundred francs at the least, and it seemed to me that no one had a better right to him than I.

Well, I was all impatience now to get back to the others, and I had just given Violette her head, when suddenly I saw something glimmering in a field by the roadside. It was the brass-work upon the chasseur hat which had flown from Montluc's head; and at the sight of it a thought made me jump in the saddle. How could the hat have flown off? With its weight, would it not have simply dropped? And here it lay, fifteen paces from the roadway! Of course, he must have thrown it off when he had made sure that I would overtake him. And if he threw it off—I did not stop to reason any more, but sprang from the mare with my heart beating the *pas-de-charge*. Yes, it was all right this time. There, in the crown of the hat was stuffed a roll of papers in a parchment wrapper bound round with yellow ribbon. I pulled it out with the one hand, and holding the hat in the other, I danced for joy in the moonlight. The Emperor would see that he had not made a mistake when he put his affairs into the charge of Etienne Gerard.

I had a safe pocket on the inside of my tunic just over my heart, where I kept a few little things which were dear to me, and into this I thrust my precious roll. Then I sprang upon Violette, and was pushing forward to see what had become of Tremeau, when I saw a horseman riding across the field in the distance. At the same instant I heard the sound of hoofs approaching me, and there in the moonlight was the Emperor upon his white charger, dressed in his grey overcoat and his three-cornered hat, just as I had seen him so often upon the field of battle.

'Well!' he cried, in the sharp, sergeant-major way of his. 'Where are my papers?'

I spurred forward and presented them without a word. He broke the ribbon and ran his eyes rapidly over them. Then, as we sat our horses head to tail, he threw his left arm across me with his hand upon my shoulder. Yes, my friends, simple as you see me, I have been embraced by my great master.

'Gerard,' he cried, 'you are a marvel!'

I did not wish to contradict him, and it brought a flush of joy upon my cheeks to know that he had done me justice at last.

'Where is the thief, Gerard?' he asked.

'Dead, sire.'

'You killed him?'

'He wounded my horse, sire, and would have escaped had I not shot him.'

'Did you recognise him?'

'De Montluc is his name, sire—a Colonel of Chasseurs.'

'Tut,' said the Emperor. 'We have got the poor pawn, but the hand which plays the game is still out of reach.' He sat in silent thought for a little, with his chin sunk upon his chest. 'Ah, Talleyrand, Talleyrand,' I heard him mutter, 'if I had been in your place and you in mine, you would have crushed a viper when you held it under your heel. For five years I have known you for what you are, and yet I have let you live to sting me. Never mind, my brave,' he continued, turning to me, 'there will come a day of reckoning for everybody, and when it arrives, I promise you that my friends will be remembered as well as my enemies.'

'Sire,' said I, for I had had time for thought as well as he, 'if your plans about these papers have been carried to the ears of your enemies, I trust you do not think that it was owing to any indiscretion upon the part of myself or of my comrades.'

'It would be hardly reasonable for me to do so,' he answered, 'seeing that this plot was hatched in Paris, and that you only had your orders a few hours ago.'

'Then how——?'

'Enough,' he cried, sternly. 'You take an undue advantage of your position.'

That was always the way with the Emperor. He would chat with you as with a friend and a brother, and then when he had wiled you into forgetting the gulf which lay between you, he would suddenly, with a word or with a look, remind you that it was as impassable as ever. When I have fondled my old hound until he has been encouraged to paw my knees, and I have then thrust him down again, it has made me think of the Emperor and his ways.

He reined his horse round, and I followed him in silence and with a heavy heart. But when he spoke again his words were enough to drive all thought of myself out of my mind.

'I could not sleep until I knew how you had fared,' said he. 'I have paid a price for my papers. There are not so many of my old soldiers left that I can afford to lose two in one night.'

When he said 'two' it turned me cold.

'Colonel Despienne was shot, sire,' I stammered.

'And Captain Tremeau cut down. Had I been a few minutes earlier, I might have saved him. The other escaped across the fields.'

I remembered that I had seen a horseman a moment before I had met the Emperor. He had taken to the fields to avoid me, but if I had known, and Violette been unwounded, the old soldier would not have gone unavenged. I was thinking sadly of his sword-play, and wondering whether it was his stiffening wrist which had been fatal to him, when Napoleon spoke again.

'Yes, Brigadier,' said he, 'you are now the only man who will know where these papers are concealed.'

It must have been imagination, my friends, but for an instant I may confess that it seemed to me that there was a tone in the Emperor's voice which was not altogether one of sorrow. But the dark thought had hardly time to form itself in my mind before he let me see that I was doing him an injustice.

'Yes, I have paid a price for my papers,' he said, and I heard them crackle as he put his hand up to his bosom. 'No man has ever had more faithful servants—no man since the beginning of the world.'

As he spoke we came upon the scene of the struggle. Colonel Despienne and the man whom we had shot lay together some distance down the road, while their horses grazed contentedly beneath the poplars. Captain Tremeau lay in front of us upon his back, with his arms and legs stretched out, and his sabre broken short off in his hand. His tunic was open, and a huge blood-clot hung like a dark handkerchief out of a slit in his white shirt. I could see the gleam of his clenched teeth from under his immense moustache.

The Emperor sprang from his horse and bent down over the dead man.

'He was with me since Rivoli,' said he, sadly. 'He was one of my old grumblers in Egypt.'

And the voice brought the man back from the dead. I saw his eyelids shiver. He twitched his arm, and moved the sword-hilt a few inches. He was trying to raise it in salute. Then the mouth opened, and the hilt tinkled down on to the ground.

'May we all die as gallantly,' said the Emperor, as he rose, and from my heart I added 'Amen.'

There was a farm within fifty yards of where we were standing, and the farmer, roused from his sleep by the clatter of hoofs and the cracking of pistols, had rushed out to the roadside. We saw him now, dumb with fear and astonishment, staring open-eyed at the Emperor. It was to him that we committed the care of the four dead men and of the horses also. For my own part, I thought

it best to leave Violette with him and to take De Montluc's grey with me, for he could not refuse to give me
back my own mare, whilst there might be difficulties
about the other. Besides, my little friend's wound had to
be considered, and we had a long return ride before us.

The Emperor did not at first talk much upon the
way. Perhaps the deaths of Despienne and Tremeau still
weighed heavily upon his spirits. He was always a reserved man, and in those times, when every hour brought
him the news of some success of his enemies or defection
of his friends, one could not expect him to be a merry
companion. Nevertheless, when I reflected that he was
carrying in his bosom those papers which he valued so
highly, and which only a few hours ago appeared to be
for ever lost, and when I further thought that it was I,
Etienne Gerard, who had placed them there, I felt that
I had deserved some little consideration. The same idea
may have occurred to him, for when we had at last left
the Paris high road, and had entered the forest, he began
of his own accord to tell me that which I should have
most liked to have asked him.

'As to the papers,' said he, 'I have already told you that
there is no one now, except you and me, who knows
where they are to be concealed. My Mameluke carried the
spades to the pigeon-house, but I have told him nothing.
Our plans, however, for bringing the packet from Paris
have been formed since Monday. There were three in
the secret, a woman and two men. The woman I would
trust with my life; which of the two men has betrayed
us I do not know, but I think that I may promise to find
out.'

We were riding in the shadow of the trees at the time,
and I could hear him slapping his riding-whip against his
boot, and taking pinch after pinch of snuff, as was his
way when he was excited.

'You wonder, no doubt,' said he, after a pause, 'why
these rascals did not stop the carriage at Paris instead of
at the entrance to Fontainebleau.'

In truth, the objection had not occurred to me, but I did not wish to appear to have less wits than he gave me credit for, so I answered that it was indeed surprising.

'Had they done so they would have made a public scandal, and run a chance of missing their end. Short of taking the berline to pieces, they could not have discovered the hiding-place. He planned it well—he could always plan well—and he chose his agents well also. But mine were the better.'

It is not for me to repeat to you, my friends, all that was said to me by the Emperor as we walked our horses amid the black shadows and through the moon-silvered glades of the great forest. Every word of it is impressed upon my memory, and before I pass away it is likely that I will place it all upon paper, so that others may read it in the days to come. He spoke freely of his past, and something also of his future; of the devotion of Macdonald, of the treason of Marmont, of the little King of Rome, concerning whom he talked with as much tenderness as any bourgeois father of a single child; and, finally, of his father-in-law, the Emperor of Austria, who would, he thought, stand between his enemies and himself. For myself, I dared not say a word, remembering how I had already brought a rebuke upon myself; but I rode by his side, hardly able to believe that this was indeed the great Emperor, the man whose glance sent a thrill through me, who was now pouring out his thoughts to me in short, eager sentences, the words rattling and racing like the hoofs of a galloping squadron. It is possible that, after the word-splittings and diplomacy of a Court, it was a relief to him to speak his mind to a plain soldier like myself.

In this way the Emperor and I—even after years it sends a flush of pride into my cheeks to be able to put those words together—the Emperor and I walked our horses through the Forest of Fontainebleau, until we came at last to the Colombier. The three spades were propped against the wall upon the right-hand side of the ruined door, and at the sight of them the tears sprang to my eyes as I thought of the hands for which they were intended. The Emperor seized one and I another.

'Quick!' said he. 'The dawn will be upon us before we get back to the palace.'

We dug the hole, and placing the papers in one of my pistol holsters to screen them from the damp, we laid them at the bottom and covered them up. We then carefully removed all marks of the ground having been disturbed, and we placed a large stone upon the top. I dare say that since the Emperor was a young gunner, and helped to train his pieces against Toulon, he had not worked so hard with his hands. He was mopping his forehead with his silk handkerchief long before we had come to the end of our task.

The first grey cold light of morning was stealing through the tree trunks when we came out together from the old pigeon-house. The Emperor laid his hand upon my shoulder as I stood ready to help him to mount.

'We have left the papers there,' said he, solemnly, 'and I desire that you shall leave all thought of them there also. Let the recollection of them pass entirely from your mind, to be revived only when you receive a direct order under my own hand and seal. From this time onwards you forget all that has passed.'

'I forget it, sire,' said I.

We rode together to the edge of the town, where he desired that I should separate from him. I had saluted, and was turning my horse, when he called me back.

'It is easy to mistake the points of the compass in the forest,' said he. 'Would you not say that it was in the north-eastern corner that we buried them?'

'Buried what, sire?'

'The papers, of course,' he cried, impatiently.

'What papers, sire?'

'Name of a name! Why, the papers that you have recovered for me.'

'I am really at a loss to know what your Majesty is talking about.'

He flushed with anger for a moment, and then he burst out laughing.

'Very good, Brigadier!' he cried. 'I begin to believe that you are as good a diplomatist as you are a soldier, and I cannot say more than that.'

So that was my strange adventure in which I found myself the friend and confident agent of the Emperor. When he returned from Elba he refrained from digging up the papers until his position should be secure, and they still remained in the corner of the old pigeon-house after his exile to St. Helena. It was at this time that he was desirous of getting them into the hands of his own supporters, and for that purpose he wrote me, as I after-wards learned, three letters, all of which were intercepted by his guardians. Finally, he offered to support himself and his own establishment—which he might very easily have done out of the gigantic sum which belonged to him —if they would only pass one of his letters unopened. This request was refused, and so, up to his death in '21, the papers still remained where I have told you. How they came to be dug up by Count Bertrand and myself, and who eventually obtained them, is a story which I would tell you, were it not that the end has not yet come.

Some day you will hear of those papers, and you will see how, after he has been so long in his grave, that great man can still set Europe shaking. When that day comes, you will think of Etienne Gerard, and you will tell your children that you have heard the story from the lips of the man who was the only one living of all who took part in that strange history—the man who was tempted by Marshal Berthier, who led that wild pursuit upon the Paris road, who was honoured by the embrace of the Emperor, and who rode with him by moonlight in the Forest of Fontainebleau. The buds are bursting and the birds are calling, my friends. You may find better things to do in the sunlight than listening to the stories of an old, broken soldier. And yet you may well treasure what I say, for the buds will have burst and the birds sung in many seasons before France will see such another ruler as he whose servants we were proud to be.

ADVENTURES OF GERARD

I. How the Brigadier Lost his Ear

It was the old Brigadier who was talking in the café.

I have seen a great many cities, my friends. I would not dare to tell you how many I have entered as a conqueror with eight hundred of my little fighting devils clanking and jingling behind me. The cavalry were in front of the Grande Armée, and the Hussars of Conflans were in front of the cavalry, and I was in front of the Hussars. But of all the cities which we visited Venice is the most ill-built and ridiculous. I cannot imagine how the people who laid it out thought that the cavalry could manœuvre. It would puzzle Murat or Lasalle to bring a squadron into that square of theirs. For this reason we left Kellermann's heavy brigade and also my own Hussars at Padua on the mainland. But Suchet with the infantry held the town, and he had chosen me as his aide-de-camp for that winter, because he was pleased about the affair of the Italian fencing-master at Milan. The fellow was a good swordsman, and it was fortunate for the credit of the French arms that it was I who was opposed to him. Besides, he deserved a lesson, for if one does not like a *prima donna*'s singing one can always be silent, but it is intolerable that a public affront should be put upon a pretty woman. So the sympathy was all with me, and after the affair had blown over and the man's widow had been pensioned, Suchet chose me as his own galloper, and I followed him into Venice, where I had the strange adventure which I am about to tell you.

You have not been to Venice? No, for it is seldom that the French travel. We were great travellers in those days. From Moscow to Cairo we had travelled everywhere, but we went in larger parties than were convenient to those whom we visited, and we carried our passports in our limbers. It will be a bad day for Europe

when the French start travelling again, for they are slow
to leave their homes; but when they have done so no one
can say how far they will go if they have a guide like our
little man to point out the way. But the great days are
gone and the great men are dead, and here am I, the last
of them, drinking wine of Suresnes and telling old tales
in a café.

But it is of Venice that I would speak. The folks there
live like water-rats upon a mud-bank; but the houses are
very fine, and the churches, especially that of St. Mark,
are as great as any I have seen. But, above all, they are
all proud of their statues and their pictures, which are
the most famous in Europe. There are many soldiers who
think that because one's trade is to make war one should
never have a thought above fighting and plunder. There
was old Bouvet, for example—the one who was killed by
the Prussians on the day that I won the Emperor's medal;
if you took him away from the camp and the canteen, and
spoke to him of books or of art, he would sit and stare at
you. But the highest soldier is a man like myself who
can understand the things of the mind and the soul. It is
true that I was very young when I joined the army, and
that the quarter-master was my only teacher; but if you
go about the world with your eyes open you cannot help
learning a great deal.

Thus I was able to admire the pictures in Venice, and
to know the names of the great men, Michael Titiens,
and Angelus, and the others, who had painted them. No
one can say that Napoleon did not admire them also, for
the very first thing which he did when he captured the
town was to send the best of them to Paris. We all took
what we could get, and I had two pictures for my share.
One of them, called 'Nymphs Surprised', I kept for myself, and the other, 'Saint Barbara', I sent as a present for
my mother.

It must be confessed, however, that some of our men
behaved very badly in this matter of the statues and the
pictures. The people at Venice were very much attached

to them, and as to the four bronze horses which stood over the gate of their great church, they loved them as dearly as if they had been their children. I have always been a judge of a horse, and I had a good look at these ones, but I could not see that there was much to be said for them. They were too coarse-limbed for light cavalry chargers, and they had not the weight for the gun-teams. However, they were the only four horses, alive or dead, in the whole town, so it was not to be expected that the people would know any better. They wept bitterly when they were sent away, and ten French soldiers were found floating in the canals that night. As a punishment for these murders a great many more of their pictures were sent away, and the soldiers took to breaking the statues and firing their muskets at the stained-glass windows. This made the people furious, and there was very bad feeling in the town. Many officers and men disappeared during that winter, and even their bodies were never found.

For myself I had plenty to do, and I never found the time heavy on my hands. In every country it has been my custom to try to learn the language. For this reason I always look round for some lady who will be kind enough to teach it to me, and then we practise it together. This is the most interesting way of picking it up, and before I was thirty I could speak nearly every tongue in Europe; but it must be confessed that what you learn is not of much use for the ordinary purposes of life. My business, for example, has usually been with soldiers and peasants, and what advantage is it to be able to say to them that I love only them, and that I will come back when the wars are over?

Never have I had so sweet a teacher as in Venice. Lucia was her first name, and her second—but a gentleman forgets second names. I can say this with all discretion, that she was of one of the senatorial families of Venice, and that her grandfather had been Doge of the town. She was of an exquisite beauty—and when I, Etienne Gerard, use such a word as 'exquisite', my friends, it has a meaning. I have judgment, I have memories, I have the means of comparison. Of all the women who have loved me there are not twenty to whom I could apply such a term as that. But I say again that Lucia was exquisite. Of the dark type I do not recall her equal unless it were Dolores of Toledo. There was a little brunette whom I loved at Santarem when I was soldiering under Massena in Portugal—her name has escaped me. She was of a perfect beauty, but she had not the figure nor the grace of Lucia. There was Agnes, also. I could not put one before the other, but I do none an injustice when I say that Lucia was the equal of the best.

It was over this matter of pictures that I had first met her, for her father owned a palace on the farther side of the Rialto Bridge upon the Grand Canal, and it was so packed with wall-paintings that Suchet sent a party of sappers to cut some of them out and send them to Paris. I had gone down with them, and after I had seen Lucia in tears it appeared to me that the plaster would crack if it were taken from the support of the wall. I said so, and the sappers were withdrawn. After that I was the friend of the family, and many a flask of Chianti have I cracked with the father and many a sweet lesson have I had from the daughter. Some of our French officers married in Venice that winter, and I might have done the same, for I loved her with all my heart; but Etienne Gerard had his sword, his horse, his regiment, his mother, his Emperor, and his career. A debonair Hussar has room in his heart for love, but none for a wife. So I thought then, my friends, but I did not see the lonely days when I should long to clasp those vanished hands, and turn my head away when I saw old comrades with their tall children standing round their chairs. This love which I had thought was a joke and a plaything—it is only now that I understand that it is the moulder of one's life, the most solemn and sacred of all things. . . . Thank you, my friend, thank you! It is a good wine, and a second bottle cannot hurt.

And now I will tell you how my love for Lucia was the cause of one of the most terrible of all the wonderful adventures which have ever befallen me, and how it was that I came to lose the top of my right ear. You have often asked me why it was missing. To-night for the first time I will tell you.

Suchet's head-quarters at that time was the old palace of the Doge Dandolo, which stands on the lagoon not far from the place of San Marco. It was near the end of the winter, and I had returned one night from the Theatre Goldini, when I found a note from Lucia and a gondola waiting. She prayed me to come to her at once as she was in trouble. To a Frenchman and a soldier there was but one answer to such a note. In an instant I was in the boat and the gondolier was pushing out into the dark lagoon. I remember that as I took my seat in the boat I was struck by the man's great size. He was not tall, but he was one of the broadest men that I have ever seen in my life. But the gondoliers of Venice are a strong breed, and powerful men are common enough among them. The fellow took his place behind me and began to row.

A good soldier in an enemy's country should everywhere and at all times be on the alert. It has been one of the rules of my life, and if I have lived to wear grey hairs it is because I have observed it. And yet upon that night I was as careless as a foolish young recruit who fears lest he should be thought to be afraid. My pistols I had left behind in my hurry. My sword was at my belt, but it is not always the most convenient of weapons. I lay back in my seat in the gondola, lulled by the gentle swish of the water and the steady creaking of the oar. Our way lay through a network of narrow canals with high houses towering on either side and a thin slit of star-spangled sky above us. Here and there, on the bridges which spanned the canal, there was the dim glimmer of an oil lamp, and sometimes there came a gleam from some niche, where a candle burned before the image of a saint. But save for this it was all black, and one could only see the water by the white fringe which curled round the long black nose of our boat. It was a place and a time for dreaming. I thought of my own past life, of all the great deeds in which I had been concerned, of the horses that I had handled, and of the women that I had loved. Then I thought also of my dear mother, and I fancied her joy when she heard the folk in the village talking about the fame of her son. Of the Emperor also I thought, and of France, the dear fatherland, the sunny France, mother of beautiful daughters and of gallant sons. My heart glowed within me as I thought of how we had brought her colours so many hundred leagues beyond her borders. To her greatness I would dedicate my life. I placed my hand upon my heart as I swore it, and at that instant the gondolier fell upon me from behind.

When I say that he fell upon me I do not mean merely that he attacked me, but that he really did tumble upon me with all his weight. The fellow stands behind you and above you as he rows, so that you can neither see him nor can you in any way guard against such an assault. One moment I had sat with my mind filled with sublime resolutions, the next I was flattened out upon the bottom of the boat, the breath dashed out of my body, and this monster pinning me down. I felt the fierce pants of his hot breath upon the back of my neck. In an instant he had torn away my sword, had slipped a sack over my head, and had tied a rope firmly round the outside of it. There was I at the bottom of the gondola as helpless as a trussed fowl. I could not shout, I could not move; I was a mere bundle. An instant later I heard once more the swishing of the water and the creaking of the oar. This fellow had done his work and had resumed his journey as quietly and unconcernedly as if he were accustomed to clap a sack over a colonel of Hussars every day of the week.

I cannot tell you the humiliation and also the fury which filled my mind as I lay there like a helpless sheep being carried to the butcher's. I, Etienne Gerard, the champion of the six brigades of light cavalry and the first swordsman of the Grand Army, to be overpowered by a single, unarmed man in such a fashion! Yet I lay quiet, for there is a time to resist and there is a time to save one's strength. I had felt the fellow's grip upon my arms, and knew that I would be a child in his hands. I waited quietly, therefore, with a heart which burned with rage, until my opportunity should come.

How long I lay there at the bottom of the boat I cannot tell; but it seemed to me to be a long time, and always there were the hiss of the waters and the steady creaking of the oars. Several times we turned corners, for I heard the long, sad cry which these gondoliers give when they wish to warn their fellows that they are coming. At last, after a considerable journey, I felt the side of the boat scrape up against a landing-place. The fellow knocked three times with his oar upon wood, and in answer to his summons I heard the rasping of bars and the turning of keys. A great door creaked back upon its hinges.

'Have you got him?' asked a voice, in Italian.

My monster gave a laugh and kicked the sack in which I lay.

'Here he is,' said he.

'They are waiting.' He added something which I could not understand.

'Take him, then,' said my captor. He raised me in his arms, ascended some steps, and I was thrown down upon a hard floor. A moment later the bars creaked and the key whined once more. I was a prisoner inside a house.

From the voices and the steps there seemed now to be several people round me. I understand Italian a great deal better than I speak it, and I could make out very well what they were saying.

'You have not killed him, Matteo?'

'What matter if I have?'

381

'My faith, you will have to answer for it to the tribunal.'

'They will kill him, will they not?'

'Yes, but it is not for you or me to take it out of their hands.'

'Tut! I have not killed him. Dead men do not bite, and his cursed teeth met in my thumb as I pulled the sack over his head.'

'He lies very quiet.'

'Tumble him out and you will find he is lively enough.'

The cord which bound me was undone and the sack drawn from over my head. With my eyes closed I lay motionless upon the floor.

'By the saints, Matteo, I tell you that you have broken his neck.'

'Not I. He has only fainted. The better for him if he never came out of it again.'

I felt a hand within my tunic.

'Matteo is right,' said a voice. 'His heart beats like a hammer. Let him lie and he will soon find his senses.'

I waited for a minute or so and then I ventured to take a stealthy peep from between my lashes. At first I could see nothing, for I had been so long in darkness and it was but a dim light in which I found myself. Soon, however, I made out that a high and vaulted ceiling covered with painted gods and goddesses was arching over my head. This was no mean den of cut-throats into which I had been carried, but it must be the hall of some Venetian palace. Then, without movement, very slowly and stealthily I had a peep at the men who surrounded me. There was the gondolier, a swart, hard-faced, murderous ruffian, and beside him were three other men, one of them a little, twisted fellow with an air of authority and several keys in his hand, the other two tall young servants in a smart livery. As I listened to their talk I saw that the small man was the steward of the house, and that the others were under his orders.

There were four of them, then, but the little steward might be left out of the reckoning. Had I a weapon I should have smiled at such odds as those. But, hand to hand, I was no match for the one even without three others to aid him. Cunning, then, not force, must be my aid. I wished to look round for some mode of escape, and in doing so I gave an almost imperceptible movement of my head. Slight as it was it did not escape my guardians.

'Come, wake up, wake up!' cried the steward.

'Get on your feet, little Frenchman,' growled the gondolier. 'Get up, I say!' and for the second time he spurned me with his foot.

Never in the world was a command obeyed so promptly as that one. In an instant I had bounded to my feet and rushed as hard as I could run to the back of the hall. They were after me as I have seen the English hounds follow a fox, but there was a long passage down which I tore. It turned to the left and again to the left, and then I found myself back in the hall once more. They were almost within touch of me and there was no time for thought. I turned towards the staircase, but two men were coming down it. I dodged back and tried the door through which I had been brought, but it was fastened with great bars and I could not loosen them. The gondolier was on me with his knife, but I met him with a kick on the body which stretched him on his back. His dagger flew with a clatter across the marble floor. I had no time to seize it, for there were half a dozen of them now clutching at me. As I rushed through them the little steward thrust his leg before me and I fell with a crash, but I was up in an instant, and breaking from their grasp I burst through the very middle of them and made for a door at the other end of the hall. I reached it well in front of them, and I gave a shout of triumph as the handle turned freely in my hand, for I could see that it led to the outside and that all was clear for my escape. But I had forgotten this strange city in which I was.

Every house is an island. As I flung open the door, ready to bound out into the street, the light of the hall shone upon the deep, still, black water which lay flush with the topmost step. I shrank back, and in an instant my pursuers were on me. But I am not taken so easily.

Again I kicked and fought my way through them, though one of them tore a handful of hair from my head in his effort to hold me. The little steward struck me with a key and I was battered and bruised, but once more I cleared a way in front of me. Up the grand staircase I rushed, burst open the pair of huge folding doors which faced me, and learned at last that my efforts were in vain.

The room into which I had broken was brilliantly lighted. With its gold cornices, its massive pillars, and its painted walls and ceilings it was evidently the grand hall of some famous Venetian palace. There are many hundred such in this strange city, any one of which has rooms which would grace the Louvre or Versailles. In the centre of this great hall there was a raised daïs, and upon it in a half circle there sat twelve men all clad in black gowns, like those of a Franciscan monk, and each with a mask over the upper part of his face.

A group of armed men—rough-looking rascals—were standing round the door and, amid them, facing the daïs was a young fellow in the uniform of the light infantry. As he turned his head I recognised him. It was Captain Auret, of the 7th, a young Basque with whom I had drunk many a glass during the winter. He was deadly white, poor wretch, but he held himself manfully amid the assassins who surrounded him. Never shall I forget the sudden flash of hope which shone in his dark eyes when he saw a comrade burst into the room, or the look of despair which followed as he understood that I had come not to change his fate but to share it.

You can think how amazed these people were when I hurled myself into their presence. My pursuers had crowded in behind me and choked the doorway, so that all further flight was out of the question. It is at such instants that my nature asserts itself. With dignity I advanced towards the tribunal. My jacket was torn, my hair dishevelled, my head was bleeding, but there was that in my eyes and in my carriage which made them realise that no common man was before them. Not a hand was raised to arrest me until I halted in front of a formidable old man whose long grey beard and masterful manner told me that both by years and by character he was the man in authority.

'Sir,' said I, 'you will perhaps tell me why I have been forcibly arrested and brought to this place. I am an honourable soldier, as is this other gentleman here, and I demand that you will instantly set us both at liberty.'

There was an appalling silence to my appeal. It is not pleasant to have twelve masked faces turned upon you and to see twelve pairs of vindictive Italian eyes fixed with fierce intentness upon your face. But I stood as a debonair soldier should, and I could not but reflect how much credit I was bringing upon the Hussars of Conflans by the dignity of my bearing. I do not think that any one could have carried himself better under such difficult circumstances. I looked with a fearless face from one assassin to another, and I waited for some reply.

It was the greybeard who at last broke the silence.

'Who is this man?' he asked.

'His name is Gerard,' said the little steward at the door.

'Colonel Gerard,' said I. 'I will not deceive you. I am Etienne Gerard, *the* Colonel Gerard, five times mentioned in despatches and recommended for the sword of honour. I am aide-de-camp to General Suchet, and I demand my instant release, together with that of my comrade in arms.'

The same terrible silence fell upon the assembly, and the same twelve pairs of merciless eyes were bent upon my face. Again it was the greybeard who spoke.

'He is out of his order. There are two names upon our list before him.'

'He escaped from our hands and burst into the room.'

'Let him await his turn. Take him down to the wooden cell.'

'If he resists us, your excellency?'

'Bury your knives in his body. The tribunal will uphold you. Remove him until we have dealt with the others.'

They advanced upon me and for an instant I thought of resistance. It would have been a heroic death, but who was there to see it or to chronicle it? I might be only postponing my fate, and yet I had been in so many bad places and come out unhurt that I had learned always to hope and to trust my star. I allowed these rascals to seize me, and I was led from the room, the gondolier walking at my side with a long naked knife in his hand. I could see in his brutal eyes the satisfaction which it would give him if he could find some excuse for plunging it into my body.

They are wonderful places, these great Venetian houses, palaces and fortresses and prisons all in one. I was led along a passage and down a bare stone stair until we came to a short corridor from which three doors opened. Through one of these I was thrust and the spring lock closed behind me. The only light came dimly through a small grating which opened on the passage. Peering and feeling, I carefully examined the chamber in which I had been placed. I understood from what I had heard that I should soon have to leave it again in order to appear before this tribunal, but still it is not my nature to throw away any possible chances.

The stone floor of the cell was so damp and the walls for some feet high were so slimy and foul that it was evident that they were beneath the level of the water. A single slanting hole high up near the ceiling was the only aperture for light or air. Through it I saw one bright star shining down upon me, and the sight filled me with comfort and with hope. I have never been a man of religion, though I have always had a respect for those who were, but I remember that night that the star shining down the shaft seemed to be an all-seeing eye which was upon me, and I felt as a young and frightened recruit might feel in battle when he saw the calm gaze of his colonel turned upon him.

Three of the sides of my prison were formed of stone, but the fourth was of wood, and I could see that it had only recently been erected. Evidently a partition had been thrown up to divide a single large cell into two smaller ones. There was no hope for me in the old walls, in the tiny window, or in the massive door. It was only in this one direction of the wooden screen that there was any possibility of exploring. My reason told me that if I should pierce it—which did not seem very difficult—it would only be to find myself in another cell as strong as that in which I then was. Yet I had always rather be doing something than doing nothing, so I bent all my attention and all my energies upon the wooden wall. Two planks were badly joined and so loose that I was certain I could easily detach them. I searched about for some tool, and I found one in the leg of a small bed which stood in the corner. I forced the end of this into the chink of the planks, and I was about to twist them outwards when the sound of rapid footsteps caused me to pause and listen.

I wish I could forget what I heard. Many a hundred men have I seen die in battle, and I have slain more myself than I care to think of, but all that was fair fight and the duty of a soldier. It was a very different matter to listen to a murder in this den of assassins. They were pushing some one along the passage, some one who resisted and who clung to my door as he passed. They must have taken him into the third cell, the one which was farthest from me. 'Help! help!' cried a voice, and then I heard a blow and a scream. 'Help! help!' cried the voice again, and then 'Gerard! Colonel Gerard!' It was my poor captain of infantry whom they were slaughtering. 'Murderers! murderers!' I yelled, and I kicked at my door, but again I heard him shout, and then everything was silent. A minute later there was a heavy splash, and I knew that no human eye would ever see Auret again. He had gone as a hundred others had gone whose names were missing from the roll-calls of their regiments during that winter in Venice.

The steps returned along the passage, and I thought that they were coming for me. Instead of that they opened the door of the cell next to mine, and they took some one out of it. I heard the steps die away up the stair. At once I renewed my work upon the planks, and within a very few minutes I had loosened them in such a way that I could remove and replace them at pleasure. Passing through the aperture I found myself in the farther cell, which, as I expected, was the other half of the one in which I had been confined. I was not any nearer to escape than I had been before, for there was no other wooden wall which I could penetrate, and the spring lock of the door had been closed. There were no traces to show who was my companion in misfortune. Closing the two loose planks behind me, I returned to my own cell, and waited there with all the courage which I could command for the summons which would probably be my death-knell.

It was a long time in coming, but at last I heard the sound of feet once more in the passage, and I nerved myself to listen to some other odious deed and to hear the cries of the poor victim. Nothing of the kind occurred, however, and the prisoner was placed in the cell without violence. I had no time to peep through my hole of communication, for next moment my own door was flung open and my rascally gondolier, with the other assassins, came into the cell.

'Come, Frenchman,' said he. He held his blood-stained knife in his great hairy hand, and I read in his fierce eyes that he only looked for some excuse in order to plunge it into my heart. Resistance was useless. I followed without a word. I was led up the stone stair and back into

388

that gorgeous chamber in which I had left the secret tribunal. I was ushered in, but to my surprise it was not on me that their attention was fixed. One of their own number, a tall, dark young man, was standing before them and was pleading with them in low, earnest tones. His voice quivered with anxiety and his hands darted in and out or writhed together in an agony of entreaty. 'You cannot do it! You cannot do it!' he cried. 'I implore the tribunal to reconsider this decision.'

'Stand aside, brother,' said the old man who presided. 'The case is decided and another is up for judgment.'

'For Heaven's sake be merciful!' cried the young man.

'We have already been merciful,' the other answered. 'Death would have been a small penalty for such an offence. Be silent and let judgment take its course.'

I saw the young man throw himself in an agony of grief into his chair. I had no time, however, to speculate as to what it was which was troubling him, for his eleven colleagues had already fixed their stern eyes upon me. The moment of fate had arrived.

'You are Colonel Gerard?' said the terrible old man.

'I am.'

'Aide-de-camp to the robber who calls himself General Suchet, who in turn represents that arch-robber Buona-parte?'

It was on my lips to tell him that he was a liar, but there is a time to argue and a time to be silent.

'I am an honourable soldier,' said I. 'I have obeyed my orders and done my duty.'

The blood flushed into the old man's face and his eyes blazed through his mask.

'You are thieves and murderers, every man of you,' he cried. 'What are you doing here? You are Frenchmen. Why are you not in France? Did we invite you to Venice? By what right are you here? Where are our pictures? Where are the horses of St. Mark? Who are you that you should pilfer those treasures which our fathers through so many centuries have collected? We were a great city when France was a desert. Your drunken, brawling, ignorant soldiers have undone the work of saints and heroes. What have you to say to it?'

He was, indeed, a formidable old man, for his white beard bristled with fury and he barked out the little sentences like a savage hound. For my part I could have told him that his pictures would be safe in Paris, that his horses were really not worth making a fuss about, and that he could see heroes—I say nothing of saints—without going back to his ancestors or even moving out of his chair. All this I could have pointed out, but one might as well argue with a Mameluke about religion. I shrugged my shoulders and said nothing.

'The prisoner has no defence,' said one of my masked judges.

'Has any one any observation to make before judgment is passed?' The old man glared round him at the others.

'There is one matter, your excellency,' said another. 'It can scarce be referred to without reopening a brother's wounds, but I would remind you that there is a very particular reason why an exemplary punishment should be inflicted in the case of this officer.'

'I had not forgotten it,' the old man answered. 'Brother, if the tribunal has injured you in one direction, it will give you ample satisfaction in another.'

The young man who had been pleading when I entered the room staggered to his feet.

'I cannot endure it,' he cried. 'Your excellency must forgive me. The tribunal can act without me. I am ill! I am mad!' He flung his hands up with a furious gesture and rushed from the room.

'Let him go! Let him go!' said the president. 'It is, indeed, more than can be asked of flesh and blood that he should remain under this roof. But he is a true Venetian, and when the first agony is over he will understand that it could not be otherwise.'

I had been forgotten during this episode, and though I am not a man who is accustomed to being overlooked

I should have been all the happier had they continued to neglect me. But now the old president glared at me again like a tiger who comes back to his victim.

'You shall pay for it all, and it is but justice that you should,' said he. 'You, an upstart adventurer and foreigner, have dared to raise your eyes in love to the grand-daughter of a Doge of Venice who was already betrothed to the heir of the Loredans. He who enjoys such privileges must pay a price for them.'

'It cannot be higher than they are worth,' said I.

'You will tell us that when you have made a part payment,' he said. 'Perhaps your spirit may not be so proud by that time. Matteo, you will lead this prisoner to the wooden cell. To-night is Monday. Let him have no food or water, and let him be led before the tribunal again on Wednesday night. We shall then decide upon the death which he is to die.'

It was not a pleasant prospect, and yet it was a reprieve. One is thankful for small mercies when a hairy savage with a blood-stained knife is standing at one's elbow. He dragged me from the room and I was thrust down the stairs and back into my cell. The door was locked and I was left to my reflections.

My first thought was to establish connection with my neighbour in misfortune. I waited until the steps had died away, and then I cautiously drew aside the two boards and peeped through. The light was very dim, so dim that I could only just discern a figure huddled in the corner, and I could hear the low whisper of a voice which prayed as one prays who is in deadly fear. The boards must have made a creaking. There was a sharp exclamation of surprise.

'Courage, friend, courage!' I cried. 'All is not lost. Keep a stout heart, for Etienne Gerard is by your side.'

'Etienne!' It was a woman's voice which spoke—a voice which was always music to my ears. I sprang through the gap and I flung my arms round her. 'Lucia! Lucia!' I cried.

It was 'Etienne!' and 'Lucia!' for some minutes, for one does not make speeches at moments like that. It was she who came to her senses first.

'Oh, Etienne, they will kill you. How came you into their hands?'

'In answer to your letter.'

'I wrote no letter.'

'The cunning demons! But you?'

'I came also in answer to your letter.'

'Lucia, I wrote no letter.'

'They have trapped us both with the same bait.'

'I care nothing about myself, Lucia. Besides, there is no pressing danger with me. They have simply returned me to my cell.'

'Oh, Etienne, Etienne, they will kill you. Lorenzo is there.'

'The old greybeard?'

'No, no, a young dark man. He loved me, and I thought I loved him until—until I learned what love is, Etienne. He will never forgive you. He has a heart of stone.'

' Let them do what they like. They cannot rob me of the past, Lucia. But you—what about you?'

'It will be nothing, Etienne. Only a pang for an instant and then all over. They mean it as a badge of infamy, dear, but I will carry it like a crown of honour since it was through you that I gained it.'

Her words froze my blood with horror. All my adventures were insignificant compared to this terrible shadow which was creeping over my soul.

'Lucia! Lucia!' I cried. 'For pity's sake tell me what these butchers are about to do. Tell me, Lucia! Tell me!'

'I will not tell you, Etienne, for it would hurt you far more than it would me. Well, well, I will tell you lest you should fear it was something worse. The president has ordered that my ear be cut off, that I may be marked for ever as having loved a Frenchman.'

Her ear! The dear little ear which I had kissed so

often. I put my hand to each little velvet shell to make certain that this sacrilege had not yet been committed. Only over my dead body should they reach them. I swore it to her between my clenched teeth.

'You must not care, Etienne. And yet I love that you should care all the same.'

'They shall not hurt you—the fiends!'

'I have hopes, Etienne. Lorenzo is there. He was silent while I was judged, but he may have pleaded for me after I was gone.'

'He did. I heard him.'

'Then he may have softened their hearts.'

I knew that it was not so, but how could I bring myself to tell her? I might as well have done so, for with the quick instinct of woman my silence was speech to her.

'They would not listen to him! You need not fear to tell me, dear, for you will find that I am worthy to be loved by such a soldier. Where is Lorenzo now?'

'He left the hall.'

'Then he may have left the house as well.'

'I believe that he did.'

'He has abandoned me to my fate. Etienne, Etienne, they are coming!'

Afar off I heard those fateful steps and the jingle of distant keys. What were they coming for now, since there were no other prisoners to drag to judgment? It could only be to carry out the sentence upon my darling. I stood between her and the door, with the strength of a lion in my limbs. I would tear the house down before they should touch her.

'Go back! Go back!' she cried. 'They will murder you, Etienne. My life, at least, is safe. For the love you bear me, Etienne, go back. It is nothing. I will make no sound. You will not hear that it is done.'

She wrestled with me, the delicate creature, and by main force she dragged me to the opening between the cells. But a sudden thought had crossed my mind.

'We may yet be saved,' I whispered. 'Do what I tell

you at once and without argument. Go into my cell. Quick!'

I pushed her through the gap and helped her to replace the planks. I had retained her cloak in my hands, and with this wrapped round me I crept into the darkest corner of her cell. There I lay when the door was opened and several men came in. I had reckoned that they would bring no lantern, for they had none with them before. To their eyes I was only a black blur in the corner.

'Bring a light,' said one of them.

'No, no; curse it!' cried a rough voice, which I knew to be that of the ruffian Matteo. 'It is not a job that I like, and the more I saw it the less I should like it. I am sorry, signora, but the order of the tribunal has to be obeyed.'

My impulse was to spring to my feet and to rush through them all and out by the open door. But how would that help Lucia? Suppose that I got clear away, she would be in their hands until I could come back with help, for single-handed I could not hope to clear a way for her. All this flashed through my mind in an instant, and I saw that the only course for me was to lie still, take what came, and wait my chance. The fellow's coarse hand felt about among my curls—those curls in which only a woman's fingers had ever wandered. The next instant he gripped my ear, and a pain shot through me as if I had been touched with a hot iron. I bit my lip to stifle a cry, and I felt the blood run warm down my neck and back.

'There, thank Heaven that's over,' said the fellow, giving me a friendly pat on the head. 'You're a brave girl, signora, I'll say that for you, and I only wish you'd have better taste than to love a Frenchman. You can blame him and not me for what I have done.'

What could I do save to lie still and grind my teeth at my own helplessness? At the same time my pain and my rage were always soothed by the reflection that I had suffered for the woman whom I loved. It is the custom of men to say to ladies that they would willingly endure any pain for their sake, but it was my privilege to show that I had said no more than I meant. I thought also how nobly I would seem to have acted if ever the story came to be told, and how proud the regiment of Conflans might well be of their colonel. These thoughts helped me to suffer in silence while the blood still trickled over my neck and dripped upon the stone floor. It was that sound which nearly led to my destruction.

'She's bleeding fast,' said one of the valets. 'You had best fetch a surgeon or you will find her dead in the morning.'

'She lies very still and she's never opened her mouth,' said another. 'The shock has killed her.'

'Nonsense; a young woman does not die so easily.' It was Matteo who spoke. 'Besides, I did but snip off enough to leave the tribunal's mark upon her. Rouse up, signora, rouse up!'

He shook me by the shoulder, and my heart stood still for fear he should feel the epaulette under the mantle.

'How is it with you now?' he asked.

I made no answer.

'Curse it! I wish I had to do with a man instead of a woman, and the fairest woman in Venice,' said the gondolier. 'Here, Nicholas, lend me your handkerchief and bring a light.'

It was all over. The worst had happened. Nothing could save me. I still crouched in the corner, but I was tense in every muscle, like a wild cat about to spring. If I had to die I was determined that my end should be worthy of my life.

One of them had gone for a lamp, and Matteo was stooping over me with a handkerchief. In another instant my secret would be discovered. But he suddenly drew himself straight and stood motionless. At the same instant there came a confused murmuring sound through the little window far above my head. It was the rattle of oars and the buzz of many voices. Then there was a crash upon the door upstairs, and a terrible voice roared: 'Open! Open in the name of the Emperor!'

The Emperor! It was like the mention of some saint which, by its very sound, can frighten the demons. Away they ran with cries of terror—Matteo, the valets, the steward, all of the murderous gang. Another shout and then the crash of a hatchet and the splintering of planks. There were the rattle of arms and the cries of French soldiers in the hall. Next instant feet came flying down the stair and a man burst frantically into my cell.

'Lucia!' he cried, 'Lucia!' He stood in the dim light, panting and unable to find his words. Then he broke out again. 'Have I not shown you how I love you, Lucia? What more could I do to prove it? I have betrayed my country, I have broken my vow, I have ruined my friends, and I have given my life in order to save you.'

It was young Lorenzo Loredan, the lover whom I had superseded. My heart was heavy for him at the time, but after all it is every man for himself in love, and if one fails in the game it is some consolation to lose to one who can be a graceful and considerate winner. I was about to point this out to him, but at the first word I uttered he gave a shout of astonishment, and, rushing out, he seized the lamp which hung in the corridor and flashed it in my face.

'It is you, you villain!' he cried. 'You French coxcomb. You shall pay me for the wrong which you have done me.'

But the next instant he saw the pallor of my face and the blood which was still pouring from my head.

'What is this?' he asked. 'How come you to have lost your ear?'

I shook off my weakness and, pressing my handkerchief to my wound, I rose from my couch, the debonair colonel of Hussars.

'My injury, sir, is nothing. With your permission we will not allude to a matter so trifling and so personal.'

But Lucia had burst through from her cell and was

pouring out the whole story while she clasped Lorenzo's arm.

'This noble gentleman—he has taken my place, Lorenzo! He has borne it for me. He has suffered that I might be saved.'

I could sympathise with the struggle which I could see in the Italian's face. At last he held out his hand to me.

'Colonel Gerard,' he said, 'you are worthy of a great love. I forgive you, for if you have wronged me you have made a noble atonement. But I wonder to see you alive. I left the tribunal before you were judged, but I understood that no mercy would be shown to any Frenchman since the destruction of the ornaments of Venice.'

'He did not destroy them,' cried Lucia. 'He has helped to preserve those in our palace.'

'One of them, at any rate,' said I, as I stooped and kissed her hand.

This was the way, my friends, in which I lost my ear. Lorenzo was found stabbed to the heart in the Piazza of St. Mark within two days of the night of my adventure. Of the tribunal and its ruffians, Matteo and three others were shot, the rest banished from the town. Lucia, my lovely Lucia, retired into a convent at Murano after the French had left the city, and there she still may be, some gentle lady abbess who has perhaps long forgotten the days when our hearts throbbed together, and when the whole great world seemed so small a thing beside the love which burned in our veins. Or perhaps it may not be so. Perhaps she has not forgotten. There may still be times when the peace of the cloister is broken by the memory of the old soldier who loved her in those distant days. Youth is past and passion is gone, but the soul of the gentleman can never change, and still Etienne Gerard would bow his grey head before her and would very gladly lose this other ear if he might do her a service.

II. How the Brigadier Captured Saragossa

HAVE I ever told you, my friends, the circumstances connected with my joining the Hussars of Conflans at the time of the siege of Saragossa, and the very remarkable exploit which I performed in connection with the taking of that city? No? Then you have indeed something still to learn. I will tell it to you exactly as it occurred. Save for two or three men and a score or two of women, you are the first who have ever heard the story.

You must know, then, that it was in the 2nd Hussars—called the Hussars of Chamberan—that I served as a lieutenant and as a junior captain. At the time I speak of I was only twenty-five years of age, as reckless and desperate a man as any in that great army. It chanced that the war had come to a halt in Germany, while it was still raging in Spain; so the Emperor, wishing to reinforce the Spanish army, transferred me as senior captain to the Hussars of Conflans, which were at that time in the 5th Army Corps under Marshal Lannes.

It was a long journey from Berlin to the Pyrenees. My new regiment formed part of the force which, under Marshal Lannes, was then besieging the Spanish town of Saragossa. I turned my horse's head in that direction, therefore, and behold me a week or so later at the French head-quarters, whence I was directed to the camp of the Hussars of Conflans.

You have read, no doubt, of this famous siege of Saragossa, and I will only say that no general could have had a harder task than that with which Marshal Lannes was confronted. The immense city was crowded with a horde of Spaniards—soldiers, peasants, priests—all filled with the most furious hatred of the French, and the most savage determination to perish before they would surrender. There were eighty thousand men in the town and only thirty thousand to besiege them. Yet we had a powerful artillery, and our Engineers were of the best.

There was never such a siege, for it is usual that when the fortifications are taken the city falls; but here it was not until the fortifications were taken that the real fighting began. Every house was a fort and every street a battle-field, so that slowly, day by day, we had to work our way inwards, blowing up the houses with their garrisons until more than half the city had disappeared. Yet the other half was as determined as ever, and in a better position for defence, since it consisted of enormous convents and monasteries with walls like the Bastille, which could not be so easily brushed out of our way. This was the state of things at the time that I joined the army.

I will confess to you that cavalry are not of much use in a siege, although there was a time when I would not have permitted any one to have made such an observation. The Hussars of Conflans were encamped to the south of the town, and it was their duty to throw out patrols and to make sure that no Spanish force was advancing from that quarter. The colonel of the regiment was not a good soldier, and the regiment was at that time very far from being in the high condition which it afterwards attained. Even in that one evening I saw several things which shocked me; for I had a high standard, and it went to my heart to see an ill-arranged camp, an ill-groomed horse, or a slovenly trooper. That night I supped with twenty-six of my new brother-officers, and I fear that in my zeal I showed them only too plainly that I found things very different to what I was accustomed to in the army of Germany. There was silence in the mess after my remarks, and I felt that I had been indiscreet when I saw the glances that were cast at me. The colonel especially was furious, and a great major named Olivier, who was the fire-eater of the regiment, sat opposite to me curling his huge black moustaches, and staring at me as if he would eat me. However, I did not resent his attitude, for I felt that I had indeed been indiscreet, and that it would give a bad impression if upon this my first evening I quarrelled with my superior officer.

So far I admit that I was wrong, but now I come to the sequel. Supper over, the colonel and some other officers left the room, for it was in a farmhouse that the mess was held. There remained a dozen or so, and a goat-skin of Spanish wine having been brought in, we all made merry. Presently this Major Olivier asked me some questions concerning the army of Germany and as to the part which I had myself played in the campaign. Flushed with wine, I was drawn on from story to story. It was not unnatural, my friends. You will sympathise with me. Up there I had been the model for every officer of my years in the army. I was the first swordsman, the most dashing rider, the hero of a hundred adventures. Here I found myself not only unknown, but even disliked. Was it not natural that I should wish to tell these brave comrades what sort of man it was that had come among them? Was it not natural that I should wish to say, 'Rejoice, my friends, rejoice! It is no ordinary man who has joined you to-night, but it is I, *the* Gerard, the hero of Ratisbon, the victor of Jena, the man who broke the square at Austerlitz'? I could not say all this. But I could at least tell them some incidents which would enable them to say it for themselves. I did so. They listened unmoved. I told them more. At last, after my tale of how I had guided the army across the Danube, one universal shout of laughter broke from them all. I sprang to my feet, flushed with shame and anger. They had drawn me on. They were making game of me. They were convinced that they had to do with a braggart and a liar. Was this my reception in the Hussars of Conflans? I dashed the tears of mortification from my eyes, and they laughed the more at the sight.

'Do you know, Captain Pelletan, whether Marshal Lannes is still with the army?' asked the major.

'I believe that he is, sir,' said the other.

'Really, I should have thought that his presence was hardly necessary now that Captain Gerard has arrived.'

Again there was a roar of laughter. I can see the ring of

faces, the mocking eyes, the open mouths—Olivier with his great black bristles, Pelletan thin and sneering, even the young sub-lieutenants convulsed with merriment. Heavens, the indignity of it! But my rage had dried my tears. I was myself again, cold, quiet, self-contained, ice without and fire within.

'May I ask, sir,' said I to the major, 'at what hour the regiment is paraded?'

'I trust, Captain Gerard, that you do not mean to alter our hours,' said he, and again there was a burst of laughter, which died away as I looked slowly round the circle.

'What hour is the assembly?' I asked, sharply, of Captain Pelletan.

Some mocking answer was on his tongue, but my glance kept it there. 'The assembly is at six,' he answered.

'I thank you,' said I. I then counted the company, and found that I had to do with fourteen officers, two of whom appeared to be boys fresh from St. Cyr. I could not condescend to take any notice of their indiscretion. There remained the major, four captains, and seven lieutenants.

'Gentlemen,' I continued, looking from one to the other of them, 'I should feel myself unworthy of this famous regiment if I did not ask you for satisfaction for the rudeness with which you have greeted me, and I should hold you to be unworthy of it if on any pretext you refused to grant it.'

'You will have no difficulty upon that score,' said the major. 'I am prepared to waive my rank and to give you every satisfaction in the name of the Hussars of Conflans.'

'I thank you,' I answered. 'I feel, however, that I have some claim upon these other gentlemen who laughed at my expense.'

'Whom would you fight, then?' asked Captain Pelletan.

'All of you,' I answered.

They looked in surprise from one to the other. Then

they drew off to the other end of the room, and I heard the buzz of their whispers. They were laughing. Evidently they still thought that they had to do with some empty braggart. Then they returned.

'Your request is unusual,' said Major Olivier, 'but it will be granted. How do you propose to conduct such a duel? The terms lie with you.'

'Sabres,' said I. 'And I will take you in order of seniority, beginning with you, Major Olivier, at five o'clock. I will thus be able to devote five minutes to each before the assembly is blown. I must, however, beg you to have the courtesy to name the place of meeting, since I am still ignorant of the locality.'

They were impressed by my cold and practical manner. Already the smile had died away from their lips. Olivier's face was no longer mocking, but it was dark and stern.

'There is a small open space behind the horse lines,' said he. 'We have held a few affairs of honour there, and it has done very well. We shall be there, Captain Gerard, at the hour you name.'

I was in the act of bowing to thank them for their acceptance when the door of the mess-room was flung open and the colonel hurried into the room, with an agitated face.

'Gentlemen,' said he, 'I have been asked to call for a volunteer from among you for a service which involves the greatest possible danger. I will not disguise from you that the matter is serious in the last degree, and that Marshal Lannes has chosen a cavalry officer because he can be better spared than an officer of infantry or of Engineers. Married men are not eligible. Of the others, who will volunteer?'

I need not say that all the unmarried officers stepped to the front. The colonel looked round in some embarrassment. I could see his dilemma. It was the best man who should go, and yet it was the best man whom he could least spare.

'Sir,' said I, 'may I be permitted to make a suggestion?'

He looked at me with a hard eye. He had not forgotten my observations at supper. 'Speak!' said he.

'I would point out, sir,' said I, 'that this mission is mine both by right and by convenience.'

'Why so, Captain Gerard?'

'By right, because I am the senior captain. By convenience, because I shall not be missed in the regiment, since the men have not yet learned to know me.'

The colonel's features relaxed.

'There is certainly truth in what you say, Captain Gerard,' said he. 'I think that you are indeed best fitted to go upon this mission. If you will come with me I will give you your instructions.'

I wished my new comrades good-night as I left the room, and I repeated that I should hold myself at their disposal at five o'clock next morning. They bowed in silence, and I thought that I could see, from the expression of their faces, that they had already begun to take a more just view of my character.

I had expected that the colonel would at once inform me what it was that I had been chosen to do, but instead of that he walked on in silence, I following behind him. We passed through the camp and made our way across the trenches and over the ruined heaps of stones which marked the old wall of the town. Within there was a labyrinth of passages, formed among the débris of the houses which had been destroyed by the mines of the Engineers. Acres and acres were covered with splintered walls and piles of brick which had once been a populous suburb. Lanes had been driven through it and lanterns placed at the corners with inscriptions to direct the wayfarer. The colonel hurried onwards until at last, after a long walk, we found our way barred by a high grey wall which stretched right across our path. Here behind a barricade lay our advanced guard. The colonel led me into a roofless house, and there I found two general officers, a map stretched over a drum in front of them, they kneeling beside it and examining it carefully by the light of a lantern. The one with the clean-shaven face and the twisted neck was Marshal Lannes, the other was General Razout, the head of the Engineers.

'Captain Gerard has volunteered to go,' said the colonel.

Marshal Lannes rose from his knees and shook me by the hand.

'You are a brave man, sir,' said he. 'I have a present to make to you,' he added, handing me a very tiny glass tube. 'It has been specially prepared by Dr. Fardet. At the supreme moment you have but to put it to your lips and you will be dead in an instant.'

This was a cheerful beginning. I will confess to you, my friends, that a cold chill passed up my back and my hair rose upon my head.

'Excuse me, sir,' said I, as I saluted, 'I am aware that I have volunteered for a service of great danger, but the exact details have not yet been given to me.'

'Colonel Perrin,' said Lannes severely, 'it is unfair to allow this brave officer to volunteer before he has learned what the perils are to which he will be exposed.'

But already I was myself once more.

'Sir,' said I, 'permit me to remark that the greater the danger the greater the glory, and that I could only repent of volunteering if I found that there were no risks to be run.'

It was a noble speech, and my appearance gave force to my words. For the moment I was an heroic figure. As I saw Lannes's eyes fixed in admiration upon my face it thrilled me to think how splendid was the début which I was making in the army of Spain. If I died that night my name would not be forgotten. My new comrades and my old, divided in all else, would still have a point of union in their love and admiration of Etienne Gerard.

'General Razout, explain the situation!' said Lannes, briefly.

The Engineer officer rose, his compasses in his hand.

He led me to the door and pointed to the high grey wall which towered up amongst the débris of the shattered houses.

'That is the enemy's present line of defence,' said he. 'It is the wall of the great Convent of the Madonna. If we can carry it the city must fall, but they have run counter-mines all round it, and the walls are so enormously thick that it would be an immense labour to breach it with artillery. We happen to know, however, that the enemy have a considerable store of powder in one of the lower chambers. If that could be exploded the way would be clear for us.'

'How can it be reached?' I asked.

'I will explain. We have a French agent within the town named Hubert. This brave man has been in constant communication with us, and he had promised to explode the magazine. It was to be done in the early morning, and for two days running we have had a storming party of a thousand Grenadiers waiting for the breach to be formed. But there has been no explosion, and for these two days we have had no communication from Hubert. The question is, what has become of him?'

'You wish me to go and see?'

'Precisely. Is he ill, or wounded, or dead? Shall we still wait for him, or shall we attempt the attack elsewhere? We cannot determine this until we have heard from him. This is a map of the town, Captain Gerard. You perceive that within this ring of convents and monasteries are a number of streets which branch off from a central square. If you come so far as this square you will find the cathedral at one corner. In that corner is the street of Toledo. Hubert lives in a small house between a cobbler's and a wine-shop, on the right-hand side as you go from the cathedral. Do you follow me?'

'Clearly.'

'You are to reach that house, to see him, and to find out if his plan is still feasible or if we must abandon it.'

He produced what appeared to be a roll of dirty brown flannel. 'This is the dress of a Franciscan friar,' said he. 'You will find it the most useful disguise.'

I shrank away from it.

'It turns me into a spy,' I cried. 'Surely I can go in my uniform?'

'Impossible! How could you hope to pass through the streets of the city? Remember, also, that the Spaniards take no prisoners, and that your fate will be the same in whatever dress you are taken.'

It was true, and I had been long enough in Spain to know that that fate was likely to be something more serious than mere death. All the way from the frontier I had heard grim tales of torture and mutilation. I enveloped myself in the Franciscan gown.

'Now I am ready.'

'Are you armed?'

'My sabre.'

'They will hear it clank. Take this knife and leave your sword. Tell Hubert that at four o'clock before dawn the storming party will again be ready. There is a sergeant outside who will show you how to get into the city. Good-night, and good luck!'

Before I had left the room the two generals had their cocked hats touching each other over the map. At the door an under-officer of Engineers was waiting for me. I tied the girdle of my gown, and taking off my busby I drew the cowl over my head. My spurs I removed. Then in silence I followed my guide.

It was necessary to move with caution, for the walls above were lined by the Spanish sentries, who fired down continually at our advanced posts. Slinking along under the very shadow of the great convent, we picked our way slowly and carefully among the piles of ruins until we came to a large chestnut tree. Here the sergeant stopped.

'It is an easy tree to climb,' said he. 'A scaling ladder would not be simpler. Go up it, and you will find that the top branch will enable you to step upon the roof of that house. After that it is your guardian angel who must be your guide, for I can help you no more.'

Girding up the heavy brown gown, I ascended the tree as directed. A half-moon was shining brightly, and the line of roof stood out dark and hard against the purple, starry sky. The tree was in the shadow of the house. Slowly I crept from branch to branch until I was near the top. I had but to climb along a stout limb in order to reach the wall. But suddenly my ears caught the patter of feet, and I cowered against the trunk and tried to blend myself with its shadow. A man was coming towards me on the roof. I saw his dark figure creeping along, his body crouching, his head advanced, the barrel of his gun protruding. His whole bearing was full of caution and suspicion. Once or twice he paused, and then came on again until he had reached the edge of the parapet within a few yards of me. Then he knelt down, levelled his musket, and fired.

I was so astonished at this sudden crash at my very elbow that I nearly fell out of the tree. For an instant I could not be sure that he had not hit me. But when I heard a deep groan from below, and the Spaniard leaned over the parapet and laughed aloud, I understood what had occurred. It was my poor, faithful sergeant who had waited to see the last of me. The Spaniard had seen him standing under the tree and had shot him. You will think that it was good shooting in the dark, but these people use *trebucos*, or blunderbusses, which are filled up with all sorts of stones and scraps of metal, so that they will hit you as certainly as I have hit a pheasant on a branch. The Spaniard stood peering down through the darkness, while an occasional groan from below showed that the sergeant was still living. The sentry looked round and everything was still and safe. Perhaps he thought that he would like to finish off this accursed Frenchman, or perhaps he had a desire to see what was in his pockets; but whatever his motive he laid down his gun, leaned forward, and swung himself into the tree.

The same instant I buried my knife in his body, and he fell with a loud crashing through the branches and came with a thud to the ground. I heard a short struggle below and an oath or two in French. The wounded sergeant had not waited long for his vengeance.

For some minutes I did not dare to move, for it seemed certain that someone would be attracted by the noise. However, all was silent save for the chimes striking midnight in the city. I crept along the branch and lifted myself on to the roof. The Spaniard's gun was lying there, but it was of no service to me, since he had the powder-horn at his belt. At the same time, if it were found it would warn the enemy that something had happened, so I thought it best to drop it over the wall. Then I looked round for the means of getting off the roof and down into the city.

It was very evident that the simplest way by which I could get down was that by which the sentinel had got up, and what this was soon became evident. A voice along the roof called 'Manuelo! Manuelo!' several times, and, crouching in the shadow, I saw in the moonlight a bearded head, which protruded from a trap-door. Receiving no answer to his summons the man climbed through, followed by three other fellows all armed to the teeth. You will see here how important it is not to neglect small precautions, for had I left the man's gun where I found it a search must have followed, and I should certainly have been discovered. As it was, the patrol saw no sign of their sentry and thought, no doubt, that he had moved along the line of the roofs. They hurried on, therefore, in that direction, and I, the instant that their backs were turned, rushed to the open trap-door and descended the flight of steps which led from it. The house appeared to be an empty one, for I passed through the heart of it and out, by an open door, into the street beyond.

It was a narrow and deserted lane, but it opened into a broader road, which was dotted with fires, round which a great number of soldiers and peasants were sleeping.

The smell within the city was so horrible that one wondered how people could live in it, for during the months that the siege had lasted there had been no attempt to cleanse the streets or to bury the dead. Many people were moving up and down from fire to fire, and among them I observed several monks. Seeing that they came and went unquestioned, I took heart and hurried on my way in the direction of the great square. Once a man rose from beside one of the fires and stopped me by seizing my sleeve. He pointed to a woman who lay motionless upon the road, and I took him to mean that she was dying, and that he desired me to administer the last offices of the Church. I sought refuge, however, in the very little Latin that was left to me. *'Ora pro nobis,'* said I, from the depths of my cowl. *'Te deum laudamus. Ora pro nobis.'* I raised my hand as I spoke and pointed forwards. The fellow released my sleeve and shrank back in silence, while I, with a solemn gesture, hurried upon my way.

As I had imagined, this broad boulevard led out into the central square, which was full of troops and blazing with fires. I walked swiftly onwards, disregarding one or two people who addressed remarks to me. I passed the cathedral and followed the street which had been described to me. Being upon the side of the city which was farthest from our attack, there were no troops encamped in it, and it lay in darkness, save for an occasional glimmer in a window. It was not difficult to find the house to which I had been directed, between the wine-shop and the cobbler's. There was no light within, and the door was shut. Cautiously I pressed the latch, and I felt that it had yielded. Who was within I could not tell, and yet I must take the risk. I pushed the door open and entered.

It was pitch-dark within—the more so as I had closed the door behind me. I felt round and came upon the edge of a table. Then I stood still and wondered what I should do next, and how I could gain some news of this Hubert, in whose house I found myself. Any mistake would cost me not only my life, but the failure of my mission. Perhaps he did not live alone. Perhaps he was only a lodger in a Spanish family, and my visit might bring ruin to him as well as to myself. Seldom in my life have I been more perplexed. And then, suddenly, something turned my blood cold in my veins. It was a voice, a whispering voice, in my very ear. 'Mon Dieu!' cried the voice in a tone of agony. 'Oh, mon Dieu! mon Dieu!' Then there was a dry sob in the darkness, and all was still once more.

It thrilled me with horror, that terrible voice; but it thrilled me also with hope, for it was the voice of a Frenchman.

'Who is there?' I asked.

There was a groaning, but no reply.

'Is that you, Monsieur Hubert?'

'Yes, yes,' sighed the voice, so low that I could hardly hear it. 'Water, water, for Heaven's sake, water!'

I advanced in the direction of the sound, but only to come in contact with the wall. Again I heard a groan, but this time there could be no doubt that it was above my head. I put up my hands, but they felt only empty air.

'Where are you?' I cried.

'Here! Here!' whispered the strange, tremulous voice. I stretched my hand along the wall, and I came upon a man's naked foot. It was as high as my face, and yet, so far as I could feel, it had nothing to support it. I staggered back in amazement. Then I took a tinder-box from my pocket and struck a light. At the first flash a man seemed to be floating in the air in front of me, and I dropped the box in my amazement. Again, with tremulous fingers, I struck the flint against the steel, and this time I lit not only the tinder, but the wax taper. I held it up, and if my amazement was lessened, my horror was increased by that which it revealed.

The man had been nailed to the wall as a weasel is nailed to the door of a barn. Huge spikes had been driven through his hands and his feet. The poor wretch was in his last agony, his head sunk upon his shoulder and his blackened tongue protruded from his lips. He was dying as much from thirst as from his wounds, and these inhuman wretches had placed a beaker of wine upon the table in front of him to add a fresh pang to his tortures. I raised it to his lips. He had still strength enough to swallow, and the light came back a little to his dim eyes.

'Are you a Frenchman?' he whispered.

'Yes. They have sent me to learn what had befallen you.'

'They discovered me. They have killed me for it. But before I die let me tell you what I know. A little more of that wine, please! Quick! Quick! I am very near the end. My strength is going. Listen to me! The powder is stored in the Mother Superior's room. The wall is pierced, and the end of the train is in Sister Angela's cell, next the chapel. All was ready two days ago. But they discovered a letter, and they tortured me.'

'Good Heavens! have you been hanging here for two days?'

'It seems like two years. Comrade, I have served France, have I not? Then do one little service for me. Stab me to the heart, dear friend! I implore you, I entreat you, to put an end to my sufferings.'

The man was indeed in a hopeless plight, and the kindest action would have been that for which he begged. And yet I could not in cold blood drive my knife into his body, although I knew how I should have prayed for such a mercy had I been in his place. But a sudden thought crossed my mind. In my pocket I held that which would give an instant and painless death. It was my own safeguard against torture, and yet this poor soul was in very pressing need of it, and he had deserved well of France.

I took out my phial and emptied it into the cup of wine. I was in the act of handing it to him when I heard a sudden clash of arms outside the door. In an instant

I put out my light and slipped behind the window-curtains. Next moment the door was flung open, and two Spaniards strode into the room—fierce, swarthy men in the dress of citizens, but with muskets slung over their shoulders. I looked through the chink in the curtains in an agony of fear lest they had come upon my traces, but it was evident that their visit was simply in order to feast their eyes upon my unfortunate compatriot. One of them held the lantern which he carried up in front of the dying man, and both of them burst into a shout of mocking laughter. Then the eyes of the man with the lantern fell upon the flagon of wine upon the table. He picked it up, held it, with a devilish grin, to the lips of Hubert, and then, as the poor wretch involuntarily inclined his head forward to reach it, snatched it back and took a long gulp himself. At the same instant he uttered a loud cry, clutched wildly at his own throat, and fell stone-dead upon the floor. His comrade stared at him in horror and amazement. Then, overcome by his own superstitious fears, he gave a yell of terror and rushed madly from the room. I heard his feet clattering wildly on the cobble-stones until the sound died away in the distance.

The lantern had been left burning upon the table, and by its light I saw, as I came out from behind my curtain, that the unfortunate Hubert's head had fallen forward upon his chest and that he also was dead. That motion to reach the wine with his lips had been his last. A clock ticked loudly in the house, but otherwise all was absolutely still. On the wall hung the twisted form of the Frenchman, on the floor lay the motionless body of the Spaniard, all dimly lit by the horn lantern. For the first time in my life a frantic spasm of terror came over me. I had seen ten thousand men in every conceivable degree of mutilation stretched upon the ground, but the sight had never affected me like those two silent figures who were my companions in that shadowy room. I rushed into the street as the Spaniard had done, eager only to leave that house of gloom behind me, and I had run as far as the cathedral before my wits came back to me. There I stopped panting in the shadow, and, my hand pressed to my side, I tried to collect my scattered senses and to plan out what I should do. As I stood there, breathless, the great brass bells roared twice above my head. It was two o'clock. Four was the hour when the storming party would be in its place. I had still two hours in which to act.

The cathedral was brilliantly lit within, and a number of people were passing in and out; so I entered, thinking that I was less likely to be accosted there and that I might have quiet to form my plans. It was certainly a singular sight, for the place had been turned into a hospital, a refuge, and a storehouse. One aisle was crammed with provisions, another was littered with sick and wounded, while in the centre a great number of helpless people had taken up their abode and had even lit their cooking fires upon the mosaic floors. There were many at prayer, so I knelt in the shadow of a pillar and I prayed with all my heart that I might have the good luck to get out of this scrape alive, and that I might do such a deed that night as would make my name as famous in Spain as it had become in Germany. I waited until the clock struck three and then I left the cathedral and made my way towards the Convent of the Madonna, where the assault was to be delivered. You will understand, you who know me so well, that I was not the man to return tamely to the French camp with the report that our agent was dead and that other means must be found of entering the city. Either I should find some means to finish his uncompleted task or there would be a vacancy for a senior captain in the Hussars of Conflans.

I passed unquestioned down the broad boulevard, which I have already described, until I came to the great stone convent which formed the outwork of the defence. It was built in a square with a garden in the centre. In this garden some hundreds of men were assembled, all armed and ready, for it was known, of course, within the town that this was the point against which the French attack was likely to be made. Up to this time our fighting all over Europe had always been done between one army and another. It was only here in Spain that we learned how terrible a thing it is to fight against a people. On the one hand there is no glory, for what glory could be gained by defeating this rabble of elderly shopkeepers, ignorant peasants, fanatical priests, excited women, and all the other creatures who made up the garrison? On the other hand there were extreme discomfort and danger, for these people would give you no rest, would observe no rules of war, and were desperately earnest in their desire by hook or by crook to do you an injury. I began to realise how odious was our task as I looked upon the motley but ferocious groups who were gathered round the watch fires in the garden of the Convent of the Madonna. It was not for us soldiers to think about politics, but from the beginning there always seemed to be a curse upon this war in Spain.

However, at the moment I had no time to brood over such matters as these. There was, as I have said, no difficulty in getting as far as the convent garden, but to pass inside the convent unquestioned was not so easy. The first thing which I did was to walk round the garden, and I was soon able to pick out one large stained-glass window which must belong to the chapel. I had understood from Hubert that the Mother Superior's room in which the powder was stored was near to this, and that the train had been laid through a hole in the wall from some neighbouring cell. I must at all costs get into the convent. There was a guard at the door, and how could I get in without explanations? But a sudden inspiration showed me how the thing might be done. In the garden was a well, and beside the well were a number of empty buckets. I filled two of these and approached the door. The errand of a man who carries a bucket of water in each hand does not need to be explained. The guard opened to let me through. I found myself in a long stone-flagged corridor lit with lanterns, with the cells of the nuns leading out from one side of it. Now at last I was on the high road to success. I walked on without hesitation, for I knew by my observations in the garden which way to go for the chapel.

A number of Spanish soldiers were lounging and smoking in the corridor, several of whom addressed me as I passed. I fancy it was for my blessing that they asked, and my 'Ora pro nobis' seemed to entirely satisfy them. Soon I had got as far as the chapel, and it was easy to see that the cell next door was used as a magazine, for the floor was all black with powder in front of it. The door was shut, and two fierce-looking fellows stood on guard outside it, one of them with a key stuck in his belt. Had we been alone it would not have been long before it would have been in my hand, but with his comrade there it was impossible for me to hope to take it by force. The cell next door to the magazine on the far side from the chapel must be the one which belonged to Sister Angela. It was half open. I took my courage in both hands, and leaving my buckets in the corridor, I walked unchallenged into the room.

I was prepared to find half a dozen fierce Spanish desperadoes within, but what actually met my eyes was even more embarrassing. The room had apparently been set aside for the use of some of the nuns, who for some reason had refused to quit their home. Three of them were within, one an elderly, stern-faced dame who was evidently the Mother Superior, the others young ladies of charming appearance. They were seated together at the far side of the room, and I saw with some amazement, by their manner and expressions, that my coming was both welcome and expected. In a moment my presence of mind had returned, and I saw exactly how the matter lay. Naturally, since an attack was about to be made upon the convent, these sisters had been expecting to be directed to some place of safety. Probably they were under vow not to quit the walls, and they had been told to remain in this cell until they had received further orders. In any case I adapted my conduct to this supposition, since it was clear that I must get them out of the room, and this would give me a ready excuse to do so. I first cast a glance at the door and observed that the key was within. I then made a gesture to the nuns to follow me. The Mother Superior asked me some question, but I shook my head impatiently and beckoned to her again. She hesitated, but I stamped my foot and called them forth in so imperious a manner that they came at once. They would be safer in the chapel, and thither I led them, placing them at the end which was farthest from the magazine. As the three nuns took their places before the altar my heart bounded with joy and pride within me, for I felt that the last obstacle had been lifted from my path.

And yet how often have I not found that this is the very moment of danger? I took a last glance at the Mother Superior, and to my dismay I saw that her piercing dark eyes were fixed, with an expression in which surprise was deepening into suspicion, upon my right hand. There were two points which might well have attracted her attention. One was that it was red with the blood of the sentinel whom I had stabbed in the tree. That alone might count for little, as the knife is as familiar as the breviary to the monks of Saragossa. But on my forefinger I wore a heavy gold ring—the gift of a German baroness whose name I may not mention. It shone brightly in the light of the altar lamp. Now, a ring upon a friar's hand is an impossibility, since they are vowed to absolute poverty. I turned quickly and made for the door of the chapel, but the mischief was done. As I glanced back I saw that the Mother Superior was already hurrying after me. I ran through the chapel door and along the corridor, but she called out some shrill warning to the two guards in front. Fortunately I had the presence of mind to call out also, and to point down the passage as if we were both pursuing the same object. Next instant I had dashed past them, sprang into the cell, slammed the heavy door, and fastened it upon the inside. With a bolt above and below and a huge lock in the centre it was a piece of timber that would take some forcing.

Even now if they had had the wit to put a barrel of gunpowder against the door I should have been ruined. It was their only chance, for I had come to the final stage of my adventure. Here at last, after such a string of dangers as few men have ever lived to talk of I was at one end of the powder train, with the Saragossa magazine at the other. They were howling like wolves out in the passage, and muskets were crashing against the door. I paid no heed to their clamour, but I looked eagerly round for that train of which Hubert had spoken. Of course, it must be at the side of the room next to the magazine. I crawled along it on my hands and knees, looking into every crevice, but no sign could I see. Two bullets flew through the door and flattened themselves against the wall. The thudding and smashing grew ever louder. I saw a grey pile in a corner, flew to it with a cry of joy, and found that it was only dust. Then I got back to the side of the door where no bullets could ever reach me—they were streaming freely into the room—and I tried to forget this fiendish howling in my ear and to think out where this train could be. It must have been carefully laid by Hubert lest these nuns should see it. I tried to imagine how I should myself have arranged it had I been in his place. My eye was attracted by a statue of St. Joseph which stood in the corner. There was a wreath of leaves along the edge of the pedestal, with a lamp burning amidst them. I rushed across to it and tore the leaves aside. Yes, yes, there was a thin black line, which disappeared through a small hole in the wall. I tilted over the lamp, and threw myself on the ground. Next instant came a roar like thunder, the walls wavered and tottered around me, the ceiling clattered down from above, and over the yell of the terrified Spaniards was heard the terrific shout of the storming column of the Grenadiers. As in a dream—a happy dream—I heard it, and then I heard no more.

When I came to my senses two French soldiers were propping me up, and my head was singing like a kettle. I staggered to my feet and looked around me. The plaster had fallen, the furniture was scattered, and there were rents in the bricks, but no signs of a breach. In fact, the walls of the convent had been so solid that the explosion of the magazine had been insufficient to throw them down. On the other hand, it had caused such a panic among the defenders that our stormers had been able to carry the windows and throw open the doors almost without resistance. As I ran out into the corridor I found it full of troops, and I met Marshal Lannes himself, who was entering with his staff. He stopped and listened eagerly to my story.

'Splendid, Captain Gerard, splendid!' he cried. 'These facts will certainly be reported to the Emperor.'

'I would suggest to your Excellency,' said I, 'that I have only finished the work that was planned and carried out by Monsieur Hubert, who gave his life for the cause.'

'His services will not be forgotten,' said the Marshal. 'Meanwhile, Captain Gerard, it is half-past four, and you must be starving after such a night of exertion. My staff and I will breakfast inside the city. I assure you that you will be an honoured guest.'

'I will follow your Excellency,' said I. 'There is a small engagement which detains me.'

He opened his eyes.

'At this hour?'

'Yes, sir,' I answered. 'My fellow-officers, whom I never saw until last night, will not be content unless they catch another glimpse of me the first thing this morning.'

'*Au revoir*, then,' said Marshal Lannes, as he passed upon his way.

I hurried through the shattered door of the convent. When I reached the roofless house in which we had held the consultation the night before, I threw off my gown, and I put on the busby and sabre which I had left there. Then, a Hussar once more, I hurried onwards to the grove which was our rendezvous. My brain was still reeling from the concussion of the powder, and I was exhausted by the many emotions which had shaken me during that terrible night. It is like a dream, all that walk in the first dim grey light of dawn, with the smouldering camp-fires around me and the buzz of the waking army. Bugles and drums in every direction were mustering the infantry, for the explosion and the shouting had told their own tale. I strode onwards until, as I entered the little clump of cork oaks behind the horse lines, I saw my twelve comrades waiting in a group, their sabres at their sides. They looked at me curiously as I approached. Perhaps with my powder-blackened face and my blood-stained hands I seemed a different Gerard to the young captain whom they had made game of the night before.

'Good-morning, gentlemen,' said I. 'I regret exceedingly if I have kept you waiting, but I have not been master of my own time.'

They said nothing, but they still scanned me with curious eyes. I can see them now, standing in a line before me, tall men and short men, stout men and thin men; Olivier, with his warlike moustache; the thin, eager face of Pelletan; young Oudin, flushed by his first duel; Mortier, with the sword-cut across his wrinkled brow. I laid aside my busby and drew my sword.

'I have one favour to ask you, gentlemen,' said I. 'Marshal Lannes has invited me to breakfast, and I cannot keep him waiting.'

'What do you suggest?' asked Major Olivier.

'That you release me from my promise to give you five minutes each, and that you will permit me to attack you all together.' I stood upon my guard as I spoke.

But their answer was truly beautiful and truly French. With one impulse the twelve swords flew from their scabbards and were raised in salute. There they stood, the twelve of them, motionless, their heels together, each with his sword upright before his face.

I staggered back from them. I looked from one to the other. For an instant I could not believe my own eyes. They were paying me homage, these, the men who had jeered me! Then I understood it all. I saw the effect that I had made upon them and their desire to make reparation. When a man is weak he can steel himself against danger, but not against emotion. 'Comrades,' I cried, 'comrades——!' but I could say no more. Something seemed to take me by the throat and choke me. And then in an instant Olivier's arms were round me, Pelletan had seized me by the right hand, Mortier by the left, some were patting me on the shoulder, some were clapping me on the back, on every side smiling faces were looking into mine; and so it was that I knew that I had won my footing in the Hussars of Conflans.

III. How the Brigadier Slew the Fox [1]

In all the great hosts of France there was only one officer towards whom the English of Wellington's army retained a deep, steady, and unchangeable hatred. There were plunderers among the French, and men of violence, gamblers, duellists, and *roués*. All these could be forgiven, for others of their kidney were to be found among the ranks of the English. But one officer of Massena's force had committed a crime which was unspeakable, unheard of, abominable; only to be alluded to with curses late in the evening, when a second bottle had loosened the

[1] This story has, by kind consent of Messrs. Smith, Elder & Co., been transferred from *The Green Flag*, so that all the Brigadier Gerard stories may appear together.

tongues of men. The news of it was carried back to England, and country gentlemen who knew little of the details of the war grew crimson with passion when they heard of it, and yeomen of the shires raised freckled fists to Heaven and swore. And yet who should be the doer of this dreadful deed but our friend the brigadier, Etienne Gerard, of the Hussars of Conflans, gay-riding, plume-tossing, debonair, the darling of the ladies and of the six brigades of light cavalry.

But the strange part of it is that this gallant gentleman did this hateful thing, and made himself the most unpopular man in the Peninsula, without ever knowing that he had done a crime for which there is hardly a name amid all the resources of our language. He died of old age, and never once in that imperturbable self-confidence which adorned or disfigured his character knew that so many thousand Englishmen would gladly have hanged him with their own hands. On the contrary, he numbered this adventure among those other exploits which he has given to the world, and many a time he chuckled and hugged himself as he narrated it to the eager circle who gathered round him in that humble café where, between his dinner and his dominoes, he would tell, amid tears and laughter, of that inconceivable Napoleonic past when France, like an angel of wrath, rose up, splendid and terrible, before a cowering continent. Let us listen to him as he tells the story in his own way and from his own point of view.

You must know, my friends (said he), that it was toward the end of the year eighteen hundred and ten that I and Massena and the others pushed Wellington backwards until we had hoped to drive him and his army into the Tagus. But when we were still twenty-five miles from Lisbon we found that we were betrayed, for what had this Englishman done but build an enormous line of works and forts at a place called Torres Vedras, so that even we were unable to get through them! They lay across the whole peninsula, and our army was so far from home that we did not dare to risk a reverse, and we had already learned at Busaco that it was no child's play to fight against these people. What could we do, then, but sit down in front of these lines and blockade them to the best of our power? There we remained for six months, amid such anxieties that Massena said afterwards that he had not one hair which was not white upon his body. For my own part, I did not worry much about our situation, but I looked after our horses, who were in great need of rest and green fodder. For the rest, we drank the wine of the country and passed the time as best we might. There was a lady at Santarem—but my lips are sealed. It is the part of a gallant man to say nothing, though he may indicate that he could say a great deal.

One day Massena sent for me, and I found him in his tent with a great plan pinned upon the table. He looked at me in silence with that single piercing eye of his, and I felt by his expression that the matter was serious. He was nervous and ill at ease, but my bearing seemed to reassure him. It is good to be in contact with brave men.

'Colonel Etienne Gerard,' said he, 'I have always heard that you are a very gallant and enterprising officer.'

It was not for me to confirm such a report, and yet it would be folly to deny it, so I clinked my spurs together and saluted.

'You are also an excellent rider.'

I admitted it.

'And the best swordsman in the six brigades of light cavalry.'

Massena was famous for the accuracy of his information.

'Now,' said he, 'if you will look at this plan you will have no difficulty in understanding what it is that I wish you to do. These are the lines of Torres Vedras. You will perceive that they cover a vast space, and you will realise that the English can only hold a position here and there. Once through the lines, you have twenty-five miles of open country which lie between them and Lisbon. It is very important to me to learn how Wellington's troops are distributed throughout that space, and it is my wish that you should go and ascertain.'

His words turned me cold.

'Sir,' said I, 'it is impossible that a colonel of light cavalry should condescend to act as a spy.'

He laughed and clapped me on the shoulder. 'You would not be a Hussar if you were not a hot-head,' said he. 'If you will listen you will understand that I have not asked you to act as a spy. What do you think of that horse?'

He had conducted me to the opening of his tent, and there was a Chasseur who led up and down a most admirable creature. He was a dapple grey, not very tall —a little over fifteen hands perhaps—but with the short head and splendid arch of the neck which comes with the Arab blood. His shoulders and haunches were so muscular, and yet his legs so fine, that it thrilled me with joy just to gaze upon him. A fine horse or a beautiful woman, I cannot look at them unmoved, even now when seventy winters have chilled my blood. You can think how it was in the year '10.

'This,' said Massena, 'is Voltigeur, the swiftest horse in our army. What I desire is that you should start to-night, ride round the lines upon the flank, make your way across the enemy's rear, and return upon the other flank, bringing me news of his dispositions. You will wear a uniform, and will, therefore, if captured, be safe from the death of a spy. It is probable that you will get through the lines unchallenged, for the posts are very scattered. Once through, in daylight you can outride anything which you meet, and if you keep off the roads you may escape entirely unnoticed. If you have not reported yourself by to-morrow night I will understand that you are taken, and I will offer them Colonel Petrie in exchange.'

Ah, how my heart swelled with pride and joy as I

sprang into the saddle and galloped this grand horse up and down to show the marshal the mastery which I had of him! He was magnificent—we were both magnificent, for Massena clapped his hands and cried out in his delight. It was not I, but he, who said that a gallant beast deserves a gallant rider. Then, when for the third time, with my panache flying and my dolman streaming behind me, I thundered past him, I saw upon his hard old face that he had no longer any doubt that he had chosen the man for his purpose. I drew my sabre, raised the hilt to my lips in salute, and galloped on to my own quarters. Already the news had spread that I had been chosen for a mission, and my little rascals came swarming out of their tents to cheer me. Ah! it brings the tears to my old eyes when I think how proud they were of their colonel. And I was proud of them also. They deserved a dashing leader.

The night promised to be a stormy one, which was very much to my liking. It was my desire to keep my departure most secret, for it was evident that if the English heard that I had been detached from the army they would naturally conclude that something important was about to happen. My horse was taken, therefore, beyond the picket line, as if for watering, and I followed and mounted him there. I had a map, a compass, and a paper of instructions from the marshal, and with these in the bosom of my tunic, and a sabre at my side, I set out upon my adventure. A thin rain was falling, and there was no moon, so you may imagine that it was not very cheerful. But my heart was light at the thought of the honour which had been done me, and the glory which awaited me. This exploit should be one more in that brilliant series which was to change my sabre into a baton. Ah, how we dreamed, we foolish fellows, young, and drunk with success! Could I have foreseen that night as I rode, the chosen man of sixty thousand, that I should spend my life planting cabbages on a hundred francs a month! Oh, my youth, my hopes, my comrades! But the wheel turns and never stops. Forgive me, my friends, for an old man has his weakness.

My route, then, lay across the face of the high ground of Torres Vedras, then over a streamlet, past a farmhouse which had been burned down and was now only a landmark, then through a forest of young cork oaks, and so to the monastery of San Antonio, which marked the left of the English position. Here I turned south and rode quietly over the downs, for it was at this point that Massena thought that it would be most easy for me to find my way unobserved through the position. I went very slowly, for it was so dark that I could not see my hand in front of me. In such cases I leave my bridle loose, and let my horse pick its own way. Voltigeur went confidently forward, and I was very content to sit upon his back, and to peer about me, avoiding every light. For three hours we advanced in this cautious way, until it seemed to me that I must have left all danger behind me. I then pushed on more briskly, for I wished to be in the rear of the whole army by daybreak. There are many vineyards in these parts which in winter become open plains, and a horseman finds few difficulties in his way.

But Massena had underrated the cunning of these English, for it appears that there was not one line of defence, but three, and it was the third which was the most formidable, through which I was at that instant passing. As I rode, elated at my own success, a lantern flashed suddenly before me, and I saw the glint of polished gun-barrels and the gleam of a red coat.

'Who goes there?' cried a voice—such a voice! I swerved to the right and rode like a madman, but a dozen squirts of fire came out of the darkness, and the bullets whizzed all round my ears. That was no new sound to me, my friends, though I will not talk like a foolish conscript and say that I have ever liked it. But at least it had never kept me from thinking clearly, and so I knew that there was nothing for it but to gallop hard and try my luck elsewhere. I rode round the English picket, and then, as I heard nothing more of them, I concluded rightly that I had at last come through their defences. For five miles I rode south, striking a tinder from time to time to look at my pocket compass. And then in an instant—I feel the pang once more as my memory brings back the moment—my horse, without a sob or stagger, fell stone dead beneath me!

I had not known it, but one of the bullets from that infernal picket had passed through his body. The gallant creature had never winced nor weakened, but had gone while life was in him. One instant I was secure on the swiftest, most graceful horse in Massena's army. The next he lay upon his side, worth only the price of his hide, and I stood there that most helpless, most ungainly of creatures, a dismounted Hussar. What could I do with my boots, my spurs, my trailing sabre? I was far inside the enemy's lines. How could I hope to get back again? I am not ashamed to say that I, Etienne Gerard, sat upon my dead horse and sank my face in my hands in my despair. Already the first streaks were whitening in the east. In half an hour it would be light. That I should have won my way past every obstacle, and then at this last instant be left at the mercy of my enemies, my mission ruined, and myself a prisoner—was it not enough to break a soldier's heart?

But courage, my friends! We have these moments of weakness, the bravest of us; but I have a spirit like a slip of steel, for the more you bend it the higher it springs. One spasm of despair, and then a brain of ice and a heart of fire. All was not yet lost. I, who had come through so many hazards, would come through this one also. I rose from my horse and considered what had best be done.

And first of all it was certain that I could not get back. Long before I could pass the lines it would be broad daylight. I must hide myself for the day, and devote the next night to my escape. I took the saddle, holsters, and bridle from my poor Voltigeur, and I concealed them among some bushes, so that no one finding him could know that he was a French horse. Then, leaving him lying there, I wandered on in search of some place where I might be safe for the day. In every direction I could see camp fires upon the sides of the hills, and already figures had begun to move around them. I must hide quickly or I was lost. But where was I to hide? It was a vineyard in which I found myself, the poles of the vines still standing, but the plants gone. There was no cover there. Beside, I should want some food and water before another night had come. I hurried wildly onwards through the waning darkness, trusting that chance would be my friend. And I was not disappointed. Chance is a woman, my friends, and she has her eye always upon a gallant Hussar.

Well, then, I stumbled through the vineyard, something loomed in front of me, and I came upon a great square house with another long, low building upon one side of it. Three roads met there, and it was easy to see that this was the *posada*, or wine-shop. There was no light in the windows, and everything was dark and silent, but, of course, I knew that such comfortable quarters were certainly occupied, and probably by someone of importance. I have learned, however, that the nearer the danger may really be the safer the place, and so I was by no means inclined to trust myself away from this shelter. The low building was evidently the stable, and into this I crept, for the door was unlatched. The place was full of bullocks and sheep, gathered there, no doubt, to be out of the clutches of marauders. A ladder led to a loft, and up this I climbed, and concealed myself very snugly among some bales of hay upon the top. This loft had a small open window, and I was able to look down upon the front of the inn and also upon the road. Then I crouched and waited to see what would happen.

It was soon evident that I had not been mistaken when I had thought that this might be the quarters of some person of importance. Shortly after daybreak an English light dragoon arrived with a despatch, and from then onwards the place was in a turmoil, officers continually riding up and away. Always the same name was upon their lips: 'Sir Stapleton—Sir Stapleton.' It was hard for me to lie there with a dry moustache and watch the great flagons which were brought out by the landlord to these English officers. But it amused me to look at their fresh-coloured, clean-shaven, careless faces, and to wonder what they would think if they knew that so celebrated a person was lying so near to them. And then, as I lay and watched, I saw a sight which filled me with surprise.

It is incredible the insolence of these English! What do you suppose Milord Wellington had done when he found that Massena had blockaded him and that he could not move his army? I might give you many guesses. You might say that he had raged, that he had despaired, that he had brought his troops together and spoken to them about glory and the fatherland before leading them to one last battle. No, Milord did none of these things. But he sent a fleet ship to England to bring him a number of fox-dogs, and he with his officers settled himself down to chase the fox. It is true what I tell you. Behind the lines of Torres Vedras these mad Englishmen made the fox-chase three days in the week. We had heard of it in the camp, and now I myself was to see that it was true.

For, along the road which I have described, there came these very dogs, thirty or forty of them, white and brown, each with its tail at the same angle, like the bayonets of the Old Guard. My faith, but it was a pretty sight! And behind and amidst them there rode three men with peaked caps and red coats, whom I understood to be the hunters. After them came many horsemen with uniforms of various kinds, stringing along the road in twos and threes, talking together and laughing. They did not seem to be going above a trot, and it appeared to me that it must indeed be a slow fox which they hoped to catch. However, it was their affair, not mine, and soon they had all passed my window and were out of sight. I waited and I watched, ready for any chance which might offer.

Presently an officer, in a blue uniform not unlike that of our flying artillery, came cantering down the road—an elderly, stout man he was, with grey side-whiskers. He stopped and began to talk with an orderly officer of dragoons, who waited outside the inn, and it was then that I learned the advantage of the English which had been taught me. I could hear and understand all that was said.

'Where is the meet?' said the officer, and I thought that he was hungering for his bifstek. But the other answered him that it was near Altara, so I saw that it was a place of which he spoke.

'You are late, Sir George,' said the orderly.

'Yes, I had a court-martial. Has Sir Stapleton Cotton gone?'

At this moment a window opened, and a handsome young man in a very splendid uniform looked out of it.

'Halloa, Murray!' said he. 'These cursed papers keep me, but I will be at your heels.'

'Very good, Cotton. I am late already, so I will ride on.'

'You might order my groom to bring round my horse,' said the young general at the window to the orderly below, while the other went on down the road.

The orderly rode away to some outlying stable, and then in a few minutes there came a smart English groom with a cockade in his hat, leading by the bridle a horse—and, oh, my friends, you have never known the perfection to which a horse can attain until you have seen a first-class English hunter. He was superb: tall, broad, strong, and yet as graceful and agile as a deer. Coal black he was in colour, and his neck, and his shoulder, and his quarters, and his fetlocks—how can I describe him all to you? The sun shone upon him as on polished ebony, and he raised his hoofs in a little playful dance so lightly and prettily, while he tossed his mane and whinnied with impatience. Never have I seen such a mixture of strength and beauty and grace. I had often wondered how the English Hussars had managed to ride over the Chasseurs of the Guards in the affair at Astorga, but I wondered no longer when I saw the English horses.

There was a ring for fastening bridles at the door of the inn, and the groom tied the horse there while he entered the house. In an instant I had seen the chance which Fate had brought to me. Were I in that saddle I should be better off than when I started. Even Voltigeur could not compare with this magnificent creature. To think is to act with me. In one instant I was down the ladder and at the door of the stable. The next I was out and the bridle was in my hand. I bounded into the saddle. Somebody, the master or the man, shouted wildly behind me. What cared I for his shouts! I touched the horse with my spurs, and he bounded forward with such a spring that only a rider like myself could have sat him. I gave him his head and let him go—it did not matter to me where, so long as we left this inn far behind us. He thundered away across the vineyards, and in a very few minutes I had placed miles between myself and my pursuers. They could no longer tell, in that wild country, in which direction I had gone. I knew that I was safe, and so, riding to the top of a small hill, I drew my pencil and note-book from my pocket, and proceeded to make plans of those camps which I could see, and to draw the outline of the country.

He was a dear creature upon whom I sat, but it was not easy to draw upon his back, for every now and then his two ears would cock, and he would start and quiver with impatience. At first I could not understand this trick of his, but soon I observed that he only did it when a peculiar noise—'Yoy, yoy, yoy'—came from somewhere among the oak woods beneath us. And then suddenly this strange cry changed into a most terrible screaming, with the frantic blowing of a horn. Instantly he went mad—this horse. His eyes blazed. His mane bristled. He bounded from the earth and bounded again, twisting and turning in a frenzy. My pencil flew one way and my note-book another. And then, as I looked down into the valley, an extraordinary sight met my eyes. The hunt was streaming down it. The fox I could not see, but the dogs were in full cry, their noses down, their tails up, so close together that they might have been one great yellow and white moving carpet. And behind them rode the horse-men—my faith, what a sight! Consider every type which a great army could show: some in hunting dress, but the most in uniforms; blue dragoons, red dragoons, red-trousered hussars, green riflemen, artillerymen, gold-slashed lancers, and most of all red, red, red, for the infantry officers ride as hard as the cavalry. Such a crowd, some well mounted, some ill, but all flying along as best they might, the subaltern as good as the general, jostling and pushing, spurring and driving, with every thought thrown to the winds save that they should have the blood of this absurd fox! Truly, they are an extraordinary people, the English! But I had little time to watch the hunt or to marvel at these islanders, for of all these mad creatures the very horse upon which I sat was the maddest. You understand that he was himself a hunter, and that the crying of these dogs was to him what the call of a cavalry trumpet in the street yonder would be to me. It thrilled him. It drove him wild. Again and again he bounded into the air, and then, seizing the bit between his teeth, he plunged down the slope, and galloped after the dogs. I swore, and tugged, and pulled, but I was powerless. This English general rode his horse with a snaffle only, and the beast had a mouth of iron. It was useless to pull him back. One might as well try to keep a Grenadier from a wine bottle. I gave it up in despair, and, settling down in the saddle, I prepared for the worst which could befall.

What a creature he was! Never have I felt such a horse between my knees. His great haunches gathered under him with every stride, and he shot forward ever faster and faster, stretched like a greyhound, while the wind beat in my face and whistled past my ears. I was wearing our undress jacket, a uniform simple and dark in itself —though some figures give distinction to any uniform— and I had taken the precaution to remove the long panache from my busby. The result was that, amidst the mixture of costumes in the hunt, there was no reason why mine should attract attention, or why these men, whose thoughts were all with the chase, should give any heed to me. The idea that a French officer might be riding with them was too absurd to enter their minds. I laughed as I rode, for, indeed, amid all the danger, there was something of comic in the situation.

I have said that the hunters were very unequally mounted, and so, at the end of a few miles, instead of being one body of men, like a charging regiment, they were scattered over a considerable space, the better riders well up to the dogs, and the others trailing away behind. Now, I was as good a rider as any, and my horse was the best of them all, and so you can imagine that it was not long before he carried me to the front. And when I saw the dogs streaming over the open, and the red-coated huntsmen behind them, and only seven or eight horse-men between us, then it was that the strangest thing of all happened, for I, too, went mad—I, Etienne Gerard! In a moment it came upon me, this spirit of sport, this desire to excel, this hatred of the fox. Accursed animal, should he then defy us? Vile robber, his hour was come! Ah, it is a great feeling, this feeling of sport, my friends, this desire to trample the fox under the hoofs of your horse. I have made the fox-chase with the English. I have also, as I may tell you some day, fought the box-fight with the Bustler, of Bristol. And I say to you that this sport is a wonderful thing—full of interest as well as madness.

The farther we went the faster galloped my horse, and soon there were but three men as near the dogs as I was.

All thought of fear of discovery had vanished. My brain throbbed, my blood ran hot—only one thing upon earth seemed worth living for, and that was to overtake this infernal fox. I passed one of the horsemen—a Hussar like myself. There were only two in front of me now—the one in a black coat, the other the blue artilleryman whom I had seen at the inn. His grey whiskers streamed in the wind, but he rode magnificently. For a mile or more we kept in this order, and then, as we galloped up a steep slope, my lighter weight brought me to the front. I passed them both, and when I reached the crown I was riding level with the little, hard-faced English huntsman. In front of us were the dogs, and then, a hundred paces beyond them, was a brown wisp of a thing, the fox itself, stretched to the uttermost. The sight of him fired my blood. 'Aha, we have you then, assassin!' I cried, and shouted my encouragement to the huntsman. I waved my hand to show him that there was one upon whom he could rely.

And now there were only the dogs between me and my prey. These dogs, whose duty it is to point out the game, were now rather a hindrance than a help to us, for it was hard to know how to pass them. The huntsman felt the difficulty as much as I, for he rode behind them and could make no progress towards the fox. He was a swift rider, but wanting in enterprise. For my part, I felt that it would be unworthy of the Hussars of Conflans if I could not overcome such a difficulty as this. Was Etienne Gerard to be stopped by a herd of fox-dogs? It was absurd. I gave a shout and spurred my horse.

'Hold hard, sir! Hold hard!' cried the huntsman.

He was uneasy for me, this good old man, but I reassured him by a wave and a smile. The dogs opened in front of me. One or two may have been hurt, but what would you have? The egg must be broken for the omelette. I could hear the huntsman shouting his congratulations behind me. One more effort, and the dogs were all behind me. Only the fox was in front.

Ah, the joy and pride of that moment! To know that I had beaten the English at their own sport. Here were three hundred all thirsting for the life of this animal, and yet it was I who was about to take it. I thought of my comrades of the light cavalry brigade, of my mother, of the Emperor, of France. I had brought honour to each and all. Every instant brought me nearer to the fox. The moment for action had arrived, so I unsheathed my sabre. I waved it in the air, and the brave English all shouted behind me.

Only then did I understand how difficult is this fox-chase, for one may cut again and again at the creature and never strike him once. He is small, and turns quickly from a blow. At every cut I heard those shouts of encouragement behind me, and they spurred me to yet another effort. And then at last the supreme moment of my triumph arrived. In the very act of turning I caught him fair with such another back-handed cut as that with which I killed the aide-de-camp of the Emperor of Russia. He flew into two pieces, his head one way and his tail another. I looked back and waved the blood-stained sabre in the air. For the moment I was exalted—superb!

Ah! how I should have loved to have waited to have received the congratulations of these generous enemies. There were fifty of them in sight, and not one of them who was not waving his hand and shouting. They are not really such a phlegmatic race, the English. A gallant deed in war or in sport will always warm their hearts. As to the old huntsman, he was the nearest to me, and I could see with my own eyes how overcome he was by what he had seen. He was like a man paralysed—his mouth open, his hand, with outspread fingers, raised in the air. For a moment my inclination was to return and embrace him. But already the call of duty was sounding in my ears, and these English, in spite of all the fraternity which exists among sportsmen, would certainly have made me prisoner. There was no hope for my mission now, and I had done all that I could do. I could see the lines of Massena's camp no very great distance off, for, by a lucky chance, the chase had taken us in that direction. I turned from the dead fox, saluted with my sabre, and galloped away.

But they would not leave me so easily, these gallant huntsmen. I was the fox now, and the chase swept bravely over the plain. It was only at the moment when I started for the camp that they could have known that I was a Frenchman, and now the whole swarm of them were at my heels. We were within gunshot of our pickets before they would halt, and then they stood in knots and would not go away, but shouted and waved their hands at me. No, I will not think that it was in enmity. Rather would I fancy that a glow of admiration filled their breasts, and that their one desire was to embrace the stranger who had carried himself so gallantly and well.

IV. How the Brigadier Saved an Army

I HAVE told you, my friends, how we held the English shut up for six months, from October, 1810, to March, 1811, within their lines of Torres Vedras. It was during this time that I hunted the fox in their company, and showed them that amidst all their sportsmen there was not one who could outride a Hussar of Conflans. When I galloped back into the French lines with the blood of the creature still moist upon my blade, the outposts who had seen what I had done raised a frenzied cry in my honour, whilst these English hunters still yelled behind me, so that I had the applause of both armies. It made the tears rise to my eyes to feel that I had won the admiration of so many brave men. These English are generous foes. That very evening there came a packet under a white flag addressed 'To the Hussar officer who cut down the fox.' Within I found the fox itself in two pieces, as I had left it. There was a note also, short but hearty as the English fashion is, to say that as I had slaughtered the fox it only remained for me to eat it. They could not know that it was not our French custom to eat foxes, and it showed their desire that he who had won the honours of the chase should also partake of the game. It is not for a Frenchman to be outdone in politeness, and so I returned it to these brave hunters, and begged them to accept it as a side-dish for their next *déjeuner de la chasse*. It is thus that chivalrous opponents make war.

I had brought back with me from my ride a clear plan of the English lines, and this I laid before Massena that very evening.

I had hoped that it would lead him to attack, but all the marshals were at each other's throats, snapping and growling like so many hungry hounds. Ney hated Massena, and Massena hated Junot, and Soult hated them all. For this reason nothing was done. In the meantime food grew more and more scarce, and our beautiful cavalry was ruined for want of fodder. With the end of the winter we had swept the whole country bare, and nothing remained for us to eat, although we sent our forage parties far and wide. It was clear even to the bravest of us that the time had come to retreat. I was myself forced to admit it.

But retreat was not so easy. Not only were the troops weak and exhausted from want of supplies, but the enemy had been much encouraged by our long inaction. Of Wellington we had no great fear. We had found him to be brave and cautious, but with little enterprise. Besides, in that barren country his pursuit could not be rapid. But on our flanks and in our rear there had gathered great numbers of Portuguese militia, of armed peasants, and of guerillas. These people had kept a safe distance all the winter, but now that our horses were foundered they were as thick as flies all round our outposts, and no man's life was worth a sou when once he fell into their hands. I could name a dozen officers of my own acquaintance who were cut off during that time, and the luckiest was he who received a ball from behind a rock through his head or his heart. There were some whose deaths were so terrible that no report of them was ever allowed to reach their relatives. So frequent were these tragedies, and so much did they impress the imagination of the men, that it became very difficult to induce them to leave the camp. There was one especial scoundrel, a guerilla chief named Manuelo, 'The Smiler', whose exploits filled our men with horror. He was a large, fat man of jovial aspect, and he lurked with a fierce gang among the mountains which lay upon our left flank. A volume might be written of this fellow's cruelties and brutalities, but he was certainly a man of power, for he organised his brigands in a manner which made it almost impossible for us to get through his country. This he did by imposing a severe discipline upon them and enforcing it by cruel penalties, a policy by which he made them formidable, but which had some unexpected results, as I will show you in my story. Had he not flogged his own lieutenant—but you will hear of that when the time comes.

There were many difficulties in connection with a retreat, but it was very evident that there was no other possible course, and so Massena began to quickly pass his baggage and his sick from Torres Novas, which was his head-quarters, to Coimbra, the first strong post on his line of communications. He could not do this unperceived, however, and at once the guerillas came swarming closer and closer upon our flanks. One of our divisions, that of Clausel, with a brigade of Montbrun's cavalry, was far to the south of the Tagus, and it became very necessary to let them know that we were about to retreat, for otherwise they would be left unsupported in the very heart of the enemy's country. I remember wondering how Massena would accomplish this, for simple couriers could not get through, and small parties would be certainly destroyed. In some way an order to fall back must be conveyed to these men, or France would be the weaker by fourteen thousand men. Little did I think that it was I, Colonel Gerard, who was to have the honour of a deed which might have formed the crowning glory of any other man's life, and which stands high among those exploits which have made my own so famous.

At that time I was serving on Massena's staff, and he had two other aides-de-camp, who were also very brave and intelligent officers. The name of one was Cortex and of the other Duplessis. They were senior to me in age, but junior in every other respect. Cortex was a small, dark man, very quick and eager. He was a fine soldier, but he was ruined by his conceit. To take him at his own valuation, he was the first man in the army. Duplessis was a Gascon, like myself, and he was a very fine fellow, as all Gascon gentlemen are. We took it in turn, day about, to do duty, and it was Cortex who was in attendance upon the morning of which I speak. I saw him at breakfast, but afterwards neither he nor his horse was to be seen. All day Massena was in his usual gloom, and he spent much of his time staring with his telescope at the English lines and at the shipping in the Tagus. He said nothing of the mission upon which he had sent our comrade, and it was not for us to ask him any questions.

That night, about twelve o'clock, I was standing outside the Marshal's headquarters when he came out and stood motionless for half an hour, his arms folded upon his breast, staring through the darkness towards the east. So rigid and intent was he that you might have believed the muffled figure and the cocked hat to have been the statue of the man. What he was looking for I could not imagine; but at last he gave a bitter curse, and, turning on his heel, he went back into the house, banging the door behind him.

Next day the second aide-de-camp, Duplessis, had an interview with Massena in the morning, after which neither he nor his horse was seen again. That night, as I sat in the ante-room, the Marshal passed me, and I observed him through the window standing and staring to the east exactly as he had done before. For fully half an hour he remained there, a black shadow in the gloom. Then he strode in, the door banged, and I heard his spurs and his scabbard jingling and clanking through the passage. At the best he was a savage old man, but when he was crossed I had almost as soon face the Emperor himself. I heard him that night cursing and stamping above my head, but he did not send for me, and I knew him too well to go unsought.

Next morning it was my turn, for I was the only aide-de-camp left. I was his favourite aide-de-camp. His heart went out always to a smart soldier. I declare that I think there were tears in his black eyes when he sent for me that morning.

'Gerard!' said he. 'Come here!'

With a friendly gesture he took me by the sleeve and he led me to the open window which faced the east. Beneath us was the infantry camp, and beyond that the lines of the cavalry with the long rows of picketed horses. We could see the French outposts, and then a stretch of open country, intersected by vineyards. A range of hills lay beyond, with one well-marked peak towering above them. Round the base of these hills was a broad belt of forest. A single road ran white and clear, dipping and rising until it passed through a gap in the hills.

'This,' said Massena, pointing to the mountain, 'is the Sierra de Merodal. Do you perceive anything upon the top?'

I answered that I did not.

'Now?' he asked, and he handed me his field-glass.

With its aid I perceived a small mound or cairn upon the crest.

'What you see,' said the Marshal, 'is a pile of logs which was placed there as a beacon. We laid it when the country was in our hands, and now, although we no longer hold it, the beacon remains undisturbed. Gerard, that beacon must be lit to-night. France needs it, the

Emperor needs it, the army needs it. Two of your comrades have gone to light it, but neither has made his way to the summit. To-day it is your turn, and I pray that you may have better luck.'

It is not for a soldier to ask the reason for his orders, and so I was about to hurry from the room, but the Marshal laid his hand upon my shoulder and held me.

'You shall know all, and so learn how high is the cause for which you risk your life,' said he. 'Fifty miles to the south of us, on the other side of the Tagus, is the army of General Clausel. His camp is situated near a peak named the Sierra d'Ossa. On the summit of this peak is a beacon, and by this beacon he has a picket. It is agreed between us that when at midnight he shall see our signal fire he shall light his own as an answer, and shall then at once fall back upon the main army. If he does not start at once I must go without him. For two days I have endeavoured to send him his message. It must reach him to-day, or his army will be left behind and destroyed.'

Ah, my friends, how my heart swelled when I heard how high was the task which Fortune had assigned to me! If my life were spared, here was one more splendid new leaf for my laurel crown. If, on the other hand, I died, then it would be a death worthy of such a career. I said nothing, but I cannot doubt that all the noble thoughts that were in me shone in my face, for Massena took my hand and wrung it.

'There is the hill and there the beacon,' said he. 'There is only this guerilla and his men between you and it. I cannot detach a large party for the enterprise, and a small one would be seen and destroyed. Therefore to you alone I commit it. Carry it out in your own way, but at twelve o'clock this night let me see the fire upon the hill.'

'If it is not there,' said I, 'then I pray you, Marshal Massena, to see that my effects are sold and the money sent to my mother.' So I raised my hand to my busby and

440

turned upon my heel, my heart glowing at the thought of the great exploit which lay before me.

I sat in my own chamber for some little time considering how I had best take the matter in hand. The fact that neither Cortex nor Duplessis, who were very zealous and active officers, had succeeded in reaching the summit of the Sierra de Merodal showed that the country was very closely watched by the guerillas. I reckoned out the distance upon a map. There were ten miles of open country to be crossed before reaching the hills. Then came a belt of forest on the lower slopes of the mountain, which may have been three or four miles wide. And then there was the actual peak itself, of no very great height, but without any cover to conceal me. Those were the three stages of my journey.

It seemed to me that once I had reached the shelter of the wood all would be easy, for I could lie concealed within its shadows and climb upwards under the cover of night. From eight till twelve would give me four hours of darkness in which to make the ascent. It was only the first stage, then, which I had seriously to consider.

Over that flat country there lay the inviting white road, and I remembered that my comrades had both taken their horses. That was clearly their ruin, for nothing could be easier than for the brigands to keep watch upon the road, and to lay an ambush for all who passed along it. It would not be difficult for me to ride across country, and I was well horsed at that time, for I had not only Violette and Rataplan, who were two of the finest mounts in the army, but I had the splendid black English hunter which I had taken from Sir Cotton. However, after much thought, I determined to go upon foot, since I should then be in a better state to take advantage of any chance which might offer. As to my dress, I covered my Hussar uniform with a long cloak, and I put a grey forage cap upon my head. You may ask me why I did not dress as a peasant, but I answer that a man of honour has no desire to die the death of a spy. It is one thing to be murdered, and it is another to be justly executed by the laws of war. I would not run the risk of such an end.

In the late afternoon I stole out of the camp and passed through the line of our pickets. Beneath my cloak I had a field-glass and a pocket pistol, as well as my sword. In my pocket were tinder, flint, and steel.

For two or three miles I kept under cover of the vineyards, and made such good progress that my heart was high within me, and I thought to myself that it only needed a man of some brains to take the matter in hand to bring it easily to success. Of course, Cortex and Duplessis galloping down the high road would be easily seen, but the intelligent Gerard lurking among the vines was quite another person. I dare say I had got as far as five miles before I met any check. At that point there is a small winehouse, round which I perceived some carts and a number of people, the first that I had seen. Now that I was well outside the lines I knew that every person was my enemy, so I crouched lower while I stole along to a point from which I could get a better view of what was going on. I then perceived that these people were peasants, who were loading two waggons with empty wine-casks. I failed to see how they could either help or hinder me, so I continued upon my way.

But soon I understood that my task was not so simple as had appeared. As the ground rose the vineyards ceased, and I came upon a stretch of open country studded with low hills. Crouching in a ditch I examined them with a glass, and I very soon perceived that there was a watcher upon every one of them, and that these people had a line of pickets and outposts thrown forward exactly like our own. I had heard of the discipline which was practised by this scoundrel whom they called 'The Smiler', and this, no doubt, was an example of it. Between the hills there was a cordon of sentries, and, though I worked some distance round to the flank, I still found myself faced by the enemy. It was a puzzle what to do. There was so little cover that a rat could hardly cross without being seen. Of course, it would be easy enough to slip through at night, as I had done with the English at Torres Vedras; but I was still far from the mountain, and I could not in that case reach it in time to light the midnight beacon. I lay in my ditch and I made a thousand plans, each more dangerous than the last. And then suddenly I had that flash of light which comes to the brave man who refuses to despair.

You remember I have mentioned that two waggons were loading up with empty casks at the inn. The heads of the oxen were turned to the east, and it was evident that those waggons were going in the direction which I desired. Could I only conceal myself upon one of them, what better and easier way could I find of passing through the lines of the guerillas? So simple and so good was the plan that I could not restrain a cry of delight as it crossed my mind, and I hurried away instantly in the direction of the inn. There, from behind some bushes, I had a good look at what was going on upon the road.

There were three peasants with red montero caps loading the barrels, and they had completed one waggon and the lower tier of the other. A number of empty barrels still lay outside the winehouse waiting to be put on. Fortune was my friend—I have always said that she is a woman and cannot resist a dashing young Hussar. As I watched, the three fellows went into the inn, for the day was hot, and they were thirsty after their labour. Quick as a flash I darted out from my hiding-place, climbed on to the waggon, and crept into one of the empty casks. It had a bottom but no top, and it lay upon its side with the open end inwards. There I crouched like a dog in its kennel, my knees drawn up to my chin; for the barrels were not very large and I am a well-grown man. As I lay there out came the three peasants again, and presently I heard a crash upon the top of me, which told that I had another barrel above me. They piled them upon the cart until I could not imagine how I was ever to get out again. However, it is time to think of crossing the Vistula when you are over the Rhine, and I had no doubt that if chance and my own wits had carried me so far they would carry me farther.

Soon, when the waggon was full, they set forth upon their way, and I within my barrel chuckled at every step, for it was carrying me whither I wished to go. We travelled slowly, and the peasants walked beside the waggons. This I knew, because I heard their voices close to me. They seemed to me to be very merry fellows, for they laughed heartily as they went. What the joke was I could not understand. Though I speak their language fairly well I could not hear anything comic in the scraps of their conversation which met my ear.

I reckoned that at the rate of walking of a team of oxen we covered about two miles an hour. Therefore, when I was sure that two and a half hours had passed— such hours, my friends, cramped, suffocated, and nearly poisoned with the fumes of the lees—when they had passed, I was sure that the dangerous open country was behind us, and that we were upon the edge of the forest and the mountain. So now I had to turn my mind upon how I was to get out of my barrel. I had thought of several ways, and was balancing one against the other, when the question was decided for me in a very simple but unexpected manner.

The waggon stopped suddenly with a jerk, and I heard a number of gruff voices in excited talk. 'Where, where?' cried one. 'On our cart,' said another. 'Who is he?' said a third. 'A French officer; I saw his cap and his boots.' They all roared with laughter. 'I was looking out of the window of the *posada* and I saw him spring into the cask like a toreador with a Seville bull at his heels.' 'Which cask, then?' 'It was this one,' said the fellow, and, sure enough, his fist struck the wood beside my head.

What a situation, my friends, for a man of my standing! I blush now, after forty years, when I think of it. To be trussed like a fowl and to listen helplessly to the rude laughter of these boors—to know, too, that my mission had come to an ignominious and even ridiculous end. I would have blessed the man who would have sent a bullet through the cask and freed me from my misery.

I heard the crashing of the barrels as they hurled them off the waggon, and then a couple of bearded faces and the muzzles of two guns looked in at me. They seized me by the sleeves of my coat, and they dragged me out into the daylight. A strange figure I must have looked as I stood blinking and gaping in the blinding sunlight. My body was bent like a cripple's, for I could not straighten my stiff joints, and half my coat was as red as an English soldier's from the lees in which I had lain. They laughed and laughed, these dogs, and as I tried to express by my bearing and gestures the contempt in which I held them, their laughter grew all the louder. But even in these hard circumstances I bore myself like the man I am, and as I cast my eye slowly round I did not find that any of the laughers were very ready to face it.

That one glance round was enough to tell me exactly how I was situated. I had been betrayed by these peasants into the hands of an outpost of guerillas. There were eight of them, savage-looking, hairy creatures, with cotton handkerchiefs under their sombreros, and many-buttoned jackets with coloured sashes round the waist. Each had a gun and one or two pistols stuck in his girdle. The leader, a great bearded ruffian, held his gun against my ear while the others searched my pockets, taking from me my overcoat, my pistol, my glass, my sword, and, worst of all, my flint and steel and tinder. Come what might I was ruined, for I had no longer the means of lighting the beacon even if I should reach it.

Eight of them, my friends, with three peasants, and I unarmed! Was Etienne Gerard in despair? Did he lose his wits? Ah, you know me too well; but they did not know me yet, these dogs of brigands. Never have I made so supreme and astounding an effort as at this very instant when all seemed lost. Yet you might guess many

445

times before you would hit upon the device by which I
escaped them. Listen and I will tell you.

They had dragged me from the waggon when they
searched me, and I stood, still twisted and warped, in the
midst of them. But the stiffness was wearing off, and
already my mind was very actively looking out for some
method of breaking away. It was a narrow pass in which
the brigands had their outpost. It was bounded on the
one hand by a steep mountain side. On the other the
ground fell away in a very long slope, which ended in a
bushy valley many hundreds of feet below. These fellows,
you understand, were hardy mountaineers, who could
travel either up hill or down very much quicker than I.
They wore *abarcas*, or shoes of skin, tied on like sandals,
which gave them a foothold everywhere. A less resolute
man would have despaired. But in an instant I saw and
used the strange chance which Fortune had placed in my
way. On the very edge of the slope was one of the wine-
barrels. I moved slowly towards it, and then with a tiger
spring I dived into it feet foremost, and with a roll of my
body I tipped it over the side of the hill.

Shall I ever forget that dreadful journey—how I
bounded and crashed and whizzed down that terrible
slope? I had dug in my knees and elbows, bunching my
body into a compact bundle so as to steady it; but my
head projected from the end, and it was a marvel that I
did not dash out my brains. There were long, smooth
slopes and then came steeper scarps where the barrel
ceased to roll, and sprang into the air like a goat, coming
down with a rattle and crash which jarred every bone in
my body. How the wind whistled in my ears, and my
head turned and turned until I was sick and giddy and
nearly senseless! Then, with a swish and a great rasping
and crackling of branches, I reached the bushes which I
had seen so far below me. Through them I broke my
way, down a slope beyond, and deep into another patch
of underwood, where striking a sapling my barrel flew to
pieces. From amid a heap of staves and hoops I crawled

out, my body aching in every inch of it, but my heart singing loudly with joy and my spirit high within me, for I knew how great was the feat which I had accomplished, and I already seemed to see the beacon blazing on the hill.

A horrible nausea had seized me from the tossing which I had undergone, and I felt as I did upon the ocean when first I experienced those movements of which the English have taken so perfidious an advantage. I had to sit for a few moments with my head upon my hands beside the ruins of my barrel. But there was no time for rest. Already I heard shouts above me which told that my pursuers were descending the hill. I dashed into the thickest part of the underwood, and I ran and ran until I was utterly exhausted. Then I lay panting and listened with all my ears, but no sound came to them. I had shaken off my enemies.

When I had recovered my breath I travelled swiftly on, and waded knee-deep through several brooks, for it came into my head that they might follow me with dogs. On gaining a clear place and looking round me, I found to my delight that in spite of my adventures I had not been much out of my way. Above me towered the peak of Merodal, with its bare and bold summit shooting out of the groves of dwarf oaks which shrouded its flanks. These groves were the continuation of the cover under which I found myself, and it seemed to me that I had nothing to fear now until I reached the other side of the forest. At the same time I knew that every man's hand was against me, that I was unarmed, and that there were many people about me. I saw no one, but several times I heard shrill whistles, and once the sound of a gun in the distance.

It was hard work pushing one's way through the bushes, and so I was glad when I came to the larger trees and found a path which led between them. Of course, I was too wise to walk upon it, but I kept near it and followed its course. I had gone some distance, and had, as I imagined, nearly reached the limit of the wood, when a strange, moaning sound fell upon my ears. At first I thought it was the cry of some animal, but then there came words, of which I only caught the French exclamation, 'Mon Dieu!' With great caution I advanced in the direction from which the sound proceeded, and this is what I saw.

On a couch of dried leaves there was stretched a man dressed in the same grey uniform which I wore myself. He was evidently horribly wounded, for he held a cloth to his breast which was crimson with his blood. A pool had formed all round his couch, and he lay in a haze of flies, whose buzzing and droning would certainly have called my attention if his groans had not come to my ear. I lay for a moment, fearing some trap, and then, my pity and loyalty rising above all other feelings, I ran forward and knelt by his side. He turned a haggard face upon me, and it was Duplessis, the man who had gone before me. It needed but one glance at his sunken cheeks and glazing eyes to tell me that he was dying.

'Gerard!' said he; 'Gerard!'

I could but look my sympathy, but he, though the life was ebbing swiftly out of him, still kept his duty before him, like the gallant gentleman he was.

'The beacon, Gerard! You will light it?'

'Have you flint and steel?'

'It is here.'

'Then I will light it to-night.'

'I die happy to hear you say so. They shot me, Gerard. But you will tell the Marshal that I did my best.'

'And Cortex?'

'He was less fortunate. He fell into their hands and died horribly. If you see that you cannot get away, Gerard, put a bullet into your own heart. Don't die as Cortex did.'

I could see that his breath was failing, and I bent low to catch his words.

'Can you tell me anything which can help me in my task?' I asked.

'Yes, yes; De Pombal. He will help you. Trust De

Pombal.' With the words his head fell back and he was dead.

'Trust De Pombal. It is good advice.' To my amazement a man was standing at the very side of me. So absorbed had I been in my comrade's words and intent on his advice that he had crept up without my observing him. Now I sprang to my feet and faced him. He was a tall, dark fellow, black-haired, black-eyed, black-bearded, with a long, sad face. In his hand he had a wine-bottle and over his shoulder was slung one of the *trebucos*, or blunderbusses, which these fellows bear. He made no effort to unsling it, and I understood that this was the man to whom my dead friend had commended me.

'Alas, he is gone!' said he, bending over Duplessis. 'He fled into the wood after he was shot, but I was fortunate enough to find where he had fallen and to make his last hours more easy. This couch was my making, and I had brought this wine to slake his thirst.'

'Sir,' said I, 'in the name of France I thank you. I am but a colonel of light cavalry, but I am Etienne Gerard, and the name stands for something in the French army. May I ask——'

'Yes, sir, I am Aloysius de Pombal, younger brother of the famous nobleman of that name. At present I am the first lieutenant in the band of the guerilla chief who is usually known as Manuelo, "The Smiler".'

My word, I clapped my hand to the place where my pistol should have been, but the man only smiled at the gesture.

'I am his first lieutenant, but I am also his deadly enemy,' said he. He slipped off his jacket and pulled up his shirt as he spoke. 'Look at this!' he cried, and he turned upon me a back which was all scored and lacerated with red and purple weals. 'This is what "The Smiler" has done to me, a man with the noblest blood of Portugal in my veins. What I will do to "The Smiler" you have still to see.'

There was such fury in his eyes and in the grin of his

449

white teeth that I could no longer doubt his truth, with that clotted and oozing back to corroborate his words.

'I have ten men sworn to stand by me,' said he. 'In a few days I hope to join your army, when I have done my work here. In the meanwhile——' A strange change came over his face, and he suddenly slung his musket to the front: 'Hold up your hands, you French hound!' he yelled. 'Up with them, or I blow your head off!'

You start, my friends! You stare! Think, then, how I stared and started at this sudden ending of our talk. There was the black muzzle, and there the dark, angry eyes behind it. What could I do? I was helpless. I raised my hands in the air. At the same moment voices sounded from all parts of the wood, there were crying and calling and rushing of many feet. A swarm of dreadful figures broke through the green bushes, a dozen hands seized me, and I, poor, luckless, frenzied I, was a prisoner once more. Thank God, there was no pistol which I could have plucked from my belt and snapped at my own head. Had I been armed at that moment I should not be sitting here in this café and telling you these old-world tales.

With grimy, hairy hands clutching me on every side I was led along the pathway through the wood, the villain De Pombal giving directions to my captors. Four of the brigands carried up the dead body of Duplessis. The shadows of evening were already falling when we cleared the forest and came out upon the mountain-side. Up this I was driven until we reached the head-quarters of the guerillas, which lay in a cleft close to the summit of the mountain. There was the beacon which had cost me so much, a square stack of wood, immediately above our heads. Below were two or three huts which had belonged, no doubt, to goatherds, and which were now used to shelter these rascals. Into one of these I was cast, bound and helpless, and the dead body of my poor comrade was laid beside me.

I was lying there with the one thought still consuming me, how to wait a few hours and to get at that pile of faggots above my head, when the door of my prison opened and a man entered. Had my hands been free I should have flown at his throat, for it was none other than De Pombal. A couple of brigands were at his heels, but he ordered them back and closed the door behind him.

'You villain!' said I.

'Hush!' he cried. 'Speak low, for I do not know who may be listening, and my life is at stake. I have some words to say to you, Colonel Gerard; I wish well to you, as I did to your dead companion. As I spoke to you beside his body I saw that we were surrounded, and that your capture was unavoidable. I should have shared your fate had I hesitated. I instantly captured you myself, so as to preserve the confidence of the band. Your own sense will tell you that there was nothing else for me to do. I do not know now whether I can save you, but at least I will try.'

This was a new light upon the situation. I told him that I could not tell how far he spoke the truth, but that I would judge him by his actions.

'I ask nothing better,' said he. 'A word of advice to you! The chief will see you now. Speak him fair, or he will have you sawn between two planks. Contradict nothing he says. Give him such information he wants. It is your only chance. If you can gain time something may come in our favour. Now, I have no more time. Come at once, or suspicion may be awakened.' He helped me to rise and then, opening the door, he dragged me out very roughly, and with the aid of the fellows outside he brutally pushed and thrust me to the place where the guerilla chief was seated, with his rude followers gathered round him.

A remarkable man was Manuelo, 'The Smiler'. He was fat and florid and comfortable, with a big, clean-shaven face and a bald head, the very model of a kindly father of a family. As I looked at his honest smile I could scarcely believe that this was, indeed, the infamous

451

ruffian whose name was a horror through the English Army as well as our own. It is well known that Trent, who was a British officer, afterwards had the fellow hanged for his brutalities. He sat upon a boulder and he beamed upon me like one who meets an old acquaintance. I observed, however, that one of his men leaned upon a long saw, and the sight was enough to cure me of all delusions.

'Good evening, Colonel Gerard,' said he. 'We have been highly honoured by General Massena's staff: Major Cortex one day, Colonel Duplessis the next, and now Colonel Gerard. Possibly the Marshal himself may be induced to honour us with a visit. You have seen Duplessis, I understand. Cortex you will find nailed to a tree down yonder. It only remains to be decided how we can best dispose of yourself.'

It was not a cheering speech; but all the time his fat face was wreathed in smiles, and he lisped out his words in the most mincing and amiable fashion. Now, however, he suddenly leaned forward, and I read a very real intensity in his eyes.

'Colonel Gerard,' said he, 'I cannot promise you your life, for it is not our custom, but I can give you an easy death or I can give you a terrible one. Which shall it be?'

'What do you wish me to do in exchange?'

'If you would die easy I ask you to give me truthful answers to the questions which I ask.'

A sudden thought flashed through my mind.

'You wish to kill me,' said I; 'it cannot matter to you how I die. If I answer your questions, will you let me choose the manner of my own death?'

'Yes, I will,' said he, 'so long as it is before midnight to-night.'

'Swear it!' I cried.

'The word of a Portuguese gentleman is sufficient,' said he.

'Not a word will I say until you have sworn it.'

He flushed with anger and his eyes swept round towards the saw. But he understood from my tone that I meant what I said, and that I was not a man to be bullied into submission. He pulled a cross from under his *zammara* or jacket of black sheepskin.

'I swear it,' said he.

Oh, my joy as I heard the words! What an end—what an end for the first swordsman of France! I could have laughed with delight at the thought.

'Now, your questions!' said I.

'You swear in turn to answer them truly?'

'I do, upon the honour of a gentleman and a soldier.' It was, as you perceive, a terrible thing that I promised, but what was it compared to what I might gain by compliance?

'This is a very fair and interesting bargain,' said he, taking a note-book from his pocket. 'Would you kindly turn your gaze towards the French camp?'

Following the direction of his gesture, I turned and looked down upon the camp in the plain beneath us. In spite of the fifteen miles, one could in that clear atmosphere see every detail with the utmost distinctness. There were the long squares of our tents and our huts, with the cavalry lines and the dark patches which marked the ten batteries of artillery. How sad to think of my magnificent regiment waiting down yonder, and to know that they would never see their colonel again! With one squadron of them I could have swept all these cut-throats off the face of the earth. My eager eyes filled with tears as I looked at the corner of the camp where I knew that there were eight hundred men, any one of whom would have died for his colonel. But my sadness vanished when I saw behind the tents the plumes of smoke which marked the head-quarters at Torres Novas. There was Massena, and, please God, at the cost of my life his mission would that night be done. A spasm of pride and exultation filled my breast. I should have liked to have had a voice of thunder that I might call to them, 'Behold it is I, Etienne Gerard, who will die in order to save the army of Clausel!' It was, indeed, sad to think that so noble a deed should be done, and that no one should be there to tell the tale.

'Now,' said the brigand chief, 'you see the camp and you see also the road which leads to Coimbra. It is crowded with your fourgons and your ambulances. Does this mean that Massena is about to retreat?'

One could see the dark moving lines of waggons with an occasional flash of steel from the escort. There could, apart from my promise, be no indiscretion in admitting that which was already obvious.

'He will retreat,' said I.

'By Coimbra?'

'I believe so.'

'But the army of Clausel?'

I shrugged my shoulders.

'Every path to the south is blocked. No message can reach them. If Massena falls back the army of Clausel is doomed.'

'It must take its chance,' said I.

'How many men has he?'

'I should say about fourteen thousand.'

'How much cavalry?'

'One brigade of Montbrun's Division.'

'What regiments?'

'The 4th Chasseurs, the 9th Hussars, and a regiment of Cuirassiers.'

'Quite right,' said he, looking at his note-book. 'I can tell you speak the truth, and Heaven help you if you don't.' Then, division by division, he went over the whole army, asking the composition of each brigade. Need I tell you that I would have had my tongue torn out before I would have told him such things had I not a greater end in view? I would let him know all if I could but save the army of Clausel.

At last he closed his note-book and replaced it in his pocket. 'I am obliged to you for this information, which shall reach Lord Wellington to-morrow,' said he. 'You have done your share of the bargain; it is for me now to perform mine. How would you wish to die? As a soldier you would, no doubt, prefer to be shot, but some think that a jump over the Merodal precipice is really an easier death. A good few have taken it, but we were, unfortunately, never able to get an opinion from them afterwards. There is the saw, too, which does not appear to be popular. We could hang you, no doubt, but it would involve the inconvenience of going down to the wood. However, a promise is a promise, and you seem to be an excellent fellow, so we will spare no pains to meet your wishes.'

'You said,' I answered, 'that I must die before midnight. I will choose, therefore, just one minute before that hour.'

'Very good,' said he. 'Such clinging to life is rather childish, but your wishes shall be met.'

'As to the method,' I added, 'I love a death which all the world can see. Put me on yonder pile of faggots and burn me alive, as saints and martyrs have been burned before me. That is no common end, but one which an Emperor might envy.'

The idea seemed to amuse him very much.

'Why not?' said he. 'If Massena has sent you to spy upon us, he may guess what the fire upon the mountains means.'

'Exactly,' said I. 'You have hit upon my very reason. He will guess, and all will know, that I have died a soldier's death.'

'I see no objection whatever,' said the brigand, with his abominable smile. 'I will send some goat's flesh and wine into your hut. The sun is sinking, and it is nearly eight o'clock. In four hours be ready for your end.'

It was a beautiful world to be leaving. I looked at the golden haze below, where the last rays of the sinking sun shone upon the blue waters of the winding Tagus and gleamed upon the white sails of the English transports. Very beautiful it was, and very sad to leave; but there are things more beautiful than that. The death that is died for the sake of others, honour, and duty, and loyalty, and love—these are the beauties far brighter than any which the eye can see. My breast was filled with admiration for my own most noble conduct, and with wonder whether any soul would ever come to know how I had placed myself in the heart of the beacon which saved the army of Clausel. I hoped so and I prayed so, for what a consolation it would be to my mother, what an example to the army, what a pride to my Hussars! When De Pombal came at last into my hut with the food and wine, the first request I made him was that he would write an account of my death and send it to the French camp. He answered not a word, but I ate my supper with a better appetite from the thought that my glorious fate would not be altogether unknown.

I had been there about two hours when the door opened again, and the chief stood looking in. I was in darkness, but a brigand with a torch stood beside him, and I saw his eyes and his teeth gleaming as he peered at me.

'Ready?' he asked.

'It is not yet time.'

'You stand out for the last minute?'

'A promise is a promise.'

'Very good. Be it so. We have a little justice to do among ourselves, for one of my fellows has been misbehaving. We have a strict rule of our own which is no respecter of persons, as De Pombal here could tell you. Do you truss him and lay him on the faggots, De Pombal, and I will return to see him die.'

De Pombal and the man with the torch entered, while I heard the steps of the chief passing away. De Pombal closed the door.

'Colonel Gerard,' said he, 'you must trust this man, for he is one of my party. It is neck or nothing. We may save you yet. But I take a great risk, and I want a definite promise. If we save you, will you guarantee that we have a friendly reception in the French camp and that all the past will be forgotten?'

'I do guarantee it.'

'And I trust your honour. Now, quick, quick, there is not an instant to lose! If this monster returns we shall die horribly, all three.'

I stared in amazement at what he did. Catching up a long rope he wound it round the body of my dead comrade, and he tied a cloth round his mouth so as to almost cover his face.

'Do you lie there!' he cried, and he laid me in the place of the dead body. 'I have four of my men waiting, and they will place this upon the beacon.' He opened the door and gave an order. Several of the brigands entered and bore out Duplessis. For myself I remained upon the floor, with my mind in a turmoil of hope and wonder.

Five minutes later De Pombal and his men were back.

'You are laid upon the beacon,' said he; 'I defy any one in the world to say it is not you, and you are so gagged and bound that no one can expect you to speak or move. Now, it only remains to carry forth the body of Duplessis and to toss it over the Merodal precipice.'

Two of them seized me by the head and two by the heels and carried me, stiff and inert, from the hut. As I came into the open air I could have cried out in my amazement. The moon had risen above the beacon, and there, clear outlined against its silver light, was the figure of the man stretched upon the top. The brigands were either in their camp or standing round the beacon, for none of them stopped or questioned our little party. De Pombal led them in the direction of the precipice. At the brow we were out of sight, and there I was allowed to use my feet once more. De Pombal pointed to a narrow, winding track.

'This is the way down,' said he, and then, suddenly, '*Dios mio*, what is that?'

A terrible cry had risen out of the woods beneath us. I saw that De Pombal was shivering like a frightened horse.

'It is that devil,' he whispered. 'He is treating another as he treated me. But on, on, for Heaven help us if he lays his hands upon us!'

One by one we crawled down the narrow goat track. At the bottom of the cliff we were back in the woods once more. Suddenly a yellow glare shone above us, and the black shadows of the tree-trunks started out in front. They had fired the beacon behind us. Even from where we stood we could see that impassive body amid the flames, and the black figures of the guerillas as they danced, howling like cannibals, round the pile. Ha! how I shook my fist at them, the dogs, and how I vowed that one day my Hussars and I would make the reckoning level!

De Pombal knew how the outposts were placed and all the paths which led through the forest. But to avoid these villains we had to plunge among the hills and walk for many a weary mile. And yet how gladly would I have walked those extra leagues if only for one sight which they brought to my eyes! It may have been two o'clock in the morning when we halted upon the bare shoulder of a hill over which our path curled. Looking back we saw the red glow of the embers of the beacon as if volcanic fires were bursting from the tall peak of Merodal. And then, as I gazed, I saw something else—something which caused me to shriek with joy and to fall upon the ground, rolling in my delight. For, far away upon the southern horizon, there winked and twinkled one great yellow light, throbbing and flaming, the light of no house, the light of no star, but the answering beacon of Mount d'Ossa, which told that the army of Clausel knew what Etienne Gerard had been sent out to tell them.

V. How the Brigadier Triumphed in England

I HAVE told you, my friends, how I triumphed over the English at the fox-hunt when I pursued the animal so fiercely that even the herd of trained dogs was unable to keep up, and alone with my own hand I put him to the sword. Perhaps I have said too much of the matter, but there is a thrill in the triumphs of sport which even warfare cannot give, for in warfare you share your successes with your regiment and your army, but in sport it is you yourself unaided who have won the laurels. It is an advantage which the English have over us that in all classes they take great interest in every form of sport. It may be that they are richer than we, or it may be that they are more idle; but I was surprised when I was a prisoner in that country to observe how widespread was this feeling, and how much it filled the minds and the lives of the people. A horse that will run, a cock that will fight, a dog that will kill rats, a man that will box—they would turn away from the Emperor in all his glory in order to look upon any of these.

I could tell you many stories of English sport, for I saw much of it during the time that I was the guest of Lord Rufton, after the order for my exchange had come to England. There were months before I could be sent back to France, and during that time I stayed with this good Lord Rufton at his beautiful house at High Combe, which is at the northern end of Dartmoor. He had ridden with the police when they had pursued me from Prince-town, and he had felt towards me when I was overtaken as I would myself have felt had I, in my own country, seen a brave and debonair soldier without a friend to help him. In a word, he took me to his house, clad me, fed me, and treated me as if he had been my brother. I will say this of the English, that they were always generous enemies, and very good people with whom to fight. In the Peninsula the Spanish outposts would present their muskets at ours, but the British their brandy flasks. And of all these generous men there was none who was the equal of this admirable milord, who held out so warm a hand to an enemy in distress.

Ah! what thoughts of sport it brings back to me, the very name of High Combe! I can see it now, the long, low, brick house, warm and ruddy, with white plaster pillars before the door. He was a great sportsman this Lord Rufton, and all who were about him were of the same sort. But you will be pleased to hear that there were few things in which I could not hold my own, and in some I excelled. Behind the house was a wood in which pheasants were reared, and it was Lord Rufton's joy to kill these birds, which was done by sending in men to drive them out while he and his friends stood outside and shot them as they passed. For my part I was more crafty, for I studied the habits of the birds, and stealing out in the evening I was able to kill a number of them as they roosted in the trees. Hardly a single shot was wasted, but the keeper was attracted by the sound of the firing, and he implored me in his rough English fashion to spare those that were left. That night I was able to place twelve birds as a surprise upon Lord Rufton's supper table, and he laughed until he cried, so overjoyed was he to see them. 'Gad, Gerard, you'll be the death of me yet!' he cried. Often he said the same thing, for at every turn I amazed him by the way in which I entered into the sports of the English.

There is a game called cricket which they play in the summer, and this also I learned. Rudd, the head gardener, was a famous player of cricket, and so was Lord Rufton himself. Before the house was a lawn, and here it was that Rudd taught me the game. It is a brave pastime, a game for soldiers, for each tries to strike the other with the ball, and it is but a small stick with which you may ward it off. Three sticks behind show the spot beyond which you may not retreat. I can tell you that it is no game for children, and I will confess that, in spite of my nine campaigns, I felt myself turn pale when first the ball flashed past me. So swift was it that I had not time to raise my stick to ward it off, but by good fortune it missed me and knocked down the wooden pins which marked the boundary. It was for Rudd then to defend himself and for me to attack. When I was a boy in Gascony I learned to throw both far and straight, so that I made sure that I could hit this gallant Englishman. With a shout I rushed forward and hurled the ball at him. It flew as swift as a bullet towards his ribs, but without a word he swung his staff and the ball rose a surprising distance in the air. Lord Rufton clapped his hands and cheered. Again the ball was brought to me, and again it was for me to throw. This time it flew past his head, and it seemed to me that it was his turn to look pale. But he was a brave man this gardener, and again he faced me. Ah, my friends, the hour of my triumph had come! It was a red waistcoat that he wore, and at this I hurled the ball. You would have said that I was a gunner, not a hussar, for never was so straight an aim. With a despairing cry—the cry of the brave man who is beaten—he fell upon the wooden pegs behind him, and they all rolled upon the ground together. He was cruel, this English milord, and he laughed so that he could not come to the aid of his servant. It was for me, the victor, to rush forwards to embrace this intrepid player, and to raise him to his feet with words of praise, and encouragement, and hope. He was in pain and could not stand erect, yet the honest fellow confessed that there was no accident in my victory. 'He did it a-purpose! He did it a-purpose!' Again and again he said it. Yes, it is a great game this cricket, and I would gladly have ventured upon it again but Lord Rufton and Rudd said that it was late in the season, and so they would play no more.

How foolish of me, the old broken man, to dwell upon these successes, and yet I will confess that my age has been very much soothed and comforted by the memory of the women who have loved me and the men whom I have

461

overcome. It is pleasant to think that five years afterwards, when Lord Rufton came to Paris after the peace,
he was able to assure me that my name was still a famous
one in the north of Devonshire for the fine exploits that I
had performed. Especially, he said, that they still talked
over my boxing match with the Honourable Baldock. It
came about in this way. Of an evening many sportsmen
would assemble at the house of Lord Rufton, where they
would drink much wine, make wild bets, and talk of
their horses and their foxes. How well I remember those
strange creatures. Sir Barrington, Jack Lupton of Barn-
staple, Colonel Addison, Johnny Miller, Lord Sadler,
and my enemy, the Honourable Baldock. They were of
the same stamp all of them, drinkers, madcaps, fighters,
gamblers, full of strange caprices and extraordinary
whims. Yet they were kindly fellows in their rough
fashion, save only this Baldock, a fat man who prided
himself on his skill at the box-fight. It was he who, by his
laughter against the French because they were ignorant
of sport, caused me to challenge him in the very sport
at which he excelled. You will say that it was foolish, my
friends, but the decanter had passed many times, and the
blood of youth ran hot in my veins. I would fight him,
this boaster; I would show him that if we had not skill,
at least we had courage. Lord Rufton would not allow it.
I insisted. The others cheered me on and slapped me on
the back. 'No, dash it, Baldock, he's our guest,' said
Rufton. 'It's his own doing,' the other answered. 'Look
here, Rufton, they can't hurt each other if they wear the
mawleys,' cried Lord Sadler. And so it was agreed.

What the mawleys were I did not know; but presently
they brought out four great puddings of leather, not
unlike a fencing-glove, but larger. With these our hands
were covered after we had stripped ourselves of our coats
and our waistcoats. Then the table, with the glasses and
decanters, was pushed into the corner of the room, and
behold us, face to face! Lord Sadler sat in the armchair
with a watch in his open hand. 'Time!' said he.

I will confess to you, my friends, that I felt at that moment a tremor such as none of my many duels have ever given me. With sword or pistol I am at home; but here I only understood that I must struggle with this fat Englishman and do what I could, in spite of these great puddings upon my hands, to overcome him. And at the very outset I was disarmed of the best weapon that was left to me. 'Mind, Gerard, no kicking!' said Lord Rufton in my ear. I had only a pair of thin dancing slippers, and yet the man was fat, and a few well-directed kicks might have left me the victor. But there is an etiquette just as there is in fencing, and I refrained. I looked at this Englishman and I wondered how I should attack him. His ears were large and prominent. Could I seize them I might drag him to the ground. I rushed in, but I was betrayed by this flabby glove, and twice I lost my hold. He struck me, but I cared little for his blows, and again I seized him by the ear. He fell, and I rolled upon him and thumped his head upon the ground. How they cheered and laughed, these gallant Englishmen, and how they clapped me on the back!

'Even money on the Frenchman,' cried Lord Sadler.

'He fights foul,' cried the enemy, rubbing his crimson ears. 'He savaged me on the ground.'

'You must take your chance of that,' said Lord Rufton coldly.

'Time,' cried Lord Sadler, and once again we advanced to the assault.

He was flushed, and his small eyes were as vicious as those of a bulldog. There was hatred on his face. For my part I carried myself lightly and gaily. A French gentleman fights, but he does not hate. I drew myself up before him, and I bowed as I have done in the duello. There can be grace and courtesy as well as defiance in a bow; I put all three into this one, with a touch of ridicule in the shrug which accompanied it. It was at this moment that he struck me. The room spun round with me. I fell upon my back. But in an instant I was on my feet again and

463

had rushed to a close combat. His ear, his hair, his nose, I seized them each in turn. Once again the mad joy of the battle was in my veins. The old cry of triumph rose to my lips. 'Vive l'Empereur!' I yelled as I drove my head into his stomach. He threw his arm round my neck, and holding me with one hand he struck me with the other. I buried my teeth in his arm, and he shouted with pain. 'Call him off, Rufton!' he screamed. 'Call him off, man! He's worrying me!' They dragged me away from him. Can I ever forget it?—the laughter, the cheering, the congratulations! Even my enemy bore me no ill will, for he shook me by the hand. For my part I embraced him on each cheek. Five years afterwards I learned from Lord Rufton that my noble bearing upon that evening was still fresh in the memory of my English friends.

It is not, however, of my own exploits in sport that I wish to speak to you to-night, but it is of the Lady Jane Dacre and the strange adventure of which she was the cause. Lady Jane Dacre was Lord Rufton's sister and the lady of his household. I fear that until I came it was lonely for her, since she was a beautiful and refined woman with nothing in common with those who were about her. Indeed, this might be said of many women in the England of those days, for the men were rude and rough and coarse, with boorish habits and few accomplishments, while the women were the most lovely and tender that I have ever known. We became great friends, the Lady Jane and I, for it was not possible for me to drink three bottles of port after dinner like those Devonshire gentlemen, and so I would seek refuge in her drawing-room, where evening after evening she would play the harpsichord and I would sing the songs of my own land. In those peaceful moments I would find a refuge from the misery which filled me, when I reflected that my regiment was left in front of the enemy without the chief whom they had learned to love and to follow. Indeed, I could have torn my hair when I read in the English papers of the fine fighting which was going on in

Portugal and on the frontiers of Spain, all of which I had missed through my misfortune in falling into the hands of Milord Wellington.

From what I have told you of the Lady Jane you will have guessed what occurred, my friends. Etienne Gerard is thrown into the company of a young and beautiful woman. What must it mean for him? What must it mean for her? It was not for me, the guest, the captive, to make love to the sister of my host. But I was reserved. I was discreet. I tried to curb my own emotions and to discourage hers. For my own part I fear that I betrayed myself, for the eye becomes more eloquent when the tongue is silent. Every quiver of my fingers as I turned over her music-sheets told her my secret. But she—she was admirable. It is in these matters that women have a genius for deception. If I had not penetrated her secret I should often have thought that she forgot even that I was in the house. For hours she would sit lost in a sweet melancholy, while I admired her pale face and her curls in the lamp-light, and thrilled within me to think that I had moved her so deeply. Then at last I would speak, and she would start in her chair and stare at me with the most admirable pretence of being surprised to find me in the room. Ah! how I longed to hurl myself suddenly at her feet, to kiss her white hand, to assure her that I had surprised her secret and that I would not abuse her confidence. But, no, I was not her equal, and I was under her roof as a castaway enemy. My lips were sealed. I endeavoured to imitate her own wonderful affectation of indifference, but, as you may think, I was eagerly alert for any opportunity of serving her.

One morning Lady Jane had driven in her phaeton to Okehampton, and I strolled along the road which led to that place in the hope that I might meet her on her return. It was the early winter, and banks of fading fern sloped down to the winding road. It is a bleak place this Dartmoor, wild and rocky—a country of wind and mist. I felt as I walked that it is no wonder Englishmen should suffer from the spleen. My own heart was heavy within me, and I sat upon a rock by the wayside looking out on the dreary view with my thoughts full of trouble and foreboding. Suddenly, however, as I glanced down the road I saw a sight which drove everything else from my mind, and caused me to leap to my feet with a cry of astonishment and anger.

Down the curve of the road a phaeton was coming, the pony tearing along at full gallop. Within was the very lady whom I had come to meet. She lashed at the pony like one who endeavours to escape from some pressing danger, glancing ever backwards over her shoulder. The bend of the road concealed from me what it was that had alarmed her, and I ran forward not knowing what to expect. The next instant I saw the pursuer, and my amazement was increased at the sight. It was a gentleman in the red coat of an English fox-hunter, mounted on a great grey horse. He was galloping as if in a race, and the long stride of the splendid creature beneath him soon brought him up to the lady's flying carriage. I saw him stoop and seize the reins of the pony, so as to bring it to a halt. The next instant he was deep in talk with the lady, he bending forward in his saddle and speaking eagerly, she shrinking away from him as if she feared and loathed him.

You may think, my dear friends, that this was not a sight at which I could calmly gaze. How my heart thrilled within me to think that a chance should have been given to me to serve the Lady Jane! I ran—oh, good Lord, how I ran! At last breathless, speechless, I reached the phaeton. The man glanced up at me with his blue English eyes, but so deep was he in his talk that he paid no heed to me, nor did the lady say a word. She still leaned back, her beautiful pale face gazing up at him. He was a good-looking fellow—tall, and strong, and brown; a pang of jealousy seized me as I looked at him. He was talking low and fast, as the English do when they are in earnest.

'I tell you, Jinny, it's you and only you that I love,' said he. 'Don't bear malice, Jinny. Let bygones be bygones. Come now, say it's all over.'

'No, never, George, never!' she cried.

A dusky red suffused his handsome face. The man was furious.

'Why can't you forgive me, Jinny?'

'I can't forget the past.'

'By George, you must! I've asked enough. It's time to order now. I'll have my rights. D'ye hear?' His hand closed upon her wrist.

At last my breath returned to me.

'Madame,' I said, as I raised my hat, 'do I intrude, or is there any possible way in which I can be of service to you?'

But neither of them minded me any more than if I had been a fly who buzzed between them. Their eyes were locked together.

'I'll have my rights, I tell you. I've waited long enough.'

'There's no use bullying, George.'

'Do you give in?'

'No, never!'

'Is that your final answer?'

'Yes, it is.'

He gave a bitter curse and threw down her hand.

'All right, my lady, we'll see about this.'

'Excuse me, sir,' said I, with dignity.

'Oh, go to blazes!' he cried, turning on me with his furious face. The next instant he had spurred his horse and was galloping down the road once more.

Lady Jane gazed after him until he was out of sight, and I was surprised to see that her face wore a smile and not a frown. Then she turned to me and held out her hand.

'You are very kind, Colonel Gerard. You meant well, I am sure.'

'Madame,' said I, 'if you can oblige me with the

gentleman's name and address I will arrange that he shall never trouble you again.'

'No scandal, I beg of you,' she cried.

'Madame, I could not so far forget myself. Rest assured that no lady's name would ever be mentioned by me in the course of such an incident. In bidding me to go to blazes this gentleman has relieved me from the embarrassment of having to invent a cause of quarrel.'

'Colonel Gerard,' said the lady, earnestly, 'you must give me your word as a soldier and a gentleman that this matter goes no farther, and also that you will say nothing to my brother about what you have seen. Promise me!'

'If I must.'

'I hold you to your word. Now drive with me to High Combe, and I will explain as we go.'

The first words of her explanation went into me like a sabre-point.

'That gentleman,' said she, 'is my husband.'

'Your husband!'

'You must have known that I was married.' She seemed surprised at my agitation.

'I did not know.'

'He is Lord George Dacre. We have been married two years. There is no need to tell you how he wronged me. I left him and sought a refuge under my brother's roof. Up till to-day he has left me there unmolested. What I must above all things avoid is the chance of a duel betwixt my husband and my brother. It is horrible to think of. For this reason Lord Rufton must know nothing of this chance meeting of to-day.'

'If my pistol could free you from this annoyance——'

'No, no, it is not to be thought of. Remember your promise, Colonel Gerard. And not a word at High Combe of what you have seen!'

Her husband! I had pictured in my mind that she was a young widow. This brown-faced brute with his 'go to blazes' was the husband of this tender dove of a woman. Oh, if she would but allow me to free her from so odious

468

an encumbrance! There is no divorce so quick and certain as that which I could give her. But a promise is a promise, and I kept it to the letter. My mouth was sealed. In a week I was to be sent back from Plymouth to St. Malo, and it seemed to me that I might never hear the sequel of the story. And yet it was destined that it should have a sequel, and that I should play a very pleasing and honourable part in it.

It was only three days after the event which I have described when Lord Rufton burst hurriedly into my room. His face was pale, and his manner that of a man in extreme agitation.

'Gerard,' he cried, 'have you seen Lady Jane Dacre?'

I had seen her after breakfast, and it was now midday.

'By Heaven, there's villainy here!' cried my poor friend, rushing about like a madman. 'The bailiff has been up to say that a chaise and pair were seen driving full split down the Tavistock Road. The blacksmith heard a woman scream as it passed his forge. Jane has disappeared. By the Lord, I believe that she has been kidnapped by this villain Dacre.' He rang the bell furiously. 'Two horses this instant!' he cried. 'Colonel Gerard, your pistols! Jane comes back with me this night from Gravel Hanger, or there will be a new master in High Combe Hall.'

Behold us then within half an hour, like two knight-errants of old, riding forth to the rescue of this lady in distress. It was near Tavistock that Lord Dacre lived, and at every house and toll-gate along the road we heard the news of the flying post-chaise in front of us, so there could be no doubt whither they were bound. As we rode Lord Rufton told me of the man whom we were pursuing. His name, it seems, was a household word throughout all England for every sort of mischief. Wine, women, dice, cards, racing—in all forms of debauchery he had earned for himself a terrible name. He was of an old and noble family, and it had been hoped that he had sowed his wild oats when he married the beautiful Lady Jane Rufton. For some months he had indeed behaved well, and then he had wounded her feelings in their most tender part by some unworthy *liaison*. She had fled from his house and taken refuge with her brother, from whose care she had now been dragged once more, against her will. I ask you if two men could have had a fairer errand than that upon which Lord Rufton and myself were riding?

'That's Gravel Hanger,' he cried at last, pointing with his crop; and there on the green side of a hill was an old brick and timber building as beautiful as only an English country house can be. 'There's an inn by the park-gate, and there we shall leave our horses,' he added.

For my own part it seemed to me that with so just a cause we should have done best to ride boldly up to his door and summon him to surrender the lady. But there I was wrong. For the one thing which every Englishman fears is the law. He makes it himself, and when he has once made it it becomes a terrible tyrant before whom the bravest quails. He will smile at breaking his neck, but he will turn pale at breaking the law. It seems, then, from what Lord Rufton told me as we walked through the park, that we were on the wrong side of the law in this matter. Lord Dacre was in the right in carrying off his wife, since she did indeed belong to him, and our own position now was nothing better than that of burglars and trespassers. It was not for burglars to openly approach the front door. We could take the lady by force or by craft, but we could not take her by right, for the law was against us. This was what my friend explained to me as we crept up towards the shelter of a shrubbery which was close to the windows of the house. Thence we could examine this fortress, see whether we could effect a lodgment in it, and, above all, try to establish some communication with the beautiful prisoner inside.

There we were, then, in the shrubbery, Lord Rufton and I, each with a pistol in the pockets of our riding-coats, and with the most resolute determination in our hearts that we should not return without the lady. Eagerly we scanned every window of the wide-spread house. Not a sign could we see of the prisoner or of anyone else; but on the gravel drive outside the door were the deep-sunk marks of the wheels of the chaise. There was no doubt that they had arrived. Crouching among the laurel bushes we held a whispered council of war, but a singular interruption brought it to an end.

Out of the door of the house there stepped a tall, flaxen-haired man, such a figure as one would choose for the flank of a Grenadier company. As he turned his brown face and his blue eyes towards us I recognised Lord Dacre. With long strides he came down the gravel path straight for the spot where we lay.

'Come out, Ned!' he shouted; 'you'll have the game-keeper putting a charge of shot into you. Come out, man, and don't skulk behind the bushes.'

It was not a very heroic situation for us. My poor friend rose with a crimson face. I sprang to my feet also and bowed with such dignity as I could muster.

'Halloa! it's the Frenchman is it?' said he, without returning my bow. 'I've got a crow to pluck with him already. As to you, Ned, I knew you would be hot on our scent, and so I was looking out for you. I saw you cross the park and go to ground in the shrubbery. Come in, man, and let us have all the cards on the table.'

He seemed master of the situation, this handsome giant of a man, standing at his ease on his own ground while we slunk out of our hiding-place. Lord Rufton had said not a word, but I saw by his darkened brow and his sombre eyes that the storm was gathering. Lord Dacre led the way into the house, and we followed close at his heels. He ushered us himself into an oak-panelled sitting-room, closing the door behind us. Then he looked me up and down with insolent eyes.

'Look here, Ned,' said he, 'time was when an English family could settle their own affairs in their own way.

471

What has this foreign fellow got to do with your sister and my wife?'

'Sir,' said I, 'permit me to point out to you that this is not a case merely of a sister or a wife, but that I am a friend of the lady in question, and that I have the privilege which every gentleman possesses of protecting a woman against brutality. It is only by a gesture that I can show you what I think of you.' I had my riding-glove in my hand, and I flicked him across the face with it. He drew back with a bitter smile and his eyes were as hard as flint.

'So you've brought your bully with you, Ned?' said he. 'You might at least have done your fighting yourself, if it must come to a fight.'

'So I will,' cried Lord Rufton. 'Here and now.'

'When I've killed this swaggering Frenchman,' said Lord Dacre. He stepped to a side table and opened a brass-bound case. 'By Gad,' said he, 'either that man or I go out of this room feet foremost. I meant well by you, Ned; I did, by George, but I'll shoot this led-captain of yours as sure as my name's George Dacre. Take your choice of pistols, sir, and shoot across this table. The barkers are loaded. Aim straight and kill me if you can, for, by the Lord, if you don't, you're done.'

In vain Lord Rufton tried to take the quarrel upon himself. Two things were clear in my mind—one that the Lady Jane had feared above all things that her husband and brother should fight, the other that if I could but kill this big milord, then the whole question would be settled for ever in the best way. Lord Rufton did not want him. Lady Jane did not want him. Therefore, I, Etienne Gerard, their friend, would pay the debt of gratitude which I owed them by freeing them of this encumbrance. But, indeed, there was no choice in the matter, for Lord Dacre was as eager to put a bullet into me as I could be to do the same service to him. In vain Lord Rufton argued and scolded. The affair must continue.

'Well, if you must fight my guest instead of myself, let

it be to-morrow morning with two witnesses,' he cried at last; 'this is sheer murder across the table.'

'But it suits my humour, Ned,' said Lord Dacre.

'And mine, sir,' said I.

'Then I'll have nothing to do with it,' cried Lord Rufton. 'I tell you, George, if you shoot Colonel Gerard under these circumstances you'll find yourself in the dock instead of on the bench. I won't act as second, and that's flat.'

'Sir,' said I, 'I am perfectly prepared to proceed without a second.'

'That won't do. It's against the law,' cried Lord Dacre. 'Come, Ned, don't be a fool. You see we mean to fight. Hang it, man, all I want you to do is to drop a handkerchief.'

'I'll take no part in it.'

'Then I must find someone who will,' said Lord Dacre. He threw a cloth over the pistols, which lay upon the table, and he rang the bell. A footman entered. 'Ask Colonel Berkeley if he will step this way. You will find him in the billiard-room.'

A moment later there entered a tall thin Englishman with a great moustache, which was a rare thing amid that clean-shaven race. I have heard since that they were worn only by the Guards and the Hussars. This Colonel Berkeley was a guardsman. He seemed a strange, tired, languid, drawling creature with a long black cigar thrusting out, like a pole from a bush, amidst that immense moustache. He looked from one to the other of us with true English phlegm, and he betrayed not the slightest surprise when he was told our intention.

'Quite so,' said he; 'quite so.'

'I refuse to act, Colonel Berkeley,' cried Lord Rufton. 'Remember, this duel cannot proceed without you, and I hold you personally responsible for anything that happens.'

This Colonel Berkeley appeared to be an authority upon the question, for he removed the cigar from his mouth and he laid down the law in his strange, drawling voice.

'The circumstances are unusual, but not irregular, Lord Rufton,' said he. 'This gentleman has given a blow, and this other gentleman has received it. That is a clear issue. Time and conditions depend upon the person who demands satisfaction. Very good. He claims it here and now, across the table. He is acting within his rights. I am prepared to accept the responsibility.'

There was nothing more to be said. Lord Rufton sat moodily in the corner, with his brows drawn down and his hands thrust deep into the pockets of his riding-breeches. Colonel Berkeley examined the two pistols and laid them both in the centre of the table. Lord Dacre was at one end and I at the other, with eight feet of shining mahogany between us. On the hearthrug, with his back to the fire, stood the tall colonel, his handkerchief in his left hand, his cigar between two fingers of his right.

'When I drop the handkerchief,' said he, 'you will pick up your pistols and you will fire at your own convenience. Are you ready?'

'Yes,' we cried.

His hand opened, and the handkerchief fell. I bent swiftly forward and seized a pistol, but the table, as I have said, was eight feet across, and it was easier for this long-armed milord to reach the pistols than it was for me. I had not yet drawn myself straight before he fired, and to this it was that I owe my life. His bullet would have blown out my brains had I been erect. As it was it whistled through my curls. At the same instant, just as I threw up my own pistol to fire, the door flew open, and a pair of arms were thrown round me. It was the beautiful, flushed, frantic face of Lady Jane which looked up into mine.

'You shan't fire! Colonel Gerard, for my sake, don't fire,' she cried. 'It is a mistake, I tell you—a mistake, a mistake! He is the best and dearest of husbands. Never

474

again shall I leave his side.' Her hands slid down my arm and closed upon my pistol.

'Jane, Jane,' cried Lord Rufton; 'come with me. You should not be here. Come away.'

'It is all confoundedly irregular,' said Colonel Berkeley.

'Colonel Gerard, you won't fire, will you? My heart would break if he were hurt.'

'Hang it all, Jinny, give the fellow fair play,' cried Lord Dacre. 'He stood my fire like a man, and I won't see him interfered with. Whatever happens, I can't get worse than I deserve.'

But already there had passed between me and the lady a quick glance of the eyes which told her everything. Her hands slipped from my arm. 'I leave my husband's life and my own happiness to Colonel Gerard,' said she.

How well she knew me, this admirable woman! I stood for an instant irresolute, with the pistol cocked in my hand. My antagonist faced me bravely, with no blenching of his sunburnt face and no flinching of his bold, blue eyes.

'Come, come, sir, take your shot!' cried the colonel from the mat.

'Let us have it, then,' said Lord Dacre.

I would, at least, show them how completely his life was at the mercy of my skill. So much I owed to my own self-respect. I glanced round for a mark. The colonel was looking towards my antagonist, expecting to see him drop. His face was sideways to me, his long cigar projecting from his lips with an inch of ash at the end of it. Quick as a flash I raised my pistol and fired.

'Permit me to trim your ash, sir,' said I, and I bowed with a grace which is unknown among these islanders.

I am convinced that the fault lay with the pistol and not with my aim. I could hardly believe my own eyes when I saw that I had snapped off the cigar within half an inch of his lips. He stood staring at me with the ragged stub of the cigar-end sticking out from his singed moustache. I can see him now with his foolish, angry eyes

475

and his long, thin, puzzled face. Then he began to talk. I have always said that the English are not really a phlegmatic or a taciturn nation if you stir them out of their groove. No one could have talked in a more animated way than this colonel. Lady Jane put her hands over her ears.

'Come, come, Colonel Berkeley,' said Lord Dacre, sternly, 'you forget yourself. There is a lady in the room.'

The colonel gave a stiff bow.

'If Lady Dacre will kindly leave this room,' said he, 'I will be able to tell this infernal little Frenchman what I think of him and his monkey tricks.'

I was splendid at that moment, for I ignored the words that he had said and remembered only the extreme provocation.

'Sir,' said I, 'I freely offer you my apologies for this unhappy incident. I felt that if I did not discharge my pistol Lord Dacre's honour might feel hurt, and yet it was quite impossible for me, after hearing what this lady had said, to aim it at her husband. I looked round for a mark, therefore, and I had the extreme misfortune to blow your cigar out of your mouth when my intention had merely been to snuff the ash. I was betrayed by my pistol. This is my explanation, sir, and if after listening to my apologies you still feel that I owe you satisfaction, I need not say that it is a request which I am unable to refuse.'

It was certainly a charming attitude which I had assumed, and it won the hearts of all of them. Lord Dacre stepped forward and wrung me by the hand. 'By George,' sir,' said he, 'I never thought to feel towards a Frenchman as I do to you. You're a man and a gentleman, and I can't say more.' Lord Rufton said nothing, but his hand-grip told me all that he thought. Even Colonel Berkeley paid me a compliment, and declared that he would think no more about the unfortunate cigar. And she—ah, if you could have seen the look she gave me, the flushed cheek, the moist eye, the tremulous lip! When I think of my beautiful Lady Jane it is at that moment that I recall her. They would have had me stay to dinner, but you will understand, my friends, that this was no time for either Lord Rufton or myself to remain at Gravel Hanger. This reconciled couple desired only to be alone. In the chaise he had persuaded her of his sincere repentance, and once again they were a loving husband and wife. If they were to remain so, it was best perhaps that I should go. Why should I unsettle that domestic peace? Even against my own will my mere presence and appearance might have their effect upon the lady. No, no, I must tear myself away—even her persuasions were unable to make me stop. Years afterwards I heard that the household of the Dacres was among the happiest in the country, and that no cloud had ever come again to darken their lives. Yet I dare say if he could have seen into his wife's mind—but there, I say no more! A lady's secret is her own, and I fear that she and it are buried long years ago in some Devonshire churchyard. Perhaps all that gay circle are gone and the Lady Jane only lives now in the memory of an old half-pay French brigadier. He at least can never forget.

VI. How the Brigadier Rode to Minsk

I WOULD have a stronger wine to-night, my friends, a wine of Burgundy rather than of Bordeaux. It is that my heart, my old soldier heart, is heavy within me. It is a strange thing, this age which creeps upon one. One does not know, one does not understand; the spirit is ever the same, and one does not remember how the poor body crumbles. But there comes a moment when it is brought home, when quick as the sparkle of a whirling sabre it is clear to us, and we see the men we were and the men we are. Yes, yes, it was so to-day, and I would have a wine of Burgundy to-night, White Burgundy—Montrachet—— Sir, I am your debtor!

It was this morning in the Champ de Mars. Your pardon, friends, while an old man tells his trouble. You saw the review. Was it not splendid? I was in the enclosure for veteran officers who have been decorated. This ribbon on my breast was my passport. The cross itself I keep at home in a leathern pouch. They did us honour, for we were placed at the saluting point, with the Emperor and the carriages of the Court upon our right.

It is years since I have been to a review, for I cannot approve of many things which I have seen. I do not approve of the red breeches of the infantry. It was in white breeches that the infantry used to fight. Red is for the cavalry. A little more, and they would ask our busbies and our spurs! Had I been seen at a review they might well have said that I, Etienne Gerard, had condoned it. So I have stayed at home. But this war of the Crimea is different. The men go to battle. It is not for me to be absent when brave men gather.

My faith, they march well, those little infantrymen! They are not large, but they are very solid and they carry themselves well. I took off my hat to them as they passed. Then there came the guns. They were good guns, well horsed, and well manned. I took off my hat to them. Then came the Engineers, and to them also I took off my hat. There are no braver men than the Engineers. Then came the cavalry, Lancers, Cuirassiers, Chasseurs, and Spahis. To all of them in turn I was able to take off my hat, save only to the Spahis. The Emperor had no Spahis. But when all of the others had passed, what think you came at the close? A brigade of Hussars, and at the charge! Oh, my friends, the pride and the glory and the beauty, the flash and the sparkle, the roar of the hoofs, and the jingle of chains, the tossing manes, the noble heads, the rolling cloud, and the dancing waves of steel! My heart drummed to them as they passed. And the last of all, was it not my own old regiment? My eyes fell upon the grey and silver dolmans, with the leopard-skin schabraques, and at that instant the years fell away from me and I saw my own beautiful men and horses, even as they had swept behind their young colonel, in the pride of our youth and our strength, just forty years ago. Up flew my cane. '*Chargez! En avant! Vive l'Empereur!*' It was the past calling to the present. But, oh, what a thin, piping voice! Was this the voice that had once thundered from wing to wing of a strong brigade? And the arm that could scarce wave a cane, were these the muscles of fire and steel which had no match in all Napoleon's mighty host? They smiled at me. They cheered me. The Emperor laughed and bowed. But to me the present was a dim dream, and what was real were my eight hundred dead Hussars and the Etienne of long ago. Enough—a brave man can face age and fate as he faced Cossacks and Uhlans. But there are times when Montrachet is better than the wine of Bordeaux.

It is to Russia that they go, and so I will tell you a story of Russia. Ah, what an evil dream of the night it seems! Blood and ice. Ice and blood. Fierce faces with snow upon the whiskers. Blue hands held out for succour. And across the great white plain the one long black line of moving figures, trudging, trudging, a hundred miles, another hundred, and still always the same white plain. Sometimes there were fir-woods to limit it, sometimes it stretched away to the cold blue sky, but the black line stumbled on and on. Those weary, ragged, starving men, the spirit frozen out of them, looked neither to right nor left, but with sunken faces and rounded backs trailed onwards and ever onwards, making for France as wounded beasts make for their lair. There was no speaking, and you could scarce hear the shuffle of feet in the snow. Once only I heard them laugh. It was outside Wilna, when an aide-de-camp rode up to the head of that dreadful column and asked if that were the Grand Army. All who were within hearing looked round, and when they saw those broken men, those ruined regiments, those fur-capped skeletons who were once the Guard, they laughed, and the laugh crackled down the column like a *feu de joie*. I have heard many a groan and cry and scream in my life, but nothing so terrible as the laugh of the Grand Army.

But why was it that these helpless men were not destroyed by the Russians? Why was it that they were not speared by the Cossacks or herded into droves, and driven as prisoners into the heart of Russia? On every side as you watched the black snake winding over the snow you saw also the dark, moving shadows which came and went like cloud drifts on either flank and behind. They were the Cossacks, who hung round us like wolves round the flock. But the reason why they did not ride in upon us was that all the ice of Russia could not cool the hot hearts of some of our soldiers. To the end there were always those who were ready to throw themselves between these savages and their prey. One man above all rose greater as the danger thickened, and won a higher name amid disaster than he had done when he led our van to victory. To him I drink this glass—to Ney, the red-maned Lion, glaring back over his shoulder at the enemy who feared to tread too closely on his heels. I can see him now, his broad white face convulsed with fury, his light blue eyes sparkling like flints, his great voice roaring and crashing amid the roll of the musketry. His glazed and featherless cocked hat was the ensign upon which France rallied during those dreadful days.

It is well known that neither I nor the regiment of Hussars of Conflans were at Moscow. We were left behind on the lines of communication at Borodino. How the Emperor could have advanced without us is incomprehensible to me, and, indeed, it was only then that I understood that his judgment was weakening, and that he was no longer the man that he had been. However, a soldier has to obey orders, and so I remained at this village, which was poisoned by the bodies of thirty thousand men who had lost their lives in the great battle. I spent the late autumn in getting my horses into condition and reclothing my men, so that when the army fell back on Borodino my Hussars were the best of the cavalry, and were placed under Ney in the rear-guard. What could he have done without us during those dreadful days? 'Ah, Gerard,' said he one evening—but it is not for me to repeat the words. Suffice it that he spoke what the whole army felt. The rear-guard covered the army, and the Hussars of Conflans covered the rear-guard. There was the whole truth in a sentence. Always the Cossacks were on us. Always we held them off. Never a day passed that we had not to wipe our sabres. That was soldiering indeed.

But there came a time between Wilna and Smolensk when the situation became impossible. Cossacks and even cold we could fight, but we could not fight hunger as well. Food must be got at all costs. That night Ney sent for me to the waggon in which he slept. His great head was sunk on his hands. Mind and body, he was wearied to death.

'Colonel Gerard,' said he, 'things are going very badly with us. The men are starving. We must have food at all costs.'

'The horses,' I suggested.

'Save your handful of cavalry, there are none left.'

'The band,' said I.

He laughed, even in his despair.

'Why the band?' he asked.

'Fighting men are of value.'

'Good!' said he. 'You would play the game down to the last card, and so would I. Good, Gerard, good!' He clasped my hand in his. 'But there is one chance for us yet, Gerard.' He unhooked a lantern from the roof of the waggon, and he laid it on a map which was stretched before him. 'To the south of us,' said he, 'there lies the town of Minsk. I have word from a Russian deserter that much corn has been stored in the town-hall. I wish you to take as many men as you think best, set forth for Minsk, seize the corn, load any carts which you may collect in the town, and bring them to me between here and

Smolensk. If you fail, it is but a detachment cut off. If you succeed, it is new life to the army.'

He had not expressed himself well, for it was evident that if we failed it was not merely the loss of a detachment. It is quality as well as quantity which counts. And yet how honourable a mission, and how glorious a risk! If mortal men could bring it, then the corn should come from Minsk. I said so, and spoke a few burning words about a brave man's duty until the Marshal was so moved that he rose and, taking me affectionately by the shoulders, pushed me out of the waggon.

It was clear to me that in order to succeed in my enterprise I should take a small force and depend rather upon surprise than upon numbers. A large body could not conceal itself, would have great difficulty in getting food, and would cause all the Russians around us to concentrate for its certain destruction. On the other hand, if a small body of cavalry could get past the Cossacks unseen it was probable that they would find no troops to oppose them, for we knew that the main Russian army was several days' march behind us. This corn was meant, no doubt, for their consumption. A squadron of Hussars and thirty Polish Lancers were all whom I chose for the venture. That very night we rode out of the camp, and struck south in the direction of Minsk.

Fortunately there was but half a moon, and we were able to pass without being attacked by the enemy. Twice we saw great fires burning amid the snow, and around them a thick bristle of long poles. These were the lances of Cossacks, which they had stood upright while they slept. It would have been a great joy to us to have charged in amongst them, for we had much to revenge, and the eyes of my comrades looked longingly from me to those red flickering patches in the darkness. My faith, I was sorely tempted to do it, for it would have been a good lesson to teach them that they must keep a few miles between themselves and a French army. It is the essence of good generalship, however, to keep one thing before one at a time, and so we rode silently on through the snow, leaving these Cossack bivouacs to right and left. Behind us the black sky was all mottled with a line of flame, which showed where our own poor wretches were trying to keep themselves alive for another day of misery and starvation.

All night we rode slowly onwards, keeping our horses' tails to the Pole Star. There were many tracks in the snow, and we kept to the line of these, that no one might remark that a body of cavalry had passed that way. These are the little precautions which mark the experienced officer. Besides, by keeping to the tracks we were most likely to find the villages, and only in the villages could we hope to get food. The dawn of day found us in a thick fir-wood, the trees so loaded with snow that the light could hardly reach us. When we had found our way out of it it was full daylight, the rim of the rising sun peeping over the edge of the great snow-plain and turning it crimson from end to end. I halted my Hussars and Lancers under the shadow of the wood, and I studied the country. Close to us there was a small farmhouse. Beyond, at a distance of several miles, was a village. Far away on the skyline rose a considerable town all bristling with church towers. This was Minsk. In no direction could I see any signs of troops. It was evident that we had passed through the Cossacks, and that there was nothing between us and our goal. A joyous shout burst from my men when I told them our position, and we advanced rapidly towards the village.

I have said, however, that there was a small farmhouse immediately in front of us. As we rode up to it I observed that a fine grey horse with a military saddle was tethered by the door. Instantly I galloped forward, but before I could reach it a man dashed out of the door, flung himself on to the horse, and rode furiously away, the crisp, dry snow flying up in a cloud behind him. The sunlight gleamed upon his gold epaulettes, and I knew that he was a Russian officer. He would raise the whole country-side if we did not catch him. I put spurs to Violette and flew after him. My troopers followed; but there was no horse among them to compare with Violette, and I knew well that if I could not catch the Russian I need expect no help from them.

But it is a swift horse indeed and a skilful rider who can hope to escape from Violette with Etienne Gerard in the saddle. He rode well, this young Russian, and his mount was a good one, but gradually we wore him down. His face glanced continually over his shoulder—a dark, handsome face, with eyes like an eagle—and I saw as I closed with him that he was measuring the distance between us. Suddenly he half turned; there were a flash and a crack as his pistol bullet hummed past my ear. Before he could draw his sword I was upon him; but he still spurred his horse, and the two galloped together over the plain, I with my leg against the Russian's and my left hand upon his right shoulder. I saw his hand fly up to his mouth. Instantly I dragged him across my pommel and seized him by the throat, so that he could not swallow. His horse shot from under him, but I held him fast, and Violette came to a stand. Sergeant Oudin of the Hussars was the first to join us. He was an old soldier, and he saw at a glance what I was after.

'Hold tight, Colonel,' said he; 'I'll do the rest.'

He slipped out his knife, thrust the blade between the clenched teeth of the Russian, and turned it so as to force his mouth open. There, on his tongue, was the little wad of wet paper which he had been so anxious to swallow. Oudin picked it out, and I let go of the man's throat. From the way in which, half strangled as he was, he glanced at the paper I was sure that it was a message of extreme importance. His hands twitched as if he longed to snatch it from me. He shrugged his shoulders, however, and smiled good-humouredly when I apologised for my roughness.

'And now to business,' said I, when he had done coughing and hawking. 'What is your name?'

'Alexis Barakoff.'

'Your rank and regiment?'

'Captain of the Dragoons of Grodno.'

'What is this note which you were carrying?'

'It is a line which I had written to my sweetheart.'

'Whose name,' said I, examining the address, 'is the Hetman Platoff. Come, come, sir, this is an important military document, which you are carrying from one general to another. Tell me this instant what it is.'

'Read it, and then you will know.' He spoke perfect French, as do most of the educated Russians. But he knew well that there is not one French officer in a thousand who knows a word of Russian. The inside of the note contained one single line which ran like this:—

'*Pustj Franzuzy pridutt v Minsk. Min gotovy.*'

I stared at it, and I had to shake my head. Then I showed it to my Hussars, but they could make nothing of it. The Poles were all rough fellows who could not read or write, save only the sergeant, who came from Memel, in East Prussia, and knew no Russian. It was maddening, for I felt that I had possession of some important secret upon which the safety of the army might depend, and yet I could make no sense of it. Again I entreated our prisoner to translate it, and offered him his freedom if he would do so. He only smiled at my request. I could not but admire him, for it was the very smile which I should have myself smiled had I been in his position.

'At least,' said I, 'tell us the name of this village.'

'It is Dobrova.'

'And that is Minsk over yonder I suppose?'

'Yes, that is Minsk.'

'Then we shall go to the village and we shall very soon find some one who will translate this despatch.'

So we rode onward together, a trooper with his carbine on either side of our prisoner. The village was but a little place, and I set a guard at the ends of the single street, so that no one could escape from it. It was necessary to call a halt and to find some food for the men and horses, since they had travelled all night and had a long journey still before them.

There was one large stone house in the centre of the village, and to this I rode. It was the house of the priest—a snuffy and ill-favoured old man who had not a civil answer to any of our questions. An uglier fellow I never met, but, my faith, it was very different with his only daughter, who kept house for him. She was a brunette, a rare thing in Russia, with creamy skin, raven hair, and a pair of the most glorious dark eyes that ever kindled at the sight of a Hussar. From the first glance I saw that she was mine. It was no time for love-making when a soldier's duty had to be done, but still, as I took the simple meal which they laid before me, I chatted lightly with the lady, and we were the best of friends before an hour had passed. Sophie was her first name, her second I never knew. I taught her to call me Etienne, and I tried to cheer her up, for her sweet face was sad and there were tears in her beautiful dark eyes. I pressed her to tell me what it was which was grieving her.

'How can I be otherwise,' said she, speaking French with a most adorable lisp, 'when one of my poor countrymen is a prisoner in your hands? I saw him between two of your Hussars as you rode into the village.'

'It is the fortune of war,' said I. 'His turn to-day; mine, perhaps, to-morrow.'

'But consider, Monsieur——' said she.

'Etienne,' said I.

'Well, then,' she cried, beautifully flushed and desperate, 'consider, Etienne, that this young officer will be taken back to your army and will be starved or frozen, for if, as I hear, your own soldiers have a hard march, what will be the lot of a prisoner?'

I shrugged my shoulders.

'You have a kind face, Etienne,' said she; 'you would not condemn this poor man to certain death. I entreat you to let him go.'

Her delicate hand rested upon my sleeve, her dark eyes looked imploringly into mine.

A sudden thought passed through my mind. I would grant her request, but I would demand a favour in return. At my order the prisoner was brought up into the room.

'Captain Barakoff,' said I, 'this young lady has begged me to release you, and I am inclined to do so. I would ask you to give your parole that you will remain in this dwelling for twenty-four hours, and take no steps to inform any one of our movements.'

'I will do so,' said he.

'Then I trust in your honour. One man more or less can make no difference in a struggle between great armies, and to take you back as a prisoner would be to condemn you to death. Depart, sir, and show your gratitude not to me, but to the first French officer who falls into your hands.'

When he was gone I drew my paper from my pocket.

'Now, Sophie,' said I, 'I have done what you asked me, and all that I ask in return is that you will give me a lesson in Russian.'

'With all my heart,' said she.

'Let us begin on this,' said I, spreading out the paper before her. 'Let us take it word for word and see what it means.'

She looked at the writing with some surprise. 'It means,' said she, 'if the French come to Minsk all is lost.' Suddenly a look of consternation passed over her beautiful face. 'Great heavens!' she cried, 'what is it that I have done? I have betrayed my country! Oh, Etienne, your eyes are the last for whom this message is meant. How could you be so cunning as to make a poor, simple-minded, and unsuspecting girl betray the cause of her country?'

I consoled my poor Sophie as best I might, and I assured her that it was no reproach to her that she should be outwitted by so old a campaigner and so shrewd a man as myself. But it was no time now for talk. This message made it clear that the corn was indeed at Minsk, and that there were no troops there to defend it. I gave a hurried order from the window, the trumpeter blew the assembly, and in ten minutes we had left the village behind us and were riding hard for the city, the gilded domes and minarets of which glimmered above the snow of the horizon. Higher they rose and higher, until at last, as the sun sank towards the west, we were in the broad main street, and galloped up it amid the shouts of the moujiks and the cries of frightened women until we found ourselves in front of the great town-hall. My cavalry I drew up in the square, and I, with my two sergeants, Oudin and Papilette, rushed into the building.

Heavens! shall I ever forget the sight which greeted us? Right in front of us was drawn up a triple line of Russian Grenadiers. Their muskets rose as we entered, and a crashing volley burst into our very faces, Oudin and Papilette dropped upon the floor, riddled with bullets. For myself, my busby was shot away and I had two holes through my dolman. The Grenadiers ran at me with their bayonets. 'Treason!' I cried. 'We are betrayed! Stand to your horses!' I rushed out of the hall, but the whole square was swarming with troops. From every side street Dragoons and Cossacks were riding down upon us, and such a rolling fire had burst from the surrounding houses that half my men and horses were on the ground. 'Follow me!' I yelled, and sprang upon Violette, but a giant of a Russian Dragoon officer threw his arms round me, and we rolled on the ground together. He shortened his sword to kill me, but, changing his mind, he seized me by the throat and banged my head against the stones until I was unconscious. So it was that I became the prisoner of the Russians.

When I came to myself my only regret was that my captor had not beaten out my brains. There in the grand square of Minsk lay half my troopers dead or wounded, with exultant crowds of Russians gathered round them.

The rest, in a melancholy group, were herded into the porch of the town-hall, a *sotnia* of Cossacks keeping guard over them. Alas! what could I say, what could I do? It was evident that I had led my men into a carefully baited trap. They had heard of our mission, and they had prepared for us. And yet there was that despatch which had caused me to neglect all precautions and to ride straight into the town. How was I to account for that? The tears ran down my cheeks as I surveyed the ruin of my squadron, and as I thought of the plight of my comrades of the Grand Army who awaited the food which I was to have brought them. Ney had trusted me, and I had failed him. How often he would strain his eyes over the snowfields for that convoy of grain which should never gladden his sight! My own fate was hard enough. An exile in Siberia was the best which the future could bring me. But you will believe me, my friends, that it was not for his own sake, but for that of his starving comrades, that Etienne Gerard's cheeks were lined by his tears, frozen even as they were shed.

'What's this?' said a gruff voice at my elbow; and I turned to face the huge, black-bearded Dragoon who had dragged me from my saddle. 'Look at the Frenchman crying! I thought that the Corsican was followed by brave men, and not by children.'

'If you and I were face to face and alone, I should let you see which is the better man,' said I.

For answer the brute struck me across the face with his open hand. I seized him by the throat, but a dozen of his soldiers tore me away from him, and he struck me again while they held my hands.

'You base hound,' I cried, 'is this the way to treat an officer and a gentleman?'

'We never asked you to come to Russia,' said he. 'If you do you must take such treatment as you can get. I would shoot you off-hand if I had my way.'

'You will answer for this some day,' I cried, as I wiped the blood from my moustache.

'If the Hetman Platoff is of my way of thinking you will not be alive this time to-morrow,' he answered, with a ferocious scowl. He added some words in Russian to his troops, and instantly they all sprang to their saddles. Poor Violette, looking as miserable as her master, was led round and I was told to mount her. My left arm was tied with a thong which was fastened to the stirrup-iron of a sergeant of Dragoons. So in most sorry plight I and the remnant of my men set forth from Minsk.

Never have I met such a brute as this man Sergine, who commanded the escort. The Russian army contains the best and the worst in the world, but a worse than Major Sergine of the Dragoons of Kieff I have never seen in any force outside of the guerillas of the Peninsula. He was a man of great stature, with a fierce, hard face and a bristling black beard, which fell over his cuirass. I have been told since that he was noted for his strength and his bravery, and I could answer for it that he had the grip of a bear, for I had felt it when he tore me from my saddle. He was a wit, too, in his way, and made continual remarks in Russian at our expense which set all his Dragoons and Cossacks laughing. Twice he beat my comrades with his riding-whip, and once he approached me with the lash swung over his shoulder, but there was something in my eyes which prevented it from falling. So in misery and humiliation, cold and starving, we rode in a disconsolate column across the vast snow-plain. The sun had sunk, but still in the long northern twilight we pursued our weary journey. Numbed and frozen, with my head aching from the blows it had received, I was borne onwards by Violette, hardly conscious of where I was or whither I was going. The little mare walked with a sunken head, only raising it to snort her contempt for the mangy Cossack ponies who were round her.

But suddenly the escort stopped, and I found that we had halted in the single street of a small Russian village. There was a church on one side, and on the other was a large stone house, the outline of which seemed to me to

be familiar. I looked around me in the twilight, and then
I saw that we had been led back to Dobrova, and that
this house at the door of which we were waiting was the
same house of the priest at which we had stopped in the
morning. Here it was that my charming Sophie in her
innocence had translated the unlucky message which had
in some strange way led us to our ruin. To think that
only a few hours before we had left this very spot with
such high hopes and all fair prospects for our mission,
and now the remnants of us waited as beaten and humiliated men for whatever lot a brutal enemy might ordain!
But such is the fate of the soldier, my friends—kisses
to-day, blows to-morrow. Tokay in a palace, ditch-water
in a hovel, furs or rags, a full purse or an empty pocket,
ever swaying from the best to the worst, with only his
courage and his honour unchanging.

The Russian horsemen dismounted, and my poor
fellows were ordered to do the same. It was already late,
and it was clearly their intention to spend the night in
this village. There were great cheering and joy amongst
the peasants when they understood that we had all been
taken, and they flocked out of their houses with flaming
torches, the women carrying out tea and brandy for the
Cossacks. Amongst others, the old priest came forth—the
same whom we had seen in the morning. He was all
smiles now, and he bore with him some hot punch on a
salver, the reek of which I can remember still. Behind
her father was Sophie. With horror I saw her clasp Major
Sergine's hand as she congratulated him upon the victory
he had won and the prisoners he had made. The old
priest, her father, looked at me with an insolent face, and
made insulting remarks at my expense, pointing at me
with his lean and grimy hand. His fair daughter Sophie
looked at me also, but she said nothing, and I could read
her tender pity in her dark eyes. At last she turned to
Major Sergine and said something to him in Russian, on
which he frowned and shook his head impatiently. She
appeared to plead with him, standing there in the flood

of light which shone from the open door of her father's house. My eyes were fixed upon the two faces, that of the beautiful girl and of the dark, fierce man, for my instinct told me that it was my own fate which was under debate. For a long time the soldier shook his head, and then, at last softening before her pleadings, he appeared to give way. He turned to where I stood with my guardian sergeant beside me.

'These good people offer you the shelter of their roof for the night,' said he to me, looking me up and down with vindictive eyes. 'I find it hard to refuse them, but I tell you straight that for my part I had rather see you on the snow. It would cool your hot blood, you rascal of a Frenchman!'

I looked at him with the contempt that I felt.

'You were born a savage, and you will die one,' said I.

My words stung him, for he broke into an oath, raising his whip as if he would strike me.

'Silence, you crop-eared dog!' he cried. 'Had I my way some of the insolence would be frozen out of you before morning.' Mastering his passion, he turned upon Sophie with what he meant to be a gallant manner. 'If you have a cellar with a good lock,' said he, 'the fellow may lie in it for the night, since you have done him the honour to take an interest in his comfort. I must have his parole that he will not attempt to play us any tricks, as I am answerable for him until I hand him over to the Hetman Platoff to-morrow.'

His supercilious manner was more than I could endure. He had evidently spoken French to the lady in order that I might understand the humiliating way in which he referred to me.

'I will take no favour from you,' said I. 'You may do what you like, but I will never give you my parole.'

The Russian shrugged his great shoulders, and turned away as if the matter were ended.

'Very well, my fine fellow, so much the worse for your fingers and toes. We shall see how you are in the morning after a night in the snow.'

'One moment, Major Sergine,' cried Sophie. 'You must not be so hard upon this prisoner. There are some special reasons why he has a claim upon our kindness and mercy.'

The Russian looked with suspicion upon his face from her to me.

'What are the special reasons? You certainly seem to take a remarkable interest in this Frenchman,' said he.

'The chief reason is that he has this very morning of his own accord released Captain Alexis Barakoff, of the Dragoons of Grodno.'

'It is true,' said Barakoff, who had come out of the house. 'He captured me this morning, and he released me upon parole rather than take me back to the French army, where I should have been starved.'

'Since Colonel Gerard has acted so generously you will surely, now that fortune has changed, allow us to offer him the poor shelter of our cellar upon this bitter night,' said Sophie. 'It is a small return for his generosity.'

But the Dragoon was still in the sulks.

'Let him give me his parole first that he will not attempt to escape,' said he. 'Do you hear, sir? Do you give me your parole?'

'I give you nothing,' said I.

'Colonel Gerard,' cried Sophie, turning to me with a coaxing smile, 'you will give *me* your parole, will you not?'

'To you, mademoiselle, I can refuse nothing. I will give you my parole, with pleasure.'

'There, Major Sergine,' cried Sophie, in triumph, 'that is surely sufficient. You have heard him say that he gives me his parole. I will be answerable for his safety.'

In an ungracious fashion my Russian bear grunted his consent, and so I was led into the house, followed by the scowling father and by the big, black-bearded Dragoon. In the basement there was a large and roomy chamber, where the winter logs were stored. Thither it was that I was led, and I was given to understand that this was to be my lodging for the night. One side of this bleak apartment was heaped up to the ceiling with faggots of firewood. The rest of the room was stone-flagged and bare-walled, with a single, deep-set window upon one side, which was safely guarded with iron bars. For light I had a large stable lantern, which swung from a beam of the low ceiling. Major Sergine smiled as he took this down, and swung it round so as to throw its light into every corner of that dreary chamber.

'How do you like our Russian hotels, monsieur?' he asked, with his hateful sneer. 'They are not very grand, but they are the best that we can give you. Perhaps the next time that you Frenchmen take a fancy to travel you will choose some other country where they will make you more comfortable.' He stood laughing at me, his white teeth gleaming through his beard. Then he left me, and I heard the great key creak in the lock.

For an hour of utter misery, chilled in body and soul, I sat upon a pile of faggots, my face sunk upon my hands and my mind full of the saddest thoughts. It was cold enough within those four walls, but I thought of the sufferings of my poor troopers outside, and I sorrowed with their sorrow. Then I paced up and down, and I clapped my hands together and kicked my feet against the walls to keep them from being frozen. The lamp gave out some warmth, but still it was bitterly cold, and I had had no food since morning. It seemed to me that every one had forgotten me, but at last I heard the key turn in the lock, and who should enter but my prisoner of the morning, Captain Alexis Barakoff. A bottle of wine projected from under his arm, and he carried a great plate of hot stew in front of him.

'Hush!' said he; 'not a word! Keep up your heart! I cannot stop to explain, for Sergine is still with us. Keep awake and ready!' With these hurried words he laid down the welcome food and ran out of the room.

'Keep awake and ready!' The words rang in my ears. I ate my food and I drank my wine, but it was neither food

494

nor wine which had warmed the heart within me. What could those words of Barakoff mean? Why was I to remain awake? For what was I to be ready? Was it possible that there was a chance yet of escape? I have never respected the man who neglects his prayers at all other times and yet prays when he is in peril. It is like a bad soldier who pays no respect to the colonel save when he would demand a favour of him. And yet when I thought of the salt-mines of Siberia on the one side and of my mother in France upon the other, I could not help a prayer rising not from my lips, but from my heart, that the words of Barakoff might mean all that I hoped. But hour after hour struck upon the village clock, and still I heard nothing save the call of the Russian sentries in the street outside.

Then at last my heart leaped within me, for I heard a light step in the passage. An instant later the key turned, the door opened, and Sophie was in the room.

'Monsieur——' she cried.

'Etienne,' said I.

'Nothing will change you,' said she. 'But is it possible that you do not hate me? Have you forgiven me the trick which I played you?'

'What trick?' I asked.

'Good heavens! is it possible that even now you have not understood it? You asked me to translate the despatch. I have told you that it meant, "If the French come to Minsk all is lost." '

'What did it mean, then?'

'It means, "Let the French come to Minsk. We are awaiting them." '

I sprang back from her.

'You betrayed me!' I cried. 'You lured me into this trap. It is to you that I owe the death and capture of my men. Fool that I was to trust a woman!'

'Do not be unjust, Colonel Gerard. I am a Russian woman, and my first duty is to my country. Would you not wish a French girl to have acted as I have done? Had

I translated the message correctly you would not have gone to Minsk and your squadron would have escaped. Tell me that you forgive me!'

She looked bewitching as she stood pleading her cause in front of me. And yet, as I thought of my dead men, I could not take the hand which she held out to me.

'Very good,' said she, as she dropped it by her side. 'You feel for your own people and I feel for mine, and so we are equal. But you have said one wise and kindly thing within these walls, Colonel Gerard. You have said, "One man more or less can make no difference in a struggle between two great armies." Your lesson of nobility is not wasted. Behind those faggots is an unguarded door. Here is the key to it. Go forth, Colonel Gerard, and I trust that we may never look upon each other's faces again.'

I stood for an instant with the key in my hand and my head in a whirl. Then I handed it back to her.

'I cannot do it,' I said.

'Why not?'

'I have given my parole.'

'To whom?' she asked.

'Why, to you.'

'And I release you from it.'

My heart bounded with joy. Of course, it was true what she said. I had refused to give my parole to Sergine. I owed him no duty. If she relieved me from my promise my honour was clear. I took the key from her hand.

'You will find Captain Barakoff at the end of the village street,' she said. 'We of the North never forget either an injury or a kindness. He has your mare and your sword waiting for you. Do not delay an instant, for in two hours it will be dawn.'

So I passed out into the starlit Russian night, and had that last glimpse of Sophie as she peered after me through the open door. She looked wistfully at me as if she expected something more than the cold thanks which I gave her, but even the humblest man has his pride, and

I will not deny that mine was hurt by the deception which she had played upon me. I could not have brought myself to kiss her hand, far less her lips. The door led into a narrow alley, and at the end of it stood a muffled figure who held Violette by the bridle.

'You told me to be kind to the next French officer whom I found in distress,' said he. 'Good luck! Bon voyage!' he whispered, as I bounded into the saddle. 'Remember "Poltava" is the watchword.'

It was well that he had given it to me, for twice I had to pass Cossack pickets before I was clear of the lines. I had just ridden past the last vedettes and hoped that I was a free man again when there was a soft thudding in the snow behind me, and a heavy man upon a great black horse came swiftly after me. My first impulse was to put spurs to Violette. My second, as I saw a long black beard against a steel cuirass, was to halt and await him.

'I thought that it was you, you dog of a Frenchman,' he cried, shaking his drawn sword at me. 'So you have broken your parole, you rascal?'

'I gave no parole.'

'You lie, you hound!'

I looked around and no one was coming. The vedettes were motionless and distant. We were all alone, with the moon above and the snow beneath. Fortune has ever been my friend.

'I gave you no parole.'

'You gave it to the lady.'

'Then I will answer for it to the lady.'

'That would suit you better, no doubt. But, unfortunately, you will have to answer for it to me.'

'I am ready.'

'Your sword, too! There is treason in this! Ah, I see it all! The woman has helped you. She shall see Siberia for this night's work.'

The words were his death-warrant. For Sophie's sake I could not let him go back alive. Our blades crossed, and an instant later mine was through his black beard and deep in his throat. I was on the ground almost as soon as he, but the one thrust was enough. He died, snapping his teeth at my ankles like a savage wolf.

Two days later I had rejoined the army at Smolensk, and was a part once more of that dreary procession which tramped onwards through the snow, leaving a long weal of blood to show the path which it had taken.

Enough, my friends; I would not reawaken the memory of those days of misery and death. They still come to haunt me in my dreams. When we halted at last in Warsaw, we had left behind us our guns, our transport, three-fourths of our comrades. But we did not leave behind us the honour of Etienne Gerard. They have said that I broke my parole. Let them beware how they say it to my face, for the story is as I tell it, and old as I am my forefinger is not too weak to press a trigger when my honour is in question.

VII. How the Brigadier Bore Himself at Waterloo

I.—THE STORY OF THE FOREST INN

OF all the great battles in which I had the honour of drawing my sword for the Emperor and for France there was not one which was lost. At Waterloo, although, in a sense, I was present, I was unable to fight, and the enemy was victorious. It is not for me to say that there is a connection between these two things. You know me too well, my friends, to imagine that I would make such a claim. But it gives matter for thought, and some have drawn flattering conclusions from it. After all, it was only a matter of breaking a few English squares and the day would have been our own. If the Hussars of Conflans, with Etienne Gerard to lead them, could not do this, then the best judges are mistaken. But let that pass. The

Fates had ordained that I should hold my hand and that the Empire should fall. But they had also ordained that this day of gloom and sorrow should bring such honour to me as had never come when I swept on the wings of victory from Boulogne to Vienna. Never had I burned so brilliantly as at that supreme moment when the darkness fell upon all around me. You are aware that I was faithful to the Emperor in his adversity, and that I refused to sell my sword and my honour to the Bourbons. Never again was I to feel my war horse between my knees, never again to hear the kettledrums and silver trumpets behind me as I rode in front of my little rascals. But it comforts my heart, my friends, and it brings the tears to my eyes, to think how great I was upon that last day of my soldier life, and to remember that of all the remarkable exploits which have won me the love of so many beautiful women, and the respect of so many noble men, there was none which, in splendour, in audacity, and in the great end which was attained, could compare with my famous ride upon the night of June 18th, 1815. I am aware that the story is often told at mess-tables and in barrack-rooms, so that there are few in the army who have not heard it, but modesty has sealed my lips, until now, my friends, in the privacy of these intimate gatherings, I am inclined to lay the true facts before you.

In the first place, there is one thing which I can assure you. In all his career Napoleon never had so splendid an army as that with which he took the field for that campaign. In 1813 France was exhausted. For every veteran there were five children—Marie Louises as we called them, for the Empress had busied herself in raising levies while the Emperor took the field. But it was very different in 1815. The prisoners had all come back—the men from the snows of Russia, the men from the dungeons of Spain, the men from the hulks in England. These were the dangerous men, veterans of twenty battles, longing for their old trade, and with hearts filled with hatred and revenge. The ranks were full of soldiers who wore two and three chevrons, every chevron meaning five years' service. And the spirit of these men was terrible. They were raging, furious, fanatical, adoring the Emperor as a Mameluke does his prophet, ready to fall upon their own bayonets if their blood could serve him. If you had seen these fierce old veterans going into battle, with their flushed faces, their savage eyes, their furious yells, you would wonder that anything could stand against them. So high was the spirit of France at that time that every other spirit would have quailed before it; but these people, these English, had neither spirit nor soul, but only solid, immovable beef, against which we broke ourselves in vain. That was it, my friends! On the one side, poetry, gallantry, self-sacrifice—all that is beautiful and heroic. On the other side, beef. Our hopes, our ideals, our dreams—all were shattered on that terrible beef of Old England.

You have read how the Emperor gathered his forces, and then how he and I, with a hundred and thirty thousand veterans, hurried to the northern frontier and fell upon the Prussians and the English. On the 16th of June Ney held the English in play at Quatre Bras while we beat the Prussians at Ligny. It is not for me to say how far I contributed to that victory, but it is well known that the Hussars of Conflans covered themselves with glory. They fought well, these Prussians, and eight thousand of them were left upon the field. The Emperor thought that he had done with them, as he sent Marshal Grouchy with thirty-two thousand men to follow them up and to prevent their interfering with his plans. Then, with nearly eighty thousand men, he turned upon these 'Goddam' Englishmen. How much we had to avenge upon them, we Frenchmen—the guineas of Pitt, the hulks of Portsmouth, the invasion of Wellington, the perfidious victories of Nelson! At last the day of punishment seemed to have arisen.

Wellington had with him sixty-seven thousand men,

but many of them were known to be Dutch and Belgian, who had no great desire to fight against us. Of good troops he had not fifty thousand. Finding himself in the presence of the Emperor in person with eighty thousand men, this Englishman was so paralysed with fear that he could neither move himself nor his army. You have seen the rabbit when the snake approaches. So stood the English upon the ridge of Waterloo. The night before, the Emperor, who had lost an aide-de-camp at Ligny, ordered me to join his staff, and I had left my Hussars to the charge of Major Victor. I know not which of us was the most grieved, they or I, that I should be called away upon the eve of battle; but an order is an order, and a good soldier can but shrug his shoulders and obey. With the Emperor I rode across the front of the enemy's position on the morning of the 18th, he looking at them through his glass and planning which was the shortest way to destroy them. Soult was at his elbow, and Ney and Foy and others who had fought the English in Portugal and Spain. 'Have a care, Sire,' said Soult, 'the English infantry is very solid.'

'You think them good soldiers because they have beaten you,' said the Emperor, and we younger men turned away our faces and smiled. But Ney and Foy were grave and serious. All the time the English line, chequered with red and blue and dotted with batteries, was drawn up silent and watchful within a long musket-shot of us. On the other side of the shallow valley our own people, having finished their soup, were assembling for the battle. It had rained very heavily; but at this moment the sun shone out and beat upon the French army, turning our brigades of cavalry into so many dazzling rivers of steel. and twinkling and sparkling on the innumerable bayonets of the infantry. At the sight of that splendid army, and the beauty and majesty of its appearance, I could contain myself no longer; but, rising in my stirrups, I waved my busby and cried, '*Vive l'Empereur!*' a shout which growled and roared and clattered

from one end of the line to the other, while the horsemen waved their swords and the footmen held up their
shakos upon their bayonets. The English remained petrified upon their ridge. They knew that their hour had
come.

And so it would have come if at that moment the
word had been given and the whole army had been permitted to advance. We had but to fall upon them and to
sweep them from the face of the earth. To put aside all
question of courage, we were the more numerous, the
older soldiers, and the better led. But the Emperor
desired to do all things in order, and he waited until the
ground should be drier and harder, so that his artillery
could manœuvre. So three hours were wasted, and it
was eleven o'clock before we saw Jerome Buonaparte's
columns advance upon our left and heard the crash of
the guns which told that the battle had begun. The loss
of those three hours was our destruction. The attack
upon the left was directed upon a farmhouse which was
held by the English Guards, and we heard the three
loud shouts of apprehension which the defenders were
compelled to utter. They were still holding out, and
D'Erlon's corps was advancing upon the right to engage
another portion of the English line, when our attention
was called away from the battle beneath our noses to a
distant portion of the field of action.

The Emperor had been looking through his glass to
the extreme left of the English line, and now he turned
suddenly to the Duke of Dalmatia, or Soult, as we soldiers preferred to call him.

'What is it, Marshal?' said he.

We all followed the direction of his gaze, some raising
our glasses, some shading our eyes. There was a thick
wood over yonder, then a long, bare slope, and another
wood beyond. Over this bare strip between the two
woods there lay something dark, like the shadow of a
moving cloud.

'I think they are cattle, Sire,' said Soult.

At that instant there came a quick twinkle from amid the dark shadow.

'It is Grouchy,' said the Emperor, and he lowered his glass. 'They are doubly lost, these English. I hold them in the hollow of my hand. They cannot escape me.'

He looked round, and his eyes fell upon me.

'Ah! here is the prince of messengers,' said he. 'Are you well mounted, Colonel Gerard?'

I was riding my little Violette, the pride of the brigade. I said so.

'Then ride hard to Marshal Grouchy, whose troops you see over yonder. Tell him that he is to fall upon the left flank and rear of the English while I attack them in front. Together we shall crush them and not a man escape.'

I saluted and rode off without a word, my heart dancing with joy that such a mission should be mine. I looked at that long, solid line of red and blue looming through the smoke of the guns, and I shook my fist at it as I went. 'We shall crush them and not a man escape.' They were the Emperor's words, and it was I, Etienne Gerard, who was to turn them into deeds. I burned to reach the Marshal, and for an instant I thought of riding through the English left wing, as being the shortest cut. I have done bolder deeds and come out safely, but I reflected that if things went badly with me and I was taken or shot the message would be lost and the plans of the Emperor miscarry. I passed in front of the cavalry therefore, past the Chasseurs, the Lancers of the Guard, the Carabineers, the Horse Grenadiers, and, lastly, my own little rascals, who followed me wistfully with their eyes. Beyond the cavalry the Old Guard was standing, twelve regiments of them, all veterans of many battles, sombre and severe, in long blue overcoats, and high bearskins from which the plumes had been removed. Each bore within the goatskin knapsack upon his back the blue and white parade uniform which they would use for their entry into Brussels next day. As I rode past them I reflected that these men had never been beaten, and, as I looked at their weather-beaten faces and their stern and silent bearing, I said to myself that they never would be beaten. Great heavens, how little could I foresee what a few more hours would bring!

On the right of the Old Guard were the Young Guard and the 6th Corps of Lobau, and then I passed Jacquinot's Lancers and Marbot's Hussars, who held the extreme flank of the line. All these troops knew nothing of the corps which was coming towards them through the wood, and their attention was taken up in watching the battle which raged upon their left. More than a hundred guns were thundering from each side, and the din was so great that of all the battles which I have fought I cannot recall more than half-a-dozen which were as noisy. I looked back over my shoulder, and there were two brigades of Cuirassiers, English and French, pouring down the hill together, with the sword-blades playing over them like summer lightning. How I longed to turn Violette, and to lead my Hussars into the thick of it! What a picture! Etienne Gerard with his back to the battle, and a fine cavalry action raging behind him. But duty is duty, so I rode past Marbot's vedettes and on in the direction of the wood, passing the village of Frishermont upon my left.

In front of me lay the great wood, called the Wood of Paris, consisting mostly of oak trees, with a few narrow paths leading through it. I halted and listened when I reached it; but out of its gloomy depths there came no blare of trumpet, no murmur of wheels, no tramp of horses to mark the advance of that great column which with my own eyes I had seen streaming towards it. The battle roared behind me, but in front all was as silent as that grave in which so many brave men would shortly sleep. The sunlight was cut off by the arches of leaves above my head, and a heavy damp smell rose from the sodden ground. For several miles I galloped at such a pace as few riders would care to go with roots below and branches above. Then, at last, for the first time I caught a glimpse of Grouchy's advance guard. Scattered parties of Hussars passed me on either side, but some distance off, among the trees. I heard the beating of a drum far away, and the low, dull murmur which an army makes upon the march. Any moment I might come upon the staff and deliver my message to Grouchy in person, for I knew well that on such a march a Marshal of France would certainly ride with the van of his army.

Suddenly the trees thinned in front of me, and I understood with delight that I was coming to the end of the wood, whence I could see the army and find the Marshal. Where the track comes out from amid the trees there is a small cabaret, where wood-cutters and waggoners drink their wine. Outside the door of this I reined up my horse for an instant while I took in the scene which was before me. Some few miles away I saw a second great forest, that of St. Lambert, out of which the Emperor had seen the troops advancing. It was easy to see, however, why there had been so long a delay in their leaving one wood and reaching the other, because between the two ran the deep defile of the Lasnes, which had to be crossed. Sure enough, a long column of troops—horse, foot, and guns —was streaming down one side of it and swarming up the other, while the advance guard was already among the trees on either side of me. A battery of Horse Artillery was coming along the road, and I was about to gallop up to it and ask the officer in command if he could tell me where I should find the Marshal, when suddenly I observed that, though the gunners were dressed in blue, they had not the dolman trimmed with red brandenburgs as our own horse-gunners wear it. Amazed at the sight, I was looking at these soldiers to left and right when a hand touched my thigh, and there was the landlord, who had rushed from his inn.

'Madman!' he cried, 'why are you here? What are you doing?'

'I am seeking Marshal Grouchy.'

'You are in the heart of the Prussian army. Turn and fly!'

'Impossible; this is Grouchy's corps.'

'How do you know?'

'Because the Emperor has said it.'

'Then the Emperor has made a terrible mistake! I tell you that a patrol of Silesian Hussars has this instant left me. Did you not see them in the wood?'

'I saw Hussars.'

'They are the enemy.'

'Where is Grouchy?'

'He is behind. They have passed him.'

'Then how can I go back? If I go forward I may see him yet. I must obey my orders and find him wherever he is.'

The man reflected for an instant.

'Quick! quick!' he cried, seizing my bridle. 'Do what I say and you may yet escape. They have not observed you yet. Come with me and I will hide you until they pass.'

Behind his house there was a low stable, and into this he thrust Violette. Then he half led and half dragged me into the kitchen of the inn. It was a bare, brick-floored room. A stout, red-faced woman was cooking cutlets at the fire.

'What's the matter now?' she asked, looking with a frown from me to the innkeeper. 'Who is this you have brought in?'

'It is a French officer, Marie. We cannot let the Prussians take him.'

'Why not?'

'Why not? Sacred name of a dog, was I not myself a soldier of Napoleon? Did I not win a musket of honour among the Vélites of the Guard? Shall I see a comrade taken before my eyes? Marie, we must save him.'

But the lady looked at me with most unfriendly eyes.

'Pierre Charras,' she said, 'you will not rest until you have your house burned over your head. Do you not understand, you blockhead, that if you fought for Napoleon it was because Napoleon ruled Belgium? He does so no longer. The Prussians are our allies and this is our enemy. I will have no Frenchman in this house. Give him up!'

The innkeeper scratched his head and looked at me in despair, but it was very evident to me that it was neither for France nor for Belgium that this woman cared, but that it was the safety of her own house that was nearest her heart.

'Madame,' said I, with all the dignity and assurance I could command, 'the Emperor is defeating the English and the French army will be here before evening. If you have used me well you will be rewarded, and if you have denounced me you will be punished and your house will certainly be burned by the provost-marshal.'

She was shaken by this, and I hastened to complete my victory by other methods.

'Surely,' said I, 'it is impossible that any one so beautiful can also be hard-hearted? You will not refuse me the refuge which I need.'

She looked at my whiskers and I saw that she was softened. I took her hand, and in two minutes we were on such terms that her husband swore roundly that he would give me up himself if I pressed the matter farther.

'Besides, the road is full of Prussians,' he cried. 'Quick! quick! into the loft!'

'Quick! quick! into the loft!' echoed his wife, and together they hurried me towards a ladder which led to a trap-door in the ceiling. There was a loud knocking at the door, so you can think that it was not long before my spurs went twinkling through the hole and the board was dropped behind me. An instant later I heard the voices of the Germans in the rooms below me.

The place in which I found myself was a single long attic, the ceiling of which was formed by the roof of the house. It ran over the whole of one side of the inn, and through the cracks in the flooring I could look down either upon the kitchen, the sitting-room, or the bar at my pleasure. There were no windows, but the place was in the last stage of disrepair, and several missing slates upon the roof gave me light and the means of observation. The place was heaped with lumber—fodder at one end and a huge pile of empty bottles at the other. There was no door or window save the hole through which I had come up.

I sat upon the heap of hay for a few minutes to steady myself and to think out my plans. It was very serious that the Prussians should arrive upon the field of battle earlier than our reserves, but there appeared to be only one corps of them, and a corps more or less makes little difference to such a man as the Emperor. He could afford to give the English all this and beat them still. The best way in which I could serve him, since Grouchy was behind, was to wait here until they were past, and then to resume my journey, to see the Marshal, and to give him his orders. If he advanced upon the rear of the English instead of following the Prussians all would be well. The fate of France depended upon my judgment and my nerve. It was not the first time, my friends, as you are well aware, and you know the reasons that I had to trust that neither nerve nor judgment would ever fail me. Certainly, the Emperor had chosen the right man for his mission. 'The prince of messengers' he had called me. I would earn my title.

It was clear that I could do nothing until the Prussians had passed, so I spent my time in observing them. I have no love for these people, but I am compelled to say that they kept excellent discipline, for not a man of them entered the inn, though their lips were caked with dust and they were ready to drop with fatigue. Those who had knocked at the door were bearing an insensible comrade, and having left him they returned at once to the ranks. Several others were carried in the same fashion and laid in the kitchen, while a young surgeon, little more than a boy, remained behind in charge of them. Having observed them through the cracks in the floor, I next turned my attention to the holes in the roof, from which I had an excellent view of all that was passing outside. The Prussian corps was still streaming past. It was easy to see that they had made a terrible march and had little food, for the faces of the men were ghastly, and they were plastered from head to foot with mud from their falls upon the foul and slippery roads. Yet, spent as they were, their spirit was excellent, and they pushed and hauled at the gun-carriages when the wheels sank up to the axles in the mire, and the weary horses were floundering knee-deep unable to draw them through. The officers rode up and down the column encouraging the more active with words of praise, and the laggards with blows from the flat of their swords. All the time from over the wood in front of them there came the tremendous roar of the battle, as if all the rivers on earth had united in one gigantic cataract, booming and crashing in a mighty fall. Like the spray of the cataract was the long veil of smoke which rose high over the trees. The officers pointed to it with their swords, and with hoarse cries from their parched lips the mud-stained men pushed onwards to the battle. For an hour I watched them pass, and I reflected that their vanguard must have come into touch with Marbot's vedettes and that the Emperor knew already of their coming. 'You are going very fast up the road, my friends, but you will come down it a great deal faster,' said I to myself, and I consoled myself with the thought.

But an adventure came to break the monotony of this long wait. I was seated beside my loophole and congratulating myself that the corps was nearly past, and that the road would soon be clear for my journey, when suddenly I heard a loud altercation break out in French in the kitchen.

'You shall not go!' cried a woman's voice.

'I tell you that I will!' said a man's, and there was a sound of scuffling.

In an instant I had my eye to the crack in the floor.

509

There was my stout lady, like a faithful watch-dog, at the bottom of the ladder; while the young German surgeon, white with anger, was endeavouring to come up it. Several of the German soldiers who had recovered from their prostration were sitting about on the kitchen floor and watching the quarrel with stolid, but attentive, faces. The landlord was nowhere to be seen.

'There is no liquor there,' said the woman.

'I do not want liquor; I want hay or straw for these men to lie upon. Why should they lie on the bricks when there is straw overhead?'

'There is no straw.'

'What is up there?'

'Empty bottles.'

'Nothing else?'

'No.'

For a moment it looked as if the surgeon would abandon his intention, but one of the soldiers pointed up to the ceiling. I gathered from what I could understand of his words that he could see the straw sticking out beween the planks. In vain the woman protested. Two of the soldiers were able to get upon their feet and to drag her aside, while the young surgeon ran up the ladder, pushed open the trap-door, and climbed into the loft. As he swung the door back I slipped behind it, but as luck would have it he shut it again behind him, and there we were left standing face to face.

Never have I seen a more astonished young man.

'A French officer!' he gasped.

'Hush!' said I. 'Hush! Not a word above a whisper.' I had drawn my sword.

'I am not a combatant,' he said; 'I am a doctor. Why do you threaten me with your sword? I am not armed.'

'I do not wish to hurt you, but I must protect myself. I am in hiding here.'

'A spy!'

'A spy does not wear such a uniform as this, nor do you find spies on the staff of an army. I rode by mistake into the heart of this Prussian corps, and I concealed myself here in the hope of escaping when they are past. I will not hurt you if you do not hurt me, but if you do not swear that you will be silent as to my presence you will never go down alive from this attic.'

'You can put up your sword, sir,' said the surgeon, and I saw a friendly twinkle in his eyes. 'I am a Pole by birth, and I have no ill-feeling to you or your people. I will do my best for my patients, but I will do no more. Capturing Hussars is not one of the duties of a surgeon. With your permission I will now descend with this truss of hay to make a couch for these poor fellows below.'

I had intended to exact an oath from him, but it is my experience that if a man will not speak the truth he will not swear the truth, so I said no more. The surgeon opened the trap-door, threw out enough hay for his purpose, and then descended the ladder, letting down the door behind him. I watched him anxiously when he rejoined his patients, and so did my good friend the land-lady, but he said nothing and busied himself with the needs of the soldiers.

By this time I was sure that the last of the army corps was past, and I went to my loop-hole confident that I should find the coast clear, save, perhaps, for a few stragglers, whom I could disregard. The first corps was indeed past, and I could see the last files of the infantry disappearing into the wood; but you can imagine my disappointment when out of the Forest of St. Lambert I saw a second corps emerging, as numerous as the first. There could be no doubt that the whole Prussian army, which we thought we had destroyed at Ligny, was about to throw itself upon our right wing while Marshal Grouchy had been coaxed away upon some fool's errand. The roar of guns, much nearer than before, told me that the Prussian batteries which had passed me were already in action. Imagine my terrible position! Hour after hour was passing; the sun was sinking towards the west. And yet this cursed inn, in which I lay hid, was like a little island amid a rushing stream of furious Prussians. It was all important that I should reach Marshal Grouchy, and yet I could not show my nose without being made prisoner. You can think how I cursed and tore my hair. How little do we know what is in store for us! Even while I raged against my ill-fortune, that same fortune was reserving me for a far higher task than to carry a message to Grouchy—a task which could not have been mine had I not been held tight in that little inn on the edge of the Forest of Paris.

Two Prussian corps had passed and a third was coming up, when I heard a great fuss and the sound of several voices in the sitting-room. By altering my position I was able to look down and see what was going on.

Two Prussian generals were beneath me, their heads bent over a map which lay upon the table. Several aides-de-camp and staff officers stood round in silence. Of the two generals one was a fierce old man, white-haired and wrinkled, with a ragged, grizzled moustache and a voice like the bark of a hound. The other was younger, but long-faced and solemn. He measured distances upon the map with the air of a student, while his companion stamped and fumed and cursed like a corporal of Hussars. It was strange to see the old man so fiery and the young one so reserved. I could not understand all that they said, but I was very sure about their general meaning.

'I tell you we must push on and ever on!' cried the old fellow, with a furious German oath. 'I promised Wellington that I would be there with the whole army even if I had to be strapped to my horse. Bülow's corps is in action, and Zeithen's shall support it with every man and gun. Forwards, Gneisenau, forwards!'

The other shook his head.

'You must remember, your Excellency, that if the English are beaten they will make for the coast. What will your position be then, with Grouchy between you and the Rhine?'

'We shall beat them, Gneisenau; the Duke and I will grind them to powder between us. Push on, I say! The whole war will be ended in one blow. Bring Pirsch up, and we can throw sixty thousand men into the scale while Thielmann holds Grouchy beyond Wavre.'

Gneisenau shrugged his shoulders, but at that instant an orderly appeared at the door.

An aide-de-camp from the Duke of Wellington,' said he.

'Ha, ha!' cried the old man; 'let us hear what he has to say.'

An English officer, with mud and blood all over his scarlet jacket, staggered into the room. A crimson-stained handkerchief was knotted round his arm, and he held the table to keep himself from falling.

'My message is to Marshal Blucher,' says he.

'I am Marshal Blucher. Go on! go on!' cried the impatient old man.

'The Duke bade me to tell you, sir, that the British army can hold its own, and that he has no fears for the result. The French cavalry has been destroyed, two of their divisions of infantry have ceased to exist, and only the Guard is in reserve. If you give us a vigorous support the defeat will be changed to absolute rout and——' His knees gave way under him, and he fell in a heap upon the floor.

'Enough! enough!' cried Blucher. 'Gneisenau, send an aide-de-camp to Wellington and tell him to rely upon me to the full. Come on, gentlemen, we have our work to do!' He bustled eagerly out of the room, with all his staff clanking behind him, while two orderlies carried the English messenger to the care of the surgeon.

Gneisenau, the Chief of the Staff, had lingered behind for an instant, and he laid his hand upon one of the aides-de-camp. The fellow had attracted my attention, for I have always a quick eye for a fine man. He was tall and slender, the very model of a horseman; indeed, there was something in his appearance which made it not unlike my own. His face was dark and as keen as that of a hawk, with fierce black eyes under thick, shaggy brows, and a moustache which would have put him in the crack squadron of my Hussars. He wore a green coat with white facings, and a horsehair helmet—a Dragoon, as I conjectured, and as dashing a cavalier as one would wish to have at the end of one's sword-point.

'A word with you, Count Stein,' said Gneisenau. 'If the enemy are routed, but if the Emperor escapes, he will rally another army, and all will have to be done again. But if we can get the Emperor, then the war is indeed ended. It is worth a great effort and a great risk for such an object as that.'

The young Dragoon said nothing, but he listened attentively.

'Suppose the Duke of Wellington's words should prove to be correct, and the French army should be driven in utter rout from the field, the Emperor will certainly take the road back through Genappe and Charleroi as being the shortest to the frontier. We can imagine that his horses will be fleet, and that the fugitives will make way for him. Our cavalry will follow the rear of the beaten army, but the Emperor will be far away at the front of the throng.'

The young Dragoon inclined his head.

'To you, Count Stein, I commit the Emperor. If you take him your name will live in history. You have the reputation of being the hardest rider in our army. Do you choose such comrades as you may select—ten or a dozen should be enough. You are not to engage in the battle, nor are you to follow the general pursuit, but you are to ride clear of the crowd, reserving your energies for a nobler end. Do you understand me?'

Again the Dragoon inclined his head. This silence impressed me. I felt that he was indeed a dangerous man.

'Then I leave the details in your own hands. Strike at no one except the highest. You cannot mistake the Imperial carriage, nor can you fail to recognise the figure of the Emperor. Now I must follow the Marshal. Adieu! If ever I see you again I trust that it will be to congratulate you upon a deed which will ring through Europe.'

The Dragoon saluted, and Gneisenau hurried from the room. The young officer stood in deep thought for a few moments. Then he followed the Chief of the Staff. I looked with curiosity from my loophole to see what his next proceeding would be. His horse, a fine, strong chestnut with two white stockings, was fastened to the rail of the inn. He sprang into the saddle, and, riding to intercept a column of cavalry which was passing, he spoke to an officer at the head of the leading regiment. Presently, after some talk, I saw two Hussars—it was a Hussar regiment—drop out of the ranks and take up their position beside Count Stein. The next regiment was also stopped, and two Lancers were added to his escort. The next furnished him with two Dragoons, and the next with two Cuirassiers. Then he drew his little group of horsemen aside, and he gathered them round him, explaining to them what they had to do. Finally the nine soldiers rode off together and disappeared into the Wood of Paris.

I need not tell you, my friends, what all this portended. Indeed, he had acted exactly as I should have done in his place. From each colonel he had demanded the two best horsemen in the regiment, and so he had assembled a band who might expect to catch whatever they should follow. Heaven help the Emperor if, without an escort, he should find them on his track!

And I, dear friends—imagine the fever, the ferment, the madness, of my mind! All thought of Grouchy had passed away. No guns were to be heard to the east. He could not be near. If he should come he would not now be in time to alter the event of the day. The sun was already low in the sky and there could not be more than two or three hours of daylight. My mission might be dismissed as useless. But here was another mission, more pressing, more immediate, a mission which meant the safety, and perhaps the life, of the Emperor. At all costs, through every danger, I must get back to his side. But how was I to do it? The whole Prussian army was now between me and the French lines. They blocked every road, but they could not block the path of duty when Etienne Gerard sees it lie before him. I could not wait longer. I must be gone.

There was but the one opening to the loft, and so it was only down the ladder that I could descend. I looked into the kitchen, and I found that the young surgeon was still there. In a chair sat the wounded English aide-de-camp, and on the straw lay two Prussian soldiers in the last stage of exhaustion. The others had all recovered and been sent on. These were my enemies, and I must pass through them in order to gain my horse. From the surgeon I had nothing to fear; the Englishman was wounded, and his sword stood with his cloak in a corner; the two Germans were half insensible, and their muskets were not beside them. What could be simpler? I opened the trap-door, slipped down the ladder, and appeared in the midst of them, my sword drawn in my hand.

What a picture of surprise! The surgeon, of course, knew all, but to the Englishman and the two Germans it must have seemed that the god of war in person had descended from the skies. With my appearance, with my figure, with my silver and grey uniform, and with that gleaming sword in my hand, I must indeed have been a sight worth seeing. The two Germans lay petrified, with staring eyes. The English officer half rose, but sat down again from weakness, his mouth open and his hand on the back of his chair.

'What the deuce!' he kept on repeating, 'what the deuce!'

'Pray do not move,' said I; 'I will hurt no one, but woe to the man who lays hands upon me to stop me. You have nothing to fear if you leave me alone, and nothing to hope if you try to hinder me. I am Colonel Etienne Gerard, of the Hussars of Conflans.'

'The deuce!' said the Englishman. 'You are the man

that killed the fox.' A terrible scowl had darkened his face. The jealousy of sportsmen is a base passion. He hated me, this Englishman, because I had been before him in transfixing the animal. How different are our natures! Had I seen him do such a deed I would have embraced him with cries of joy. But there was no time for argument.

'I regret it, sir,' said I; 'but you have a cloak here and I must take it.'

He tried to rise from his chair and reach his sword, but I got between him and the corner where it lay.

'If there is anything in the pockets——'

'A case,' said he.

'I would not rob you,' said I; and raising the coat I took from the pockets a silver flask, a square wooden case, and a field-glass. All these I handed to him. The wretch opened the case, took out a pistol, and pointed it straight at my head.

'Now, my fine fellow,' said he, 'put down your sword and give yourself up.'

I was so astonished at this infamous action that I stood petrified before him. I tried to speak to him of honour and gratitude, but I saw his eyes fix and harden over the pistol.

'Enough talk!' said he. 'Drop it!'

Could I endure such a humiliation? Death were better than to be disarmed in such a fashion. The word 'Fire!' was on my lips when in an instant the Englishman vanished from before my face, and in his place was a great pile of hay, with a red-coated arm and two Hessian boots waving and kicking in the heart of it. Oh, the gallant landlady! It was my whiskers that had saved me.

'Fly, soldier, fly!' she cried, and she heaped fresh trusses of hay from the floor on to the struggling Englishman. In an instant I was out in the courtyard, had led Violette from her stable, and was on her back. A pistol bullet whizzed past my shoulder from the window, and I saw a furious face looking out at me. I smiled my contempt and spurred out into the road. The last of the Prussians had passed, and both my road and my duty lay clear before me. If France won, all was well. If France lost, then on me and on my little mare depended that which was more than victory or defeat—the safety and the life of the Emperor. 'On, Etienne, on!' I cried. 'Of all your noble exploits, the greatest, even if it be the last, lies now before you!'

II.—THE STORY OF THE NINE PRUSSIAN HORSEMEN

I TOLD you when last we met, my friends, of the important mission from the Emperor to Marshal Grouchy, which failed through no fault of my own, and I described to you how during a long afternoon I was shut up in the attic of a country inn, and was prevented from coming out because the Prussians were all around me. You will remember also how I overheard the Chief of the Prussian Staff give his instructions to Count Stein, and so learned the dangerous plan which was on foot to kill or capture the Emperor in the event of a French defeat. At first I could not have believed in such a thing, but since the guns had thundered all day, and since the sound had made no advance in my direction, it was evident that the English had at least held their own and beaten off all our attacks.

I have said that it was a fight that day between the soul of France and the beef of England, but it must be confessed that we found the beef was very tough. It was clear that if the Emperor could not defeat the English when alone, then it might, indeed, go hard with him now that sixty thousand of these cursed Prussians were swarming on his flank. In any case, with this secret in my possession, my place was by his side.

I had made my way out of the inn in the dashing manner which I have described to you when last we met,

and I left the English aide-de-camp shaking his foolish
fist out of the window. I could not but laugh as I looked
back at him, for his angry red face was framed and frilled
with hay. Once out on the road I stood erect in my
stirrups, and I put on the handsome black riding-coat,
lined with red, which had belonged to him. It fell to the
top of my high boots, and covered my tell-tale uniform
completely. As to my busby, there are many such in the
German service, and there was no reason why it should
attract attention. So long as no one spoke to me there was
no reason why I should not ride through the whole of the
Prussian army; but though I understood German, for I
had many friends among the German ladies during the
pleasant years that I fought all over that country, still I
spoke it with a pretty Parisian accent which could not
be confounded with their rough, unmusical speech. I
knew that this quality of my accent would attract attention, but I could only hope and pray that I would be
permitted to go my way in silence.

The Forest of Paris was so large that it was useless to
think of going round it, and so I took my courage in both
hands and galloped on down the road in the track of the
Prussian army. It was not hard to trace it, for it was
rutted two feet deep by the gunwheels and the caissons.
Soon I found a fringe of wounded men, Prussians and
French, on each side of it, where Bülow's advance had
come into touch with Marbot's Hussars. One old man
with a long white beard, a surgeon, I suppose, shouted at
me, and ran after me still shouting, but I never turned
my head and took no notice of him save to spur on faster.
I heard his shouts long after I had lost sight of him
among the trees.

Presently I came up with the Prussian reserves. The
infantry were leaning on their muskets or lying exhausted on the wet ground, and the officers stood in
groups listening to the mighty roar of the battle and
discussing the reports which came from the front. I hurried past at the top of my speed, but one of them rushed

out and stood in my path with his hand up as a signal to me to stop. Five thousand Prussian eyes were turned upon me. There was a moment! You turn pale, my friends, at the thought of it. Think how every hair upon me stood on end. But never for one instant did my wits or my courage desert me. 'General Blucher!' I cried. Was it not my guardian angel who whispered the words in my ear? The Prussian sprang from my path, saluted and pointed forwards. They are well disciplined, these Prussians, and who was he that he should dare to stop the officer who bore a message to the general? It was a talisman that would pass me out of every danger, and my heart sang within me at the thought. So elated was I that I no longer waited to be asked, but as I rode through the army I shouted to right and left, 'General Blucher! General Blucher!' and every man pointed me onwards and cleared a path to let me pass. There are times when the most supreme impudence is the highest wisdom. But discretion must also be used, and I must admit that I became indiscreet. For as I rode upon my way, ever nearer to the fighting line, a Prussian officer of Uhlans gripped my bridle and pointed to a group of men who stood near a burning farm. 'There is Marshal Blucher. Deliver your message!' said he, and sure enough my terrible old grey-whiskered veteran was there within a pistol shot, his eyes turned in my direction.

But the good guardian angel did not desert me. Quick as a flash there came into my memory the name of the general who commanded the advance of the Prussians. 'General Bülow!' I cried. The Uhlan let go my bridle. 'General Bülow! General Bülow!' I shouted as every stride of the dear little mare took me nearer my own people. Through the burning village of Plancenoit I galloped, spurred my way between two columns of Prussian infantry, sprang over a hedge, cut down a Silesian Hussar who flung himself before me, and an instant afterwards, with my coat flying open to show the uniform below, I passed through the open files of the tenth of the line and was back in the heart of Lobau's corps once more. Outnumbered and outflanked, they were being slowly driven in by the pressure of the Prussian advance. I galloped onwards, anxious only to find myself by the Emperor's side.

But a sight lay before me which held me fast as though I had been turned into some noble equestrian statue. I could not move, I could scarce breathe, as I gazed upon it. There was a mound over which my path lay, and as I came out on the top of it I looked down the long shallow valley of Waterloo. I had left it with two great armies on either side and a clear field between them. Now there were but long, ragged fringes of broken and exhausted regiments upon the two ridges, but a real army of dead and wounded lay between. For two miles in length and half a mile across the ground was strewed and heaped with them. But slaughter was no new sight to me, and it was not that which held me spell-bound. It was that up the long slope of the British position was moving a walking forest—black, tossing, waving, unbroken. Did I not know the bearskins of the Guard? And did I not also know, did not my soldier's instinct tell me, that it was the last reserve of France; that the Emperor, like a desperate gamester, was staking all upon his last card? Up they went and up—grand, solid, unbreakable, scourged with musketry, riddled with grape, flowing onwards in a black, heavy tide, which lapped over the British batteries. With my glass I could see the English gunners throw themselves under their pieces or run to the rear. On rolled the crest of the bearskins, and then, with a crash which was swept across to my ears, they met the British infantry. A minute passed, and another, and another. My heart was in my mouth. They swayed back and forwards; they no longer advanced; they were held. Great Heaven! was it possible that they were breaking? One black dot ran down the hill, then two, then four, then ten, then a great, scattered, struggling mass, halting, breaking, halting, and at last shredding out and rushing madly downwards. 'The Guard is beaten! The Guard is beaten!' From all around me I heard the cry. Along the whole line the infantry turned their faces and the gunners flinched from their guns.

'The Old Guard is beaten! The Guard retreats!' An officer with a livid face passed me yelling out these words of woe. 'Save yourselves! Save yourselves! You are betrayed!' cried another. 'Save yourselves! Save yourselves!' Men were rushing madly to the rear, blundering and jumping like frightened sheep. Cries and screams rose from all around me. And at that moment, as I looked at the British position, I saw what I can never forget. A single horseman stood out black and clear upon the ridge against the last red angry glow of the setting sun. So dark, so motionless against that grim light, he might have been the very spirit of Battle brooding over that terrible valley. As I gazed he raised his hat high in the air, and at the signal, with a low, deep roar like a breaking wave, the whole British army flooded over their ridge and came rolling down into the valley. Long steel-fringed lines of red and blue, sweeping waves of cavalry, horse batteries rattling and bounding—down they came on to our crumbling ranks. It was over. A yell of agony, the agony of brave men who see no hope, rose from one flank to the other, and in an instant the whole of that noble army was swept in a wild, terror-stricken crowd from the field. Even now, dear friends, I cannot, as you see, speak of that dreadful moment with a dry eye or with a steady voice.

At first I was carried away in that wild rush, whirled off like a straw in a flooded gutter. But, suddenly, what should I see amongst the mixed regiments in front of me but a group of stern horsemen, in silver and grey, with a broken and tattered standard held aloft in the heart of them! Not all the might of England and of Prussia could break the Hussars of Conflans. But when I joined them it made my heart bleed to see them. The major, seven captains, and five hundred men were left upon the field.

Young Captain Sabbatier was in command, and when I asked him where were the five missing squadrons he pointed back and answered: 'You will find them round one of those British squares.' Men and horses were at their last gasp, caked with sweat and dirt, their black tongues hanging out from their lips; but it made me thrill with pride to see how that shattered remnant still rode knee to knee, with every man, from the boy trumpeter to the farrier-sergeant, in his own proper place. Would that I could have brought them on with me as an escort for the Emperor! In the heart of the Hussars of Conflans he would be safe indeed. But the horses were too spent to trot. I left them behind me with orders to rally upon the farmhouse of St. Aunay, where we had camped two nights before. For my own part I forced my horse through the throng in search of the Emperor.

There were things which I saw then, as I pressed through that dreadful crowd, which can never be banished from my mind. In evil dreams there comes back to me the memory of that flowing stream of livid, staring, screaming faces upon which I looked down. It was a nightmare. In victory one does not understand the horror of war. It is only in the cold chill of defeat that it is brought home to you. I remember an old Grenadier of the Guard lying at the side of the road with his broken leg doubled at a right angle. 'Comrades, comrades, keep off my leg!' he cried, but they tripped and stumbled over him all the same. In front of me rode a Lancer officer without his coat. His arm had just been taken off in the ambulance. The bandages had fallen. It was horrible. Two gunners tried to drive through with their gun. A Chasseur raised his musket and shot one of them through the head. I saw a major of Cuirassiers draw his two holster pistols and shoot first his horse and then himself. Beside the road a man in a blue coat was raging and raving like a madman. His face was black with powder, his clothes were torn, one epaulette was gone, the other hung dangling over his breast. Only when I came close to him did I recognise that it was Marshal Ney. He howled at the flying troops and his voice was hardly human. Then he raised the stump of his sword—it was broken three inches from the hilt. 'Come and see how a Marshal of France can die!' he cried. Gladly would I have gone with him, but my duty lay elsewhere. He did not, as you know, find the death he sought, but he met it a few weeks later in cold blood at the hands of his enemies.

There is an old proverb that in attack the French are more than men, in defeat they are less than women. I knew that it was true that day. But even in that rout I saw things which I can tell with pride. Through the fields which skirt the road moved Cambronne's three reserve battalions of the Guard, the cream of our army. They walked slowly in square, their colours waving over the sombre line of the bearskins. All around them raged the English cavalry and the black Lancers of Brunswick, wave after wave thundering up, breaking with a crash, and recoiling in ruin. When last I saw them the English guns, six at a time, were smashing grape-shot through their ranks, and the English infantry were closing in upon three sides and pouring volleys into them; but still, like a noble lion with fierce hounds clinging to its flanks, the glorious remnant of the Guard, marching slowly, halting, closing up, dressing, moved majestically from their last battle. Behind them the Guards' battery of twelve-pounders was drawn up upon the ridge. Every gunner was in his place, but no gun fired. 'Why do you not fire?' I asked the colonel as I passed. 'Our powder is finished.' 'Then why not retire?' 'Our appearance may hold them back for a little. We must give the Emperor time to escape.' Such were the soldiers of France.

Behind this screen of brave men the others took their breath, and then went on in less desperate fashion. They had broken away from the road, and all over the country-side in the twilight I could see the timid, scattered, frightened crowd who ten hours before had formed the finest army that ever went down to battle. I with my splendid mare was soon able to get clear of the throng, and just after I passed Genappe I overtook the Emperor with the remains of his Staff. Soult was with him still, and so were Drouot, Lobau, and Bertrand, with five Chasseurs of the Guard, their horses hardly able to move. The night was falling, and the Emperor's haggard face gleamed white through the gloom as he turned it towards me.

'Who is that?' he asked.

'It is Colonel Gerard,' said Soult.

'Have you seen Marshal Grouchy?'

'No, Sire. The Prussians were between.'

'It does not matter. Nothing matters now. Soult, I will go back.'

He tried to turn his horse, but Bertrand seized his bridle. 'Ah, Sire,' said Soult, 'the enemy has had good fortune enough already.' They forced him on among them. He rode in silence with his chin upon his breast, the greatest and the saddest of men. Far away behind us those remorseless guns were still roaring. Sometimes out of the darkness would come shrieks and screams and the low thunder of galloping hoofs. At the sound we would spur our horses and hasten onwards through the scattered troops. At last, after riding all night in the clear moonlight, we found that we had left both pursued and pursuers behind. By the time we passed over the bridge at Charleroi the dawn was breaking. What a company of spectres we looked in that cold, clear, searching light, the Emperor with his face of wax, Soult blotched with powder, Lobau dabbled with blood! But we rode more easily now and had ceased to glance over our shoulders, for Waterloo was more than thirty miles behind us. One of the Emperor's carriages had been picked up at Charleroi, and we halted now on the other side of the Sambre, and dismounted from our horses.

You will ask me why it was that during all this time I had said nothing of that which was nearest my heart, the need for guarding the Emperor. As a fact, I had tried to speak of it both to Soult and to Lobau, but their minds were so overwhelmed with the disaster and so distracted by the pressing needs of the moment that it was impossible to make them understand how urgent was my message. Besides, during this long flight we had always had numbers of French fugitives beside us on the road, and, however demoralised they might be, we had nothing to fear from the attack of nine men. But now, as we stood round the Emperor's carriage in the early morning, I observed with anxiety that not a single French soldier was to be seen upon the long, white road behind us. We had outstripped the army. I looked round to see what means of defence were left to us. The horses of the Chasseurs of the Guard had broken down, and only one of them, a grey-whiskered sergeant, remained. There were Soult, Lobau, and Bertrand; but, for all their talents, I had rather, when it came to hard knocks, have a single quartermaster-sergeant of Hussars at my side than the three of them put together. There remained the Emperor himself, the coachman, and a valet of the household who had joined us at Charleroi—eight all told; but of the eight only two, the Chasseur and I, were fighting soldiers who could be depended upon at a pinch. A chill came over me as I reflected how utterly helpless we were. At that moment I raised my eyes, and there were the nine Prussian horsemen coming over the hill.

On either side of the road at this point are long stretches of rolling plain, part of it yellow with corn and part of it rich grass land watered by the Sambre. To the south of us was a low ridge, over which was the road to France. Along this road the little group of cavalry was riding. So well had Count Stein obeyed his instructions that he had struck far to the south of us in his determination to get ahead of the Emperor. Now he was riding from the direction in which we were going—the last in which we could expect an enemy. When I caught that first glimpse of them they were still half a mile away.

'Sire!' I cried, 'the Prussians!'

They all started and stared. It was the Emperor who broke the silence.

'Who says they are Prussians?'

'I do, Sire—I, Etienne Gerard!'

Unpleasant news always made the Emperor furious against the man who broke it. He railed at me now in the rasping, croaking, Corsican voice which only made itself heard when he had lost his self-control.

'You were always a buffoon,' he cried. 'What do you mean, you numskull, by saying that they are Prussians? How could Prussians be coming from the direction of France? You have lost any wits that you ever possessed.'

His words cut me like a whip, and yet we all felt towards the Emperor as an old dog does to its master. His kick is soon forgotten and forgiven. I would not argue or justify myself. At the first glance I had seen the two white stockings on the forelegs of the leading horse, and I knew well that Count Stein was on its back. For an instant the nine horsemen had halted and surveyed us. Now they put spurs to their horses, and with a yell of triumph they galloped down the road. They had recognised that their prey was in their power.

At that swift advance all doubt had vanished. 'By heavens, Sire, it is indeed the Prussians!' cried Soult. Lobau and Bertrand ran about the road like two frightened hens. The sergeant of Chasseurs drew his sabre with a volley of curses. The coachman and the valet cried and wrung their hands. Napoleon stood with a frozen face, one foot on the step of the carriage. And I—ah, my friends, I was magnificent! What words can I use to do justice to my own bearing at that supreme instant of my life! So coldly alert, so deadly cool, so clear in brain and ready in hand. He had called me a numskull and a buffoon. How quick and how noble was my revenge! When his own wits failed him, it was Etienne Gerard who supplied the want.

To fight was absurd; to fly was ridiculous. The Emperor was stout, and weary to death. At the best he was never a good rider. How could he fly from these, the picked men of an army? The best horseman in Prussia was among them. But I was the best horseman in France. I, and only I, could hold my own with them. If they were on *my* track instead of the Emperor's, all might still be well. These were the thoughts which flashed so swiftly through my mind that in an instant I had sprung from the first idea to the final conclusion. Another instant carried me from the final conclusion to prompt and vigorous action. I rushed to the side of the Emperor, who stood petrified, with the carriage between him and our enemies. 'Your coat, Sire! your hat!' I cried. I dragged them off him. Never had he been so hustled in his life. In an instant I had them on and had thrust him into the carriage. The next I had sprung on to his famous white Arab and had ridden clear of the group upon the road.

You have already divined my plan; but you may well ask how could I hope to pass myself off as the Emperor. My figure is as you still see it, and his was never beautiful, for he was both short and stout. But a man's height is not remarked when he is in the saddle, and for the rest one had but to sit forward on the horse and round one's back and carry oneself like a sack of flour. I wore the little cocked hat and the loose grey coat with the silver star which was known to every child from one end of Europe to the other. Beneath me was the Emperor's own white charger. It was complete.

Already as I rode clear the Prussians were within two hundred yards of us. I made a gesture of terror and despair with my hands, and I sprang my horse over the bank which lined the road. It was enough. A yell of exultation and of furious hatred broke from the Prussians. It was the howl of starving wolves who scent their prey. I spurred my horse over the meadow-land and looked back under my arm as I rode. Oh, the glorious moment when one after the other I saw eight horsemen come over the bank at my heels! Only one had stayed behind, and I heard shouting and the sounds of a struggle. I remembered my old sergeant of Chasseurs, and I was sure that number nine would trouble us no more. The road was clear, and the Emperor free to continue his journey.

But now I had to think of myself. If I were overtaken the Prussians would certainly make short work of me in their disappointment. If it were so—if I lost my life—I should still have sold it at a glorious price. But I had hopes that I might shake them off. With ordinary horse-men upon ordinary horses I should still have had no difficulty in doing so, but here both steeds and riders were of the best. It was a grand creature that I rode, but it was weary with its long night's work, and the Emperor was one of those riders who do not know how to manage a horse. He had little thought for them, and a heavy hand upon their mouths. On the other hand Stein and his men had come both far and fast. The race was a fair one.

So quick had been my impulse, and so rapidly had I acted upon it, that I had not thought enough of my own safety. Had I done so in the first instance I should, of course, have ridden straight back the way we had come, for so I should have met our own people. But I was off the road and had galloped a mile over the plain before this occurred to me. Then when I looked back I saw that the Prussians had spread out into a long line, so as to head me off from the Charleroi road. I could not turn back, but at least I could edge towards the north. I knew that the whole face of the country was covered with our flying troops, and that sooner or later I must come upon some of them.

But one thing I had forgotten—the Sambre. In my excitement I never gave it a thought until I saw it, deep and broad, gleaming in the morning sunlight. It barred my path, and the Prussians howled behind me. I gal-loped to the brink, but the horse refused the plunge. I spurred him, but the bank was high and the stream deep. He shrank back trembling and snorting. The yells of triumph were louder every instant. I turned and rode for my life down the river bank. It formed a loop at this part, and I must get across somehow, for my retreat was blocked. Suddenly a thrill of hope ran through me, for I saw a house on my side of the stream and another on the farther bank. Where there are two such houses it usually means that there is a ford between them. A sloping path led to the brink, and I urged my horse down it. On he went, the water up to the saddle, the foam flying right and left. He blundered once and I thought we were lost, but he recovered and an instant later was clattering up the farther slope. As we came out I heard the splash behind me as the first Prussian took the water. There was just the breadth of the Sambre between us.

I rode with my head sunk between my shoulders in Napoleon's fashion, and I did not dare to look back for fear they should see my moustache. I had turned up the collar of the grey coat so as partly to hide it. Even now if they found out their mistake they might turn and overtake the carriage. But when once we were on the road I could tell by the drumming of their hoofs how far distant they were, and it seemed to me that the sound grew perceptibly louder, as if they were slowly gaining upon me. We were riding now up the stony and rutted lane which led from the ford. I peeped back very cautiously from under my arm and I perceived that my danger came from a single rider, who was far ahead of his comrades. He was a Hussar, a very tiny fellow, upon a big black horse, and it was his light weight which had brought him into the foremost place. It is a place of honour; but it is also a place of danger, as he was soon to learn. I felt the holsters, but, to my horror, there were no pistols. There was a field-glass in one and the other was stuffed with papers. My sword had been left behind with Violette. Had I only my own weapons and my own little mare I could have played with these rascals. But I was not entirely unarmed. The Emperor's own sword hung to the saddle. It was curved and short, the hilt all crusted with gold—a thing more fitted to glitter at a review than to serve a soldier in his deadly need. I drew it, such as it was, and I waited my chance. Every instant the clink and clatter of the hoofs grew nearer. I heard the panting of the horse, and the fellow shouted some threat at me. There was a turn in the lane, and as I rounded it I drew up my white Arab on his haunches. As we spun round I met the Prussian Hussar face to face. He was going too fast to stop, and his only chance was to ride me down. Had he done so he might have met his own death, but he would have injured me or my horse past all hope of escape. But the fool flinched as he saw me waiting, and flew past me on my right. I lunged over my Arab's neck and buried my toy sword in his side. It must have been the finest steel and as sharp as a razor, for I hardly felt it enter, and yet his blood was within three inches of the hilt. His horse galloped on and he kept his saddle for a hundred yards before he sank down with his face on the mane, and then dived over the side of the neck on to the road. For my own part, I was already at his horse's heels. A few seconds had sufficed for all that I have told.

I heard the cry of rage and vengeance which rose from the Prussians as they passed their dead comrade, and I could not but smile as I wondered what they could think of the Emperor as a horseman and a swordsman. I glanced back cautiously as before, and I saw that none of the seven men stopped. The fate of their comrade was nothing compared to the carrying out of their mission. They were as untiring and as remorseless as bloodhounds. But I had a good lead, and the brave Arab was still going well. I thought that I was safe. And yet it was at that very instant that the most terrible danger befell me. The lane divided, and I took the smaller of the two divisions because it was the more grassy and the easier for the horse's hoofs. Imagine my horror when, riding through a gate, I found myself in a square of stables and farm-buildings, with no way out save that by which I had come! Ah, my friends, if my hair is snowy white, have I not had enough to make it so?

To retreat was impossible. I could hear the thunder of the Prussians' hoofs in the lane. I looked round me, and Nature has blessed me with that quick eye which is the first of gifts to any soldier, but most of all to a leader of cavalry. Between a long, low line of stables and the farmhouse there was a pig-sty. Its front was made of bars of wood four feet high; the back was of stone, higher than the front. What was beyond I could not tell. The space between the front and the back was not more than a few yards. It was a desperate venture, and yet I must take it. Every instant the beating of those hurrying hoofs was louder and louder. I put my Arab at the pig-sty. He cleared the front beautifully, and came down with his forefeet upon the sleeping pig within, slipping forward upon his knees. I was thrown over the wall beyond, and fell upon my hands and face in a soft flower-bed. My horse was upon one side of the wall, I upon the other, and the Prussians were pouring into the yard. But I was up in an instant, and had seized the bridle of the plunging horse over the top of the wall. It was built of loose stones, and I dragged down a few of them to make a gap. As I tugged at the bridle and shouted the gallant creature rose to the leap, and an instant afterwards he was by my side and I with my foot on the stirrup.

An heroic idea had entered my mind as I mounted into the saddle. These Prussians, if they came over the pig-sty, could only come one at once, and their attack would not be formidable when they had not had time to recover from such a leap. Why should I not wait and kill them one by one as they came over? It was a glorious thought. They would learn that Etienne Gerard was not a safe man to hunt. My hand felt for my sword, but you can imagine my feelings, my friends, when I came upon an empty scabbard. It had been shaken out when the horse had tripped over that infernal pig. On what absurd trifles do our destinies hang—a pig on one side, Etienne Gerard on the other! Could I spring over the wall and get the sword? Impossible! The Prussians were already in the yard. I turned my Arab and resumed my flight.

But for a moment it seemed to me that I was in a far worse trap than before. I found myself in the garden of the farmhouse, an orchard in the centre and flower-beds all round. A high wall surrounded the whole place. I reflected, however, that there must be some point of entrance, since every visitor could not be expected to spring over the pig-sty. I rode round the wall. As I expected, I came upon a door with a key upon the inner side. I dismounted, unlocked it, opened it, and there was a Prussian Lancer sitting his horse within six feet of me.

For a moment we each stared at the other. Then I shut the door and locked it again. A crash and a cry came from the other end of the garden. I understood that one of my enemies had come to grief in trying to get over the pig-sty. How could I ever get out of this cul-de-sac? It was evident that some of the party had galloped round, while some had followed straight upon my tracks. Had I my sword I might have beaten off the Lancer at the door, but to come out now was to be butchered. And yet if I waited some of them would certainly follow me on foot over the pig-sty, and what could I do then? I must act at once or I was lost. But it is at such moments that my wits are most active and my actions most prompt. Still leading my horse, I ran for a hundred yards by the side of the wall away from the spot where the Lancer was watching. There I stopped, and with an effort I tumbled down several of the loose stones from the top of the wall. The instant I had done so I hurried back to the door. As I expected, he thought I was making a gap for my escape at that point, and I heard the thud of his horse's hoofs as he galloped to cut me off. As I reached the gate I looked back, and I saw a green-coated horseman, whom I knew to be Count Stein, clear the pig-sty and gallop furiously with a shout of triumph across the garden. 'Surrender, your Majesty, surrender!' he yelled; 'we will give you quarter!' I slipped through the gate, but had no time to lock it on the other side. Stein was at my very heels, and the Lancer had already turned his horse. Springing upon my Arab's back, I was off once more with a clear stretch of grass land before me. Stein had to dismount to open the gate, to lead his horse through, and to mount again before he could follow. It was he that I feared rather than the Lancer, whose horse was coarse-bred and weary. I galloped hard for a mile before I ventured to look back, and then Stein was a musket-shot from me, and the Lancer as much again, while only three of the others were in sight. My nine Prussians were coming down to more manageable numbers, and yet one was too much for an unarmed man.

It had surprised me that during this long chase I had seen no fugitives from the army, but I reflected that I was considerably to the west of their line of flight, and that I must edge more towards the east if I wished to join them. Unless I did so it was probable that my pursuers, even if they could not overtake me themselves, would keep me in view until I was headed off by some of their comrades coming from the north. As I looked to the eastward I saw afar off a line of dust which stretched for miles across the country. This was certainly the main road along which our unhappy army was flying. But I soon had proof that some of our stragglers had wandered into these side tracks, for I came suddenly upon a horse grazing at the corner of a field, and beside him, with his back against the bank, his master, a French Cuirassier, terribly wounded and evidently at the point of death. I sprang down, seized his long, heavy sword, and rode on with it. Never shall I forget the poor man's face as he looked at me with his failing sight. He was an old, grey-moustached soldier, one of the real fanatics, and to him this last vision of his Emperor was like a revelation from on high. Astonishment, love, pride—all shone in his pallid face. He said something—I fear they were his last words—but I had no time to listen, and I galloped on my way.

All this time I had been on the meadow-land, which was intersected in this part by broad ditches. Some of them could not have been less than from fourteen to fifteen feet, and my heart was in my mouth as I went at each of them, for a slip would have been my ruin. But whoever selected the Emperor's horses had done his work well. The creature, save when it balked on the bank of the Sambre, never failed me for an instant. We cleared everything in one stride. And yet we could not shake off those infernal Prussians. As I left each watercourse behind me I looked back with renewed hope, but it was only to see Stein on his white-legged chestnut flying over it as lightly as I had done myself. He was my enemy, but I honoured him for the way in which he carried himself that day.

Again and again I measured the distance which separated him from the next horseman. I had the idea that I might turn and cut him down, as I had the Hussar, before his comrade could come to his help. But the others had closed up and were not far behind. I reflected that this Stein was probably as fine a swordsman as he was a rider, and that it might take me some little time to get the better of him. In that case the others would come to his aid and I should be lost. On the whole, it was wiser to continue my flight.

A road with poplars on either side ran across the plain from east to west. It would lead me towards the long line of dust which marked the French retreat. I wheeled my horse, therefore, and galloped down it. As I rode I saw a single house in front of me upon the right, with a great bush hung over the door to mark it as an inn. Outside there were several peasants, but for them I cared nothing. What frightened me was to see the gleam of a red coat, which showed that there were British in the place. However, I could not turn and I could not stop, so there was nothing for it but to gallop on and to take my chance. There were no troops in sight, so these men must be stragglers or marauders, from whom I had little to fear.

As I approached I saw that there were two of them sitting drinking on a bench outside the inn door. I saw them stagger to their feet, and it was evident that they were both very drunk. One stood swaying in the middle of the road. 'It's Boney! So help me, it's Boney!' he yelled. He ran with his hands out to catch me, but luckily for himself his drunken feet stumbled and he fell on his face in the road. The other was more dangerous. He had rushed into the inn, and just as I passed I saw him run out with his musket in his hand. He dropped upon one knee, and I stooped forward over my horse's neck. A single shot from a Prussian or an Austrian is a small matter, but the British were at that time the best shots in Europe, and my drunkard seemed steady enough when he had a gun at his shoulder. I heard the crack, and my horse gave a convulsive spring which would have unseated many a rider. For an instant I thought he was killed, but when I turned in my saddle I saw a stream of blood running down the off hind-quarter. I looked back at the Englishman, and the brute had bitten the end off another cartridge and was ramming it into his musket, but before he had it primed we were beyond his range. These men were foot-soldiers and could not join in the chase, but I heard them whooping and tally-hoing behind me as if I had been a fox. The peasants also shouted and ran through the fields flourishing their sticks. From all sides I heard cries, and everywhere were the rushing, waving figures of my pursuers. To think of the great Emperor being chivied over the countryside in this fashion! It made me long to have these rascals within the sweep of my sword.

But now I felt that I was nearing the end of my course. I had done all that a man could be expected to do—some would say more—but at last I had come to a point from which I could see no escape. The horses of my pursuers were exhausted, but mine was exhausted and wounded also. It was losing blood fast, and we left a red trail upon the white, dusty road. Already his pace was slackening, and sooner or later he must drop under me. I looked back, and there were the five inevitable Prussians—Stein, a hundred yards in front, then a Lancer, and then three others riding together. Stein had drawn his sword, and he waved it at me. For my own part I was determined not to give myself up. I would try how many of these Prussians I could take with me into the other world. At this supreme moment all the great deeds of my life rose in a vision before me, and I felt that this, my last exploit, was indeed a worthy close to such a career. My death would be a fatal blow to those who loved me, to my dear mother, to my Hussars, to others who shall be nameless. But all of them had my honour and my fame at heart, and I felt that their grief would be tinged with pride when they learned how I had ridden and how I had fought upon this last day. Therefore I hardened my heart and, as my Arab limped more and more upon his wounded leg, I drew the great sword which I had taken from the Cuirassier, and I set my teeth for my supreme struggle. My hand was in the very act of tightening the bridle, for I feared that if I delayed longer I might find myself on foot fighting against five mounted men. At that instant my eye fell upon something which brought hope to my heart and a shout of joy to my lips.

From a grove of trees in front of me there projected the steeple of a village church. But there could not be two steeples like that, for the corner of it had crumbled away or been struck by lightning, so that it was of a most fantastic shape. I had seen it only two days before, and it was the church of the village of Gosselies. It was not the hope of reaching the village which set my heart singing with joy, but it was that I knew my ground now, and that farmhouse not half a mile ahead, with its gable end sticking out from amid the trees, must be that very farm of St. Aunay where we had bivouacked, and which I had named to Captain Sabbatier as the rendezvous of the Hussars of Conflans. There they were, my little rascals, if I could but reach them. With every bound my horse grew weaker. Each instant the sound of the pursuit grew louder. I heard a gust of crackling German oaths at my very heels. A pistol bullet sighed in my ears. Spurring frantically and beating my poor Arab with the flat of my sword I kept him at the top of his speed. The open gate of the farmyard lay before me. I saw the twinkle of steel within. Stein's horse's head was within ten yards of me as I thundered through. 'To me, comrades! To me!' I yelled. I heard a buzz as when the angry bees swarm from their nest. Then my splendid white Arab fell dead under me, and I was hurled on to the cobble-stones of the yard, where I can remember no more.

Such was my last and most famous exploit, my dear friends, a story which rang through Europe and has made the name of Etienne Gerard famous in history. Alas! that all my efforts could only give the Emperor a few weeks more liberty, since he surrendered upon July 15th to the English. But it was not my fault that he was not able to collect the forces still waiting for him in France, and to fight another Waterloo with a happier ending. Had others been as loyal as I was the history of the world might have been changed, the Emperor would have preserved his throne, and such a soldier as I would not have been left to spend his life in planting cabbages or to while away his old age telling stories in a café. You ask me about the fate of Stein and the Prussian horsemen! Of the three who dropped upon the way I know nothing. One you will remember that I killed. There remained five, three of whom were cut down by my Hussars, who, for the instant, were under the impression that it was indeed the Emperor whom they were defending. Stein was taken, slightly wounded, and so was one of the Uhlans. The truth was not told to them, for we thought it best that no news, or false news, should get about as to where the Emperor was, so that Count Stein still believed that he was within a few yards of making that tremendous capture. 'You may well love and honour your Emperor,' said he, 'for such a horseman and such a swordsman I have never seen.' He could not understand why the young colonel of Hussars laughed so heartily at his words—but he has learned since.

VIII. *The Last Adventure of the Brigadier*

I WILL tell you no more stories, my dear friends. It is said that man is like the hare, which runs in a circle and comes back to die at the point from which it started. Gascony has been calling to me of late. I see the blue Garonne winding among the vineyards and the bluer ocean towards which its waters sweep. I see the old town also, and the bristle of masts from the side of the long stone quay. My heart hungers for the breath of my native air and the warm glow of my native sun. Here in Paris are my friends, my occupations, my pleasures. There all who have known me are in their grave. And yet the south-west wind as it rattles on my windows seems always to be the strong voice of the motherland calling her child back to that bosom into which I am ready to sink. I have played my part in my time. The time has passed. I must pass also. Nay, dear friends, do not look sad, for what can be happier than a life completed in honour and made beautiful with friendship and love? And yet it is solemn also when a man approaches the end of the long road and sees the turning which leads him into the unknown. But the Emperor and all his Marshals have ridden round that dark turning and passed into the beyond. My Hussars, too—there are not fifty men who are not waiting yonder. I must go. But on this the last night I will tell you that which is more than a tale—it is a great historical secret. My lips have been sealed, but I see no reason why I should not leave behind me some account of this re-markable adventure, which must otherwise be entirely lost, since I, and only I of all living men, have a know-ledge of the facts.

I will ask you to go back with me to the year 1821. In that year our great Emperor had been absent from us for six years, and only now and then from over the seas we heard some whisper which showed that he was still alive. You cannot think what a weight it was upon our hearts for us who loved him to think of him in captivity eating his giant soul out upon that lonely island. From the moment we rose until we closed our eyes in sleep the thought was always with us, and we felt dishonoured that he, our chief and master, should be so humiliated without our being able to move a hand to help him. There were many who would most willingly have laid down the remainder of their lives to bring him a little ease, and yet all that we could do was to sit and grumble in our cafés and stare at the map, counting up the leagues of water which lay between us. It seemed that he might have been in the moon for all that we could do to help him. But that was only because we were all soldiers and knew nothing of the sea.

Of course, we had our own little troubles to make us bitter, as well as the wrongs of our Emperor. There were many of us who had held high rank and would hold it again if he came back to his own. We had not found it possible to take service under the white flag of the Bourbons, or to take an oath which might turn our sabres against the man whom we loved. So we found ourselves with neither work nor money. What could we do save gather together and gossip and grumble, while those who had a little paid the score and those who had nothing shared the bottle? Now and then, if we were lucky, we managed to pick a quarrel with one of the Garde du Corps, and if we left him on his back in the Bois we felt that we had struck a blow for Napoleon once again. They came to know our haunts in time, and they avoided them as if they had been hornets' nests.

There was one of these—the Sign of the Great Man— in the Rue Varennes, which was frequented by several of the more distinguished and younger Napoleonic officers.

Nearly all of us had been colonels or aides-de-camp, and when any man of less distinction came among us we generally made him feel that he had taken a liberty. There were Captain Lepine, who had won the medal of honour at Leipzig; Colonel Bonnet, aide-de-camp to Macdonald; Colonel Jourdan, whose fame in the army was hardly second to my own; Sabbatier of my own Hussars, Meunier of the Red Lancers, Le Breton of the Guards, and a dozen others. Every night we met and talked, played dominoes, drank a glass or two and wondered how long it would be before the Emperor would be back and we at the head of our regiments once more. The Bourbons had already lost any hold they ever had upon the country, as was shown a few years afterwards, when Paris rose against them and they were hunted for the third time out of France. Napoleon had but to show himself on the coast, and he would have marched without firing a musket to the capital, exactly as he had done when he came back from Elba.

Well, when affairs were in this state there arrived one night in February, in our café, a most singular little man. He was short but exceedingly broad, with huge shoulders, and a head which was a deformity, so large was it. His heavy brown face was scarred with white streaks in a most extraordinary manner, and he had grizzled whiskers such as seamen wear. Two gold ear-rings in his ears, and plentiful tattooing upon his hands and arms, told us also that he was of the sea before he introduced himself to us as Captain Fourneau, of the Emperor's navy. He had letters of introduction to two of our number, and there could be no doubt that he was devoted to the cause. He won our respect, too, for he had seen as much fighting as any of us, and the burns upon his face were caused by his standing to his post upon the *Orient*, at the Battle of the Nile, until the vessel blew up underneath him. Yet he would say little about himself, but he sat in the corner of the café watching us all with a wonderfully sharp pair of eyes and listening intently to our talk.

One night I was leaving the café when Captain Fourneau followed me, and touching me on the arm he led me without saying a word for some distance until we reached his lodgings. 'I wish to have a chat with you,' said he, and so conducted me up the stair to his room. There he lit a lamp and handed me a sheet of paper which he took from an envelope in his bureau. It was dated a few months before from the Palace of Schönbrunn at Vienna. 'Captain Fourneau is acting in the highest interests of the Emperor Napoleon. Those who love the Emperor should obey him without question—Marie Louise.' That is what I read. I was familiar with the signature of the Empress, and I could not doubt that this was genuine.

'Well,' said he, 'are you satisfied as to my credentials?'

'Entirely.'

'Are you prepared to take your orders from me?'

'This document leaves me no choice.'

'Good! In the first place, I understand from something you said in the café that you can speak English?'

'Yes, I can.'

'Let me hear you do so.'

I said in English, 'Whenever the Emperor needs the help of Etienne Gerard, I am ready night and day to give my life in his service.'

Captain Fourneau smiled.

'It is funny English,' said he, 'but still it is better than no English. For my own part I speak English like an Englishman. It is all that I have to show for six years spent in an English prison. Now I will tell you why I have come to Paris. I have come in order to choose an agent who will help me in a matter which affects the interests of the Emperor. I was told that it was at the café of the Great Man that I would find the pick of his old officers, and that I could rely upon every man there being devoted to his interests. I studied you all, therefore, and I have come to the conclusion that you are the one who is most suited for my purpose.'

I acknowledged the compliment. 'What is it that you wish me to do?' I asked.

'Merely to keep me company for a few months,' said he. 'You must know that after my release in England I settled down there, married an English wife, and rose to command a small English merchant ship, in which I have made several voyages from Southampton to the Guinea coast. They look on me there as an Englishman. You can understand, however, that with my feelings about the Emperor I am lonely sometimes, and that it would be an advantage to me to have a companion who would sympathise with my thoughts. One gets very bored on these long voyages, and I would make it worth your while to share my cabin.'

He looked hard at me with his shrewd grey eyes all the time that he was uttering this rigmarole, and I gave him a glance in return which showed him that he was not dealing with a fool. He took out a canvas bag full of money.

'There are a hundred pounds in gold in this bag,' said he. 'You will be able to buy some comforts for your voyage. I should recommend you to get them in Southampton, whence we will start in ten days. The name of the vessel is the *Black Swan*. I return to Southampton to-morrow, and I shall hope to see you in the course of next week.'

'Come now,' said I, 'tell me frankly what is the destination of our voyage?'

'Oh, didn't I tell you?' he answered. 'We are bound for the Guinea coast of Africa.'

'Then how can that be in the highest interests of the Emperor?' I asked.

'It is in his highest interests that you ask no indiscreet questions and I give no indiscreet replies,' he answered, sharply. So he brought the interview to an end, and I found myself back in my lodgings with nothing save this bag of gold to show that this singular interview had indeed taken place.

There was every reason why I should see the adventure to a conclusion, and so within a week I was on my way to England. I passed from St. Malo to Southampton, and on inquiry at the docks I had no difficulty in finding the *Black Swan*, a neat little vessel of a shape which is called, as I learned afterwards, a brig. There was Captain Fourneau himself upon the deck, and seven or eight rough fellows hard at work grooming her and making her ready for sea. He greeted me and led me down to his cabin.

'You are plain Mr. Gerard now,' said he, 'and a Channel Islander. I would be obliged to you if you would kindly forget your military ways and drop your cavalry swagger when you walk up and down my deck. A beard, too, would seem more sailor-like than those moustaches.'

I was horrified by his words, but, after all, there are no ladies on the high seas, and what did it matter? He rang for the steward.

'Gustav,' said he, 'you will pay every attention to my friend, Monsieur Etienne Gerard, who makes this voyage with us. This is Gustav Kerouan, my Breton steward,' he explained, 'and you are very safe in his hands.'

This steward, with his harsh face and stern eyes, looked a very warlike person for so peaceful an employment. I said nothing, however, though you may guess that I kept my eyes open. A berth had been prepared for me next the cabin, which would have seemed comfortable enough had it not contrasted with the extraordinary splendour of Fourneau's quarters. He was certainly a most luxurious person, for his room was new-fitted with velvet and silver in a way which would have suited the yacht of a noble better than a little West African trader. So thought the mate, Mr. Burns, who could not hide his amusement and contempt whenever he looked at it. This fellow, a big, solid red-headed Englishman, had the other berth connected with the cabin. There was a second mate named Turner, who lodged in the middle of the ship, and there were nine men and one boy in the crew, three of whom, as I was informed by Mr. Burns, were Channel

Islanders like myself. This Burns, the first mate, was much interested to know why I was coming with them.

'I come for pleasure,' said I.

He stared at me.

'Ever been to the West Coast?' he asked.

I said that I had not.

'I thought not,' said he. 'You'll never come again for that reason, anyhow.'

Some three days after my arrival we untied the ropes by which the ship was tethered and we set off upon our journey. I was never a good sailor, and I may confess that we were far out of sight of any land before I was able to venture upon deck. At last, however, upon the fifth day I drank the soup which the good Kerouan brought me, and I was able to crawl from my bunk and up the stair. The fresh air revived me, and from that time onwards I accommodated myself to the motion of the vessel. My beard had begun to grow also, and I have no doubt that I should have made as fine a sailor as I have a soldier had I chanced to be born to that branch of the service. I learned to pull the ropes which hoisted the sails, and also to haul round the long sticks to which they are attached. For the most part, however, my duties were to play écarté with Captain Fourneau, and to act as his companion. It was not strange that he should need one, for neither of his mates could read nor write, though each of them was an excellent seaman. If our captain had died suddenly I cannot imagine how we should have found our way in that waste of waters, for it was only he who had the knowledge which enabled him to mark our place upon the chart. He had this fixed upon the cabin wall, and every day he put our course upon it so that we could see at a glance how far we were from our destination. It was wonderful how well he could calculate it, for one morning he said that we should see the Cape Verd light that very night, and there it was, sure enough, upon our left front the moment that darkness came. Next day, however, the land was out of sight, and Burns, the mate, explained to me that we should see no more until we came to our port in the Gulf of Biafra. Every day we flew south with a favouring wind, and always at noon the pin upon the chart was moved nearer and nearer to the African coast. I may explain that palm oil was the cargo which we were in search of, and that our own lading consisted of coloured cloths, old muskets, and such other trifles as the English sell to the savages.

At last the wind which had followed us so long died away, and for several days we drifted about on a calm and oily sea under a sun which brought the pitch bubbling out between the planks upon the deck. We turned and turned our sails to catch every wandering puff, until at last we came out of this belt of calm and ran south again with a brisk breeze, the sea all round us being alive with flying fishes. For some days Burns appeared to be uneasy, and I observed him continually shading his eyes with his hand and staring at the horizon as if he were looking for land. Twice I caught him with his red head against the chart in the cabin, gazing at that pin, which was always approaching and yet never reaching the African coast. At last one evening, as Captain Fourneau and I were playing écarté in the cabin, the mate entered with an angry look upon his sunburned face.

'I beg your pardon, Captain Fourneau,' said he. 'But do you know what course the man at the wheel is steering?'

'Due south,' the captain answered, with his eyes fixed upon his cards.

'And he should be steering due east.'

'How do you make that out?'

The mate gave an angry growl.

'I may not have much education,' said he, 'but let me tell you this, Captain Fourneau, I've sailed these waters since I was a little nipper of ten, and I know the line when I'm on it, and I know the doldrums, and I know how to find my way to the oil rivers. We are south of the line now, and we should be steering due east instead of due south if your port is the port that the owners sent you to.'

'Excuse me, Mr. Gerard. Just remember that it is my lead,' said the captain, laying down his cards. 'Come to the map here, Mr. Burns, and I will give you a lesson in practical navigation. Here is the trade wind from the south-west and here is the line, and here is the port that we want to make, and here is a man who will have his own way aboard his own ship.' As he spoke he seized the unfortunate mate by the throat and squeezed him until he was nearly senseless. Kerouan, the steward, had rushed in with a rope, and between them they gagged and trussed the man, so that he was utterly helpless.

'There is one of our Frenchmen at the wheel. We had best put the mate overboard,' said the steward.

'That is safest,' said Captain Fourneau.

But that was more than I could stand. Nothing would persuade me to agree to the death of a helpless man. With a bad grace Captain Fourneau consented to spare him, and we carried him to the after-hold, which lay under the cabin. There he was laid among the bales of Manchester cloth.

'It is not worth while to put down the hatch,' said Captain Fourneau. 'Gustav, go to Mr. Turner, and tell him that I would like to have a word with him.'

The unsuspecting second mate entered the cabin, and was instantly gagged and secured as Burns had been. He was carried down and laid beside his comrade. The hatch was then replaced.

'Our hands have been forced by that red-headed dolt,' said the captain, 'and I have had to explode my mine before I wished. However, there is no great harm done, and it will not seriously disarrange my plans. Kerouan, you will take a keg of rum forward to the crew and tell them that the captain gives it to them to drink his health on the occasion of crossing the line. They will know no better. As to our own fellows, bring them down to your pantry so that we may be sure that they are ready for business. Now, Colonel Gerard, with your permission we will resume our game of écarté.'

It is one of those occasions which one does not forget. This captain, who was a man of iron, shuffled and cut, dealt and played as if he were in his café. From below we heard the inarticulate murmurings of the two mates, half smothered by the handkerchiefs which gagged them. Outside the timbers creaked and the sails hummed under the brisk breeze which was sweeping us upon our way. Amid the splash of the waves and the whistle of the wind we heard the wild cheers and shoutings of the English sailors as they broached the keg of rum. We played half a dozen games, and then the captain rose. 'I think they are ready for us now,' said he. He took a brace of pistols from a locker, and he handed one of them to me.

But we had no need to fear resistance, for there was no one to resist. The Englishman of those days, whether soldier or sailor, was an incorrigible drunkard. Without drink he was a brave and good man. But if drink were laid before him it was a perfect madness—nothing could induce him to take it with moderation. In the dim light of the den which they inhabited, five senseless figures and two shouting, swearing, singing madmen represented the crew of the *Black Swan*. Coils of rope were brought forward by the steward, and with the help of two French seamen (the third was at the wheel) we secured the drunkards and tied them up, so that it was impossible for them to speak or move. They were placed under the fore-hatch, as their officers had been under the after one, and Kerouan was directed twice a day to give them food and drink. So at last we found that the *Black Swan* was entirely our own.

Had there been bad weather I do not know what we should have done, but we still went gaily upon our way with a wind which was strong enough to drive us swiftly south, but not strong enough to cause us alarm. On the evening of the third day I found Captain Fourneau gazing eagerly out from the platform in the front of the vessel. 'Look, Gerard, look!' he cried and pointed over the pole which struck out in front.

A light blue sky rose from a dark blue sea, and far away, at the point where they met, was a shadowy something like a cloud, but more definite in shape.

'What is it?' I cried.

'It is land.'

'And what land?'

I strained my ears for the answer, and yet I knew already what the answer would be.

'It is St. Helena.'

Here, then, was the island of my dreams! Here was the cage where our great Eagle of France was confined! All those thousands of leagues of water had not sufficed to keep Gerard from the master whom he loved. There he was, there on that cloud-bank yonder over the dark blue sea. How my eyes devoured it! How my soul flew in front of the vessel—flew on and on to tell him that he was not forgotten, that after many days one faithful servant was coming to his side! Every instant the dark blur upon the water grew harder and clearer. Soon I could see plainly enough that it was indeed a mountainous island. The night fell, but still I knelt upon the deck, with my eyes fixed upon the darkness which covered the spot where I knew that the great Emperor was. An hour passed and another one, and then suddenly a little golden twinkling light shone out exactly ahead of us. It was the light of the window of some house—perhaps of his house. It could not be more than a mile or two away. Oh, how I held out my hands to it!—they were the hands of Etienne Gerard, but it was for all France that they were held out.

Every light had been extinguished aboard our ship, and presently, at the direction of Captain Fourneau, we all pulled upon one of the ropes, which had the effect of swinging round one of the sticks above us, and so stopping the vessel. Then he asked me to step down to the cabin.

'You understand everything now, Colonel Gerard,' said he, 'and you will forgive me if I did not take you into my complete confidence before. In a matter of such importance I make no man my confidant. I have long planned the rescue of the Emperor, and my remaining in England and joining their merchant service was entirely with that design. All has worked out exactly as I expected. I have made several successful voyages to the West Coast of Africa, so that there was no difficulty in my obtaining the command of this one. One by one I got these old French man-of-war's men among the hands. As to you, I was anxious to have one tried fighting man in case of resistance, and I also desired to have a fitting companion for the Emperor during his long homeward voyage. My cabin is already fitted up for his use. I trust that before to-morrow morning he will be inside it, and we out of sight of this accursed island.'

You can think of my emotion, my friends, as I listened to these words. I embraced the brave Fourneau, and implored him to tell me how I could assist him.

'I must leave it all in your hands,' said he. 'Would that I could have been the first to pay him homage, but it would not be wise for me to go. The glass is falling, there is a storm brewing, and we have the land under our lee. Besides, there are three English cruisers near the island which may be upon us at any moment. It is for me,' therefore, to guard the ship and for you to bring off the Emperor.'

I thrilled at the words.

'Give me your instructions!' I cried.

'I can only spare you one man, for already I can hardly pull round the yards,' said he. 'One of the boats has been lowered, and this man will row you ashore and await your return. The light which you see is indeed the light of Longwood. All who are in the house are your friends, and all may be depended upon to aid the Emperor's escape. There is a cordon of English sentries, but they are not very near to the house. Once you have got as far as that you will convey our plans to the Emperor, guide him down to the boat, and bring him on board.'

The Emperor himself could not have given his instructions more shortly and clearly. There was not a moment to be lost. The boat with the seaman was waiting alongside. I stepped into it, and an instant afterwards we had pushed off. Our little boat danced over the dark waters, but always shining before my eyes was the light of Longwood, the light of the Emperor, the star of hope. Presently the bottom of the boat grated upon the pebbles of the beach. It was a deserted cove, and no challenge from a sentry came to disturb us. I left the seaman by the boat and began to climb the hillside.

There was a goat-track winding in and out among the rocks, so I had no difficulty in finding my way. It stands to reason that all paths in St. Helena would lead to the Emperor. I came to a gate. No sentry—and I passed through. Another gate—still no sentry! I wondered what had become of this cordon of which Fourneau had spoken. I had come now to the top of my climb, for there was the light burning steadily right in front of me. I concealed myself and took a good look round, but still I could see no sign of the enemy. As I approached I saw the house, a long, low building with a veranda. A man was walking up and down upon the path in front. I crept nearer and had a look at him. Perhaps it was this cursed Hudson Lowe. What a triumph if I could not only rescue the Emperor, but also avenge him! But it was more likely that this man was an English sentry. I crept nearer still, and the man stopped in front of the lighted window, so that I could see him. No; it was no soldier, but a priest. I wondered what such a man could be doing there at two in the morning. Was he French or English? If he were one of the household I might take him into my confidence. If he were English he might ruin all my plans. I crept a little nearer still, and at that moment he entered the house, a flood of light pouring out through the open door. All was clear for me now, and I understood that not an instant was to be lost. Bending myself double I ran swiftly forward to the lighted window. Raising my head I peeped through, and there was the Emperor lying dead before me!

My friends, I fell down upon the gravel walk as sense-less as if a bullet had passed through my brain. So great was the shock that I wonder that I survived it. And yet in half an hour I had staggered to my feet again, shiver-ing in every limb, my teeth chattering, and there I stood staring with the eyes of a maniac into that room of death.

He lay upon a bier in the centre of the chamber, calm, composed, majestic, his face full of that reserve power which lightened our hearts upon the day of battle. A half-smile was fixed upon his pale lips, and his eyes, half-opened, seemed to be turned on mine. He was stouter than when I had seen him at Waterloo, and there was a gentleness of expression which I had never seen in life. On either side of him burned rows of candles, and this was the beacon which had welcomed us at sea, which had guided me over the water, and which I had hailed as my star of hope. Dimly I became conscious that many people were kneeling in the room; the little Court, men and women, who had shared his fortunes, Bertrand, his wife, the priest, Montholon—all were there. I would have prayed too, but my heart was too heavy and bitter for prayer. And yet I must leave, and I could not leave him without a sign. Regardless of whether I was seen or not, I drew myself erect before my dead leader, brought my heels together, and raised my hand in a last salute. Then I turned and hurried off through the darkness, with the picture of the wan, smiling lips and the steady grey eyes dancing always before me.

It had seemed to me but a little time that I had been away, and yet the boatman told me that it was hours. Only when he spoke of it did I observe that the wind was blowing half a gale from the sea and that the waves were roaring in upon the beach. Twice we tried to push out our little boat, and twice it was thrown back by the sea.

The third time a great wave filled it and stove the bottom. Helplessly we waited beside it until the dawn broke, to show a raging sea and a flying scud above it. There was no sign of the *Black Swan*. Climbing the hill we looked down, but on all the great torn expanse of the ocean there was no gleam of a sail. She was gone. Whether she had sunk, or whether she was recaptured by her English crew, or what strange fate may have been in store for her, I do not know. Never again in this life did I see Captain Fourneau to tell him the result of my mission. For my own part I gave myself up to the English, my boatman and I pretending that we were the only survivors of a lost vessel—though, indeed, there was no pretence in the matter. At the hands of their officers I received that generous hospitality which I have always encountered, but it was many a long month before I could get a passage back to the dear land outside of which there can be no happiness for so true a Frenchman as myself.

And so I tell you in one evening how I bade good-bye to my master, and I take my leave also of you, my kind friends, who have listened so patiently to the long-winded stories of an old broken soldier. Russia, Italy, Germany, Spain, Portugal, and England, you have gone with me to all these countries, and you have seen through my dim eyes something of the sparkle and splendour of those great days, and I have brought back to you some shadow of those men whose tread shook the earth. Treasure it in your minds and pass it on to your children, for the memory of a great age is the most precious treasure that a nation can possess. As the tree is nurtured by its own cast leaves, so it is these dead men and vanished days which may bring out another blossoming of heroes, of rulers, and of sages. I go to Gascony, but my words stay here in your memory, and long after Etienne Gerard is forgotten a heart may be warmed or a spirit braced by some faint echo of the words that he has spoken. Gentlemen, an old soldier salutes you and bids you farewell.

THE GREAT SHADOW

I. The Night of the Beacons

I⊤ is strange to me, Jack Calder of West Inch, to feel that though now, in the very centre of the nineteenth century, I am but five-and-fifty years of age, and though it is only once in a week, perhaps, that my wife can pluck out a little grey bristle from over my ear, yet I have lived in a time when the thoughts and the ways of men were as different as though it were another planet from this. For when I walk in my fields I can see, down Berwick way, the little fluffs of white smoke which tell me of this strange, new, hundred-legged beast with coals for food and a thousand men in its belly, for ever crawling over the border. On a shiny day I can see the glint of the brass-work as it takes the curve near Corriemuir. And then, as I look out to sea, there is the same beast again, or a dozen of them, maybe, leaving a trail of black in the air and of white in the water, and swimming in the face of the wind as easily as a salmon up the Tweed. Such a sight as that would have struck my good old father speechless with wrath as well as surprise, for he was so stricken with the fear of offending the Creator that he was chary of contradicting Nature, and always held the new thing to be nearly akin to the blasphemous. As long as God made the horse, and a man, down Birmingham way, the engine, my good old dad would have stuck by the saddle and the spurs.

But he would have been still more surprised if he had seen the peace and kindliness which reign now in the hearts of men, and the talk in the papers and at the meetings that there is to be no more war—save, of course, with blacks and suchlike. For when he died we had been fighting with scarce a break, save for two short years, for very nearly a quarter of a century. Think of it, you who live so quietly and peacefully now. Babies who were born in the war grew to be bearded men with babies of their own, and still the war continued. Those who had served and fought in their stalwart prime grew stiff and bent, and yet the ships and the armies were struggling. It was no wonder that folk came at last to look upon it as the natural state, and thought how queer it must seem to be at peace. During that long time we fought the Dutch, we fought the Danes, we fought the Spanish, we fought the Turks, we fought the Americans, we fought the Montevideans, until it seemed that in this universal struggle no race was too near of kin or too far away to be drawn into the quarrel. But most of all it was the French whom we fought, and the man whom of all others we loathed and feared and admired was the great captain who ruled them.

It was very well to draw pictures of him, and sing songs about him, and make as though he were an impostor, but I can tell you that the fear of that man hung like a black shadow over all Europe, and that there was a time when the glint of a fire at night upon the coast would set every woman upon her knees, and every man gripping for his musket. He had always won. That was the terror of it. The fates seemed to be behind him. And now we know that he lay upon the northern coast with a hundred and fifty thousand veterans, and the boats for their passage. But it is an old story how a third of the grown folk of our country took up arms, and how our little one-eyed, one-armed man crushed their fleet. There was still to be a land of free thinking and free speaking in Europe.

There was a great beacon ready on the hill by Tweedmouth, built up of logs and tar-barrels, and I can well remember how night after night I strained my eyes to see if it were ablaze. I was only eight at the time, but it is an age when one takes a grief to heart, and I felt as though the fate of the country hung in some fashion upon me and my vigilance. And then one night as I looked, I suddenly saw a little flicker on the beacon hill—a single red tongue of flame in the darkness. I remember how I rubbed my eyes, and pinched myself, and rapped my knuckles against the stone window-sill to make sure that I was indeed awake. And then the flame shot higher, and I saw the red quivering line upon the water beyond, and I dashed into the kitchen, screeching to my father that the French had crossed and the Tweedmouth light was aflame. He had been talking to Mr. Mitchell, the law-student from Edinburgh, and I can see him now as he knocked his pipe out at the side of the fire, and looked at me from over the top of his horn spectacles.

'Are you sure, Jock?' says he.

'Sure as death,' I gasped.

He reached out his hand for the Bible upon the table, and opened it upon his knee as though he meant to read to us, but he shut it again in silence and hurried out. We went too, the law-student and I, and followed him down to the gate which opens out upon the highway. From there we could see the red light of the big beacon, and the glimmer of a smaller one to the north of us, at Ayton. My mother came down with two plaids to keep the chill from us, and we all stood there until morning, speaking little to each other, and that little in a whisper. The road had more folk on it than ever passed along it at night before, for many of the yeomen up our way had enrolled themselves in the Berwick Volunteer regiments, and were riding now as fast as hoof could carry them for the muster. Some had a stirrup cup or two before parting, and I cannot forget one who tore past on a huge white horse, brandishing a great rusty sword in the moonlight. They shouted to us, as they passed, that the North Berwick Law-fire was blazing, and that it was thought that the alarm had come from Edinburgh Castle. There were a few who galloped the other way, couriers for Edinburgh, and the laird's son, and Master Clayton, the deputy sheriff, and suchlike. And among others there was one, a fine-built heavy man on a roan horse, who pulled up at our gate and asked some question about the road. He took off his hat to ease himself, and I saw that he had

559

a kindly, long-drawn face, and a great high brow that shot away up into tufts of sandy hair.

'I doubt it's a false alarm,' says he. 'Maybe I'd ha' done well to bide where I was, but now I've come so far I'll break my fast with the regiment.' He clapped spurs to his horse, and away he went down the brae.

'I ken him weel,' said our student, nodding after him. 'He's a lawyer in Edinburgh, and a braw hand at the stringin' of verses. Wattie Scott is his name.' None of us had heard of it then, but it was not long before it was the best-known name in Scotland, and many a time we thought of how he speered his way of us on the night of the terror.

But early in the morning we had our minds set at ease. It was grey and cold, and my mother had gone up to the house to make a pot of tea for us, when there came a gig down the road with Dr. Horscroft, of Ayton, in it, and his son Jim. The collar of the doctor's coat came over his ears, and he looked in a deadly black humour, for Jim, who was but fifteen years of age, had trooped off to Berwick at the first alarm with his father's new fowling-piece. All night his dad had chased him, and now there he was, a prisoner, with the barrel of the stolen gun sticking out from behind the seat. He looked as sulky as his father, with his hands thrust into his side-pockets, his brows drawn down, and his lower lip thrust out.

'It's all a lie,' shouted the doctor, as he passed. 'There has been no landing, and all the fools in Scotland have been gadding about the roads for nothing.' His son Jim snarled something up at him on this, and his father struck him a blow with his clenched fist on the side of his head, which sent the boy's chin forward upon his breast as though he had been stunned. My father shook his head, for he had a liking for Jim, but we all walked up to the house again, nodding and blinking, and hardly able to keep our eyes open, now that we knew that all was safe, but with a thrill of joy at our hearts such as I have only matched once or twice in my lifetime.

Now all this has little enough to do with what I took my pen up to tell about; but when a man has a good memory and a little skill he cannot draw one thought from his mind without a dozen others trailing out behind it. And yet, now that I come to think of it, this had something to do with it after all; for Jim Horscroft had so deadly a quarrel with his father that he was packed off to Birtwhistle's Berwick Academy; and as my father had long wished me to go there, he took advantage of this to send me also. But before I say a word about this school I shall go back to where I should have begun, and give you a hint as to who I am, for it may be that these words of mine may be read by some folk beyond the Border country who never heard of the Calders of West Inch.

It has a brave sound, West Inch, but it is not a fine estate with a braw house upon it, but only a great hard-bitten, wind-swept sheep-run, fringing off into links along the sea-shore, where a frugal man might, with hard work, just pay his rent and have butter instead of treacle on Sundays. In the centre there is a grey-stoned, slate-roofed house with a byre behind it, and '1708' scrawled in stone-work over the lintel of the door. There for more than a hundred years our folk have lived, until, for all their poverty, they came to take a good place among the people, for in the country parts the old yeoman is often better thought of than the new laird.

There was one queer thing about the house of West Inch. It has been reckoned by engineers and other knowing folk that the boundary line between the two countries ran right through the middle of it, splitting our second best bedroom into an English half and a Scotch half. Now the cot in which I always slept was so placed that my head was to the north of the line and my feet to the south of it. My friends say that if I had chanced to lie the other way, my hair might not have been so sandy nor my mind of so solemn a cast. This I know, that more than once in my life, when my Scotch head could see no way out of a

561

danger, my good thick English legs have come to my help and carried me clear away. But at school I never heard the end of this, for they called me 'Half-and-half,' and 'The Great Briton,' and sometimes 'Union Jack.' When there was a battle between the Scotch and the English boys, one side would kick my shins and the other cuff my ears, and then they would both stop and laugh as though it were something funny.

At first I was very miserable at the Berwick Academy. Birtwhistle was the first master, and Adams the second, and I had no love for either of them. I was shy and backward by nature, and slow at making a friend either among masters or boys. It was nine miles as the crow flies, and eleven and a half by road from Berwick to West Inch, and my heart grew weary at the heavy distance that separated me from my mother; for, mark you, a lad of that age pretends that he has no need of his mother's caresses, but ah, how sad he is when he is taken at his word! At last I could stand it no longer, and I determined to run away from the school and make my way home as fast as I might. At the very last moment, however, I had the good fortune to win the praise and admiration of every one from the head-master downwards, and to find my school life made very pleasant and easy for me. And all this came of my falling by accident out of a second-floor window.

This is how it happened. One evening I had been kicked by Ned Barton, who was the bully of the school, and this injury coming on top of all my other grievances caused my little cup to overflow. I vowed that night, as I buried my tear-stained face beneath the blankets, that the next morning would either find me at West Inch, or well on the way to it. Our dormitory was on the second floor, but I was a famous climber and had a fine head for heights. I used to think little, young as I was, of swinging myself, with a rope round my thighs, off the West Inch gable, and that stood three-and-fifty feet above the ground. There was not much fear, then, but that I could make my way out of Birtwhistle's dormitory. I waited a weary while until the coughing and tossing had died away, and there was no sound of wakefulness from the long line of wooden cots. Then I very softly rose, slipped on my clothes, took my shoes in my hand, and walked tiptoe to the window. I opened the casement and looked out. Underneath me lay the garden, and close by my hand was the stout branch of a pear-tree. An active lad could ask no better ladder. Once in the garden, I had but a five-foot wall to get over, and then there was nothing but distance between me and home. I took a firm grip of a branch with one hand, placed my knee upon another one, and was about to swing myself out of the window, when in a moment I was as silent and as still as though I had been turned to stone.

There was a face looking at me from over the coping of the wall. A chill of fear struck to my heart at its whiteness and its stillness. The moon shimmered upon it, and the eyeballs moved slowly from side to side, though I was hidden from them behind the screen of the pear-tree. Then in a jerky fashion this white face ascended until the neck, shoulders, waist, and knees of a man became visible. He sat himself down upon the top of the wall, and with a great heave he pulled up after him a boy about my own size, who caught his breath from time to time as though to choke down a sob. The man gave him a shake, with a few rough whispered words, and then the two dropped together down into the garden. I was still standing balanced with one foot upon the bough and one upon the casement, not daring to budge for fear of attracting their attention, for I could hear them moving stealthily about in the long shadow of the house. Suddenly, from immediately beneath my feet, I heard a low, grating noise, and the sharp tinkle of falling glass.

'That's done it,' said the man's eager whisper, 'there is room for you.'

'But the edge is all jagged,' cried the other in a weak quaver.

563

The fellow burst out into an oath that made my skin pringle.

'In with you, you cub,' he snarled, 'or——' I could not see what he did, but there was a short, quick gasp of pain.

'I'll go! I'll go!' cried the little lad, but I heard no more, for my head suddenly swam, my heel shot off the branch, I gave a dreadful yell, and came down with my ninety-five pounds of weight right upon the bent back of the burglar. If you ask me, I can only say that to this day I am not quite certain whether it was an accident, or whether I designed it. It may be that, while I was thinking of doing it, chance settled the matter for me. The fellow was stooping with his head forward, thrusting the boy through a tiny window, when I came down upon him just where the neck joins the spine. He gave a kind of whistling cry, dropped upon his face, and rolled three times over, drumming on the grass with his heels. His little companion flashed off in the moonlight, and was over the wall in a trice. As for me, I sat yelling at the pitch of my lungs, and nursing one of my legs, which felt as if a red-hot ring were welded round it.

It was not long, as may be imagined, before the whole household, from the head-master to the stable-boy, was out in the garden with lamps and lanterns. The matter was soon cleared, the man carried off on a shutter, and I borne, in much state and solemnity, to a special bedroom, where the small bone of my leg was set by Surgeon Purdie—the younger of the two brothers of that name. As to the robber, it was found that his legs were palsied, and the doctors were of two minds as to whether he would recover the use of them or not; but the law never gave them a chance of settling the matter, for he was hanged after Carlisle assizes, some six weeks later. It was proved that he was the most desperate rogue in the north of England, for he had done three murders at the least, and there were charges enough against him upon the sheet to have hanged him ten times over.

Well, now, I could not pass over my boyhood without

telling you about this, which was the most important thing that happened to me. But I will go off upon no more side-tracks, for when I think of all that is coming, I can see very well that I shall have more than enough to do before I have finished. For when a man has only his own little private tale to tell, it often takes him all his time; but when he gets mixed up in such great matters as I shall have to speak about, then it is hard on him, if he has not been brought up to it, to get it all set down to his liking. But my memory is as good as ever, thank God, and I shall try to get it all straight before I finish.

It was this business of the burglar that first made a friendship between Jim Horscroft, the doctor's son, and me. He was cock boy of the school from the day he came, for within the hour he had thrown Barton, who had been cock before him, right through the big black-board in the class-room. Jim always ran to muscle and bone, and even then he was square and tall, short of speech, and long in the arm, much given to lounging with his broad back against walls, and his hands deep in his breeches pockets. I can even recall that he had a trick of keeping a straw in the corner of his mouth, just where he used afterwards to hold his pipe. Jim was always the same, for good and for bad, since first I knew him.

Heavens! How we all looked up to him! We were but young savages, and had a savage's respect for power. There was Tom Carndale, of Appleby, who could write alcaics as well as mere pentameters and hexameters. Yet nobody would give a snap for Tom. And there was Willie Earnshaw, who had every date from the killing of Abel on the tip of his tongue, so that the masters themselves would turn to him if they were in doubt; yet he was but a narrow-chested lad, over long for his breadth, and what did his dates help him when Jack Simons, of the lower third, chivied him down the passage with the buckle end of a strap. But you didn't do things like that with Jim Horscroft. What tales we used to whisper about his strength; how he put his fist through the oak panel of the

game-room door. How, when Long Merridew was carrying the ball, he caught up Merridew, ball and all, and
ran swiftly past every opponent to the goal. It did not
seem fit to us that such a one as he should trouble his
head about spondees and dactyls, or care to know who
signed the Magna Charta. When he said in open class
that King Alfred was the man, we little boys all felt that
very likely it was so, and that, perhaps, Jim knew more
about it than the man who wrote the book.

Well, it was this business of the burglar that drew his
attention to me, for he patted me on my head, and said
that I was a spunky little devil, which blew me out with
pride for a week on end. For two years we were close
friends, for all the gap that the years had made between
us, and, though in passion or in want of thought he did
many a thing that galled me, yet I loved him like a
brother, and wept as much as would have filled an ink-
bottle when at last, after two years, he went off to Edinburgh to study his father's profession. Five years after that
I did bide at Birtwhistle's, and when I left I had become
cock myself, for I was as wiry and as tough as whalebone,
though I never ran to weight and sinew, like my great
predecessor. It was in jubilee year that I left Birtwhistle's,
and then for three years I stayed at home, learning the
ways of the cattle; but still the ships and the armies were
wrestling, and still the great shadow of Bonaparte lay
across the country.

How could I guess that I, too, should have a hand in
lifting that shadow for ever from our people?

II. Cousin Edie of Eyemouth

SOME years before, when I was still but a lad, there had
come over to us, upon a five weeks' visit, the only daughter of my father's brother. Willie Calder had settled at
Eyemouth as a maker of fishing-nets, and he had made

more out of twine than ever we were like to do out of the whin-bushes and sand-links of West Inch. So his daughter, Edie Calder, came over with a braw red frock and a five-shilling bonnet, and a kist full of things that brought my dear mother's eyes out like a parten's. It was wonderful to see her so free with money, and she but a slip of a girl, paying the carrier-man all that he asked and a whole twopence over, to which he had no claim. She made no more of drinking ginger-beer than we did of water, and she would have her sugar in her tea and butter with her bread just as if she had been English. I took no great stock of girls at that time, for it was hard for me to see what they had been made for. There were none of us at Birtwhistle's that thought very much of them; but the smallest laddies seemed to have the most sense, for, after they began to grow bigger, they were not so sure about it. We little ones were all of one mind that a creature that couldn't fight and was carrying tales, and couldn't so much as shy a stone without flapping its arm like a rag in the wind, was no use for anything. And then the airs that they would put on, as if they were mother and father rolled into one, for ever breaking into a game with, 'Jimmy, your toes come through your boot,' or, 'Go home, you dirty boy, and clean yourself,' until the very sight of them was wearisome.

So when this one came to the steading at West Inch I was not best pleased to see her. I was twelve at the time (it was in the holidays) and she eleven, a thin, tallish girl, with black eyes and the queerest ways. She was for ever staring out in front of her, with her lips parted as if she saw something wonderful; but when I came behind her and looked the same way, I could see nothing but the sheep's trough or the midden, or father's breeches hanging on a clothes-line. And then, if she saw a lump of heather or bracken, or any common stuff of that sort, she would mope over it as if it had struck her sick, and cry, 'How sweet! How perfect!' just as though it had been a painted picture. She didn't like games, but I used to make her play 'tig' and suchlike; but it was no fun, for I could always catch her in three jumps, and she could never catch me, though she would come with as much rustle and flutter as ten boys would make. When I used to tell her that she was good for nothing, and that her father was a fool to bring her up like that, she would begin to cry, and say that I was a rude boy, and that she would go home that very night, and never forgive me as long as she lived. But in five minutes she had forgotten all about it. What was strange was, that she liked me a deal better than I did her, and she would never leave me alone, but she was always watching me and running after me, and then saying, 'Oh, here you are!' as if it were a surprise.

But soon I found that there was good in her, too. She used sometimes to give me pennies, so that once I had four in my pocket all at the same time. But the best part of her was the stories that she could tell. She was sore frightened of frogs; so I would bring one to her, and tell her that I would put it down her neck unless she told a story. That always helped her to begin; but when once she was started it was wonderful how she would carry on. And the things that had happened to her, they were enough to take your breath away. There was a Barbary Rover that had been at Eyemouth, and he was coming back in five years, in a ship full of gold, to make her his wife. And then there was a wonderful knight, who had been there also, and he had given her a ring which he said he would redeem when the time came. She showed me the ring, which was very like the ones upon my bed-curtain, but she said that this one was virgin gold. I asked her what the knight would do if he met the Barbary Rover, and she told me that he would sweep his head from his shoulders. What they could all see in her was more than I could think. And then she told me that she had been followed on her way to West Inch by a disguised prince. I asked her how she knew it was a prince, and she said by his disguise. Another day she said that her father was preparing a riddle, and that when it was ready it would be put in the papers, and any one who guessed it would have half his fortune and his daughter. I said that I was good at riddles, and that she must send it to me when it was ready. She said it would be in the *Berwick Gazette*, and wanted to know what I would do with her when I won her. I said that I would sell her by public roup for what she would fetch; but she would tell me no more stories that evening, for she was very tetchy about some things.

Jim Horscroft was away when Cousin Edie was with us, but he came back the very week she went, and I mind how surprised I was that he should ask any questions or take any interest in a mere lassie. He asked me if she were pretty; and when I said that I hadn't noticed, he laughed and called me a mole, and said my eyes would be opened some day. But very soon he came to be interested in something else, and I never gave Edie another thought until, one day, she just took my life in her hands, and twisted it as I could twist this quill.

That was in 1813, after I had left school, when I was already eighteen years of age, with a good forty hairs on my upper lip, and every hope of more. I had changed since I left school, and was not so keen on games as I had been, but found myself instead lying about on the sunny side of the braes, with my own lips parted and my eyes staring just the same as Cousin Edie's used to do. It had satisfied me, and filled my whole life, that I could run faster and jump higher than my neighbour, but now all that seemed such a little thing, and I yearned, and looked up at the big arching sky, and down at the flat blue sea, and felt that there was something wanting, but could never lay my tongue to what that something was. And I became quick of temper, too, for my nerves seemed all of a fret; and when my mother would ask me what ailed me, or my father would speak of my turning my hand to work, I would break into such sharp, bitter answers as I have often grieved over since. Ah, a man may have more than one wife, and more than one child, and more than one friend, but he can never have but the one mother, so let him cherish her while he may.

One day, when I came in from the sheep, there was my father sitting with a letter in his hands, which was a very rare thing with us, except when the factor wrote for the rent. Then, when I came nearer to him, I saw that he was crying, and I stood staring, for I had always thought that it was not a thing that a man could do. I can see him now, for he had so deep a crease across his brown cheek that no tear could pass it, but must trickle away sideways, and so down to his ear, hopping off on to the sheet of paper. My mother sat beside him, and stroked his hand like she did the cat's back when she would soothe it.

'Aye, Jeannie,' said he, 'poor Willie's gone. It's from the lawyer, and it was sudden, or they'd ha' sent word of it. Carbuncle, he says, and a flush o' blood to the head.'

'Ah, well, his trouble's over,' said my mother.

My father rubbed his ears with the table-cloth. 'He's left a' his savings to his lassie,' said he, 'and, by gom, if she's not changed from what she promised to be, she'll soon gar them flee. You mind what she said of weak tea under this very roof, and it at seven shillings the pound.'

My mother shook her head, and looked up at the flitches of bacon that hung from the ceiling.

'He doesn't say how much, but she'll have enough and to spare, he says. And she's to come and bide with us, for that was his last wish.'

'To pay for her keep,' cried my mother, sharply. I was sorry that she should have spoken of money at that moment, but then, if she had not been sharp, we should all have been on the roadside in a twelvemonth.

'Aye, she'll pay, and she's coming this very day. Jock, lad, I'll want you to drive to Ayton and meet the evening coach. Your Cousin Edie will be in it, and you can fetch her over to West Inch.'

And so off I started, at quarter-past five, with Souter

Johnnie, the long-haired fifteen-year-old, and our cart with the new-painted tail-board, that we only used on great days. The coach was in, just as I came, and I, like a foolish country-lad, taking no heed to the years that had passed, was looking about among the folk in the inn-front for a slip of a girl with her petticoats just under her knees. And as I slouched past, and craned my neck, there came a touch to my elbow, and there was a lady, dressed all in black, standing by the steps, and I knew that it was my Cousin Edie.

I knew it, I say, and yet, had she not touched me, I might have passed her a score of times and never known it. My word, if Jim Horscroft had asked me then if she were pretty or no, I should have known how to answer him! She was dark, much darker than is common among our Border lassies, and yet with such a faint flush of pink breaking through her dainty colour, like the deeper flush at the heart of a sulphur rose. Her lips were red and kindly and firm, and even then, at the first glance, I saw that light of mischief and mockery that danced away at the back of her great dark eyes. She took me then and there as though I had been her heritage, put out her hand and plucked me. She was, as I have said, in black, dressed in what seemed to me to be a wondrous fashion, with a black veil pushed up from her brow.

'Ah, Jack,' said she, in a mincing English fashion that she had learned at the boarding-school. 'No, no, we are rather old for that——' This because I, in my awkward fashion, was pushing my foolish brown face forward to kiss her, as I had done when I saw her last. 'Just hurry up, like a good fellow, and give a shilling to the conductor, who has been exceedingly civil to me during the journey.'

I flushed up red to the ears, for I had only a silver four-penny in my pocket. Never had my lack of pence weighed so heavily upon me as just at that moment. But she read me at a glance, and there, in an instant, was a little mole-skin purse with a silver clasp thrust into my

571

hand. I paid the man, and would have given it back, but she would still have me keep it.

'You shall be my factor, Jack,' said she, laughing. 'Is this our carriage? How funny it looks. And where am I to sit?'

'On the sacking,' said I.

'And how am I to get there?'

'Put your foot on the hub,' said I; 'I'll help you.' I sprang up, and took her two little gloved hands in my own. As she came over the side, her breath blew in my face, sweet and warm, and all that vagueness and unrest seemed in a moment to have been shredded away from my soul. I felt as if that instant had taken me out from myself, and made me one of the race. It took but the time of the flicking of the horse's tail, and yet something had happened, a barrier had gone down somewhere, and I was leading a wider and a wiser life. I felt it all in a gush, but, shy and backward as I was, I could do nothing but flatten out the sacking for her. Her eyes were after the coach which was rattling away to Berwick, and suddenly she shook her handkerchief in the air.

'He took off his hat,' said she; 'I think he must have been an officer. He was very distinguished-looking; perhaps you noticed him—a gentleman on the outside, very handsome, with a brown overcoat.'

I shook my head, with all my flush of joy changed to foolish resentment.

'Ah, well, I shall never see him again. Here are all the green braes, and the brown, winding road, just the same as ever. And you, Jack—I don't see any great change in you, either. I hope your manners are better than they used to be. You won't try to put any frogs down my back, will you?'

I crept all over when I thought of such a thing. 'We'll do all we can to make you happy at West Inch,' said I, playing with the whip.

'I'm sure it's very kind of you to take a poor, lonely girl in,' said she.

'It's very kind of you to come, Cousin Edie,' I stammered. 'You'll find it very dull, I fear.'

'I suppose it is a little quiet, Jack. Not many men about, as I remember it.'

'There is Major Elliott, up at Corriemuir. He comes down of an evening, a real brave old soldier, who had a ball in his knee under Wellington.'

'Ah, when I speak of men, Jack, I don't mean old folks with balls in their knees. I meant people of our own age, that we could make friends of. By the way, that crabbed old doctor had a son, had he not?'

'Oh, yes, that's Jim Horscroft, my best friend.'

'Is he at home?'

'No; he'll be home soon. He's still at Edinburgh, studying.'

'Ah, then we'll keep each other company until he comes, Jack. And I'm very tired, and I wish I was at West Inch.'

I made old Souter Johnnie cover the ground as he had never done before or since, and in an hour she was seated at the supper-table, where my mother had laid out not only butter, but a glass dish of gooseberry jam which sparkled and looked fine in the candle-light. I could see that my parents were as overcome as I was at the difference in her, though not in the same way. My mother was so set back by the feather thing that she had round her neck that she called her Miss Calder instead of Edie, until my cousin, in her pretty, flighty way, would lift her forefinger to her whenever she did it. After supper, when she had gone to her bed, they could talk of nothing but her looks and her breeding.

'By the way, though,' says my father, 'it does not look as if she were heart-broke about my brother's death.'

And then, for the first time, I remembered that she had never said a word about the matter since I had met her.

III. The Shadow on the Waters

IT was not very long before Cousin Edie was queen of West Inch, and we all her devoted subjects from my father down. She had money and to spare, though none of us knew how much. When my mother said that four shillings the week would cover all that she would cost, she fixed on seven shillings and sixpence of her own free will. The south room, which was the sunniest and had the honeysuckle round the window, was for her; and it was a marvel to see the things that she brought from Berwick to put into it. Twice a week she would drive over. And the cart would not do for her; for she hired a gig from Angus Whitehead, whose farm lay over the hill. And it was seldom she went without bringing something back for one or other of us. It was a wooden pipe for my father, or a Shetland plaid for my mother, or a book for me, or a brass collar for Rob, the collie. There was never a woman more free-handed.

But the best thing that she gave us was just her own presence. To me it changed the whole country-side; and the sun was brighter, and the braes greener, and the air sweeter from the day she came. Our lives were common no longer, now that we spent them with such a one as she; and the old, dull, grey house was another place in my eyes since she had set her foot across the door-mat. It was not her face, though that was winsome enough; nor her form, though I never saw the lass that could match her. But it was her spirit; her queer, mocking ways; her fresh, new fashion of talk; her proud whisk of the dress and toss of the head, which made one feel like the ground beneath her feet; and then the quick challenge in her eye, and the kindly word that brought one up to her level again.

But never quite to her level either. To me she was always something above and beyond. I might brace myself and blame myself, and do what I would, but still I could not feel that the same blood ran in our veins, and

574

that she was but a country lass as I was a country lad. The more I loved her the more frightened I was at her; and she could see the fright long before she knew the love. I was uneasy to be away from her; and yet, when I was with her, I was in a shiver all the time for fear my stumbling talk might weary her or give her offence. Had I known more of the ways of women I might have taken less pains.

'You're a deal changed from what you used to be, Jack,' said she, looking at me sideways from under her dark lashes.

'You said that when first we met,' said I.

'Ah, I was speaking of your looks then, and of your ways now. You used to be so rough with me, and so imperious, and would have your own way, like the little man that you were. I can see you now with your tangled brown hair and your mischievous eyes. And now you are so gentle and quiet and soft-spoken.'

'One learns to behave,' says I.

'Ah, but, Jack, I liked you so much better as you were.'

Well, when she said that I fairly stared at her, for I had thought that she could never have quite forgiven me for the way I used to carry on. That any one out of a daft-house could have liked it was clean beyond my understanding. I thought of how, when she was reading by the door, I would go up on the moor, with a hazel switch, and little clay balls at the end of it, and sling them at her until I made her cry. And then I thought of how I caught an eel in the Corriemuir burn, and chivied her about with it, until she ran screaming under my mother's apron, half mad with fright, and my father gave me one on the ear-hole with the porridge-stick, which knocked me and my eel under the kitchen dresser. And these were the things that she missed? Well, she must miss them, for my hand would wither before I could do them now. But for the first time I began to understand the queerness that lies in a woman, and that a man must not reason about one, but just watch and try to learn.

We found our level after a time, when she saw that she had just to do what she liked and how she liked, and that I was as much at her beck and call as old Rob was at mine. You'll think that I was a fool to have had my head so turned, and maybe I was; but, then, you must think how little I was used to women, and how much we were thrown together. Besides, she was a woman in a million, and I can tell you that it was a strong head that would not be turned by her.

Why, there was Major Elliott, a man that had buried three wives, and had twelve pitched battles to his name. Edie could have turned him round her finger like a damp rag—she, only new from the boarding-school. I met him hobbling from West Inch, the first time after she came, with pink in his cheeks and a shine in his eye that took ten years from him. He was cocking up his grey moustaches at either end, and curling them into his eyes, and strutting out with his sound leg as proud as a piper. What she had said to him, the Lord knows, but it was like old wine in his veins.

'I've been up to see you, laddie,' said he, 'but I must go home again now. My visit has not been wasted, however, as I had an opportunity of seeing *la belle cousine*. A most charming and engaging young lady, laddie.' He had a formal, stiff way of talking, and was fond of jerking in a bit of the French, for he had picked some up in the Peninsula. He would have gone on talking of Cousin Edie, but I saw the corner of a newspaper thrusting out of his pocket, and I knew that he had come over, as was his way, to give me some news, for we heard little enough at West Inch.

'What is fresh, major?' I asked.

He pulled the paper out with a flourish. 'The allies have won a great battle, my lad,' says he. 'I don't think "Nap" can stand up long against this. The Saxons have thrown him over, and he's been badly beat at Leipzig. Wellington is past the Pyrenees, and Graham's folk will be at Bayonne before long.'

I chucked up my hat. 'Then the war will come to an end at last,' I cried.

'Aye, and time, too,' said he, shaking his head gravely. 'It's been a bloody business. But it is hardly worth while for me to say now what was in my mind about you.'

'What was that?'

'Well, laddie, you are doing no good here; and, now that my knee is getting more limber, I was hoping that I might get on active service again. I wondered whether, maybe, you might like to do a little soldiering under me.'

My heart jumped at the thought. 'Aye, would I!' I cried.

'But it'll be clear six months before I'll be fit to pass a board, and it's long odds that Boney will be under lock and key before that.'

'And there's my mother,' said I. 'I doubt she'd never let me go.'

'Ah, well, she'll never be asked to now,' he answered, and hobbled on his way.

I sat down among the heather, with my chin on my hand, turning the thing over in my mind, and watching him in his old brown clothes, with the end of a grey plaid flapping over his shoulder, as he picked his way up the swell of the hill. It was a poor life this at West Inch, waiting to fill my father's shoes, with the same heath, and the same burn, and the same sheep, and the same grey house for ever before me. But over there—over the blue sea— ah, there was a life fit for a man. There was the major, a man past his prime, wounded and spent, and yet planning to get to work again; whilst I, with all the strength of my youth, was wasting it upon these hill-sides. A hot wave of shame flushed over me, and I sprang up, all in a tingle to be off and play a man's part in the world.

For two days I turned it over in my mind, and on the third there came something which first brought my resolutions to a head, and then blew them all to nothing, like a puff of smoke in the wind.

I had strolled out in the afternoon with Cousin Edie

and Rob, until we found ourselves on the brow of the slope which dips away down to the beach. It was late in the fall, and the links were all bronzed and faded, but the sun still shone warmly, and a south breeze came in little hot pants, rippling the broad blue sea with white curling lines. I pulled an armful of bracken to make a couch for Edie, and there she lay in her listless fashion, happy and contented, for of all folk that I have ever met she had the most joy from warmth and light. I leaned on a tussock of grass, with Rob's head upon my knee, and there, as we sat alone in peace in the wilderness, even there we saw suddenly thrown upon the waters in front of us the shadow of that great man over yonder, who had scrawled his name in red letters across the map of Europe.

There was a ship coming up with the wind—a black, sedate old merchantman—bound for Leith as likely as not. Her yards were square, and she was running with all sail set. On the other tack, coming from the north-east, were two great, ugly, lugger-like craft, with one high mast each, and a big, square, brown sail. A prettier sight one would not wish to see than the three craft dipping along upon so fair a day, but of a sudden there came a spurt of flame and a whirl of blue smoke from one lugger, then the same from the second, and a rap-rap-rap from the ship. In a twinkling hell had elbowed out heaven, and there on the water were hatred and savagery and the lust for blood.

We had sprung to our feet at the outburst, and Edie put her hand, all in a tremble, upon my arm.

'They are fighting, Jack,' she cried. 'What are they? Who are they?'

My heart was thudding with the guns, and it was all that I could do to answer her for the catch of my breath.

'It's two French privateers, Edie,' said I. '*Chasse-marées*, they call them, and yon's one of our merchant ships, and they'll take her as sure as death, for the major says that they've always got heavy guns, and are as full of men as an egg's full of meat. Why doesn't the fool make back for Tweedmouth bar?'

But not an inch of canvas did she lower, floundering on in her stolid fashion, while a little black ball ran up to her peak, and the rare old flag streamed suddenly out from the halliard. Then again came the rap-rap-rap of her little guns, and the boom-boom of the big carronades in the bows of the lugger. An instant later the three ships met, and the merchantman staggered on like a stag with two wolves hanging to its haunches. The three became but a dark blur amid the smoke, with the top spars thrusting out in a bristle, and from the heart of that cloud came the quick, red flashes of flame, and such a devil's racket of big guns and small, cheering, and screaming, as was to din in my head for many a week. For a stricken hour the hell-cloud moved slowly across the face of the water, and still, with our hearts in our mouths, we watched the flap of the flag, straining to see if it were yet there. And then suddenly the ship, as proud and black and high as ever, shot on upon her way, and as the smoke cleared we saw one of the luggers squattering like a broken-winged duck upon the water, and the other working hard to get the crew from her before she sank.

For all that hour I had lived for nothing but the fight. My cap had been whisked away by the wind, but I had never given it a thought. Now, with my heart full, I turned upon Cousin Edie, and the sight of her took me back six years. There was the vacant, staring eye and the parted lips, just as I had seen them in her girlhood, and her little hands were clenched until the knuckles gleamed like ivory.

'Ah, that captain!' said she, talking to the heath and the whin-bushes. 'There is a man—so strong, so resolute! What woman would not be proud of a man like that!'

'Aye, he did well!' I cried, with enthusiasm.

She looked at me as if she had forgotten my existence.

'I would give a year of my life to meet such a man,' said she. 'But that is what living in the country means. One never sees anybody but just those who are fit for nothing better.'

I do not know that she meant to hurt me, though she was never very backward at that; but, whatever her intention, her words seemed to strike straight upon a naked nerve.

'Very well, Cousin Edie,' I said, trying to speak calmly. 'That puts the cap on it. I'll take the bounty in Berwick to-night.'

'What, Jack? You be a soldier?'

'Yes, if you think that every man that bides in the country must be a coward.'

'Oh, you'd look so handsome in a red coat, Jack, and it improves you vastly when you are in a temper. I wish your eyes would always flash like that, for it looks so nice and manly. But I am sure that you are joking about the soldiering.'

'I'll let you see if I'm joking.' Then and there I set off running over the moor, until I burst into the kitchen where my father and mother were sitting on either side of the ingle.

'Mother,' I cried, 'I'm off for a soldier.'

Had I said that I was off for a burglar they could not have looked worse over it, for in those days among the decent, canny folks it was mostly the black sheep that were herded by the sergeant. But, my word, those same black sheep did their country some rare service too! My mother put up her mittens to her eyes, and my father looked as black as a peat-hole.

'Hoots, Jock, you're daft,' says he.

'Daft or not, I'm going.'

'Then you'll have no blessing from me.'

'Then I'll go without.'

At this my mother gave a screech, and throws her arms about my neck. I saw her hand, all hard, and worn, and knuckly with the work that she had done for my up-bringing, and it pleaded with me as words could not have done. My heart was soft for her, but my will was as hard as a flint edge. I put her back in her chair with a kiss, and then ran to my room to pack my bundle. It was already growing dark, and I had a long walk before me; so I thrust a few things together and hastened out. As I came through the side-door some one touched my shoulder, and there was Edie in the gloaming.

'Silly boy!' said she. 'You are not really going?'

'Am I not? You'll see.'

'But your father does not wish it, nor your mother.'

'I know that.'

'Then why go?'

'You ought to know.'

'Why then?'

'Because you make me.'

'I don't want you to go, Jack.'

'You said it. You said that the folk in the country were fit for nothing better. You always speak like that. You think no more of me than of those doos in the cot. You think I'm nobody at all. I'll show you different.' All my troubles came out in hot little spurts of speech. She coloured up as I spoke, and looked at me in her queer, half-mocking, half-petting fashion.

'Oh, I think so little of you as that,' said she. 'And that is the reason why you are going away. Well then, Jack, will you stay if I am—if I am kind to you?'

We were face to face, and close together, and in an instant the thing was done. My arms were round her, and I was kissing her, and kissing her, and kissing her, on her mouth, her cheeks, her eyes, and pressing her to my heart, and whispering to her that she was all, all, to me, and that I could not be without her. She said nothing, but it was long before she turned her face aside, and when she pushed me back it was not very hard.

'Why, you are quite your rude, old, impudent self,' said she, patting her hair with her two hands. 'You have tossed me, Jack. I had no idea that you would be so forward.'

But all my fear of her was gone, and a love ten-fold hotter than ever was boiling in my veins. I took her up again, and kissed her, as if it were my right.

'You are my very own now,' I cried. 'I shall not go to Berwick, but I'll stay and marry you.'

But she laughed when I spoke of marriage. 'Silly boy! Silly boy!' said she, with her forefinger up, and then when I tried to lay hands on her again she gave a little dainty courtesy and was off into the house.

IV. The Choosing of Jim

AND then there came ten weeks which were like a dream, and are so now to look back upon. I would weary you were I to tell you what passed between us, but oh! how earnest and fateful and all-important it was at the time. Her waywardness, her ever-varying moods, now bright, now dark like a meadow under drifting clouds, her causeless angers, her sudden repentances, each in turn filling me with joy or sorrow—these were my life, and all the rest was but emptiness. But ever deep down behind all my other feelings was a vague disquiet—a fear that I was like the man who set forth to lay hands upon the rainbow, and that the real Edie Calder, however near she might seem, was, in truth, for ever beyond my reach.

For she was so hard to understand—or, at least, she was so for a dull-witted country lad like me. For if I would talk to her of my real prospects, and how, by taking in the whole of Corriemuir, we might earn a hundrew good pounds over the extra rent, and maybe be able to build out the parlour at West Inch, so as to make it fine for her when we married, she would pout her lip and droop her eyes, as though she scarce had patience to listen to me. But if I would let her build up dreams about what I might become, how I might find a paper which proved me to be the true heir of the laird, or how, without joining the army, which she would by no means hear of, I showed myself to be a great warrior until my name was in all folk's mouth, then she would be as blithe as the May. I would keep up the play as well as I could, but soon some luckless word would show that I was only plain Jock Calder of West Inch, and out would come her lip again in scorn of me. So we moved on, she in the air and I on the ground, and if the rift had not come in one way it must in another.

It was after Christmas, but the winter had been mild, with just frost enough to make it safe walking over the peat-bogs. One fresh morning Edie had been out early, and she came back to breakfast with a fleck of colour on her cheeks.

'Has your friend, the doctor's son, come home, Jack?' says she.

'I heard that he was expected.'

'Ah, then it must have been him that I met on the muir.'

'What? You met Jim Horscroft?'

'I am sure it must be he. A splendid-looking man, a hero, with curly black hair, a short, straight nose, and grey eyes. He had shoulders like a statue, and as to height —why, I suppose that your head, Jack, would come up to his scarf-pin.'

'Up to his ear, Edie,' said I impatiently. 'That is, if it was Jim. But tell me, had he a brown wooden pipe stuck in the corner of his mouth?'

'Yes, he was smoking. He was dressed in grey, and he has a grand, deep, strong voice.'

'Ho, ho, you spoke to him?' said I.

She coloured a little, as if she had said more than she meant. 'I was going where the ground was a little soft, and he warned me of it,' she said.

'Ah, it must have been dear old Jim,' said I. 'He should have been a doctor years back if his brains had been as strong as his arm. Why, heart alive! here is the very man himself!' I had seen him through the kitchen window, and now I rushed out with my half-eaten bannock in my hand to greet him. He ran forward, too, with his great hand out and his eyes shining.

583

'Ah, Jock!' he cried, 'it's good to see you again. There are no friends like the old ones.' Then suddenly he stuck in his speech, and stared, with his mouth open, over my shoulder. I turned, and there was Edie, with such a merry, roguish smile, standing in the door. How proud I felt of her, and of myself too, as I looked at her.

'This is my cousin, Miss Edie Calder, Jim,' said I.

'Do you often take walks before breakfast, Mr. Horscroft?' she asked, still with that roguish smile.

'Yes,' said he, staring at her with all his eyes.

'So do I, and generally over yonder,' said she; 'but you are not very hospitable to your friend, Jack. If you do not do the honours I shall have to take your place for the credit of West Inch.'

Well, in another minute we were in with the old folk, and Jim had his plate of porridge ladled out for him, but hardly a word would he speak, but sat, with his spoon in his hand, staring at Cousin Edie. She shot little twinkling glances across at him all the time, and it seemed to me that she was amused at his backwardness, and that she tried by what she said to give him heart.

'Jack was telling me that you were studying to be a doctor,' said she. 'But oh! how hard it must be, and how long it must take before one can gather so much learning as that.'

'It takes me long enough,' Jim answered ruefully, 'but I'll beat it yet.'

'Ah, but you are brave. You are resolute. You fix your eyes on a point, and you move on towards it, and nothing can stop you.'

'Indeed, I've little to boast of,' said he. 'Many a one who began with me has put up his plate years ago, and here am I but a student still.'

'That is your modesty, Mr. Horscroft. They say that the bravest are always humble. But then, when you have gained your end, what a glorious career—to carry healing in your hands, to raise up the suffering, to have for one's sole end the good of humanity.'

Honest Jim wriggled in his chair at this. 'I'm afraid I have no such very high motives, Miss Calder,' said he. 'It's to earn a living, and to take over my father's business, that I do it. If I carry healing in one hand I have the other out for a crown-piece.'

'How candid and truthful you are!' she cried, and so they went on, she decking him with every virtue, and twisting his words to make him play the part, in the way that I knew so well. Before she was done I could see that his head was buzzing with her beauty and her kindly words. I was thrilled with pride to think that he should think so well of my kin.

'Isn't she fine, Jim?' I could not help saying when we stood alone outside the door, he lighting his pipe before he set off home.

'Fine!' he cried. 'I never saw her match.'

'We're going to be married,' said I.

The pipe fell out of his mouth, and he stood staring at me. Then he picked it up, and walked off without a word. I thought that he would likely come back, but he never did, and I saw him far off walking up the brae with his chin on his chest.

But I was not to forget him, for Cousin Edie had a hundred questions to ask me about his boyhood, about his strength, about the women that he was likely to know; there was no satisfying her. And then again, later in the day, I heard of him, but in a less pleasant fashion.

It was my father who came home in the evening with his mouth full of poor Jim. He had been deadly drunk since mid-day, had been down to Westhouse Links to fight the gypsy champion, and it was not certain that the man would live through the night. My father had met Jim on the high-road, dour as a thunder-cloud, and with an insult in his eye for every man that passed him. 'Guid sakes!' said the old man. 'He'll make a fine practice for himsel' if breaking bones will do it.' Cousin Edie laughed at all this, and I laughed because she did, but I was not so sure that it was funny.

On the third day afterwards I was going up Corriemuir by the sheep-track, when who should I see striding down but Jim himself. But he was another man from the big, kindly fellow who had supped his porridge with us the other morning. He had no collar nor tie, his vest was open, his hair matted, and his face mottled, like a man who has drunk heavily overnight. He carried an oak stick, and he slashed at the whin-bushes on either side of the path.

'Why, Jim!' said I.

But he looked at me in the way that I had often seen at school when the devil was strong in him, and when he knew that he was in the wrong, and yet set his will to brazen it out. Not a word did he say, but he brushed past me on the narrow path, and swaggered on, still brandishing his stick and cutting at the bushes.

Ah well, I was not angry with him. I was sorry, very sorry, and that was all. Of course I was not so blind but that I could see how the matter stood. He was in love with Edie, and he could not bear to think that I should have her. Poor devil! how could he help it! Maybe I should have been the same. There was a time when I should have wondered that a girl could have turned a strong man's head like that, but I knew more about it now.

For a fortnight I saw nothing of Jim Horscroft, and then came the Thursday which was to change the whole current of my life.

I had woke early that day, and, with a little thrill of joy, which is a rare thing to feel when a man first opens his eyes. Edie had been kinder than usual the night before, and I had fallen asleep with the thought that maybe at last I had caught the rainbow, and that, without any imaginings or make-believes, she was learning to love plain Jack Calder of West Inch. It was this thought, still at my heart, which had given me that little morning chirrup of joy. And then I remembered that if I hastened I might be in time for her, for it was her custom to go out with the sunrise.

But I was too late. When I came to her door it was half open and the room empty. Well, thought I, at least I may meet her and have the homeward walk with her. From the top of the Corriemuir hill you may see all the country round; so, catching up my stick, I swung off in that direction. It was bright but cold, and the surf, I remember, was booming loudly, though there had been no wind in our parts for days. I zigzagged up the steep pathway, breathing in the thin, keen morning air, and humming a lilt as I went, until I came out, a little short of breath, among the whins upon the top. Looking down the long slope of the farther side. I saw Cousin Edie as I had expected, and I saw Jim Horscroft walking by her side.

They were not far away, but too taken up with each other to see me. She was walking slowly, with the little petulant cock of her dainty head which I knew so well, casting her eyes away from him, and shooting out a word from time to time. He paced along beside her, looking down at her and bending his head in the eagerness of his talk. Then, as he said something, she placed her hand, with a caress, upon his arm, and he, carried off his feet, plucked her up and kissed her again and again. At the sight I could neither cry out nor move, but stood, with a heart of lead and the face of a dead man, staring down at them. I saw her hand passed over his shoulder, and that his kisses were as welcome to her as ever mine had been.

Then he set her down again, and I found that this had been their parting, for indeed in another hundred paces they would have come in view of the upper windows of the house. She walked slowly away, with a wave back once or twice, and he stood looking after her. I waited until she was some way off, and then down I came, but so taken up was he that I was within a hand's touch of him before he whisked round upon me. He tried to smile as his eyes met mine.

'Ah, Jock,' said he, 'early afoot!'

'I saw you,' I gasped, and my throat had turned so dry that I spoke like a man with a quinsy.

'Did you so,' said he, and he gave a little whistle. 'Well, on my life, Jock, I'm not sorry. I was thinking of coming up to West Inch this very day and having it out with you. Maybe it's better as it is.'

'You've been a fine friend,' said I.

'Well, now, be reasonable, Jock,' said he, sticking his hands into his pockets and rocking to and fro as he stood. 'Let me show you how it stands. Look me in the eye, and you'll see that I don't lie. It's this way. I had met Edie—Miss Calder, that is—before I came that morning, and there were things which made me look upon her as free, and, thinking that, I let my mind dwell on her. Then you said that she wasn't free, but was promised to you, and that was the worst knock I've had for a time. It clean put me off, and I made a fool of myself for some days, and it's a mercy I'm not in Berwick jail. Then by chance I met her again—on my soul, Jock, it was chance for me —and when I spoke of you she laughed at the thought. It was cousin and cousin, she said, but as for her not being free, or you being more to her than a friend, it was fool's talk. So you see, Jock, I was not so much to blame after all, the more so as she promised that she would let you see by her conduct that you were mistaken in thinking that you had any claim upon her. You must have noticed that she has hardly had a word for you these last two weeks.'

I laughed bitterly. 'It was only last night,' said I, 'that she told me that I was the only man in all this earth that she could ever bring herself to love.'

Jim Horscroft put out a shaking hand and laid it on my shoulder, while he pushed his face forward to look into my eyes.

'Jock Calder,' said he, 'I never knew you to tell a lie. You are not trying to score trick against trick, are you? Honest now, between man and man.'

'It's God's truth,' said I.

He stood looking at me, and his face had set like that of a man who is having a hard fight with himself. It was a long two minutes before he spoke.

'See here, Jock,' said he, 'this woman is fooling us both. D'you hear, man?—she's fooling us both. She loves you at West Inch, and she loves me on the brae-side, and in her devil's heart she cares a whin-blossom for neither of us. Let's join hands, man, and send the hell-fire hussy to the right-about.'

But this was too much. I could not curse her in my own heart, and still less could I stand by and hear another man do it, not though it was my oldest friend.

'Don't you call names!' I cried.

'Ach! you sicken me with your soft talk. I'll call her what she should be called.'

'Will you, though?' said I, lugging off my coat. 'Look you here, Jim Horscroft, if you say another word against her I'll lick it down your throat if you were as big as Berwick Castle. Try me, and see!'

He peeled off his coat down to the elbows, and then he slowly pulled it on again.

'Don't be such a fool, Jock,' said he. 'Four stone and five inches is more than mortal man can give. Two old friends mustn't fall out over such a—well, there, I won't say it. Well, by the Lord! if she hasn't nerve for ten!'

I looked round, and there she was, not twenty yards from us, looking as cool and easy and placid as we were hot and fevered.

'I was nearly home,' said she, 'when I saw you two boys very busy talking, so I came all the way back to know what it was about.'

Horscroft took a run forward and caught her by the wrist. She gave a little squeal at the sight of his face, but he pulled her towards where I was standing.

'Now, Jock, we've had tomfoolery enough,' said he. 'Here she is. Shall we take her word as to which she likes? She can't trick us now that we're both together.'

'I am willing,' said I.

'And so am I. If she goes for you I swear I'll never so much as turn an eye on her again. Will you do as much for me?'

'Yes, I will.'

'Well, then, look here, you! We're both honest men and friends, and we tell each other no lies, and so we know your double ways. I know what you said last night. Jock knows what you said to-day. D'you see? Now, then, fair and square! Here we are before you, once and have done. Which is it to be, Jock or me?'

You would have thought that the woman would have been overwhelmed with shame, but, instead of that, her eyes were shining with delight, and I dare wager that it was the proudest moment of her life. As she looked from one to the other of us, with the cold morning sun glittering on her face, I had never seen her look so lovely. Jim felt it also, I am sure, for he dropped her wrist, and the harsh lines were softened upon his face.

'Come, Edie! Which is it to be?' he asked.

'Naughty boys! to fall out like this,' she cried. 'Cousin Jack, you know how fond I am of you.'

'Oh, then, go to him!' said Horscroft.

'But I love nobody but Jim. There is nobody that I love like Jim.' She snuggled up to him, and laid her cheek against his breast.

'You see, Jock!' said he, looking over her shoulder.

I did see, and away I went for West Inch, another man from the time that I left it.

V. The Man from the Sea

WELL, I was never one to sit groaning over a cracked pot; if it cannot be mended, then it is the part of a man to say no more of it. For weeks I had an aching heart; indeed, it is a little sore now, after all these years and a happy marriage, when I think of it. But I kept a brave face on me, and above all I did as I had promised that day on the hillside. I was a brother to her, and no more, though there were times when I had to put a hard curb upon myself; for even now she would come to me with her coaxing ways, and with tales about how rough Jim was, and how happy she had been when I was kind to her, for it was in her blood to speak like that, and she could not help it.

But for the most part she and Jim were happy enough. It was all over the country-side that they were to be married when he had passed his degree, and he would come up to West Inch four nights a week to sit with us. My folk were pleased enough about it, and I tried to be pleased too.

Maybe at first there was a little coolness between him and me. There was not quite the old schoolboy trust between us. But then, when the first smart was passed, it seemed to me that he had acted openly, and that I had no just cause for complaint against him. So we were friendly enough, and as for her, he had forgotten all his anger, and would have kissed the print of her shoe in the mud. We used to take long rambles together, he and I, and it is about one of those that I now want to tell you.

We had passed over Bramston Heath and round the clump of firs which screens the house of Major Elliott from the sea-wind. It was spring now, and the year was a forward one, so that the trees were well leaved by the end of April. It was as warm as a summer day, and we were the more surprised when we saw a huge fire roaring upon the grass-plot before the major's door. There was half a fir-tree in it, and the flames were spouting up as high as the bedroom windows. Jim and I stood staring; but we stared the more when out came the major, with a great quart pot in his hand, and at his heels his old sister, who kept house for him, and two of the maids, and all four began capering about the fire. He was a douce, quiet man, as all the country knew; and here he was, like Old Nick at the carlins' dance, hobbling round, and waving his drink above his head. We both set off running, and he waved the more when he saw us coming.

'Peace!' he roared. 'Huzza, boys! Peace!'

And at that we both fell to dancing and shouting too, for it had been such a weary war, as far back as we could remember, and the shadow had lain so long over us that it was wondrous to feel that it was lifted. Indeed, it was too much to believe, but the major laughed our doubts to scorn.

'Aye, aye, it is true,' he cried, stopping, with his hand to his side. 'The Allies have got Paris, Boney has thrown up the sponge, and his people are all swearing allegiance to Louis the Eighteenth.'

'And the Emperor?' I asked, 'will they spare him?'

'There's some talk of sending him to Elba, where he'll be out of mischief's way. But his officers—there are some of them who will not get off so lightly. Some deeds have been done during these last twenty years that have not been forgotten. There are a few old scores to be settled. But it's peace, peace!' and away he went once more, with his great tankard, hopping round his bonfire.

Well, we stayed some time with the major, and then away we went down to the beach, Jim and I, talking about this great news and all that would come of it. He knew a little and I knew less, but we pieced it all together and talked about how the prices would come down; how our brave fellows would return home; how the ships could go where they would in peace; and how we could pull all the coast beacons down, for there was no enemy now to fear. So we chatted as we walked along the clean, hard sand, and looked out at the old North Sea. How little did Jim know at that moment, as he strode along by my side so full of health and of spirits, that he had reached the extreme summit of his life, and that from that hour all would, in truth, be upon the downward slope.

There was a little haze out to sea, for it had been very misty in the early morning, though the sun had thinned it. As we looked seaward we suddenly saw the sail of a small boat break out through the fog, and come bobbing along towards the land. A single man was seated in the sheets, and she yawed about as she ran, as though he were of two minds whether to beach her or no. At last, determined, it may be, by our presence, he made straight for us, and her keel grated upon the shingle at our very feet. He dropped his sail, climbed out, and pulled her bows up on to the beach.

'Great Britain, I believe?' said he, turning round and facing us.

He was a man somewhat above middle height, but exceedingly thin. His eyes were piercing and set close together, a long, sharp nose jutted out from between them, and beneath was a bristle of brown moustache as wiry and stiff as a cat's whiskers. He was well dressed in a suit of brown with brass buttons, and he wore high boots, which were all roughened and dulled by the sea-water. His face and hands were so dark that he might have been a Spaniard, but as he raised his hat to us we saw that the upper part of his brow was quite white, and that it was from without that he had his swarthiness. He looked from one to the other of us, and his grey eyes had something in them which I had never seen before. You could read the question, but there seemed to be a menace at the back of it, as if the answer were a right and not a favour.

'Great Britain?' he asked again, with a quick tap of his foot on the shingle.

'Yes,' said I, while Jim burst out laughing.

'England? Scotland?'

'Scotland. But it's England past yonder trees.'

'*Bon!* I know where I am now. I've been in a fog without a compass for nearly three days, and I didn't thought I was ever to see land again.' He spoke English glibly enough, but with some strange turn of speech from time to time.

'Where did you come from, then?' asked Jim.

'I was in a ship that was wrecked,' said he shortly. 'What is the town down yonder?'

'It is Berwick.'

'Ah, well, I must get stronger before I can go further.'
He turned towards the boat, and as he did so he gave a
lurch, and would have fallen had he not caught the
prow. On this he seated himself, and looked round him
with a face that was flushed and two eyes that blazed
like a wild beast's.

'*Voltigeurs de la Garde!*' he roared, in a voice like a
trumpet-call, and then again, '*Voltigeurs de la Garde!*'
He waved his hat above his head, and suddenly pitching
forward upon his face on the sand, he lay all huddled
into a little brown heap.

Jim Horscroft and I stood and stared at each other.
The coming of the man had been so strange, and his
questions, and now this sudden turn. We took him by
a shoulder each and turned him upon his back. There
he lay, with his jutting nose and his cat's whiskers, but
his lips were bloodless, and his breath would scarce shake
a feather.

'He's dying, Jim,' I cried.

'Aye, for want of food and water. There's not a drop
or a crumb in the boat. Maybe there's something in the
bag.' He sprang in and brought out a black leather bag,
which, with a large blue coat, was the only thing in the
boat. It was locked, but Jim had it open in an instant. It
was half full of gold-pieces.

Neither of us had ever seen so much before—no, nor a
tenth part of it. There must have been hundreds of them,
all bright new British sovereigns. Indeed, so taken up
were we that we had forgotten all about their owner,
until a groan took our thoughts back to him. His lips
were bluer than ever, and his jaw had dropped. I can see
his open mouth now, with its row of white, wolfish teeth.

'My God! he's off,' cried Jim. 'Here, run to the burn,
Jock, for a hatful of water. Quick, man, or he's gone! I'll
loosen his things the while.'

Away I tore, and was back in a minute with as much
water as would stay in my Glengarry. Jim had pulled
open the man's coat and shirt, and we doused the water

over him, and forced some between his lips. It had a good effect, for after a gasp or two he sat up, and rubbed his eyes slowly, like a man who is waking from a deep sleep. But neither Jim nor I were looking at his face now, for our eyes were fixed on his uncovered chest.

There were two deep red puckers in it, one just below the collar-bone, and the other about half-way down on the right side. The skin of his body was extremely white up to the brown line of his neck, and the angry crinkled spots looked the more vivid against it. From above I could see that there was a corresponding pucker in the back at one place but not at the other. Inexperienced as I was, I could tell what that meant. Two bullets had pierced his chest—one had passed through it, and the other had remained inside.

But suddenly he staggered up to his feet, and pulled his shirt to, with a quick, suspicious glance at us.

'What have I been doing?' he asked. 'I've been off my head. Take no notice of anything I may have said. Have I been shouting?'

'You shouted just before you fell.'

'What did I shout?'

I told him, though it bore little meaning to my mind. He looked sharply at us, and then he shrugged his shoulders.

'It's the words of a song,' said he. 'Well, the question is, what am I to do now? I didn't thought I was so weak. Where did you get the water?'

I pointed towards the burn, and he staggered off to the bank. There he lay down upon his face, and he drank until I thought he would never have done. His long, skinny neck was outstretched like a horse's, and he made a loud, supping noise with his lips. At last he got up, with a long sigh, and wiped his moustache with his sleeve.

'That's better,' said he. 'Have you any food?'

I had crammed two bits of oatcake into my pocket when I left home, and these he crushed into his mouth

595

and swallowed. Then he squared his shoulders, puffed out his chest, and patted his ribs with the flat of his hands.

'I am sure that I owe you exceedingly well,' said he. 'You have been very kind to a stranger. But I see that you have had occasion to open my bag?'

'We hoped that we might find wine or brandy there when you fainted.'

'Ah, I have nothing there but just my little—how do you say it?—my savings. They are not much, but I must live quietly upon them until I find something to do. Now one could live very quietly here, I should say. I could not have come upon a more peaceful place, without, perhaps, so much as a gendarme nearer than that town.'

'You haven't told us yet who you are, where you come from, nor what you have been,' said Jim bluntly.

The stranger looked him up and down with a critical eye. 'My word! but you would make a grenadier for a flank company,' said he. 'As to what you ask, I might take offence at it from other lips, but you have a right to know, since you have received me with so great a courtesy. My name is Bonaventure de Lapp. I am a soldier and a wanderer by trade, and I have come from Dunkirk, as you may see painted upon the boat.'

'I thought that you had been shipwrecked?' said I.

But he looked at me with the straight gaze of an honest man.

'That is right,' said he. 'But the ship went from Dunkirk, and this is one of her boats. The crew got away in the long-boat, and she went down so quickly that I had no time to put anything into her. That was on Monday.'

'And to-day's Thursday. You have been three days without bite or sup.'

'It is too long,' said he. 'Twice before I have been for two days, but never quite so long as this. Well, I shall leave my boat here, and see whether I can get lodgings in any of these little grey houses upon the hillsides. Why is that great fire burning over yonder?'

'It is one of our neighbours who has served against the French. He is rejoicing because peace has been declared.'

'Oh! you have a neighbour who has served, then? I am glad, for I, too, have seen a little soldiering here and there.' He did not look glad, but he drew his brows down over his keen eyes.

'You are French, are you not?' I asked, as we all walked up the hill together, he with his black bag in his hand, and his long blue cloak slung over his shoulder.

'Well, I am of Alsace,' said he. 'And you know they are more German than French. For myself, I have been in so many lands that I feel at home in all. I have been a great traveller. And where do you think that I might find a lodging?'

I can scarcely tell now, on looking back with the great gap of five-and-thirty years between, what impression this singular man had made upon me. I distrusted him, I think, and yet I was fascinated by him also, for there was something in his bearing, in his look, and his whole fashion of speech which was entirely unlike anything that I had ever seen. Jim Horscroft was a fine man, and Major Elliott was a brave one, but they both lacked something that this wanderer had. It was the quick, alert look, the flash of the eye, the nameless distinction which is so hard to fix. And then, we had saved him when he lay gasping on the shingle, and one's heart always softens towards what one has once helped.

'If you will come with me,' said I, 'I have little doubt that I can find you a bed for a night or two, and by that time you will be better able to make your own arrangements.'

He pulled off his hat, and bowed with all the grace imaginable. But Jim Horscroft pulled me by the sleeve and led me aside.

'You're mad, Jock,' he whispered. 'The fellow's a common adventurer. What do you want to get mixed up with him for?'

But I was always as obstinate a man as ever laced his

boots, and if you jerked me back it was the finest way of sending me to the front.

'He's a stranger, and it's our part to look after him,' said I.

'You'll be sorry for it,' said he.

'Maybe so.'

'If you don't think of yourself you might think of your cousin.'

'Edie can take very good care of herself.'

'Well, then, the devil take you, and you may do what you like,' he cried, in one of his sudden flushes of anger. Without a word of farewell to either of us he turned off upon the track that led up towards his father's house.

Bonaventure de Lapp smiled at me as we walked on together.

'I didn't thought he liked me very much,' said he. 'I can see very well that he has made a quarrel with you because you are taking me to your home. What does he think of me then? Does he think, perhaps, that I have stole the gold in my bag, or what is it that he fears?'

'Tut! I neither know nor care,' said I. 'No stranger shall pass our door without a crust and a bed.' With my head cocked, and feeling as if I was doing something very fine, instead of being the most egregious fool south of Edinburgh, I marched on down the path, with my new acquaintance at my elbow.

VI. A Wandering Eagle

MY father seemed to be much of Jim Horscroft's opinion, for he was not over warm to this new guest, and looked him up and down with a very questioning eye. He set a dish of vinegared herrings before him, however, and I noticed that he looked more askance than ever when my companion ate nine of them, for two were always our portion. When at last he had finished, Bonaventure de

Lapp's lids were drooping over his eyes, for I doubt not that he had been sleepless as well as foodless for these three days. It was but a poor room to which I led him, but he threw himself down upon the couch, wrapped his big blue cloak around him, and was asleep in an instant. He was a very high and strong snorer, and, as my room was next to his, I had reason to remember that we had a stranger within our gates.

When I came down in the morning I found that he had been beforehand with me, for he was seated opposite my father at the window-table in the kitchen, their heads almost touching, and a little roll of gold-pieces between them. As I came in my father looked up at me, and I saw a light of greed in his eyes such as I had never seen before. He caught up the money with an eager clutch, and swept it into his pocket.

'Very good, mister,' said he. 'The room's yours, and you pay always on the third of the month.'

'Ah, and here is my first friend,' cried De Lapp, holding out his hand to me with a smile which was kindly enough, and yet had that touch of patronage which a man uses when he smiles to his dog. 'I am myself again now, thanks to my excellent supper and good night's rest. Ah, it is hunger that takes the courage from a man. That most, and cold next.'

'Aye, that's right,' said my father. 'I've been out on the moors in a snow-drift for six-and-thirty hours, and I ken what it is like.'

'I once saw three thousand men starve to death,' remarked De Lapp, putting out his hands to the fire. 'Day by day they got thinner and more like apes, and they did come down to the edge of the pontoons where we did keep them, and they howled with rage and pain. The first few days their howls went over the whole city, but after a week our sentries on the bank could not hear them, so weak they had fallen.'

'And they died?' I exclaimed.

'They held out a very long time. Austrian grenadiers

599

they were, of the corps of Starowitz, fine, stout men, as big as your friend of yesterday, but when the town fell there were but four hundred alive, and a man could lift them three at a time, as if they were little monkeys. It was a pity. Ah, my friend, you will do me the honours with madame and with mademoiselle.'

It was my mother and Edie, who had come into the kitchen. He had not seen them the night before; but now it was all I could do to keep my face as I watched him, for, instead of our homely Scottish nod, he bent up his back like a louping trout, and slid his foot, and clapped his hand over his heart in the queerest way. My mother stared, for she thought he was making fun of her, but Cousin Edie fell into it in an instant, as though it had been a game, and away she went in a great courtesy, until I thought she would have had to give it up, and sit down right there in the middle of the kitchen floor. But no, she was up again as light as a piece of fluff, and we all drew up our stools and started on the scones and milk and porridge.

He had a wonderful way with women, that man. Now, if I were to do it, or Jim Horscroft, it would look as if we were playing the fool, and the girls would have laughed at us; but with him it seemed to go with his style of face and fashion of speech, so that one came at last to look for it. For when he spoke to my mother or to Cousin Edie— and he was never backward in speaking—it would always be with a bow and a look as if it would hardly be worth her while to listen to what he had to say; and when they answered he would put on a face as though every word she said was to be treasured up and remembered for ever. And yet, even while he humbled himself to a woman, there was always a proud sort of look at the back of his eye, as if he meant to say that it was only to them that he was so meek, and that he could be stiff enough upon occasion. As to my mother, it was wonderful the way that she softened to him, and in half an hour she had told him all about her uncle, who was a surgeon in Carlisle, and the highest of any upon her side of the house. She spoke to him about my brother Rob's death, which I had never heard her mention to a soul before, and he looked as if the tears were in his eyes over it—he who had just told us how he had seen three thousand men starved to death. As to Edie, she did not say much, but she kept shooting little glances at our visitor, and once or twice he looked very hard at her.

When he had gone to his room, after breakfast, my father pulled out eight golden pounds, and laid them on the table.

'What think ye of that, Martha?' said he.

'You've sold the two black tups after all?'

'No, but it's a month's pay for board and lodging from Jock's friend, and as much to come every four weeks.'

But my mother shook her head when she heard it. 'Two pounds a week is over-much,' said she. 'And it is not when the poor gentleman is in distress that we should put such a price on his bit food.'

'Tut!' cried my father. 'He can very well afford it, and he with a bagful of gold. Besides, it's his own proposing.'

'No blessing will come from that money,' said she.

'Why, woman, he's turned your head wi' his foreign trick of speech,' cried my father.

'Aye, and it would be a good thing if Scottish men had a little more of that kindly way,' she said, and that was the first time in all my life that I had ever heard her answer him back.

He came down soon, and asked me whether I would come out with him. When we were in the sunshine he held out a little cross made of red stones, one of the bonniest things that ever I had set eyes upon.

'These are rubies,' said he, 'and I got it at Tudela, in Spain. There were two of them, but I gave the other to a Lithuanian girl. I pray that you will take this as a memory of your exceeding kindness to me yesterday. It will fashion into a pin for your cravat.'

I could but thank him for the present, which was of more value than anything I had ever owned in my life.

'I am off to the upper muir to count the lambs,' said I. 'Maybe you would care to come up with me and see something of the country?'

He hesitated for a moment, and then he shook his head.

'I have some letters,' he said, 'which I ought to write as soon as possible. I think that I will stay at quiet this morning and get them written.'

All forenoon I was wandering over the links, and you may imagine that my mind was turning all the time upon this strange man, whom chance had drifted to our doors. Where did he gain that style of his, that manner of command, that haughty, menacing glint of the eye? And his experiences, to which he referred so lightly, how wonderful the life must have been which had put him in the way of them. He had been kind to us, and gracious of speech, but still I could not quite shake myself clear of the distrust with which I had regarded him. Perhaps, after all, Jim Horscroft had been right, and I had been wrong, about taking him to West Inch.

When I got back he looked as though he had been born and bred in the steading. He sat in the big wooden-armed ingle-chair, with the black cat on his knee. His arms were out, and he held a skein of worsted from hand to hand, which my mother was busily rolling into a ball. Cousin Edie was sitting near, and I could see by her eyes that she had been crying.

'Hullo! Edie,' said I; 'what's the trouble?'

'Ah! mademoiselle, like all good and true women, has a soft heart,' said he; 'I didn't thought it would have moved her or I should have been silent. I have been talking of the suffering of some troops of which I knew something, when they were crossing the Guadarama Mountains in the winter of 1808. Ah, yes, it was very bad, for they were fine men and fine horses. It is strange to see men blown by the wind over the precipices, but the ground was so slippy, and there was nothing to which they could hold. So companies all linked arms, and they did better in that fashion; but one artilleryman's hand came off as I held it, for he had had the frost-bite for three days.'

I stood staring, with my mouth open.

'And the old grenadiers, too, who were not so active as they used to be, they could not keep up; and yet if they lingered the peasants would catch them, and crucify them to the barn-doors with their feet up and a fire under their heads, which was a pity for these fine old soldiers. So when they could go no farther, it was interesting to see what they would do. For they would sit down, and say their prayers, sitting on an old saddle, or their knapsacks, maybe, and then take off their boot and their stocking, and lean their chin on the barrel of their musket. Then they would put their toe on the trigger, and pouf! it was all over, and there was no more marching for those fine old grenadiers. Oh! it was very rough work up there on the Guadarama Mountains.'

'And what army was this?' I asked.

'Oh! I have served in so many armies that I mix them up sometimes. Yes, I have seen much of war. Apropos, I have seen your Scotch men fight, and very stout *fantassins* they make; but I thought from them that the folk over here all wore—how do you say it?—petticoats.'

'Those are the kilts, and they wear them only in the Highlands.'

'Ah, on the mountains. But there is a man out yonder. Maybe he is the one who your father said would carry my letters to the post.'

'Yes, he is farmer Whitehead's man. Shall I give them to him?'

'Well, he would be more careful of them if he had them from your hand.' He took them from his pocket, and gave them over to me. I hurried out with them, and as I did so my eyes fell upon the address of the topmost one. It was written very large and clear.

'A S. Majesté
'Le Roi du Suède
'Stockholm.'

I did not know very much French, but I had enough to make that out. What sort of eagle was this which had flown into our humble little nest?

VII. *The Corriemuir Peel-tower*

WELL, it would weary me, and I am very sure that it would weary you also, if I were to attempt to tell you how life went with us after this man came under our roof, or the way in which he gradually came to win the affections of every one of us. With the women it was quick work enough, but soon he had thawed my father, too, which was no such easy matter, and had gained Jim Horscroft's good-will as well as my own. Indeed, we were but two great boys beside him, for he had been everywhere and seen everything, and of an evening he would chatter away in his limping English until he took us clean away from the plain kitchen and the little farm-steading, to plunge us into courts and camps and battle-fields, and all the wonders of the world. Horscroft had been sulky enough with him at first, but De Lapp, with his tact and his easy ways, soon drew him round until he had quite won his heart, and Jim would sit with Cousin Edie's hand in his, and the two be quite lost in listening to all that he had to tell us. I will not tell you all this, but even now, after so long an interval, I can trace how, week by week and month by month, by this word and that deed, he moulded us all as he wished.

One of his first acts was to give my father the boat in which he had come, reserving only the right to have it back in case he should have need of it. The herring were down on the coast that autumn, and my uncle, before he

604

died, had given us a fine set of nets, so the gift was worth many a pound to us. Sometimes De Lapp would go out in the boat alone, and I have seen him for a whole summer day rowing slowly along, and stopping every half-dozen strokes to throw over a stone at the end of a string. I could not think what he was doing until he told me of his own free will.

'I am fond of studying all that has to do with the military,' said he, 'and I never lose a chance. I was wondering if it would be a difficult matter for the commander of an army corps to throw his men ashore here.'

'If the wind were not from the east,' said I.

'Ah, quite so, if the wind were not from the east. Have you taken soundings here?'

'No.'

'Your line-of-battle ships would have to lie outside, but there is water enough for a forty-gun frigate right up within musket range. Cram your boats with *tirailleurs*, deploy them behind these sand-hills, then back with the launches for more, and a stream of grape over their heads from the frigate. It could be done! It could be done!' His moustaches bristled out more like a cat's than ever, and I could see by the flash of his eyes that he was carried away by his dream.

'You forget that our soldiers would be upon the beach,' said I indignantly.

'Ta, ta, ta!' he cried. 'Of course it takes two sides to make a battle. Let us see now! Let us work it out! What could you get together? Shall we say twenty, thirty thousand? A few regiments of good troops. The rest, pouf!— conscripts, bourgeois with arms, how do you call them— volunteers.'

'Brave men!' I shouted.

'Oh yes, very brave men, but imbecile; ah, *mon Dieu!* it is incredible how imbecile they would be. Not they alone, I mean, but all young troops. They are so afraid of being afraid that they would take no precaution. Ah, I have seen it! In Spain I have seen a battalion of conscripts attack a battery of ten pieces. Up they went, ah, so gallantly, and presently the hillside looked, from where I stood, like—how do you say it in English?—a raspberry tart, and where was our fine battalion of conscripts? Then another battalion of young troops tried it, all together in a rush, shouting and yelling, but what will shouting do against a *mitraille*?—and there was our second battalion laid out on the hillside. And then the foot-chasseurs of the Guard, old soldiers, were told to take the battery, and there was nothing fine about their advance, no column, no shouting, nobody killed, just a few scattered lines of *tirailleurs* and *pelotons* of support, but in ten minutes the guns were silenced and the Spanish gunners cut to pieces. War must be learned, my young friend, just the same as the farming of sheep.'

'Pooh!' said I, not to be outcrowed by a foreigner. 'If we had thirty thousand men on the line of the hill yonder you would come to be very glad that you had your boats behind you.'

'On the line of the hill?' said he, with a flash of his eyes along the ridge. 'Yes, if your man knew his business he would have his left about your house, his centre on Corriemuir, and his right over near the doctor's house, with his *tirailleurs* pushed out thickly in front. His horse, of course, would try to cut us up as we deployed on the beach. But once let us form, and we should soon know what to do. There's the weak point, there at the gap. I would sweep it with my guns, then roll in my cavalry, push the infantry on in grand columns, and that wing would find itself up in the air. Eh, Jack, where would your volunteers be?'

'Close at the heels of your hindmost man,' said I, and we both burst out into the hearty laugh with which such discussions usually ended.

Sometimes, when he talked, I thought he was joking, and at other times it was not quite so easy to say. I well remember one evening that summer when he was sitting in the kitchen with my father, Jim, and me, after the women had gone to bed, he began about Scotland and its relation to England.

'You used to have your own king, and your own laws made at Edinburgh,' said he; 'does it not fill you with rage and despair when you think that it all comes to you from London now?'

Jim took his pipe out of his mouth. 'It was we who put our king over the English, so if there's any rage it should have been over yonder,' said he.

This was clearly news to the stranger, and it silenced him for the moment.

'Well, but your laws are made down there, and surely that is not good,' he said at last.

'No, it would be well to have a Parliament back in Edinburgh,' said my father; 'but I am kept so busy with the sheep that I have little enough time to think of such things.'

'It is for fine young men like you two to think of it,' said De Lapp. 'When a country is injured it is to its young men that it looks to avenge it.'

'Aye, the English take too much upon themselves sometimes,' said Jim.

'Well, if there are many of that way of thinking about, why should we not form them into battalions and march them upon London?' cried De Lapp.

'That would be a rare little picnic,' said I, laughing; 'and who would lead us?'

He jumped up, bowing, with his hand on his heart in his queer fashion. 'If you would allow me to have the honour!' he cried, and then, seeing that we were all laughing, he began to laugh also, but I am sure that there was really no thought of a joke in his mind.

I could never make out what his age could be, nor could Jim Horscroft either. Sometimes we thought that he was an oldish man that looked young, and at others that he was a youngish man who looked old. His brown, stiff, close-cropped hair needed no cropping at the top where it thinned away to a shining curve. His skin, too.

was intersected by a thousand fine wrinkles, lacing and interlacing, and was all burned, as I have already said, by the sun. Yet he was as lithe as a boy, and he was as tough as whalebone, walking all day over the hills, or rowing on the sea, without turning a hair. On the whole, we thought that he might be about forty-five, though it was hard to see how he could have seen so much of life in the time. But one day we got talking of ages, and then he surprised us.

I had been saying that I was just twenty, and Jim said that he was twenty-seven.

'Then I am the most old of the three,' said De Lapp.

We laughed at this, for by our reckoning he might almost have been our father.

'But not by so much,' said he, arching his brows. 'I was nine-and-twenty in December.'

And it was this even more than his talk which made us understand what an extraordinary life it must have been that he had led. He saw our astonishment, and laughed at it.

'I have lived. I have lived,' he cried. 'I have spent my days and my nights. I led a company in a battle where five nations were engaged when I was but fourteen. I made a king turn pale at the words I whispered in his ear when I was twenty. I had a hand in remaking a kingdom and putting a fresh king upon a fresh throne the very year that I came of age. *Mon Dieu!* I have lived my life.'

That was the most that I ever heard him confess of his past life, and he only shook his head and laughed when we tried to get something more out of him. There were times when we thought that he was but a clever impostor —for what could a man of such influence and talents be loitering here in Berwickshire for?—but one day there came an incident which showed us that he had, indeed, a history in the past.

You will remember that there was an old officer of the Peninsular War who lived no great way from us, the same who danced round the bonfire with his sister and the two maids. He had gone up to London on some business about his pension and his wound money and the chance of having some work given him, so that he did not come back until late in the autumn. One of the first days after his return he came down to see us, and there for the first time he clapped eyes on De Lapp. Never in my life did I look upon so astonished a face, and he stared at our friend for a long minute without so much as a word. De Lapp looked back at him equally hard, but there was no recognition in his eyes.

'I do not know who you are, sir,' he said at last, 'but you look at me as if you had seen me before.'

'So I have,' answered the major.

'Never to my knowledge.'

'But I'll swear it!'

'Where, then?'

'At the village of Astorga, in the year '8.'

De Lapp started, and stared again at our neighbour. '*Mon Dieu!* what a chance!' he cried; 'and you were the English *parliamentaire*. I remember you very well indeed, sir. Let me have a whisper in your ear.' He took him aside, and talked very earnestly with him in French for a quarter of an hour, gesticulating with his hands, and explaining something, while the major nodded his old grizzled head from time to time. At last they seemed to come to some agreement, and I heard the major say '*parole d'honneur*' several times, and afterwards '*fortune de la guerre*', which I could very well understand, for they gave you a fine up-bringing at Birtwhistle's. But after that I always noticed that the major never used the same free fashion of speech that we did towards our lodger, but bowed when he addressed him, and treated him with a wonderful deal of respect. I asked the major more than once what he knew about him, but he always put it off, and I could get no answer out of him.

Jim Horscroft was at home all that summer, but late in the autumn he went back to Edinburgh again for the winter session, and as he intended to work very hard, and get his degree next spring if he could, he said that he would bide up there for the Christmas. So there was a great leave-taking between him and Cousin Edie, and he was to put up his plate and to marry her as soon as he had the right to practise. I never knew a man love a woman more fondly than he did her, and she liked him well enough in a way, for indeed in the whole of Scotland she would not find a finer-looking man; but when it came to marriage I think she winced a little at the thought that all her wonderful dreams should end in nothing more than in being the wife of a country surgeon. Still, there was only Jim and me to choose out of, and she took the best of us.

Of course, there was De Lapp also, but we always felt that he was of an altogether different class to us, and so he didn't count. I was never very sure at that time whether Edie cared for him or not. When Jim was at home they took little notice of each other. After he was gone they were thrown more together, which was natural enough, as he had taken up so much of her time before. Once or twice she spoke to me about De Lapp as though she did not like him, and yet she was uneasy if he were not in in the evening, and there was no one so fond of his talk or with so many questions to ask him as she. She made him describe what queens wore, and what sort of carpets they walked on, and whether they had hair-pins in their hair, and how many feathers in their hats, until it was a wonder to me how he could find an answer to it at all. And yet an answer he always had, and was so ready and quick with his tongue, and so anxious to amuse her, that I wondered how it was that she did not like him better.

Well, the summer and the autumn and the best part of the winter passed away, and we were still all very happy together. We got well into the year 1815, and the great emperor was still eating his heart out at Elba, and all the ambassadors were wrangling together at Vienna as to what they should do with the lion's skin, now that they had so fairly hunted him down. And we, in our little corner of Europe, went on with our petty, peaceful business, looking after the sheep, attending the Berwick cattle-fairs, and chatting at night round the blazing peat-fire. We never thought that what all these high and mighty people were doing could have any bearing upon us, and as to war—why, everybody was agreed that the great shadow was lifted from us for ever, and that, unless the Allies quarrelled among themselves, there would not be a shot fired in Europe for another fifty years.

There was one incident, however, that stands out very clearly in my memory—I think that it must have happened about the February of this year—and I will tell it to you before I go any further.

You know what the Border peel-castles are like, I have no doubt. They were just square keeps, built every here and there along the line, so that the folk might have some place of protection against raiders and moss-troopers. When Percy and his men were over the Marches, then the people would drive some of their cattle into the yard of the tower, shut up the big gate, and light a fire in the brazier at the top, which would be answered by all the other peel-towers, until the lights would go twinkling up to the Lammermuir hills, and so carry the news on to the Pentlands and to Edinburgh. But now, of course, all these old keeps were warped and crumbling, and made fine nesting-places for the wild birds. Many a good egg have I had for my collection out of the Corriemuir peel-tower.

One day I had been a very long walk, away over to leave a message at the Laidlaw Armstrongs, who live two miles on this side of Ayton. About five o'clock, just before the sunset, I found myself on the brae-path, with the gable end of West Inch peeping up in front of me, and the old peel-tower lying on my left. I turned my eyes on the keep, for it looked so fine with the flush of the level sun beating full upon it, and the blue sea stretching out behind. And as I stared I suddenly saw the face of a man twinkle for a moment in one of the holes in the wall.

Well, I stood and wondered over this, for what could anybody be doing in such a place, now that it was too early for the nesting season? It was so queer that I was determined to come to the bottom of it; so, tired as I was, I turned my shoulder on home, and walked swiftly towards the tower. The grass stretches right up to the very base of the wall, and my feet made little noise until I reached the crumbling arch where the old gate used to be. I peeped through, and there was Bonaventure de Lapp, standing inside the keep, and peeping out through the very hole at which I had seen his face. He was turned half away from me, and it was clear that he had not seen me at all, for he was staring with all his eyes over in the direction of West Inch. As I advanced, my foot rattled the rubble that lay in the gateway, and he turned round with a start and faced me.

He was not a man whom you could put out of countenance, and his face changed no more than if he had been expecting me there for a twelvemonth, but there was something in his eyes which let me know that he would have paid a good price to have me back on the brae-path again.

'Hullo!' said I, 'what are you doing here?'

'I may ask you that,' said he.

'I came up because I saw your face at the window.'

'And I because, as you may well have observed, I have very much interest for all that has to do with the military, and of course castles are among them. You will excuse me for one moment, my dear Jack,' and he stepped out suddenly through the hole in the wall, so as to be out of my sight.

But I was very much too curious to excuse him so easily. I shifted my ground swiftly, to see what it was that he was after. He was standing outside, and waving his hand frantically, as in a signal.

'What are you doing?' I cried, and then, running out to his side, I looked across the moors, to see whom he was beckoning to.

'You go too far, sir,' said he angrily; 'I didn't thought you would have gone so far. A gentleman has the freedom to act as he choose, without your being the spy upon him. If we are to be friends, you must not interfere in my affairs.'

'I don't like these secret doings,' said I, 'and my father would not like them, either.'

'Your father can speak for himself, and there is no secret,' said he curtly. 'It is you, with your imaginings, that make a secret. Ta, ta, ta! I have no patience with such foolishness.' And, without so much as a nod, he turned his back upon me and started walking swiftly to West Inch.

Well, I followed him, and in the worst of tempers, for I had a feeling that there was some mischief in the wind, and yet I could not for the life of me think what it all meant. Again I found myself puzzling over the whole mystery of this man's coming, and of his long residence among us. And whom could he have expected to meet at the peel-tower? Was the fellow a spy? and was it some brother spy who came to speak with him there? But that was absurd. What could there be to spy about in Berwickshire? And besides, Major Elliott knew all about him, and he would not show him such respect if there were anything amiss.

I had just got as far as this in my thoughts when I heard a cheery hail, and there was the major himself, coming down the hill from his house, with his big bulldog, Bounder, held in leash. This dog was a savage creature, and had caused more than one accident on the country side, but the major was very fond of it, and would never go out without it, though he kept it tied with a good, thick thong of leather. Well, just as I was looking at the major, waiting for him to come up, he stumbled with his lame leg over a branch of gorse, and in recovering himself he let go his hold of the leash, and in an instant there was the beast of a dog flying down the hillside in my direction.

I did not like it, I can tell you, for there was neither stick nor stone about, and I knew that the brute was dangerous. The major was shrieking to it from behind, and I think that the creature thought that he was hallooing it on, so furiously did it rush. But I knew its name, and I thought that maybe that might give me the privileges of acquaintanceship; so, as it came at me with bristling hair and its nose screwed back between its two red eyes, I cried out, 'Bounder! Bounder!' at the pitch of my lungs. It had its effect, for the beast passed me with a snarl, and flew along the path on the traces of Bonaventure de Lapp.

He turned at the shouting, and seemed to take in the whole thing at a glance, but he strolled along as slowly as ever. My heart was in my mouth for him, for the dog had never seen him before, and I ran as fast as my feet would carry me to drag it away from him. But somehow, as it bounded up and saw the twittering finger and thumb which De Lapp held out behind him, its fury died suddenly away, and we saw it wagging its thumb of a tail and clawing at his knee.

'Your dog, then, major?' said he, as its owner came hobbling up. 'Ah, it is a fine beast—a fine, pretty thing!'

The major was blowing hard, for he had covered the ground nearly as fast as I had.

'I was afraid lest he might have hurt you,' he panted.

'Ta, ta, ta!' cried De Lapp. 'He is a pretty, gentle thing. I always love the dogs. But I am glad that I have met you, major, for here is this young gentleman, to whom I owe very much, who has begun to think that I am a spy. Is it not so, Jack?'

I was so taken aback by his words that I could not lay my tongue to an answer, but coloured up and looked askance, like the awkward country lad that I was.

'You know me, major,' said De Lapp; 'and I am sure that you will tell him that this could not be.'

'No, no, Jack! Certainly not! Certainly not!' cried the major.

'Thank you,' said De Lapp. 'You know me, and you do me justice. And yourself, I hope that your knee is better, and that you will soon have your regiment given you.'

'I am well enough,' answered the major; 'but they will never give me a place unless there is war, and there will be no more war in my time.'

'Oh! you think that?' said De Lapp, with a smile. 'Well, *nous verrons!* We shall see, my friend!' He whisked off his hat, and, turning briskly, he walked off in the direction of West Inch. The major stood looking after him with thoughtful eyes, and then asked me what it was that had made me think that he was a spy. When I told him he said nothing, but he shook his head, and looked like a man who was ill at ease in his mind.

VIII. *The Coming of the Cutter*

I NEVER felt quite the same to our lodger after that little business at the peel-tower. It was always in my mind that he was holding a secret from me; indeed, that he was all a secret together, seeing that he always hung a veil over his past. And when, by chance, that veil was for an instant whisked away, we always caught just a glimpse of something bloody and violent and dreadful upon the other side. The very look of his body was terrible. I bathed with him once in the summer, and I saw then that he was haggled with wounds all over. Besides seven or eight scars and slashes, his ribs on one side were twisted out of shape, and a part of one of his calves had been torn away. He laughed in his merry way when he saw my face of wonder.

'Cossacks! Cossacks!' said he, running his hand over his

615

scars. 'And the ribs were broke by an artillery tumbril. It is very bad to have the guns pass over one. Now, with cavalry it is nothing. A horse will pick its steps, however fast it may go. I have been ridden over by fifteen hundred cuirassiers and by the Russian hussars of Grodno, and I had no harm from that. But guns are very bad.'

'And the calf?' I asked.

'Poof! It is only a wolf-bite,' said he. 'You would not think how I came by it! You will understand that my horse and I had been struck, the horse killed, and I with my ribs broken by the tumbril. Well, it was cold—oh, bitter, bitter!—the ground like iron, and no one to help the wounded, so that they froze into such shapes as would make you smile. I, too, felt that I was freezing, so what did I do? I took my sword, and I opened my dead horse, so well as I could, and I made space in him for me to lie, with one little hole for my mouth. *Sapristi!* It was warm enough there. But there was not room for the entire of me, so my feet and part of my legs stuck out. Then in the night, when I slept, there came the wolves to eat the horse, and they had a little pinch of me also, as you can see; but after that I was on guard with my pistols, and they had no more of me. There I lived, very warm and nice, for ten days.'

'Ten days!' I cried. 'What did you eat?'

'Why, I ate the horse. It was what you call board and lodging to me. But, of course, I have sense to eat the legs and live in the body. There were many dead about who had their water-bottles, so I had all I could wish. And on the eleventh day there came a patrol of light cavalry, and all was well.'

It was by such chance chats as these—hardly worth repeating in themselves—that there came light upon himself and his past. But the day was coming when we should know all, and how it came I shall try now to tell you.

The winter had been a dreary one, but with March came the first signs of spring, and for a week on end we had sunshine and winds from the south. On the seventh Jim Horscroft was to come back from Edinburgh, for though the session ended with the first, his examination would take him a week. Edie and I were out walking on the sea-beach on the sixth, and I could talk of nothing but my old friend, for, indeed, he was the only friend of my own age that I had at that time. Edie was very silent, which was a rare thing with her, but she listened, smiling, to all that I had to say.

'Poor old Jim!' said she, once or twice, under her breath. 'Poor old Jim!'

'And if he has passed,' said I, 'why then, of course, he will put up his plate, and have his own house, and we shall be losing our Edie.' I tried to make a jest of it, and to speak lightly, but the words still stuck in my throat.

'Poor old Jim!' said she again, and there were tears in her eyes as she said it. 'And poor old Jock!' she added, slipping her hand into mine as we walked. 'You cared for me a little bit once also, didn't you, Jock? Oh! is not that a sweet little ship out yonder?'

It was a dainty cutter of about thirty tons, very swift, by the rake of her masts and the lines of her bow. She was coming up from the south under jib, foresail, and mainsail, but, even as we watched her, all her white canvas shut suddenly in, like a kittiewake closing her wings, and we saw the splash of her anchor just under her bowsprit. She may have been rather less than a quarter of a mile from the shore—so near that I could see a tall man with a peaked cap, who stood at the quarter with a telescope to his eye, sweeping it backwards and forwards along the coast.

'What can they want here?' asked Edie.

'They are rich English from London,' said I, for that was how we explained everything that was above our comprehension in the Border counties. We stood for the best part of an hour watching the bonny craft, and then, as the sun was lying low on a cloud-bank and there was a nip in the evening air, we turned back to West Inch.

617

As you come to the farm-house from the front you pass up a garden, with little enough in it, which leads out by a wicket gate to the road—the same gate at which we stood on the night when the beacons were lit, the night that we saw Walter Scott ride past on his way to Edinburgh. On the right of this gate, on the garden side, was a bit of a rockery, which was said to have been made by my father's mother many years before. She had fashioned it out of water-worn stones and sea-shells, with mosses and ferns in the chinks. Well, as we came in through the gate, my eyes fell upon this stone-heap, and there was a letter stuck in a cleft stick upon the top of it. I took a step forward to see what it was, but Edie sprang in front of me, and, plucking it off, she thrust it into her pocket.

'That's for me,' said she, laughing.

But I stood looking at her, with a face which drove the laugh from her lips.

'Who is it from, Edie?' I asked.

She pouted, but made no answer.

'Who is it from, woman?' I cried. 'Is it possible that you have been as false to Jim as you were to me?'

'How rude you are, Jack!' she cried. 'I do wish that you would mind your own business.'

'There is only one person that it could be from,' I cried. 'It is from this man De Lapp.'

'And suppose that you are right, Jack?'

The coolness of the woman amazed and enraged me. 'You confess it!' I cried. 'Have you, then, no shame left?'

'Why should I not receive letters from this gentleman?'

'Because it is infamous.'

'And why?'

'Because he is a stranger.'

'On the contrary,' said she, 'he is my husband.'

IX. *The Doings at West Inch*

I CAN remember that moment so well. I have heard from others that a great sudden blow has dulled their senses. It was not so with me. On the contrary, I saw and heard and thought more clearly than I had ever done before. I can remember that my eyes caught a little knob of marble as broad as my palm, which was embedded in one of the grey stones of the rockery, and I found time to admire its delicate mottling. And yet the look upon my face must have been strange, for Cousin Edie screamed, and leaving me she ran off to the house. I followed her, and tapped at the window of her room, for I could see that she was there.

'Go away, Jack, go away!' she cried. 'You are going to scold me. I won't be scolded! I won't open the window! Go away!'

But I continued to tap. 'I must have a word with you,' I cried.

'What is it, then?' she asked, raising the sash about three inches. 'The moment you begin to scold I shall close it.'

'Are you really married, Edie?'

'Yes, I am married.'

'Who married you?'

'Father Brennan, at the Roman Catholic chapel at Berwick.'

'And you a Presbyterian!'

'He wished it to be in a Catholic church.'

'When was it?'

'On Wednesday week.'

I remembered, then, that on that day she had driven over to Berwick, while De Lapp had been away on a long walk, as he said, among the hills.

'What about Jim?' I asked.

'Oh! Jim will forgive me.'

'You will break his heart and ruin his life.'

'No, no; he will forgive me.'

619

'He will murder De Lapp. Oh, Edie! how could you bring such disgrace and misery upon us?'

'Ah, now you are scolding!' she cried, and down came the window.

I waited some little time and tapped, for I had much still to ask her; but she would return no answer, and I thought that I could hear her sobbing. At last I gave it up, and was about to go into the house, for it was nearly dark now, when I heard the click of the garden gate. It was De Lapp himself.

But as he came up the path he seemed to me to be either mad or drunk. He danced as he walked, cracked his fingers in the air, and his eyes blazed like two will-o'-the-wisps. *'Voltigeurs!'* he shouted—*'voltigeurs de la garde!'*—just as he had done when he was off his head, and then suddenly *'En avant! en avant!'* and up he came, waving his walking-cane over his head. He stopped short when he saw me looking at him, and I dare say he felt a bit ashamed of himself.

'Hallo, Jack!' he cried, 'I didn't thought anybody was there. I am in what you call the high spirits to-night.'

'So it seems!' said I, in my blunt fashion. 'You may not feel so merry when my friend, Jim Horscroft, comes back to-morrow.'

'Ah, he comes back to-morrow, does he? And why should I not feel merry?'

'Because, if I know the man, he will kill you.'

'Ta, ta, ta!' cried De Lapp. 'I see that you know of our marriage. Edie has told you. Jim may do what he likes.'

'You have given us a nice return for having taken you in.'

'My good fellow,' said he, 'I have, as you say, given you a very nice return. I have taken Edie from a life which is unworthy of her, and I have connected you by marriage with a noble family. However, I have some letters which I must write to-night, and the rest we can talk over to-morrow when your friend Jim is here to help us.' He stepped towards the door.

620

'And this was whom you were awaiting at the peel-tower!' I cried, seeing light suddenly.

'Why, Jack, you are becoming quite sharp,' said he, in a mocking tone, and an instant later I heard the door of his room close and the key turn in the lock. I thought that I should see him no more that night, but a few minutes later he came into the kitchen where I was sitting with the old folk.

'Madame,' said he, bowing down with his hand to his heart in his own queer fashion, 'I have met with much kindness in your hands, and it shall always be in my heart. I didn't thought I could have been so happy in the quiet country as you have made me. You will accept this small souvenir, and you, also, sir, you will take this little gift which I have the honour to make to you.' He put two paper packets down upon the table at their elbows, and then, with three more bows to my mother, he walked from the room.

His present was a brooch with a green stone set in the middle, and a dozen little shining white ones all round it. We had never seen such things before, and did not know how to set a name to them, but they told us afterwards at Berwick that the big one was an emerald and that the others were diamonds, and that they were worth more than all the lambs we had that spring. My dear old mother has been gone now this many a year, but that bonny brooch sparkles at the neck of my eldest daughter when she goes out into company, and I never look at it that I do not see the keen eyes, and the long, thin nose, and the cat's whiskers of our lodger at West Inch. As to my father, he had a fine gold watch with a double case, and a proud man was he as he sat with it in the palm of his hand, his ear stooping to hearken to the tick. I do not know which was best pleased, and they would talk of nothing but what De Lapp had given them.

'He's given you something more,' said I, at last.

'What then, Jock?'

'A husband for Cousin Edie,' said I.

They thought I was daffing when I said that, but when they came to understand that it was the real truth, they were as pleased as if I had told them that she had married the laird. Indeed, poor Jim, with his hard drinking and his fighting, had not a very bright name on the country-side, and my mother had often said that no good could come of such a match. Now De Lapp was, for all we knew, steady and quiet and well-to-do; and as to the secrecy of it, secret marriages were very common in Scotland at that time, when only a few words were needed to make man and wife, so nobody thought much of that. The old folk were as pleased, then, as if their rent had been lowered, but I was still sore at heart, for it seemed to me that my friend had been cruelly dealt with, and I knew well that he was not a man who would easily put up with it.

X. *The Return of the Shadow*

I WOKE with a heavy heart the next morning, for I knew that Jim would be home before long, and that it would be a day of trouble. But how much trouble that day was to bring, or how far it would alter the lives of all of us, was more than I had ever thought in my darkest moments. But let me tell you it all, just in the order that it happened.

I had to get up early that morning, for it was just the first flush of the lambing, and my father and I were out on the moors as soon as it was fairly light. As I came out into the passage a wind struck upon my face, and there was the house-door wide open and the grey light drawing another door upon the inner wall. And when I looked again, there was Edie's room open also, and De Lapp's too, and I saw in a flash what that giving of presents meant upon the evening before. It was a leave-taking, and they were gone.

My heart was bitter against Cousin Edie as I stood looking into her room. To think that for the sake of a new-comer she could leave us all without one kindly word or as much as a hand-shake. And he, too! I had been afraid of what would happen when Jim met him, but now there seemed to be something cowardly in this avoidance of him. I was angry and hurt and sore, and I went out into the open without a word to my father, and climbed up on to the moors to cool my flushed face.

When I got up to Corriemuir I caught my last glimpse of Cousin Edie. The little cutter still lay where she had anchored, but a row-boat was pulling out to her from the shore. In the stern I saw a flutter of red, and I knew that it came from her shawl. I watched the boat reach the yacht, and the folk climb on to her deck. Then the anchor came up, the white wings spread once more, and away she dipped right out to sea. I still saw that little red spot on the deck, and De Lapp standing beside her. They could see me also, for I was outlined against the sky, and they both waved their hands for a long time, but gave it up at last when they found that I would give them no answer.

I stood with my arms folded, feeling as glum as ever I did in my life, until their cutter was only a square, flickering patch of white among the mists of the morning. It was breakfast-time, and the porridge upon the table, before I got back, but I had no heart for the food. The old folk had taken the matter coolly enough, though my mother had no word too hard for Edie, for the two had never had much love for each other, and less of late than ever.

'There's a letter here from him,' said my father, pointing to a note folded up on the table. 'It was in his room. Maybe you would read it to us.' They had not even opened it, for, truth to tell, neither of the good folk were very clever at reading ink, though they could do well with a fine large print.

It was addressed, in big letters, to 'The good people of

West Inch,' and this was the note which lies before me, all stained and faded, as I write:

'MY FRIENDS,—I didn't thought to have left you so suddenly, but the matter was in other hands than mine. Duty and honour have called me back to my old comrades. This you will doubtless understand before many days are passed. I take your Edie with me as my wife, and it may be that in some more peaceful time you will see us again at West Inch. Meanwhile accept the assurance of my affection, and believe me that I shall never forget the quiet months which I spent with you at the time when my life would have been worth a week at the utmost had I been taken by the Allies. But the reason of this you may also learn some day.

'Yours,
'BONAVENTURE DE LISSAC,
'Colonel des Voltigeurs de la Garde, et aide-de-camp de S. M. l'Empereur Napoleon.'

I whistled when I came to these words, written under his name; for though I had long made up my mind that our lodger could be none other than one of those wonderful soldiers of whom we had heard so much, who had forced their way into every capital of Europe, save only our own, still I had little thought that our roof covered Napoleon's own aide-de-camp and a colonel of his Guard.

'So,' said I, 'De Lissac is his name, and not De Lapp. Well, colonel or no, it is as well for him that he got away from here before Jim laid hands upon him. And time enough too,' I added, peeping out at the kitchen window, 'for here is the man himself coming through the garden.'

I ran to the door to meet him, feeling that I would have given a deal to have him back in Edinburgh again. He came running, waving a paper over his head, and I thought that maybe he had had a note from Edie, and that it was all known to him. But, as he came up, I saw that it was a big, stiff, yellow paper, which crackled as he waved it, and that his eyes were dancing with happiness.

'Hurrah! Jock,' he shouted. 'Where is Edie? Where is Edie?'

'What is it, man?' I asked.

'Where is Edie?'

'What have you there?'

'It's my diploma, Jock. I can practise when I like. It's all right. I want to show it to Edie.'

'The best you can do is to forget all about Edie,' said I.

Never have I seen a man's face change as his did when I said these words.

'What! What d'ye mean, Jock Calder?' he stammered. He let go his hold of the precious diploma as he spoke, and away it went over the hedge and across the moor, where it stuck flapping on a whin-bush, but he never so much as glanced at it. His eyes were bent upon me, and I saw the devil's spark glimmer up in the depths of them.

'She is not worthy of you,' said I.

He gripped me by the shoulder. 'What have you done,' he whispered. 'This is some of your hanky-panky. Where is she?'

'She's off with that Frenchman who lodged here.' I had been casting about in my mind how I could break it gently to him; but I was always backward in speech, and I could think of nothing better than this.

'Oh!' said he; and stood nodding his head and looking at me, though I knew very well that he could neither see me, nor the steading, nor anything else. So he stood for a minute or more, with his hands clenched and his head still nodding. Then he gave a gulp in his throat, and spoke in a queer, dry, rasping voice.

'When was this?' said he.

'This morning.'

'Were they married?'

'Yes.'

He put his hand against the door-post to steady himself.

'Any message for me?'

'She said that you would forgive her.'

'May God blast my soul on the day I do. Where have they gone to?'

'To France, I should judge.'

'His name was De Lapp, I think?'

'His real name is De Lissac, and he is no less than a colonel in Boney's Guards.'

'Ah, he would be in Paris likely! That is well. That is well!'

'Hold up!' I shouted. 'Father! father! Bring the brandy!'

His knees had given way for an instant, but he was himself again before the old man came running with the bottle.

'Take it away!' said he.

'Have a soop, Mister Horscroft,' cried my father, pressing it upon him. 'It will give you fresh heart!'

He caught hold of the bottle, and sent it flying over the garden hedge.

'It's very good for those who wish to forget,' said he; 'I am going to remember.'

'May God forgive you for sinfu' waste,' cried my father aloud.

'And for well-nigh braining an officer of His Majesty's infantry,' said old Major Elliott, putting his head over the hedge. 'I could have done with a nip after a morning's walk, but it is something new to have a whole bottle whiz past my ear. But what is amiss, that you all stand round like mutes at a burying?'

In a few words I told him our trouble, while Jim, with a grey face and his brows drawn down, stood leaning against the door-post. The major was as glum as we by the time I had finished, for he was fond both of Jim and of Edie.

'Tut, tut!' said he. 'I feared something of the kind ever since that business of the peel-tower. It's the way with the French. They can't leave the women alone. But at least De Lissac has married her, and that's a comfort. But it's no time now to think of our own little troubles, with all Europe in a roar again, and another twenty years' war before us, as like as not.'

'What d'ye mean?' I asked.

'Why, man, Napoleon's back from Elba, his troops have flocked to him, and Louis has run for his life. The news was in Berwick this morning.'

'Great Lord!' cried my father. 'Then the weary business is all to do over again.'

'Aye, we thought we were out from the shadow, but it's still there. Wellington is ordered from Vienna to the Low Countries, and it is thought that the emperor will break out first on that side. Well, it's a bad wind that blows nobody any good. I've just had news that I'm to join the Seventy-first as senior major.'

I shook hands with our good neighbour on this, for I knew how it had lain on his mind that he should be a cripple, with no part to play in the world.

'I am to join my regiment as soon as I can, and we shall be over yonder in a month, and in Paris, maybe, before another one is over.'

'By the Lord, then, I'm with you, major!' cried Jim Horscroft. 'I'm not too proud to carry a musket, if you will put me in front of this Frenchman.'

'My lad, I'd be proud to have you serve under me,' said the major. 'And as to De Lissac, where the emperor is, he will be.'

'You know the man,' said I; 'what can you tell us of him?'

'There is no better officer in the French army, and that is a big word to say. They say that he would have been a marshal, but he preferred to stay at the emperor's elbow. I met him two days before Corunna, when I was sent with a flag to speak about our wounded. He was with Soult then. I knew him again when I saw him.'

'And I will know him again when I see him,' said Horscroft, with the old dour look on his face.

And then at that instant, as I stood there, it was

627

suddenly driven home to me how poor and purposeless a life I should lead while this crippled friend of ours and the companion of my boyhood were away in the fore-front of the storm. Quick as a flash my resolution was taken.

'I'll come with you, too, major,' I cried.

'Jock! Jock!' said my father, wringing his hands.

Jim said nothing, but he put his arm half round me, and hugged me. The major's eye shone, and he flourished his cane in the air.

'My word! but I shall have two good recruits at my heels,' said he. 'Well, there's no time to be lost, so you must both be ready for the evening coach.'

And this was what a single day brought about, and yet years pass away so often without a change. Just think of the alteration in that four-and-twenty hours. De Lissac was gone. Edie was gone. Napoleon had escaped. War had broken out. Jim Horscroft had lost everything, and he and I were setting out to fight against the French. It was all like a dream, until I tramped off to the coach that evening, and looked back at the grey farm-steading, and at the two little dark figures—my mother, with her face sunk in her Shetland shawl, and my father, waving his drover's stick to hearten me upon my way.

XI. *The Gathering of the Nations*

AND now I come to a bit of my story that clean takes my breath away as I think of it, and makes me wish that I had never taken the job of telling it in hand. For when I write I like things to come slow and orderly and in their turn—like sheep coming out of a paddock. So it was at West Inch; but now that we were drawn into a larger life, like wee bits of straw that float slowly down some lazy ditch until they suddenly find themselves in the dash and swirl of a great river, then it is very hard for me, with my simple words, to keep pace with it all. But you can find the cause and reason of everything in the books about history, and so I shall just leave that alone, and talk about what I saw with my own eyes and heard with my own ears.

The regiment to which our friend had been appointed was the Seventy-first Highland Light Infantry, which wore the red coat and the trews, and had its depot in Glasgow town. There we went, all three, by coach, the major in great spirits and full of stories about the Duke and the Peninsula, while Jim sat in the corner, with his lips set and his arms folded, and I knew that he killed De Lissac three times an hour in his heart. I could tell it by the sudden glint of his eyes and the grip of his hand. As to me, I did not know whether to be glad or sorry; for home is home, and it is a weary thing, however you may brazen it out, to feel that half Scotland is between you and your mother.

We were in Glasgow next day, and the major took us down to the depot, where a soldier, with three stripes on his arm and a fistful of ribbons from his cap, showed every tooth he had in his head at the sight of Jim, and walked three times round him, to have the view of him as if he had been Carlisle Castle. Then he came over to me, and felt my muscle, and was nigh as pleased as with Jim.

'These are the sort, major; these are the sort,' he kept on saying. 'With a thousand of these we could stand up to Boney's best.'

'How do they run?' asked the major.

'A poor show,' said he, 'but they may lick into shape. The best men have been drafted to America, and we are full of militiamen and recruities.'

'Tut, tut!' said the major. 'We'll have old soldiers and good ones against us. Come to me if you need any help, you two.' And so, with a nod, he left us, and we began to understand that a major who is your officer is a very different person from a major who happens to be your neighbour in the country.

Well, well, why should I trouble you with these things? I could wear out a good quill pen just writing about what we did, Jim and I, at the depot in Glasgow, and how we came to know our officers and our comrades, and how they began to know us. Soon came the news that the folk at Vienna, who had been cutting up Europe as if it had been a jigget of mutton, had flown back, each to his own country, and that every man and horse in their armies had their faces towards France.

We heard of great reviews and musterings in Paris too, and then that Wellington was in the Low Countries, and that on us and on the Prussians would fall the first blow. The government was shipping men over to him as fast as they could, and every port along the east coast was choked with guns and horses and stores. On the third of June we had our marching-orders also, and on the same day we took ship from Leith, reaching Ostend the night after. It was my first sight of a foreign land, and, indeed, most of my comrades were the same, for we were very young in the ranks. I can see the blue water now, and the curling surf-line, and the long, yellow beach, and queer windmills twisting and turning—a thing that a man would not see from one end of Scotland to the other. It was a clean, well-kept town, but the folk were under-sized, and there was neither ale nor oatmeal cakes to be bought amongst them.

From there we went on to a place called Bruges, and from there to Ghent, where we picked up with the Fifty-second and the Ninety-fifth, which were the two regiments that we were brigaded with. It's a wonderful place for churches and stonework, is Ghent; and, indeed, of all the towns we were in, there was scarce one but had a finer kirk than any in Glasgow. From there we pushed on to Ath, which is a little village on a river, or a burn rather, called the Dender. There we were quartered—in tents mostly, for it was fine, sunny weather—and the whole brigade set to work at its drill from morning till evening. General Adams was our chief, and Reynell was our colonel, and they were both fine old soldiers; but what put heart into us most was to think that we were under the Duke, for his name was like a bugle-call. He was at Brussels with the bulk of the army, but we knew that we should see him quick enough if he were needed.

I had never seen so many English together, and, indeed, I had a kind of contempt for them, as folk always have if they live near a border. But the two regiments that were with us now were as good comrades as could be wished. The Fifty-second had a thousand men in the ranks, and there were many old soldiers of the Peninsula among them. They came from Oxfordshire for the most part. The Ninety-fifth were a rifle regiment, and had dark-green coats instead of red. It was strange to see them loading, for they would put the ball in a greasy rag and then hammer it down with a mallet, but they could fire both farther and straighter than we. All that part of Belgium was covered with British troops at that time, for the Guards were over near Enghien, and there were cavalry regiments on the farther side of us. You see, it was very necessary that Wellington should spread out all his force, for Boney was behind the screen of his fortresses, and, of course, we had no means of saying on what side he might pop out, except that he was pretty sure to come the way that we least expected him. On the one side he might get between us and the sea, and so cut us off from England; and on the other he might shove in between the Prussians and ourselves. But the Duke was as clever as he, for he had his horse and his light troops all round him, like a great spider's web, so that the moment a French foot stepped across the border he could close up all his men at the right place.

For myself, I was very happy at Ath, and I found the folk very kindly and homely. There was a farmer, of the name of Bois, in whose fields we were quartered, who was a real good friend to many of us. We built him a wooden barn among us in our spare time, and many a time I and Jeb Seaton, my rear-rank man, have hung out his washing, for the smell of the wet linen seemed to take us both straight home as nothing else could do. I have often wondered whether that good man and his wife are still living, though I think it hardly likely, for they were of a hale middle-age at the time. Jim would come with us too sometimes, and would sit with us smoking in the big Flemish kitchen, but he was a different Jim now to the old one. He had always had a hard touch in him, but now his trouble seemed to have turned him to flint, and I never saw a smile upon his face, and seldom heard a word from his lips. His whole mind was set on revenging himself upon De Lissac for having taken Edie from him, and he would sit for hours, with his chin upon his hands, glaring and frowning, all wrapped in the one idea. This made him a bit of a butt among the men at first, and they laughed at him for it; but when they came to know him better they found that he was not a good man to laugh at, and then they dropped it.

We were early risers at that time, and the whole brigade was usually under arms at the first flush of dawn. One morning—it was the sixteenth of June—we had just formed up, and General Adams had ridden up to give some order to Colonel Reynell, within a musket-length of where I stood, when suddenly they both stood staring along the Brussels road. None of us dared move our heads, but every eye in the regiment whisked round, and there we saw an officer, with the cockade of a general's aide-de-camp, thundering down the road as hard as a great dapple-grey horse could carry him. He bent his face over its mane, and flogged at its neck with the slack of the bridle, as though he rode for very life.

'Hullo, Reynell,' says the general. 'This begins to look like business. What do you make of it?' They both cantered their horses forward, and Adams tore open the despatch which the messenger handed to him. The envelope had not touched the ground before he turned, waving the letter over his head as if it had been a sabre.

'Dismiss!' he cried. 'General parade and march in half an hour.'

Then, in an instant, all was buzz and bustle, and the news on every lip. Napoleon had crossed the frontier the day before, had pushed the Prussians before him, and was already deep in the country to the east of us with a hundred and fifty thousand men. Away we scuttled to gather our things together and have our breakfast, and in an hour we had marched off and left Ath and the Dender behind us forever. There was good need for haste, for the Prussians had sent no news to Wellington of what was doing, and though he had rushed from Brussels at the first whisper of it, like a good old mastiff from its kennel, it was hard to see how he could come up in time to help the Prussians.

It was a bright, warm morning, and as the brigade tramped down the broad Belgian road the dust rolled up from it like the smoke of a battery. I tell you that we blessed the man that planted the poplars along the sides, for their shadow was better than drink to us. Over across the fields, both to the right and the left, were other roads, one quite close and the other a mile or more from us. A column of infantry was marching down the near one, and it was a fair race between us, for we were each walking for all we were worth. There was such a wreath of dust round them that we could only see the gun-barrels and the bearskins breaking out here and there, with the head and shoulders of a mounted officer coming out above the cloud, and the flutter of the colours. It was a brigade of the Guards, but we could not tell which, for we had two of them with us in the campaign. On the far road there was also dust and to spare, but through it there flashed every now and then a long twinkle of brightness, like a hundred silver beads threaded in a line, and the breeze brought down such a snarling, clanging, clashing kind of music as I had never listened to. If I had been left to myself it would have been long before I knew what it was, but our corporals and sergeants were all old soldiers, and I had one trudging along with his halbert at my elbow, who was full of precept and advice.

'That's heavy horse,' said he. 'You see that double twinkle. That means they have helmet as well as cuirass. It's the Royals or the Enniskillens or the Household. You can hear their cymbals and kettles. The French heavies are too good for us. They have ten to our one, and good men, too. You've got to shoot at their faces, or else at their horses. Mind you that when you see them coming, or else you'll find a four-foot sword stuck through your liver to teach you better. Hark! hark! hark! there's the old music again!'

And as he spoke there came the low grumbling of a cannonade away somewhere to the east of us, deep and hoarse, like a roar of some blood-daubed beast that thrives on the lives of men. At the same instant there was shouting of 'Heh! heh! heh!' from behind, and somebody roared, 'Let the guns get through!' Looking back, I saw the rear companies split suddenly in two and hurl themselves down on either side into the ditch, while six cream-coloured horses, galloping two and two, with their bellies to the ground, came thundering through the gap with a fine twelve-pound gun whirling and creaking behind them. Following were another and another, four-and-twenty in all, flying past us with such a din and clatter, the blue-coated men clinging on to the guns and the tumbrils, the drivers cursing and cracking their whips, the manes flying, the mops and buckets clanking, and the whole air filled with the heavy rumble and the jingling of chains. There was a roar from the ditches and a shout from the gunners, and we saw a rolling grey cloud before us, with a score of busbies breaking through the shadow. Then we closed up again, while the growling ahead of us grew louder and deeper than ever.

'There's three batteries there,' said the sergeant. 'There's Bull's and Webber Smith's, but the other is new. There's some more on ahead of us, for here's the track of a nine-pounder, and the others were all twelves.

Choose a twelve if you want to get hit, for a nine mashes you up, but a twelve snaps you like a carrot'—and then he went on to tell about the wonderful wounds that he had seen, until my blood ran like iced water in my veins, and you might have rubbed all our faces in pipe-clay and we should have been no whiter. 'Aye, you'll look sicklier yet when you get a hatful of grape into your tripes,' said he; and then, as I saw some of the old soldiers laughing, I began to understand that this man was trying to frighten us, so I began to laugh also, and the others as well, but it was not a very hearty laugh either.

The sun was almost above us when we stopped at a little place called Hal, where there is an old pump from which I drew and drank a shako full of water—and never did a mug of Scotch ale taste as sweet. More guns passed us here, and Vivian's hussars, three regiments of them, smart men with bonny brown horses, a treat to the eye. The noise of the cannons was louder than ever now, and it tingled through my nerves just as it had done years before when, with Edie by my side, I had seen the merchant ship fight with the privateers. It was so loud now that it seemed to me that the battle must be going on just beyond the nearest wood, but my friend, the sergeant, knew better.

'It's twelve to fifteen miles off,' said he. 'You may be sure that the general knows that we are not wanted, or we should not be resting here at Hal.'

What he said proved to be true, for a minute later down came the colonel with orders that we should stack arms and bivouac where we were, and there we stayed all day, while horse and foot and guns, English, Dutch, and Hanoverians, were streaming through. The devil's music went on till evening, sometimes rising into a roar, sometimes sinking into a grumble, until about eight o'clock in the evening it stopped altogether. We were eating our hearts out, as you may think, to know what it all meant, but we knew that what the Duke did would be for the best, so we just waited in patience.

Next day the brigade remained at Hal in the morning, but about mid-day came an orderly from the Duke, and we pushed on once more until we came to a little village called Braine something, and there we stopped, and time, too, for a sudden thunder-storm came on, and a plump of rain that turned all the roads and the fields into bog and mire. We got into the barns at this village for shelter, and there we found two stragglers, one from a kilted regiment and the other a man of the German Legion, who had a tale to tell that was as dreary as the weather.

Boney had thrashed the Prussians the day before, and our fellows had been sore put to it to hold their own against Ney, but had beaten him off at last. It seems an old, stale story to you now, but you cannot think how we scrambled round those two men in the barn, and pushed and fought, just to catch a word of what they said, and how those who had heard were in turn mobbed by those who had not. We laughed and cheered and groaned all in turn, as we were told how the Forty-fourth had received cavalry in line, how the Dutch-Belgians had fled, and how the Black Watch had taken the lancers into their square, and then had killed them at their leisure. But the lancers had had the laugh on their side when they crumpled up the Sixty-ninth and carried off one of the colours. To wind it all up, the Duke was in retreat, in order to keep in touch with the Prussians, and it was rumoured that he would take up his ground and fight a big battle just at the very place where we had been halted.

And soon we saw that this rumour was true, for the weather cleared towards evening, and we were all out on the ridge to see what we could see. It was such a bonny stretch of corn and grazing land, with the crops just half green and half yellow, and fine rye as high as a man's shoulder. A scene more full of peace you could not think of, and look where you would over the low, curving, corn-covered hills, you could see the little village steeples pricking up their spires among the poplars. But slashed right across this pretty picture was a long trail of marching men, some red, some green, some blue, some black, zigzagging over the plain and choking the roads, one end so close that we could shout to them as they stacked their muskets on the ridge at our left, and the other end lost among the woods as far as we could see. And then on other roads we saw the teams of horses toiling and the dull gleam of the guns, and the men straining and swaying as they helped to turn the spokes in the deep, deep mud. As we stood there, regiment after regiment and brigade after brigade took position on the ridge, and ere the sun had set we lay in a line of over sixty thousand men, blocking Napoleon's way to Brussels. But the rain had come swishing down again, and we of the Seventy-first rushed off to our barn once more, where we had better quarters than the greater part of our comrades, who lay stretched in the mud, with the storm beating upon them, until the first peep of day.

XII. The Shadow on the Land

IT was still drizzling in the morning, with brown, drifting clouds and a damp, chilly wind. It was a queer thing for me as I opened my eyes to think that I should be in a battle that day, though none of us ever thought it would be such a one as it proved to be. We were up and ready, however, with the first light, and as we threw open the doors of our barn we heard the most lovely music that I had ever listened to playing somewhere in the distance. We all stood in clusters hearkening to it, it was so sweet and innocent and sad-like. But our sergeant laughed when he saw how it had pleased us all.

'Them are the French bands,' said he; 'and if you come out here you'll see what some of you may not live to see again.'

Out we went—the beautiful music still sounding in

our ears, and stood on a rise just outside the barn. Down below, at the bottom of the slope, about half a musket shot from us, was a snug tiled farm with a hedge and a bit of an apple-orchard. All round it a line of men in red coats and high fur hats were working like bees, knocking holes in the wall and barring up the doors.

'Them's the light companies of the Guards,' said the sergeant. 'They'll hold that farm while one of them can wag a finger. But look over yonder, and you'll see the camp-fires of the French.'

We looked across the valley at the low ridge upon the farther side, and saw a thousand little yellow points of flame, with the dark smoke wreathing up slowly in the heavy air. There was another farm-house on the farther side of the valley, and as we watched we suddenly saw a little group of horsemen appear on a knoll beside it and look across at us. There were a dozen hussars behind, and in front five men, three with helmets, one with a long, straight, red feather in his hat, and the last with a low cap.

'By God!' cried the sergeant. 'That's him! That's Boney, the one with the grey horse. Aye, I'll lay a month's pay on it.'

I strained my eyes to see him, this man who had cast that great shadow over Europe which darkened the nations for five-and-twenty years, and which had even fallen across our out-of-the-world little sheep-farm, and had dragged us all—myself, Edie, and Jim—out of the lives that our folk had lived before us. As far as I could see he was a dumpy, square-shouldered kind of man, and he held his double glasses to his eyes with his elbows spread very wide out on each side. I was still staring when I heard the catch of a man's breath by my side, and there was Jim, with his eyes glowing like two coals and his face thrust over my shoulder.

'That's he, Jock,' he whispered.

'Yes, that's Boney,' said I.

'No, no; it's he. This De Lapp or De Lissac, or whatever his devil's name is. It is he.'

Then I saw him at once. It was the horseman with the high red feather in his hat. Even at that distance I could have sworn to the slope of his shoulders and the way he carried his head. I clapped my hand upon Jim's sleeve, for I could see that his blood was boiling at the sight of the man, and that he was ready for any madness. But at that moment Bonaparte seemed to lean over and say something to De Lissac, and the party wheeled and dashed away, while there came the bang of a gun and a white spray of smoke from a battery along the ridge. At the same instant the assembly was blown in our village, and we rushed for our arms and fell in. There was a burst of firing all along the line, and we thought that the battle had begun, but it came really from our fellows cleaning their pieces, for their priming was in some danger of being wet from the damp night.

From where we stood it was a sight now that was worth coming over the seas to see. On our own ridge was the checker of red and blue, stretching right away to a village over two miles from us. It was whispered from man to man in the ranks, however, that there was too much of the blue and too little of the red, for the Belgians had shown on the day before that their hearts were too soft for the work, and we had twenty thousand of them for comrades. Then even our British troops were half made up of militiamen and recruits, for the pick of the old Peninsular regiments were on the ocean in transports, coming back from some fool's quarrel with our kinsfolk of America. But for all that we could see the bearskins of the Guards, two strong brigades of them, and the bonnets of the Highlanders, and the blue of the old German Legion, and the red lines of Pack's brigade, and Kempt's brigade, and the green-dotted riflemen in front; and we knew that, come what might, these were men who would bide where they were placed, and that they

639

had a man to lead them who would place them where they should bide.

Of the French we had seen little, save the twinkle of their fires and a few horsemen here and there on the curves of the ridge; but as we stood and waited there came suddenly a grand blare from their bands, and their whole army came flooding over the low hill which had hid them—brigade after brigade, and division after division—until the broad slope in its whole length and depths was blue with their uniforms and bright with the glint of their weapons. It seemed that they would never have done, still pouring over and pouring over, while our men leaned on their muskets and smoked their pipes, looking down at this grand gathering and listening to what the old soldiers, who had fought the French before, had to say about them. Then, when the infantry had formed in long, deep masses, their guns came whirling and bounding down the slope, and it was pretty to see how smartly they unlimbered and were ready for action. And then, at a stately trot, down came the cavalry— thirty regiments at the least, with plume and breastplate, twinkling sword and fluttering lance—forming up at the flanks and rear in long, shifting, glimmering lines.

'Them's the chaps,' cried our old sergeant. 'They're gluttons to fight, they are. And you see them regiments with the great high hats in the middle, a bit behind the farm? That's the Guard—twenty thousand of them, my sons, and all picked men—grey-headed devils that have done nothing but fight since they were as high as my gaiters. They've three men to our two, and two guns to our one, and, by God! they'll make you recruities wish you were back in Argyle Street before they have finished with you.' He was not a cheering man, our sergeant, but then he had been in every fight since Corunna, and had a medal with seven clasps upon his breast, so that he had a right to talk in his own fashion.

When the Frenchmen had arranged themselves just out of cannon-shot we saw a small group of horsemen,

all in a blaze with silver and scarlet and gold, ride swiftly
between the divisions; and as they went a roar of cheering burst out from either side of them, and we could see
arms outstretched to them and hands waving. An instant
later the noise had died away, and the two armies stood
facing each other in absolute deadly silence—a sight
which often comes back to me in my dreams. Then of
a sudden there was a lurch among the men just in front
of us, a thin column wheeled off from the dense blue
clump, and came swinging up towards the farm-house
which lay below us. It had not taken fifty paces before
a gun banged out from an English battery on our left,
and the battle of Waterloo had begun.

It is not for me to tell you the story of that battle, and
indeed I should have kept far enough away from such
a thing had it not happened that our own fates—those
of the three simple folk who came from the border
country—were all just as much mixed up in it as those
of any king or emperor of them all. To tell the honest
truth, I have learned more about that battle from what
I have read than from what I saw, for how much could
I see with a comrade on either side, and a great white
cloudbank at the very end of my fire-lock? It was from
books and the talk of others that I learned how the
heavy cavalry charged, how they rode over the famous
cuirassiers, and how they were cut to pieces before they
could get back. From them, too, I learned all about the
successive assaults, and how the Belgians fled, and how
Pack and Kempt stood firm. But of my own knowledge
I can only speak of what we saw during that long day
in the rifts of the smoke and the lulls of the firing, and
it's just of that that I will tell you.

We were on the right of the line and in reserve, for the
Duke was afraid that Boney might work round on that
side and get at him from behind, so our three regiments,
with another British brigade and the Hanoverians, were
placed there to be ready for anything. There were two
brigades of light cavalry, too, but the French attack was

all from the front, so it was late in the day before we were really wanted.

The English battery which fired the first gun was still banging away on our left, and a German one was hard at work upon our right, so that we were wrapped round with the smoke, but we were not so hidden as to screen us from a line of French guns opposite, for a score of round shot came piping through the air and plumped right into the heart of us. As I heard the scream of them pass my ear, my head went down like a diver, but our sergeant gave me a prod in the back with the handle of his halbert.

'Don't be so blasted polite,' said he. 'When you're hit you can bow once and for all.'

There was one of those balls that knocked five men into a bloody mash, and I saw it lying on the ground afterwards, like a crimson foot-ball. Another went through the adjutant's horse with a plop, like a stone in the mud, broke its back, and left it lying like a burst gooseberry. Three more fell farther to the right, and by the stir and cries we could tell that they had all told.

'Ah, James, you've lost a good mount,' says Major Reed, just in front of me, looking down at the adjutant, whose boots and breeches were all running with blood.

'I gave a cool fifty for him in Glasgow,' said the other. 'Don't you think, major, that the men had better lie down, now that the guns have got our range?'

'Tut!' said the other. 'They are young, James, and it will do them good.'

'They'll get enough of it before the day's done,' grumbled the other, but at that moment Colonel Reynell saw that the Rifles and the Fifty-second were down on either side of us, so we had the order to stretch ourselves out too. Precious glad we were when we could hear the shot whining like hungry dogs within a few feet of our backs. Even now a thud and a splash every minute or so, with a yelp of pain and a drumming of boots upon the ground, told us that we were still losing heavily.

A thin rain was falling, and the damp air held the smoke low, so that we could only catch glimpses of what was doing just in front of us, though the roar of the guns told us that the battle was general all along the lines. Four hundred of them were all crashing at once now, and the noise was enough to split the drum of your ear. Indeed, there was not one of us but had a singing in his head for many a long day afterwards. Just opposite us, on the slope of the hill, was a French gun, and we could see the men serving her quite plainly. They were small, active men with very tight breeches and high hats with great, straight plumes sticking up from them, but they worked like sheep-shearers, ramming and sponging and training. There were fourteen when I saw them first, and only four left standing at the last, but they were working away just as hard as ever.

The farm that they called Hougoumont was down in front of us, and all morning we could see that a terrible fight was going on there, for the walls and the windows and the orchard hedges were all flame and smoke, and there rose such shrieking and crying from it as I never heard before. It was half burned down, and shattered with balls, and ten thousand men were hammering at the gates, but four hundred guardsmen held it in the morning and two hundred held it in the evening, and no French foot was ever set within its threshold. But how they fought, those Frenchmen! Their lives were no more to them than the mud under their feet. There was one —I can see him now—a stoutish, ruddy man on a crutch. He hobbled up alone in a lull of the firing to the side gate of Hougoumont, and he beat upon it, screaming to his men to come after him. For five minutes he stood there, strolling about in front of the gun-barrels which spared him, but at last a Brunswick skirmisher in the orchard flicked out his brains with a rifle-shot. And he was only one of many, for all day, when they did not

643

come in masses they came in twos and threes, with as brave a face as if the whole army were at their heels.

So we lay all morning looking down at the fight at Hougoumont; but soon the Duke saw that there was nothing to fear upon his right, and so he began to use us in another way. The French had pushed their skirmishers past the farm, and they lay among the young corn in front of us, popping at the gunners, so that three pieces out of six on our left were lying with their men strewed in the mud all round them. But the Duke had his eyes everywhere, and up he galloped at that moment, a thin, dark, wiry man, with very bright eyes, a hooked nose, and a big cockade on his cap. There were a dozen officers at his heels, all as merry as if it were a fox-hunt; but of the dozen there was not one left in the evening.

'Warm work, Adams,' said he as he rode up.

'Very warm, your grace,' said our general.

'But we can outstay them at it, I think. Tut! tut! we cannot let skirmishers silence a battery. Just drive those fellows out of that, Adams.'

Then first I knew what a devil's thrill runs through a man when he is given a bit of fighting to do. Up to now we had just lain and been killed, which is the weariest kind of work. Now it was our turn, and, my word, we were ready for it. Up we jumped, the whole brigade, in a four-deep line, and rushed at the corn-field as hard as we could tear. The skirmishers snapped at us as we came, and then away they bolted like corn-crakes, their heads down, their backs rounded, and their muskets at the trail. Half of them got away, but we caught up the others, the officer first, for he was a very fat man who could not run fast. It gave me quite a turn when I saw Rob Stewart on my right stick his bayonet into the man's broad back and heard him howl like a damned soul. There was no quarter in that field, and it was butt or point for all of them. The men's blood was aflame, and little wonder, for those wasps had been stinging all morning without our being able so much as to see them.

And now, as we broke through the farther edge of the corn-field we got in front of the smoke, and there was the whole French army in position before us, with only two meadows and a narrow lane between us. We set up a yell as we saw them, and away we should have gone, slap at them, if we had been left to ourselves, for silly young soldiers never think that harm can come to them until it is there in their midst. But the Duke had cantered his horse beside us as we advanced, and now he roared something to the general, and the officers all rode in front of our line, holding out their arms for us to stop. There was a blowing of bugles, a pushing and a shoving, with the sergeants cursing and digging us with their halberts, and in less time than it takes me to write it there was the brigade in three neat little squares, all bristling with bayonets and in *échelon*, as they call it, so that each could fire across the face of the other.

It was the saving of us, as even so young a soldier as I was could very easily see. And we had none too much time either. There was a low, rolling hill on our right flank, and from behind this there came a sound like nothing on this earth so much as the beat of the waves on Berwick coast when the wind blows from the east. The earth was all shaking with that dull, roaring sound, and the air was full of it. 'Steady, Seventy-first, for God's sake, steady!' shrieked the voice of our colonel behind us, but in front was nothing but the green, gentle slope of the grassland, all mottled with daisies and dandelions.

And then suddenly, over the curve, we saw eight hundred brass helmets rise up, all in a moment, each with a long tag of horsehair flying from its crest, and then eight hundred fierce brown faces, all pushed forward, and glaring out from between the ears of as many horses. There was an instant of gleaming breast-plates, waving swords, tossing manes, fierce red nostrils opening and shutting, and hoofs pawing the air before us, and then down came the line of muskets, and our bullets smacked up against their armour like the clatter of a hailstorm upon a window. I fired with the rest, and then rammed down another charge as fast as I could, staring out through the smoke in front of me, where I could see some long, thin thing, which flapped slowly backwards and forwards. A bugle sounded for us to cease firing, and a whiff of wind came to clear the curtain from in front of us, and then we could see what had happened.

I had expected to find half that regiment of horse lying on the ground; but whether it was that their breast-plates had shielded them, or whether, being young and a little shaken at their coming, we had fired high, our volley had done no very great harm. About thirty horses lay about, three of them together within ten yards of me, the middle one right on its back, with its four legs in the air, and it was one of these that I had seen flapping through the smoke. Then there were eight or ten dead men, and about as many wounded, sitting dazed on the grass for the most part, though one was shouting '*Vive l'Empereur!*' at the top of his voice. Another fellow who had been shot in the thigh—a great, black-moustached chap he was, too—leaned his back against his dead horse, and, picking up his carbine, fired as coolly as if he had been shooting for a prize, and hit Angus Myers, who was only two from me, right through the forehead. Then he out with his hand to get another carbine that lay near, but before he could reach it big Hodgson, who was the pivot-man of the grenadier company, ran out and passed his bayonet through his throat, which was a pity, for he seemed to be a very fine man.

At first I thought that the cuirassiers had run away in the smoke, but they were not men who did that very easily. Their horses had swerved at our volley, and they had raced past our square and taken the fire of the two other ones beyond. Then they broke through a hedge, and coming on a regiment of Hanoverians who were in line, they treated them as they would have treated us if we had not been so quick, and cut them to pieces in an instant. It was dreadful to see the big Germans running and screaming, while the cuirassiers stood up in their stirrups to have a better sweep for their long, heavy swords, and cut and stabbed without mercy. I do not believe that a hundred men of that regiment were left alive, and the Frenchmen came back across our front, shouting at us and waving their weapons which were crimson down to the hilts. This they did to draw our fire, but the colonel was too old a soldier, for we could have done little harm at the distance, and they would have been among us before we could reload.

These horsemen got behind the ridge on our right again, and we knew very well that if we opened up from the squares they would be down upon us in a twinkle. On the other hand, it was hard to bide as we were, for they had passed the word to a battery of twelve guns which formed up a few hundred yards away from us, but out of our sight, sending their balls just over the brow and down into the midst of us, which is called a plunging fire. And one of their gunners ran up on to the top of the slope and stuck a handspike into the wet earth, to give them a guide, under the very muzzles of the whole brigade, none of whom fired a shot at him, each leaving him to the other. Ensign Samson, who was the youngest subaltern in the regiment, ran out from the square and pulled down the handspike, but quick as a jack after a minnow a lancer came flying over the ridge, and he made such a thrust from behind that not only his point but his pennon, too, came out between the second and third buttons of the lad's tunic. 'Helen! Helen!' he shouted, and fell dead on his face, while the lancer, blown half to pieces with musket-balls, toppled over beside him, still holding on to his weapon, so that they lay together with that dreadful bond still connecting them.

But when the battery opened there was no time for us to think of anything else. A square is a very good way of meeting a horseman, but there is no worse one of taking a cannon-ball, as we soon learned when they began to cut red seams through us, until our ears were weary of the slosh and splash when hard iron met living flesh and blood. After ten minutes of it we moved our square a hundred paces to the right, but we left another square behind us, for a hundred and twenty men and seven officers showed where we had been standing. Then the guns found us out again, and we tried to open out into line, but in an instant the horsemen—lancers they were this time—were upon us from over the brae. I tell you we were glad to hear the thud of their hoofs, for we knew that that must stop the cannon for a minute, and give us a chance of hitting back. And we hit back pretty hard, too, that time, for we were cold and vicious and savage, and I, for one, felt that I cared no more for the horsemen than if they had been so many sheep on Corriemuir. One gets past being afraid or thinking of one's own skin after a while, and you just feel that you want to make some one pay for all you have gone through. We took our change out of the lancers that time, for they had no breast-plates to shield them, and we cleared seventy of them out of their saddles at a volley. Maybe if we could have seen seventy mothers weeping for their lads we should not have felt so pleased over it, but then men are just brutes when they are fighting, and have as much thought as two bull-pups when they've got one another by the throttle.

Then the colonel did a wise stroke, for he reckoned that this would stave off the cavalry for five minutes, so he wheeled us into line and got us back into a deeper hollow, out of reach of the guns, before they could open again. This gave us time to breathe, and we wanted it too, for the regiment had been melting away like an icicle in the sun. But bad as it was for us, it was a deal worse for some of the others. The whole of the Dutch-Belgians were off by this time helter skelter, fifteen thousand of them, and there were great gaps left in our line, through which the French cavalry rode as pleased them best. Then the French guns had been too many and too good for ours, and our heavy horse had been cut to bits, so that things were none too merry with us. On the other hand, Hougoumont, a blood-soaked ruin, was still ours, and every British regiment was firm, though, to tell the honest truth, as a man is bound to do, there were a sprinkling of red coats among the blue ones who made for the rear. But these were lads and stragglers, the faint hearts that are found everywhere, and I say again that no regiment flinched. It was little we could see of the battle, but a man would be blind not to know that all the fields behind us were covered with flying men. But then, though we on the right wing knew nothing of it, the Prussians had begun to show, and Napoleon had set twenty thousand of his men to face them, which made up for ours that had bolted, and left us much as we began. That was all dark to us, however, and there was a time when the French horsemen had flooded in between us and the rest of the army, that we thought we were the only brigade left standing, and had set our teeth with the intention of selling our lives as dearly as we could.

At that time it was between four and five in the afternoon, and we had had nothing to eat, the most of us, since the night before, and were soaked with rain into the bargain. It had drizzled off and on all day, but for the last few hours we had not had a thought to spare either upon the weather or our hunger. Now we began to look round and tighten our waistbelts, and ask who was hit and who was spared. I was glad to see Jim, with his face all blackened with powder, standing on my right rear, leaning on his fire-lock. He saw me looking at him, and shouted out to know if I were hurt.

'All right, Jim,' I answered.

'I fear I'm here on a wild-goose chase,' said he, gloomily, 'but it's not over yet. By God, I'll have him or he'll have me!' He had brooded so much on his wrong, had poor Jim, that I really believe it had turned his head, for he had a glare in his eyes as he spoke that was hardly human. He was always a man that took even a little thing to heart, and since Edie had left him I am sure that he was no longer his own master.

It was at this time that we saw two single fights which they tell me were common enough in the battles of old, before men were trained in masses. As we lay in the hollow, two horsemen came spurring along the ridge in front of us, riding as hard as hoof could rattle. The first was an English dragoon, his face right down on his horse's mane, with a French cuirassier, an old grey-headed fellow, thundering behind him on a big, black mare. Our chaps set up a hooting as they came flying on, for it seemed shame to see an Englishman run like that; but as they swept across our front we saw where the trouble lay. The dragoon had dropped his sword and was unarmed, while the other was pressing him so close that he could not get a weapon. At last, stung maybe by our hooting, he made up his mind to chance it. His eye fell on a lance beside a dead Frenchman, so he swerved his horse to let the other pass, and hopping off cleverly enough, he gripped hold of it. But the other was too tricky for him, and was on him like a shot. The dragoon thrust up with the lance, but the other turned it and sliced him through the shoulder-blade. It was all done in an instant, and the Frenchman cantered his horse up the brae, showing his teeth at us over his shoulder like a snarling dog.

That was one to them, but we scored one for us presently. They had pushed forward a skirmish-line whose fire was towards the batteries on our right and left rather than on us, but we sent out two companies of the Ninety-fifth to keep them in check. It was strange to hear the crackling kind of noise that they made, for both sides were using the rifle. An officer stood among the French skirmishers, a tall, lean man with a mantle over his shoulders, and as our fellows came forward he ran out midway between the two parties and stood as a fencer would, with his sword up and his head back. I can see him now, with his lowered eyelids, and the kind of sneer that he had upon his face. On this the subaltern of the Rifles, who was a fine, well-grown lad, ran forward and drove full tilt at him with one of the queer crooked swords that the riflemen carry. They came together like two rams, for each ran for the other, and down they tumbled at the shock, but the Frenchman was below. Our man broke his sword short off, and took the other's blade through his left arm, but he was the stronger man, and he managed to let the life out of his enemy with the jagged stump of his blade. I thought that the French skirmishers would have shot him down, but not a trigger was drawn, and he got back to his company with one sword through his arm and half of another in his hand.

XIII. The End of the Storm

OF all the things that seem strange in that great battle, now that I look back upon it, there was nothing that was queerer than the way in which it acted on my comrades. For some took it as though it had been their daily meat, without question or change, and others pattered out prayers from the first gun-fire to the last, and others again cursed and swore in a way that was creepy to listen to. There was one, my own left-hand mate, Mike Threading-ham, who kept telling about his maiden aunt, Sarah, and how she had left the money which had been promised to him for a home for the children of drowned sailors. Again and again he told me this story, and yet, when the battle was over, he took his oath that he had never opened his lips all day. As to me, I cannot say whether I spoke or not, but I know that my mind and my memory were clearer than I can ever remember them, and I was thinking all the time about the old folk at home, and about Cousin Edie with her saucy, dancing eyes, and De Lissac with his cat's whiskers, and all the doings at West Inch which had ended by bringing us here on the plains

651

of Belgium as a cock-shot for two hundred and fifty cannons.

During all this time the roaring of those guns had been something dreadful to listen to, but now they suddenly died away, though it was like the lull in a thunder-storm when one feels that a worse crash is coming hard at the fringe of it. There was still a mighty noise on the distant wing, where the Prussians were pushing their way onwards, but that was two miles away. The other batteries, both French and English, were silent, and the smoke cleared so that the armies could see a little of each other. It was a dreary sight along our ridge, for there seemed to be just a few scattered knots of red, and the lines of green where the German Legion stood, while the masses of the French appeared to be as thick as ever, though, of course, we knew that they must have lost many thousands in these attacks. We heard a great cheering and shouting from among them, and then suddenly all their batteries opened together with a roar which made the din of the earlier part seem nothing in comparison. It might well be twice as loud, for every battery was twice as near, being moved right up to point-blank range, with huge masses of horse between and behind them to guard them from attack.

When that devil's roar burst upon our ears there was not a man down to the drummer-boys who did not understand what it meant. It was Napoleon's last great effort to crush us. There were but two more hours of light, and if we could hold our own for those, all would be well. Starved and weary and spent, we prayed that we might have strength to load and stab and fire while a man of us stood upon his feet.

His cannon could do us no great hurt now, for we were on our faces, and in an instant we could turn into a huddle of bayonets if his horse came down again. But behind the thunder of the guns there arose a sharper, shriller noise, whirring and rattling, the wildest, jauntiest, most stirring kind of sound.

'It's the *pas-de-charge*,' cried an officer. 'They mean business this time.'

And as he spoke we saw a strange thing. A Frenchman, dressed as an officer of hussars, came galloping towards us on a little bay horse. He was screeching *'Vive le Roi! Vive le Roi!'* at the pitch of his lungs, which was as much as to say that he was a deserter, since we were for the king and they for the emperor. As he passed us he roared out in English, 'The Guard is coming! The Guard is coming!' and so vanished away to the rear like a leaf blown before a storm. At the same instant up there rode an aide-de-camp with the reddest face that ever I saw upon mortal man.

'You must stop 'em or we are done,' he cried to General Adams, so that all our company could hear him.

'How is it going?' asked the general.

'Two weak squadrons left out of six regiments of heavies,' said he, and began to laugh like a man whose nerves are overstrung.

'Perhaps you would care to join in our advance. Pray consider yourself quite one of us,' said the general, bowing and smiling as if he were asking him to a dish of tea.

'I shall have much pleasure,' said the other, taking off his hat, and a moment afterwards our three regiments closed up and the brigade advanced in four lines over the hollow where we had lain in square, and out beyond the point whence we had seen the French army.

There was little of it to be seen now, only the red belching of the guns flashing quickly out of the cloud-bank, and the black figures, stooping, straining, mopping, sponging, working like devils, and at devilish work. But through the cloud that rattle and whir rose louder and louder, with a deep-mouthed shouting and the stamping of thousands of feet. Then there came a broad black blur through the haze, which darkened and darkened, until we could see that it was a hundred men abreast, marching swiftly towards us, with high fur hats upon their heads and a gleam of brass-work over their brows. And behind that hundred came another hundred, and behind that another, and on and on, coiling and writhing out of the cannon-smoke, like a monstrous snake, until there seemed to be no end to the mighty column. In front ran a spray of skirmishers and behind them the drummers, and up they all came together at a kind of tripping step, with the officers clustering thickly at the sides and waving their swords and cheering. There were a dozen mounted men, too, at their front, all shouting together, and one with his hat held aloft upon his sword-point. I say again that no men upon this earth could have fought more manfully than the French did upon that day.

It was wonderful to see them, for, as they came onward, they got ahead of their own guns, so that they had no longer any help from them, while they got in front of the two batteries which had been on either side of us all day. Every gun had their range to a foot, and we saw long red lines scored right down the dark column as it advanced. So near were they, and so closely did they march, that every shot ploughed through ten files of them, and yet they closed up, and came on with a swing and dash that was fine to see. Their head was turned straight for ourselves, while the Ninety-fifth overlapped them on one side and the Fifty-second on the other.

I shall always think that, if we had waited so, the Guard would have broken us, for how could a four-deep line stand against such a column? But at that moment Colburne, the colonel of the Fifty-second, swung his right flank round so as to bring it on the side of the column, which brought the Frenchmen to a halt. Their front line was forty paces from us at the moment, and we had a good look at them. It was funny to me to remember that I had always thought of Frenchmen as small men, for there was not one of that first company who could not have picked me up as if I had been a child, and their great hats made them look taller yet. They were hard, wizened, wiry fellows, too, with fierce, puckered eyes and

bristling moustaches—old soldiers who had fought and
fought week in, week out, for many a year. And then, as
I stood with a finger upon the trigger, waiting for the
word to fire, my eye fell full upon the mounted officer,
with his hat upon his sword, and I saw that it was De
Lissac.

I saw it, and Jim did, too. I heard a shout, and saw
him rush forward madly at the French column. And, as
quick as a thought, the whole brigade took their cue
from him, officers and all, and flung themselves upon
the Guard in front, while our comrades charged them
on the flanks. We had been waiting for the order, and
they all thought now that it had been given; but, you
may take my word for it, Jim Horscroft was the
real leader of the brigade when we charged the Old
Guard.

God knows what happened during that mad five
minutes. I remember putting my musket against a blue-
coat, and pulling the trigger, and that the man could
not fall, because he was so wedged in the crowd; but I
saw a horrid blotch upon the cloth, and a thin curl of
smoke from it, as if it had taken fire. Then I found
myself thrown up against two big Frenchmen, and so
squeezed together, the three of us, that we could not
raise a weapon. One of them, a fellow with a very large
nose, got his hand up to my throat, and I felt that I was
a chicken in his grasp. '*Rendez-vous, coquin, rendez-
vous!*' said he, and then suddenly doubled up with a
scream, for some one had stabbed him in the bowels
with a bayonet. There was very little firing after the first
sputter, but there was the crash of butt against barrel,
the short cries of stricken men, and the roaring of the
officers. And then, suddenly, they began to give ground,
slowly, sullenly, step by step, but still to give ground.
Ah, it was worth all we had gone through, the thrill of
that moment, when we felt that they were going to
break. There was one Frenchman before me, a sharp-
faced, dark-eyed man, who was loading and firing as

quietly as if he were at practice, dwelling upon his aim, and looking round first to try and pick off an officer. I remember that it struck me that to kill so cool a man as that would be a good service, and I rushed at him, and drove my bayonet into him. He turned as I struck him, and fired full into my face, and the bullet left a weal across my cheek which will mark me to my dying day. I tripped over him as he fell, and, two others tumbling over me, I was half smothered in the heap. When, at last, I struggled out and cleared my eyes, which were half full of powder, I saw that the column had fairly broken, and was shredding into groups of men who were either running for their lives, or were fighting back to back, in a vain attempt to check the brigade, which was still sweeping onward. My face felt as if a red-hot iron had been laid across it, but I had the use of my limbs, so, jumping over the litter of dead and mangled men, I scampered after my regiment, and fell in upon the right flank.

Old Major Elliott was there, limping along, for his horse had been shot, but none the worse in himself. He saw me come up, and nodded, but it was too busy a time for words. The brigade was still advancing, but the general rode in front of me, with his chin upon his shoulder, looking back at the British position.

'There is no general advance,' said he. 'But I'm not going back.'

'The Duke of Wellington has won a great victory,' cried the aide-de-camp, in a solemn voice, and then, his feelings getting the better of him, he added, 'if the damned fool would only push on!'—which set us all laughing in the flank company.

But now any one could see that the French army was breaking up. The columns and squadrons which had stood so squarely all day were now all ragged at the edges, and where there had been thick fringes of skirmishers in front, there were now a spray of stragglers in the rear. The Guard thinned out in front of us as we pushed on, and we found twelve guns looking us in the face, but we were over them in a moment, and I saw our youngest subaltern, next to him who had been killed by the lancer, scribbling great 71's with a lump of chalk upon them, like the school-boy that he was. It was at that moment that we heard a noise of cheering behind us, and saw the whole British army flood over the crest of the ridge, and come pouring down upon the remains of their enemies. The guns, too, came bounding and rattling forward, and our light cavalry—as much as was left of it—kept pace with our brigade upon the right. There was no battle after that. The advance went on without a check, until our army stood lined upon the very ground which the French had held in the morning. Their guns were ours, their foot were rabble, spread over the face of the country, and their gallant cavalry alone was able to preserve some sort of order, and to draw off unbroken from the field. Then at last, just as the night began to gather, our weary and starving men were able to let the Prussians take the job over, and to stack their arms upon the ground that they had won. That was as much as I saw or can tell you about the battle of Waterloo, except that I ate a two-pound rye loaf for my supper that night, with as much salt meat as they would let me have, and a good pitcher of red wine, until I had to bore a new hole at the end of my belt, and then it fitted me as tight as a hoop to a barrel. After that I lay down in the straw, where the rest of my company were sprawling, and in less than a minute I was in a dead sleep.

XIV. The Tally of Death

DAY was breaking, and the first grey light had just begun to steal through the long, thin slits in the walls of our barn, when some one shook me hard by the shoulder, and up I jumped. I had the thought, in my stupid, sleepy brain, that the cuirassiers were upon us, and I gripped hold of a halbert that was leaning against the wall; but then, as I saw the long lines of sleepers, I remembered where I was, but I can tell you that I stared when I saw that it was none other than Major Elliott that had roused me up. His face was very grave, and behind him stood two sergeants, with long slips of paper and pencils in their hands.

'Wake up, laddie,' said the major, quite in his old, easy fashion, as if we were back on Corriemuir again.

'Yes, major,' I stammered.

'I want you to come with me. I feel that I owe something to you two lads, for it was I that took you from your homes. Jim Horscroft is missing.'

I gave a start at that, for, what with the rush and the hunger and the weariness, I had never given a thought to my friend since the time that he had rushed at the French Guards with the whole regiment at his heels.

'I am going out to take a tally of our losses,' said the major, 'and if you care to come with me, I shall be very glad to have you.'

So off we set, the major, the two sergeants, and I, and, oh! but it was a dreadful, dreadful sight—so much so that even now, after so many years, I had rather say as little of it as possible. It was bad to see in the heat of fight, but now, in the cold morning, with no cheer or drum-tap or bugle-blare, all the glory had gone out of it, and it was just one huge butcher's shop, where poor devils had been ripped and burst and smashed, as though we had tried to make a mock of God's image. There, on the ground, one could read every stage of yesterday's fight, the dead footmen that lay in squares, and the fringe of dead horsemen that had charged them, and above, on the slope, the dead gunners who lay round their broken pieces. The Guard's column had left a streak right up the field like the trail of a snail, and at the head of it the blue-coats were lying heaped upon the red ones, where that fierce tug had been, before they took their backward step.

And the very first thing I saw, when I got there, was Jim himself. He was lying on the broad of his back, his face turned up towards the sky, and all the passion and the trouble seemed to have passed clean away from him, so that he looked just like the old Jim as I had seen him in his cot a hundred times when we were schoolmates together. I had given a cry of grief at the sight of him, but when I came again to look upon his face, and to see how much happier he looked in death than I could ever have hoped to see him in life, it was hard to mourn for him. Two French bayonets had passed through his chest, and he had died in an instant, and without pain, if one could believe the smile upon his lips.

The major and I were raising his head, in the hope that some flutter of life might remain, when I heard a well-remembered voice at my side, and there was De Lissac, leaning upon his elbow, among a litter of dead Guardsmen. He had a great blue coat muffled round him, and his hat, with the high red plume, was lying on the ground beside him. He was very pale and had dark blotches under his eyes, but otherwise he was as he had ever been, with the keen, hungry nose, the wiry moustache, and the close-cropped head, thinning away to baldness upon the top. His eyelids had always drooped, but now one could hardly see the glint of his eyes from beneath them.

'Halloo, Jack!' he cried. 'I didn't thought to have seen you here, and yet I might have known it, too, when I saw friend Jim.'

'It is you that have brought all this trouble,' said I.

'Ta, ta, ta!' he cried, in his old, impatient fashion. 'It is all arranged for us. When I was in Spain I learned to believe in fate. It is fate which has sent you here this morning.'

'This man's blood lies at your door,' said I, with my hand on poor Jim's shoulder.

659

'And mine on his, so we have paid our debts.' He flung open his mantle as he spoke, and I saw with horror that a great black lump of clotted blood was hanging out of his side.

'This is my thirteenth and last,' said he, with a smile. 'They say that thirteen is an unlucky number. Could you spare me a drink from your flask?'

The major had some brandy-and-water. De Lissac supped it up eagerly. His eyes brightened, and a little fleck of colour came back into each of his haggard cheeks.

'It was Jim did this,' said he. 'I heard some one calling my name, and there he was, with his gun against my tunic. Two of my men cut him down just as he fired. Well, well, Edie was worth it all. You will be in Paris in less than a month, Jack, and you will see her. You will find her at number eleven of the Rue Miromesnil, which is near to the Madelaine. Break it very gently to her, Jack, for you cannot think how she loved me. Tell her that all I have is in the two black trunks, and that Antoine has the keys. You will not forget?'

'I will remember.'

'And madame, your mother? I trust that you have left her very well. And monsieur too, your father? Bear them my distinguished regards.' Even now, as death closed in upon him, he gave the old bow and wave as he sent his greetings to my mother.

'Surely,' said I, 'your wound may not be so serious as you think. I could bring the surgeon of our regiment to you.'

'My dear Jack, I have not been giving and taking wounds this fifteen years without knowing when one has come home. But it is well, for I know that all is ended for my little man, and I had rather go with my *voltigeurs* than remain to be an exile and a beggar. Besides, it is quite certain that the Allies would have shot me, so I have saved myself from that humiliation.'

'The Allies, sir,' said the major, with some heat, 'would be guilty of no such barbarous action.'

But De Lissac shook his head with the same sad smile.

'You do not know, major,' said he. 'Do you suppose that I should have fled to Scotland and changed my name if I had not more to fear than my comrades in Paris? I was anxious to live, for I was sure that my little man would come back. Now I had rather die, for he will never head an army again. But I have done things that could not be forgiven. It was I that led the party that took and shot the Duc d'Enghien. It was I—ah, *mon Dieu, Edie, Edie, ma chérie!*' He threw out both his hands, with all the fingers feeling and quivering in the air. Then he let them drop heavily in front of him, and his chin fell forward upon his chest. One of our sergeants laid him gently down, and the other stretched the big blue mantle over him, and so we left those two whom fate had so strangely brought together, the Scotchman and the Frenchman, lying silently and peacefully within hand's touch of each other upon the blood-soaked hillside near Hougoumont.

XV. *The End of It*

AND now I have very nearly come to the end of it all, and precious glad I shall be to find myself there, for I began this old memory with a light heart, thinking that it would give me some work for the long summer evenings, but as I went on I wakened a thousand sleeping sorrows and half-forgotten griefs, and now my soul is all as raw as the hide of an ill-sheared sheep. If I come safely out of it, I will swear never to set pen to paper again, for it is so very easy at first, like walking into a shelving stream, and then, before you can look round, you are off your feet and down in a hole, and can struggle out as best you can.

We buried Jim and De Lissac with four hundred and thirty-one others of the French Guards and our own light infantry in a single trench. Ah, if you could sow a brave man as you sow a seed, there should be a fine crop of heroes coming up there some day! Then we left that bloody battlefield behind us for ever, and with our brigade we marched on over the French border on our way to Paris.

I had always been brought up during all these years to look upon the French as very evil folk, and as we only heard of them in connection with fightings and slaughterings by land and by sea, it was natural enough to think that they were vicious by nature and ill to meet with. But then, after all, they had only heard of us in just the same fashion, and so, no doubt, they had just the same idea of us. But when we came to go through their country and to see their bonny little steadings, and the douce, quiet folk at work in the fields, and the women knitting by the road-side, and the old granny with a big white smutch smacking the baby to teach it manners, it was all so homelike that I could not think why it was that we had been fearing and hating these good people for so long. But I suppose that, in truth, it was really the man who was over them that we hated, and now that he was gone, and his great shadow was cleared from the land, all was brightness once more.

We jogged along happily enough through the loveliest country that ever I set my eyes on, until we came to the great city, where we thought that maybe there would be a battle, for there are so many folk in it that if only one in twenty comes out it would make a fine army. But by that time they had seen that it was a pity to spoil the whole country just for the sake of one man, and so they had told him that he must shift for himself in the future. The next we heard was that he had surrendered to the British, and that the gates of Paris were open to us, which was very good news to me, for I could get along very well just on the one battle that I had had.

But there were plenty of folk in Paris now who loved Boney, and that was natural when you think of the glory that he had brought them, and how he had never asked his army to go where he would not go himself. They had stern enough faces for us, I can tell you, when we marched in, and we of Adams' brigade were the very first who set foot in the city. We passed over a bridge which they call Neuilly, which is easier to write than to say, and then through a fine park, the Bois de Boulogne, and so into the Champs d'Elysées. There we bivouacked, and pretty soon the streets were so full of Prussians and English that it became more like a camp than a city.

The very first time that I could get away I went with Rob Stewart, of my company—for we were only allowed to go about in couples—to the Rue Miromesnil. Rob waited in the hall, and I was shown upstairs, and as I put my foot over the mat there was Cousin Edie, just the same as ever, staring at me with those wild eyes of hers. For a moment she did not recognise me, but when she did she just took three steps forward and sprang at me with her two arms round my neck.

'Oh, my dear old Jack!' she cried, 'how fine you look in a red coat!'

'Yes, I am a soldier now, Edie,' said I, very stiffly, for as I looked at her pretty face I seemed to see behind it that other face which had looked up to the morning sky on the Belgian battlefield.

'Fancy that!' she cried. 'What are you then, Jock? A general? a captain?'

'No, I am a private.'

'What! Not one of the common people who carry guns?'

'Yes, I carry a gun.'

'Oh, that is not nearly so interesting,' said she, and she went back to the sofa from which she had risen. It was a wonderful room, all silk and velvet and shiny things, and I felt inclined to go back to give my boots another rub. As Edie sat down again I saw that she was all in black, and so I knew that she had heard of De Lissac's death.

'I am glad to see that you know all,' said I, 'for I am a

clumsy hand at breaking things. He said that you were to keep whatever was in the boxes, and that Antoine had the keys.'

'Thank you, Jock, thank you,' said she. 'It was like your kindness to bring the message. I heard of it nearly a week ago. I was mad for the time—quite mad. I shall wear mourning all my days, although you can see what a fright it makes me look. Ah, I shall never get over it. I shall take the veil and die in a convent.'

'If you please, madame,' said a maid, looking in, 'the Count de Beton wishes to see you.'

'My dear Jock,' said Edie, jumping up, 'this is very important. I am so sorry to cut our chat short, but I am sure that you will come to see me again, will you not, when I am less desolated. And would you mind going out by the side door instead of the main one. Thank you, you dear old Jock; you were always such a good boy, and did exactly what you were told.'

And that was the last I was ever to see of Cousin Edie. She stood in the sunlight with the old challenge in her eyes and flash of her teeth, and so I shall always remember her, shining and unstable like a drop of quicksilver. As I joined my comrade in the street below I saw a fine carriage and pair at the door, and I knew that she had asked me to slip out so that her grand new friends might never know what common people she had been associated with in her childhood. She had never asked for Jim, nor for my father and mother, who had been so kind to her. Well, it was just her way, and she could no more help it than a rabbit can help wagging its scut, and yet it made me heavy-hearted to think of it. Two months later I heard that she had married this same Count de Beton, and she died in child-bed a year or two later.

And as for us, our work was done, for the great shadow had been cleared away from Europe, and should no longer be thrown across the breadth of the lands, over peaceful farms and little villages, darkening the lives which should have been so happy. I came back to Corrie-muir after I had bought my discharge, and there, when my father died, I took over the sheep-farm, and married Lucy Deane, of Berwick, and have brought up seven children who are all taller than their father, and take mighty good care that he shall not forget it. But in the quiet, peaceful days that pass now, each as like the other as so many Scotch tups, I can hardly get the young folks to believe that even here we have had our romance, when Jim and I went a-wooing, and the man with the cat's whiskers came up from the sea.